ADA LEWIS

Jenny

WILLIAM HEINEMANN LTD
MELBOURNE :: LONDON :: TORONTO

To my mother
and father

LONDON

May 1748

TODAY, as I came out of Mr. Currie's glove shop, I saw a harlot being whipped through the street at the tail of a wagon. It is a thing you may see any day in Bridewell, if you have a fancy for such sights. I do not. But there was such a press of people gathered to watch her pass that I could not reach my sedan chair, and so had to wait perforce with the others.

It was a scene of curious contrasts, such as Mr. Hogarth rejoices in. Smoky, dirty old London, turning for once a springtime face —blue sky above the roof-tops, little white clouds drifting just above the chimneys like idling birds, sunshine gilding house fronts and shops with rare charm. And down below, affronting the sunlight, man at his ugliest, in a righteous mood.

All sorts and quality of persons were in the crowd I watched from the step of Mr. Currie's shop. Apprentices in dirty smocks, maids with cap and cloth, had run from their work into the street to see the fun. A filthy beggar woman, scarred and eyelids puckered from smallpox, carried a basket of fresh violets with which she jostled ladies of quality, such as the hoop-skirted dame directly below me. Though dressed handsomely, in the face she was nearly as scarred as the beggar. Smallpox, next to death itself, is the Great Leveller. She peered as eagerly as the others, and her little black page, eyes bugging with curiosity, was letting her long velvet cloak trail in the dirty street while he stood on tiptoe to see.

Making up the bulk of the crowd were respectable shopkeepers and their wives, come out to enjoy the spectacle while pointing a moral to their youthful maids.

And not one among them—not one!—to look sorry or show

any pity. The women primmed their lips and said, "Serve her right, the nasty hussy!" The men grinned and shouted lewdly, bidding the executioner lay on stoutly and warm Madam's back for her. They did not hesitate to throw *their* stones—these good people. I daresay some of the women were as bad as she, and among the men were more than likely former customers of hers—but they none of them hesitated.

As the wagon bumped slowly by, dragging the poor wretch who could scarcely stand any more, let alone walk, I turned my face aside. But I could not shut out the sounds—the wet thump of the whip, each stroke followed by a cry from the victim, less like a human cry than the pitiful howl of a tortured dog, the slow roll and rattle of the wheels along the cobblestones, the coarse unfeeling mockery of the crowd.

I longed to stop up my ears, and stood sick and sorry till the procession passed and my chairmen brought the chair to the step. I had meant to visit another shop or two, but instead I bid them take me home. I had had enough of my fellow man for one day.

Surely a very common sight to distress me so? An edifying sight too, as the moralists and clergymen would tell us. Perhaps so. And once I daresay I would have regarded it with no more than a shrug and a grimace, for I never liked cruelty as so many people do. But it is different now. Different, because once I saw the faces of the mob turned thus on me—jeering, curious, insolent, cruel. It's a sight you don't forget. And because once I saw before me no better fate than hers, to end perhaps with just such a walk in the sunlight, with the whip on *my* shoulders.

It's not that I am afraid. But once you have seen the face of disaster, you are marked. Afterwards you do not see things as other people do. All those others, watching a harlot whipped, had laughed or jeered or gloated or gravely approved, according to their natures, viewing a spectacle, a thing apart from them. But I—all I could think was, *'There, but for the grace of God, goes Jenny Archer . . .'*

I am not yet twenty years old. When I look into my glass the

2

face that looks back at me is a girl's face still—small pointed chin; mischievous curling mouth, readier to laugh or kiss than to cry; nose not so bad, pert but shapely; eyes large and well-shaped though more green than the blue I would wish them to be, but with long and heavy fair lashes and pretty-shaped fair brows. The complexion is good—very good, in truth—clear and bright, with a high pure colour in the cheeks for which I do not yet have to thank my rouge pot. Though, alas! I have to pay for that complexion by the wretchedly unfashionable colour of my hair, shining defiant even now through all the coating of powder my maid has put on it—the gleaming red of a copper kettle when firelight strikes sparks out of it.

For the rest—a tongue too quick, a figure too slight but shapely nevertheless, pretty small feet, hands as thin and square-fingered as a boy's—this is Jenny Archer, and I have looked out of her eyes and smiled with that curling mouth and spoken with that quick tongue for nearly twenty years now, and I do not know her yet. I have by heart every tint and line of that pretty girl's face, and yet it looks back at me, smiling and enigmatic, forever a stranger. That is why I can paint it truthfully, faults and graces both, without either pride or shame. For the real Jenny, the Jenny that matters, is somewhere else deep down inside of me, a being entirely apart from the shape that houses her.

I wonder if everybody else is as conscious as I am of that secret inward self? Or do they know only the stranger that smiles back at them from their glass? Is it just because I once knew a time when there was nothing left to me but that stubborn inward self— the last friend of all?

I have promised never to think of those old dark days again. But today, seeing that wretched woman, somehow it all comes back to me and it seems as though I must remember it once more, just as it was. For though there is not a mark to show for it any- where on that young smiling face in my mirror, there is a mark— deep down. I do not suppose it will ever come off, not for all the forgetting in the world.

But I have promised to try, and I will, only I *must* remember, just this once more, what Jenny Archer was and what she might have been . . .

I was born in my father's house, Archfield, in the county of Essex, England, in the early years of the reign of George II, who still sits on the throne despite the great dissatisfaction of many of his subjects at seeing him there, and his own self-expressed preference for his native Hanover. The fashions that now prevail —powdered hair, hooped skirts, tight stays, low bodices and high heels—were just developing then, and look to be fixed for ever now, though fashion, like love, is always unaccountable.

Archfield is a big comfortable country house, of no particular style, standing in its own grounds, with something that may be called a park, and boasting a rent-roll larger than anybody else's for some miles round. There have been Squire Archers at Archfield for nearly two hundred years, some good, some bad, like most families. My grandfather, I believe, was a very respectable gentleman. Nor do I know any ill of my grandmother. I cannot imagine what they did to deserve a son like my father.

I was about eight years old, learning my history lesson, when I declared to my startled stepmother—"I *hate* Henry the Eighth. He is just like Papa."

I was whipped for my impertinence, but not before I had caught unwilling agreement in her glance. Really, there was no denying it. They were both big men, seeming larger than life size because they were so blustery and loud-spoken, given to alternate fits of rage and gusty good humour. Both were huge eaters, indeed greedy in everything, lusting after every well-formed female they saw, amorous but capable of great cruelty when crossed. Both were domestic tyrants. And both had six wives. The only difference was that my father outlived all of his.

I was fifteen when my last stepmother died. I had liked her least of any. I thought her stern and unyielding but perhaps that was because I had reached a difficult age, no longer child but not yet grown. I learned later that she thought she discerned dangerous signs of a wanton nature in me, and hoped by chastisement to curb it. She was a capable woman, and had she lived

4

there is no saying what she might have accomplished; but, as I say, she died.

I was a little sorry, but chiefly pleased to have more freedom and return to some of my old gypsy ways which she had forbidden.

My little sisters cried. They were not hers—she had no children—but they could scarcely remember any other mother. I pitied them, remembering my own bitter grief when Caroline died. She was my father's fourth wife and I loved her dearly. Perhaps, if she had lived, she might have done more with me than anybody. I had something of my father's stubbornness. I would do anything for anybody for the asking, and nothing for the bidding.

My father was furiously annoyed at his last wife's death. The house was never run decently unless there was a mistress, he declared, but he was getting damned sick and tired of going to market every few years.

My eldest sister Valentine offered to manage the house for him, but he told her to find a house of her own. She was his favourite, the only one of his children he liked, but his comfort came first, and it was true she was not much of a housewife.

He then proposed to several young ladies of the neighbourhood, but for the first time in his life met with refusals. He was getting older, and there was not as much money as there had been, and all those daughters to marry off!

He came stamping home from his last effort, cursing and swearing at all women, especially the fool who had just died and put him to all this trouble. We children kept out of his way, I can tell you. The servants couldn't, and cuffs, blows and yelps sounded all over the house.

At last he worked out a solution satisfactory to everybody. He chose a good sensible woman from the village, made her house-keeper, and took her to bed with him to give her prestige over the other servants. She was hard-working and docile, and made no attempt to control us children, so it worked out very well.

The only wife my father had ever respected was his first, my sister Valentine's mother. She was better born than he, for one thing, and then she had the only son who lived—my brother Neal. Of course my father was younger then and more easily impressed. I daresay he would have treated her like the others, in time, but she died too soon, and so he always remembered her as the best of the lot. When he was drunk, he would cry about her. When he was angry with the others, he would tell them what fools and sluts they were, compared to her.

My own mother had the worst time. She was a country girl, just yeoman stock, and he married her in a hurry to console himself for his first wife's death, and then despised her because she was so different. She was the beauty of the countryside when he married her, but that didn't last long. The servants decried her because she was not much better born than they; the neighbouring wives snubbed her; my father abused her; and her babies died. I was the only one who lived and she didn't herself live long enough to be sure of that. I have no recollection of her at all, but those who knew her have told me she was very pretty, merry and spirited even to the last. I fancy Jenny—my Jenny—owes her a good deal.

I had a bad time myself until my first stepmother came. The servants took out their scorn on me, and my father always hated me. But his new wife thought it a shame, and saw to it I was decently cared for. After her death, the servants were in the habit of treating me tolerably; and then Caroline came, and for a few years I was happy.

Now two more wives had come and gone their way to the churchyard, and there were five little girls younger than I, and Valentine was beginning to make a companion of me because she had to have some confidante, and there was nobody else. She and my father were quarrelling—she despised his mistress.

"Fat slut! Why should *she* run the house?"

"She does it very well," I pointed out reasonably.

"That's well enough, but why does he have to take her to bed with him? Everybody is laughing about Squire Archer and his new love, and laying bets whether he'll marry her or not."

"I'm sure he won't. But I suppose he has to have somebody."

6

"It's perfectly disgusting!" Val flashed. "And pray how does a chit like you know so much about it?"

That was silly. How could I not know? The servants were always doing it—in the barn, the garden, the hall and corners at night—wherever they could find a place. It was hard for them to save enough money to be married, and at night they were locked into separate attics.

For that matter, I spent the first few years of my life sleeping in a truckle bed rolled out from under the big bed where my father slept with his wife or one of the maids. And then there were the animals—you'd have to be blind to live in the country and not know how babies come!

But I did not say so to my sister. I was very proud of her confidence, and had no wish to quarrel. Instead, I imitated her in everything, trying to copy her walk and scornful air, and I was even haughty to poor Minnie, the housekeeper, though she was always kind to me. I thought it would please Valentine, and it did.

She was six years older than I—a tall, fair girl, very proud, carrying her height with a kind of graceful arrogance that I imitated in vain. She was said to greatly resemble her mother, who had been a notable beauty of her day, and my father was proud of her accordingly.

He always boasted so much about Val's beauty and what a good marriage he would make for her, perhaps with a lord, that his neighbours had a good laugh at his expense when she only got a London merchant—not really a gentleman at all, and horridly ugly, though very rich.

But of course my father would never have agreed to such a match if Valentine hadn't burned her cakes in the baking of them, as the saying is.

It was greatly his fault, too. There was only one man in the neighbourhood that he liked. That was Harvey Underhill, who owned Underhill Grange on the other side of Ashton, a large town about five miles from our own little village. There had been Underhills there so long that he was often spoken of as the

7

'Squire' in that part of the country, and, next to my father, he owned more land and better horses than anybody we knew. He had been married young, to a wealthy woman older than himself, and he was a very young man still when she began to ail and at last became a confirmed invalid, scarcely ever leaving her bed. My father was always saying it was a damned shame Harvey and Valentine couldn't make a match of it. Why the devil should *his* wives die and that sickly slut of Harvey's linger on?

All the same, Mrs. Underhill didn't die and my father should have known better than to encourage Val to make eyes at Harvey and spend half her time at the Grange, sitting in the drawing-room or riding with Harvey, while his wife lay upstairs in bed.

Harvey was a tall, good-looking young man with a hot, bold eye. People are always ready to believe scandal about a man whose wife is an invalid——especially a man who looks at other women as Harvey did.

The odd part of it is that although I think my sister liked him better than any man she knew, she didn't give him what he wanted. I didn't believe her when she said so, and neither did anybody else. But later when my brother-in-law told me so, I did believe it, because he was obviously so surprised himself.

Harvey Underhill was just the kind of man my father *would* admire. He could ride a horse half to death hunting, dance all night at a ball, then go off hunting again, without so much as a yawn. He could drink as much as my father, and hold it better. He once killed a groom with his fists, and he had duelled with a lord. And he had that loud, ferocious good humour that men, and some women, seem to admire so much.

My father always thought whatever he wanted was bound to happen. He really persuaded himself Mrs. Underhill would die, so that it didn't matter how much time Val spent with Harvey. And then of course she didn't die, and people began to talk, and one day Harvey's father-in-law arrived. Next Sunday at church Harvey bowed stiffly and hurried out after the Collect so that he shouldn't meet us in the church door. He didn't come to Archfield for a week. And when Val at last went to the Grange, the old man met her and said, "Young woman, tell your father to

8

keep you at home till he finds a husband for you. And this time choose one that isn't taken already."

She was fool enough to tell my father that. I think she hoped he would challenge Mr. Egerton or Harvey to a duel. Instead, for making a fool of him, he beat her with a riding whip till she screamed. It was Minnie who ran in and pulled him off, but Val only hated her the worse for it. She locked herself in her room and wouldn't even let me in. I could hear her crying, and walking up and down.

She begged and begged my father to let her off going to the next Assembly Ball in Ashton, but he wouldn't do it, and I think he was right. One should always outface scandal. If she had stayed at home, they would say she was getting rid of a baby.

So she went, and Mr. Dangerfield, up from London for a few days to visit friends in Ashton, saw her there and danced with her. He called after church on Sunday, was invited to dinner Monday, and proposed on Tuesday. My father accepted him. When he told Val, she said she'd rather die, and he went at her again with the riding whip till she gave in.

After that I think she hated everybody, and Mr. Dangerfield most of all, worse even than Harvey or my father.

Mr. Dangerfield was really very ugly. He was small and pale, with very narrow shoulders, and big protruding eyes the colour of unripe gooseberries. His lips were big, too, and very full and red, and he wetted them continually, so they were always chapped. His face was shaped like a bun, flat and the same size all the way down. It was the colour of a doughy bun too. He had quite a nicely shaped nose but somehow it just seemed to make the rest of him look worse. Val told me he was quite bald—she pushed his wig off once, when he was trying to make love to her.

He was always trying to make love to her, and she never would stand it. She treated him abominably. She made fun of him all the time, and said really cruel things about his appearance, and made him run errands for her like a servant. He pretended not to mind. "High spirits, my dear sir, high spirits!" he said to my father, who called him an ass to his face. He despised Dangerfield,

9

now that he was safely caught, as much as Val did, and said so even more brutally.

"The man's a born cuckold," he told Val. "If you can't manage him and have your fun at the same time you're a bigger fool than he is. I don't know what the devil you're complaining about."

But I didn't agree at all. Val and my father never understood anybody else because they never noticed anybody but themselves, but I had plenty of time to watch Mr. Dangerfield, and I thought Val was rash to treat him in the way she did.

"I don't think he's a fool at all," I told her, "and he'll take it out on you after you're married if you treat him like this now."

Val thought this such a good joke that she told Dangerfield. He seemed to take it as a very good joke too. Next day he told my father he didn't think he cared to take Miss Jenny into his household, as he had at first agreed. I was at a difficult age, he said, and Val wasn't old enough to manage me.

My father was furious. He had hoped to get rid of me by sending me along with Val. He caught me in the hall, pulled me into the library, and gave me a terrific beating. I bit him on the hand, but it didn't help, it just made things worse. And he locked the door, so even Minnie couldn't help me.

Val was sorry for what she had done, and very kind to me, but I think she was a little frightened at finding out Mr. Dangerfield wasn't such a fool after all, and her wedding was only two days off, so she couldn't think much about anything else.

"See what my father did to me, because of you," I said, pulling my dress off my shoulder to show Mr. Dangerfield.

He clicked with his tongue, but when I looked up at him to see if he was sorry I saw that he was staring down the front of my dress instead of the back.

"I had no idea you were such a young lady, Miss Jenny!" he said. His gooseberry eyes stuck out farther than ever. "Your clothes don't do you justice, my dear. Such pretty little white titties!" And before I knew what he was doing, he pushed his hand down my dress and grabbed one of them.

I gave him such a whack in the face that he bit his tongue, and ran away. After that I felt sorrier for Val than ever, and we spent all the last two days locked in her room together.

"I shall die, Jenny, I shall die!" she said, over and over again.

"Kick him hard," I said, showing her where. One of the maids showed me. She did it to a man who caught her in the lane one night, and she said he yelled so that you could hear him a mile away. "I wish you could kick him to death, the stinking beast!"

"I wish I could kill myself, but I'm afraid," Val said, and it was the first time I ever heard her admit to being afraid of anything.

I tried to encourage her, but I thought Mr. Dangerfield so horrid I couldn't think of very much to say that was cheerful.

"I wish I'd bitten out my tongue before I told him what you said." Val was crying worse than ever. "Then I'd have you with me. But he said your eyes were too sharp—he didn't want a spy in his own household. He said you'd be a bad influence."

"Well, it can't be helped now," I said. "And I'm sorry, Val, but I don't think I want to live with him."

"Oh God, how I wish I didn't have to!" she said, despairingly.

But of course she did. They were married very early in the morning. She looked beautiful, and white enough to be dead. He looked worse than ever in a new suit of clothes practically the same colour as his gooseberry eyes. He had a fine new carriage, too, and all the maids said how lucky Miss Val was.

We watched them out of sight. I kept waving, but Val didn't look back. Perhaps he wouldn't let her. I wondered whether he'd wait till London or take her at the first inn they stopped at.

"Now, you little devil," my father said to me, "you can begin to earn your keep. You can take your sister's keys and help Minnie in the house, and if she has trouble with you I'll have your hide, so take care."

Actually I rather enjoyed it. With Val gone, I didn't think about her so much; I was just as sorry for her as ever, but it didn't bother me as much, and I even got to thinking perhaps she was having a good time in London. I liked Minnie, and I didn't mind

11

learning how to manage the house. It gave me something to do that really seemed to matter. I always hated needlework and tinkling on the spinet, but I liked working with Minnie in the still-room and the linen room.

Minnie was a good gossip too, and told me many things. She was very sensible about men. She said she was sorry for Val but Mr. Dangerfield would probably soon tire of her and then it wouldn't be so bad.

"I hear the ladies in London all have fine lovers, and Miss Val's such a beauty she'll surely have the best of any. But she'd better learn not to make rows with men. They don't like it and you never get your way, unless they are poor weak things."

"How *do* you get your way, Minnie?"

"Oh, there's lots of ways! Wait till you've got the man in bed and coax it out of him there. Or feed him and see he's got plenty of wine, and sit on his knee. Or pretend you're sickly and can't give him what he wants till he gives you whatever it is *you* want. Oh, there's lots of ways! As long as he thinks he's master, a man'll give you almost anything."

Helping Minnie, I didn't have as much time to run outdoors or gypsy about with the stable boys as I used to do, but now and then, when the sun shone and I could hear the cuckoos calling from way over by Ashton Wood, I'd run off for the day. Minnie never told my father, but she used to warn me I'd get into trouble romping with the rough boys.

"One of them will tumble you on your back in a ditch some day, Miss Jenny, and where will you be then?"

"In a ditch," I said pertly. "Oh, Minnie, don't be foolish! They're just boys!"

"It's the boys that are the hot ones," she said, wisely. "Well, do as you please, miss, but take care!"

I was angry at what she said. It seemed to spoil my pleasure. Now and then, when one of the boys would say something, or look at my front, I'd remember her words, and then I'd stay in the house for a while. But I didn't really believe any of the boys would treat me like that. They had their village girls, and they were afraid of my father besides.

12

One fine day I'd been working with the maids in the dairy, churning butter. We got a fine lot of it, and I put some on a plate to take to the house for dinner that day, while the maids shaped the rest for market.

Running through the stable yard, I saw the head groom step out of a stall and beckon to me.

"Look here, Miss Jenny!" he said. His voice was excited.

I thought one of the dogs had littered. I put down the plate of butter in the shade and followed John Groom into the stall. It was quite dark, and the other men were out, exercising the horses.

"Where are the puppies, John?" I asked, peering into the gloom. "I don't see any."

"Oh, I have something better than that to show you, miss!" he said. His voice was queer, and I turned round. He had the front of his breeches open.

"Don't you dare touch me!" I said. I could hardly speak; I couldn't believe what was happening.

"Oh, come on, miss!" he said, trying to make a joke of it. "Don't be upset. I thought you might like to see what a man looked like. Young misses often do."

It was so funny, I could hardly help laughing, and yet I was frightened, and angry too.

"I'll scream! I'll tell my father!"

"You do, and I'll tell him about the way you go off ramshackling with those boys!" he said. "You're not so shy with *them*!"

He was too absurd, standing there arguing, with his breeches gaping. I tried not to look, but I couldn't quite help it. The boys used to show me when they were younger, but not recently.

And then he tried to grab me. I remember wrestling with him, and the funny part is that all I could think of was how wet and nasty the straw would be to lie on. The next thing, somebody gave John an almighty kick in the behind that sent him staggering away from me, and there stood Minnie with the plate of butter in her hand.

She called him names I'd never heard before, and then she took

13

me by the wrist and jerked me out of there, and took me in the house. I began to laugh and cry, trying to tell her about it, and she dosed me with my father's best brandy.

"The nasty toad! He'll be off the place by tonight. You'll see! Your father will have his hide for this."

"For what?" my father said, stamping into the kitchen with his dogs at his heels as usual. Then he saw me drinking the best brandy, and for a while he cursed and yelled so that Minnie couldn't make herself heard.

Finally he calmed down enough to let her tell what had happened. He didn't take it at all as I expected. I thought he'd probably fall on me and beat me, and then rush out and flay John.

Instead, he looked at me sideways, scowling, and said, "Is that all? Hell, she's probably been in the straw before!"

"Master!" Minnie cried, scandalised. "What a thing to say! And she just seventeen years old!"

"Hell, her mother was fifteen when she went in the hay with me," he said, speaking in that ugly sneering tone with which he always did speak of my mother. "And she was ready, too. This one is another bitch. You can see it to look at her. John might as well have her as anybody."

"Sir," Minnie said, in a queer shocked voice, "you are a bad man."

And she marched me upstairs and put me to bed, to get over my fright and the strong dose of brandy. What is more, she locked me in and took the key, while I slept. After that, I always had one of the maids to sleep with me.

"Guard yourself, Miss Jenny," Minnie said. "Your father hates you, God forgive him, and it's my belief he'd as soon give you to a groom as anybody. I'm not saying he put John up to it, for such wickedness ought to be beyond any father, but John's still here, I notice, and not a bit ashamed of himself either."

She shook her head. "This is no place for you, miss. But while you're here, don't you go about any more without one of us goes with you."

So I didn't, but it was very wearisome, and I couldn't forget my father's hatred of me, and his contempt. He was always saying that my mother was a bitch and that I was no get of his. I don't think anybody believed him, but I sometimes wondered, because he hated me so.

One day there was a thundering knock on the front door. As the maids were all busy, I ran to answer it. I was in a plain gown with a great apron over it, and my hair tied up with a ribbon, so I was cast into great confusion by seeing a handsome young gentleman waiting at the door.

He took me for one of the maids, of course, and chucked me under the chin, smiling. He was dressed in a beautiful riding suit, and smelled of scent. I had never seen anybody so handsome— tall and fair with bright blue eyes—but somehow he looked familiar, and that puzzled me.

"Well, my dear, aren't you going to let me in?" he smiled. "Where's my father "

And then of course I realised it was my half-brother, Neal. I had not seen him for years, not since I was a child. He and my father quarrelled like a pair of tomcats, and as soon as my brother was eighteen and came into his own money, from his mother's family, he left home and went to London. He was only a boy then, weedy, with a bad skin, rustic and clumsy. No wonder I hadn't recognised this handsome gallant! He did not look at all like the boy I remembered. It was his strong resemblance to Val that had puzzled me.

He mistook my surprise for shyness and kissed me, lightly. It was odd, being kissed by a handsome strange young man, even if it *was* my brother.

I blushed—I could feel it all over my face—and he chuckled.

"What's your name, child?" he asked. "And what is a pretty innocent thing like you doing in my father's house?"

"Oh, Neal, don't you know me?" I said, laughing, and blushing still more. "I'm Jenny."

"Jenny!" he said. "Good Lord!" He tossed his hat and whip on the long bench that ran along one side of the hall, and took me by the shoulders, turning my face to the light from the door. "So it is!" he said, marvelling. "I should have known you by

15

those red curls. But you've got so pretty, and nearly grown-up. Little Jenny!"

And then his face grew suddenly black as thunder, so that I was frightened, thinking he saw something ugly or amiss in me.

"God damn and blast my father to everlasting hell," he said, deliberately. His fingers on my shoulders hurt me with their pressure. "A lovely, innocent thing like you———!"

I suppose he saw then that he was frightening me, for his hands relaxed their grip, and he tried to smile.

"Sweet sister, don't be frightened! I am not angry with you, only with myself. I should have come before. But I thought of you still as a baby." He put his arm around my shoulders and began to walk down the hall, looking around him. "Same old place," he said. "Good Lord, I daresay it has not changed these fifty years. Same old smell!"

"I think it's all those animals," I said, looking up at the rows of animal heads decorating both sides of the wide hall, tribute to the bloody skills of Archers long dead.

He laughed. "How I used to hate them when I was a little fellow! They frightened me. All those glass eyes—the candle-light used to shine in them and make them seem to be alive. They'll come down when I'm master here! All the same, it's not a bad old house, if my father were out of it."

"He hates me," I said, sorrowfully.

His arm tightened around my shoulders. "He hates everything that is good and innocent. Never mind, Jenny, I shall take you away."

"Oh, Neal, if you only would!" I said, looking up at him adoringly. He was tall, like Val, and like my father too, but where my father was bulky and massive, Neal was slim as a girl. For his journey, he wore his own hair, clubbed back at the neck with a black ribbon in the new fashion, which I had never seen before, and which I thought mighty handsome and becoming. It was fairer even than Val's, silver hair without the sunny lights, and to me he appeared handsome and awe-inspiring as an angel.

"Of course I shall," he said masterfully. "I should have done

16

it long ago. You shall come and keep house for me in London, and I'll find a good husband for you when you are older."

I could not speak for the bliss of thinking about it. I cuddled up to him, and kissed his hand, at which he laughed, a little embarrassed.

"No, no, Jenny! You ought to hate me for neglecting you so long. The truth is, I hoped never to come home again till my father had been carried out feet first."

I was a little shocked, but I could not think of blaming him; I knew how brutal my father used to be to him.

"I was near to coming down to kill him when I saw the man he married Val to," my brother went on. "Good Lord! *My* sister to be married to a stinking City merchant. And I used to think he was fond of Val."

"Do you see her? How is she?" I asked eagerly.

"I go there sometimes. He sets a good table and has good wine. She seems well enough. Dressed to kill—he don't stint her anything, I'll say that for the fellow. They see lots of people. Not the right sort, but what can you expect, with a husband like that?"

"I was going to stay with them, but he wouldn't have me and now I'm so glad!" I said, clinging to him as though he might vanish if I let go.

"Oh," he smiled, "we'll do better for you than that."

I understood the source of my brother's anger when I found out that Minnie had sent for him on my account, telling him quite plainly why he ought to come. Of course she could not read or write, but she went to the parson and he wrote the letter for her. He expressed himself as greatly shocked by what she had to say, but she insisted on his putting it all down. As she told me after-wards, she thought it might be as well the parson should know what was going on. Not that he would ever dare interfere with my father, but he might tell others who would.

This was a very bold thing for Minnie to do. My father would have thrown her straight out of the house if he had dreamed she had anything to do with it. But my brother, to protect her,

17

pretended he had come at Val's request to bring me to her for a visit.

My father did not come home until late—after dark. Neal whiled the day away with Minnie and myself, putting all the maids into a flutter with his handsome face and gallant ways. He seemed quite taken with Minnie, and she could not dote enough on him. My father was by no means so well pleased to see him, but he had had a good day's sport with his gun and was in a good humour—for him.

So, having heard Neal's explanation, he graciously gave his consent to my departure by saying, "Take the little slut, and welcome."

Men are such damned fools! Instead of accepting this as part of my father's ordinary manner of speech, and securing the consent he wanted, my brother chose to resent his language on my behalf. He rebuked my father, my father swore at him, my brother swore back, and in ten minutes they were yelling and shouting at one another so that they could be heard all over the countryside.

It ended with my father ordering Neal out of the house, and my brother assuring him he would never again set foot in it till he came there as its master. He then repeated that he intended to take me with him, at which my father instantly said he would not part with me and Neal might go to the devil.

Of course there was nothing my brother could do. He had no legal power over me till my father should be dead. He flung out of the house in a rage, and galloped off to spend the night at the village inn, while my father rushed upstairs and threw all Neal's clothes out of the window.

Neal's servant gathered up all of them eventually and followed his master to the inn, while my father went raging to Minnie to tell her all about it. As she told me next day, she quaked for fear my brother, in his fury, had let slip his source of information. But Neal was not so indiscreet as that, and my father never knew.

When I heard what had happened, I wept with dismay. Neal was gone, my father now determined to keep me out of spite, and life seemed so hopeless I was ready to throw myself in Ashton Pond.

Minnie told me not to give up hope. "Your Papa is obstinate as a donkey," said she, "but your brother has plenty of Old Nick in him too, and I daresay he'll manage to get hold of you somehow. Don't you fret!"

I did fret, but not for long, for one of the servants brought me a note secretly from Neal, bidding me slip away if I could and travel up to London with him tomorrow evening. If I could not, he wrote, he would return to London by himself and think out some scheme to get hold of me. I was not to despair, but to guard myself and stay close to Minnie.

Of course I immediately determined to break out of the house and go with him, and I enlisted Minnie's aid.

I don't think I can ever remember seeing my father cold sober, but he was not usually drunk before midday, and very seldom roaring drunk till after dinner, when he had finished his second bottle and occasionally begun a third. If he had a boon companion, like Harvey Underhill, he would drink himself under the table and sleep there until the menservants dragged him out and poured water over his head in the morning. If he were alone, he was usually able to get himself to bed, or at least with only Minnie's assistance.

Minnie calculated that my brother would not begin his journey till the moon rose, which that night would be about ten. My father was seldom in bed before that hour, but she promised to do what she could to make him hopelessly drunk early, so that I could slip out without his missing me till next day.

Ordinarily the house was locked up about nine, when all work was finished. The servants gathered in the kitchen for supper, and then went to bed, the men and women being locked into separate lofts to sleep. My father, like many lecherous men, was very strict as to the morals of others. Consequently the servants had become wonderfully adept at making the most of every few minutes of leisure, and of every private nook and cranny a big old house like Archfield afforded, and I do not know what my father's scheme accomplished except to send him to bed with the virtuous knowledge that he was the only person in it enjoying himself at that hour.

The keys to the sleeping lofts and to the outer doors had never been given to Minnie. They were kept by my father, and given in his absence, or incapacity, to his own servant, who acted as spy on the rest of the household and could be trusted not to help in any deceits.

I had to get out of the house, therefore, before the locking up took place at nine.

Minnie was very clever about her plans. She ordered a dinner of salt fish, cured ham, pork pie and rhubarb. My father washed this down with his second bottle, and soon afterwards found himself so thirsty that he opened a third. Minnie, contrary to her usual custom, sat down to take a glass with him and amused him so well with her gossip that he got deep into the third bottle. When he rose to lock the house, as the clocks struck nine, he abruptly sat down again, and shouted for Alfred, his servant.

I, with a bundle of clothes under my cloak, was hiding in the shadow of the stairs. I heard Alfred come down and go into the dining-room to get the keys. Until now there had been a constant to-ing and fro-ing of servants, till I began to despair. But at my father's bellow for Alfred there was a concerted rush towards the kitchen, so as not to be late for supper, and I took my courage in my hands and tiptoed to the front door.

There was one terrible moment when it squeaked on its hinges and I looked round in terror, expecting to see Alfred and hear him call my father. But my father was having trouble getting the keys out of his pocket, and Alfred was delayed.

I slipped out, pulling the door closed after me. Not daring to cross the lawn for fear Alfred might look out, I crouched in the bushes by the front door. Presently I heard him shooting the bolts, turning the key, and putting up the chain, and then the sound of his receding footsteps. Instantly, I slipped out of the bushes and ran across the lawn and down the avenue, turning right, outside the gates, into the lane which led to the village.

It would be lying to say I wasn't frightened. I had heard so many horrid stories from the servants—all about ghosts, and murderers, and sinister beggars, and the Lord knows what not—that my teeth chattered with fright to be out in this dangerous night by myself. A glimpse of something white made me jump a foot, and I nearly dropped dead when an owl suddenly shot out of the bushes and sailed over my head.

But I kept thinking about Neal, and London, and seeing Val again, and about how awful it would be if I had to go back! and I kept on steadfastly, running as long as I could, and then walking fast. Being so frightened kept me from thinking about how odd it was that I was leaving home like this, and probably never would come back here again. I was glad in a way, and in a way I wasn't. But mostly all I could think about was getting to the inn and being with Neal.

Once the lights of the village were in sight, I stopped being frightened and began to be hopeful and excited. I set off running again, and arrived at the inn so breathless I could only pant out Neal's name.

The serving man looked at me queerly. He was on his way from the tap room with a tray of mugs filled with beer, and he stood holding it and staring at me.

"Mr. Archer, miss?" he said, stupidly. "Whatever do you want with him?"

I stamped my foot at him. I knew what he must be thinking. Of course they didn't know me here; I had never before been inside the doors.

"Never mind! I want him. Where is he?"

"Why, miss," the fool said stolidly, "he's gone to London."

"*Gone!*" I cried. "Oh, no—he can't be gone—he *can't*! Without me! When did he go?"

"About twenty minutes ago, miss," the man said, grinning, I suppose, at my apparent desertion.

And with that, I sat down on a bench and burst into tears. Twenty minutes!

The landlord came into the hall and asked, "What's this?" I looked up, the tears running down my face, and he exclaimed, "Good Lord, it's Miss Archer!" He turned on the fellow with the beer mugs, now gaping at me in astonishment, and told him to get about his business. To me he said, "Come into a private room, miss. Shall I get you a glass of cordial?"

I got up and stumbled after him. He was very kind. He made me sit in a comfortable chair and fetched me a glass of cordial with his own hands.

I sipped the cordial and said, sobbingly, "I c-can't pay you. I haven't any money."

"You're most kindly welcome, miss," the landlord assured me. He got plenty of business from my father. "I'm sorry you missed your brother; he was looking for you earlier. To be sure, he never thought you'd come as late as this!"

"I c-couldn't get away. Oh, I wish I were dead!"

The landlord considered me in silence for a minute. Then he said slowly, "Was it your brother's plan to take you to London, miss, may I ask?"

I hesitated. He said, encouragingly, "You may tell me, Miss Archer. I shan't run to your father, you may be sure."

So I told him: how my brother and father had quarrelled, how my father had at first agreed and then refused, and that I had run away to join Neal.

"But if you did go with him, the Squire would only follow you to London and take you back," he pointed out.

I shook my head. "No, he wouldn't take that much trouble. He hates me; he wants to get rid of me; he would be glad never to see me again. But he'll stop me now if he can, to spite Neal."

"But you think if you were with Mr. Archer in London, the Squire'd let you bide?"

"Yes, or if I were with my sister. Mrs. Dangerfield, you know."

"I daresay Mrs. Dangerfield would be very glad to see you again, miss," the man said civilly. He considered, while I finished my cordial. It gave me a sort of courage, and I gazed hopefully at Mr. Jones.

"Look here, Miss Archer," he said at last, evidently making up his mind. "Your father is no man to cross, and at best it's a bad business coming between a father and daughter. But I've heard

22

tales of how things go on in that house and, if you'll pardon my saying so, a young lady like you is better out of it."

By now I was really hopeful. I sat forward in excitement, fixing my eyes on him, and he seemed to get more enthusiastic when he saw how eagerly I hung on every word.

"The nearest coach stop is at Ashton," he said. "Would you be afraid to travel by coach?"

"Oh no! Why should I be?"

"Well, it's not thought very genteel, miss, and there are sometimes rough characters to be met with. Still, you could go in charge of the coachman, and you'd be safe enough, if you didn't mind the roughness."

"I don't, I don't, but I haven't any money!"

"Well, miss, I can lend you that. Your brother can pay me back. I'd send you properly in a chaise, miss, but if I did that your Pa would be sure to hear of it and there'd be the devil and all to pay with him."

"Oh no, I don't care about a chaise at all. The coach will do if only you will be so good and kind as to lend me the money! Oh, I shall bless you all my life!"

"Tut, miss," he said, smiling, "there's no need to be all that obliged. Only be sure not to tell your Papa who helped you off, and that will do me."

"Never; never; I'll die first!"

He shook his head at me doubtfully. "I doubt you're too young and enthusiastic, miss, to go wandering around the country alone. 'Tisn't proper, that I know."

"But I'll soon be in London. And there I will be quite safe, you know. Only how am I to get to Ashton?"

"There's a carter in the public room this minute," Mr. Jones said, reflectively. "He'll leave at moonrise and he could drop you at the coach stop in Ashton. He's a close-mouthed chap, and married, with six children; you'll be safe enough with him. The coach goes through Ashton about midnight, and there'll be others waiting for it no doubt. You'll not have a long wait in any case."

After all the landlord's warning, my coach journey to London

23

was quiet and uneventful. Nobody treated me roughly or made improper advances. The carter—who never spoke a word from beginning to end except "Evening, miss; good-bye, miss; you're welcome"—set me down at the coach stop in Ashton. There was a couple with a sleepy child waiting there. They were very civil to me, though obviously curious, and I was not at all afraid in their company.

When the coach came, I paid for my ticket, and one of the inside passengers offered to ride on top and let me have his seat. I thanked him very warmly; he said, "Not at all," and paid me no further attention. I sat between an old country woman with a basket of eggs, going to visit her married son in London, and a fat snoring gentleman who slept all the way with the head of his cane boring into his stomach.

It was exceedingly warm and close in the coach, and I soon got drowsy myself, and slept in spite of my excitement and the dreadful roughness of the road. The sun in my face woke me, and as I yawned and stretched I realised that we were now rattling over paved streets. We were in London.

I was frantic to see out, but was so squeezed in between my fat companions that I could see little, and had to contain myself in patience until we reached the coaching inn, drawing up with a flourish in the courtyard.

It was then about eight in the morning, and the place was a bustle of activity in which I felt forlorn and lost.

The fat old gentleman woke as we stopped, observed my dismay, and gallantly handed me out of the coach, begging me to do him the favour of breakfasting with him at the inn. He seemed kind and fatherly, and I was very hungry. As I hesitated what to do, the coachman came up to me, touching his beaver with the butt of his whip.

"I ask your pardon, miss, but I saw you get on in Ashton. Are you travelling alone"

I said, "Yes," while the fat gentleman glared at him.

"And is there nobody to meet you, miss?"

"No, they don't know I'm coming, but I have a brother and sister in London."

24

"Then, miss, if I may make so bold, let me order you a chair and you go at once to where they live. A coaching inn is no place for a young genteel female."

I agreed meekly. The old gentleman, who was probably very innocent and very kind, stumped off in a huff. Presently the coachman secured a decent sort of sedan chair for me—the first time I had ever ridden in one, though I had occasionally seen them in Ashton—and gave the address to the man. I had wits enough to fee him for his pains, and he nodded kindly and told the men to take good care of me.

I had to give my brother-in-law's address, for I had not the faintest idea where Neal lived. The men grunted, for, as I later learned, it was half-way across London, but took up the poles, sending me lurching first forward and then back, and I went jolting off, thrilled to bursting with the success of my adventure, and lost in the wonder of being carried through the streets of London. I used to think Ashton a great place, especially at fair time, but Lord! how London did eclipse anything I ever heard or dreamed of.

One cannot see much from the windows of a hired sedan chair, whose glass is all dirty and smoked from constant exposure to the city's horrid sooty fogs. I saw enough, however, to feel that I had not lived in vain if I had lived to see London. Even so early, the streets were crowded with vehicles and people. There were vendors everywhere, crying their wares in harsh husky voices. Servants were washing steps clean of muck, not caring at all how they splashed the passer-by. Sweeps drove their grimy little apprentices before them, crying for "Chimneys to clean!" One old woman flower-seller trotted beside my chair for a long distance, holding up a bunch of violets and grinning at me hopefully. I kept shaking my head and making gestures of despair, but she trotted along like a racehorse, and was still grinning when she gave up. I would gladly have bought some, but discovered I had not the faintest idea how to stop my bearers or open the sedan chair.

It was truly an odd feeling to be thus carted along by strange men through a strange city, without any power of stopping, starting or directing my own course. It seemed hours before we arrived at Dangerfield's house, and I suspect that they did bring me the long way round in hope of increasing their fee. If so, they had their pains for nothing, for I had scarcely a penny beyond the sum for which the coachman had providently compacted.

When I opened my purse and showed them there was no more money, the men finally went off grumbling. I rang the bell and asked for Mrs. Dangerfield. A staring but civil maidservant took me upstairs. It was as easy as that.

My first thought was that Val looked much older, though so beautiful. In her loose dressing-gown I could see that she was breeding, and wondered if she were glad. Mr. Dangerfield was just as horrid as ever. He kept asking me if no one had molested me in the coach, and expressing his concern that I should travel in such a shocking way.

"Well, no harm has come of it, so why make such a riot?" Val said impatiently. She treated him in the same way as she used to, and that was a relief to me. I thought perhaps he'd managed to make her afraid of him somehow.

"It's enough to ruin Miss Jenny's reputation," Mr. Dangerfield said solemnly, shaking his head. "Your brother will be wild when he hears of it."

And sure enough he was, scolding till he made me cry, when he was kind to me again. Val watched impatiently. She was dressed for the day by the time Neal arrived and in her hoops you couldn't see anything except that she was a little sway-backed when she walked.

"You men are all alike," she said impatiently. "You think no woman can be safe with any other man."

"We know ourselves, sister," Neal said, now in a high good humour again. "I would think poorly of myself if I saw a pretty morsel like my sweet sister Jenny all unprotected, and did not try to have a bite out of her."

Val turned away with a shrug. "It's a pretty thing to be a gentleman," she said, disdainfully. "You are too much with your rakish friends, brother."

26

This naturally did not please Neal. He pointedly ignored her, asking, "Now, sweet Jenny, would you rather stay here with Val and her stinking cit, or come keep house for me?"

I looked hesitantly at Val. I did not want to offend her, but I would much rather live with Neal.

She gave an exasperated sigh. "Don't be a fool, brother! Or do you plan to hire a companion for her? A pretty reputation she'll have left, after a week in an establishment like yours!

"She'll be the only *mistress* in it, anyhow," Neal retorted, but he yielded, to my dismay. "I don't want to bring in some old woman to keep you company, child," he explained kindly. "That would sink all our pleasure. But Val is right—a bachelor establishment is no place for a young female. You'd better stay here with her, but I'll come often to see you."

"That's more than you ever do for me," Val said jealously. "I see Jenny is your new fancy!"

"Isn't she a pretty, adorable, innocent thing? That lovely, lovely hair and eyes blue as speedwells!"

"Her eyes are green," Val said, coldly. "As for her hair—red has been out of fashion since Queen Elizabeth's day and well you know it. It's lucky we can powder it—Jenny, are you *never* going to stop eating? You'll be fat in no time if you eat like that."

"I haven't had any breakfast," I explained, while Neal exclaimed:

"Fat! Jenny! A blasphemy! She's a sprite made out of fire and moonlight."

I enjoyed Neal's compliments, but did not take them seriously, for I saw they were chiefly to tease Val.

When we were alone, Val was very kind to me, in spite of her shrewish ways with the men. She had her maid Betty cut and dress my hair and take in one of her gowns to fit me. I hardly knew myself afterwards, and fancied I looked very elegant, Mr. Dangerfield soon disillusioned me.

"This will never do," he said, surveying me. "You and your

sister are too unlike, my dear," he said to Val. "What suits you makes Miss Jenny look like an elf in hoops."

I discovered there was one thing that Mr. Dangerfield knew about, and that was dress. He always looked horridly himself, but that was the fault of his Maker and not his tailor. He knew all about colours and materials and style. It was his business, of course. He owned one of the largest silk warehouses in London, and prided himself on selling to the most beautiful and fashionable women in society. He was quite different when he talked on this subject. Even Val listened to him, and took his advice. He taught her just what she ought to wear, and how best to have her gowns cut, and I will say for him that he stinted her in nothing. It gratified him that his wife should dress as handsomely and look as beautiful as any lady in London.

Nothing would do now but we must go down to the warehouse at once and buy me a new wardrobe. Val was nothing loath and I was naturally eager. For a few minutes I really felt quite grateful to Mr. Dangerfield. Then, as he handed me into the carriage, he tried to put his hand on me, and after that I hated him again. He never could let a woman alone, but must always be eyeing and feeling her. His hand was perpetually in Val's bosom or under her skirts.

She endured this with a sort of weary contempt, as though an insect crawled upon her that she was too indifferent to crush. I think he liked this. He was always looking round secretly at me to see if his fondling her would arouse me. It was not ten minutes before I thought him more odious than ever.

In his warehouse, however, he was all business, handing Val and myself about with great solicitude. I fancy he was a tyrannical master—the serving-men seemed very much afraid of him and jumped if he only looked their way.

But I never saw anybody quite so bold or so right about fashion and fabrics.

Light silks and muslins for me, he said, all pure bright colours —primrose, silver and green, and lute-strings striped in gold and lavender, and brocades very soft and fine with a small delicate flower pattern. He would not let me have any material that was heavy or ornate. He shuddered at the very thought of red upon me, but allowed me to choose a delicate muslin the shade of a pale wild rose, which he said becomingly matched my cheeks.

He ordered material enough for half a dozen gowns—morning wear, riding dress, *négligée*, and formal dress. As I was virtually destitute, Val also set aside plenty of linen for my body clothes, and several pairs of fine stockings. We had to go elsewhere for stays, shoes, ribbons, fans, etc., but at the end of the day they had bespoke for me a very complete wardrobe, and I was quite out of breath with expectation.

My body linen was promised for next day, but it would be several days before my gowns were finished. In the meantime, I would have to draw upon Val's wardrobe, whether suitable or not.

Mr. Dangerfield did not confine his generosity to me. He chose a magnificent brocade of red patterned in a leafy gold for Val, with an underskirt of white satin. She was tall enough and fair enough to carry such clothes, for which I envied her.

Dangerfield even ordered a flowered velvet made up as a waist-coat for Neal, though Val shrugged and said he would not like it.

He was not a stingy man. He poured out money and presents on those around him. But I couldn't help thinking that it was less because he wanted to make others happy than that he liked them to be under an obligation to him. I did not like the proprietary airs he assumed towards me with each new purchase for my wardrobe.

It was strange that Val wasn't afraid of him, when I was, but then I think she never saw people very clearly. She didn't see that if he let her treat him as she did, it was because it gave him some sort of horrid pleasure. If it hadn't, he would have stopped it soon enough.

In the next few days I met most of the people who frequented the Dangerfield house, and I must confess that at first I was quite dazzled by them. They talked perpetually of Lady This and the Duchess of That, tattling so much scandal peppered with high-sounding names that I supposed they themselves must be in the first rank of fashion.

But when I ventured to say this to Neal, he nearly split himself with derision.

"These people! Lord, child, there isn't a decent name among them, except one or two of the men, and *they* only come because Val is handsome and Dangerfield sets a good table. If they had anything better to do, you wouldn't see them here."

"But, Neal——! I'm sure you must be wrong. Lady Townshend—they called her by her first name."

"Yes, and that's the worst-bred thing you can do. Always remember that. You ought always to call Val and me 'Sister' and 'Brother', except when we're alone. And never let anybody call you Jenny." He burst out laughing. "Called her by name! Lord, that's a good one. Do you know the King because you can call him by name? As for Lady Townshend, she's the worst rake in London, that's true, but she hasn't fallen so low as to let any of Val's friends inside her door. She only sins with the *ton*. Of course it's a true story. Everybody in London is telling it."

I was abashed by his scorn. "If they are so vulgar, why does Val see them?"

"Because she can't do better," he said gruffly, abruptly sobered. "It's one thing to be Miss Archer. The Archers are good enough for anybody, I hope, even though we haven't a title—on our father's side anyhow. But it's another thing to be Mrs. Dangerfield. He's not a gentleman. He's nothing but a City merchant, whose grandfather sold ribbons from a hand-barrow, and all his money won't wipe him clean enough for the *bon ton*. The people you see here are all third rate and worse. Poor Val!"

"But you, Neal?"

"That's different. I'll be Squire Archer myself some day. We're landed gentry, and we've never been anything else. Too good for this rackety crew!" He looked troubled. "You ought not to stay here, Jenny. It's better than home, but not good enough. You'll never marry decently if you stay here. That's why it's so important for a girl, especially——"

He stopped short, but I knew what he was thinking. A girl in my position could not afford to take chances. My father might be Squire Archer, but my sister was married to a City man, and my mother was only pretty Mollie Lake, daughter of a farmer who touched his forelock to the gentry when he met them, even on his own land.

I did not resent the reminder. I had scarcely been in London a week, but already I saw that it was the way of the world. As far as Society went, you were either *in* or *out*. If in, you were virtually unassailable. It did not matter how outrageously Lady Townshend might rake it about town, she would be courted and accepted as Lady Townshend still.

If you were out, hardly even a brilliant marriage could bring you in. I stood dangerously close to that chasm marked 'out'. And in the society I now frequented, I would not find the good marriage to make me safely 'in'. It was like a child's game. You could easily, if you had spirit, make it seem ridiculous. But all same, the stakes were high and the penalties severe.

"I shouldn't mind marrying a City man," I said, cautiously, so as not to vex Neal. "One who was nice himself, you know— not like Dangerfield. Some of them are gentlemen."

"Certainly," Neal said. He prided himself on his broad-mindedness. "But don't you see, child, *they* want to marry lords' daughters. And nowadays, when money is everything, plenty of them are doing it, too."

"Yes, I see," I said, fascinated by the rules of the game. Of course a man who stood nearly if not quite 'out' would need a girl more securely 'in' than I.

"Of course what I ought to do," Neal said, pursuing his own thoughts, "is arrange to have you live with me."

"If only you were married!" I said, wistfully.

But he interrupted with a vehement protest against any thought so awful. My father had been married so early and often it seemed strange to think of Neal as nearly five-and-twenty and not married yet. Perhaps it was seeing so much of it that had given Neal such a distaste for it.

Once the glamour of Val's friends had worn off and I had begun to see them through Neal's disillusioning eyes, I soon perceived for myself that many of them were certainly very vulgar. The men were better than the women, on the whole, enjoying as they did better education and a broader experience of life. Some of the women were so common and talked so bawdy I could scarcely believe my ears. The servants at Archfield used to talk rudely enough, but it was with an open, guffawing vulgarity that might sometimes offend but never was unnatural. The whispering, sniggering nastiness of Val's friends was something new to me.

I call them her 'friends'. Actually, her relationship with most of them was curious. She moved like a queen among them, fair, proud and indifferent. She had a queen's own gift for being deaf to what she did not want to hear. Dispensing dinners, teas, suppers, music and cards with indifference to them all, she quarrelled with none, remaining totally aloof. Very often, I think, she did not even hear the conversation around her, retreating into her own thoughts as she used to do when she was a girl and anything displeased or distressed her.

If any of them approached her too familiarly, she froze them with a scorn so absolute that they hardly even recognised it, only retreating confused to mutter that "Mrs. Dangerfield carries herself so mighty high there is no saying where you are with her." I could have told them that they were *nowhere* with her; she hardly even remembered their names between one visit and the next.

Scarcely any of them liked her—any of the women, that is— but they were all afraid of her, and in that society fear was virtually the only emotion which could compel respect.

Me they made much of at first, while I was still of a mind to be impressed by their airs and graces. As I grew less impressionable, they liked me less, and left me more alone. I am not of a quarrelsome disposition, however, and as I could not possibly emulate Val's haughtiness, they preferred me and consequently I had to endure a good deal of the impertinent familiarity she escaped. I did not think I ought to quarrel with my host's friends, so often held my tongue when I would rather have spoken out. Val's manner towards them all astonished me a good deal, but I couldn't help admiring it when I saw how effective it was. Neal's treat-

32

ment of them was much like hers but as a handsome young man he was pardoned almost everything, by the women at least.

Certainly it was not the most agreeable society in which I could have found myself. I often sighed for my old dreams of the great world, in which all the women were gracious and lovely, and all the men gallant and well-bred.

The same taint—the outward luxury and inward dirt—permeated Dangerfield's house itself. It was big and new, a tall narrow house after the London fashion, built in a section of the city just coming into fashion, especially among rich merchants like himself. (The fact that a lord lived only two doors away was supposed to cast some special virtue on our location, though he never spoke to any of us, and snarled if anybody dared speak to him.) The house was luxuriously furnished and, be it said to Dangerfield's credit, in good taste. There were plenty of servants; too many, indeed, for they had an excess of leisure in which to gossip and spy on their master and mistress. I was often astounded at their rude pert ways. They openly despised their master because he was not a gentleman. Val they disliked but feared, and she could have ordered them much better had she cared to take the trouble.

Loath as I was to find fault with her in anything, I could not help seeing she was a bad housekeeper, and allowed conditions to exist which Minnie would never have endured for a moment. Though she was so delicate and proud in her personal habits, she was curiously blind to the sluttish disorder—slicked over sometimes but never really cleaned—which prevailed in her house. So long as she was herself clean and beautiful, and her comfort not interfered with, she was oblivious to the horrors in the corners.

I was not. I had been too well taught by Minnie. I would gladly have played housekeeper for Val, but she was jealous of her prerogative as mistress of the house. And I daresay the servants would not have obeyed me, even had she been willing to turn over her authority to me. Nevertheless, at first I tried to effect some reforms, but very soon received such broad hints to desist that I gave over and let them all do as they would.

Oddly enough, I think Dangerfield was the only one who

33

appreciated my attempts. But he showed his appreciation by criticism of Val, and I would not listen.

I myself was given a pretty, tiny bedroom just above Val's, high up in the house. From its window I had a fine view of London and never tired of staring out at the stretching sea of roofs and chimneys and pointed gables, the great dome of St. Paul's rising in the distance, a round unchanging cloud upon the horizon.

It was a great change from the country to which I was used, but I liked it. It excited me. I always thought people preferable to things, and surely there were more people gathered together under the roofs of London than anywhere else in the world? I did not believe there could be, or ever had been, a greater city in the world. I used to hang at my window by the hour, wondering about all those other people under those many roofs, inventing stories for them and longing to know the true ones. It all seemed new and charming to me, turning a smiling face.

"We must make up a frolic for your sister, my dear," Mr. Dangerfield said to Val one day. He had come home to dine and found quite a party of acquaintances to sit down with him. It was the usual crowd—Mr. Collins, another merchant; Fred Hays, a young attorney; Mrs. Morrow, a vulgar good-natured neighbour, and her nieces, Miss Andrews and Miss Kitty Andrews, daughters of a wealthy brewer. They had brought with them a young man who seemed to be courting either or both of them impartially. His name was Gentry, and, as Val wickedly whispered, it seemed the only genteel thing about him. He was dreadfully common, it was true, but seemed good-natured and kind, which gave him, in my eyes, a decided advantage over most of his companions. Neal, by the by, was not of the party.

Dangerfield's proposal for a frolic was warmly seconded by his guests. They were always restless and in want of occupation. The women, especially, perpetually were yawning and wishing for something new to do. Londoners born, no place of pleasure was novel to them, but the idea that everything would be new to me gave the suggestion a fillip, and there were quite heated disputes about which spot to choose.

34

Mr. Dangerfield professed to leave it to his guests, but I noted that it was his choice, as usual, which was finally fixed on. He thought Miss Archer would like Ranelagh because it was both smart and genteel, and Ranelagh was then found to be everybody's favourite—I suppose because nobody wanted to be thought lacking in those qualities.

At least an hour after dinner was spent in argument, and another hour while the ladies ran in and out of Val's chamber to renew their paint, but as we dined at two, it was thought a little early for Ranelagh, and accordingly the whole party stopped to take tea at an agreeable inn near the river.

We took a large table, of course, and very noisy our party was. Except for Val and myself, every woman in it seemed to wish to draw every eye upon herself by being louder and gayer than the others. I never heard such a *cackling* in my life. The men, taking wine instead of tea, soon became loud in their turn, and began to lay bets on the colour of our garters. The very waiters viewed us with contempt.

During all this tediousness, I saw Val moving restlessly, sometimes half turning her head, as though she were conscious of somebody staring at her. Craning round the back of her chair, I saw a party of gentlemen lounging at a little distance, very coolly surveying us all while they whispered together with smiles of derision, but chiefly staring, with a sort of bold admiration, at Valentine, who only looked more beautiful and more a lady beside her vulgar companions.

"Val," I whispered, "those men are looking at you."

"I know it," she said petulantly. "Mr. Dangerfield, I am tired of this place—let us go on."

"Your guests have not yet finished, my dear," he returned placidly, and continued to beg Mrs. Morrow for a sight of her garter, which he vowed was sure to be a heavenly blue to match her eyes. Mrs. Morrow, whose legs were exceedingly fat, as I knew from seeing her on the close-stool, was wise enough to reply only with giggles.

Presently one of the party of gentlemen observing us rose and came strolling over to our table. He made our party in general a handsome bow, and addressing himself to Mr. Collins, the wine merchant, asked whether he were not the gentleman with whom he had done some business the other day.

Almost suffocated by the distinction, Mr. Collins struggled to his feet and made an answering bow, so like a caricature of the first that I giggled aloud.

Our visitor flickered a very bright, knowing glance in my direction, with something almost like a wink, but answered Mr. Collins's stammers affably and sat down between him and Mrs. Morrow, who made room for him most eagerly. While he conversed readily with the others, he continued to look at Val, and also at myself.

Presently Mr. Dangerfield ventured to ask him whether his companions would not join our party.

"I am sure they would be most happy," he said promptly. "Pray, sir, why not ask them yourself?"

Val made signs at her husband to prevent him, but he ignored her, and approached the other table with so many bows and hesitancies and anxious smirks that I could hardly keep from laughing, while they regarded him with unconcealed derision.

They were not slow to accept the invitation, however, but I saw that no introductions were made. If they had been, the gentlemen would have to recognise us as acquaintances another time. As it was, they were under no obligation, at another time, to notice any of us. It was one of the oddest things I had observed about Society: how you could be constantly in company and carry on a conversation with someone to whom you were never introduced. It was for the person of higher rank to indicate that such an introduction would be agreeable. Gentlemen like this would never condescend to a motley group such as ours.

From their addressing one another, however, I soon made out that the gentleman who had first joined us was a Mr. Parker, while his companions were Captain Alverson and Lord Dutton.

When my brother-in-law understood that it was a real lord sitting at his table and drinking his wine, his delight became more than he could contain. He nodded and smirked and writhed his thick red lips in constant smiles. At last, greatly daring, he ventured to ask his lordship to take wine with him.

Dutton gave him a long insolent stare and then, very indifferently, allowed Dangerfield to fill his glass. Without speaking, Dutton looked towards Val and raised his glass. Mr. Dangerfield seemed quite carried away at the honour. Val smiled faintly, and looked another way. I could tell that she was conscious of Lord Dutton's stare, and she could not well help but be, seeing it was never anywhere else but on her face or bosom.

Personally, I thought there was little to choose between Lord Dutton and my brother-in-law in the matter of looks. My lord was very tall and thin, so thin that he had an almost death's-head appearance, enhanced by his pale complexion and lacquer-black eyes and eyebrows. His face was badly scarred on one cheek from his eye to his mouth. He was magnificently dressed, with an even bizarre splendour, and had a lordliness of manner which I thought as odious as it was ungentlemanly. It was excused, however, if not justified, by the absolute cringing deference paid him by every member of our party except Val and myself. Captain Alverson himself, a weedy bad-featured youth, was almost as slavish. Mr. Parker appeared to remain somewhat aloof, watching the scene with very bright, very dark eyes that missed nothing and spared no one. Compared to his companions, he was attractive, but I hated him on principle with the others.

Dutton came of a good family, I later heard, but had undermined his constitution and his reputation as well by violent excesses, and was now so notorious that it was said he could not marry even if he would. I have never seen anyone whose appearance so ideally matched his character. Upon the whole, I think villains are quite as likely to be handsome and smiling; but Lord Dutton might have stepped right upon the stage in the role of First Murderer. And yet he had had women without number, and not all of them bought mistresses either.

Beyond one long stare, he paid me no attention—nor indeed anyone but Val—and eventually wearying of the sport, for Val would not speak to him more than she could help, rose and carried off his companions. I heard Mr. Parker, however, enquire of Mr.

37

Collins our destination, and suspected them of an intention to follow us to Ranelagh.

After our party had discussed at length the charm, good breeding and infinite condescension of the lord and his friends, we at last rose from the table, not without a quarrel over the bill between Dangerfield and the landlord, and packed ourselves again into the coaches for the short drive to Ranelagh Gardens.

Ranelagh, when we finally reached it, was certainly a dazzling sight to my eyes. For a while I was lost to everything in wondering admiration of the great rotunda, the blazing lights of hundreds of candles, the tiers of boxes, the crowds of elegantly dressed people (as many of them courtesans as ladies, but I did not know that), and the sweetness of the music being played by the orchestra in the centre of the rotunda.

In spite of the crowds which seemed so immense to me, it was actually not a fashionable night, and Mr. Dangerfield at length secured us a box in the first tier. With an awed voice, he told us that Lady Townshend was no more than three boxes away, and pointed out the Duke and Duchess of Richmond strolling arm-in-arm around the parade of the rotunda like any loving couple.

One of the charms of Ranelagh was that everybody went there. In our party Mr. Dangerfield was greatly in demand, for he alone knew the really fashionable ladies as well as the famous courtesans. As often as not, her grace or her ladyship was brushing skirts with somebody's fancy-piece out of the opera, and nobody seemed to be the worse for it. My brother-in-law, thanks to his business, could not only tell us about them all, but say whether they had purchased their gowns at his warehouse and how much the silks had cost.

After a while I became a little bored with inactivity, and asked Val in a whisper if this were all.

She asked if I would like to walk round the orchestra, as half the assembly was doing, while the other half sat still and stared at them.

I eagerly said I would and we formed a walking party, which

Fred Hays, both the Misses Andrews and of course Mr. Gentry joined. Mr. Collins remained in the box to stare his fill at the lords and ladies. Mrs. Morrow was too fat to like walking, and Mr. Dangerfield gallantly elected to keep her company. I think he was still in hopes of seeing that garter.

The crowd was too great to admit of our walking abreast. The Andrewses with their attendant gallant soon fell behind, while Mr. Hays played the swain to Val and me.

I was not much interested in his gallantries, which were chiefly directed to Val, and preferred to look about me. I soon saw that this was what everybody did, and decided—quite correctly—that Ranelagh was so popular because it offered such unparalleled opportunities both to see and be seen.

There were numerous gentlemen walking alone, all of them ogling the ladies pretty freely. They stared hard at Val, and I came in for my share too. Those strolling in pairs often passed comments quite loudly enough to be heard, which I thought very rude. Nobody else seemed to notice it, or be offended by the relentless staring—often with the help of an eyeglass—that made me feel so exposed.

I had rather resented Val's putting a piece of lace into the bosom of my gown, but by the time I had strolled half round the parade I wished I were muffled up to the ears in a stuff gown. Even that would hardly have sufficed to save my modesty. Some of those gentlemen's stares could have pierced a suit of armour!

We had been strolling for some time, and Mr. Hays was beginning to hint at a return to our box and supper, when we were accosted very freely by the same trio who had joined us at the inn. Val received their compliments coldly, and of course I followed suit, but Mr. Hays was so flattered at being in company with these fine gentlemen that he was ready to play gull to anything they proposed.

Lord Dutton offered his arm to Val. She refused it with a slight curtsey, attempting to remain with Mr. Hays, but he, poor fool, was so eager to give way to the lord that he absolutely disengaged his arm, stammering some idiotic gallantry or other.

At the same moment, Mr. Alverson shouldered him from Val's

other side, while Mr. Parker adroitly took his place by me. I really cannot say how it was done without being so obtrusive that everybody around would notice, but it *was* done and there stood Mr. Hays, looking more foolish than ever, finding himself as summarily dismissed as a footman.

He was not unconscious of the slight, for he grew red; but chose not to resent it and, muttering something about the box, and supper, made a bow and walked off.

Val immediately cried, "By your leave, Mr. Hays, my sister and I will go with you."

Either he did not or would not hear—at any rate, he did not wait for us.

Lord Dutton took Val's hand and attempted to lead her on. She resisted, saying politely but decidedly, "Your pardon, my lord, but I prefer to return to my box. My sister and I are weary of walking, and we have not supped yet."

"Why, then," he said, with the coolest effrontery, "pray let me offer you some refreshment. Supper is already laid in my box."

But Val stood her ground. She and I had both heard some of the stories about Dutton with which Dangerfield was enlightening Collins in the coach.

"I am with my husband and a party of friends, my lord, as you know. I must remain with them." And resisting all of his attempts to take her hand, she began to walk towards our box.

I caught a flash of amusement in Parker's dark eyes. I suppose he was not used to see his friend so snubbed when he condescended to a merchant's wife.

Dutton himself was quite undisturbed.

"Why, then, ma'am, rather than lose the pleasure of your company I will accept your husband's invitation and join your party."

"I heard no invitation, my lord!" Val exclaimed, too astonished to be polite.

He raised his eyebrows languidly. "Did you not? But I feel sure I was not mistaken." He added, with delicate insolence, "If you think we shall be too large a party for your box, ma'am, I daresay my friends can find some other occupation."

40

I stole a glance at Mr. Parker to see how he bore this slight, but found him looking merely amused.

Val, however, frowned. "Certainly not, my lord," she said, putting up her lovely little head with the haughtiness I so much admired. "If there was an invitation it was undoubtedly meant for all your party. Sir, will you accompany me?"

And, turning away from Dutton, she calmly took Captain Alverson's arm, leaving Dutton either to seize the other or follow on behind. Alverson, who seemed to be a perfect puppet to Dutton's jerking, glanced round at him with an air of apology which almost made me giggle, but could not well shake Val off.

Mr. Parker turned to me, offering his arm. "May I have the honour, ma'am?" he asked formally, but with a twinkle in his eye.

Mind you, I was wearing one of Val's gowns, none of my own being finished yet, and I was very conscious of Dangerfield's remarks on my appearance in it. I did not like that twinkle, as though Mr. Parker thought we made a humorous couple, or as though he played at grown-up with a child.

As I say, I had already observed some peculiarities of Society and one of them was that a gentleman could scarcely refuse any reasonable request that a lady chose to make him. He might tease her, make love to her, pay her offensive compliments and attempt still more offensive gallantries. He could make her conspicuous by his pursuit, as Dutton did. But when she asked an outright favour of him, he was virtually bound to oblige her.

In reply to Mr. Parker's offer, therefore, I looked up at him most demurely and said, "La, sir, I am not at all tired and have no mind for supper after all that tea. I should like to go round the room again, if you will accompany me."

Mr. Parker's dark gaze rested on me for a moment. There was considerable speculation in it, as well as amusement. Then he said obligingly, "Your pleasure is mine, madam."

Val glanced round as if to forbid me, but I winked at her, and I suppose she thought I could scarcely come to harm in such a crowd, for she merely said, "Pray, sister, do not weary yourself. I daresay the gentleman wants his supper, if you do not."

41

She then walked on with Alverson, Dutton following like a horrid black shadow behind; and Mr. Parker and I began to stroll onward with the movement of the crowd.

I determined to give Mr. Parker all the trouble of making conversation, if there was to be any, so I hung primly on his arm without speaking. He glanced at me once or twice mischievously, but I affected to ignore it, staring timidly down at the floor.

Presently he enquired politely, "Pray, ma'am, how do you like Town?"

I simpered foolishly. "La, sir, vastly well!"

He blinked slightly, as well he might. "I am happy to hear it. Is your stay to be a long one?"

"Oh yes, sir; I am come here to live."

"I am transported to hear it," he said, in thrilling tones. "To see so much beauty, charm and wit, and then have it snatched away—that would be a grievous blow indeed!"

I looked up startled and met a wickedly infectious grin. That was a little too much. I *snatched* my arm out of his and exclaimed rudely, "I wish, sir, I *could* give you a grievous blow but I daresay it would be thought very ill-bred here in all this company."

He burst out into a sudden laugh, throwing his head back. I saw then that he was younger than I had supposed, escaping as yet those marks of dissipation that made so many men appear older than their years. Not particularly tall, he had a good, tight-knit figure and carried himself like a man assured of health and vigour. He had a pleasant brown face, with eyes very dark indeed, eyelashes short but thick and black, with well-shaped brows. His nose was good, shapely and not too small; his mouth curled up on one side, and still more so when he smiled. All in all, he was an agreeable man in appearance, if he had not so odious an expression of teasing amusement. Perhaps I would not even have minded that, if I had not so greatly mistrusted his motives.

"If the impulse is overmastering, madam," he offered, "we could step outside. One may do many things in the dark that are considered ill-bred in public."

I glared at him. "Yes, and I daresay you know them all," I

said, nastily, "but I would not set foot outside with you for anything. And you can tell your friend Lord Dutton that my sister will not have anything to do with *him* either."

Mr. Parker regarded me thoughtfully. "Pray, madam," he advised, "keep your voice down. It will do your sister's reputation no good to be coupled with my lord's, even in the most negative fashion."

"Is he as bad as that?" I asked, sobered. "And yet you go about with him, and help him make fools of people!"

"Miss Archer, you are most irreverently confusing me with your Maker."

I bit my lip. "It seems to me," I said shrewishly, "that you look as foolish as anybody. How can you bear to help him, and then be sent off when he doesn't want you, like a—a footman?"

"What do you mean?" he said, blankly, and then smiled. "Oh, yes—about the invitation. My dear Miss Archer, surely you have heard that all is fair in love as in war?"

"I don't know anything about it," I answered sullenly. It provoked me that he could turn all my shafts away so smilingly.

"Then perhaps you will allow me to instruct you?" he offered, suggestively.

Of course I should have returned a light answer, but I did not know how yet. Instead I said passionately, "Don't you dare! Don't you dare try to make a fool of me! I think you are odious— all of you!"

Seeing that he was struggling not to laugh, I was angrier than ever. "Sir," I said, through my teeth, trying to imitate Val's grand air, "pray take me back to my party."

"We are just half-way around," he said, obligingly. "Would you rather go forward or back? 'Tis no object to me, but you might prefer to see the half you have not yet seen."

I felt a great fool and was ready to cry with vexation. Yet I had a half-ashamed recollection that I had begun this by being so pert with him, and so could scarcely complain. I walked on, therefore, in silence, my cheeks burning.

After a pause, Mr. Parker said abruptly, "Is your brother-in-law a sensible man, Miss Archer?"

"No—I don't know," I said, startled into speech. "I don't know what kind of man he is, except that he is as horrid as can be."

Parker gave another boyish snort of laughter. "Upon my word, ma'am," he said, "you are most refreshingly outspoken. Is there any gentleman of your acquaintance of whom you *do* approve?"

"There is my brother," I said, and thought of him longingly. How I wished he would appear at that moment to save me from this teasing young man and send that horrid Dutton about his business.

"I had forgotten," Parker said, musingly. "Neal Archer is your brother, of course. You do not much resemble him. Mrs. Dangerfield and he are more like."

"Well, they had the same mother."

"And you had not?"

"Their mother was Lady Evelyn Clarke," I replied, shortly. "Mine was Mollie Lake. Her father was Farmer Lake and my father took her out of the dairy. So if you wish to think me common, sir, you may."

I knew how angry Neal would be, or even Val, to hear me thus expose to the world how lowborn my mother was—for no doubt Mr. Parker would find the fact amusing enough to repeat. I could not conceive why I had done it, except as a kind of defiance.

Mr. Parker's answer, however, was unexpected. "Indeed, Miss Archer, that is about the last word I should apply to you. A creature more *un*common it has never been my lot to meet before."

And though he was smiling, I could not take offence at his words, for I saw they were only teasingly and not insultingly meant. I returned to our box in a better humour with him, therefore, and only afterwards remembered all the dreadful things I had blurted out, and hated both myself and him for them.

Next morning Val lay late abed, complaining of a headache. I felt well, only languid and sleepy, and curled up on the end of her bed to talk. I was dying to discuss last night with her, but Val was disinclined.

"Spare me, Jenny! I have heard enough on that subject from

my husband. He was pleased to complain of my incivility to Lord Dutton."

She met my wondering glance and gave a hard little laugh, twisting one fair curl around her finger. Most of last night's powder had come off; it shone like a gold ring round her white finger.

"What do you think, Jenny?" she said. "Sometimes I fancy you are cleverer than I am about people. Is my husband more knave or fool?"

I shook my head. It was beyond me. He could not be ignorant of Dutton's reputation. In his way, Dangerfield was very well-informed about the great world.

"He does love a lord," Val mused, "but——"

"I hate him!" I said viciously.

"Who—Dutton?"

"No. Mr. Dangerfield."

Val shrugged. Then her gaze suddenly sharpened. "Does he molest you, Jenny? Fumble you?" I was silent, and after an instant she laughed again, bitterly. "Of course he does! Mind you lock your bedroom door at night!"

"I'm your sister!" I said, shocked.

She shrugged her pretty bare shoulders. Her bosom, from breeding, was very full, but I thought its look was spoiled by the great brown stains round the nipples. Val had assured me that would disappear when the baby was born if she did not nurse it, and she had no mind to, for the ruin of her shape.

"Oh," she said, contemptuously, "my husband has a taste for all sorts of nastiness; that would not trouble him at all. I had better find you a husband, Jenny! You've grown mighty captivating all of a sudden, and there's something about you that seems to make the men stare. Dangerfield says red hair always means wantonness."

She gave a sudden giggle. "He asked me: Do red-haired females have the same colour hair—everywhere? Men are mighty curious about us poor females, Jenny—as much as we about them!"

I could not help laughing too, but said wistfully, "I wish I were tall and fair like you, Val, and Neal."

45

"That reminds me——" Val began, frowning. But what it reminded her of I was never to learn, for the servant came in to announce Mrs. Allison.

"Mrs. Allison Who can she be?" Val said, puzzled. "Has she something to sell?"

"Oh, la, no, ma'am! She's a fine lady, and came in a French sedan chair with four servants in livery."

"Lord!" Val said. "I had better see her, then. Jenny, straighten the bed, will you? Betty, tidy my hair and bring me that lace cap—and for God's sake push that thing under the bed." She winked at me. "I'll have my salon in bed," she said, "like a duchess. Very well, Betty, that will do; beg the lady to step upstairs."

Mrs. Allison brought an aura of ruined magnificence with her. She was dressed for the morning as for a Court ball and was all covered with jewels. Her fingers were stiff with them right down to the knuckles. Her hair was arranged in exquisite short curls around her head, thickly powdered. The heavy layer of paint on her face could not restore its youth, nor entirely conceal the marks of ill-temper and dissipation. She was heavily scented, but had wine on her breath, and there was a fine tremor of her hands that made the jewels flash and wink. I saw that Val noticed it, and exchanged an expressive glance with her. When you see such a tremor in a man who is not old, it means hard and heavy drinking. It was not likely to mean anything different in a female.

The woman had a drunkard's voice too—deep and hoarse—though that may have been as much from snuff. She carried a gold and enamel snuffbox in her hand and dipped in it freely. Val and I both refused its offer, though I was dying to know what it was like.

And yet, with it all, she was a lady. Or had, at any rate, been bred a lady. The ease, the self-assurance, the manner—you could not mistake it. Women like Dangerfield's friends imitated it in vain.

"Don't mention it, my dear," she said, when Val made her apologies for receiving her in bed. "It is an unconscionably

46

early hour to call and I apologise for it. I am not often abroad so early myself."

She had very sharp eyes and I do not think there was much about Val or myself that escaped her notice. She spoke little to me, as I remained demurely and properly in the background, but looked at me as often as at Val,

"But I had a great curiosity to see the beautiful Mrs. Dangerfield," she continued. "I have heard much of you, my dear. I know your brother."

"I am afraid Neal is a partial witness," Val smiled.

"Not only from him." Mrs Allison returned the smile. "From others too. And now I see for myself. Of course, child, you ought to be in the front rank of fashion, by right. But, Lord! what can be done with your husband?"

"Nothing, I very much fear," Val said. She seemed amused by her visitor, but a little watchful, sitting upright against the pillows Betty had piled behind her. It was strange to see the contrast between them: Val so young and beautiful, without any adornment at all, and Mrs. Allison so adorned in vain, with youth gone and beauty going. And yet I could see she had once been as beautiful as, or more than, Val.

Mrs. Allison shook her head regretfully. "What possessed your father to marry you to the wretch?"

"Money, I suppose," Val said, with composure. "My father never has enough, and Dangerfield is rich. I daresay he paid him."

"It's a pity," Mrs. Allison said. She sounded genuinely sympathetic. "You can only hope for a fever to carry him off—and meanwhile I daresay you manage to amuse yourself. He must be away a good deal?" There was a world of insinuation in her tone.

Val sat up a little straighter. "I don't care for my husband, madam; that is true. I will not dissemble. But neither do I care to amuse myself in the way you suppose!"

"La, child, don't be vexed!" Mrs. Allison laughed, most provokingly. "If true, 'tis a miracle."

"It is true, ma'am. Though what business it is of yours, I don't know!"

"No business at all," she replied coolly. "I find you interesting,

47

my dear, and I pity you. I should be the last to throw stones at any woman. But if you *are* honest, then your husband has a better bargain than he had any right to expect!"

Val suddenly burst out laughing. "Lord, ma'am, I have only been married a year!" She rang the bell and Betty appeared. "Bring us chocolate and fruit and cake," she ordered. "Or would you rather take a glass of wine, ma'am?"

"Infinitely," Mrs. Allison said, frankly. She took her glass of wine and a plate of rich cakes, but waved away the fruit. Val, always hungry for fruit nowadays, seized a peach and bit into it greedily.

Mrs. Allison shifted her attention to me. "Your sister is a pretty child," she said, as though I were six years old. "That red hair will prove beguiling to some men. Those who have a taste for it cannot resist it!" She gave a fleeting, wicked smile. "Have you a notion to marry her, ma'am?"

"I have a notion to it," Val answered frankly, "but not much choice here. I won't have her marry as I did. Perhaps Neal can find her a husband."

"Has she a dowry?"

"Not a penny."

"Then I fear it may prove difficult. Men are sadly mercenary these days. There are too many women."

"We will see. My sister is but seventeen years old."

"Charming," Mrs. Allison said, perfunctorily. "But it is you, my dear Mrs. Dangerfield, who chiefly concern me."

"I am obliged to you, madam; but why should I be of any concern to you?"

"Because you are of much concern to one who is dear to me."

Val cast me a quick glance, and I know we were both of the same mind: Can this raddled creature be in love with Neal?

God knows whether she read our thoughts. There was not much she missed. She gave a hoarse knowing laugh that made us both colour, and said, "Surely you can guess, my dear! Or have you so *many* admirers? I can well believe it!"

Val opened her blue eyes very wide, looking steadily at the woman.

"I do not know who you can mean,' she said coldly.

Mrs. Allison leaned back in her chair, holding her wine-glass with an unsteady hand. She must have had a good deal to drink before she came, and these were big glasses, filled to the brim with my brother-in-law's best Madeira. I saw a faint film of sweat on her forehead and upper lip.

"La, child, how very coy! You may be frank with me. Of course I mean Dutton. He's my brother, you know."

"I did not know," Val said. I think she was suddenly very angry, for she added, coarsely, "Do you always bawd for him?"

Nothing could shake Mrs. Allison's composure. "Don't be rude, my dear," she advised, in the tone of a governess mildly rebuking a naughty charge. " 'Tis ill-bred, and besides it shows you are touched somewhere. Now I'll wager you are not as indifferent to Dutton as you would like to appear."

"Upon my word, Ma'am," Val cried, her voice shaking with anger, "you are monstrously bold! Have you come here merely to affront me?"

"On the contrary."

"Then let me say you are quite mistaken in me. I am not flattered by your brother's regard, not in the least. I know his reputation too well. Is it so blown on he can no longer find mistresses among his own quality? Must he sink so low as to pursue a merchant's wife? Let me tell you, madam, I am not to be had for the asking. My husband loves a lord, but I don't give a damn for one! Your brother is odious and insolent, and I think worse of him now than I did before."

I thought Val delivered this speech very well—as good as a play —and, what is more, she meant it. But Mrs. Allison's reply was merely a slow, provoking smile.

"And I must beg, ma'am, to let the servant show you out. I do not care to receive offers from your brother through you or anybody else."

"I have made you no offers, my dear," Mrs. Allison pointed out reasonably. "You are jumping to conclusions."

"Am I?" Val said, intently. She let her hand fall from the bell-rope. "Then suppose you tell me what your brother does propose, and what your own purpose is."

"Merely and solely to make your acquaintance, my dear Mrs. Dangerfield. It is natural that I should speak of my brother. I do not deny that he admires you—he quite raves of your beauty——"

"For heaven's sake, madam, spare me!" Val interrupted rudely. "Do you take me for a fool?"

"Somewhat," Mrs. Allison retorted equably. "A gentleman falls in love with you, and you take it for an insult! It is an insult many women pray for."

"Love is one thing. Duttons' *admiration* is another. I consider it an insult, and it is."

Mrs. Allison remained calm, looking at her levelly. "You do unwisely to make an enemy of us," she answered at last. "We are not so blown upon yet that we cannot expect civility from a little merchant's wife."

"Madam, if I am rude you have driven me to it. Tell me frankly—did you not come here this morning with the intention of making me an offer from your brother? And expecting me to jump at it? How much was included, pray?" Val seemed to have lost her anger; she leaned back on her pillows, pulling at her tumbled curls, smiling with a trace of mischief, showing all her bosom right through the lace. "A settlement, I suppose? Jewels, perhaps? Custom for my husband? Or was it just the honour of his lordship's attention that you thought sufficient for the merchant's wife?"

Mrs. Allison's knowing eyes dwelt on her with frank appreciation. "On my word, child," she said, "you are a very good match for my brother or any other gentleman. I will not deny that I thought to find you something quite different. I shall tell my brother he had better do his wooing in person."

"It is always better," Val said, still laughing. "But you will do better to advise him not to trouble at all. There are plenty of women in the world to tumble into bed with him. It will be a long fall that brings me there, I assure you."

"One never knows," Mrs. Allison remarked equivocally. She turned her regard on me. "What about you, my little miss?" she asked cheerfully. "You have a pretty, merry, wanton look. Have you a mind to find out how a man is made? My brother is not so set on your sister but what a pretty slip like you would please him."

"Get out!" Val cried. She seized the bell rope and tugged it furiously. "My little sister . . . Get out, you bitch, you—you bawd! If your brother dares to look at Jenny, I'll—I'll kill him!"

"Why, here's a mighty noise!" Mrs. Allison shrugged. "Are you jealous, my dear?"

Val controlled herself with difficulty. "How much does your brother pay you to fill his bed?" she asked insolently.

Mrs. Allison did not answer. Instead, she surveyed Val once more and said, drawlingly, "You know, my dear, I have many talents. If you are tired of that burden you are carrying, come to see me. I can always find the means to help my friends with these little problems."

"Good God!" Val whispered. As Betty curtsied in the doorway, she bade her show Mrs. Allison out. And the lady made her farewell compliments to us with the most unstudied naturalness, as though nothing but the time of day and Court tittle-tattle had passed between us.

When she was gone, Val suddenly fell back on her pillows and burst into tears. Astonished and dismayed, I ran to her and tried to comfort her.

"What a terrible woman! Just the sort of sister he *would* have! Oh, Val, don't cry! You were splendid!"

"Did you hear what she said?" Val whispered. Her golden head lay in my arms, the tears wetting them. "She offered——" A great shudder took her and she was silent.

"To get rid of the baby," I acknowledged. "I know. But why should that upset you?" I hesitated, and asked awkwardly, "Do you want the baby so much?"

Val raised her head, her eyes blazing. "*Want* it?" she said, between her teeth. "*His* child? Would *you*?"

"No. But then——"

"She knew that. She guessed it. I could see she did. When she made the offer, she knew how much it would tempt me. Bitch! Bitch!" my sister sobbed. She could not lie still; she writhed to

51

and fro, in painful disorder. "I hate it! Oh God, Jenny, how I hate it! And when it is born, I know what it will be—a little white worm, as *he* is! And I am so sick and weary of it, and I want my shape again, and it never gives me any rest—— Oh God, God, I wish I were dead!"

But Val used often to wish that, even in the old days, and I never took much heed of it.

My new clothes came home that day and it was wonderful to see how they changed me. Mr. Dangerfield knew one subject, at any rate. Delicate materials, clear pure colours, cut and fashion— all were perfect for me. I looked quite a different person—no longer so much the little sister to Val.

I thought the bodices all cut amazingly low, though at Ranelagh I had seen some fashionable ladies whose bosoms were scarcely covered at all, pushed up by their stays till the nipples showed above their gowns. I was not quite in that condition, but it would have been a perilous undertaking to lean over; and I had to practise my curtseys so that my bodice did not gape too much as I bent my knee.

Betty, who had really a very good hand, cut my hair into the shorter curls now fashionable, and Mr. Dangerfield brought me all sorts of pretty trifles—heeled shoes, fans, handkerchiefs, lace aprons, lace caps, neck ribbons. I was overwhelmed; I hated to take so much from him, but he would not be argued with; he gave and gave more. To do him justice, he dealt with Val quite as lavishly, and she had several rings as fine as anything Mrs. Allison wore.

He heard about her visit. His valet was certainly his spy, and I suppose the other servants were ready to tell him all they knew. He expressed himself as highly gratified by her visit, and urged Val to return it at once. When she refused, he was furiously angry. Then she told him bluntly Mrs. Allison's purpose.

Instead of raging, he appeared highly amused, even flattered, at Dutton's attention. He complimented Val on her beauty, told her jestingly that at any rate in her condition Dutton could not put a cuckoo in the nest, and assured her a number of times that he was not jealous. Val shrugged despairingly, glanced at me, as much as to say 'What is one to do with the fool?' and finally agreed to return the visit.

She merely sent in word by the servant, however; we did not stay to be asked in. She told Dangerfield that Mrs. Allison was out. Whether he knew better or not, he did not quarrel with her about it. He insisted on Val's obeying him to the letter but was not so rash as to expect obedience to the spirit.

To me he remarked, "Your sister is a cold female, my dear. I suppose you thought she and Harvey Underhill were lovers? I know your esteemed Papa thought so, or he would not have been in such a hurry to push her into my arms."

"What did you think?" I asked contemptuously.

"Oh, I took it for granted," he grinned. "Imagine my surprise when on the wedding night—I don't want to offend your maiden ears, my dear, so shall we merely say I found her intact? Your famous Mr. Underhill is not so bold a gentleman as his reputation. But neither is my wife so amorous as that bosom of hers would make you think. Now you, my pretty sister——" He grinned again, more odiously than before, reaching out to take hold of me. "If you were my wife, I would not trust you so freely. You have a wanton's eyes, my dear, and a charming waggle to your tail that makes every man want to——"

"If I were your wife," I said, evading him, "I would deceive you with every man that asked me. Let me alone, you toad, or I'll scream the house down!"

"Fine gratitude for all your pretty things, miss! A fortune I have spent on you!"

"You can have it all back!" I cried. I pulled the ribbon off my neck and threw it at him, and my lace apron, and, stooping, pulled off my shoes and threw them both at him too. He dodged them, laughing, and crying, "May I help you with the dress, my love?"

But finding myself near the door, I ran out, slamming it almost on his fingers, and up to Val's room, where she stared in amazement to see me half undressed.

When I returned to my own room, I found all the things neatly

53

laid on my bed, and the toe of one slipper filled with money. I was greatly tempted to throw *that* in his face, too, but it was the first money I had held in my hand since coming to London—almost the first in my life—and I could not bring myself to part with it. If he wanted to pay for nothing but a slap in the face, that was his affair.

The one taste Dangerfield and my sister shared in common was a passion for the theatre. Both loved a good play—or a bad one, for that matter. Val dearly loved the opera too, but he did not care so much for that, though he liked to ogle the dancers and tell which lord each one of them belonged to.

Consequently, we were sure of being at Covent Garden Theatre or the Haymarket at least once a week, and Dangerfield always sent a servant ahead to secure us good places.

I enjoyed the fun of going, of dressing up and seeing everybody, and sometimes I liked the play, but I never cared much for sitting still, and often I thought the plays very dull indeed, if not down-right silly.

Dangerfield could pass a starving beggar child in the street and make a joke about it, but he would sit at some sentimental play with the tears streaming down his face. I used to get fits of giggles over it, and poke Val to take notice, but she would poke me back to be still. She threw herself into the play as though she were willing herself out of her own life into a dream, and she resented anything that brought her back to reality.

I could not help sympathising with her, but I could not share her absorption. I wanted activity and amusement. Like Ranelagh. I was always longing to go back, but Val seemed to have taken a dislike to the place.

If she thought to avoid Dutton by avoiding Ranelagh, however, she underestimated him.

One night at the theatre we ran into Mrs. Allison upon the stairs. She greeted us as cordially as though we were dear acquaintances. I saw her taking a survey of Dangerfield, and I am sure she wondered more than ever at Val's obduracy after seeing her husband.

54

No doubt she told her brother, for thereafter as often as we were there, we were almost certain to see Dutton stroll in and take up a position where he could stare at Val, and approach her in the intervals. He rarely remained for long, since the plays seemed to bore him as much as they did me, but he always spoke to her before he left, and always looked his fill before he went away. Between the acts he would come and sit or stand near her, now and then speaking to her in such a low voice no one else could hear—saying God knows what, for Val would not repeat it.

Dangerfield was like a cat on hot bricks whenever this happened. He was flattered at being seen in Dutton's company. He did, as Val said, love a lord! On the other hand, in spite of his boasted indifference, he did not enjoy seeing the notorious rake so close to his wife, murmuring into her ear and staring down the front of her dress. If Dutton would have talked to him, I think my brother-in-law could have borne anything, but for all the notice his lordship paid him, Dangerfield might as well have been at home and in bed.

Neither did Lord Dutton honour me with much attention. When he was in pursuit of a woman, he did not deviate from his single-minded purpose. I believe this was the secret of much of his success. It was to some extent flattering, it was a little frightening, and it achieved its aim by sheer weight of persistence.

Val did not seem much affected by it. She treated him with the most complete indifference. She acknowledged his bow, she bade him good-evening and good-night, and she heard all his compliments (or obscenities) without so much as changing colour or fluttering her eyelashes. Any other man would have been chilled into positive dislike of her, I think, but it was only fuel to Dutton's fire. A man who spends all his life in pursuit of women must be interested by any change from easy acquiescence.

Often Lord Dutton had Alverson with him, sometimes other men, and often he was alone. But he never again had Mr. Parker in his company and I wondered at it, until Neal accidentally enlightened me.

Neal occasionally joined us at the theatre, of which he also was fond, though he pretended to be bored. It was always much more amusing when Neal was there. Even Val would laugh and sparkle as she used to do, and Dangerfield was thrust into the background. Not even Dutton ignored Dangerfield more completely than my brother did, and Dangerfield did not love him for it.

In the intervals Neal would point out interesting or fashionable personages, and tell the latest scandal. Dangerfield listened quite as eagerly as Val or I; his own sources were good but not as near the bone as Neal's, so gossip came to his warehouse a little delayed. I daresay Neal's revelations were very useful to him, and enabled him to play the man of fashion among his fellow merchants.

At any rate, one evening Val asked about one little actress, a charmingly pretty, painted little piece, who seemed to be looking a trifle downcast lately. We saw them all so often, we were as well acquainted with their moods and expressions as our own.

"Oh, she is moping after George Parker," Neal said, laughingly.

"After Mr. Parker?" I said, quickly. "Why?"

"She has been his fancy-piece this six months, and now he has fought a duel about her, and since the other fellow seemed likely to die poor George was chased overseas. But the would-be lover is recovering, so we'll soon have Parker back, I daresay. I've missed him—a very merry, good fellow in company."

"Who was the other man?" Val asked.

"Ned Fisher—but you don't know him. A sort of hanger-on of the Marquess of Sylvester. Calls himself a gentleman, and I believe he was born one, but I can't abide him."

"But Miss Kitty could?" Val suggested.

"No, she couldn't; that was just it. The fellow annoyed and frightened her, and at last George warned him off, and Fisher wouldn't take warning—just like him, he wouldn't care whether a girl could abide him or not!—and was insulting, and so it came to a duel. Old George is a famous hand with the foils, and the pistol too, for that matter, so Ned was a fool to drive him to it and would have been rightly served by a full quittance, but of course it would have been a damned nuisance for Parker. As it is, he thought it best to cross the Channel, but Alverson says he'll soon be back."

56

"He takes after Dutton evidently," Val remarked, referring to his lordship's notoriety as a duellist.

"I can't imagine any man being fool enough to fight about an actress!" I said, crossly.

Val glanced at me quickly, with a little smile. "Why, Jenny!" she said. "You sound quite vexed! I do believe you were a trifle catched by Mr. Parker."

"No, I wasn't! I think he is odious—almost as bad as Dutton. I dislike him very much," I said warmly.

Neal, who had looked vexed at Val's suggestion, smiled again, putting his arm around my shoulders. "We'll find a better lover for my sweet Jenny than George Parker. He's nothing but a younger son, and rolled up at that."

"I thought you liked him so well," Val said, reminding him in that aggravating way people have of throwing one's words in one's teeth.

"So I do," Neal shrugged, "but not as a lover for Jenny."

"I think," Val said, scornfully, "you would not like *any* lover for Jenny. You are jealous. You want her to care for no one but you."

"That is true," he admitted laughingly, looking at me teasingly with the beautiful blue eyes so like Val's. "I must have my pretty sister all to myself, now that I have discovered her."

"That's very well," Val said, "but you will tire of your fancy, as you always do, and meanwhile Jenny needs a husband."

"Then she shall have one. I won't be a dog in the manger. Let me see, who shall we choose?" And he began suggesting all sorts of improbable people, from Beggar Joe to the Prince of Wales, so that even Val had to laugh reluctantly.

As for me, I was well content without a husband, since what I had seen of marriage did not incline me towards it. As long as I was Neal's favourite now, I did not worry about the future. I adored him; I would have done anything to please him; I dressed and spoke and behaved according to his liking when I was with him. Val said scornfully that I was no more than his puppet. But I think she was jealous; for she had been first with him till I came, and he was her own true-born brother. He made no secret

57 c

of his preference now, and it flattered me beyond reason. Why should I want a husband, when I had Neal? If only he would have me to live with him! But though he often spoke of it, he never took any steps towards making it possible, and I feared too much to lose his favour to tease him about it.

The days were growing long now, and the evenings warm, the kind of weather that brings all of London out after the day's work to take pleasure upon the river or in the gardens.

Dangerfield did not like the water; he was afraid of it, and even the slightest motion made him sick. But Neal, Val and I loved it madly. Night after night Neal would hire a boat to take us up and down the river, or across to Vauxhall Gardens. Sometimes Dangerfield refused to accompany us; sometimes he came along, looking liverish and unhappy. When he did, Neal delighted in bribing the watermen to race other boats or perform daring feats that Val and I thrilled to, and that frightened Dangerfield till he was green.

Even on the river, Dutton's pursuit continued. He had a launch with his own watermen in livery, and constantly teased Val to join him for an evening on the river. She would not do so, and Neal approved, though otherwise he seemed to think Dutton's unsuccessful chase a very good joke.

"But if you are seen in his boat, sister, everybody will think the next step is his bed."

"I have not the slightest inclination to get into either," Val assured him.

"Though, on my word, after Dangerfield I should think *any* change would be welcome."

Val jerked her shoulder pettishly. We were crossing to Vauxhall, on a lovely June evening, and the westering sun shone on the flame-coloured silk cloak she wore and on the golden hair bared by the loose hood and turned them both to a blaze of sunset brilliance.

"You men are all alike, brother," she said. "You think no woman can be happy unless she is coupling with one of you. We are not so hot-blooded. It is no pleasure to *me*, I assure you!"

"Not with Dangerfield," Neal laughed. "But I daresay Dutton could show you a thing or two."

Val turned her face away. The sunset dazzled me so that I could not be sure whether or not there were tears glittering in her eyes.

"Are you against me, too, Neal?" she said, unsteadily. "*Must I be a whore?*"

In one of his sudden changes of mood, Neal dropped his mockery and scrambled to her side, drawing her affectionately into his arms rubbing his cheek against the unpowdered golden head.

"Sweet sister!" he said, with that crooning gentleness he often used to me. It made me a little jealous to hear him. "No one shall say that of you to me—not even you yourself. As for Dutton, I'll warn him off, if you like."

"No, no!" Val cried impatiently. She seemed restive in his embrace. "For God's sake, Neal, do nothing so foolish! You would provoke a duel as likely as not, and be killed, and what would be said of me then?"

Neal was silent, drawing away. Val saw she had vexed him, and laid her hand over his. They had the same hands, long and fine and nervous.

"And Jenny and I would break our hearts," she added softly. "What would become of us, Neal, without you?"

This pacified him, and we landed at Vauxhall in a very good humour with one another, Neal taking a hand of each. Val threw off her mood of bitterness and became as gay as I. She was very fond of Vauxhall—I think because it lay across the river, and the rippling tides of the Thames, which Dangerfield hated to venture, stood like a shield between her and the husband and home she hated.

It was a clear cloudless evening and the light lingered long. Val, in a great hoop that concealed her condition, smiling and merry, took many eyes, and so, to tell the truth, did I.

"How long the sun lingers!" Val remarked.

"It is caught in Jenny's hair," Neal answered, smiling, "and cannot go to bed for kissing of her. See how it burns there, with how lovely a light. The colour of your cloak, Val."

59

But Val did not reply. I thought she pressed closer to him, and, following the direction of her eyes, I saw Dutton regarding us from a few yards' distance. He was dressed, as usual, in modish fashion and, had he looked a shade less deadly, might have appeared handsome, except for that long scar down his cheek from eye to lip. Neal told me that it had been given him—deliberately—in a duel, by a wronged husband. Dutton had laid his adversary in the grave, but he would carry that mark to his own.

I saw that Val did not wish to draw Neal's attention to Dutton, so I said nothing. Neal, as it happened, was ogling a pair of pretty girls with their father, and saw nothing else. Dutton rarely approached Val when Neal was near, and now contented himself with a bow. All would have passed without incident if the gentleman walking on Dutton's right hand had not suddenly observed us.

Leaving Dutton, who paused, he came directly up to us, smiling gaily and saluting Val and myself.

"Mrs. Dangerfield, your servant! Miss Archer, your most humble admirer!"

"Good Lord! George Parker! Ned Fisher must be on the mend," Neal cried, joyfully greeting him. "Welcome back, George. You are acquainted with my sisters, I see."

"We met at Ranelagh," Mr. Parker said, smiling mischievously at me. I returned a stony glance, having decided upon adopting this manner if I should ever chance to meet him again.

"Will you join us?" Neal asked. "Or are you pre-engaged?"

"Only to Dutton."

Neal frowned a little. "He has not waited for you," he pointed out, and glancing round I saw Dutton strolling on, indolently swinging his cane and surveying from head to foot every female he passed.

"Then I will be most happy to join you," Mr. Parker said pleasantly, and fell into step beside me as we walked on. I would not look at him, nor speak, but Neal gaily questioned him about Paris and whether he had made any conquests there.

"Not I," Mr. Parker said. "In truth, I did not hang out for any. French ladies upon the whole seem plain beside our own, and their husbands jealous. I had no mind to get embroiled in more quarrels."

"How ungallant of you!" Neal laughed. "Surely a gentleman should always be ready to undertake as many quarrels as there are ladies to favour him."

Mr. Parker grinned. "I am a peaceful man by nature," he pointed out. "Nor do ladies force their favours on me as they do on you, Neal, you handsome dog."

My brother laughed again, not displeased, but cried warningly, "No tales, George, no tales! Remember we are with my sisters."

"I never tell tales," Parker drawled languidly, "to sisters, wives, or anybody." And changing the subject he remarked, "Is it only that I have been away, or is Vauxhall mightily crowded tonight?"

"It's been like this for a fortnight," Neal said. "It's the fine weather."

The paths were so crowded, in fact, that walking four abreast was not possible, and Neal and Val presently walked ahead, leaving me to follow behind with Mr. Parker. For a while we strolled in silence, neither saying anything, unless Parker replied to some remark Neal would pass over his shoulder.

But it was such a lovely evening! and Vauxhall was so pretty with the lights beginning to twinkle among the trees; and it was so pleasant to be there, hearing the music sweetly from a distance and feeling the air soft against my face, that I could not remain sulky for ever. And at the sight of the cascade, though I had seen it before, I could not help crying out at its ravishing prettiness.

Mr. Parker peered down at me. "Ah!" he said, solemnly. "It is Miss Archer, after all. I had begun to wonder if it was some changeling."

"What do you mean by that?"

He surveyed me with that mischievous teasing smile. "New dress," he said, "your hair newly cut, everything modish, including your manner, which is so fine-ladyish it has quite chilled me to the bone. I would not have known you but by the hair and——"

"Never mind my hair!" I snapped. "I hate red hair! I wish I might keep it always powdered."

"I am very glad you do not."

"I look much better. Powder is vastly becoming to me. Everybody says so. But Val says it is foolish to wear it for an evening's stroll. *She* likes to go without because her hair is so pretty."

"Mrs. Dangerfield's hair is beautiful but yours is still more so. I am excessively partial to red hair."

"Oh, are you?" I said disagreeably. "Mademoiselle Kitty has black hair."

His arm stiffened under my hand. "Neal has been telling tales, I see," he said coolly. "Did he also tell you, Miss Archer, that it is not at all the thing to refer to such matters?"

"Why? Are you ashamed of it? Why should you be, if you cared enough to fight a duel over her?"

He glanced down at me with a sudden glint in the dark eyes. "If you must know," he said, deliberately, "I *am* a little ashamed to have risked my life, and come near to taking another man's, in such a cause."

"Then why did you?"

"Because she is a good little soul and had accepted my protection. Sometimes, Miss Archer, a man must fight whether he likes the cause or not."

"Oh, I remember," I said, scornfully. "You have a peaceful nature."

"I wish I could say the same for yours," Mr. Parker replied, equably. "You are the most quarrelsome, sharp-tongued little shrew I ever met with."

He said this so calmly, in so matter-of-fact a manner, that I was quite stunned. After a pause, I admitted meekly:

"I suppose I am. I beg your pardon. I know I ought not to have said anything about your fancy lady, and I never will again."

"Lord save us!" Mr. Parker exclaimed. Coming to a standstill, he took my hand in his, looking down at me laughingly. "What a metamorphosis! Who would have thought she could coo so like a dove? Miss Archer, I ask *your* pardon for my impertinences."

"Oh no, I am very bad-tempered," I said eagerly. "And I don't know why, but I am always trying to quarrel with you."

Mr. Parker regarded me thoughtfully. "Some people would say that meant you were attracted to me, Miss Archer. Hate is akin to love, you know."

"I know," I said, thinking of certain things I had seen. I added dryly, "Do not be alarmed, Mr. Parker. You are in no danger of having *my* favours forced upon you, believe me!"

"And believe me, my angel, I would put up only a very token struggle!"

I supposed that he was joking, but did not want him to be in any doubt as to my sentiments, and therefore replied directly, "It is only that you provoke me. You tease me as though—as though you were my brother."

"Your brother! I have not the smallest wish to seem like your brother, I assure you."

"But you do," I assured him innocently, delighted at having found means to provoke him at last.

"Oh, my God!" Mr. Parker said feelingly. He stopped short again, staring down at me. It was quite dark now, and we were strolling far from the lights. "Miss Archer, you are either very innocent or very malicious."

I concealed my delight and said demurely, "I don't know what you are talking about, sir."

Before I could stop him, he put a hand under my chin and lifted my face to his kiss. I was too startled to struggle, and his mouth was hard on mine for a moment before he let me go.

"*Brother*, Miss Archer?" he said softly and ironically.

I was furious with myself for having felt how pleasant his lips were. I did not know how much I had yielded to him, unconsciously, but I disliked very much that triumphant tone in his voice.

"You take advantage, sir," I said, as coldly as I could. "Be pleased to remember I am not Mademoiselle Kitty nor anybody else from the opera."

"Willingly, so long as you remember *I* am not Neal."

I looked up at him, blazing with anger against that com-

63

placency. "There is only one thing I care to remember about you, Mr. Parker. You are a friend of Lord Dutton's, one of his party."

"And does that damn me utterly?"

"Yes!" I said fiercely. "You are as bad as he is. You are a rake and—and a duellist, and you think all women should fall into your arms."

"My dearest girl!"

"And I've disliked you since the first moment I saw you. I wish you would let me alone! I wish you would!"

As I turned furiously away from him, he caught me by the wrist.

"Wait! Do you really mean that?" His tone was greatly altered, and I felt a curious reluctance to answer, and yet did so, sullenly—"Yes!"

He let go my hand. "Very well, Miss Archer," he said quietly. "Lord knows I've no wish to appear another Dutton in your eyes. I'll leave you alone, if you wish it. But I must find your brother and make my excuses."

I followed him silently, biting my lip. Mr. Parker did not speak again, until he bade me good-night as he left me with Val and Neal.

"Why did Mr. Parker leave so suddenly?" Val asked, surprised.

"Oh, I daresay there is some riot or other afoot," Neal answered for me, gazing rather enviously after Mr. Parker. "He and his friends are always taking part in some rash scheme."

"He has a very rash look in his eyes sometimes," Val said, looking at me laughingly. "I rather like it. You didn't quarrel with him, did you, Jenny?"

"No," I said, shortly. I had never felt so let down in my life. "But I detest him; I never want to see him again!"

Val raised one eyebrow, but was too kind to laugh. "Perhaps it's just as well," she said, lightly. "He's an attractive wretch and if he's one of Dutton's crowd he is no man for you, Jenny!"

I was too chagrined to answer her; and instead complained pettishly that I was cold.

"Because you're too vain to wear a cloak over that new finery!"

64

Val exclaimed impatiently. "I told you it would grow cold when the sun went down. Here—take my cardinal!"

"But *you* will be cold," I said, hesitating.

"No, I won't. I've been suffocatingly hot ever since I began to breed. Only for Lord's sake let us stay out of the light, for the colour will clash odiously with your hair!"

I was sick of hearing about my hair, and as Val and Neal again linked arms and walked on, I walked rather sullenly after them. Vauxhall suddenly seemed intolerably flat. They were deep in conversation, and I dropped farther and farther behind, vexed at being ignored, and feeling of a good deal less consequence since I had lost a companion of my own.

It would serve them right, I thought darkly, watching them stroll obliviously ahead, disregarding my feelings, if they were to lose me. And I meditated darkly on how frightened they would be, though not giving much thought to my own dismay in such a case.

For Vauxhall Gardens were large and rambling, parts of them deliberately darkened, and in the great crowds it was not difficult to get astray from your own party. Even with Neal, Val and I had never dared do more than peep into the famous Dark Alleys.

These long hedged alleys, with the trees meeting overhead, without a single light showing, filled with the sound of giggling and struggling and other things more suggestive still, were notorious. No woman went into them unless she were prepared to be affronted; and no gentleman took a lady there unless his intentions were dishonourable. Reputations have been lost by a single stroll through those dark mazes.

When I was married, I thought, I would get my husband to bring me here, and see what the dark alleys hid, and kiss with him in the dark like any amorous couple. If he were that sort of husband——

Meditating on this interesting subject, I dropped farther behind Neal and Val than I realised. Some man, passing, spoke to me insolently, and that startled me back to myself. I saw my brother and sister far ahead, just going into another of the lighted avenues, and I was quite surprised to see how near I had come to

65

really losing them. Vexed as I was that they could so stroll on without noticing me, I still did not hesitate to pluck up my skirts and run after them. It was quite dark now, and no matter what I had been threatening to myself, I did not at all relish the idea of being lost here.

People stared as I ran, threading my way among them, and men called out rude jokes, but I paid no heed, putting on a good sprint. Crossing a patch of lawn with one bound, I ran into the farther avenue and saw Val and Neal just before me, arms linked, heads together. I felt an instant pang of jealousy, and now that my fright was over, was really wrathful to have been so forgotten.

I came up behind them, therefore, and gave Val a good pinch in the arm, to punish her.

She gave a furious little scream, swinging round—and, my God! it was not Val.

"What the devil?" the gentleman exclaimed, also turning. And it was not Neal, nor even like him; though the height and a similarity of dress had deceived me in the flickering light.

"The little slut pinched me!" the woman screamed.

Horrified and humiliated, I could only stammer: "N-no, I d-didn't—I mean—I thought you were somebody else. I t-thought you were my s-sister."

"Damn your sister!" the horrid wretch shrieked. "Look at my arm! Ten to one she's a pickpocket. Have you your watch safe, my love?"

The gentleman, with an oath, clapped his hand to his pocket, while people began to gather around. The word 'Pickpocket' always makes a crowd ugly and there were mutterings. Somebody suggested going for a constable.

I drew myself up as haughtily as I could, feeling very trembly about the knees. "I ask your pardon, madam, for the error," I said, trying to imitate Val's cool haughtiness. "I mistook you for my sister."

Meanwhile the gentleman, having discovered that his watch, fob and snuffbox were intact, and after giving me a pretty good stare, up and down, intervened on my behalf.

"Keep your temper, my love," he said to the screaming shrew

66

on his arm. (How could I ever have mistaken this dyed, raddled slut for my beautiful sister?) "The young lady is obviously a person of quality. And in any case, pickpockets do not advertise their presence by pinching their victims," he added, shrewdly. Over her head he winked at me, giving his head a quick suggestive jerk.

I did not stay for more warning. I curtsied briefly, with no reply but an oath from the woman, and walked quickly away. The crowd, seeing no excitement to be had, let me through, but two or three loose men in it followed me, talking loudly and trying to take my hand. Vauxhall is the last place in London where an unprotected female should wander alone.

Where, in God's name, were Neal and Val? It was obvious that for the last few minutes I had been following the wrong couple, and they perhaps had been equally deceived into thinking me near them.

My only thought was to retrace my steps to where I had seen them last. I was a good deal confused by all the people, and by the glimmering lights that shone here and there among the trees. My three tormentors followed close behind me, too, and vexed and humiliated me so that I hardly knew what I was doing. I was ready to burst into tears with fright and chagrin, but controlled myself, and tried to think what I should do if my brother and sister did not soon appear. They would look for me, doubtless, but meanwhile what was I to do? It would be best to choose a well-lighted place and wait; but to stand still was to invite attention of the most undesirable kind.

Otherwise, the best thing I could do would be to appeal to some respectable party for help, and remain with them until my brother reappeared.

The only difficulty was to find such a respectable party. It was growing late, and family parties had long since left the groves.

Most of all, however, I wanted to shake my pursuers. Hearing them laugh loudly behind me, I glanced round and saw that they had stopped to insult and jostle a pair of foolish girls walking on the look-out for men.

Now was my chance! I saw near-by a long dark alley, hardly more than a lane between high bushes, bending sharply at one end.

So far as I could see, there was not a soul in it. Again I picked up my skirts and fled, as swiftly and silently as I could. At the corner the lane turned sharply in between its hedges and continued another few yards, coming to an abrupt halt at the foot of a wall.

I rounded the corner and stood still. Far off the music and laughter of the crowds drifted to me. I heard the raucous shouting of that wretched trio, finding I had evaded them. If they came down the alley, what should I do? I was in a cul-de-sac and my heart beat thickly at the thought I had run myself into such a trap. Too late I realised the folly of leaving the lights and the crowds for any reason whatever. *There,* I could only be teased and annoyed. *Here,* I could be——

I dared not complete the thought; I shivered and grew cold, drawing Val's cloak tightly round me. That sulky fit of mine was likely to cost me dearly and I swore if I got out of this whole and unmolested, I would never let go of Neal's arm again.

My three noisy fellows were blundering around in the distance. One of them started down the alley, and my heart absolutely stood still. But the others, bored with a profitless pursuit, drew him off, and presently their voices died away in the distance, lost in the general murmur.

I drew a long breath of relief, and pulling my cloak well over my face, so that nobody should see who I was when I came out of the dark lane, started quickly forward and turned the corner.

And there, bulking large and dark against the lights at the end of the lane, were three men.

I gave a little cry—I could not even get breath enough to scream—and shrank back. One of them said in a low voice, "Do not be frightened, and don't scream," and I suddenly realised that these were not my old pursuers. These were quiet men, cloaked and masked, and frightened me far more.

"Let me pass!" I said, my voice shaking. "What do you want? Let me go!"

One of them muttered something, very low, and suddenly there was a spark, as flint and tinder were struck. I started back from the suddenness of it, and heard the quiet voice say, "No, there is no mistake. Quickly, now!"

Against the distant lights of the garden, I saw them move in upon me, and flung up my hands to keep them off, trying to scream. But the scream would not come, and in a moment it was too late.

They flung a heavy cloak around my head and shoulders, gagging and almost stifling me, and one of them picked me up. When I began to kick and struggle, the cloth was brutally tightened around my head till my breath was cut off and I went limp, my head swimming, stars flashing in front of my eyes.

After that, I don't remember much. I'm not sure how they got me out of the garden. I have some idea I was lifted over the wall, but I'm not sure. There was a coach, and a long jolting ride, but I was hardly aware of it. I was half fainting and half suffocated, and wholly out of my wits with terror.

The first thing I heard was the sound of men's voices, quarrelling furiously.

"I tell you, you damned fools, this is not the one!"

Something about the voice was familiar. I languidly opened my eyes. I was lying on a bed, covered over with Val's cloak, and for a moment felt too ill and dizzy to care where I was, or what was happening to me. And then I *did* recognise the voice and sat up with a jerk, recovering all my senses in the same moment.

"Lord Dutton!"

His lordship jerked round, regarding me with a baleful gaze.

"Yes!" he said. He looked like a devil, his face so white, his eyes and brows so black, and that long scar showing livid all down one cheek. "And you! you damnable tiresome little bitch—what the devil are you doing in your sister's cloak?"

I gaped at him. This seemed to enrage him further, for he burst into a perfect fury of oaths, and turned on the men so savagely they gave up their defence and slunk speechlessly out of the room.

Lord Dutton rounded again on me. He walked to the bed, seized me by the wrist, as I shrank from him, and pulled me

69

roughly to my feet. Still holding my wrists with one hand, he slapped me hard across the cheek with the other.

"Take that," he said, "for a damned interfering little slut!"

To this point I had been too surprised and far too frightened to feel resentment. Now sheer rage possessed me. I dragged my hands free and flew at Lord Dutton like a fury, screaming and yelling with rage, kicking, striking, biting, scratching. I sobbed with rage, all my pent-up fright and humiliation pouring out of me.

Lord Dutton seemed momentarily taken aback by my on-slaught and gave ground before me, automatically defending himself. Then, as I really hurt him, he yelped a curse and gave me a backhanded box across the face that knocked me spinning to the rug.

Shocked into sanity, I lay there and stared at him, incredulous at my own behaviour and quite worn out by it. He stared back at me, nursing his bitten hand for a moment, his lips drawn down and the pulses in his cheek muscles working in and out. Then he gave a sharp bark of laughter and bent down, picking me up and seating me, none too gently, in a chair.

From a decanter on the table he poured me a glass of wine and took one himself, throwing his head back as he drained it right to the bottom in one long gulp.

It was strong wine, and I had no intention of following his example, but a swallow or two did me good. It made me feel less queer and exhausted, and dulled the pain of my bruises.

On the other hand, I grew more afraid. Looking around me, cautiously, I saw that I was apparently in Lord Dutton's bedroom, a chamber as dark and fantastic as its owner. Oriental rugs covered the floor, there were Oriental hangings, very sombre and magnificent, on the walls. A large carved screen stood in front of the fireplace, and I think scents had been put on the fire, for the air was full of a curious sweetish odour, not very pleasant. Like Dutton, the whole room had a disagreeably theatrical effect. It seemed most horridly a place where frightening things could happen. As for the great bed in the corner, with its crimson and gold hangings, I hardly dared look at it.

"Upon my word, ma'am," Lord Dutton said at last, in that odious, drawling, sneering voice of his, "I seem to have netted more than I bargained for. What a little tigress! I'm sure your sister would not have proved so obdurate."

"You were going to abduct Val!" I cried, aghast. Of course it was obvious, but the full realisation only dawned on me in that moment. "Good God! Why, even you can't do that!"

This seemed to amuse him. "Evidently not," he said, "with the bunglers that serve me. But if you mean I do not dare to do it, there you sit to give yourself the lie. And all because of that damned cloak! I pointed out your sister, but those idiots evidently did not trouble to look at her face so closely as her dress. May I ask why the devil you are wearing her cardinal, by the way?"

"I was cold, and she gave it to me." I was cold now, and drank deeply of the wine. It was a mellow golden Canary, and warmed me through with false courage.

"I suppose you know, Lord Dutton, that abduction is a criminal offence? Even for a peer?"

"Are you threatening me, child?" he said, silkily.

I looked up at him and was suddenly sobered.

"No," I said. "I only want—I—Lord Dutton, please send me home! I'll say nothing of what has happened! I swear I won't! I'll say I was lost in the garden and you found me and took me home."

"It's not a good story but we can try it," Dutton grinned. "Though I warn you frankly, my dear, that when it is known you have spent an hour alone with me, your reputation will be blasted for ever. You can swear, and I can swear, but no one will believe either of us. My poor child, you are ruined!"

I knew it was too probably true, but that was the least of my concerns at the moment. My only thought was to escape him before it entered his head to ruin me in fact as well as by report.

He drank another glass of wine, again at one draught. Nothing seemed to affect him at all. Picking up his cloak from a chair, he looked round for mine.

"The sooner we try it, the better, at any rate," he remarked, and crossed the room to get Val's cardinal from the bed, while I

71

watched him, shaking all over, and unable to believe that I would escape so easily.

I don't know whether my fear touched him somehow, and put the thing into his mind; or whether it was the sight of Val's cloak that reminded him of his disappointment; but the devil suddenly came uppermost again.

"No!" he said, and flung both cloaks on the floor. "I'm damned if I will! If you're old enough to run about Vauxhall alone, you're old enough to take the consequences. I'm not going to bed with a cloak instead of a woman, like some damned poet!"

He turned round on me that white damnable death's-head, the nostrils flaring.

"Look here, child," he said in a deadly quiet voice, "you might as well have the name with the fame. And don't make a fuss, or I shall have to hurt you again. You can reproach me all you like—afterwards—but don't annoy me now."

I jumped up and stood like a bird before a snake as he came at me with that soft deadly violence. And then all the shrieks I had been stifling came out in one mighty yell that must have startled the whole house. A door flew open and a servant popped his head in, his mouth and eyes gaping.

"Shut the door, you damned idiot!" his master shouted, and threw the decanter at him.

The fellow dodged, the decanter splintered in the hall beyond, and for a moment the door was clear.

I ran as I never ran in all my life before, and as I ran I prayed, "O God, don't let the front door be locked—don't let the door be locked!"

I flew down the stairs without touching any, I think, and reached the big front door before Dutton or his servant had rounded the landing. There was a bolt driven home and I thrust it back with frantic hands. If the door were also locked with a key, I was undone.

But locking-up had not yet been done for the night, and I flung open the door and ran out into the darkness, wasting not one moment to appeal to anyone in that damned house.

.   .   .   .   .

The streets were dark and quiet. I saw no help anywhere, but neither was there any hindrance, and fear spurred me so that I ran like a racehorse. Ran and ran till my desperate lungs forced me to a standstill. Then at last, when I was driven to bay, I turned round and saw that I had clean outrun pursuit, if indeed there had been any. More than likely Dutton had not cared enough to run the risks and indignities of such a chase. Or perhaps I had been so quick they had simply lost sight of me at once.

I was safe from Dutton, and I leaned against a wall and sobbed for breath, my lungs making horrid little dry crackling sounds, like burning paper. I felt as though I could not go another step.

But Lord! what was I to do? I was alone in London in the middle of the night. I had no idea where I was—in what locality, even. I did not know whether I were on the north or south side of the Thames. Was Vauxhall near, or had they brought me back across the river to Dutton's home? Or to some house which he kept private for such adventures as this?

If the house had been Dutton's town residence, then I knew vaguely where I must be, for I had heard talk of his living near Queen Anne Street. I was half-way across town from Danger-field's house. I knew not a soul anywhere near. What in heaven's name was I to do?

I do not think that ordinarily I am timid—at least for a female. But you must admit there is something very terrifying in being suddenly set down alone, in the middle of a black night, in a place utterly strange. I have had dreams like that, and waked so frightened that at first I neither knew who I was nor where I was. Such a dream was this—only there was no waking.

I had no money, even if I could find a coach for hire at this time of night. The street appeared to be a respectable one, but how could I wake a respectable household in the middle of the night to ask for assistance? They would think me thief or strumpet, or worse, and very likely call the watch and have me taken to prison.

Equally, I could not set out to walk home, even if I knew the

73

direction. My thin shoes were half worn out by an evening at Vauxhall.

And yet it was still worse to think of spending the night in the streets. Indeed, I dared not. As well walk in a den of wolves as walk the streets of London at night, alone, unprotected, and helpless.

Only one thing remained, therefore. I must walk on till I met with the watch, tell my predicament, and beg their assistance. They would probably do their best, in hope of a reward, and at any rate I would be under some sort of protection, feeble as it was.

When I had come to this conclusion, and regained my breath, I began to walk on as fast as I could, looking about me all the time, with a heart that jumped like a rabbit at any sound. That long dark walk from my father's house to the inn had not been half so dangerous as this. The very sound of my own feet frightened me, echoing from the houses so that I turned round a hundred times, fancying myself followed.

Luckily it was a very clear night, the stars large and bright. The laws require each householder to burn a light before his door, but it is not one in a hundred that complies, and, to tell the truth, I was more afraid in the light, which made me so conspicuous.

Nevertheless, I kept my heart up and walked on quickly. Oh, how I longed to hear the call of the watch! And if I had prayed in the dark alley at Vauxhall, I prayed ten times as hard now. "Oh God," I petitioned fervently, "please forgive my thinking so much about my shape and the colour of my hair and whether gentlemen will like me, and what it feels like to have a lover, and the extra cream tart I stole from the pantry yesterday, and my calling Mr. Dangerfield an odious put and a stinking toad, for though he *is* both he is also my brother-in-law and a fellow Christian and I ought not to do it. And forgive my being so rash and foolish as to get myself into this mess. I will never do it again if You will please *please* be so kind, Dear God, as to get me out of it. And make Neal forgive me. Amen."

It seemed as though God had answered my prayers at once, for no sooner had I concluded than I saw the wavering lantern

74

of the watch approaching down the street, and heard the far-off hoarse cry that proclaimed it was close on one o'clock of a fine clear night.

I suppressed a longing to run as fast as I could towards the light, and walked on sedately, only a little quicker. I did not wish to appear frenzied or hysterical—the old men who go the rounds of the watch are very timid and cautious, and I feared to frighten them off. As I hurried, I rehearsed the speech with which I would address them, beginning in a very dignified way, "My good men———"

But suddenly I heard a sound that struck my soul with the greatest terror I had yet known. Not very distant, perhaps a hundred yards away on a side street, there was a sudden outburst of noisy laughter and yelling, and sounds as though a barrel was being rolled down to the street to the accompaniment of wild whoops.

There are in London certain bands of wild young men, chiefly of good family and thus nearly invulnerable to the law, who delight to roam about the town at night playing all sorts of cruel and wicked pranks. And doing some deeds too cruel and too wicked to be called anything but crimes. They call themselves Mohocks, after the Red Indians of America, and, from all I have heard, I think I would prefer capture by the savages to mishandling by our Mohocks.

Val had told me the beastliest stories—women teased and tormented, their petticoats thrown over their heads or their clothes stripped off altogether—yes, even rape. And of shops broken and burned, their owners beaten for trying to interfere; even gentlemen attacked and rolled in the mire, and their noses slit if they resisted; while the members of the watch had suffered from them so cruelly that they no more dared try to control or arrest them than to stand the attack of wild beasts.

Even as I stood still, my heart palpitating, wondering if it could indeed be the Mohocks, and if they were coming this way, I saw the lantern of the watch come to an agitated halt and then begin a hasty retreat.

At that moment I would have bargained even for Dutton. My

best chance, no doubt, was to try to conceal myself in the garden or on the steps of some house, but by this time I had fairly lost my wits with fright.

I took to my heels, running after the watch, and the Mohocks, sighting me, gave a wild whoop and set out in pursuit. Their deserted barrel rolled down the street, hopping and crashing from one stone to another until it ran into a wall and broke all to pieces.

'Tis amazing what fright will do. A moment since, I had been limping along, half dead with fatigue, hardly able to put one foot before the other. And now I was running as fleetly as ever— so fast that I rapidly overtook the two old watchmen, who could barely dodder along.

I flung myself panting on the nearest old man, clutching him in terror. "Please help me!" I panted. "The Mohocks—oh God, protect me!"

Instead of offering me aid, the old wretch cursed and swore most vilely at me, trying to thrust me away, and hurting me cruelly. His companion, meanwhile, went tottering on as fast as he could without staying for either of us.

The miserable old coward was angry enough to kill me for bringing the Mohocks on him. At any other time, I might have thought it ludicrous indeed for the representative of law and order to be striking and cursing an unfortunate female for imploring his protection and making it impossible for him to run away from the criminals. But now I was simply beside myself, and did not care how much he hurt me, clinging to him with frantic hands.

"Oh God, sir, you *must* help me—you *must*! Oh, tell them to leave me alone!" I shrieked, while he mumbled and cursed, the lantern swaying and swinging overhead, dripping boiling wax on us both.

Then, with a blood-curdling yell, the Mohocks were upon us, linking arms and dancing around us in a parody of a Maypole, laughing and jeering obscenely, pretending to think us lovers, and urging the old man to lift my petticoats and take what the lady was so obviously ready to give.

76

He ceased even to curse at me and stood trembling with his eyes shut, holding himself upright only by the pole of his lantern. I stood helplessly beside him, dazed and so driven to bay that I could only think how I longed to have a knife, to kill at least the first one to lay hands on me.

The Mohocks danced and yelled until one man broke free of the circle and seized me. With cruel experienced fingers he gripped my wrists in one hand, holding them behind my back. With the other hand he jerked up my face, and kissed me, a horrible lusting kiss that forced my lips apart, his great wet tongue thrusting into my mouth.

I writhed and struggled, but had no more hope to escape than a kitten in the clutches of some cruel boy. He kissed and pawed me, tearing my dress in his eagerness to get a hand into my bosom, till he was tired, while I struggled and sobbed and kicked in vain. And the other monsters encouraged him with hoarse cries, kicking and beating the old watchman by way of diversion.

At last one exclaimed, in a kind of astonishment, "By God, I'm thirsty!" Instantly the others took up the shout and they all set off running, the brute that held me dragging me by one wrist. When they found their barrel broken, and the wine leaked out, they were full of drunken lamentations.

My captor, who seemed to be some sort of leader, cursed and swore, and then announced that they would go to Mother Polly's. This met with instant acclamation and off they set again, running, jumping and shouting like maniacs escaped from Bedlam—or like devils loose out of hell.

I had to run with them, perforce, or be dragged along the stones. I was so exhausted I could hardly keep my feet. Once I stumbled and went to my knees. My companion paused to haul me up again, but with a good box on the ear to teach me to be more careful.

Mother Polly's proved to be a tavern set discreetly down a dark alley, showing only a very dim light over the door. The door was open, however, and as we came whooping and hallooing in, a woman very decently dressed met us to ask our pleasure.

"Drink, beautiful Polly, drink!" my brute sang out, dropping

77

hold of me to catch her around the neck and kiss her, to which she submitted with perfect indifference.

She was a woman neither young nor old, dressed in a plain goodly fashion, with a neat cap on her head and a white apron over a dress of black watered silk. But the lace at her neck was real, and the stones were real that winked and glittered in her ears and on her fingers. She had a pale, smooth face, but it was not the smoothness of youth, rather the hardness of a cruel nature that has never known enough emotion to be marked by it. Her eyes too were pale, hard as glass. All the while the man kissed and fondled her, she was looking at me with no friendly glance.

Still, she *was* a woman, and presumably mistress here. As my beast turned away from her, reaching for me again, I sprang from his grasp and ran to her other side, holding out my hands to her beseechingly.

"For God's sake, madam, save me from these cruel men!"

"Cruel!" my captor quoted, with a loud hoarse laugh. "Lord, child, I'll be kinder when I've had a drink! Shall have no complaint of me, I guarantee it!"

"Madam!" I implored the woman, in a low voice. "For God's sake, help me! I am a decent young female that has been stolen away from her family. Only help me, and my brother will reward you!"

She looked me up and down—I would say scornfully, but that her glance did not hold even that much of feeling.

"You've found a pretty little harlot, my lord!" she said. "But what ails the little fool?"

"No, no!" I screamed. "I'm *not* a harlot—I'm *not!* I tell you I am a lady—my family will have you hanged if you lay a finger on me!"

At this they all laughed terribly; even the atrocious Polly condescending to smile.

I burst into tears, wild with rage and fear. "Oh God, will nobody help me?" As 'my lord' lunged at me, I caught the woman by one arm, holding on with all the strength of my terror. "Only help me, and you shall have a great reward—I swear it—I swear it on the Bible! My sister is married to Mr. Dangerfield the

78

merchant—he is very rich and will give you anything you ask for my safe return——"

"Mr. Dangerfield!" the woman echoed, suddenly looking very hard at me. "Are you kin to him?" Then she shrugged, smiling, "More likely a dismissed servant!"

But I saw I had struck the right note at last, and I would not be dragged from her, but babbled Dangerfield's name over and over again, promising her such rewards that he would have been ruined to redeem them.

Naturally all this had not gone forward without making a considerable uproar in the tavern, and two or three of the private doors opened, the occupants gazing out in curiosity at the scene. Some of them appeared to be gentlemen, sitting with friends at drink or play. But I had had my fill of trying to appeal to men. I pinned all my hopes to the woman's cupidity, which I was shrewd enough to see had been greatly aroused.

You must not suppose 'my lord' had been idle all this while, but I clung so frantically to Madam Polly that he could not tear me away without injuring her as well. Most of his friends had already rushed straight into the tap room and could be heard a mile off, yelling for liquor and baiting the tapster.

Suddenly a voice behind me said, "What the devil is all this talk of Dangerfield?" And then, in a tone of utter amazement, "Good God, it is little Jenny Archer!"

It was Harvey Underhill, Val's old lover.

With an exclamation of indignation, he thrust off the man who was pulling at me, putting his arm protectively around my shoulders. And at that, now that I was safe, I did what any well-conducted young female would have done long since, and fainted.

When I opened my eyes again, I found myself wrapped in a man's cloak, lying in a strange man's arms.

Bewildered, and still filled with a sense of terror, I gave a little cry and tried to free myself, but his arms tightened around me gently.

"Lie still; don't be frightened," he said soothingly. "You are

79

safe now." Supporting me with one arm, he took a glass of wine from the table and made me drink from it till I had drunk nearly all.

"There!" he said, smilingly. "That's better! I never saw such a pale little face—you frightened us all. Poor Harvey thought you were dead."

"Where is Harvey?" I asked faintly.

"He is having a little discussion with your late companions," he said, looking grim. "No—don't be frightened; they're not duelling. They have all been quite sufficiently alarmed; and Madam Polly is in fear of her neck. Harvey will have them in here to apologise presently."

"I don't care about that," I said, forlornly. "'I only want to go home! I want Val!" and the tears welled up in my eyes at the thought of how badly I wanted her.

"Don't cry!" he said coaxingly. "We have sent for a coach; we'll take you home directly."

He had a very pleasant coaxing voice and was so kind that I checked my tears to look at him better.

I thought then, and I say now, that a handsomer man than Robert Haywood never stepped the earth. A young god or angel could not have appeared to me more dazzlingly beautiful, and I stared at him with all my eyes, stricken with the wonder of him.

He was very fair, fair as the old Saxons were said to be, not pale or ashen blond, but golden, with thick closely curling hair, straight brows, and long curling lashes brighter even than his hair. His eyes were blue as a child's, and with all that gold made him look like a medieval illustration of some knightly saint. For, beautiful as he was, you would never mistake him for anything but a true man. He had a build that any man might envy—and that women loved almost better than his face.

I gazed at this beautiful young man with wide, bedazzled eyes, and he looked down at me very kindly, the light making his hair so bright you might have minted coins from it.

"What a pretty child you are, Miss Jenny!" he said, smilingly. He had a smile that would have seduced the angels. "On my word, I can hardly find it in my heart to blame that Mohock too much."

"Horrid wretch!" I said, but I did not put much feeling into it. The thought that he found me pretty and enticing made me friends with all the world.

He laughed very heartily at the thought of my lord's present chagrin. "To find such a beautiful little actress—" He used the word, I suppose, to spare my feelings, but I knew what he meant! "And then to discover her a lady of quality with a protector ready at hand to defend her!"

"Oh—dear Harvey," I murmured. "Can they be fighting, do you think?" Not that I cared in the least. Lying thus closely wrapped in his arms I was quite content to stay there, caring little for Harvey or the distress of those at home, or anything else.

Harvey came in almost as I spoke, however, followed by my lord, who appeared half sober and half sulky, and very ill-at-ease in both characters. He was a burly young man, heavy-set, with thick red neck and round face. Even his eyes were red, from liquor. Beside him, Harvey appeared handsomer than I remembered him, and as for Mr. Haywood, they hardly seemed to be of the same species.

Mr. Haywood had been holding me in his arms on a bench in front of the fire, in one of the little private rooms. He now assisted me to sit up beside him, and I found myself so much less comfortable at once that I looked very sullenly indeed upon my former tormentor.

"I find, ma'am," said he very stiffly, "that I have mistook your quality and offered you an affront by mistake, for which I now tender you my apologies, though under the same circumstances I daresay I should make the same mistake again."

I stared at him in amazement, the colour coming into my cheeks at so insulting an apology. He could hardly have said plainer that the fault was not his, and that finding me in such a situation was excuse enough for his own conduct.

I could see Harvey signalling me from behind my lord's back, but I was too angry to pay any attention.

"I don't doubt you would," I said haughtily, "if by circumstances you mean being most monstrously the worse for liquor and running about London like a wild Indian. How should you tell a lady from a—an actress—or know how to assist a young female in distress?"

"Jenny!" Harvey cried imploringly. Mr. Haywood gave an ill-suppressed laugh. My lord's face became still redder.

"I was *not* drunk. A little promising, I grant you, but not clean bowled by any means. And by circumstances I mean, madam, as you very well know, that decent young ladies do not run about London unattended in the middle of the night. This gentleman assures me you are merely young and misguided. I trust your friends will keep you in better restraint hereafter. In fact," he said, bursting with wrath, "I hope your brother will know how to lesson you! By God, I would, if you were my sister! Over my knee and a belt on your bare bottom, ma'am, would cure you of such frolics!"

"Would you, sir!" I gasped. "I suppose you are brute enough to do so, and Lord help your sister, if you have one!"

"I have, madam, and she is safe at home, where she belongs to be."

"While her brother roves about London like a Bedlamite!" I cried furiously. "Lord, sir, you set her a mighty fine example!"

"My lord," said poor Harvey, "the young lady is over-wrought——"

"The young lady, sir is a damned little shrew and I wish you joy of her!" my lord shouted. "She is bold enough now with you to support her! You should have seen her weeping and begging for mercy, meek and mild as a dove, when she thought herself undone!"

"I do not think, my lord," Mr. Haywood said, very seriously and unexpectedly, "that it becomes you to boast of it."

My lord whirled on him, glad enough to fasten a quarrel where he could get more satisfaction of it.

"What are *you* to Miss, may I ask?"

"A friend, I hope," he said, smiling down at me so that I nearly melted on the spot.

"Another?" my lord sneered. "Upon my word, for so young a lady she seems to have a monstrous wide acquaintance!"

"What do you mean by that, my lord?" Mr. Haywood

demanded, sternly. "Any young lady in so distressed a situation could command my friendship—and ought, my lord, to be able to count upon that of any decent man."

I thought this a mighty fine speech indeed, but it seemed so likely to lead to a quarrel, and I was so terrified for him, that I burst into tears, being partly driven to them by fatigue. For, in truth, I was more undone than I knew, and felt all the time upon the brink of hysterics.

This damped them all. Mr. Haywood rushed for another glass of wine, Harvey rang for smelling salts, and my lord stood looking at me with something of a hangdog expression.

I saw myself gaining so much by tears that I continued them as long as I could make them seem natural, being careful not to rub too much at my eyes, to make them red and spoil their prettiness in Mr. Haywood's opinion.

When my sobs showed signs of running down my lord said, with a return to his first sulky, half-apologetic manner, "I seem to be doing more harm than good. I repeat, madam, that I am sorry to have frightened you and am glad that you have come to no worse harm of it."

He then coldly wished us all good-night, and was going away, when some of my native wit returned—having been more bemused by Mr. Haywood than by all the frights of the evening. I saw in a sudden flash of clarity that I was sending away unappeased a man who, between pique and injured self-esteem, had it in his power to do me much ill in the eyes of the world. No doubt he owed me a handsomer apology than he had cared to make, but these lords carry everything with such a high hand that it was a wonder he had been brought to apologise at all. And it was true that in his eyes I must seem to have merited by folly, if not worse, all the distress he had brought on me.

So I jumped up off the bench and ran after him, trailing Harvey's cloak, with which they had covered my own torn and dirtied dress. Val's cardinal, of course, had been left behind in my flight from Dutton.

"My lord!" I said appealingly. As he turned round, looking at me glumly, I put one hand on his arm, holding the cloak up tight under my chin with the other, for I was half naked beneath.

My voice was a good deal broken with the passage of sobs and I did not scruple to let it quaver as much as it would. "My lord, I—I ask your pardon if I have been shrewish with you, but I was so frightened—I am distracted near out of my wits—I hardly know what I do——"

The tears came spilling over again, but through them I saw his lordship regard me with quite an altered countenance.

"Pray don't distress yourself further, ma'am," he said, more softly, though still stiffly. "I am sorry to have been the source of so much alarm to you."

I looked up at him imploringly, still clinging to his arm. It vexed me sorely to coax him like this, when I would like to have boxed his ears for the anguish he had caused me. My lips and bosom were still sore from his mishandling. But I could not help being gratified to see how well a little show of distress could befriend me. Truly, one catches more flies with honey than vinegar—particularly if they be of the male sex.

"I fear you think me very naughty," I murmured brokenly. "I know—I feel how strange my situation must appear—how impossible to explain—but if you had the patience—if you would believe me——"

"You may be sure, madam, that I will believe anything you do me the honour of explaining, but I beg you to believe that no explanations are necessary. I could never think ill of one so young and lovely."

Talk of cooing like a dove! True, he made the speech with a heavy gallantry that robbed it of all feeling, but all the same—— I blinked my eyes at him in genuine astonishment and said bluntly, "But I should like to tell you, if you will only listen, for I am sure you must be wondering very much how I came to be in such a pass."

"Madam, I shall be honoured by your confidence."

With which, he led me by the hand back to my bench and seated me like a duchess. I was gratified to observe Harvey Underhill staring at me quite amazed; but Mr. Haywood, the handsome wretch, had his hand over his lips, and his eyes laughed at me. I had not fooled him for an instant. I could not help thinking, even then, that he was a man who knew too much about women.

They say it is the devil who puts lies upon our lips. I hope this is not so, for I have always found that lies come very readily to mine. But only when it is necessary; I have never been one to fib for the love of it.

It was certain that I had to lie on this occasion. I was not yet very worldly, and certainly not very wise, but I had a certain amount of native sense and I saw at once I could not tell the whole of my story truthfully. For my life, I dared not tell of Dutton. To begin with, my reputation would be ruined at once, even as he himself had warned me. No one would believe I had been in his house and had escaped unravished. Abduction was a very serious offence, even for a lord, and if I could prove the charge against him, he might even be driven to flee overseas. But what good would that do me, if I proved my own ruin along with his crime?

And I had a thought more serious than this. Dutton was infamous as a duellist who had more than once killed his opponent, escaping all punishment by merely going to France for a time. If Neal were to learn what had happened to me, I knew he would call Dutton out. God forbid that I should ever have my brother's death on my hands!

But in suppressing all reference to Dutton, I was left with a great hiatus in my story, which I had to fill somehow, making it sound convincing and yet too vague for anybody to disprove. Upon the whole, I think I did pretty well, considering everything.

I told all that had happened at Vauxhall, just as it did happen, up to the point of the abuction. I explained my natural mistake, and my doubt how to find Neal and Val again. But instead of the truth, I remembered the thing I had considered doing, and said that I had appealed to a passing couple for aid.

They treated me kindly at first, I said with a pathetic sigh. While I remained with the lady, the man had searched the gardens for my brother. When he could not find him, the gentleman suggested my brother and sister had probably left the gardens, hoping to find me at home before them. There were always chairs and coaches for hire outside the gardens, and they might think that I had thus returned home. The gentleman then suggested that they drive me home, and the lady cordially supported him.

"I was very much frightened at Vauxhall alone," I said, looking appealingly at my lord. "The men affronted me and I did not know what to do. So I went with this couple, who seemed very kind and quite respectable."

He wagged his head gravely. "Aye, but I warrant they were nothing of the sort," he said ominously. "Lord, child! Vauxhall is filled with pimps and bawds seeking young innocents like you. 'Tis notorious."

Thus neatly guided in my tale, I sighed, "Alas, my lord, if only I had your knowledge of the world! But indeed I was quite taken in. And at first they offered me no affront. But when we had crossed the Bridge and come into the City, I saw that we were not going the right way. I thought the coachman had mistaken, and told the gentleman so. He reassured me, and called out something. But Lord! what was my fright to discover we merely went faster, and quite in the wrong direction."

Harvey Underhill scowled; my lord swore. I ventured a glance at Mr. Haywood, who stood leaning against the mantel, looking impossibly handsome with the firelight flickering over his golden head. He wore an appropriately sympathetic expression, but there was something in his bright glance that made me hastily avert my own.

I continued my story, explaining how they had at first reassured and then threatened me, how they had taken my purse, but still promised to bring me home at last. Taking advantage of the coachman's pulling up to let a wagon cross before him, I suddenly tore open the door, jumped out into the street, and ran for my life.

"So I escaped them," I explained, "but found myself quite lost, and at a great distance from home, and with no money to hire assistance. I was afraid to ring at any house, so walked on, hoping to meet with the watch——"

86

"As well call on a mouse for protection!" my lord exclaimed scornfully. Then he grew extremely red. "Upon my word, ma'am, I am chagrined to recall my behaviour," he said, and this time he sounded as though he really meant it.

I judged this was the time to strike, and said appealingly, "Indeed, my lord, I will never think of it again and I hope you won't. I am afraid many persons might still think the worst of me, should they hear the story."

Heavy as he was, he took the hint quickly enough. "They shan't hear of it from me, my dear," he assured me. "My friends are too drunk to remember, and Polly's mouth is shut. I shall see that it remains so."

I thanked him with genuine gratitude this time. He then made an offer which I was ready to jump at, but which did not please Harvey. "I'll go home with you," my lord said, "and stand surety for your story, so that they will not deal harshly with you."

Remembering the treatment he had recommended for me, I could hardly help giggling, and Mr. Haywood winked at me.

But I was very ready to take his offer, knowing how Mr. Dangerfield loved a lord. Harvey Underhill, however, politely declined it, and I thought he scowled when my lord bade me goodnight very graciously, and begged to have the honour of sending to know how I did next day.

"Now, Miss Archer, I have ordered a coach and I shall take you home," Harvey said, when we were at last rid of my lord. "There's not the least need in the world for you to come with us, Bob."

"I think I'll be as obtuse as my lord in taking a hint," Mr. Haywood said, laughing.

"My dear fellow, these people will have been quite distracted over Jenny. The fewer of us involved, the better for their feelings."

"The thought does you credit," Haywood said lazily. He pushed himself away from the hearth with easy grace and came forward to take my hand. I felt ready to bite Harvey for his kind consideration for Val. It was Val he thought of, I knew, and for her sake I was cheated of a coach ride in the dark with Robert Haywood.

"Good-night, Miss Archer," Mr. Haywood said, looking down at me with that bright blue glance that made my bones turn to water. "I hope I may claim the same privilege as Lord Gould, and send tomorrow to learn how you do."

I curtsied as well as I could for the encumbrance of Harvey's great cloak, and longed to say, "Come yourself, sir," but contented myself with as speaking a glance as possible.

And then, as Harvey turned away, Robert suddenly bent down so that his cheek brushed mine and whispered, "Some day, when we are better acquainted, I will ask you what *really* happened at Vauxhall!"

I was so shaken by the touch of his face against mine that I hardly noticed his words till I recalled them in the coach afterwards, and sat torn between dismay and laughter. It was frightening to be seen through so easily! And yet it was curiously thrilling too.

I did not even notice the dark streets for seeing his face, nor hear Harvey's conversation for remembering the low coaxing voice. He had called me pretty; yes, and beautiful; and though men said those things easily, not meaning them, in that voice you believed them, or did not even care whether they were true.

When we arrived at Dangerfield's we saw the house all lit up, late as it was, with servants running in and out, and such an air of disorder everywhere you might have guessed some disaster had occurred.

At the sight of me, one maid went into hysterics and two or three of the men rushed off to find Dangerfield and my brother, who were searching all over town for me. There was not a servant left with sense enough to offer us any service.

Val heard the riot and came running downstairs, crying, "Oh, Jenny, Jenny!"

Then she saw Harvey and turned as red as she had been white before. She took hold of me very hard by the hand, as though she could never let me go, but stared all the while at Harvey, looking most strangely. And I had grown so wise in one night that I knew, with a pang of pity for her, that she had loved Harvey Underhill, and loved him still.

As for him, he stared too, growing flushed. She was dressed still as she had been at Vauxhall, having neither been to bed nor even taken off her clothes since they realised I was lost. With the colour burning up bright in her cheeks she looked more beautiful than ever.

Watching them both, I began to gabble out my story, talking very fast so that neither of them need say anything, but only stand and stare upon one another. I told the same tale I had done before, only glossing over my treatment at the hands of Lord Gould, and saying of course very handsome things about Harvey's rescue of me.

When I finished, Val, still holding fast to my hand, went forward a step and made him a great curtsey, smiling a strange, almost wild, smile.

"So, Harvey," she said, "I have you to thank for saving my sister. It is strange to think on, is it not?"

"It is as if God meant it," he answered hoarsely, looking at her as though he would eat her with his eyes.

"God or the Devil," Val said, and she gave a little laugh, so that I shivered to hear her.

"It makes no difference to me," he answered hotly, "so that we are brought together again."

Val suddenly grew very pale. "To what purpose?" she said coldly, though that hot, feverish clutch upon my hand told a different story. "We parted before because you had a wife. That was reason enough then. Now I have a husband, and we have two good reasons to part instead of one."

"No," he said, in a low voice. "There is still one only. Alice is dead." And he thrust out his arm so that we might see the mourning band on it.

"Dead!" Val whispered. Her hand grew suddenly cold and slack in mine. "Dead! So soon?"

And I knew what she meant. So soon—and so late.

Harvey knew also. He tore his eyes from her and stared

89   D

sullenly at the floor. "Yes," he said, "so soon. Six months after you were married. You need not have waited so long, after all."

Val gazed at him almost frantically. "Good God! Do you mean by that to reproach me?" She looked round on me as if to make me judge between them. "Jenny! Do you hear him? And it was he—he who fell away from me! Who let himself be herded like a beast that has strayed out of the fold! And left me without a word!"

"Valentine——"

"Do you remember the last time I came to your house? And was driven away like a whore who has thieved what belonged to an honest woman? Where were you then, Harvey? Watching from behind some curtain? You were not so sorrowful to be parted from me then."

"I was from home," he said hoarsely. "I did not know. I heard afterwards—it was too late. I could not mend and might make all worse. You had a right to marry—— But oh, Val! if you had only waited a little longer!"

I could have wrung my hands over the two of them, driving each other wild with reproaches.

"Wait?" Val said, in a low savage voice. "For what? For your wife to die, and let all say that I had driven you to murder her? For my father to half kill me, or send me out of the house? For you to decide in the end, maybe, that you wanted goods not so shopworn as I? And now you come to me boldly—now that you are free and the sin is not yours. You're a coward, Harvey Underhill! A coward and a fool, and it is God's punishment on me that I must love you . . . That I must love you . . ."

I think she had nearly driven him from her with that cruel speech, but she repeated those last few words in a tone so low and hopeless and desperate that the tears came to my eyes and Harvey simply put me aside and took her by the hands.

"My darling," he said, "it is all true, but God be my witness—I loved you then, I love you now, and never shall love anybody else."

I heard Val whisper something, I could not tell what, and then they were locked in each other's arms—there in the very hall of

90

the house, with servants everywhere and Dangerfield perhaps even now upon the doorstep.

I stood aghast at such folly. It was such wild careless work as this that had brought them to ruin in the first place. Short of going into the streets at noon, they could have chosen no place more conspicuous to expose themselves.

However I soon saw that nothing would part them, once they began to kiss, and I did not know what to do but remain with them, so that no one could say anything worse had passed.

To tell the truth, I was vexed as well as dismayed. Here was I, the heroine of the occasion, having passed from one danger to another, the whole household thinking me murdered or worse—receiving no more attention than the cat that has strolled home after a pleasant evening upon the roofs!

I stood, tired, hungry and thirsty, first upon one foot and then on the other, ready to cry with vexation and anxiety, and yet in my heart not able to blame them either. Only to envy them.

Lord knows when they would have separated, or what might have come of it, but that Val suddenly grew very faint, almost unconscious in Harvey's arms.

He was much alarmed, and would have carried her up to her chamber, but I prevented him. That would make a pretty story, truly!

I told him to carry her to the sofa in the drawing-room and cover her with a shawl. While he hung over her, out of his wits with love and anxiety, I ran about beating up the fire, fetching salts and spirits, berating the servants into some sort of order, and wondering all the while to see myself, having expected to be put to bed and waited upon as an invalid the moment I entered the house.

When Val had recovered a little, I warned Harvey very seriously to go, and she had wit enough to second me. He was very unwilling, but obeyed us at last. Why men have so little sense when they are in love, I shall never understand, but so it is. Whereas women who are stupid enough ordinarily can show the cunning of the devil in carrying off a love affair. I suppose it is because men are accustomed to take what they want, and women to contrive for it.

Mrs. Betty, my sister's woman, helped me put her mistress to bed. She was a sly-faced creature, and I would not willingly have trusted her an inch, but I had to have help, for Val was really ill.

" 'Tis to be hoped she does not come on with a miscarriage," the woman said to me, reproachfully. "La, such a to-do! We thought you abducted, miss, or worse."

"I was lost," I snapped, not being of a mind to hear reproaches from a slut like her. "But no harm has come of it to me, and I daresay my sister will take none. If you fools tended her better, instead of rioting about the house, your master would be better served."

She tossed her head, and muttered something which I took to be insolence of some kind, directed more at Val than at me.

I took her up very sharply. "Speak up, if you have anything to say. And say what you have to say to your mistress, instead of sneaking behind her back carrying tales." I added nastily, "He is not so fond of you but what I can carry the day against you, and tell a tale worth any of yours."

This quelled her, for though I knew she had lain with Dangerfield from time to time, she had also tumbled with the footmen, and Lord knows who else beside, being a harlot by nature.

Then, to pacify her, I gave her a ribbon of mine and a piece of Val's lace, and thus struck a truce. Mrs. Betty had a nose for intrigue, and had seen and heard enough of Harvey's arrival to know there might be more profit coming to her through this source, and so agreed, without plainly saying so, to hold her tongue for the time being.

At last, seeing Val asleep, I was able to get to bed myself. It was by now about three, and I felt as though I had been awake for days and days. My thin little shoes were quite worn through, and my feet sore and bruised from walking almost barefoot upon the street. I ached all over, as though I had had a beating from my father. And, worst of all, I was oppressed with a queer sense of disaster, without knowing why.

So at first I tossed and could not sleep, and then suddenly fell into a deep sleep. And in that sleep I had a dream, and in the dream I saw the face of disaster, which in my waking was still turned from me. When the day came at last that I saw it, I knew that I had seen it before. And yet it was a very simple, harmless dream, to haunt me so.

I saw Harvey Underhill, sitting very still in a chair, with a sweet gentle smile on his face giving him a look almost child-like. He was gazing down at a baby that he held in his lap, and though I could not see its face, I knew that it was Val's child. It was all bound up from head to foot in fine white cloth, as though it were dressed for christening, but with no lace or finery.

This was a pleasant picture enough, and yet it frightened me very much in my dream, for I knew Dangerfield would be angry to see Harvey hold his child and look at it so fondly, as though he loved it. I tried to step forward and take the baby away, but Val came up behind me and held me. She held me so tightly, with her little hands, that I could not shake her off, and she kept saying, "No, no, let them go together. Why should *he* have everything?" I was angry at her folly, and kept striking at her furiously, trying to get to Harvey and take the child from him, but she paid no heed to my blows, seeming to laugh at me. And then Neal's voice spoke in my ear, only strange and deep, trembling with emotion, not like his ordinary voice at all. "Leave them, Jenny," he said, "leave them and come with me. I will take care of you; come with me. There is nobody but us, now . . ."

I woke from this dream shivering and trembling from an un-known terror, and found that Neal's voice was no dream but reality, and that was what had wakened me.

He knelt beside my bed, saying my name over and over, with a kind of sob in it like a man distracted.

As I stirred and opened my eyes, he lifted his head. "Jenny!" he said, as though he cried in pain. And then he caught me up in his arms, holding me so fiercely that I gasped for breath. "Jenny! Jenny, my darling!"

93

He buried his face upon my shoulder and I could feel the hot tears wet through the stuff of my gown and run down my neck.

He held me so tightly that I could not even move to put my arms around his neck, or comfort him. Wakened suddenly from sleep like this, and taken by surprise, I was almost frightened by his vehemence. And he hurt me in his passion—my breast was bruised and his fingers bit cruelly into my flesh.

"Neal!" I gasped. "Oh, brother, pray!—you are hurting me—let me go!"

As suddenly as he had snatched me up, he dropped me. He had brought a lighted candle with him by which I saw his face, all distorted. As he towered over me, I thought he was going to strike me, and shrank from him in terror.

"Hurt you!" he said savagely. "I am of a mind to kill you! By God, I have been near to killing myself. Tell me, tell me now——" He took me again by the arms in that fierce, cruel grasp. "If you lie to me, I'll strangle you! Are you innocent still? Have you spent the night on the streets and come off intact? Or did you find out tonight how a man is made, sweet sister?"

I was absolutely terrified of him. He had been drinking, but it was something beside drink that made him so wild.

And then, with that dreadful suddenness, he changed again, dropping his head beside mine on the pillow, throwing his arm across my body.

"Forgive me, Jenny!" he whispered. "Forgive me, sweet sister! I am mad—I have been out of my mind—thinking—thinking what might happen to you—— And it was my fault. I lost sight of you. It was all my fault. It was as though I betrayed you. I saw your sweetness violated—— Oh God, I have been in hell!"

He sobbed like a child, lying there beside me on the pillow, and now it was my turn to draw him into my arms and try to comfort him.

In bits and snatches, while he grew quieter, I told him my story—only not the true version, you may be sure. Indeed, I concealed much that I had told the others, and even at that it was almost more than he could bear, and I had to break off to soothe and comfort him.

"I'm not hurt, Neal! See, I am well and whole! And no one has done me any harm. I was much frightened, I own, but, thank God, I have come safely off. Was it not strange that Harvey should be there to help me?"

"I would it had been I," Neal said jealously. "There would have been somebody dead, I swear it!"

"Then I'm glad it was not you," I answered resolutely. "There had been no hurt done that anybody should be killed for it. And promise me—Neal, you *must* promise me!—that you will carry it no further, nor try to find those people who deceived me, nor do anything foolish."

"Find them!" he said, between his teeth. "I'll see them on the same gallows yet! They must be known at Vauxhall."

Well, there was no danger of his being able to find the villainous pair of my story, since I had made them of whole cloth, as the saying is. But I was terrified that any enquiry at Vauxhall might put him upon Dutton's trail.

I begged and pleaded with him, therefore, to let it all go. He was very unwilling, but when I represented to him that the less that was known of the story the better for my reputation, he reluctantly gave his promise.

"I'll call on Harvey Underhill tomorrow, and give him my thanks."

"Yes, do," I said, thankful to turn his thoughts into safer channels. "Indeed, he was very brave and very good to me."

Neal lay beside me silent for a moment. Then he said, as though absently, "Did you know this Underhill well in the old days?"

"Oh yes," I said. "You know he was for ever riding and riot-ing about with my father. And then, of course, Val——" But I paused, finding myself in difficulty.

He raised himself sharply on one elbow, gazing down at me. The candle was at his back, so that his face was shadowed. But I felt his eyes closely searching my face.

95

"Val?" he said. "I remember now—I heard something of this. So this was the hot lover that drove my father to marrying her off? It's Harvey we have to thank for a brother-in-law like Dangerfield?"

"It was not Harvey's fault," I defended him. "My father should have known better, and so should Val. They were too much together and people began to talk, and that vexed my father, so he made her marry Dangerfield. But there was nothing wrong between them."

"No?" Neal said coolly. "And if there was, my dear little innocent sister, how should you know of it? Would they tell you?"

"Dangerfield told me himself that Val was—that she had not had a lover."

"And Underhill? Why did *he* not marry her?"

"He had a wife already. But she is dead now."

"Indeed?" Neal said remotely. He lay down again and was silent for so long that I had nearly drifted off when he spoke.

"And this is the chivalrous gentleman who rescued you tonight?"

I had already told him so several times, and repeated "Yes!" impatiently, vexed at being wakened. I was dreadfully sleepy and the windows were growing grey with morning.

"And are you fond of him, Jenny?" Neal went on, his own voice seeming sleepy. "You like this Harvey?"

I saw enough trouble ahead without there being ill-feeling between Harvey and Neal, so roused myself to answer warmly. I extolled Harvey's virtues—his good humour, his bold riding, easy friendliness, kindness to his invalid wife, etc., etc.

"He's a handsome fellow, I suppose?" Neal murmured, his voice half smothered in the pillow.

"Oh yes," I said, though in truth I did not care much for Harvey's kind of good looks. He had a hot brown look about him, a reddish cast to hair and skin and eyes, that made him seem like a big handsome animal, full of good-humoured lusting, but not much else. "Tall and handsome . . ."

96

Neal's hand slowly crept up from my shoulder and dropped across my throat like a caress. It lay there, uncomfortably heavy, yet I did not like to put it off.

"It is like an old romance, sister," he said, with something like a smile in his voice. "A tall handsome gentleman, a friend from the past, riding up like a knight on a white horse when the maiden is in greatest need . . ." His voice dropped to a whisper. "And what did you give him, sweet sister, as a reward? This old friend, this hot lover of Val's, what did you give him?"

"Give him?" I said, bewildered. "What do you mean, brother?" And then suddenly I uttered a choked cry and my hands came up, clutching, as his hand caught me round the throat.

"You know what I mean!" Neal whispered savagely into my ear. I could feel his breath, very hot, upon my neck and cheek. "You are not so innocent as that! You were alone with him—he had saved you—and you, perhaps, had always lusted after him——Had you not, Jenny? You remembered him so well! And then did he take you, Jenny, for his reward? Or did you give it willingly? Did he put up your skirts, or did you? And was it pleasant, Jenny, and would you like to do it again some day? Nay, sweet sister, stop struggling and answer me! *Answer me, you little bitch!*"

I would have screamed, but I had no breath; I would have jumped from bed, but he was too strong for me. I writhed and gasped, unable even to speak, my hands tearing at that clutch around my throat.

And then there came again that great swing of the pendulum. He let me go, abruptly, and sat up on the edge of the bed, his head in his hands.

I lay back, gulping in the sweet air, my hands at my throat. I was too dazed even to be frightened. I said, in a whisper, "Neal, you are surely mad!"

"Yes," he said, after a pause. "Yes, I believe I am—sometimes. I am sane and sober now. Forgive me, Jenny; did I hurt you? Forgive me—did I frighten you?"

"It was not that!" I said, still staring at his back, unbelieving that all this had passed between us. "It was the things you

97

said—— Do you think me so easy a harlot, Neal? Or a decent gentleman so great a villain?"

"I do not think at all," he said, in that quiet voice, his head bent down. "I only feel. I love you too much, little sister. You must remember that and excuse the rest."

"Neal," I said, "I swear to you that no harm has come to me tonight, and that Harvey did not so much as offer to kiss me! Good Lord, he doesn't care for *me*!"

"Don't talk of it, Jenny. I was mad. We will not talk of it any more. I know you are little and innocent still. Who could look in your eyes and doubt you? It is only that I know how evil men can be."

He rose and bent over me, tucking me in gently, as though I were a little child. His handsome face was all smoothed out and peaceful in the grey dawn light.

"Go to sleep, my darling," he said. "Do not think any more tonight of me or any man. We are all villains in our hearts, that is why no man will trust another. But you are safe, thanks be to God, and hereafter I will see that you remain so."

"Yes, Neal," I said, meekly, from under the bedclothes.

The greatest joke was that Mr. Dangerfield did not get home at all until noon the next day. He drove up to the door in a hired coach, looking exceedingly green and ill-at-ease. He was very sick upon the stairs, and sick again in Val's room so that she screamed with disgust and fled, leaving a servant to clean the mess. His valet brought him a glass of flat ale, which settled his stomach and restored him a good deal.

"Lord, my dear!" he said, staggering into my bedroom, where Val had taken refuge. "I cannot imagine how I came to be so over-set."

Val surveyed him, wrinkling up her pretty nose. "You are in a horrid pickle, sir! Pray, where did you spend the night?"

He rolled his eyes in a way to make you laugh, though he was so ill I could not but pity him. "I will not offend your ears, my love."

"I wish you would not offend my nose," Val said roundly.

98

"For the Lord's sake, change your clothes! Your reek makes me ill."

No man likes to be told that he stinks, however true it may be, and he was provoked into the sulks, saying that this was all the thanks he got for running about the whole night long after that little devil Jenny.

"And there she sits," he said, focusing those great gooseberry eyes (more unripe than ever!) upon me, not without difficulty. "Sweet little innocent! Pray, Miss Jenny, what's *your* story? How many gentlemen got a hand under *your* skirts last night?"

"Don't be vile, sir," Val said, haughtily. "My sister and I are not accustomed to such language." (I used to marvel sometimes to hear her talking to Dangerfield! I think she almost believed herself that we had been brought up innocent and sheltered. Whereas we had both been called worse names by our father than by any man since. Yes, and sat at table when he was drunk and heard his stories, enough to make a stable-boy blush.)

But it was strange how she could cow Dangerfield when she put on this tone. I suppose it reminded him of the great ladies whom he served every day in his warehouse. And then too he had the essential character of a bully. Fear him, shrink from him, and he would follow you to twist your arm. Face him down boldly and scornfully, and he would give ground before you.

At this point he sulked and muttered, saying that this was pretty thanks for searching about London all night, in danger of robbery and murder and Lord knows what else.

It was usually my part in their quarrels to make such peace as I was able. I accordingly intervened now to thank him prettily for his care of me. This soothed him a little, and he was very ready to hear my story.

He was also very ready to blame me for what was not my fault, and showed his usual nasty eagerness to believe the worst. I sustained this as best I could, and was just working up to a glowing description of Harvey's rescue, when we heard a thundering double knock on the front door.

99

"Oh Lord!" Val said. "Who can this be? Well, we can't see anybody now, that's plain."

Mrs. Betty came in, her eyes round. "My Lord Gould's compliments to Miss Archer, and he hopes she does not find herself the worse today." Then she dropped all pretence and gasped, "My lord's own chariot, ma'am! and his own servant, fine as a gentleman, to deliver the message!"

The change in Mr. Dangerfield was ludicrous. As I reluctantly explained that this lord had been the leader of the Mohocks, all his blame turned to rapturous congratulations. Insulted by a lord? Manhandled by a peer? Good God, was ever girl so fortunate!

He raved on in this style, asking Betty a thousand questions about my lord's equipage, etc., until Val could bear it no longer, and said curtly:

"The man sounds a great brute. He ought to be made to pay damages."

The very thought shattered Mr. Dangerfield. He faintly requested her not to talk like a damned fool, and eagerly asked me if I thought my lord was the least bit catched by me.

Remembering all that had passed between us, I could hardly keep from bursting out laughing, as I demurely replied, "He did seem rather catched at one time, sir, but it went off."

"Still, he has sent to enquire. That's very handsome! You must take your sister about, my dear, where Lord Gould is likely to see her again. Do you think he would ever do us the honour of dining here?"

This delight of my brother-in-law's with my lord's condescension tided us over a very awkward moment—the arrival of Harvey Underhill. Bold as always, he had evidently resolved to take the high hand and call at once with the freedom of an old acquaintance.

Mr. Dangerfield was by no means glad to see him. He was too proud of his own hospitality to refuse it to anyone, especially to a gentleman with a good property. But he grew sullen and silent, saying no more to Harvey than necessary, and though he had planned to go to his warehouse, he changed his mind and remained at home the whole afternoon.

Val always said her husband was a fool, but it was not so. He was free enough of her favours to such a one as Dutton, seeing plainly that she hated and detested him, so that he might safely allow what she would never grant. But he was quite otherwise with Harvey Underhill. And, seeing it, I realised again what I had guessed from the first—that he was more than shrewd in his own way, and that those who discounted him too lightly might find themselves surprised.

I was in despair to see how plainly Val and Harvey *did* discount him. From the first they scarcely troubled to conceal their feelings; and as for their disdain, they made that plain enough. It was just what I would have expected of Harvey. Big, bold and handsome, he laughed openly at the comic figure of the shopkeeper husband, thin, puny and ugly. He did not even make a pretence of propitiating him. He gazed at Val as though they were alone in the world, and spoke to Dangerfield only to snub or deride him.

I could not help thinking this very rude as well as very foolish of Harvey. It is ill-natured to insult a man in his own house, before his own wife, where he can scarcely resent it. Not that Dangerfield was the man to carry his resentment to an open quarrel. Harvey was safe enough there. But what of Val?

I thought to myself that Harvey would make a proper lover, no doubt, when the advantage lay his way. But if difficulties pressed, he did not seem likely to prove a resourceful support. Indeed, he had already proved the contrary.

Obviously, however, it was of no use now to remind Val of that. It remained to smooth things over, and outwit Dangerfield if possible, and I resolved to have a talk with Harvey as soon as an opportunity presented itself.

Meanwhile, I thrust myself very much forward, laughed and chattered, forced Harvey to go over the tale with me again and again, praised him lavishly, and did as much as I could to come between them and distract Dangerfield's attention.

Val reproached me for it afterwards, and I tore my hair in despair.

"How *can* you be so foolish? You had no care before of your reputation with Harvey, and look what came of it! Do you *want* to be ruined? I'm only trying to save you, and you haven't wit enough to see it."

"I want to be happy!" poor Val wailed. "Only let us alone, Jenny! What does it matter if I am ruined? I can't be more unhappy, and Harvey will take care of me."

"*Will* he?" I asked, grimly. "And of Dangerfield's child too?"

That gave her pause. "I don't suppose I can stop you," I went on. "If you must have Harvey, you must."

"Do you think me very dishonest, Jenny?" Val asked, colouring. "But Dangerfield—— Jenny, I caught him with Betty the first week we were married! Why should he care? He doesn't love me."

"Husbands are strange that way," I said, sagely.

"I don't care!" Val cried. And then she said, not very convincingly, "I only want to be loved a little. I do not mean to ruin myself, I assure you."

"You may find Harvey too hot to hold," I warned her. "But anyhow you can't go on like this. If he will, Harvey had better pretend to be catched by me."

"Aye, Jenny, that's a good thought!" Val said eagerly. "Then he can come as often as he likes." She clouded. "But you are so pretty, Jenny! Suppose he should come to like you best? I shall grow to be fat and awkward, with this damned thing in me, and you are so little and slender!"

I groaned. "Val, for heaven's sake! *I* don't want Harvey and he thinks of nobody but you. Indeed, I doubt he can act well enough to make a pretence of it, but we can try."

"He'll do it for me, Jenny," Val said confidently, and from tears she went into laughter, describing how Harvey had held her hand between their chairs while Dangerfield was scolding the servant about the wine.

I fancied I knew a good deal of love, but in truth I knew so little as to marvel at this flightiness of hers. I did not see why one could not be practical in love. No more need be said to explain that I did not yet know the meaning of the word.

There was one person only to whom I told the true story of what happened at Vauxhall, and that was Val. I could not let her remain ignorant of the lengths to which Dutton's passion for her might carry him.

Swearing her to secrecy, I told it all while she listened in amazement. She agreed that Neal must never hear of it, and promised to take care not to expose herself to a second attempt by Dutton.

"Do you think he would dare?"

"He would dare anything," I said, positively. "He boasts of it. I think he is more than a little mad."

"I have always thought so," Val answered, "but I am not afraid of him."

I was silent. It is well to be brave; but sometimes it is well also to know when to be afraid. I was very much afraid of Dutton.

Up to this time Neal, though he spoke scornfully of Val's acquaintances and scoffed at the idea of my marrying a merchant like Dangerfield, had not done much to introduce me to other society. It was too much trouble, I suppose. He liked better to have Val and myself with him alone.

But now he and Val had several discussions concerning my future which resulted in my introduction to a society hitherto unknown to me. And which had some results also very foreign to what they planned.

I fancy it was not without difficulty that Neal obtained the *entrée* for me that he wanted. A young man like himself, handsome, agreeable, able to make a good figure in the world, with a well-sounding name and a claim to aristocracy through his mother, will always find a welcome in good society. His halfsister, the daughter of Mollie Lake and granddaughter of Farmer Lake, was not so welcome. My residence in a merchant's house was held to be much against me too. Luckily he was a favourite of a rich and fashionable lady, Mrs. Sylvester, who had no daughters of her own to marry and who, hearing of his difficulty, good-naturedly offered to sponsor my introduction to the world.

She had a handsome house in Queen Anne Street, and proposed that I should stay with her for a while, but I would not leave Val. Neal was vexed with me, and Val urged me. She made a very good pretence, but I saw through it.

"I don't care if I never go into Society. I don't care if I never marry. I won't leave Val now," I said, and Neal had to give in.

Fortunately Mrs. Sylvester did not feel herself eternally polluted by the fact that I stepped into her carriage from a merchant's house.

"I'm glad you won't leave your sister, my dear," she said, on my introduction to her. "I'm sure she needs you. So many young females would cut their sister's throat for an introduction to Society that I'm glad to see one who has a little natural affection. We shan't get on the worse for it, I assure you."

I thanked her most sincerely for her kindness, and repeated her words to Neal with some triumph.

He shrugged. "Vastly good-humoured of her," he said, with that sneering touch he could affect when he was crossed or vexed in any way. "It's to be hoped others will be as charitable. But if you suppose the same men will call on you at Dangerfield's as would seek you out in Queen Anne Street, you are mistaken."

"Then they may go to hell!" I said, roundly, and at this he inexplicably laughed and was in a good humour with me again.

Mrs. Sylvester took me visiting with her among the ladies of her acquaintance—to have me looked over and approved, I suppose, since I was of such doubtful antecedents.

I cannot say I enjoyed it, feeling all my pride rebel; but for Neal's sake I choked down my feelings and went about as dutifully as any proper miss. Mrs. Sylvester was helpful in her advice, and by sticking close to her, doing all she did, and saying as little as possible (which was the first rule in her book) I did not much miscarry.

The result was that Mrs. Sylvester was able to get me an invitation to a large private ball. To appear there, she assured me, was to be accepted in a general way by Society, since the hostess was known to be extremely careful of her company.

"After that, my dear, it all depends on you. Only do not forget that, while it is pleasant to be admired by the gentlemen, it is absolutely imperative to be accepted by the females. If the men admire you too boldly, or too extravagantly, the women will draw off. The old ones will fear for their daughters—and their sons!—and the young ones will be jealous. A young lady with a good family to back her can afford to become a toast. You, my dear, will do very much better to avoid too much success of that kind."

There was so much good sense in this, though unpalatable as good sense is apt to be, that I could not resent it.

"I will try, ma'am," I said meekly.

She gave me a sudden mischievous twinkle. "You are a clever child," she said. "You will not miscarry from lack of wit. That is why I speak frankly to you. You will never make the excuse that you *could not help it*. A clever girl can avert anything, even being a toast."

Her commendation flattered me. So did the assumption that I might aspire to be a belle—a toast—if I wished. I resolved to be very decorous indeed, if not downright inconspicuous.

But I was not so demure that I forgot to care about my dress. Even Dangerfield, much impressed by my sudden elevation, had a hand in ordering it; and Val, Mrs. Betty and I thought and talked of nothing else for days.

For a dance my hair was powdered, of course, curled all round my face with a thick cluster of curls at the nape. Val painted my face and tied a black velvet ribbon round my throat to show off my white skin. I wore a gown of silvery rose brocade over a skirt of pale green satin. My petticoat was also of pale green, with a fringe to show, and I had lace on my sleeves, which came just below the elbows, and on the bodice of the gown. The gown was cut, as the fashion was, scandalously low, with a thin silk handkerchief put in to save my modesty from total exposure. Val hung her pearl ear-rings in my ears; and with fan, lace handkerchief and gold scent bottle (Neal's gift on the great occasion) I felt elegant indeed.

Mrs. Sylvester, herself handsomely dressed in red brocade over a magnificent white satin skirt, complimented me upon my appearance as I got into her coach.

"Now, Miss Archer," she said briskly, "remember what I have told you. At a private ball you may dance with any gentleman who presents himself as a partner, whether you have been introduced to him or not. If you refuse one partner, you cannot dance afterwards without giving offence, so be careful not to catch a gentleman's eye until you are sure you like his appearance. You may sit down a dance or two with him, if you are tired, so long as you remain in plain view. If your partner becomes too warm or particular in his compliments, ask him to fetch you something— an ice, or a drink of water, or anything, to give him time to recollect himself. If he persists, ask to be taken to me for a while. I shall be in the card-room and you may sit with me if you are annoyed. It will also serve to remind the gentleman that you are not without protection. But if you wish to dance again, you must dance with him."

To this point I had been bold and eager, but as we joined the line of carriages before the house, and I began to con over my lessons, my heart suddenly failed me. As we entered the house I positively slunk behind Mrs. Sylvester's ample skirts, and would gladly have remained hidden there all night. For once in my life I felt as Missish as I ought.

Mrs. Sylvester, however, had no intention of keeping me on her hands all night. She was panting to take her place at the card-tables, but was too good-natured to do so until I had been provided with a partner.

She chose our places skilfully, therefore, taking two seats somewhat isolated, where we should be sure to be seen, and near a group of gentlemen who stood chatting beneath the musicians' gallery.

The men eyed me, and all the other young females, very complacently as we sat waiting like so many sheep for our shepherds. At that sight, my courage began to rise again.

Besides, I had never been in so beautiful a house, nor in such fine company, even at Ranelagh. It was a great house and the ballroom could accommodate, I believe, as many as forty couples. It seemed to me all of London must be there, though Mrs. Sylvester assured me it was not so.

We had arrived in good time for the dancing, which did not commence until eleven o'clock. To be late, Mrs. Sylvester said, unless one was pre-engaged or an acknowledged belle, was to run the risk of losing a good partner.

I remembered her advice about not catching anybody's eye until I was sure I wanted to encourage him, but I looked around as unobtrusively as I could. It did not take me long to separate the sheep from the goats. I would take *him* or *him*, but I would rather sit down all night than dance with *him*!

As time passed, I began to grow less particular. One gentleman after another passed me by to bow before other young ladies, and the sets were rapidly filling up. Plenty of men eyed me, and obviously discussed me, but whether it was because I did not please them, or looked too nervous, or was unknown, none approached me.

Till then, it had never occurred to me that I might fail to get a partner. Or, almost worse, only secure one through somebody's good offices, to make up a set when all the more favoured young ladies had been chosen.

A most horrid feeling of panic swept over me. I dared not look at Mrs. Sylvester, for fear she might be sympathising with me, or impatient at my lack of success. I fancied the other girls were talking and tittering over me among themselves. Most of them were acquainted, making up sets and chatting in groups. My isolation was deadly. I felt as though I stood alone under a great light, with everybody staring at me in derision.

If there is one thing I am sure of, it is that in Society success breeds success; and the reverse. I have seen pretty girls passed over because they looked worried or anxious, or chanced not to secure partners at first. And thereafter their chances grew successively less with each appearance; and their obvious anxiety increased; and in turn their charms diminished. It is a fatal circle. Whereas to begin well is everything.

I felt this instinctively, but what could I do? I could not spring from my seat and fasten myself upon a gentleman as he walked by. Once or twice I ventured an encouraging glance, even a faint smile. Judge of my chagrin when the gentleman did not respond! *That* was worse than anything and made me hot with shame.

Finally, when all the most attractive men had selected their partners and taken their places, a very plain simpering young man came up to Mrs. Sylvester with a bow, and begged to wish her a good evening. She responded graciously and they chatted. My heart beat with hope—I was so frantic by now I was ready to dance with anybody, anybody at all. Short, too thin or too fat, bad skin, no chin—I was past all reckoning of such items. All I cared for was the sum total—a man, any man, just so that he could hobble through a dance and give me the credit of having a partner.

Mrs. Sylvester's acquaintance was a very thin, reedy young gentleman with a receding chin and large drooping nose. Under other circumstances, I should have viewed him with disdain. Or, at most, pity.

Now I was positively brought so low that I prayed he might do me the infinite honour to ask for my hand. I prayed for his condescension as—I blush to say—I have prayed for few things before or since. And at the same time I hated him for being so necessary to me, and myself for being so desperate.

The sets were nearly formed, the musicians were tuning their instruments, and still that odious young man continued to chat, disregarding all of Mrs. Sylvester's pretty plain hints about Miss Archer. I forced myself to seem to take an interest in his conversation. I smiled, I simpered, I made play with my fan, and used my eyes as encouragingly as I could.

Suddenly I met his glance directly. He had very small pale eyes. They were bright at the moment with a glinting malicious satisfaction. I realised that he was perfectly aware of my situation, of my desperate anxiety, and was thoroughly enjoying himself. Perhaps women had been unkind to him; or perhaps he was naturally malicious; I do not know. But that he found this situation both amusing and gratifying was obvious.

I was quite paralysed with anger and chagrin. He looked at me with that bright, knowing stare, and then remarked to Mrs. Sylvester, with more bows, smirks and compliments than I can remember, " 'Pon my honour, ma'am, this has been a great pleasure! But I believe my partner is awaiting me. And perhaps I keep Miss Archer from dancing?"

His malice was so apparent that I saw Mrs. Sylvester redden with annoyance. If this wretched creature turned and left me without asking me to dance, I might as well cut my throat as hope to receive any other offer. That, and his insolence, was past bearing. My resentment broke over bounds.

I rose abruptly, so that they both looked at me startled. "Indeed, sir," I said crisply, "you do, and as your partner must be very eager indeed, pray do not let me detain you from her another moment. Ma'am," turning to the astonished Mrs. Sylvester with a curtsey, "pray excuse me. I will seek you out by and by."

And with that I walked straight out of the ballroom.

I had no thought in my head but to escape. I could not go home alone, but I could find the card-room and sit there while Mrs. Sylvester had her game. Anything was better than suffer such humiliation.

I hurried out of the ballroom in such disorder that I blundered straight into a gentleman and had to clutch him with both hands to save myself from falling.

I was in such a rage with every man alive by this time that I could cheerfully have hit him for being in my way. As for him, I had stepped very hard on his toe with a high heel, and I could hear him curse under his breath.

"Your pardon, sir!" I snapped.

"Not at all, madam," he returned through his clenched teeth. And then, recognising him, I exclaimed, "Mr. Parker!" while he burst out laughing and said cheerfully, "Miss Archer, my toes are always at *your* service."

"I hope I didn't hurt you."

"You did, very much," he said, with his odious frankness, "but I forgive you, for the unexpected pleasure of seeing you here."

"Why shouldn't I be here?" I said, ruffling.

"No reason at all, except that I did not know you were acquainted with Mrs. Hamilton. Are you here with your sister?"

"No, with Mrs. Sylvester. Do you know her? Neal has asked her to take me into Society."

"I see. But why are you running the other way in such a hurry?"

"I—I was going to the card-room."

Mr. Parker adjusted his handsome lace cravat—somewhat disordered by our encounter—and gazed at me thoughtfully.

"I have seen gamesters rushing on their ruin," he remarked, "but never in *quite* such haste. Are you so passionately fond of cards, Miss Archer? For my part, when I am at a ball I prefer to dance."

I hesitated and coloured. "So do I," I said, in a small voice. "But I have no partner."

Lord knows what it was that always made me blurt out to Mr. Parker something I might better have left unsaid. There was not the least need in the world to tell him the brutal truth. And yet, under the teasing yet friendly gaze of those bright dark eyes, out it came like a cork from a bottle. I had quite forgotten already how angry I had been with him at Vauxhall.

"No partner!" Mr. Parker echoed, in surprise. "What's the matter—are they all blind in there?"

There was in this something so soothing to my vanity that I asked appealingly, "*Do* I look as I should? Mrs. Sylvester said so—but of course she's not a man. And it was Mr. Dangerfield who chose my dress, and I'm sure he knows, except that he's not a gentleman," I added, suddenly doubtful.

"Miss Archer," Mr. Parker said gravely, "speaking as a man and also—I hope—as a gentleman, you look not only as you should, but downright ravishing."

I felt myself blush, and said shyly, "Thank you very much."

"Not at all," Mr. Parker said. He shook down his ruffles and settled the dark blue satin coat over his square shoulders. "And now that is settled, madam, I have the honour to propose myself as your partner for the evening."

"Oh!" I said foolishly. And then I drew back, feeling very self-conscious. "Please don't," I said. "I'd much rather sit in the card-room with Mrs. Sylvester."

Mr. Parker threw back his head in a laugh so heartily infectious that one of the footmen at the door grinned in sympathy before he could check himself.

"Good Lord!" he said. "What a set-down! Is my company as odious to you as all that?"

"No, no," I protested, in dismay. "That's not what I meant! Oh, you know it wasn't! Pray don't tease me. I meant that— that I don't want you to take pity on me."

"Miss Archer, *do* you want a good box on the ear?" he demanded. "Then don't talk nonsense but for heaven's sake come along before all the sets are made up."

I must say that I have rarely felt such satisfaction as I did on returning to the ballroom on Mr. Parker's arm. Though he could be so odiously provoking he was certainly as a partner all that any lady could desire. He was not angelically handsome like Robert Haywood, or even Neal, but in his own teasing way he was an attractive devil, and he handed me to a set with a manner that nobody, I think, could have bettered.

It is an ignoble confession to make, but I felt more obliged to him for saving me from the horrors of social failure than I had to Harvey Underhill for rescuing me from the Mohocks. And what's more, I think most women, if they told the truth, would choose rather to be insulted and manhandled than passed over as not worthy of attention. In the balance of life and death, maybe, the stings of Society should not count for much. But Lord! how the stings are poisoned at the time.

We met Mrs. Sylvester in the door, just coming to seek me. She was a woman of much poise, and did not seem in the least surprised to meet me with Mr. Parker, but, civilly wishing me much enjoyment, told me I would find her in the card-room whenever I was weary of dancing.

I suppose I thought every eye was upon us, when it was really not so. But as Mr. Parker appeared to be well known, and I was virtually a stranger to everybody, there was in fact some curiosity in seeing us together. The young ladies stared at me and simpered at him. The gentlemen greeted him and ogled me with increased interest. I had the greatest satisfaction in ignoring them all, and concentrating my entire attention on my partner.

All, that is, I could spare from the dance itself. I had never danced in public before and though I knew the steps perfectly well, I found it quite a different matter at a ball from hopping about at home with one of my sisters or the village dancing master.

I survived the first dance, however, without going amiss or making any fatal *faux pas*. The next dance was livelier and I began to enjoy myself. It might be more alarming to dance with a man than with my sisters, but a good deal more interesting. And Mr. Parker danced well, just as I would have expected from the way he carried himself.

We did not talk much. He spoke now and then, but seemed chiefly content to watch me smilingly, while I concentrated on the work in hand.

"Are you enjoying yourself, Miss Archer?"

"Oh yes! So much!"

"The air is full of compliments. Don't you hear them?"

"I don't care about them now," I said scornfully.

Mr. Parker applauded this spirit and we went down another dance with much *éclat*.

"Are you tired, Miss Archer?"

"No, not at all," I said, trying not to pant for breath.

"Well, I am. And dying of thirst as well. Shall we see what there is for supper?"

He seemed to know the house remarkably well. First he led the way to a charming little room, scarcely bigger than a cupboard, with long doors opening to a balcony overlooking the garden.

Then, settling us both very comfortably, he coolly rang the bell and desired a servant to bring us some supper and a bottle of wine.

"Not that sickly stuff for the ladies. Some of the good claret."

"I see you make yourself at home!" I said, half amazed, half admiring, as the servant bowed and withdrew.

"Well, you see, in a manner of speaking I *am* at home here," Mr. Parker explained, almost apologetically. "Mrs. Hamilton is my mother's sister. And as she is the only one of my relations who can tolerate me, I am here a good deal."

"Why don't the others like you?" I asked, impressed.

"I can't understand it either," Mr. Parker replied, choosing to suppose I spoke in wonder.

I could not help laughing. "You are so strange! Are you never serious?"

"Never for very long at a time. Neither are you, Jenny, I suspect."

I wriggled in discontent, suddenly diverted. "I do so hate my name! It's so monstrously *rustic*!"

"It is a charming little name that just suits you. However, if you prefer it, I will call you Jane."

"If you must use my first name," I said, with dignity, "pray use the right one. My name is *Jennifer*, not Jane."

"That is charming too, and since you have given me your permission——"

"No, no, I didn't mean to," I said hastily. "I don't think you ought. Neal says one must never do so."

"Your brother is a very proper-minded young man. Do you always do as he says?"

"Certainly," I said, hoping God would forgive me the lie. "He knows best—and besides, he is my guardian."

"Is he? Even to your disposition in marriage?" Mr. Parker enquired. He leaned back on the little gilt sofa, watching me. The open windows let in a draught that made the candle flames dance. The flickering light made his expression hard to read; now he seemed to be smiling, teasing, and then for a moment there was an odd gentleness in his glance.

113

"Well, I suppose so. My father is alive, but he hates me, and so——"

"Hates you! Good God, why?"

I shook my head. "I don't know. He always has. He was very unkind to my mother after he married her, and he has always hated me. That is why Neal brought me away to London —because my father used me so scornfully."

Mr. Parker started to say something, and then checked himself, shutting his lips with a firmness that made his chin look very square, deepening the cleft in it.

The servant returned with our supper and the wine. It had been hours since I dined and I fell to my plate with eagerness. The claret was delicious too, light and tingling. After a couple of glasses I began to feel rather tingling also, and Mr. Parker firmly put the bottle out of my reach.

"That's enough. You're an explosive mixture even when sober, Miss Jennifer, and Lord knows what we might expect of you drunk."

"I am *not* drunk. A little promising, I grant you, but not clean bowled." As Mr. Parker gazed at me in astonishment, I burst into giggles. "That's what Lord Gould said. Do you know my lord?"

"I do," Mr. Parker said, dryly. "And I can only say, Miss Archer, that I'm surprised at you."

"I couldn't help it," I said, giggling again. "I—I fell into an acquaintance with him."

"Then, if I were you, I would fall straight out again," my companion said emphatically.

I drew myself up haughtily. "Pray, sir, who are you to advise me as to my acquaintances?"

Mr. Parker sighed. "Take a glass of water, ma'am. It will serve to dilute the wine."

"I don't want to. I feel deliciously!"

"Come into the air, then," he suggested, and I followed him through the open doors to the balcony.

It was a warm June evening; the air moved softly against my hot cheeks. Distantly we could hear the music from the ballroom and below us somewhere there was the clink of dishes in the kitchen. The moon was just rising; there was a pale pearly light all over Mrs. Hamilton's charming little garden.

I leaned my arms on the railing and gazed down into the garden. There was a subdued sound of giggling and a young couple, servants by their dress, bounced out of the bushes, laughing and struggling. In the middle of the grass plot the young man caught the girl and gave her a hearty kiss; she replied with an equally hearty box on the ear, and they went strolling into the house in complete accord with each other.

"Do you suppose they are happy?" I asked dreamily. The wine had made me feel very odd—everything seemed much clearer than usual, and yet nothing seemed to matter as much. "Servants, I mean, and people like that."

Mr. Parker leaned beside me. The soft light darkened his coat to black. I held my hand up to it to see how white the fingers looked.

"As happy as anyone, perhaps," he answered, after a pause. "Are *you* happy, Jenny?"

I considered. "I don't know. I've never thought about it."

"Then perhaps you are." He turned and smiled down at me. "You have such merry eyes, Jenny! Do you know how inviting they are?"

I looked up at him in silence. I saw by the change in his face that he meant to kiss me, and instinctively I shut my eyes, tipping up my face.

I don't know whether it was the claret, or the moonlight, or what, but when he kissed me I suddenly forgot that I felt toward him as a brother. Putting my arms around his neck I kissed him back, and felt quite ready to go on kissing him all night.

It was he who put me away from him. "Jenny!" he said, in a strange low voice. "Jenny! *Do* you know what you are doing?"

I stared at him puzzled. God knows what he read in my expression, but he gave a sudden hard laugh and put me quite out of his arms, stepping back.

"No, it's not love," he said. "It's only claret. Damn it!"

115

If he had slapped me, I don't think I could have felt more sharply or unjustly rebuffed. For a moment I was too astonished to speak, and in that moment came near to the ignominy of tears. Then my pride belatedly took the shock, and anger came boiling up to save me.

"Love you! I?" I forced a little affected laugh, unnatural even to my own ears. "La, Mr. Parker, you are very vain. Do you suppose I love all the men I kiss?"

I wanted to hit him—hard—but until it was said I didn't quite realise how it would sound. Then, except that I was too angry, I might have wished it unsaid again. I had not meant to make him look at me quite like that.

"I see," he said, after a slight but very unpleasant pause. "I had no idea you were so experienced, Miss Archer. In that case, it was not even the claret, but merely—habit?"

I did not quite understand him, but I shrank instinctively from the tone of his words.

"I don't know what you mean," I said, breathlessly, "but I shouldn't have come here with you. I wish I hadn't—I wish I hadn't danced with you. I don't want to dance any more. I want to go to Mrs. Sylvester."

I thought he hesitated a moment. Then he gave his characteristic slight shrug, and ironically offered me his arm. I took it in silence, and in silence he led me to the door of the card-room. But just as I turned away, he caught me for a moment by the hand.

"Jenny!" he said, and there was the old teasing note in his voice, with something of a new softness. "I believe I *am* a fool, after all."

It was almost an apology; it was certainly a peace offering. It was very nearly irresistible. But my pride had been hardening. I drew my hand away, without looking at him, and walked silently into the card-room, leaving him at the door.

I suppose he was angered again in his turn at my sullenness, for he did not follow me. But it was not all anger, not all pride, on my part. There was a kind of fear too, that he could so easily hurt me—that he could hurt me so much.

Mrs. Sylvester was deep in a game of loo. She glanced up from the cards in her hand and nodded absently, as I slipped into a chair behind hers.

"Have you been enjoying yourself, my dear?"

"Yes, ma'am," I said, in a subdued voice. "But I am tired; I should like to sit down a little."

"To be sure, child," she said, and was deep in the game again in a moment. The other players had not even looked up from the table.

I had been too deeply offended by Mr. Parker to recover in a hurry, but gradually the strangeness of the scene caught my interest.

There was no noise, no conversation, no laughter—only the whisper of the cards, an occasional word from one of the players, and the subdued sound of violins from the ballroom. Did anyone so much as cough, there were reproachful glances, as though one giggled aloud in church.

Candlelight sparkled on jewels as the ladies played their cards. The powdered heads bent and nodded. Under the soft light the rosy hues of brocade were reflected in the many pearls, and coloured even the grey and white heads with a pinkish tint. The card-room itself was papered in the newest fashion, with an elaborate Chinese print. It was strange to look from the animated scenes upon the wall to the fixed immobility of the players.

The *beau monde* has but one serious occupation, and that is gambling. Dancing is for the very young, love is for the amorous, but cards are universal. I think it is because gambling is the one excitement left to them, the one amusement that does not pall by repetition. Its fever is intermittent, but once in he blood you are tainted for ever.

Down at Will's and White's the men gambled away their fortunes, their homes, their estates. Their horses even, and their dogs. Sometimes, it was whispered, the favours of their wives. Daughters and sons were contracted in marriage to pay off gambling debts of their parents.

Here, in my lady's parlour, the women played very nearly as deep and some of the diamonds were paste because the real stones had gone to pay their debts of honour. Fortunes ran like water from these pretty jewelled fingers.

Mrs. Sylvester's luck was out. She plunged deep—I swear, my teeth chattered to hear the sums she pledged. And yet, when she lost, her face was as unmoved, her smile as natural, as though she were fortune's darling. She was a rich woman, of course. Here and there, as I glanced around me, I saw fingers that trembled as they laid down the cards. But it was all smooth and unruffled upon the surface.

"La!" I heard one pretty woman cry. "I am undone. I have never seen the cards so cross with me. But 'tis nothing to what my husband will be."

"Lord, child!" her opponent retorted. "Do you look to your husband to pay your gambling debts?"

"To be sure," she replied pertly. "What else is one good for?"

This raised a laugh all round. I edged my chair so that I could look and listen, for the other voice was one I knew—hoarse, mocking, knowing—Mrs. Allison's.

She smiled in appreciation of her pretty friend's wit, but answered, not troubling to lower her voice, "Aye, but a lover pays more readily and is good for other things beside. Never put yourself in the power of a husband, my dear!"

"But the power of a lover?" the pretty lady smiled, not at all offended.

"A lover can only make himself disagreeable. Or desert you. A husband can send you to the country."

"Lord, I would as soon die!" the little lady cried, and all the others echoed her, in apparent sincerity.

I was looking too fixedly at Mrs. Allison. It made her turn round, as a hard stare at one's back often will, I don't know why.

I did not much wish to catch her glance, but could not avoid it, and she bowed and smiled cordially, while the others stared. Presently she raised one jewelled finger and beckoned.

I obeyed reluctantly. I had a kind of horror of her since that scene at Val's.

She was more magnificently dressed than ever, her hands so stiff with rings up to the knuckles that she could scarcely hold the cards. Her face had been more lacquered than painted, and the thick coat had cracked around her mouth. Her neck and bosom were white-leaded, and as I stood above her I could look into her bodice and see that the nipples had been rouged. Flakes of powder and paint lay over the shoulders of her beautiful brocade dress, and there were stiff dark spots here and there on the skirt where she had dripped food or wine with that unsteady drunkard's hand. She was not drunk now; she had been at cards so long that she was comparatively sober; but her breath had an unpleasing sour-winish smell. And yet with it all there was a kind of compelling vitality about her that made her the centre of the company, and the features of her ruined face were beautiful still under the cracking mask of red and white.

"What's the matter, child, that you don't dance?" she asked. "Or have you a mind to play?" And she moved as though to make room for my chair beside hers.

"No, thank you, I don't play," I said hastily.

The pretty woman who had been complaining of her losses tossed her head, looking at me with unfriendly eyes, her lips curling scornfully. "Why not? Are you a Methodist?" she asked contemptuously.

"No, madam," I said, my courage rising as it always does when I am directly attacked. "But having neither husband nor lover, I cannot afford it."

"True for you, child!" Mrs. Allison said, bursting into mirth. "Come, my lady," she added, as my adversary glared at me like a spiteful little cat, "you must not quarrel with this young lady, for she is sister to a favourite of yours."

"My footman, you mean?" my lady said, so insolently I was ready to slap her face.

But this was going a little too far, even for this sharp-tongued company, and somebody near-by said, "Shame!" quite audibly.

"Why, no, child," Mrs. Allison said, composedly. "This young lady is Miss Archer. Make your curtsey to Lady Fairlie, my dear."

I think Lady Fairlie was greatly vexed at having brought this introduction on herself, and she acknowledged my curtsey with the curtest of nods. There was a little natural colour in her face, and I vowed to plague Neal about her at the first opportunity.

"Oh, la, Mr. Archer is a killing devil!" another lady exclaimed. "Now I do believe I see a likeness in the young lady. But why is your handsome brother not here tonight, child?"

"He has company better to his liking somewhere else, I daresay," a handsome brunette said, with a glance of pure malice at Lady Fairlie. "Pray, child," she said, turning to me graciously, "convey Miss Bertram's compliments to Mr. Archer and bid him remember my aunt's *fête champêtre* this Thursday. Or, if it seems like to rain, it will be on Thursday next."

I curtsied my acknowledgement. I saw Mrs. Allison whisper something in Miss Bertram's ear, and the young lady immediately called out, "Aye, and bid him bring you, Miss Archer. My aunt will be monstrous well pleased to see you there."

I thanked her, somewhat shyly, though I liked the bold friendly way she smiled at me, and the obvious pleasure she took in spiting Lady Fairlie.

My lady rose, spilling cards on the table. "If we are not to play," she said, disagreeably, "I will order my chair."

Mrs. Allison laughed at her back. "Poor Betty Fairlie!" she cried, in malicious sympathy. "To be twice disappointed in a week! She hoped to dance with your brother, my dear," she added, turning to me, "but he did not accompany you, it seems. And yesterday, at Lady Townshend's, that handsome wretch Bob Haywood scarcely spoke to her, but hung all the while over Miss Elin."

My ears fairly pricked at the name, while Miss Bertram laughed, and somebody else said, "Ah—the new heiress? I wish her joy of him!"

"She will have the handsomest husband in England," Mrs. Allison shrugged. "She is not much amiss herself, and has thirty thousand pounds; it will do very well. Lady Townshend is all on fire to bring it off, having a fondness for Haywood."

"Which of us does not?" Miss Bertram cried, and I laughed with the others, wishing rather to cry, and thinking that the colour in my face must tell a tale to everybody.

Miss Elin . . . an heiress! So that was why he had never sent to enquire after my health, or come himself. A whole fortnight . . .

"I have a mind to watch the dancing," Mrs. Allison said, rising. "Will you come with me, child? Surely you have a partner eagerly waiting for you somewhere?"

"I have been dancing, but I don't care to dance any more," I said, not at all wanting to accompany her.

"Then let us watch for a few minutes, while I tell all the scandal," said she, and I did not know how to refuse.

Mrs. Sylvester, seeing me go, cried after me that if I were tired of dancing, she would go home presently . . . another game or two. Of course I said politely that I was in no hurry; I would wait upon her convenience; and Mrs. Allison bore me off.

"How is your sister, my dear?" she asked, seating herself upon a sofa in an embrasure of the ballroom, and drawing me beside her.

I said, coldly, that Val was well.

Mrs. Allison, I found, was one who always took the bull boldly by the horns. She said directly, "You think me no friend to her, child, and perhaps not to you either, is that it?"

I was much disconcerted by this, but after a pause answered with equal bluntness, "We think you too good a friend to your brother, madam, if you will pardon my saying so."

"You may say what you please, my dear," she said, smiling wolfishly. It was only when she smiled that I saw any likeness to Lord Dutton. "It's a privilege I reserve to my friends. And I mean to be your friend, child, whether you will or no."

"Indeed, madam, I am honoured. But——"

Her careless glance swept over the dancers. "I don't care much for young ladies as a general rule," she said coolly. "Young misses that simper and look priggishly at a plain word, and then giggle behind their fans at obscenities. Prim virgins that will scarcely look a man in the face, and run screaming if he tries to take their hand, and pretend they don't know how a baby is got, and then have their footmen strip for them in their bedrooms. Women become honester when they are married, at any rate. But I think you have been bred differently, Miss Archer; you are bold enough, and honest enough, and no fool."

I was startled by the venom of her words, but flattered, in spite of myself, at being taken up as an exception. And I had suffered enough that evening from these same young ladies, and their admirers, to hear her rail at them unmoved.

She turned and looked at me directly. "Have you a mind to marry, child?"

Much taken aback, I said hesitantly, "Why, I must marry some day, madam, I suppose, but—I am in no hurry."

She grimaced. "I cannot blame you. But since you must marry, I suppose you are like the others and would ruin yourself to advantage. 'Tis why your brother sends you here, of course."

"I suppose it is, madam. But I do not think I shall find a husband here."

"Why not? You are pretty enough."

"I have no fortune, and it seems they do not want a wife without," I said bitterly, thinking of Robert Haywood.

Mrs. Allison's sharp eyes considered me so knowingly that I coloured again, feeling as though she could read my very thoughts.

"Some men have fortunes of their own," she said, "and may marry to please themselves. It takes clever management, I own. Perhaps I can be of help to you."

I was silent, and, after a quizzical glance, she took up the fan that lay closed in her lap. "Look here, child," she said, "here is a moral for you."

She spread out the fan. It was painted with a sweetly pretty scene of a party picnicking rustically by a little river, with a charming shepherdess and her flock in the background. Mrs. Allison cast me a quick look, and then turned the fan over.

I started, in spite of myself, and blushed. It was as indecent a picture as ever I saw—a naked lady, not a thing upon her but some jewels and a ribbon round her neck, and a blackamoor, her servant evidently, in a position so compromising that it did not need the pleased smirk upon the lady's face nor the labouring grimace upon his to show what was being done.

Mrs. Allison gave a short laugh, and snapped the fan closed. "There is life for you, my dear, upon one piece of painted chicken-skin," she said calmly. "Here you look upon the pretty side. The ladies are clothed; the gentlemen are polite; obscenities are only hinted at; indecency is taken into a dark corner. Only do not forget the other side, Miss Archer. That is where most young ladies fall into error. They forget that we are all naked underneath our clothes. And clothes are easily taken off."

"But where is the moral, madam, exactly?"

"This, child. If you take a man at his face value, see him only with his clothes and his company manners on, you will never understand him. But remember what they are like naked, and what lies in his mind under all the pretty compliments he pays you, and it is ten to one but you can make him run so mad after you that he will buy you even with a wedding ring to get what he wants."

"It is not pretty," I said slowly.

"Why, no," she laughed. "Life is not pretty, Miss Archer. Have you ever looked about you? I could show you parts of London as bad as hell. And scenes that make my lady and her blackamoor seem like two children playing innocently together."

"I don't want to hear of it."

She shrugged. "I daresay not. You are romantic, child, like all girls. But you know *something*, and you are bold." She gave me that sudden wolfish smile. "It was a bold thing, my dear, to escape my brother as you did."

I started away from her. "You—you know about that?"

"Yes, I know. You are wise to have kept it to yourself."

I looked at her with abhorrence. "And you, madam—was it you arranged it all?"

She burst out laughing. "Good Lord, no! Do you think I take part in my brother's mad frolics? He told me of it afterwards—as he tells me most things. No, no, it was his friends who arranged it."

"His friends?" I echoed, in a low voice. "What friends, madam?"

"Perhaps I ought not to tell you."

"I will not repeat it, madam. You know I can keep a secret."

"True. And you should be warned. But cannot you guess?"

I licked my dry lips. "Alverson?"

"Oh—he is the servant only," she laughed. "It was George Parker, of course."

I started to my feet, looking down at her through a dimness in my eyes. "No! I don't believe it! He is—he would not do that."

She gazed at me in surprise. "Why, child, have you a liking for Parker? I would not have told you. But, my dear, of course he did not mean any harm to *you*."

I reseated myself abruptly. "No. Only to my sister. And she, being out of the *beau monde*, is fair game."

"Child," Mrs. Allison said gravely, "you are touched. I am sorry."

Numbly, looking into my lap, I shook my head. "It is just that I feel such a fool."

"Why should you? Only be warned."

Well, I was warned. And I was remembering, so clearly, how Neal had laughed, seeing Parker hurry away from us at Vauxhall, and wagered that there was some frolic afoot "now that George had returned."

After a pause, Mrs. Allison said, "He is very much in debt to my brother. They gamble high, and Parker is ruined. He had a pretty little fortune from his mother—she was a Richmond—but it is all gone. What fools men are! So he is in some sense subservient to my brother."

It seemed to me that was worse than if he had done it in sheer wildness, or wanton cruelty. Anything was better than to do an evil deed because you are servant to a man you owe money. Why didn't he take a horse and rob upon the highway, as other gentlemen had done? Thieving would be better than this; or hanging, for that matter.

I thought of his bright, dark, teasing face, and I remembered the reverse of Mrs. Allison's fan. She had driven home the moral in one sharp lesson.

After a pause I said, "I do not care for Parker, or any man. But I am sorry he is such a villain."

"And I suppose you consider my brother another?"

"How can I help it?" I said, suppressing a shudder. "Dear Mrs. Allison, if you have any influence over him, for God's sake induce him to leave my sister alone! She has troubles enough, and she will never, never care for him. It will only end in his doing some violence, and surely you would not wish to see him ruined."

"By no means. I will do my best, though my brother is very stubborn for what he wants." After a pause, she added, "You know, my dear, you ought to be grateful to him."

"Why, madam?"

"Because, in running away from his arms, you have run into Lord Gould's."

"A rare privilege!" I cried sarcastically.

She could not but laugh, but shook her head. "No, no, you must not be ironical on him. I design him for your husband."

I gaped at her. "Me, madam! Good God, why? And why should you interest yourself?"

"I must amuse myself somehow," she shrugged. "Match-making is a great amusement. And I am a complete hand at it, as you shall see. I have taken a fancy to you, my dear; I like your pretty face and your spirit. And when you are my Lady Gould, no doubt if you are so inclined you may find a way to thank me."

"No doubt," I said, dryly. "But I cannot suppose Lord Gould would ever think of me, and I am not very much inclined toward him."

"You could do worse and are not likely to do better," she said bluntly. "He is a baron; you would be my lady; there is a good fortune; and he has only one sister to marry off. Moreover, he is just the kind of blustering fool to be easily managed by a clever wife."

She waited, and smiled when I made no answer. "Think of

it, child," she said, rising. "And if you are minded that way, bespeak my help. I am told the gentleman was much catched by you."

"How do you know so much?" I asked wonderingly.

"My dear, I have not lived these twenty years in London for nothing. I daresay I know as much of what goes on as any person in it. If you wish to know something, enquire of me; it is ten to one but I can help you.—And here is Mrs. Sylvester, in search of you, so I will bid you good-night."

She curtsied to Mrs. Sylvester and walked off, leaving my mind in a perfect whirl.

"My dear, are you ready to go?" Mrs. Sylvester asked.

I very thankfully said that I was.

"But you must say good-night to your partner. Where is the wretch?" she asked laughingly. "Have you quarrelled with him, Miss Archer?"

I stammered something, and she hailed a passing servant and bade him go in search of Mr. Parker, for Miss Archer wanted to go home.

I would have given anything to avoid seeing him again, but Mrs. Sylvester was a stickler for etiquette. I could not escape.

He did not keep us waiting long. He appeared in company with a handsome elderly lady whom I recognised as our hostess, Mrs. Hamilton.

I thought she regarded me with some curiosity as I curtsied to her; and not altogether, perhaps, with favour; but she asked kindly if I had enjoyed myself.

"My dear aunt," Mr. Parker said, grandly, "she has been *my* partner."

"I know that, nephew; that is why I asked," the old lady retorted dryly. But there was an affectionate twinkle in her eye as she rebuked him; it was plain she favoured him highly.

I managed to say whatever was suitable; we bade Mrs. Hamilton good-night; and Mr. Parker handed us downstairs to the coach.

There was a little delay while Mrs. Sylvester entered and seated herself, during which Mr. Parker said to me in a low

126

voice, "Why do we always quarrel when we meet, Jenny?"

"Sir," I said, as icily as I could, "perhaps it is because you presume too much."

But it was very hard to give Mr. Parker a set-down. He said, in an awed voice that made me boil with rage, "What a goddess-like mien, Miss Archer! You make me quite quake with fear. Still," he added cheerfully, "it is better to displease by presuming too much than attempting too little!"

I thought this a reminder of my luckless situation when he encountered me, and was angrier still. In a voice I could hardly control, I said, "Will you answer me one question, sir?"

"Certainly, madam."

"Do you owe gambling debts to Lord Dutton?"

I had really startled him at last. I saw a dark look come across his face, and thought at first he did not mean to answer. Then, with forced lightness, he said:

"That is another improper question, Miss Archer. Where did you hear that, may I ask?"

"Does it matter?" I said, wearily. "If you do not answer me, I shall know it is true."

"I am not afraid to answer," he said, with a little touch of sternness. "Yes, it is true. I owe him money. Do you wish to know how much?"

I had earned the rebuke, but had not spirits enough left to resent it. "No," I said, turning away. "I do not want to know anything more." And I mounted into the carriage before he could speak again.

He stood in the lighted doorway as we drove away. I looked back once, and then sat silent in the corner of the carriage. Mrs. Sylvester nodded in her corner. It was very late. The moon was going down, and the coachman drove cautiously. It seemed a long time before I reached home.

"Good-night, my dear," Mrs. Sylvester said, rousing herself. "I am glad you enjoyed yourself, and had such an agreeable partner."

"Yes," I said steadily. "It was very good fortune. I had a very pleasant evening. My thanks to you, madam."

And I went into the house with a smile on my face to say the same thing to the sleepy maid who waited for me. I was not going to cry for George Parker.

I had judged him rightly the first time I ever met him. How could I have been such a fool as to let his teasing ways disarm me? He was a friend of Dutton's, a rake among rakes. They thought girls like myself fair game. Not for marriage! Then they looked for heiresses and young ladies with great names. But for sport, for another conquest to boast of afterwards. That was all his teasing attention to me meant. Underneath he was as bad as or worse than the others. What a fool I was! My face burned as I thought how I had kissed him . . . No wonder he thought me a wanton little fool! But he should never have the chance to despise me again . . . His mother was a Richmond. He would never think Mollie Lake's daughter good enough for anything but his mistress.

I tossed and turned in bed till the windows were brightening with dawn. My first appearance in Society had not been a very happy one. But I told myself sternly I had learned a valuable lesson, from which I would profit hereafter. I was not going to cry for George Parker. . . .

During the two weeks I had been gadding with Mrs. Sylvester I had seen Neal but seldom. He seemed almost to avoid me since that awful night at Vauxhall, and this made me unhappy. On the morning after the ball, however, he came to the house so early that he found Val still in bed while I curled on the end of the bed telling her about my experiences.

I do not know what I might have told her alone, but with Neal there I painted a picture sufficiently unlike the truth to please him.

But it seemed I could not please Neal these days. He scowled when he heard who my partner had been and said, "Good Lord, you had better have stayed at home! He's a younger son and ruined ten times over to boot. I've told you that before." He shot a vexed glance at Val, adding angrily, "But my sisters prefer rakes, it seems."

Val coloured with resentment, pushing herself up on her pillows. "What do you mean by that?"

He shrugged maddeningly. Her eyes flashed. "I suppose you mean Harvey? Why do you hate him so?"

"Because I know the sort of man he is. And if he comes sniffing round Jenny I shall know what to say to him. *Your* business, Val, is your own—and your husband's. I only hope you know what you are doing."

"I know very well. And you can run tattling to Dangerfield, if you like."

"Oh, go to the devil!" he said, and flung out of the house. Val's hit had not been without point, for if he and Dangerfield were united in no other thought, they were at one in dislike of Harvey.

Harvey had tried to carry out my suggestion and make it seem that he came to the house only to pay court to me. But a worse actor I never saw; he would not have fooled a child. He only succeeded in firing Neal's suspicion without allaying Dangerfield's.

The truth was, I think, Harvey was proud of his passion for Val, and of her infatuation for him, and would have preferred to vaunt it. He despised Dangerfield so much I believe he would have lain with Val in his presence without feeling any alarm for the consequences for himself.

For the consequences that might affect Val, he evidently never gave them a thought. Wives were expected to cuckold their husbands, and deceive them afterwards. It was a stupid woman who could not evade the consequences. And Harvey, being essentially very thick-headed himself, had the greatest admiration for Val's cleverness, and thought she could manage any situation.

I will do Harvey so much justice as to admit that Val joined and encouraged him in taking Dangerfield's resentment lightly. She hated him so much, she could not but wish to despise him. This I thought very dangerous, and it did not ease my mind to see Neal and Dangerfield leagued together for once.

129

Neal was evidently ashamed of his ill-humour, for he returned presently and made himself agreeable. None of us referred to the quarrel. He was pleased by Miss Bertram's invitation, and still more pleased by my being included. Wishing to flatter him still further, I told him about Lady Fairlie's disappointment. Val laughed; he got rather red and bid me hold my tongue; yet I think he was not ill-pleased.

There was much I might have told Val in private about Mrs. Hamilton's ball. Especially I would like to have consulted her about Mrs. Allison's conversation with me. But I could not talk to Val now unless we talked of Harvey or her husband. She was as obsessed by hatred of one as by love for the other, and I do not know which I thought more ominous to her future happiness.

Moreover, as the weather grew hot and she grew larger, she was so uncomfortable that I spent most of my time trying to devise ways to ease or amuse her, and tried not to trouble her with any concerns of my own.

"This—*thing*!" she said, pressing down hard on her belly. "It kicks and torments me. Oh God, how glad I shall be to be rid of it! Till August—and then I shall be slim and pretty again, and then——"

She flung herself back on her pillows, her hands clenched, and I turned away from the look of naked misery and hunger, and despair.

"Do you really think he loves me, Jenny?" she asked presently. It was not that she doubted, but she could not have enough of hearing it. She was starving for it.

"I suppose he does," I said, slowly. "But he does not have much care for you—for your reputation."

Val opened her eyes indignantly. "Why—he has hardly so much as kissed me yet!"

"He is very rude to Dangerfield."

"Oh—well!" she said, and laughed.

"Val," I said seriously, "you think Dangerfield will bear anything. But you are wrong. He is evil; he is dangerous."

She laughed again. "Oh, Jenny! He delights to hurt a little, I know, but he dare not strike too hard. He is a coward and a fool. I can control him. I threatened to kill myself once, and he has been cowed by it ever since."

And, say what I would, I could not change her. No older sister will take seriously advice from a younger. Especially if one be wife and the other virgin. When a woman has slept with one man she thinks she knows them all, and most particularly that one. Val told me I did not know Dangerfield as she did, and what could I say?

As it did not rain upon the Thursday, Neal and I attended Miss Bertram's *fête champêtre*. I especially looked forward to a day in the open air of the country. London in the heat was beginning to oppress me.

We met early at Miss Bertram's house, where she lived with her aunt, Lady Frances Gray. Lady Frances was nominally the mistress of the house, but Miss Bertram possessed the fortune and she pulled the strings which animated her aunt—a very old faded lady with a thin surprised voice and round doll's eyes. The house itself was handsome, and Miss Bertram made a sprightly hostess. She soon had us packed into coaches and taken to the river. There we entered barges, especially engaged by the day, and went up-river to Richmond, where servants sent ahead awaited us with lunch.

The party was a large one. I recognised a few of the guests, and Neal knew nearly everybody. But I had one acquaintance there that he did not.

My throat grew dry, my heart thudded against my ribs, as I recognised Robert Haywood and received his smiling bow, with a meaning glance of conspiracy that made me go weak in the knees.

I had tried hard to hate him for his neglect, but could not manage it. Now, when I saw him again, I was as lost as ever. He was handsomer even than I remembered him.

I was not the only female to be so dazzled. Neal, accustomed to be a good deal spoiled for his handsome looks, soon became jealous of Mr. Haywood and cast fulminating glances in his direction. The other men, equally neglected, drew together; while

Mr. Haywood, his guinea-yellow curls bared, his height and magnificent build set off by tight riding dress, was surrounded by adoring females and scarcely had time to cast a glance occasionally in my direction.

I'll be damned if I make one of his harem, I said to myself, and pointedly stood aside. As a result, I was soon honoured by a good deal of attention from the jealous gentlemen, and before I knew it, Robert and I had a sort of rival court, each striving to outdo the other.

Now this was not without its amusing side! and I drank up the admiration greedily, but it effectually separated Mr. Haywood and myself. We drove to the river in separate coaches; we travelled in separate barges. Ours carried the musicians, and my admirers sang very loudly and chiefly out of tune, while one tried to hold my hand and another, sitting in the bottom of the barge, got a little familiar with my ankle.

Though Miss Bertram seemed as catched by Mr. Haywood as anybody, I suppose she realised that this arrangement was not likely to make her party a success. On our arrival, she reorganised the party so forcefully that the rival courts were broken up. There was dancing, and since Mr. Haywood could have but one partner at a time, the ladies found themselves compelled to pay some attention to the other men.

He danced with Miss Bertram first, and then—the party being informal—sought other partners. But he did not approach me. I had no lack—I danced with whoever asked me, laughed, chattered, was prodigiously gay, and could have wept with disappointment all the while.

Lunch was spread. I sat between a Guards officer and a witty Mr. Cory, and flirted my hardest with them both. Neal watched me jealously, but after several glasses of wine he mellowed and became tolerably absorbed in Miss Bertram. It was not long before they went strolling into the woods to look for flowers, and this was a signal for everybody to go a-walking.

I strolled demurely between my two admirers, a little flown with wine and not paying much attention to their conversation. The wood was pleasant and cool. There were flowers in the

132

sunny spots and I picked these, arranging them into a nosegay. Listening dreamily to the high-flown compliments of the Guards officer and the wit of Mr. Cory, I wondered who was picking flowers for Robert Haywood.

Suddenly there was a prodigious uproar at the spot where we had lunched. We ran back, together with everybody else, to see what was going on, and found that a flock of goats had overrun our picnic site and were busily engaged in eating everything, whether edible or not—ladies' hats, the blankets, everything.

The gentlemen joined the servants in trying to drive them off, while the ladies stood laughing and crying out for their injured finery. Everybody cursed the absent goatherd whose carelessness had let the beasts stray.

As I stood laughing heartily, for the goats lowered their heads and butted and behaved most gallantly, I felt my hand suddenly seized.

"Be quick!" Mr. Haywood whispered, and before I knew what was happening, he had pulled me away, out of sight of the others.

Hand in hand we ran through the wood, laughing and panting, till we stumbled into a sheltered little nook hidden all round by bushes.

Here, with no words at all, he tried to take me eagerly into his arms, but I held him off in punishment for his previous neglect.

"Jenny, don't be cruel!" he said, reproachfully. "I have been at immense pains to get you away from those two fools!"

"You, sir! You have not even looked at me. It was all those goats——"

"Well, and who do you think bribed the goatherd, child?" he asked.

I burst out laughing. "You didn't? Oh, that is famous!"

"Then give me my kiss," he said, triumphantly, and would not take No for an answer. I am afraid I did not say it very convincingly. He was so incredibly handsome! It dazzled the eyes to look at him, the sun burning on his fair, unpowdered head, the brilliant blue eyes full of laughing triumph. His cheek was warm against mine, his mouth experienced, his arms ardent . . .

I drew away at last, staring at him dizzily. "Why didn't you ask me to dance?" I said, stupidly—the first thing that came into my mind.

"Because the less anyone knows of our acquaintance, the better," he said calmly.

I was puzzled, but he gave me no time to think, kissing me again, and still more passionately.

"Darling Jenny! My little love!" He kissed my neck and shoulders and, before I could stop him, pulled my dress off one shoulder and kissed the exposed breast.

"No!" I said, pantingly. "Please! Don't!" I struggled to get free my hands. Those kisses filled my mind with fright and doubt, but my flesh understood them perfectly. It frightened me to feel how I responded to him. My very body seemed to arch towards him even as I tried to thrust him away.

He let me go at last, after a slight struggle, standing smiling down at me with an air half indulgent, half triumphant, while I rearranged my dress with trembling fingers.

"I—I think I must go back. My brother will miss me."

"Not yet. Sit down here with me. Don't be frightened, Jenny! I won't hurt you. Only let me hold you a little—so."

He kissed me till I was half out of my wits, but still I struggled to keep him within bounds.

"You mustn't! Please! Suppose someone should see us."

"No one will find us here. Please, Jenny—let me see them—they are so lovely!" He laughed exultantly. "Don't be shy, my darling! Why do you think God made you like this? To please me—as I could please you, if you would let me."

"No!"

"Stubborn one!" he whispered. His breath brushed my skin, warm and soft as lips. "You want to, you know you do! Jenny, you must say Yes to me some day! Why must you say No?"

I could not, or would not, answer. I said reproachfully, "You never came. You said you would. You don't care for me, or you would have come long ago."

He laid his head against my shoulder, holding me by one hand thrust so strongly under my breast that my heartbeats must have struck upon his fingers and told him all he wanted to know. The golden head was irresistible; to save my life I could not help putting my face against it.

"Jenny, I wanted to come. You are such a beguiling little creature—I think you have bewitched me. I have thought of you—often. But what was the use? I cannot court you honestly, as I should wish, as your brother would expect."

"Why not? You—you are not married?"

"No, no," he assured me, sounding amused. "But, you see, my dearest, we are of the same kind. We are adventurers. You have no money, neither have I. What would marriage between us mean, but ruin for one another?"

"I don't know," I said slowly. "I have not thought about it." Nor had I. I suppose it was very unworldly of me, but it had never entered my head to think that I could only marry a rich man.

"Little one, are you vexed with me? Don't be. I would be charmed to marry you, if I could."

"But as you can't, you want me to be your whore." I spoke in bitterness, and he moved protestingly.

"Jenny, that is an ugly word for a beautiful thing."

"It is the common word. It *is* what you want of me, isn't it?"

"I want you to love me."

I was silent. If this was love, this painful enchantment, this fierce arching yearning, then he had his wish. And if it was not, what then was it, and what was I? I had used an ugly word to provoke him, but, once spoken, I could not get the sound of it out of my ears.

At last I said hesitantly, "My brother-in-law is very rich. He is fond of me. Perhaps he might give me a dowry."

Robert stirred alertly. "Dangerfield? Yes, he is rich, I know. But your sister is with child. He will have a family. Why should he give you anything?"

To my own astonishment, I began to lie. I said that Danger-field doted on me, that he had so much he could not spend it all, that he poured money and gifts on me. I said my brother too had money of his own, and no wife, and that my father, if my husband pleased him, would not let me go without a dowry.

And all the while I listened to myself in amazement, knowing there was not one word of truth in the whole. I could not stop myself; I seemed bewitched. I could not understand myself at the time. I see it more clearly now. I wanted him, just as he said I did. But I was not honest enough to face it plainly. I had to dress it with lies, to give it the plausibility of an honest courtship. It was myself I was trying to deceive, not him.

But he pretended to be deceived. He agreed with it all; we lay whispering and planning. And he had his share of hope to offer— how, if his sickly elder brother died, the estate would all come to him; and how there was an elderly aunt, who promised him her fortune.

Of course I knew that he lied, as well as I knew it of myself. I knew already that the man I held in my arms was no true lover. He had not cared to seek me out, even to ruin me, until chance threw me again in his way and I made it all easy for him. It was not his fault; I do not blame him. He had been honest enough to begin with—saying in so many words that he would be glad to ruin me though I was not rich enough to marry. It was only when he saw that I *must* have my dream, that he acquiesced, and lied to please me.

But I could not admit that. For if I did, then I ought never to see him again. And I was bewitched. Having lain in his arms, I felt as though I could not live until I lay there again. Call it by whatever name you will, it had taken possession of me.

We were to meet again soon, at a masquerade, and I think I only half lived the hours between. I forgot Val and Harvey and the rest of the world; I lived in that little green hollow among the bushes, and felt again his lips and his hands, and kissed once more the short curling hair of his temples, and blew wantonly into his ear to make him stop my breath with his lips . . .

It was to please him that I designed my dress for the masquerade so wanton that Val, when she saw it, was shocked.

"Lord, child, you are half naked!"

136

"It is a shepherdess dress," I said, defensively.

Dangerfield walked around me, licking his horrid full red lips. "Who would not be sheep, with such a shepherdess?" he smirked. "Lord, to be an old ram!"

"Don't be so disgusting!" Val snapped. "I say it is indecent. She is not to go out in it. Why, Jenny, you have nothing on top but that little laced bodice, and it is laced so broad I can see almost everything."

Dangerfield looked over my shoulder, smacking his lips, which was his way of making a joke. I could have killed him, letting his slug's glance travel where Robert was to lie.

"'Tis charming," said he. "And only one skirt, I warrant you."

"Jenny, go upstairs and put a hoop on!"

"A shepherdess in hoops!" Dangerfield tittered. "No, no, my dear, that will never do. Let Miss Jenny alone. She knows what she is doing, I daresay." His glance met mine full, and I saw so much obscene knowledge in it that I shrank from him. His lips broadened in a smile. He bent close to my shoulder, whispering, "Who is the lucky man, Miss Jenny? I wish *I* might have the lifting of that skirt!"

As I pulled away from him his big horse's teeth nipped at my shoulder. "Well, well!" he said. "I shall have to make do with your sister."

"Leave her alone!" I said fiercely. "She's not well."

"Oh, come!" he grinned. "Women have to give up *that* excuse when they are breeding! 'Tis the best part of the business. Run along, Miss Jenny, and have a merry party. Don't begrudge us our simple pleasures here at home!"

Val, coming in with a full cloak to wrap me up in, said crossly, "Well, I only hope Neal doesn't refuse to take you, when he sees you!"

But I took good care that he did not see me without my cloak, and when we were fairly into the masquerade it was impossible for him even to find me, so riotously everything was managed.

These masquerades were the wildest things imaginable! The heavy masks covered so much of the face that it was really possible to be disguised. Couples were wandering all over the house, locked in compromising embraces in every shadowy corner. I am sure if Neal had dreamed how wild the company was, he would never have brought me. But the invitation had come through Robert's contriving, and Neal had no idea until it was too late that the respectable lady in whose name the invitation had been made was actually lying-in in the country, while my lord's mistress and her friends made up the party.

I learned afterwards that Neal spent most of the evening— when he could escape the bold importunities of the pretty, wanton, masked ladies—searching for me, without any success. And when at last he did find me, I was placidly sitting at cards upstairs with my lord and a few sober friends. As I had observed before, Robert was an experienced contriver.

It was such a hot night that all the doors and windows were left open, in hope of getting a cool breath from the garden. The sound of our dancing and mirth must have carried right to the street. The very porter at the door was so drunk he could not open his eyes. It was not long before the party had grown to a great size, and I daresay above half the guests were uninvited, and very likely even unknown to my lord and his mistress. You could tell that by the number of people who were not in costume, although all were masked. Masks are easily procured, and few people went abroad on errands of gallantry without one.

The instant we arrived, I was swept away from Neal's side by a great crowd of people. My cloak being twitched off my shoulders, the cry went up, "A shepherdess, a shepherdess! Here is Phyllis! Where is the shepherd?"

There was a ready response from half a dozen men, all dressed in different guise, but all ready to swear themselves shepherds. I was seized upon, rudely enough, by first one and then another, with much laughter and numerous coarse sallies.

I fought them off as best I could, striving to keep my temper. I had brought this on myself by the inviting indecency of my costume, and could only endure it and hope that Robert would come soon to rescue me.

Neal was detained in another room or the Lord knows what might have come of it! He would have been mad with rage to see me so mishandled.

Suddenly all my assailants were thrust aside by a sturdy hand, and I was swept out of the hurly-burly by a man's ungentle grip. Loud laughter and cheering followed us, but the maskers were not yet drunk enough to be quarrelsome and no one tried seriously to prevent us.

In the comparative quiet of the supper room we came to a halt. Gasping for breath, I tried to tighten the laces of my little green bodice, seeing for the first time how true Val had spoken when she said it left me half naked.

I knew my rescuer, and would not speak to him. But he took off his mask, regarding me in a cool impersonal sort of way that made me boil with rage.

"That's a very pretty dress," he said, watching my efforts "but haven't you forgotten something? A trifle of lace, or something like that?"

"Mr. Parker," I said, between my teeth, "I wish you would mind your affairs and let me mind mine. You are no guardian of mine!"

"Your guardians seem so very remiss in their care for you," George Parker said. "Here, let me tie that for you."

I struck down his hand. "Don't touch me!"

"Good Lord!" he said, in amazement. "What has come over you? One would think I was Dutton, at the very least."

I looked up at him, raging and ashamed. "I had as lief you were! If I must be insulted by a villain, let it be the lion rather than the jackal!"

He became very still at that. I was almost frightened when I saw his face. I had meant to anger him, to hurt him if I could, but I had not meant to make him look at me like that.

"Miss Archer," he said, "I am no man's jackal. What do you mean by that?"

To avoid his eyes, I looked down, jerking and knotting my ties hastily. "You know best," I muttered.

His hands closed on my shoulders in a hard grip. "No, I do

not know," he said, between his teeth. "Are you merely striving to insult me; or have you a meaning? Speak up—I *will* know!"

I pulled at my mask. It was stifling me. "Then you had better know," I said, in a low voice, "that it was not my sister you arranged to abduct the other night, but me—and it is no thanks to you that I am not ruined by Dutton this moment."

His hands slowly dropped from my shoulders. I had the queerest feeling that his friendship fell away with them, and left me forlorn and deserted.

"Who told you that?" he asked, in a low voice that matched my own. And then, as I was silent, "Never mind. What does it matter? The same friend, I suppose, who told you I owed Dutton money. And was it for that, that I was supposed to do Dutton's dirty work?"

Mutely, I nodded. The mask's knotted ribbons slipped at last and I pulled it off, breathlessly. But I might as well have kept it on. I could not look up and meet his eyes.

"And you believed that, Jenny? Yes, I see you did."

I could not speak; and he was silent for a long while.

"You had better put on your mask, Miss Archer," he said, at last, in a tone quite changed and cool. "Ladies at such affairs as this never take them off."

I obeyed him, silently, and he replaced his own mask with steady fingers.

"There," he said, with a slight hard laugh. "Now we are masked and ready for the world again. It is indecent, you know, to bare one's true face, though fashionable to bare everything else. That has been our trouble, Miss Archer. We have spoken too honestly together. We cannot go on from here but to love or hate. And with you, I judge, it must be hate?"

"I am sorry if I have misjudged you," I whispered. I could lower myself no further. And it was not low enough.

"Oh," he said brutally, "you have not been so much amiss. I am bad enough, in all conscience. I am not come to be a pimp yet, that is all. But I suppose it is natural you should think me no better than Dutton."

I hesitated, biting my lips. I wanted to apologise. If he had spoken gently, or even reproachfully, it would have been easy. But he was angry, frowning at me with those black brows drawn down. I felt that he wanted to master me. And looking at that square chin I knew a kind of fear of him. If I gave way to him now, I thought obscurely, I should never be mistress of myself again.

I said at last, haughtily, "You are a friend of Lord Dutton's. Why should I think you are any different?"

"Why, indeed? But, you know, Jenny, somehow I thought you would."

There was still anger, but there was something else at last. I turned to him quickly, and saw that he was watching me eagerly through the slits of his mask. I wonder—if I had said then, "I'm sorry," and nothing more—I wonder what would have happened!

But, as luck would have it, there was a sudden noise of a new arrival at the door, and I paused an instant, looking instinctively towards the disturbance. I saw the light fall on a tall golden head, and my heart gave a sudden surprised lurch. Robert caught my glance, and recognised me instantly. He raised one hand in a slight salute. The little gesture had a curious intimacy, though it was so slight.

Beside me I heard Parker draw a quick breath. Guiltily, with colour flooding my face around the edges of the mask, I turned back to him, and saw the jut of his chin more pronounced than ever. Above the black lines of the mask the black brows met in almost as straight a line.

"So," he said. "The beautiful Mr. Haywood has made another conquest."

"I don't know what you mean! I have only met him——"

"Met, and been conquered. London is paved with the hearts he has broken. Now I understand why you have been so hard on me. I can hardly compare with all that blue and gold—that beauty's complexion—those long eyelashes—— "

"He is handsomer than you are, that's true," I said. I was trembling with rage and a kind of despair, feeling myself driven farther into a quarrel for which I had no heart. "But I thought only women were so petty as to be jealous for *that*."

"I am not jealous," he retorted stiffly. "I am only sorry to see you have no better sense than the others." He shrugged. "Oh, well," he said, with infuriating condescension, "you'll get over it, I suppose, without coming to any harm. Half the females in London are sighing for him. But, to tell the truth, Jenny, I thought you had better taste."

"You think, I suppose, I ought to sigh for you!" I cried, remembering resentfully how I had kissed him. "Well, let me tell you, if you were the last man——"

He flung up his hand. "Spare me, for God's sake! You are speaking by the book tonight. Next you will tell me he is a better man than I am."

"Well, he is!"

"No, my dear. He is prettier, but he is not a better man. And if I were a woman, I should prefer a lover less beautiful than myself. It balances Nature better."

"He is not my lover!"

"You wish he were," said Mr. Parker, with abominable prescience. "You heave your bosom and sigh and blush every time he looks at you. You are on your knees with adoration. Good God," he added, unnecessarily, "it's enough to make one sick! That all women should be such fools!".

I literally could not speak with wrath. He made me a fine ironical bow. "I leave you to the free enjoyment of your adoration, my dear. I won't try to prevent you. But if you should become tired of it, you might let me know. Unless, of course, you have heard any more stories about me in the meantime."

"I told you I was sorry!"

He looked down at me grimly. "I can forgive you for that," he said. "But I won't find it easy to forgive you for preferring Haywood."

He turned on his heel and was swallowed up at once in the riotous crowd. I stood looking after him, feeling very uncomfortable indeed. Angry as I was, there was no warmth in my anger. Instead, I had a horrid cold feeling in the pit of my stomach that seemed to be spreading upward towards my heart. When he fought his way to the door, and was gone, I felt as though suddenly somebody had put out the lights.

An arm caught me strongly around the waist, and Robert whispered in my ear, "Who the devil was that? I was about to loose the goats on him!"

"No one of importance," I said, wearily. I leaned back in his arm, and let him lead me away to dance. So long as he was my friend, why should I care for George Parker?

But there was a soreness at my heart still, which made me laugh too much, and dance too feverishly, and drink too much iced wine. Far too much, for my inexperienced head. It tasted so delicious on that hot night, after the exercise of dancing, and I did not realise how strong it was until half-way through a set my head reeled, and I had to clutch at Robert to save myself from falling.

"So hot . . ." I said breathlessly, shutting my eyes.

I heard people around us laughing. Robert picked me up off my feet. It was delicious to lie in his arms, feeling as though I floated on air, and knowing that he would take care of me, and get me away from all these hot, noisy people.

He carried me outside. The air was warm, but the freshness soothed me. I opened my eyes and saw a great moon sailing slowly overhead, so large and bright that I felt as though I could touch it. I put up my hand towards it, but by some curious association my dark fingers against the milky light made me think of how I had laid my hand against Parker's dark coat to show off its whiteness.

I gave a sudden startled sob, and turned my face into Robert's shoulder.

"My darling!" he said softly. He put his strong hand on my chin and turned my face back to the light. I don't think he even saw that I was crying. He laid his lips down upon mine and kissed me till I was half senseless, my head falling back on his arm.

Wine, kisses, moonlight . . . the world swung round and round dizzily. My limbs had no strength in them; I could not even hold up my head. I was vaguely aware that he was caressing me more boldly and ardently than ever, but I was too dreamy to repulse him. Hot as it was, I began to shiver. The thrills ran through me, one after another, shaking me to my finger-tips. And all the while my head went round, so that I felt as though the moon were sometimes above us, and sometimes below, and all the universe was dancing wildly . . .

Somewhere in the shadows near us another couple fondled and giggled. Robert swore under his breath, and suddenly took me up again in his arms.

"Come!" he said. "We'll go where there is no one but ourselves."

In a dreamy trance, I lay motionless in his arms, feeling leaves and vines trail over my face as he threaded his way though the garden. Turning my head languidly, I saw that there was a little ornamental lake glimmering in one corner of the garden, with a tiny pleasure house in the centre, reached only by a narrow arched stone bridge.

I felt Robert cross the stones cautiously and pause before the door. There was the soft jangle of a key, the creak of a lock, and in a moment he kicked the door open and was carrying me across the threshold.

It did not occur to me to wonder then how he knew of this place, and had the key. Nor with whom he had come here before.

For it was plain he knew it well. Feeling his way carefully, he crossed the room and laid me upon the bed. Then closing and relocking the door, he struck flint and tinder and lit the candles that stood upon the table.

It was a little hexagon, a six-sided room such as are used as summer-houses in many fashionable gardens. In this case, however, it had been designed for other purposes. The pretty, tiny room, scarcely bigger than a bird-house, was all hung with rosy tapestries and furnished charmingly with white and gilt furniture. The round ceiling was painted with very realistic scenes from the love-life of the gods and the floor was inlaid with an exceedingly indecent mosaic, which I afterwards learned had been brought at immense expense from some ancient villa near Rome. The bed itself was shaped like a golden swan, very beautifully designed, though something of an absurdity in itself.

All this I learned about later. At the moment I saw nothing but the man who stood beside the table, looking at me with smiling eyes. My head swung dizzily; all my senses were flown with wine. I had no wits, no honour, no decency left. I rose on my elbow and stretched out my arms to him like any wanton. And he, with a low laugh, as triumphant as tender, came to me, one hand reaching for the laces of my bodice . . .

. . . There was just one curious moment, when I opened my eyes and thought I saw George Parker looking at me, the dark eyes burning black with scorn. It was only an illusion, and yet it was curiously real, vanishing in an instant as I gave a little cry, half pain, half protest. Robert mistook me, and seized me so passionately that I could not resist him. In a moment everyone and everything in the world was forgotten, burnt up in that moment of surrender that yet was triumph . . .

Afterwards I wept, as I suppose women always do. He comforted me tenderly, and presently from sorrow and tenderness we came to love again . . .

I slept, exhausted and drowsy with wine. It was Robert's kiss that awakened me and I started up, suddenly quite sober and aghast at what I had done.

Fully dressed, he sat beside me on the bed, holding my little green bodice in his hands, smiling as he met my horrified glance. "I hated to wake you, Jenny. You were sleeping so happily! But it is getting late and you must be dressed."

He laughed, as my hands flew to cover myself. "Darling, I have covered every inch of you with kisses! Why should you hide from me now? Have you forgotten in your sleep how much we love each other?"

Then, seeing me quite speechless with fright and reaction, he brought me a tiny glass filled to the brim with a golden liquor. The little house was well equipped with all things for the pleasures of love.

The drink's sweet fiery comfort steadied me a little. And when he kissed me again, I knew with a sinking heart that never, never could I deny him now.

He had carefully removed my dress, so that it should show no tell-tale rumples, and he now assisted me to put it on again.

"I am a good abigail," he said, laughing, finding a comb to get the tangles out of my hair.

"Yes," I said, bitterly. It was terrible to me that he should boast of his experience. And he knew this house so well, and all that it contained—wine to promote love, cosmetics to repair its ravages, keys to lock out the world—how many times had he come here before me, and how often would he come again without me?

But when he caressed me, I forgot all my bitterness and clung to him, mad for him. He had left the candles burning, so that we should not sleep too sound, I suppose, and in their golden light he looked like some god come down from the sky to love the daughters of men. So much more beautiful, and like a god, than the painted gods upon the ceiling! How could I help desiring him —the beautiful body, the beautiful face, the infinitely experienced caresses—how could I help it?

Afterwards, masked again, we strolled in the garden, drifting reluctantly towards the house. "We must meet whenever we can," he whispered. "I will find the way. I have many friends— they know how to manage these things."

I did not doubt it, and my lip curled at the thought. But I had no room for scorn; I was as bad as any of them now. I had given myself to him utterly. What use was it to look back? I had done the thing and it could not be undone.

I turned resolutely away from regret. I had burnt my bridges; I was Robert Haywood's mistress. I could not be anyone else's now.

But even then, try as I would to drive it away, there came the ghost of another love, a dark-eyed ghost that looked at me scornfully and tormented me, and would not let me alone.

It was incredible to me that no one should observe any change

146

in me. But Val was so wrapped in her own love, her own troubles, that I believe she scarcely even saw anyone else. As for Neal, he was wrathful with me, true, but simply because he had taken me to an indecent place, and not because he had any really ill thoughts of me. Finding me so demurely occupied at cards, what could he say? It was my lord himself who remarked that Miss Archer had found the party a little too rompish for her. "But she must be greatly fatigued," he added, smiling at me, "for we have been sitting at cards these three hours. I'm afraid you are a careless brother, Mr. Archer!"

This so effectually took the wind out of Neal's sails that I could have laughed, had I not been almost too guilty to look at him. My lord, no doubt, was in league with Robert Haywood, and he lied with that careless ease which is so much more convincing than earnestness. But I was not yet used to deceit, least of all with my own brother.

I was very much afraid of Neal. He had behaved so strangely when he merely thought I *might* have committed a sin, there was no saying what violence he would do if he knew it to be true, and of my own free will. He was likely to kill me, and Haywood afterwards.

But Neal never guessed. He scolded me all the way home for running off and hiding myself, but he was not really angry, only relieved and vexed with his own anxiety. As we parted for the night, he kissed me, and I almost shrank from him, thinking surely he could taste those other kisses on my bruised lips. But he was absorbed in his own thoughts. I believe he had been carried away with one of the wantons at the masquerade, and felt guilty at having forgotten me in her arms.

So we said good-night, each hiding our own secret and guilty toward the other. Not the least part of my guilt was that I no longer loved him best.

Next day I drooped about the house in a languor, longing for Robert again, yet afraid of what I had already done. I scarcely noticed Harvey as he came and went, and only roused myself to fend off Dangerfield's obscene curiosity. He, of them all, being always upon the look, may have guessed my secret, but I could not be sure. He was always lewd and knowing in his glances. It might be only my conscience. In any case, if he guessed he could not *know*, and it suited him to remain silent.

Upon the following day Mrs. Allison called to take me for an airing. Val shrugged when I told her.

"If you like her, Jenny!"

"Oh," I said, uncomfortably, "I do not exactly *like* her, but——"

The truth was, I had begun to wonder at hearing nothing from Robert, and hoped by going abroad to give him some opportunity to meet or speak with me. Or at least to catch a glimpse of him somewhere. I was beginning to understand something of Val's restless fever when Harvey was not with her.

"Well, child?" Mrs. Allison said, as we settled ourselves for the drive. "Have you thought more about my Lord Gould?"

"No," I admitted, truthfully. "Not at all."

She paused for a while, contemplating her jewelled hands with a faint smile. Then she said coolly, "Yet you may have better cause to look for a husband soon, Miss Archer, than you have now."

I started, and looked at her frightened. She said she knew everything—but how *could* she know?

She smiled upon me, that cruel wolfish smile. "La, my dear, there's no cause to blush! It is done every day. I knew, as soon as I saw you, you would not long remain an innocent. I never knew red hair that did not mark a wanton!"

I gasped breathlessly, "How did you—— Does anyone else know?"

"By no means, child. I am the discreetest woman alive. As for how I know, your lover told me, to be sure."

"Judas!" I gasped, falling back as though I had been struck.

"Nonsense. He must have help, and so must you, and he came where he knew he might be sure of it. We are old friends, Robert Haywood and I," the lady said, calmly taking a pinch of snuff. "I shall contrive everything very prettily. You need have no care."

I did not know which way to look. I loathed the woman

148

beside me with such loathing that I was almost sick. Her paint, her winey breath, her hoarse knowing voice, her laugh—my God, she was but a bawd after all, and this was not the first time he had used her!

"La, my dear, don't be so modest," she said, surveying me cruelly. "'Tis not a crime to be ruined so pleasantly! You have the prettiest gentleman in London to be your lover. It is a thousand pities you can't marry, but both of you must have money, and neither of you has any."

"I—I may have some one day," I stammered, sore and humiliated.

"Pooh! Don't try to gull me with your fairy stories. You have not a penny and he has a mountain of debts. One of these days he must take Miss Elin, or some other heiress, and we must find a husband for you. Meanwhile, you may have an agreeable time together, and maybe even repeat it after marriage, if you carry it off discreetly and he does not weary of you."

I think till this moment I had never realised quite what I had done. The woman's changed manner toward me told it all. I was damaged goods now—to be handled roughly and got off the counter by any cheat imaginable. And my ears were not innocent any more—she spoke to me in the hoarse voice of one initiate to another. We were harlots together, and, oh God, God, I could not deny it!

She brought me to her house, and of course he was waiting there. After we had all taken wine together, she left us with some coarse jests, and though for a moment I tried to deny him, I was soon enough in his arms. What comfort was there left for me anywhere else?

Through all that hot July and early August, we met and loved and kept our secret. One by one the fashionables left London, and that made our meetings easier. While Mrs. Sylvester was still in town, I was often called to be with her, and could not escape without offence to a woman who had befriended me. Or without giving rise to suspicion.

But towards the end of July, Mrs. Sylvester's great chariot

rolled out of London on its way to her country house. In September she would visit Bath; she would not be in town again until the first of October. She offered to take me to Bath with her, expressing concern that Val and I must remain in the hot, fever-ridden city. But though I thanked her for her kind offers, I said I must remain with my sister.

And it was true, too, for Val's time was coming near and I dreaded it almost as much as she. My own mother had died in childbed, so had Caroline, so had all of my stepmothers but one. And Val's detestation of the child to come frightened me; it was so ill and unnatural a way to face her ordeal.

There was no one to whom I could talk. Robert had no interest in such matters. He said, "Don't worry, my love, women have babies every day. A few grunts, and it will soon be over."

"I wonder how *you* would bear it," I cried indignantly, but he merely laughed at the thought, teasing and kissing me, and asking whether there were any signs I might follow my sister's example.

How he could make a joke of it passed my understanding. I lived in terror of it. For the first time in my life, I welcomed the signs that told me I was still safe. And so often and passionately had we loved, and so worn was I, between guilt and desire and contriving and lying, that I almost welcomed the excuse to avoid him for a few days and remain at home with Val.

We had come close together again, though there were so many secrets between us now. With her great increase in the last month had come a release from desire for Harvey; she was totally absorbed now by her own miseries. At last she begged Harvey to go out of town for a month or two, and he reluctantly did so, returning to his own home.

I thought how my father would laugh to know how easily I had been ruined. He had always called me a born harlot, and said I would go into the hay with the first man that asked me, and I bitterly thought that he was right.

And yet, when I saw Robert again, I could not help but glory in my love and wonder how any woman could resist him. Not many had done so, I was certain, and I had come to be so sure of him that I gloried in his past triumphs, and believed him when he laid them all at my feet and swore that no woman had ever meant anything to him compared to me.

Few of Val's acquaintances left town; they were City people, without country estates, not fashionable enough for Bath or Tunbridge Wells. They professed to prefer London without a 'crowd' and pretended they did not mind the heat and stink of summer.

I did. With all my heart I longed for the country, and once or twice Robert took me on the river with him, going as far as Richmond, where we lounged and played in the meadows.

Val was grown too large to care for any outing, so Neal no longer took us upon the river. He seemed rather to avoid the house. Val's misery troubled him; and there had come a distance between him and me for which there seemed no cause, though God knows I knew there was one. But Neal did not know. It was more that he avoided me for some reason of his own, and it came so pat to help my deceits that I did not strive much against it. I wondered at it a little, but nothing touched me now unless through Robert.

Among those who came to say good-bye to Val was Lord Dutton. He had not been to the house since the night of my abduction. Val laid it to his guilty conscience; I attributed it to Mrs. Allison's good offices. We were both wrong, of course, but, from whatever cause, the slackening in his pursuit was welcome.

Harvey chanced to be there when Dutton called, and I saw the two men measure each other: Harvey hotly, my lord with his cold snake-like glance. Because of Harvey, he said nothing in particular to either of us, though I thought his look dwelt more on me than it used to. I was very glad to hear that he was going out of town, and so was Val, who had to soothe Harvey's suspicions. It is odd how men can smell a rival—look at Dangerfield's instant detestation of Harvey!

With Harvey gone, and Dutton, and most of the others who had caused us dismay, we spent that last fortnight before Val's lying-in in something like peace. I heard Parker was gone also, to his father's house in Suffolk. I had not seen him since the masquerade and would have been glad, I thought, never to see him again. I thought of him as little as I could; I lost myself, drowned myself, in Robert's arms.

Robert was tenderer to me than ever before. I had grown hardened in wrong-doing and had more joy of it. What would come must come, and meanwhile I was happy and had a lover that a queen might envy me.

Moreover, I argued, we were not so very sinful; we loved and would marry if we could. And we were both free; there was no adultery in it.

Now and then I ventured to ask him if we could not somehow marry. He was always gentle and loving, and swore we would some day. I came almost to believe it. I had come, indeed, to believe anything that he told me. I could not think what life would be without him, and therefore I believed him when he said we would always be together.

Val never liked my going about so much with Mrs. Allison, but I reasoned her out of it. She could not take me about herself, in her condition, I argued; and Mrs. Sylvester was gone; and with Dutton out of town, what harm could Mrs. Allison do? She was a fashionable woman; she knew everybody in the *beau monde*; nobody thought any the worse of her for having such a brother.

But to myself I used to think, "Oh God, she is worse than he, and you are right, Val, you are right—she is vile and evil and degraded; she is dirt and it soils me even to come near her; I am sickened by everything she says and does—but she is the only way to Robert, the only way. And I would walk in dirt to my knees to come to him."

It seemed to me strange that Val, often so unperceptive about people, had discerned Mrs. Allison's true quality at once; while I, who fancied myself shrewder, had been for a time deceived.

Yet, though I loathed and despised her—and feared her too, not a little—there was a queer relief in her company. It was partly because she knew it all; with her I could throw off all pretence. And partly also because she *was* so entirely depraved.

152

There was no shame in her, no remorse, seemingly no memory even of any time when she might have been innocent, or a child. Bad as many people are, you meet few who have totally left behind them all that they once knew of good. Even in the wretched poor, who have known nothing but degradation and vileness from birth, there are flickers of something better—remorse, regret, at worst, fear. They have not wholly forgotten God.

And it is just that, I think, that makes the society of most wicked people so painful, rather even than the things they do—the hidden regret, the secret fear, the remorse glossed over with bravado—shame that takes the shape of defiance.

With Mrs. Allison there was nothing of that. Nothing. If ever a woman sold her soul and gloried in it, it was she.

And with my lover there was no remorse or regret either. He was not so much devilish as pagan. Life was simple to him. He lived it as each impulse prompted, and knew no more of guilt than an animal.

I think I may say that I soon came to know him, whether I would admit it or not, through and through. He was a practised seducer who knew every trick in the game, but he did not play it with any malice or calculation. He simply wished to give and receive pleasure, and had learned the words and caresses most likely to gain his objective, as a beautiful animal learns to show off its graces to advantage so as to be prized and petted.

And he lied in the same way—not to deceive for any special advantage, but simply to make things pleasant. For himself, by nature, I think he would always have been perfectly honest. Certain facts were apparent; he saw them quite clearly and had no wish to conceal them. But he had learned by experience, no doubt, that the women who loved him were less honest—or more loving. They required lies to be happy, and he had simply learned to oblige them.

He had tried to be honest with me; I had insisted on lies; and therefore he lied, expertly, convincingly, and with the kindest motives. He was really fond of me. He wanted me to be happy. He was incapable of feeling a stronger emotion.

And I knew it all, saw it with eyes that never had been more clear, and turned away and would not believe that there was nothing in him to love, except his beauty and good nature and amorous skill.

But because he *was* so beautiful, and we were young and loved with passion, and he brought to it all there was in him—I really believe he cared for nothing else, wine, or gaming, or hunting, or anything but love—there was a glamour about those hours, an enchantment, that I could only feel and cannot now explain.

And, like all enchantments, it broke one day as completely and inexorably as any bubble.

We lay together, one drowsy summer afternoon, in the little summer-house where we had first known each other. He had a key to the garden; we used to come and go by a door behind the pavilion, so that no one in the house knew we were there. My lord and his mistress had gone out of town; while his wife still remained with the children in the country. There were only a few servants in the house, and they never came into the garden.

The pretty room was now as familiar to me as my own. I lay drowsily looking at it, the light filtering through the heavy green silk curtains, and thought how I should always remember it for the happiness it had brought me.

Robert lay beside me. It was so hot that he lay stripped and panting, his arms flung above his head, while I wore only a thin chemise, my gown and petticoats tossed heedlessly over a chair.

I rose on one elbow to see him better. I never tired of looking at him. From head to toe, there was not a flaw—only the perfection of line and running muscle and long, fine, powerful bones. The hair that curled over his chest and under his arms was only a shade less bright than the golden head, and all the things that used to revolt me in other men—my father and the menservants and Dangerfield—seemed in him beautiful. Even his sweat did not offend me. It had the healthy untainted odour of a fine animal. He loved his body as passionately as I did, and cleaned and conditioned it as I never knew anyone to do before.

When I bent and kissed the hollow at the base of his throat, he made a sleepy sound and pulled me to him ardently.

"Darling!" he whispered into my hair. "How beautiful you are . . ."

"Not half as beautiful as you," I answered regretfully. I wished to be as perfect as he, and saw many flaws in myself. I had a pretty shape—long slim legs, good rounded hips flowing smoothly into a soft little waist, a fine bosom, high and well carried. But my neck and shoulders were too thin—as though I were a very young girl—and my arms too thin, the wrists and hands boyish instead of being plump and helpless.

"Such a lovely little face . . ." he whispered. "You are more beautiful, Jenny, since I began to love you!"

It was true. It was as though a touch of magic had been laid upon my face, softening away the thinness, perfecting the shape, pulsing colour into the lips, putting a mysterious darkness into the eyes. How could anyone, I sometimes thought, look upon that face and not know that I was loved? I was not beautiful; I never should be; but for this little while enchantment put its mask upon my face and hid all the flaws.

We were very happy, that long silent summer's afternoon. Hardly a sound penetrated our little room under the trees. We seemed shut away in a shell, a shell tinted with the colours of an opal—rose and green, white and gold.

He was so loving to me, it was all so dream-like, so perfect, that I went away in a daze of happiness, my old sorrows and guilts forgotten, as pagan in bliss as he.

"Tomorrow?" I whispered, as we parted outside the garden wall; he to walk to his lodgings, I to go to Mrs. Allison's carriage, waiting around the corner this past hour.

And he smiled, bending his head for one last kiss, murmuring, "How can I stay away from you even that long, sweet Jenny?"

To my surprise, Mrs. Allison was waiting in the carriage. Ordinarily she remained at home, sending me in the coach and ordering it to pick me up again in a few hours, wherever Robert and I had chosen to meet. I marvelled sometimes that she should so patiently accommodate us; I was not so simple as to think she did it all for friendship. No doubt Robert paid her; he always seemed to have plenty of ready money.

"Get in, my dear," she said. "I have a fancy for an airing, and will drive you home."

I mounted beside her, apologising, somewhat perfunctorily, for keeping her waiting. Some of my bliss scattered at the sight of her; I had so wanted the quiet drive home alone!

"Oh," she said, with that detestable smile, "I do not complain. I know lovers cannot be hurried. I daresay you were well occupied!"

I put my fan up beside my face, as though to shield it from the hot light of the setting sun, and was silent.

I felt that she was looking at me, though I would not meet her eyes, and presently she laughed contemptuously.

"Lord!" she said. "What cowards men are!"

Startled, I turned to glance at her, and something in her look frightened me suddenly, so that I stammered, "What—— Who do you mean, madam?"

"I mean your handsome lover, my dear," she answered, still with that same rough contempt. "I can see by your face that he was too cowardly to tell you."

"Tell me what?" I said slowly. A clutch seemed to fasten on my heart; I lost my breath.

She shrugged. "Only that he is going away—tonight or early tomorrow—you will not see him again. He is going to Bath. Miss Elin is there with her guardian; he has lately received some encouragement; and goes to make all secure."

God knows, it was brutally done. It was enough to kill me. I do not know now which I despise the more—the cruelty that so rejoiced in hurt, or the cowardice that left me exposed to it.

I gave a cry and caught her by the arm. "No! You are lying. He would not—— You are lying!"

She smiled. To my dying day, I shall never forget that smile. It was the first time I knew she hated me.

"Be calm, my dear," she advised, in a tone of cool contempt that was past bearing.

156

I stared at her incredulously, and then suddenly flung myself on the door, striving to undo the catch, to jump into the street.

She gave an exclamation, and pulled me back with strong hands.

"Are you trying to kill yourself, you little fool?"

"Let me out! I must go back! I must see him! You are lying—what lies have you told him? I must go back—tell them to turn back, or let me out!"

"Be still!" she said, sharply, and gave me a shake that fairly rattled the teeth in my head. "Do you want the servants to hear—the people in the street?"

I tried to force her hands away. She was trying to kill me, and she thought I would care whether the servants heard!

"You *must* be quiet," she said, between her teeth. She wrenched at my wrists so cruelly I cried out in pain, and gave me a box across the ear that half stunned me.

"I think you're mad!" she said, as I fell back, my hand to my cheek. "Good Lord, no wonder he was afraid to tell you! Why, you're clean out of your wits about him—greensick!"

The blow brought me somewhat to my wits; the tone of unutterable scorn did more. I put my hands over my face and sat silent. It could not be true—and yet I knew, by some sure instinct, that it *was* true. Knew it with the first word she uttered, seeing his face still before me, hearing him murmur, "How can I stay away from you even that long, sweet Jenny?"

"Oh God!" I whispered. "Oh God!"

"That's better," Mrs. Allison approved, with sharp malice. "Turn to prayer, my dear, it's very soothing. Lord! I thought I had driven you clean out of your wits."

I pressed my fingers hard upon my eyes. If I died for it, I would not give her the satisfaction to see me cry.

I think she waited for the tears, as an executioner for the first cries of his victim, but when they did not come, she went on, in that cool tone of advice:

"Now, child, you have been fond and foolish long enough. I thought you a girl of some wit. You must have known it could not last. Lord knows, we both told you so often enough!"

I bit my lip to keep silent. I was trapped in this damned prison; I could not escape her malice; but I could at least keep still and give her the scant satisfaction of talking to herself.

"I hope you remember," she continued, "that it was not by *my* advice you came to be ruined. I offered to help you to a husband, you may recall. But you preferred to let Bob Haywood tumble you for nothing." She laughed jeeringly. "That was your choice, my dear. Not mine. So pray let me have no high tragedy rants from you. I have been your friend, and will be so still, if you are sensible."

After a silence, she said coldly, "What, sullen! Lord, what an unreasonable little toad! Though I suppose I must make allowance for your broken heart, child. It *is* broken, I daresay, and your faith shattered, and you wish you were dead, and all the rest of it."

In a way, I suppose her scorn was good for me. It made me come alive again. I writhed in secret, as though she had been flogging me, but sat outwardly still and silent, behind the shelter of my hands.

"You will get over it," she assured me. "You are not the first girl ruined by Bob Haywood, and you won't be the last. But it was mighty pleasant while it lasted, wasn't it?"

My silence at last enraged her; she struck at my hands with her fan, cutting the knuckles with its sharp edge.

"Don't sit there as though you had been struck silly!" she cried, ferociously enough. "Or are you ashamed to show your face to me?"

That brought my hands down in a hurry, and found my tongue as well.

"I could never be ashamed to show my face to *you*, madam," I said, as quietly as I could, "whatever evil or folly I had done."

She burst out laughing, as though I had paid her a compliment.

"Thank God, you haven't lost your tongue! Come, Miss Archer, keep your tongue and your temper and we may pull through this comfortably yet."

She leant back in her corner, snuffing with relish at her scent bottle. It was terribly hot; the air in the carriage was close and fetid. It made me sick to sit so close to her, to smell her rank, winey smell, to feel her hot, heavy thigh against mine.

"Lord, it's hot!" she said. "Well, child, are you sensible yet? Can you listen to me?"

"Say whatever you have to say to me, madam. It will be your last opportunity."

"Oh, is that the way of it?" she cried. "Now you will be haughty! You are not out of the woods, you know. I can ruin you with a word. It will pay you better to be friends with me."

I shut my lips; and she shrugged.

"Perhaps, miss, you have forgotten something else? You may be with child this moment. How will you deal with *that*, pray tell?"

I turned and looked at her at last, full in the face. "There is always the river, madam," I said. "Believe me, at the worst I would prefer it."

"Ah!" she said softly. If I had not been so outraged, so sickened, I think I might have shrunk from the almost gleeful malice of her glance. I had declared myself her enemy, and she was not sorry to take up the challenge. Whatever she had pretended before, whatever the cause of her long patience with me, she was not sorry to have it over.

"Well, I will remind you of that, my dear, when the time comes to jump," she said, with that jovial malice I had once mistaken for good humour. "Meanwhile, I wish you and your sister both a safe delivery."

After that, she too was silent; we rode the rest of the way without speaking.

The sun was going down, hot and brassy, in a sulphur-coloured sky. It is rare that London is not hazed over with smoke, and the sky on that hot summer evening was heavy and harsh with it, burning up in fiery tints like the end of the world. You could fairly taste the metal of its burning upon your tongue and feel its heat on your cheek. To the end of my days I shall remember that day, dying so ugly and violent a death, like all my happiness. I shall never be so happy or so old, I think, that the remembrance of it does not come back on me with a taint of sickness and pain.

As I entered the house, a maid came flying to me.

"Thank God you've come, miss! We've been sending all over town for you. Where have you been? The mistress's time has come—she's took hard!"

I stood quite still, staring at her. I was so dazed I could scarcely take in what she meant. And when I did, for a minute all I could think was, 'Oh God, I can't—I can't bear any more! I *must* get some rest!'

It was only for a minute. Then all my love and care for Val came back on me in a rush, putting everything else for the time out of my head. I flung aside my hat and fan and ran upstairs to her, frantic with anxiety.

The midwife had already come, and she and Mrs. Betty were busy about Val. Dangerfield was also in my sister's room, looking pale, and very much in the way. He was perpetually asking Val how she felt, and the midwife whether it would be an easy birth. The woman replied to him contemptuously—if at all—pushing him to one side.

He began to reproach me at sight with being away so long. But Val called to me, and I pushed past him and dropped on my knees beside her bed, jerking impatiently at my hoop to get it out of my way.

"Dearest Val! Are you all right? Is it very bad yet?"

"Oh Jenny! I'm so glad you've come!" Val gasped, clutching at me with hot frightened hands. "I can't bear it! I didn't think it would be as bad as this!"

"You haven't even begun to feel it yet," the midwife told her scornfully. She was a huge woman, ham-fisted as a man. Standing with those great doubled fists on her thick hips, she stared down at Val with contemptuous calculation. "Lord knows how long you may be about this business. I'm going to have my dinner. I'm hungry. Now miss has come, she may see what she can do with you."

Jerking her head at me to follow her, she walked with a heavy tread to the door.

"Keep her quiet, if you can," she commanded. "She's been screeching and throwing herself about like a madwoman every time a pain comes. She'll be worn out before the time comes for her to do some work."

"Do you think it will go easily with her?" I whispered anxiously. Val's white face, shining with sweat, frightened me.

"Lord, no! She's no broader than a boy. We'll hear some rare screaming before this is over, I warrant you," the horrible woman said, and went off to her dinner. No doubt, with good appetite.

Full of anxiety, I went back to Val. Even as I took her hand, a pain came over her. She gasped and cringed, the perspiration starting out at the roots of her hair. She bore down on my hand, shutting her eyes and grinding her teeth. When it was over, she lay still with shut eyes, and I wiped the sweat from her face. Already it seemed to me that her face had grown thinner, the bones showing more sharply.

She had begun to feel her pains, Mrs. Betty told me in a whisper, just after I had gone with Mrs. Allison, and had been suffering now these three hours.

I felt a horrible pang of guilt as I remembered how I had passed most of those three hours. While Val had wanted me! And then I thought of what had followed, and winced from a stab of pain more unbearable still.

But perhaps it was not true. Here, away from Mrs. Allison, I could almost believe it all a lie. He *could* not be so faithless. As soon as I could, I would write to him, send to him—and then, then I would know. Perhaps he would come to me. I could almost hear him laugh, feel his hands on me—"How could you think I would leave you, sweetest Jenny?"

With an effort, I forced my thoughts away. Val must come first with me now.

I coaxed her to let me go for a little while, and ran up to my room to change my dress. I put off my hoops and prettinesses, and donned an old stuff gown, very simple and loose, and tied back my hair from my face with a clean ribbon. But even then I had to pause to look at myself stripped in the little mirror. Smooth skin, white body, high firm breasts that he had kissed and adored so often—there was not a sign to show that body had known a lover, except, perhaps, one dark little bruise low down under one breast. Even that was fading. I pressed my hand upon it fiercely, to make it worse. . . . It was not possible that he should leave me. She had lied. He loved me; he thought me lovely; he would never, *never* leave me; he had said so a thousand times!

So I reminded myself, passionately, striving to force back the fears that threatened me. But all the while a little voice whispered maliciously in my ear—"Miss Elin has thirty thousand pounds. Thirty thousand pounds!"

I could see that Dangerfield's presence fretted my sister very much, but I could not induce him to go. He was curious, I think. He viewed Val's suffering with a mixture of fascination and repugnance which I found sufficiently ugly.

"Lord, I am sure she is very bad!" he said again and again. "Look at her, Miss Jenny, does she not look very bad? And so monstrously big! If the child is as big as that, I cannot see how it shall ever come forth, do you? And to think I am to blame for it all!" He forced remorse into his voice, but looked positively complacent upon the thought.

Luckily, Val paid him no heed. She was used to ignoring him, and she was totally absorbed in her own sufferings.

At last Dangerfield bethought himself of his own dinner and went off, promising to have me brought something on a tray. When it came, I tried to get Val to eat, knowing she would need her strength, but she could not.

"I am sick—I am sick," she moaned, pushing me away. "And so hot! Oh Lord, must that fire be lit?"

It was true it was suffocating in the room. The windows were shut, and the midwife had given orders to keep the fire up. As fast as Mrs. Betty piled bedclothes upon my sister, she kicked them off, and I at last told the maid to stop.

"It is hotter than midsummer in here," I said, fanning Val as hard as I could. "Put a screen before the fire, for God's sake!"

"Midwife said she was to be kept warm," Mrs. Betty protested. "But Lord! it is hot!" She was sweating, and smelled so rank I finally sent her out of the room on a pretext.

"Thank God!" Val muttered. "She stinks like a sick cat. She turns my stomach. Oh God——here it comes! Oh God!" She clung to me fiercely till it was over, drawing up her knees in agony.

"They are worse," she whispered. "Much worse . . . I'm sure the baby is coming . . . Where is that woman?"

"Darling Val," I said, trying to get her to drink a glass of wine, "the baby won't come for hours, I'm afraid. It's so long between pains."

"So long!"

"Oh Val, dearest, you know they must come every minute, and oftener. Don't you remember——" But I checked myself, remembering how Caroline's hoarse cries had haunted the house for hours, driving even the hardened servants out of doors. After her death I used to start up crying from my sleep, thinking I could hear them still.

"Oh God, I can't bear it!" Val whispered. "I can't bear it, if it's worse than this—— Oh Jenny, you don't know! I thought I would be brave, but I can't—I can't! Oh God!" She stiffened, a look of terror twisted her face. "It's coming! It's coming! Oh Christ!"

And I dropped the fan and held her in my arms, twisting and shuddering as the convulsion took her, the whole body racked to free itself of this burden it had carried so long.

The midwife took her time about dinner, but Val seemed thankful she was gone. Between pains she complained of the woman, saying she was hard-handed and cruel and unsympathetic. "And like a man—I had as lief be mauled by a great man—Jenny, couldn't we send her away? You used to help at home, when I ran off and put my fingers in my ears. Couldn't you help me?"

I was terror-stricken at the very thought. They had always

sent me out at the last. I begged Val to be patient; the woman was said to be one of the best midwives in London.

She was a rough, coarse creature, certainly. When I saw how Val shrank from her, I was almost ready to send her away myself. But I did not dare. It was going to be bad enough. I couldn't take the responsibility alone.

Mrs. Holl, as her name was, came up to Val and laid one hand upon her belly. Energetically picking her teeth with one hand, she kept the other upon Val until a pain had come and gone. Val clutched at me, while the woman's hard pressure kept her still in bed.

"It's coming slow," was Mrs. Holl's verdict. "Don't give her too much of that wine. She's got to work."

Acting on her orders, I tied a long strip of tough linen to one of the bed-posts and put the end into Val's hands.

"Hold to that," the woman ordered. "And when the pain comes, pull on it, and push down with your belly."

"I can't!" Val gasped. "It hurts so!"

"It'll hurt worse before it's better," the woman assured her. "If you want it over with, you'd best work a little."

With which, kicking aside the screen, she settled herself before the fire, asking me to ring for a glass of Geneva. "With a bit of hot water, love, for I've got to keep my strength up."

Seeing me look blank, she added impatiently, "Hollands, child, Hollands! For the Lord's sake, have you never heard of parliament water before?"

I exchanged a glance with Val and rang the bell, ordering hot gin and water for Mrs. Holl. It was Dangerfield himself who brought it up. He had obviously wined well at dinner and was in a state of maudlin sentiment. He pressed the glass into the midwife's hand, tearfully imploring her to take good care of his darling wife.

She took the glass and contemptuously pushed him away. He reeled and fell beside Val's bed. Pulling her hand to his lips, he slobbered over it, half crying, imploring her not to die. Between kisses, he promised her everything—she should have her own carriage—a running footman—a sedan chair with carriers in

164

livery—anything! He would never refuse her anything, his darling, his poppet, his love, if only she would not die and leave him.

I thought Val would be sick. "Jenny, take him away!" she gasped. "He's drunk. Oh God, I *shall* die if he——"

She broke off, and stiffened, her hand clenching unconsciously upon Dangerfield's. Then she cried out, a short hard cry, almost more of protest than of pain. Her lips curled back from her teeth, her eyes seemed to sink into her head. Agony in an instant wiped all the beauty from her face. And when it was over, she sank back motionless, unconscious for a moment.

The sight sobered Dangerfield out of his dramatics. He staggered to his feet, letting her hand slip out of his. Almost humbly, he turned round to the midwife.

"She looks bad," he said, blinking his great gooseberry eyes in fright. He looked down in astonishment at his hand where Val's little fingers had bitten so deep that there were livid marks on the flesh.

Mrs. Holl drained her glass, smacked her lips, and rose, with the reluctant air of one called to duty.

"Of course she does," she said, roughly. "Have you never seen a woman labour before? It's little you men think of your pleasures when we women have to pay for them."

"But—but she won't really die?" Dangerfield stammered. His pale, bun-shaped face was all slack, the jaw dropping. A muscle worked at one corner of his mouth, jumping queerly.

I almost felt sorry for him, but that I felt so much sorrier for Val. In his own horrid way, he loved her; or at any rate valued her so that the thought of losing her was dismaying to him. It was not much, but perhaps it was the best he could do. So ugly, so unloved himself, how could he do more?

"She may or she may not," Mrs. Holl replied, quite unmoved. "You can't do any good, anyhow. She doesn't want you, that's plain, so you'd best get out."

"I shall stay if I wish. She's my wife," Dangerfield blustered. But he looked with a kind of horror toward Val, as though he feared she might turn on him and accuse him of her death.

I went up to him and laid my hand upon his arm, though I shrank always from touching him.

"Come back a little later, sir," I whispered. "And please, if you have not done so, send for Neal."

He looked at me blankly, and then nodded violently. "Aye, aye! I'll go for him myself." As he went out of the room, he stumbled in his walk like a man half dazed.

Mrs. Holl grinned. "Frightened," she said tersely. "Do him good. A frightened husband is a good husband, I say. The beasts!"

The brutality of the woman disgusted me. But we had to depend on her, Val and I. In a whisper, I asked imploringly:

"*Is* she very bad?"

"Now don't you begin to fret! She'll do well enough. You keep your head and do as I tell you and we'll pull her through," Mrs. Holl retorted confidently. Then she coughed hoarsely once or twice, and asked if she could have a drop more Hollands, just to keep down the cold on her chest.

"Best to keep the bottle here, my dear. We'll give your sister a drop now and then."

When Mrs. Betty brought the gin, I pulled her outside, shutting the door.

"Is this drunken beast the best we can do?" I demanded fiercely. "Aren't there other midwives?"

Mrs. Betty rolled her eyes. "La, miss, she *is* a rough one. You should hear her stories—fair turned my stomach at supper, they did! But they do say she has the best hand with a bad case in all of London. And as for drinking, miss—Lord, they all do that! Keeps them going!"

"I'll see what Neal says," I promised myself, wishing with all my heart that he would come and comfort me. I was horribly afraid for Val.

But Neal, when he came, was not much comfort to me. Indeed, I had to comfort him. He gave one glance of horror at Val's distorted face, and when she screamed, turned ashen and fairly fled the room.

I found him outside, sitting on the stairs.

"Jesus!" he whispered, as I sat down beside him and put my head on his shoulder. "Will she die, Jenny?"

"I don't know," I answered wearily. He put his arm around me, but not protectively, rather as though he clung to me. "She can't die," he said forlornly. "So lovely and so young . . . Jenny, you can't let her die!" He took me by the shoulders, looking at me intently. His fair hair fell over his forehead, his blue eyes burned on mine. With his pallor, his evident anguish, he looked more like Val than I had ever seen him. "Make her stay, Jenny!" he said, so queerly that my hair crept. "Hold her here. You can do it, I know. You have so much life in you—— If I were dying, you could call me back, Jenny. I know you could. I would never leave you." And then, with a kind of sob, he caught me into his arms and held me passionately, as though he too could draw life from me.

There rose, behind us, a long low cry, hoarse and wavering. It was less like a scream than the stifled howl of an animal in agony. We both started apart at the sound.

"Jesus!" Neal said, getting violently to his feet. "I can't stand this. Jenny, I can't stand it!" he repeated pathetically, as though he were ashamed and appealed to me for understanding.

I touched him gently on the shoulder, as he stood below me. "Only stay near enough so that I can call you, if——" I stopped, and he turned his convulsed face away. "Do you remember Caroline?" I added, in a low voice.

"Do I not!" After a pause, he said, more quietly, "It was her death drove me from home. I remember my father complaining at the noise she made, and going out to ride over to Underhill's 'to get away from the damned caterwauling.'" Neal's voice was bleak with remembered bitterness. "It was then I decided to leave home. . . . Even Dangerfield isn't as bad as that."

"Where is he?"

"Downstairs, getting drunk. I think I'll do the same, Jenny. Only not here—I can't stand to be with him. I brought my man William to help—he'll know where to find me. And Tommy—he can run errands for you."

"Tommy?" I said quickly, remembering the bright face of my

167

brother's little page. "Is he here? Will you send him to me? I do have an errand."

When Tommy came bounding upstairs, I had my note written. I gave it to him, with all the money I had in the world—the money Dangerfield had given me once.

"Tommy, will you do something for me? And not tell anybody? Even your master?"

"I'll do anything, Miss Jenny. And I'll not tell anybody, not if I die for it," the boy said, his eyes shining.

"Then take this note, Tommy——" and I told him where. "Don't try to run all the way—take a hackney coach. You can keep all the money that's left over. And don't give my note to anybody but the gentleman himself—into his hand. You know him, don't you?"

Tommy nodded. He knew everybody. "I'll do it easy," he promised. "I'll be back in an hour." He grinned at me cockily, and swaggered a little. I could see he was much flattered to be made part of an intrigue. But when I stooped down and kissed him, he turned red as fire and fled, muttering something incoherent, so that even then I could not help smiling a little.

When midnight came, Val had been in labour nine hours, and in hard labour for more than two. Her cries never stopped now.

Mrs. Holl was a dirty, drunken, hard-voiced woman. She had seemed indifferent and almost contemptuous towards Val before. I would not have known her now. The hard voice was sunk low, soft with endearments; the powerful hands worked unceasingly to ease my sister; she held her when I no longer had the strength to do it; and all the while ordering Mrs. Betty and me about, seeing everything, watchful of every turn, nursing Val's failing strength with doses of brandy and gin, urging her to keep up, to try, to try once more—it would soon be over now.

Mrs. Betty and I worked like slaves under her direction. The dapper lady's-maid was dapper no longer. She was as sweaty and as frightened as I.

"God!" she whispered to me. "I'll never go through this, miss, never, for any man, I swear it!"

168

And I, thinking that I might be with child even now, seeing myself nine months hence in such an agony as this, turned cold at the thought, in a room as hot as hell.

There came a moment when the cries stopped and there was a brief cessation in the pains. Val sank instantly into a sleep like a coma, and Mrs. Holl, shaking her head, lowered herself groaning into a chair and begged for gin. She had earned it, God knows; I poured it for her myself with a shaking hand, and took a swallow of brandy, at her urging, and gave Betty some.

"Best to get some air, miss," Mrs. Holl said briefly. "And say your prayers, if you believe in 'em. We haven't seen the worst yet."

"Oh Christ!" Mrs. Betty whimpered, and I turned and went out, staggering, thinking that I could not bear much more.

Little Tommy was sitting on the stairs outside, his tow head bowed upon his arms. I was so dazed with fatigue that for a moment I could not think of what I wanted him to tell me.

At the sound of the door closing behind me, his head jerked up and he looked at me, his face so pale that all the freckles stood out like bruises.

"Miss Val?" he said, and his lip trembled. "Is Miss Val——?" He stopped as though he could not ask the question; I only shook my head.

My legs trembled under me as though I had just learned to walk. I had to lean on the wall and on the stair-rail, and when I had dropped down beside Tommy I felt as though I could never get up again.

"Tommy—you ought not to be here. Why do you not go downstairs? There is nothing anyone can do."

"I was waiting for you, Miss Jenny," he whispered. "I've been waiting this hour and more. I didn't dare to knock——" his voice trailed away.

And then, and not until then, I remembered the errand on which I had sent him. It seemed very long ago. An hour in that room was like eternity.

He was looking at me anxiously, but dropped his eyes as soon as they met mine.

I turned my own head away, resting my face against the cool wood of the banister. My head ached as though it would split; the brandy had made it worse.

"You gave him my note, Tommy?" I said, in a low voice. And then, "Was there no answer?"

I felt him wriggle beside me. "Tell me, Tommy," I said. "I must know. Was he gone?"

"No, Miss Jenny," he said reluctantly. "He was there. But——" He wriggled again, scraping his feet together; he was in misery; he could no more look at me than if he had been guilty of some crime.

I waited till I could speak quite steadily. "You must tell me everything, Tommy. Indeed, you must. Please! Don't think that I——" I stopped and had to steady my voice again. "It's only that I'm so tired, and anxious for my sister. But please, tell me just what happened."

"Yes, ma'am," Tommy muttered. Suddenly he flew out, in a rage. "I wouldn't take his money—his dirty money! I'd as lief cut my throat!"

I shut my eyes. The pain pounded and pounded inside my head. Every time my heart beat, the throb came in my head. And there was such a pain in my heart too—the two of them together were almost more than I could bear. So he was false after all; so false that even the boy scorned him.

"Why did he offer you money, Tommy?"

Poor lad, he was in such misery. I think he would 'as lief cut his throat' as tell me. But he blurted it all out at last.

"I went there, Miss Jenny, in a coach, just as you told me, and when I told his man—the servant, you know—that it was a message from a lady, he laughed and let me in. He wanted the note, but I wouldn't give it to him. So he laughed and told me to go in."

I could hear the man's knowing laughter. How many messengers had come there, I wondered, with how many messages such as mine? Loving, desperate, offering all, begging him to come back, imploring him to say he was still true—— I felt the red come up into my face at the thought I had sent a boy upon such an errand, for his sake as much as for my own.

"And then, Tommy?"

"Then I went in," he said, reluctantly. "I saw him, Miss Jenny—in a blue coat, ever so handsome, with no powder on his hair. So I knew it was himself, and I gave him the note, as you bade me."

He seemed almost to choke, and paused, but I could prompt him no more. I could see, too plainly, the golden head in the candlelight, and the eyes bluer than his coat, and his smile— Had he smiled when he read my note, or was he merely bored, it was such an old story?

The boy went on with a rush, to get it over: "He read it, Miss Jenny, once or twice, frowning a bit as though he found it hard to read, and then he turned it over in his fingers, and looked down at it, and folded it up neat, and then smoothed it out again, like he was thinking. And then, quite sudden, miss, he folded it up the way it had been, and warmed a knife in the candle, and pressed the seal down again, and he held it out to me. And he said, 'Take it back to your mistress and tell her you could not deliver it. Tell her Mr. Haywood had already gone out of town. Do you understand?' And I took the note, miss, not knowing what to do or say, but all confused-like. And then, Miss Jenny, he held out a piece of money! And it was a guinea—I saw how it shone in the candle! And he said, 'This is for you, my lad, if you tell your mistress I was already gone——'" Tommy's hesitation was gone now; the words came boiling out of him, stumbling and angry. "And I took the money, Miss Jenny, and I called him a name, the worst I could think of, and I threw the money in his face. And then I turned and ran, as fast as I could, and got clean away, and come back here, and——"

His voice dwindled; he muttered: "As if I would take his dirty money to tell you lies!"

After a long, long pause, I asked. "What did you do with the note, Tommy?"

"I burnt it, miss, in the kitchen fire."

171

"Thank you, Tommy," I whispered, and felt the boy's hand upon my shoulder as I bowed my head down into my arms.

"If I were a man I would kill him!" he muttered fiercely, at last.

I shook my head upon my arms. "He is not worth it, Tommy." And the bitterest of all my pain was that there should be so much contempt in it. That he should leave me, throw me off so lightly—even that was not so bad. But that he should be such a coward!

After a while I roused myself, and got haltingly to my feet. The boy jumped up and gave me his shoulder, chivalrously refraining from looking at my face. In that moment of humiliation it was strange how the boy's gallantry touched and mended me.

"Tommy," I said gently, "I am so much obliged to you. I will never forget your kindness. It was a sorry errand I sent you on. Do not think of it any more."

I saw the red come into his face, though he kept his head down.

"I'd die for you, Miss Jenny," he said, hoarsely. "Before God, I would! I wish I was a man! I wish——"

He pulled away from my hand and went rushing and stumbling downstairs and out of sight. I could hear him crying as he went. It was strange that Tommy could cry, and not I. But maybe not so strange, when I come to think on it. Love is a painful, sore thing, whether at twelve or twenty; God forbid that I should ever make light of it.

The hours came and went. Two or three times William, my brother's servant, came upstairs for news and went away looking troubled. At the last visit, he said that his master was in the house; he had thought it best to call him away from the tavern.

"He won't come upstairs, miss, unless there's news——" He hesitated and I shook my head.

The man lingered, looking at me sympathetically. "Is Mrs. Dangerfield no better, miss?"

I leaned against the wall, too tired to stand upright.

"She is dying, I think——" I couldn't say anything more.

He gave a low troubled exclamation and was silent for a while.

Dully, I wondered why William did not go. But as long as he stood there, I felt unable to make the effort to go back, to open that door again—

At last, in a very low voice, almost a whisper, he said, "Miss— I have heard— There was a lady once brought to bed at the house where I was before— And she laboured for hours and the child could not be brought to birth— At last the husband could bear it no longer, but went out and got someone and brought him to the house— A man, it was, and the women all cried out upon letting him in to the lady. But the husband, my master, would have it so. And the man he had brought sent everybody away, the maids and all the women, even the midwife, and he and another man who came with him shut and locked the door and left the key in the lock, so nobody could even peep in. And the people listening heard the lady crying out, and then one great scream, that frightened them all, and then nothing. But presently the man came out and called the women, and when they went in, the baby had been born and the mother still lived. Then the gentleman gave them a great deal of money and they went away, as secret as they had come. It was my lady's own maid who told me, and she was there all the while and saw it all. And she told me, she said they brought something with them that clinked under their cloaks, and she thought it knives, or such-like, and she talked to the other servants, and some of them had heard that these men—brothers they are, miss—were often called for such hard cases as your sister, miss, and they had some secret, that they would tell nobody, and they send everybody away and deliver the baby themselves, when it cannot come by any natural means."

I stared at him breathlessly, grasping at any hope. "William! But—knives? And they do not kill the mother?"

"No, no, miss! That's the secret. Only sometimes the baby dies."

I had long since ceased to think of the baby—or to think of it only as a horrible, swollen monster that was killing my sister by inches, and not a human soul to consider at all.

"William, do you know where these men may be found?"

"I could find out, miss, I think," he answered, a shade evasively. "But it will take a great deal of money."

"Come with me," I said quickly, and I ran downstairs. A moment since I could scarcely walk, but hope activated me again.

I found Dangerfield in the drawing-room, dead drunk, snoring in his chair with his head thrown back. Neal, William, told me, was in the dining-room; he was playing cards with some of the servants and was like a wild man, so that none of them dared to refuse, or complain of being sleepy.

I shook Dangerfield until his teeth rattled, but could not rouse him. Then, without the slightest compunction, I went through his pockets till I found his purse. He never carried large sums, for fear of robbers, but I thrust the purse into William's hands.

"Has my brother any money?"

"Not much, miss, I fancy," the man said apologetically.

"Get it all, whatever he has. I have none———" I drew in my breath, remembering how I had spent what little I had. I looked around the room desperately, but saw nothing of value. "Well, you must give them that, William, and promise them whatever more they ask. Tell them it is Mrs. Dangerfield—everybody has heard of *him*. He will pay them anything—tell them that."

William hesitated. "I don't like it, miss— Will you take it on you, if I get them, to let them come to the lady?"

"Yes, yes," I said, pushing him towards the door. "I will take it all upon me—the money, the responsibility, everything! Only hurry, for God's sake! William, she is dying, and God! such a death!"

And then I went back to Val, and held her swollen hands in mine, and wetted her lips with wine and water, and wiped the sweat from her ghastly face and listened to those croaking groans more terrible than any screams.

"I doubt it's much good, miss," the midwife said to me, wiping her wet face with the back of her reddened hand. "It won't come, do what I will. I've done all I know, miss."

I nodded. It was true. She had done everything I had ever heard of, and more. She had tried all the superstitions, and used all the tricks. She had done things that made me sick, remembering. But there was one thing she could not do, and that was to stretch Val's slender body enough to let this great monstrous thing out.

"It will kill her, if it comes," she said, shaking her head. "But I doubt she'll die with it still in her, and we'll lose the baby too. I've never seen labour so hard as this, with no more to show for it."

I was silent. If there was nothing she could do, I wished she would go and leave us alone. But she was resolved to try one or two things more, and she waddled off to restore herself with her favourite drink.

There were brief intervals when Val was conscious, and intervals also when she was so far gone that she could not speak, nor answer me when I spoke to her. But never was she out of pain; there was no unconsciousness merciful enough for that.

Once she whispered, "Jenny . . . do not tell *him* . . . how I died . . ." I knew she meant Harvey, and mutely kissed the little broken hand. And once she said, very loudly and strongly, "Do not let *him* come to me . . . not even when I am dead!" And this time I knew she was not speaking of Harvey. The old detestation of her husband was strong as ever, even now. Of course I promised, would promise anything. But still I could not help pitying Dangerfield a little.

I do not know how long a time passed. I think I had forgotten everything, when suddenly Mrs. Betty came whispering to me that William was outside and would speak with me.

I started up, and rushed out. At first I thought he had returned alone, and my heart sank with despair. Then he made a queer little gesture, of both fear and repugnance, and I saw two men standing behind him, out of the light, like two shadows.

"I've brought them, miss," he whispered. "But I doubt I should——"

I had no time for his doubts or fears. I put him aside and went up to the two men. They stood close together, dressed just alike in black cloaks hanging down to their feet—despite the heat of that August night—with hats pulled low over their foreheads.

They were masked. In the dark they looked like two great birds, gazing at me unwinkingly through the slits in the masks, and I confess that at any other time I would have quailed in terror. But at that moment I did not care where I looked for help, or wonder from what darkness I had called it up.

"My sister is dying," I said. "The baby will not come. Can you help her? Her husband is rich, very rich—the merchant Dangerfield. He will pay you anything, if you save her. Anything!"

My voice shook; I gazed at them imploringly.

One of them said curtly, "We can probably save the mother, but cannot always save the child. Will you absolve us of all blame?"

"Yes, yes! I will sign something—do anything you say! It is my sister—never mind the baby!"

"We should speak to the husband," he said, doubtfully:

"He is downstairs; he is drunk," I said, trying to control myself. "Will not I do? Or—or her brother? Will he do?"

They conferred in low tones; and at last agreed to speak to Neal. I sent William running for him, and remained myself with the men.

You could hear Val, and I said, hoarsely: "That is my sister. Do you hear her? How can you refuse to help her?"

The one who had spoken before said, not unkindly, "We are sorry for your sister, madam. But this could be a hanging matter for us. We must have authority."

"I suppose so," I said wearily, and we waited in silence for Neal.

He looked ghastly, and I saw how he shrank as Val's horrible sounds reached his ears. Like William, he looked with mingled fear and detestation at the two dark figures. But I went and clung to him imploringly, saying that anything, *anything* was better than to do nothing, and that Mrs. Holl could do no more.

"Let them try, Neal, please let them try! They say they can save her. What difference does it make if the baby dies? They will both die if——"

"What will you do to my sister?" Neal said, looking at them

176

with burning eyes in his white face. I could feel how his arm jerked in mine at every sound that came from behind the closed door.

"That is our secret, sir," said the first speaker. "We will not divulge it to anyone. We cannot promise anything. But the secret has been long in our family and we have aided many women in sore labour. It may be we can aid your sister. Only the child may die in our doing so. That you must accept, or we cannot go on."

"Damn the baby!" Neal said, shuddering. "Only, my sister—I *must* know what you mean to do."

"Then we cannot help you," the man said firmly. "It is our secret. Sir, we could refer you to many, many successes of ours, but there is not time. We are sorry for the poor lady, but our secret must remain our own."

He added, with a flash of contempt or amusement. "There is nothing devilish in it, sir, nothing that smacks of brimstone. It is not supernatural. It is a simple thing, neither of Heaven nor Hell, but merely man's ingenuity. We have been sprinkled with holy water before, and exorcised many times; we are Christian men and there is no devil's hand in our business."

"For God's sake, Neal!" I whispered.

Neal hesitated a moment, and then threw up his hands, with a desperate gesture. "Go on, gentlemen," he said. "So you save my sister, I do not care what your methods are."

"And the child's death, if it must be?"

"I hold you absolved, and will so hold you in any court in the land, taking the blame upon myself, so help me God, and upon my honour, and in the presence of these witnesses," Neal answered, formally.

The men looked at William and myself; we both nodded, as taking witness, and they seemed satisfied.

"We will do our best, then," one said briskly. "Only all others must be sent away, and the door locked."

"See to it, Jenny," Neal whispered. "I—I will wait for you here."

I went in, and shortly told Mrs. Holl and Mrs. Betty that they must step outside. The maid went gladly; the midwife protested.

"You can do no more; you have said so. I have brought some-one else to help," I said briefly. "Never fear, you will be paid. Only go. And bid the nurse be ready." For I dared not show before this stranger that we thought the child would be born dead.

When she heard she would be paid, she was pacified; she went out too, and I heard her say, "Aye, gentlemen, I have heard of you; you would take our practice from us; and ruin us poor women who have not your devil's means." The door shut upon the man's quiet reply.

I knelt down by Val and took both her hands. She slowly turned her head upon the pillow and stared at me with wild eyes, so sunken as to be almost lost in her ravaged, swollen face. I laid my cheek down upon hers, gently kissing her.

"Val—I have brought some men here. They will help you. It will soon be over. Are you willing?"

She could not speak; I do not know whether she really even heard me. I wrung my hands from hers and got up, leaving her faintly calling after me. I *had* to leave her . . .

Outside, I said to the men: "Go in. There is no one there. For God's sake, be quick as you can!" And then I suddenly caught one by the arm, making him start, so that I heard some-thing chink under his cloak—something hidden, something that rang like metal.

"Do not let her die without me," I whispered. "I will say nothing of your secrets. I swear it! Only do not let her die without me."

"My dear, if we can help it, she will not die. Be patient," the man said, not without gentleness.

They vanished into Val's room, two strange black figures that must have seemed to her like the phantasms of a tortured dream. We heard the door close and the key turn in the lock.

Mrs. Holl grumbling that she was not wanted, waddled off in search of a new bottle of Geneva. Mrs. Betty, looking scared, followed her downstairs. I bade her rouse her master, if she could. I thought it only right to try.

Neal stayed, holding me gripped within his arm as though he

thought some devilish power might snatch me away. And William, looking quite blanched with anxiety, remained also, leaning against the wall, praying half aloud.

I do not know how long we waited there. I do not think it can have been very long. But it seemed for ever.

The sounds inside died away; it was deathly silent. William knelt down and put his eye first at the keyhole, and then at the crack of the door, but rose shaking his head. "They have put a cloak over the door; I can see nothing," he muttered to Neal, who mutely nodded, tightening his grip on me.

Suddenly there came an awful shriek from Val—I would not have believed she had so much strength left to her. I started and clung to Neal, who swore softly and steadily under his breath. Poor William sank to his knees, this time in good earnest, and prayed as volubly as Neal cursed.

After that single, terrible scream there was silence again. I thought numbly, 'She is dead—they have killed her—I have killed Val." But it did not seem real; I was too exhausted to take in anything. Only, quite plainly, I saw her dead; the sight haunted me for a long time afterwards.

And then we heard another sound—the last sound, I do believe, that any of us expected to hear—a sound I had long since ceased to hope or pray for. It was the feeble, mewling cry of a baby.

"Good God!" Neal whispered. William, a great grin on his face, started up from his knees. "They've done it, sir!" he said. "They've saved the baby too."

"But Val?" I whispered, and ran to the door, softly calling to be let in. A man's voice answered briefly, telling me all was well. They made me wait another five minutes, and then unlocked the door.

There was no change in them. They were still cloaked and masked as before; only there was the smell of fresh blood on them; it is a smell not easy to wash away.

"You may go in," they said to me. "You had better get a nurse; the child is living."

I heard Neal eagerly questioning them; he led them away,

promising they should be paid anything they liked; and I ran in to Val.

She lay as if asleep or dead. A terror came on me as I first saw her. It was the ghastly face I had seen while I waited. But when I laid my hands upon her, she was warm, and she stirred and moaned.

And then that little mewling cry came again, and I saw they had dried the child, and wrapped it in a clean cloth, and laid it in its cradle.

The thing that caught my eyes first was such a mark as I never saw on any other newborn infant—deep purplish indentations at each temple, as though a cruel, powerful finger and thumb had been laid upon its head to drag it out. A little more, and the head itself would have been crushed. I touched my finger cautiously to the mark, and felt how deep it was, and broader than my thumb. There was something here, I felt sure, beyond what was natural, but I could not guess what.

The child's head was big, bigger than normal. No wonder it had forced so cruel a course. It was a big baby altogether, but seemed none too strong, uttering very feebly its mewling cry. At any rate they had not killed it; and, by the grace of God, it had not killed my sister.

The nurse for the baby came hurrying upstairs and fell to making a great to do over it. "La, la, what a fine child! Oh, what a fine big boy! La, my sweeting, you have cost your mother dear, but how she will rejoice at such a fine great son! Look here, miss, is not your nephew a splendid boy?"

Till this moment I had not even thought to enquire its sex. Looking at it, as she wiped its face, I gave a sudden, half-hysterical laugh.

"It is Dangerfield himself! My God! Poor Val!"

The woman looked at me scandalised and began rocking and soothing the baby. Stifling my laughter, which was nearer to tears, I turned back to Val and presently the nurse put down the baby and came to help me.

It was a great relief to me to get Val clean and beautiful again, to wash the stains off her pale body, and comb out her damp, tangled hair. I could not rest till it was done, and all the mess cleaned away out of the room, and herbs put to burning on the coals of the fire. It seemed to me I would never get the smell of blood out of my head, but the herbs helped. The nurse would not let me open a window, but I opened the door. God knows it was hot enough.

"Now, miss," the nurse said kindly, "you'd best get some sleep. Your eyes are fair burned into your head. I'll watch over your sister."

I thanked her, but there was one thing still to be done. I went staggering downstairs, and a sleepy servant told me that my brother was gone; he had taken the men away in a carriage.

The man civilly wished me joy of my sister's delivery, and asked whether it were a boy or girl.

"It's a boy," I said feebly, "and tomorrow you shall all drink my sister's health."

"Why, it's tomorrow now, miss," the man smiled, and pulled back a curtain to show me daylight.

"Oh Lord!" I said, astonished. "I'm so tired."

"Indeed, miss, you look it. Best let me help you upstairs."

"First I must tell your master," I said. "Is he still in here?" pointing toward the drawing-room door.

"Yes, miss," the man said, with a grin, "but I think you'd better wait——"

But I thought how glad Dangerfield would be to hear the news, if I could rouse him, and I would not be turned away.

When I opened the door, I blinked for a moment in the dimness, the curtains all drawn, and sniffed at the stink of spilled wine.

I had last seen Dangerfield asleep in a chair, and I looked there first, coming into the room a little way. Then I heard snores from the floor, near the hearth, and looked there. It was dusky, but not too dark for me to see.

This was why the man had grinned, and tried to stop me.

I had sent Mrs. Betty to rouse her master. She had roused him, evidently, but not as I had anticipated. They lay there together, both fallen into drunken slumber, half naked, in a relationship that not even innocence could have mistaken.

It was a pretty sight for the morning sun to shine on.

I stood looking at it for a moment in silence. And then I turned and went out, closing the door behind me. No doubt the servants had been already, to stare and titter, but I would not further expose him. God help her, he was my sister's husband.

"Your master is fast asleep," I said, looking at the man so levelly his titter died on his lips. "Best to leave him alone. Keep the house quiet, for my sister is sleeping, and very ill yet. No!" I said, as he approached, "I don't need your arm."

And I went upstairs alone, slowly, he following me with his eyes, and a kind of shuddering abhorrence on me of everything and everyone in that vile tainted house.

My sister was not yet twenty-three. She recovered quickly from her ordeal. In a week she was more beautiful than ever, and in a fortnight entirely well. She could not—or would not—nurse the child, and so her figure too was soon restored. A wet nurse was obtained, and the baby survived, though it was never a lively child. It cried a great deal, and was languid in its kickings, a heavy, fat child, so pale that it looked like a great white grub lying in the rose-lined cradle.

I thought now the baby was born that Val would be fond of it, but this was not so. If anything, her aversion was greater than it had been when she carried the child.

Next day, when they showed it to her, she exclaimed bitterly, "Good God, did I endure all that for *this*?" And when the nurse, much shocked, protested that it was a fine boy, Val said simply, with a grimace, "Aye, it looks just as I thought it would. It is Dangerfield all over again."

"Well, and I'm sure, ma'am, it could do worse than resemble its father!" the woman said tartly, and carried the baby back to its cradle.

Val made a face at her back. "Has he seen it?" she enquired. "I suppose he is pleased?"

"He is delighted," I said shortly, and told her to stop talking and rest. I did not wish to talk or even think of Dangerfield.

.   .   .   .   .

On the whole, I thought it a pity Val liked the child so little. It would have given her an interest, perhaps reconciled her to some extent to her husband. Odious as he was, he *was* her husband, and it would be better if they could live amicably together.

Unfortunately, however, the effect was just otherwise. Val, as usual, did not trouble to conceal her sentiments. The nurses were scandalised; they did nothing but talk of her unnaturalness. The servants, thinking to ingratiate themselves with their master, joined in crying it against her. She had few friends in the house and many enemies; she had never troubled to conciliate any of them; and they had had a far easier time when Dangerfield was unmarried.

It seemed always to be my fortune to have my emotions in sympathy with Val and my reason opposed. Loathing Dangerfield as I did, I could not help sympathising with her aversion for the creature who was so like him. But neither could I help wishing she would not express it so freely. It was unkind to the poor child, who could not help himself; it was impolitic—seeming so cruel and unnatural—and it put all the right on Dangerfield's side.

He was dotingly fond of the child, and his resentment of Val's scornful indifference was no more than natural.

"One would think the boy a monster!" he cried one day when she had refused to take it, saying that it was dirty and that it smelt nasty.

And when Val provokingly shrugged, as though she refrained from making the obvious reply, he flew into a terrible fury, cursing and swearing at her, saying that it was she who was the monster, a cruel, unnatural mother, a bitch——

"Though even a bitch will give her pups suck!" he shouted. "You're too afraid to ruin those pretty tits of yours! By God, ma'am, a whore would make a better mother than you."

"I daresay you have cause to know," Val murmured languidly.

Mr. Dangerfield's mother had been of questionable virtue, and had run off from her husband and child to vanish in the half-world of London. It was a cruel answer, and caught the man upon a spot so sore he could not conceal his wince. He grew strangely pale, glared at her in silence for a moment, then turned and went out without a word.

I expostulated with her when he was gone. She shrugged again, fretfully.

"I was not thinking of her," she said. "I was thinking of his own whores. You can tell him so, Jenny, if you think it will make him feel better."

I gazed at her speechlessly. Sometimes I could have sworn at her myself.

"Hardly, I should suppose," I said, when I had recovered my breath. "Anyhow, it's too late. Once a thing is said, you can't explain it. I wish to God you'd remember that sometimes, Val, and hold your tongue!"

All of Val's acquaintances visited her during her lying-in to congratulate her on a safe delivery. They seemed to me more vulgar than ever, but then I was out of sorts with the world.

The women gushed tediously over the baby. Despite its unwholesome looks and continual fretful crying, they declared he was the finest boy in the world.

"La, ma'am," Miss Kitty Andrews cried, seeing the wet nurse coming in one day to give the baby suck, "how can you bear to watch her? I vow if it were my boy my heart would break to see it!"

Val stared and shrugged; the nurse nodded approval. This, she seemed to say, was the way a mother ought to feel. It was evident she had often been gratified by jealous effusions in the past. Val's indifference belittled her importance.

Miss Andrews said, impatiently, "For God's sake, Kitty, don't talk so sloppy!" To me she whispered, "My sister can scarcely wait to get in that condition; did you ever hear of such a fool?"

It appeared that Mr. Gentry, long hovering between the two sisters, had at last fixed upon the younger. This sore affront to Miss Andrews had caused bitterness between the sisters. Miss Kitty wore a perpetual simpering smile of complacency which even I, completely indifferent to her triumphs, found maddening.

Secure in her own success, she showed herself kindly willing to make allowance for her sister's disappointment. Naturally this was almost more than Miss Andrews could bear. Too bad-tempered to pretend indifference, she had to content herself with spite.

Having recently been disappointed in love myself, I suppose I ought to have found more sympathy with Miss Andrews's state of mind. We might even have become friends, whispering our wrongs in each other's ears. But I was arrogant enough to think there was a world of difference between her loss and mine.

Indeed, I had no friends among them. I snubbed Miss Kitty's gushing confidences; I was indifferent to her sister's malice; they bored or offended me with every word they spoke. Mrs. Morrow was as vulgar as she was good-natured. And so with all of them.

I was wrong, I think now, to be so censorious. One or two among them were deserving of my better interest, and none, probably, of such whole-hearted condemnation. But even now, looking back on it, I cannot but see they were a set of very common, tedious, small-minded people. They were ill-educated, excessively ignorant and still more excessively prejudiced. As they never read and never met anyone of superiority to correct their opinions, they considered themselves complacently as very well able to pronounce on any subject and be listened to. Apeing the manners of Society, they also imitated its faults and dissipations, without grace, wit or humour to make them tolerable.

Val, if possible, despised them more than I, and showed it more. They endured her pride because her husband was rich and entertained freely, but behind her back they spoke angrily of her airs and gossiped about her. Some of them were not above bribing her servants to carry tales.

She and I would have been wiser to placate these people. Taken one by one, their stings were not serious. But attacking all at once, they had considerable power to do harm.

Once, perhaps, I might have seen that. Once I would not have been so sullen against the world. But I was wrapped up in my own sore misery and supported Val where once I would have tried to advise her differently. Between us, we alienated them all.

G

When the day came that they could openly speak ill of us, I learned that we had not one friend among them. I suppose one cannot blame them; I do not know that we had ever shown them any greater charity.

In great heat and petty irritations, August wore away. One day I woke to hear a wind in the eaves and, looking out, saw the skies for once swept clear of fog and smoke, as brightly blue as though they looked down on country fields. It was September, and suddenly autumn was in the air. Even here in the city you could feel it; it stung the cheek and sent the leaves whispering down across the roofs and along the gutters.

To me it brought back life. The sore spot in my heart was still sore, but I could bear that. It was the soreness of my mind that had driven me wild—the bitterness, the reproaches that I would never make to him, the eternal wondering what I might have done differently to have held him—and all the while knowing perfectly well that it had been doomed from the first. And from the first I had known it. When I tried to deny it, I lied to myself. That was what I hated. It was so weak, and false, and foolish.

The September winds blew all that away. I saw that I had loved too easily, and loved the wrong man, but I no longer despised myself for it. I did not even despise him any more. We are as we are made. He was for the beguilement of women. God, making him so beautiful, had given him that gift, and not any other. It was not his fault. It was as unreasonable to expect Robert to hold true to one woman as to think an artist should paint one picture only.

It may be partly that September brought me another relief. Somehow I had never *felt* that I was with child, nor shown any of the early symptoms, but God knows I was thankful to have it confirmed. Neither the river nor Mrs. Allison need confront me now.

"What a heavenly colour you have, Jenny!" Val said languidly one morning as I ran into her room, bringing her a handful of roasted nuts I had bought from a street-vendor. "You were so

186

peaked this summer I thought you might be going into a decline."

I laughed, throwing myself down in a chair. I had walked for an hour in the streets, with Mrs. Betty an unwilling companion. My blood was racing, my cheeks tingled, I felt as though my body had shaken itself free of some fever, and were renewed.

"Oh, it was so hot! How could I not decline? But now—Val, you ought to go out more, it is you who are pale now. Come, walk with me tomorrow!"

"I hate to walk!" Val declared pettishly. "I'll go with you for a drive if you like."

"It's not the same, but it's better than nothing. Let's drive down to Richmond with Neal, and picnic. Or perhaps he will take us on the river again."

"Isn't it too cold for the river?"

"Too cold! Val, it is only September! You should feel the sun —how warm!"

"Yes, and I felt your hands when you came in," my sister retorted. "But a picnic at Richmond sounds pleasant. Ask Neal when he comes today. Shall we make up a party?"

"Oh no. Who should we ask?"

"Lord knows. I wish September were over; I wish everybody had come back to town! I am so tired of these City people."

"You are missing Lord Dutton," I teased her.

Val affected to shudder. "I prefer Fred Hays. Even Mr. Gentry. Even—" she gave a wicked giggle "—Mr. Danger-field."

I was suddenly sobered. "Val, for God's sake guard your tongue! They listen to everything we say."

"Who?"

"The servants!" I said impatiently. "Don't you know that? They tell him everything."

"What of it? He knows how I feel. I have told him so myself often enough. I am not afraid of him."

I sat silent. She laughed at me.

"He is a worm, Jenny, a worm! A horrid, white, writhing worm! There is not enough red blood in him for resentment."

"Even a worm may turn," I reminded her. "Val, why provoke him? He is out of humour with you now."

"Not so much out of humour that he fails to honour me every night," she said, showing her pretty white teeth in a grimace. "Jenny, let me alone! If *you* had to lie with him—— I take what revenge I can. Believe me, he has his own weapons—he lets me feel the weight of them every night."

Remembering Mrs. Betty, I asked hesitantly, "Every night, Val? I should not have thought he cared enough for that."

"He likes to make me suffer. It is the only way he can. I would not care if he struck me. But to have to lie with him every night—God!"

I put out my hand abruptly to stop her; Mrs. Betty was tapping at the door.

She came in with a little flurry, casting a queer, knowing glance towards Val. "Oh madam!" she said, in a tone at once excited and malicious. "It's Mr. Underhill. He's come back to town already. Shall I bid him come up?"

"Harvey!" I said, and turned quickly to look at my sister.

For a moment I thought Val could not have heard. She lay upon her bed staring straight before her, without making any response. Then slowly a smile touched her lips, a strange, secretive smile, at once sweet and seductive. She rose from the sofa, her loose morning dress falling about her in long azure folds.

"No," she said, "I shall go down." She did not look at me, nor speak again to Betty. The maid had to move out of her way as she went to the door. Once I saw a serving-girl walk in her sleep. It was with just that blind, concentrated determination, as though set upon some goal that we could not see.

My heart sank within me. In all these long weeks since he went away, Val had scarcely said one word of Harvey. Now, seeing the effect of his return upon her, I knew why. So now it was upon us—the trouble and danger that I had long foreseen—and I felt a queer foreboding that there was nobody but myself to stand between my sister and disaster.

"So Harvey Underhill has come back," Neal said. We were

188

walking side by side on a long terrace above the river. It was a lovely day. The blue of the sky caught reflections in the dark shadows of the river, with swirls of silver like sequins on a dress. The sun was warm on our shoulders. It was one of those days when everything looks bright and new, just as at some parties everybody looks attractive.

"Yes."

"I wonder how our dear brother Dangerfield will enjoy the part of the Deceived Husband," Neal continued, in the idly amused tone of one who comments on a scandal in which he is not concerned.

But I looked up at him, and saw a constriction around his mouth, as though he tasted something bad.

"I wish he *were* deceived," I said doubtfully.

"You think he knows, sister?"

"Of course he knows!" I cried, my anxiety making me impatient. "He is not such a fool as you and Val think. And if he were," I added wearily, "he would still guess. Indeed, I would not be surprised if Val told him."

Neal gave a short bark of laughter. His fair boyish face was strained; he looked older, and consequently handsomer than ever. He was very like Robert, I thought, not for the first time. Neal was not so handsome, of course; nobody was. But very like, all the same—tall, fair, blue-eyed.

"Neither would I," he said. "Do you know, Jenny, our sister Val is really a very unfeminine creature? There is no deceit in her; she hates like a man, and loves like a man—straight and to the point."

"Yes," I answered, looking at the river. A boat went by, its pennant gaily fluttering. A crowd of young people were aboard, singing; some of them waved to us, and I waved in return. Neal did not notice them. Watching the boat out of sight, I went on slowly, "Perhaps, you know, men and women were meant to be more alike. Perhaps they were so, once. Men can afford to be straight and to the point. But we have no power any more, and so we must use guile—like slaves, who must please or be whipped."

Neal looked down at me in surprise. "Good heavens, Jenny!"

"It is true, you know," I told him. "Val hated Dangerfield like—like a snake—from the beginning. But my father made her marry him. Do you know how, Neal? He beat her until she couldn't bear it any longer. I suppose she could have drowned herself or taken poison. Otherwise she hadn't much choice."

Neal cursed under his breath, his face ugly. He hated my father so—I ought not to have told him. Some day he would have to go back and live in that house.

"Anyhow," I went on quickly, "it is done. And now—— Neal, what do you think Dangerfield will do?"

"What can a man do, when his wife cuckolds him? Look the other way and pretend he does not see. You have that much power over us, Jenny. You can make us look such damned fools!"

"Then you think he will do nothing?" I persisted.

"What *can* he do?" Neal repeated, shrugging.

I shook my head. I was remembering Dangerfield's white face of malice. It was of no use to tell me he was too despicable to fear. The wasp is a small thing, but there are people who will die of its sting.

We walked on a while, Neal scowling moodily before him. Suddenly he said, "There's one thing I'm determined on, at any rate. I shall take you away from there."

I stopped still in my surprise, looking up at him, my hand still tucked in his arm, so that he paused also.

"You, Neal!"

"Yes. I should have done it long before. I wanted to. You and Val dissuaded me. Sometimes I think you love her better than you do me."

I knew that jealous, sullen tone, and said quickly, "Nonsense, brother! You know yourself you did not really want me. You would have to get an old woman for me. It would be a trouble. You said so."

"I always want you, sweet Jenny," he said, gently. "It is true there are difficulties—— But I won't wait any longer. That house is no place for you."

"I don't think I ought to leave Val alone," I protested, in a low voice.

His arm jerked irritably under my hand. "Get it into your head, Jenny," he said, in a strained voice, "that Val is older than you are, that she is married, and that she knows very well what she is doing. It is absurd for you to think you can protect her."

It was absurd, but I felt it all the same.

"I think—I feel that she is in danger," I said, with difficulty.

He gave a hard, impatient laugh. "There is some danger her next brat won't look like Dangerfield," he said. "Other than that, what can happen? I'm here to see he doesn't try to shut her up, or any tricks of that kind. After all, she gave him a boy of his own, the first one. What more can any husband ask? There are plenty of gentlemen in town who would like to be sure of even that much, I can tell you!"

The sun was going down, the azure and silver of the Thames beginning to take on darker tints of purple and wine.

"Are there *no* constant husbands or wives in London, Neal?" I asked.

He laughed again, more cheerfully. "A few, I suppose. Good Lord, child, you don't suppose Dangerfield is faithful to Val, do you?" He smiled down at me indulgently.

I was silent. I had no wish for Neal to know how very unlike I was to the innocent young sister he supposed me. I wondered, with a shiver of dread, how he would feel towards me if he knew the truth. Would he think me soiled, spoilt, no longer his sweet Jenny? What would become of me if I lost Neal too?

God knows I was sick of Dangerfield's house—sick of the very sight and smell of it, the greenish face of its master, the whispering malice of the servants, the anxiety and distaste I had always felt there, the memories I had, the despair I had known——

But, Val! Could I go, and leave her there, with all her rashness, her folly, her honesty, so frighteningly vulnerable and so blindly bold? Who would bribe Mrs. Betty and coax Dangerfield and drum some sense into Harvey?

"I *can't* leave Val!" I repeated desperately.

I thought Neal would storm at me, would use that sarcastic

bitterness that made me so miserable, saying that I did not love him. Instead he looked at me thoughtfully and asked:

"Would you go if Val wished it?"

"Wished it!" I repeated blankly. "Why should she wish it?"

There was something almost of triumph in his glance.

"Dearest Jenny," he said, "can't you see that she thinks of no one but Harvey now? And you are trying to stop her——"

"No. I know I can't do that."

"Trying to check her, then, to make *her* use self-control. When all she wants is to be left alone. She is blind, deaf and dumb to everything but Harvey. She would jump off a cliff to get to him. She'll get over this, or he'll leave her. Then she will need you again. Now all she needs is Harvey. He is her only cure. Don't you see, Jenny, she doesn't want you there? You only worry her. She does not want to think about anybody else—even you."

It was not quite the truth; but it was so near true that I had no reply. It made me unhappy, but I could not blame Val. I knew more about love now. When it is at its height, the whole world is your enemy, and you have only one friend and desire no other.

The leaves were coming off the trees now. They blew across our path, rustling over the stones of the terrace. They blew into the river, whirling and dancing over its surface for a little while, then dipping, floating, sinking . . . carried away on the tide to sea, their bright day done, the dark water closing over them for ever.

I shivered and drew close to Neal.

"Are you cold, sweet sister?"

"A little. Let us go home."

"And you will ask Val what she really wishes?"

"Yes," I said. "I will ask her."

Neal was set on this thing as I never had seen him set on anything. I suppose he knew that he was safe in referring me to Val, for he at once began to make arrangements. He moved to larger, better lodgings in New Bond Street, near Burlington Gardens, where there was room for me and my companion. He even found the companion—an elderly lady, Mrs. Frye, a great-aunt of his through his mother, Lady Evelyn Clarke. She was widowed, had no children, and had long been reduced to the charity of a nephew. Judging by the alacrity with which she jumped at Neal's offer, the charity must have been more in name than in spirit. At the opportunity of earning her bread, she instantly packed her goods and came down from Norfolk in the coach of a young gentlewoman coming to London. Almost before I knew what was happening, Mrs. Frye was installed in New Bond Street and Neal was pestering me to come and give her something to do.

I felt as though I had been caught up in a twist of wind and carried off my feet. There seemed to be nothing left to my decision. I had only to pack up and go.

"It's not that I want you to leave me, dearest Jenny!" Val explained, caressing me. "What shall I do without you?"

That was precisely my anxiety. I said, as tactfully as I could, "I don't like to leave you alone, Val. I think you ought to have somebody with you beside the servants."

"Oh, but I shall see you every day! You shall come and sit with me every day. Or, better still, I shall come to you. Then I can get away from this house for a while."

And meet Harvey somewhere coming or going, I thought grimly. Just as I used to do with Mrs. Allison and Robert. Dear God! But that was better than flaunting Harvey in the house.

I could see it was true, what Neal said. She did not really want me there; I knew too much and watched her too closely. Even though I said nothing, I made her feel nervous and guilty, and she wanted only to be happy. I knew—I knew only too well.

"You will have such good opportunities at Neal's," Val went on brightly. "He knows everybody, you know; and Mrs. Frye is very well connected. I'm sure you'll marry very well indeed, and you know, Jenny, you are nearly eighteen; you ought to be thinking of marriage and you won't want to marry as I did."

I agreed, with a sigh. I did not want to force her to tell me she wished me away. It would be easier to give up lies if they did not make relationships so much smoother!

"But you must come or send every day, Val, or I shall come to you. I must know how you get on. And I wish you could get rid of Mrs. Betty. I don't trust her."

"Get rid of Betty!" Val cried, with horror. "Heavens, no, my dear, Dangerfield would be furious! Good God, what do I care if she sleeps with him, if it keeps him satisfied, and away from *me*?"

I could not but admit the sense of that. But still I disliked and distrusted the woman; I wished Val had a maid who was devoted to her rather than the master.

I had a maid of my own soon. I was used to doing for myself, and thought Mrs. Frye could assist me a little with the finishing touches, but Neal would not have it. I was his sister and must have a proper maid of my own. And Mrs. Frye was our kinswoman, she ought not to do a servant's work. I demurred, because I knew Neal could not afford it; he was so extravagant. He would not listen to me, however; he increased his household still further, by another maid and footman, and had the drawing-room new furnished.

"So you're leaving us, Miss Jenny," Mr. Dangerfield said to me the night before my departure.

"Yes, sir."

"We shall miss you," he said, his gosoeberry eyes glinting at me. "But you've grown a mighty handsome young lady, my dear, and I suppose your brother thinks he can do better for you than we can."

"My brother wishes a companion, sir, that is all. I hope you do not think my leaving casts disrepute on anybody."

"Oh," he said, in his ugly way, half fawning, half snarling, "I know what Mr. Archer thinks of me! But I hope, my dear Miss Jenny, that you won't be brought to agree with him, once you leave us."

He took my hand. It cost me a shudder, but I let him keep it, and even managed to say, "You have been very kind to me, sir. I am not ungrateful, indeed."

He pressed my hand, squinting up his eyes in that awful smile he meant to be so killing.

"I'm sure, my dear Miss Jenny, we've always been good friends."

I gulped. "Yes, sir. I hope we always shall. My sister is very dear to me, you know; I should not like to be unfriends with her husband."

There came into his protruding eyes that disconcerting glint of shrewdness that I saw there but seldom, but never could forget when I heard others call him a fool.

"My dear wife and I are of good accord," he said, with a simper. "I trust we shall always remain so. Of course, Miss Jenny, you will come to see us? Your brother must not have you altogether to himself."

"I shall come often, sir," I said, curtseying, and in doing so at last managing to free my hand.

"Good!" he said. "Good! Your sister has need of companionship too, you know. I daresay she is often lonely when I am away at my business. What do you think?"

I opened my eyes very wide at him. "Lonely, sir? Do you think so? She has so many friends! I am sure she is never a moment alone! The Misses Andrews are for ever here, and Mrs. Morrow——"

He smiled. "You are a very clever young lady, Miss Jenny," he said, and walked off, leaving me much disconcerted.

Before I left her, I begged Val to be discreet. She listened with that provoking, dreamy smile—I was sure she did not hear a word I said—and agreed to everything.

"And you think Dangerfield is a fool," I concluded, desperately, "but he is not! Believe me, Val, if you never believe me about anything else. He knows about you and Harvey. I think he will put up with it, if you are careful. But if you are foolish —and you and Harvey are so dreadfully rash!—and make people laugh at him as a cuckold, he will do something to hurt you, I know he will. I wish you could care about the baby a little," I ended sadly.

And she smiled and promised everything, and vowed she was sure she would love the child when it was a little older, and not such a mewling, puking, sickly creature.

I went to look at the boy before I went to bed. The nurse regarded me with unfriendly eyes. She was Val's enemy and mine.

"Pray, miss, don't wake him," she said, sharply. "I had trouble enough getting him off. Poor lamb, he cries something terrible. I'm sure, miss, you come to see him seldom enough; you might come when he is awake!"

I paid her no heed, but bent over the cradle. I was ashamed of myself, but he was so repulsive! His arms and legs were like scraggly little pieces from an uncooked fowl; he had lost all his early fat. He looked so *raw*, so underdone. Baby birds affect me the same way. They are indecent; they ought not to come into the world so half-finished. He had puked a little, there was a dried scurf of vomit down his chin and on his night-clothes. His bowels were continually disturbed; no matter how often he was cleaned a sick, disgusting smell came from him.

And yet he was my sister's son. Part of her was in him, and part of me too, in a queer distant way. There is always that tug-of-kinship, because you feel, however reluctantly, that something of yourself lives and dies with each tie of blood.

Perhaps he might be a handsome child. He looked horribly like Dangerfield now, but ugly babies do not always' remain so, and Val was so beautiful. I wondered if I could ever forget the aversion I felt for him now, and learn to love him.

I could not bring myself to kiss him; I pretended it might wake him. I just touched one dark-red little hand lightly, and went away, leaving the nurse muttering insolently to my back. Perhaps she loved him. It was very well, if it were so. He was a tiny, helpless thing; it was not his fault he was so horrid to look upon and had tortured his mother so cruelly. Somebody ought to love him. His father was only proud of having a son; and his mother would scarcely go near him.

I left Dangerfield's house on a dark day of rain. Most of the servants were civil enough to bid me good-bye, and Val came to the door in her morning gown to wave. She promised to come and see my new home that very afternoon. It was absurd for me to have that frightened, desolate feeling, as though I left her deserted in that dark, cold house. She had driven me away, but I ought not to have gone. I ought not to have left her. I never felt it more surely than at that moment.

So surely, that at the end of the street I knocked upon the glass of my sedan chair. But when the men stopped and asked my orders, I told them Nothing, to go on. What could I do? I could not control Val, nor placate Dangerfield. Neal's plans were all made; he would never forgive me. We cannot live one another's lives. It is all most of us can do to manage our own.

I sat very still, looking out at London in the rain. An autumn rain can be the darkest, dreariest thing in the universe. The remaining leaves hang dark and sodden, the gutters are full of horrid messes from the summer, the browning lawns and gardens turn the colour of mud. And cold! The cold crept through me to the bone on that short journey. I envied the chairmen, even in the wet, for a chance to stir their blood.

But there was a warm welcome for me at my new home. Neal was there, full of excited gaiety, and little Mrs. Frye, and my new maid, a pleasant-faced sturdy country girl, and all of my brother's servants, a cheerful, willing crew compared to Dangerfield's spoiled, sullen staff. Neal would even have the chairmen brought in to celebrate my arrival, and he and Mrs. Frye and I drank so much mulled wine we all grew very merry. The fire crackled on the hearth; everything was new and handsome. I would not look at the rain, coming down the glass of the windows like eternally pouring tears.

Our new lodgings occupied the whole first floor of a large house. The servants used the kitchen below, and slept in the attics above; otherwise we were a complete household to ourselves. The landlord came up to pay me his compliments and assure me whatever we needed he would be glad to provide. He looked plump and prosperous. He had a pretty wife, his third, much

197

younger than himself, and a baby small enough to be the child of his oldest son. All his older married children were frequently there; we sometimes dimly heard the sound of their cheerful dinners; and I always liked to hear it. In fact, in Neal's absence I very often ran downstairs and passed an hour with young Mrs. Brown and her stepchildren. Her own baby was about eight months old; fat, fair and beguiling. I felt guilty because I could love it so much more easily than my own sad little nephew.

I had my own chamber, with a small dressing-room separating it from Mrs. Frye's chamber. She often spoke of the joy of having a room of her own, however small; she had shared with two maids and the children at her nephew's house. Rose, my maid, slept in the dressing-room. She was too attractive and ignorant to be let sleep in the attics near the menservants. William, in particular, was young and handsome and had, I too much feared, learned bad habits from his master.

Little Tommy, the page, had recently suffered a bad attack of measles, and had been sent home to his parents in the country to recover. I was sorry, missing his bright face, and yet in a way I was just as glad, too, not to have constantly before me a reminder of that ghastly August night.

Neal's room was next to mine on the street side; we developed a code of knocking that amused us both like children. He would tap softly on the wall in the morning, and, upon my reply, would come lounging in to drink chocolate with me and tease Rose the maid, who turned the colour of her name at every word he addressed her.

We were very happy. Like most men, he enjoyed a feminine influence in his house. I daresay he had a mistress established elsewhere, but he could not have spent much time with her, he was so much with me. Whenever he was in the house, he was sure to be in my company. He would follow me even into the kitchen to watch me mix him a syllabub. He swore nobody else could make one to his taste, and indeed I had the knack of making them very sweet and strong. I learned this, and many other housewifely turns, from Minnie, good soul! I was not sorry to have a house of my own to show off in, and have the ordering of, and yet to have no tie of husband or children.

Mrs. Frye, ostensibly designated the housekeeper, never interfered with me. She had had plenty of *that* work, I daresay, earning her nephew's charity, and was glad enough to sit back and take her ease, with no duties more arduous than sitting with me in the drawing-room or driving out to take the air or shop. Neal gave me money to buy her several good plain silks, and she had some fine lace of her own.

"My nephew's wife seemed to think I ought to give it to her," she said, drawing herself up, "but that I would *not* do. When one is a lady, my dear, one must show some marks of it, or the servants, you know—— *You* shall have it, love, when I am gone."

She was an old lady of surprising spirit, considering the cruelly lowering circumstances of her life since her husband's death left her penniless.

"If I had had children, my love, I daresay one of them would have been kind to me. Though one cannot always tell. My nephew was not *un*kind, only thoughtless, and I was an expense to him. But the woman he married, my dear—for I *cannot* call her a lady—used to try my temper very sorely, very sorely indeed. I did not always give in to her, no indeed!" And the old lady would sit up straight as a rod, with a peppery flash of her bright old eyes.

I admired her spirit. It is hard to be old, and dependent. It is hard enough when one is young. Mrs. Frye showed the quality of her breeding—*she* was a lady, undeniably. I believe Neal thought she would be a harmless, timid old soul to lend me a decent countenance without troubling anyone. But she was far brisker and more amusing than that. I found her delightful to talk to; she had once known very good company and was full of merry tales. A clean-mouthed old lady, she had that matter-of-fact acceptance of all things of life, whether disagreeable, dirty or strange, that is so individual to old people. You could not have shocked her, but she could be disgusted.

I told her something of my sister's situation—nothing of

Harvey, of course—and she heard my stories of Dangerfield with a wrinkle of repugnance on her fine old nose.

"Odious man!" said she. "Your sister should never have been married to such a creature."

She was very small, wiry, and straight. In her girlhood she had sat six hours a day at the backboard. I do not believe she could have bent her spine in a slouch if she had tried. She had a little brownish face, quite wrinkled, with a puckered-up mouth to conceal her missing teeth. In spite of those, her smile had much charm still. She must have been delightfully pretty once; she had that indefinable manner that none but belles, I think, ever do have, compounded partly of assurance and partly of charm.

Calling her his kinswoman, Neal was charming to her. She did love a handsome, gallant young man! He liked to tease and compliment her, to hear her pretty tinkling old laughter, with a rap on his arm from her fan. He saw to it that the servants were mannerly towards her, and when they saw that both he and I were fond of her, they grew even deferential.

"My dear," she once said to me, "you and your brother have true good breeding. You treat an old woman who has nothing as prettily as though she were rich and fashionable."

I kissed her. "Who would not, madam?"

"Many would not. I wish I *were* rich for your sake, my love."

"I wish you were too," I teased her. "Then you could give me a dowry and some fine gentleman would marry me."

"Ah!" she cried, shaking her head at me. "You need not be concerned for that, child. You will make a fine match yet."

With me for his hostess, Neal began to entertain often. I think the house was a pleasant one to visit. Everything was of the best, if I do say it, and the company that came there was always good. Talk never grew bawdy, and yet the atmosphere was free and merry. We danced a good deal, played cards rather less, very often amused ourselves with old games, and even ventured to try our hand at plays, using the drawing-room doors to make a stage of one half of the room. Neal and I were both accounted good at play-acting, and Mrs. Frye took all the old lady parts with such spirit and verve that I suspect she had never lost a certain girlish hankering for the stage. We went to the theatre often and she laughed and cried at everything.

There was only one rule Mrs. Frye laid down for my benefit, and I knew it was a wise one: never to have two parties in a row without ladies. An occasional bachelor dinner for some of Neal's intimates, with cards afterwards, and Mrs. Frye and myself discreetly withdrawing at an early hour, was allowable. But the next time we must have women.

This did not present any difficulties. Val came as often as she could. (Neal refused to invite Dangerfield, so whenever they had company at home she had to remain.) Miss Bertram had always treated me with good nature, and was delighted to have the opportunity to make eyes at Neal. Through her, I met other young ladies of fashion. And when Mrs. Sylvester came to town, I had all the company I wanted.

My obligation to her was very great, and I tried to repay it as best I could. She seemed to enjoy our entertainments, and came often, always with a pretty young friend or niece or companion of some kind.

As for the men, there was no lack of them. Neal knew all the young bucks in town. Handsome, good-natured, independently situated, and hospitable, he had always been a favourite. They were a little shy of his new establishment at first, thinking their fun would be spoiled, I suppose. But when they found his wine as good, his dinners even better, and plenty of freedom to drink and play afterwards, they went so far as to beg invitations. And when they discovered there were plenty of pretty girls at the more sedate evenings, they flocked to them also. Good food and pretty women will always draw the men like flies.

I myself enjoyed a good deal of success, and learned how to handle men in all stages of intoxication and love. With the consciousness that Mrs. Frye and Neal were there to support me, I learned to flirt without going too far, to cool a rake with a glance or a word, turn off a compliment with a smile, and repel a quiz with wit. My own wits had never been without quickness, nor my tongue without readiness. But I remembered an older lesson still, and whenever I felt myself growing too sharp in my wit, or too quick with my tongue, I would check myself and be gentle and appealing. I had not forgotten how I tamed Lord Gould by such manners. They were not as natural to me as laughter and teasing, but what is the use of being born with some wit if one cannot learn the manner most pleasing to others?

Among the New Bond Street visitors were inevitably some that I had known from Val's drawing-room. Lord Dutton was one. I could not imagine why he came, unless it was because he knew he was not wanted. He took the devil's own delight in the discomfiture of others, and upon my word I had almost as soon see the devil himself seated in my drawing-room as Lord Dutton, with his death's-head arrogance.

Neal received him coolly at first. Without knowing my particular reason for hating and fearing Dutton, he was aware that his lordship was not a desirable companion for any decent female. He had not specially objected to Dutton's pursuit of Val, but he watched jealously whenever his lordship spoke to me.

Lord Dutton was a clever man. I had never before seen him try to be agreeable, but he took a good deal of trouble to placate Neal. He was amazingly successful. It was not long before Neal was swearing that Dutton was not so black as he was painted.

I could have told him differently. But my tongue was effectually tied. I knew how quarrelsome Neal was where any affront to me was concerned. Even after all these months he might feel it necessary to call Dutton out. The very thought of it filled me with terror. My brother, like most gentlemen, was a fair shot and swordsman. But Dutton was a killer. They said he practised for hours every day with sword and pistol. It was also said that though he had so far escaped punishment for his duels—fleeing overseas for a few months and then returning when the scandal blew over—one more death at his hands would make England too hot to hold him. That would be small comfort for me when Neal was dead. Men *are* such fools about their honour!

I knew better than to think any little drawback such as sure death or exile would prevent a gentleman from taking up a challenge, or making one.

So I had no choice but to accept Dutton with the best grace I could. One word from me to Neal would effectually banish his lordship, but I dared not say that word. It was a very galling situation.

Nor did Dutton make it any better by letting me know he was aware exactly how matters stood. I cannot say exactly how he conveyed this—he was clever, as I have said, and I do not think I am slow to take a hint. He had a manner of looking from me to Neal, and smiling, that filled me with rage and apprehension.

His manner to me was altogether very subtle. He spoke to me seldom, always in a tone of high-flown compliment. He never seemed to notice me much, so that Neal's guard was quite down. If there were other women present, he was invariably more attentive to any of them than to me. But he watched me, without seeming to do so, watched me incessantly, so that after an evening in his company my nerves were jangling and my mouth dry. There is a peculiar persecution in being covertly regarded. It makes one feel hunted. I could not be natural when he was of the company. I would talk too much or not enough, be affectedly gay, or sit in the sullens.

I hated him for it, and he knew it; and that, I suppose, was reason enough for him to come so often and take so much seeming pleasure in our company.

Mrs. Frye was shrewd enough to observe my dislike of Dutton, and shared it so thoroughly that she actually spoke to Neal about his lordship coming so often. My brother, however, could be very stubborn in his sweet-tempered way. Dutton had done him favours, and was not so bad a fellow as scandal painted him. He could not see any cause for offence in his lordship's attentions. He was sorry his sweet sister did not like Dutton, but females had these whimsies, and he supposed I would get over it.

As a matter of fact, I would have been much cleverer if I had pretended to like Dutton better than I did. Neal would have been much readier to cut his visits short. He did not care how many gentlemen admired me, but he was apt not to like the men I favoured. I was not long in finding this out. I had always known Neal was jealous, but did not realise how much until the day I casually said I thought Mr. Cory the wittiest man in London.

"And as agreeable as he is witty, which is *not* common," Mrs. Frye added.

I agreed enthusiastically. Neal was silent. Soon after, he remarked that of all the odious bores on earth, the self-professed wit was the worst. Next time Mr. Cory came Neal did not so much as smile all evening, though his friend was as entertaining as ever. He cold-shouldered him so conspicuously that Cory was at first surprised, then distressed, and at last angry.

I believe they had some high words at the end of the evening. After that, Mr. Cory came but seldom, and I was deprived of his amusing companionship. Worse still, my drawing-room was deprived of his wit, which had kept the company in a roar, and our parties suffered for it.

I was mightily vexed with Neal. The falling-out had followed so obviously upon my praise that I could not miss the connection. I was foolish enough to tax him with it, and he was so bitterly angry that I was almost frightened. I ended at last by bursting into tears, which always stopped his anger.

He took me in his arms and called me his sweet sister. I cried on his shoulder, and we were reconciled. But Cory did not return, and I learned my lesson.

After that, I kept my opinions to myself, at least when they were too favourable. Once I remarked to Mrs. Frye that I wondered how my brother expected me to marry, when he would not allow me to like anybody.

Her glance at me was almost startled, and she hesitated over her reply. "Oh," she said at last, "brothers are often jealous, and sisters too, but I daresay Mr. Archer will not gainsay you if you have a serious liking, or an opportunity to marry to advantage."

There was something in her manner which led me to drop the subject. She was uncomfortable, and made me so. Fond as I was of her——and a kinswoman too——I did not wish to seem to complain of Neal to her.

Another former acquaintance of mine who turned up unexpectedly was Lord Gould, the Mohock. Since the day he had so signally honoured me by sending to enquire after my health, I had not seen him. He was not a man often met with in respectable houses, and under the ægis of Mrs. Sylvester I had been nowhere else.

He came to New Bond Street, however, and sponsored by the very last person I expected to see there——Mrs. Allison.

When her name was brought in, I was first tempted to deny myself. On second thought, I decided to receive her, just to show her how perfectly happy, respectable and prosperous I was.

She had not changed a bit. She swam in, as over-dressed, over-jewelled and half-tipsy as ever, and with the same air of cool assurance. She greeted me as though we had parted yesterday the best of friends. It was impossible to affront her. Before long I found myself, unwillingly, falling into her game again.

"Upon my word, Miss Archer, I must congratulate you. You are handsomer than ever," said she, looking my figure up and down with a knowing smile. Then meeting me full in the face, she said, "I am glad to see you have come off so well, my dear. I knew you would be sensible once that little pain was over and forgotten."

It seemed to me that I could taste the metallic flavour of that day's pain in my mouth still. I could have struck her for the allusion.

But I had grown wiser. I had learned the smooth double-meaning tongue of the fashionable drawing-room. I smiled, and said:

"Oh, everything like that is forgotten."

She smiled and nodded in return, taking it, I knew, to mean that her odious part in it was forgotten also. How could she, I wondered, remembering how she had shown me, at last, just how much she hated me? Under all the paint and the smiles the hatred was still there; neither of us could forget it.

But clever people are often deceived, particularly if they think you less clever than themselves. It was evident that she was determined to resume an appearance of friendship with me, and she seized eagerly upon the amnesty I offered.

"To be sure, child; you are a sensible girl. As you know, I always thought so."

She looked at me sharply as she spoke, as though to discover how "sensible" I might have become.

I offered her another glass of wine and, fanning myself, said obligingly, "I hope I shall not again forfeit your good opinion, madam."

It was almost too unbelievable. I saw how closely she watched me. But I looked as innocent as I knew how, and I suppose she wished to believe me.

"Excellent, my dear! Then perhaps you will listen to me more patiently than you did to the proposal I made you before."

"What proposal?" I asked curtly. It made me sick to feel how my heart turned at the very thought she might bring me word from Robert. I had thought myself cured, and now the mere sight of her had infected me again.

Before she could answer, I realised that of course she could not be speaking of Robert. I hoped to God I had not in any way betrayed myself. When she spoke of a "little pain" I remembered how much she had enjoyed it. I would die rather than let her know that any of it remained.

If the thought of Robert had not made me so stupid, I might have guessed who she meant, but, as it was, she had to speak out plainly.

"I told you before, my dear, that Lord Gould was much struck with you. I fancy you are just such a girl as might catch him."

I could not help myself; I laughed aloud. "Good Lord, ma'am! Are you still driving that pig to market?"

She was not affronted. "That's a humorous rustical way of putting it, child," she smiled, "but I can tell you that if a pig could make his mate my lady there would be plenty of girls eager to share his straw."

I shrugged. "I don't doubt it. But the fact is, madam, I am not so anxious as all that to be married. I am not even so eager to be my lady."

206

"You had better marry when you get the chance. How old are you? Nearly eighteen? The years go fast, my dear. As for being my lady, *that* satisfaction remains when complexion and lovers are gone."

"Very well, madam," I said. "I will not dispute with you. No doubt you know the world better than I. As for Lord Gould's disposition to be catched, I know nothing of it. If he has to be brought to his courting, he cannot be very eager."

"On the contrary, I am his ambassadress."

"Are you indeed?" I said dryly. "And pray, madam, what do you gain by all this?"

She looked a little pained by my bluntness, but, to do her justice, she never refused plain-speaking.

"Lord Gould's gratitude, my dear, and yours. He is exceedingly rich and my poor husband, alas! has left me very ill provided-for."

I opened my eyes. "Good Lord!" I said bluntly. "You wear a fortune on your fingers."

She surveyed her jewelled hands with complacency. "I cannot have enough of such baubles. They are my weakness, child; you have found me out. I understand the Gould family jewels are very handsome."

I followed her glance, raising my eyebrows in an unspoken question. She smiled, turning round a great heavy-set ruby on her middle finger. I do not like rubies, but the thing was magnificent and must have been worth a fortune.

"When Miss Carter became the bride of the *very* rich Mr. Washington, she was good enough to let me choose a little keepsake from her jewel box. My own jeweller assures me I made an excellent selection. And this rose-cut diamond—do you like diamonds? I thought so, all red-haired women do—that was a charming gift made me by Lord Gerould after I introduced the heiress Miss Alexander to him."

"She must have had a handsome fortune," I said, laughing despite myself at the woman's cool effrontery.

"Only twenty thousand pounds, but it saved Gerould from the Jews. He was a handsome, killing devil!" she said, with a reminiscent sigh. "He has settled down in the country now and

Lord! how dull he must be. But it was better than being sold up."

"Well," I said, thinking myself safe in making the promise, "on the day I become Lady Gould you shall have the run of my jewel box. But I hope you will choose rubies, for I don't like them."

"I will leave you the diamonds, my dear. They are magnificent and will become you brilliantly. The Goulds have always been generous to their womenfolk."

So she had the last word after all. It may be in the nature of some women to spurn the thought of diamonds, but it was not in mine. I could not despise Mrs. Allison too much for her weakness. Whenever I looked at those rings of hers I could not help thinking how well some of them would look on my fingers. There is no denying that the vision of a lapful of diamonds made the memory of Lord Gould more palatable.

"All he wants, my dear, is an assurance that he will be welcome and that little romp of his will not be held against him!"

I shrugged. "He is quite welcome to come, if he pleases. I do not answer for anything else."

"That is quite sufficient," she assured me, and departed in evident satisfaction with her mission.

Employing Mrs. Allison as his go-between did not increase my inclination towards Lord Gould, but I kept my word and received him courteously, if not warmly, when he called in her company a few days later.

He was just as I remembered him, a heavy-set, red-faced young man, with a small choleric blue eye, except that he was sober. Our previous acquaintance had run such a curious course that it was impossible for us to meet again with ease. Mrs. Allison took charge capably, however; she played go-between as expertly as she had once played bawd. My lord took several glasses of wine and began to appear more comfortable. He would not look me directly in the face, but I caught him stealing little side-glances at me.

Conscious of appearing at my best, I sustained his glances with ease. Our positions were changed. It was I who took command now. I was cool and composed at first, saying little, making considerable play with my fan, and seeming unconscious of his glances. As my lord began to warm up with wine, I grew cooler still in tone, but allowed a certain provocation to enter my glance whenever it met his.

As he was taking leave, I curtsied deeply and said, with a smile, softly:

"My lord, you have been a long time coming to enquire after my health. But I shall forgive you, if you do not wait so long again for a second visit."

"By God, ma'am, you'll have no complaint on that score, I promise you," he said, with a sudden high flush that made me remember him as he was before. It evidently betokened an amorous state of mind, for I saw how his glance lingered in the low cut of my bodice. It did not make me love him more to remember how rudely his hand had once thrust there, but I was not the less inclined to captivate him if I could. It would be an agreeable revenge!

I saw that Mrs. Allison too regarded me with approval; even with admiration. I had suffered such sore humiliations at both their hands I could not help rejoicing. Revenge is not a pretty ambition, but I cannot but think it a very natural one!

Gould was as good as his word. He became a constant visitor. I used every trick I knew to torment him, and had the satisfaction presently to see that he was getting in a frame of mind where he did not know what to do. He blustered and grew angry, went away swearing he would never come back, and came back to find me as tormenting as ever. I would be sweet and soft with him one moment, cold and haughty the next; I surrounded myself with admirers when he came and teased him from behind the barrier; next time I would refuse myself to everybody else and let him sit close to me and even sometimes hold my hand, while Mrs. Frye, stitching sedately near-by, kept him from going any further. And then again I would laugh at him, and flout him, and refuse to give him even my hand in farewell.

If I had really cared to keep him, I would never have gone so far. I would never use such tactics on a man I cared for. To tell the truth, I rather despised them. They were theatrical and silly. I went through my paces as consciously as a professional coquette. But since I had as lief he went as stayed, I practised every trick I knew on him, and was rather astonished to see what success I had. He was thick-headed, and slow in his thinking, so that I fairly danced circles around him. A big clumsy bear, he shook his head angrily at my torments, but came steadily after me, with something almost formidable in his lumbering persistence. As long as I kept out of his reach, I was safe, but it amazed me to see how doggedly he followed.

No matter what Mrs. Allison might say, to flatter my vanity, I did not believe he had any intention of making me an honourable offer. He was vain of his name and knew himself to be a good catch. I was a penniless nobody, with nothing but my brother's name to back me, and he only a half-brother. For I soon discovered that Lord Gould knew my background—my mother a mere farmer's daughter, without pretence to breeding or fashion.

With a queer pang, I asked him, "Did Mr. Parker tell you that?"

He looked surprised, in his heavy way. "George? No. Why should he? He does not think to marry you, surely?"

"Good God, no," I said, as airily as I could. "Mr. Parker looks for a lady of fortune, you know."

"I thought he must," my lord said. He shook his head mournfully. "Poor old George is damned near sold-up. He is a younger son, and Papa won't pay any more bills."

"Actresses are expensive, I daresay," I said, venomously.

"Miss Kitty, you mean?" my lord grinned. "Pretty little piece. But I heard somebody else was keeping her now. Poor George likely can't afford her." He looked at me with a glint of appreciation. "Can't afford you either, m'dear."

"I wouldn't have Mr. Parker!" I cried, angrily.

"Why not? The best of good fellows! Everybody likes him, especially the ladies."

"Well, I don't. He is a friend of Dutton's, for one thing."

"Well, I don't like Dutton either, but George is different. And

I tell you what, he isn't the sort of fellow to go around carrying tales. I don't know how he should know about your Mama——"

"I told him myself."

"How damned peculiar," Lord Gould commented, regarding me curiously. "But, as it happens, I found out for myself. Like to know, you know."

"Why should your lordship be interested?" I asked, coolly.

But his lordship thrust one tongue into his cheek in a very vulgar manner, with that tiresome grin, and did not reply. He had a certain heavy cunning, having been much pursued. It was not easy to corner him.

Dishonourable proposals he made me in plenty—couched so artfully that I could laugh them off, and yet could not claim to be insulted. But a plain, "Madam, will you be my wife?" was never forthcoming. I did not believe that it would ever be. And though I knew what my answer must be, finding him as distasteful as I did, yet it angered me to be disdained, especially for my poor mother's sake.

The first of November was Neal's birthday. We had a large party in his honour. Among the ladies were Val, Mrs. Sylvester, Miss Bertram, and a pretty friend of hers, a Miss Collins. The gentlemen included little Mr. Franklin, who had an obvious and rather touching adoration for Val, an attractive Guards officer named Woodford who was wooing Miss Bertram in friendly rivalry to Neal, and Lord Gould. I was not particularly anxious to include him among the special friends who were coming to dinner, but he hinted so broadly for the invitation that I had not aplomb enough to refuse.

"Do you know, my dear, I think his lordship is a good deal catched by you?" Mrs. Frye remarked, after he had departed. She never said such things merely to please and flatter. Indeed, I thought there was considerable warning in her tone.

I laughed. "Oh, he is courting an heiress! I am merely a distraction."

"I believe him to be *distracted*, indeed!" she replied meaningly. "You torment him very prettily, my dear. I do not mean to criticise in the least, but suppose his feelings should become serious?"

"What, a lord to love *me*! Plain Miss Archer, without money, titled relations, or anything! A sister married to a man in commerce! A mother with low connections! Good God, Mrs. Frye, you forget yourself! Aren't you afraid of a thunderbolt, for suggesting such a thing?"

She smiled, but said, "Do not protest too much, my dear. Matches of great inequality are made every day."

"Are they? I think one reads of them only in romances. In life, lords marry the daughters of lords, and rich men marry ladies with large dowries. As for me, I shall be well satisfied to marry a plain gentleman, if there is any that will have me."

"Do not speak so loweringly of yourself, my love! You are very beguiling. I sometimes wonder if you know *how* beguiling. You are not so handsome as Mrs. Dangerfield—you see I speak frankly—but you have a *something*, a charm of manner, a provocative air, I do not know quite how to call it, that is better than beauty. You are more admired, I believe, than she, by those who are much in your company. I cannot find anything strange in the thought that *any* man, be he lord or gentleman, should wish to secure your affections."

"That is because you love me," I said, embracing her. "Believe me, the men are not so easily beguiled as you think. I daresay there are plenty of them that would hop into bed with me, but not so many, I fear, to offer to go into church with me."

"I wish I knew what makes you so bitter, my dear!" little Mrs. Frye sighed. "Has someone made you unhappy?"

"I? I do not love any man in the world except my brother. As for marriage, I have seen enough of it to have no illusions. My stepmothers were all, I think, unhappy. Val is married to the most odious man in London. If there were any other future for a woman, I would never think of it again. As it is, I suppose I must marry somebody. But my ambitions do not fly as high as Lord Gould, I assure you!"

"Perhaps I ought not to have spoken of it," she said, doubtfully. "I would not wish to put the idea into your head, for I must agree that it is unlikely. But Lord Gould is rich, and his own master. He has no family to object, should he wish to please himself. I only wanted you to think, my love, what your answer would be, should the offer be made."

"*Think* of it, ma'am? Good heavens, as if there could be any thought! To marry a baron—rich, not very old, not dead drunk above once a night, nor having more than one poplolly, I daresay, at a time. What an opportunity! What else *could* I do, but say Yes and swoon at the honour?"

"My dear, I am serious. He is no worse than many men, and it is a great opportunity."

"So am I serious. I detest Lord Gould and would not marry him if he were King of England."

"You would not have the chance then, my dear," she said, quite matter-of-factly. But when I laughed, and hugged her again, she added wistfully, "It's not that I *wish* it for you, my love! I don't care so very much for Lord Gould myself. But it means *so* much to have a position and security in this world."

And I, remembering the years of her servitude in her nephew's house, was too much touched to laugh any more, but promised seriously and soberly to think on the matter, and meanwhile to modify my teasing ways somewhat, for fear of discouraging Lord Gould utterly.

"I would not have any young woman *encourage* a man she did not mean to accept. That would be most unladylike and unkind. But there is no need to run to opposite extremes.

This, the most worldly advice I ever received from Mrs. Frye, I promised to follow, but without considering the matter very seriously. Lord Gould was a man whose vanity did not allow him to take his rank lightly, though he behaved in a manner so little calculated to make it respected. I thought him a man as little likely to marry for love—as much for consequence—as anybody I knew.

Val arrived early for dinner, looking dazzlingly beautiful and happy. Harvey had rooms not far from us and I knew she visited him whenever she came to me. Dangerfield had called her cold, but I do not think Harvey found her so. (My father was right, I suppose, when he used to say we were both wantons.)

I repeat that it never occurred to us to include Dangerfield in any of our parties. We would have affronted half our guests if we had done so. I sometimes wondered that he would let her go so often without him. I suppose he was vain of the company she met. No doubt he had his own enjoyments at home among the maids.

Val made a little face when I asked after him, in duty bound. "Thank God, he is going to Liverpool on business, and will be gone a month. Think of it, Jenny, a whole month without him! I am mad with joy, only thinking of it."

I congratulated her, but begged her to be careful. "He will leave spies, you may be sure."

She shrugged superbly. "Let them spy! I do not care what they tell him. Of course he knows about Harvey. But what can he do? He tells me to my face that Mrs. Betty is better company than I. It would serve him rightly if I deceived him with one of the footmen! And the boy is his, at any rate; he cannot deny that."

"Not with that face!" I agreed, heartlessly. "But, Val, take care all the same! He is more jealous than you think!"

"Ah, if it were only for that, I would lie with every man in London to spite him! But it is only Harvey that I——" She paused, and a wonderful colour came into her face. I envied her. Sinful or not, I envied her."

"Is Dutton still after you?" I asked, curiously.

She hesitated. "I hardly know. Yes, that sounds strange, but it is the truth. He comes, and talks, and looks, but makes no more offers. He knows about Harvey, I daresay, and thinks he will have his turn later. But that will be never, Jenny, never! Oh God, if only I had not married Dangerfield. Harvey and I might have been so happy!"

I could not deny it. Six months only she need have waited for his wife to die. It is not pretty, to wait thus for an unfortunate woman's death, but it was no more than natural, and in a few years, who would remember? And now it was all awry.

"Harvey loved me first. His is the first right," Val continued, in a low voice. "Dangerfield *bought* me. He knew how I hated him. He liked it. It stimulates him—God!" She rubbed at her mouth in a sudden violent motion, as though wiping away the taste of sickness. It was a queer, startling gesture, almost ugly. It frightened me. It seemed to me that her hatred of Dangerfield was passing beyond what was reasonable—or, at any rate, what could reasonably be endured. How could she go on like this?

"It's of no use to talk of *right*, Val," I said, at last. "You are married to Dangerfield, not Harvey."

"If I could get a divorce——" Val suggested, in a low voice.

I turned the matter over in my mind. "I don't know. It is very difficult."

"If I ran away from him, *he* could get a divorce," my sister said slowly.

"Yes, and a pretty business that would be! He will never let you go, Val, don't think of it."

"I think of nothing else," she said, defiantly. "But I am all in doubt. You do not know, Jenny, what I endure! You don't know——" she dropped her voice almost to a whisper—"what I feel for Harvey." And that same wonderful light came across her face.

He is not worth it, I thought wearily. But the words had no meaning, I knew. I understood better than she thought I did. I knew, only too well, that deserving has nothing to do with loving. They may come together, or they may not. But all the same, Harvey was not worth it.

We were very merry at dinner. We drank so many toasts that we all became a little flown, and I allowed Lord Gould to hold my hand under the table, and fumble for my foot with his. His face always became highly flushed with wine. When he leaned over me, his breath was hot and heavy in my face, and his eyes roamed in a fashion that made me remember how he had once mishandled me. I believe he had long since forgotten that episode —except perhaps to regret that Harvey had appeared before he had his will of me—but I never could help remembering it when he pressed me so ardently, and it gave me a secret disgust of him I could not conquer. I could imagine him in bed, and the very thought brought a hot colour into my face.

Lord Gould chose to misinterpret this blush, and hung over me more passionately than ever. I saw one or two meaning glances cast our way, and Neal, from being very merry, suddenly became silent and sullen, glaring at his lordship.

It was a relief to catch Mrs. Frye's glance and rise from the table with the other ladies, leaving the gentlemen to the soothing influence of port and Madeira.

They soon followed us to the drawing-room, however, and when the rest of the company arrived to spend the evening, we set to at dancing, while Mrs. Frye led the older ladies to cards in the dining-room, which had been quickly cleared for this purpose.

My partner was Lord Gould, and God knows I soon wearied of him. In the dance I had him all to myself, with no escape unless we sat down together, which would be a change but no relief.

He was for ever pressing me away from the dance, trying to get me to go upon the stairs with him, or into one of the bed-rooms. I longed to box his ears, but dared make no scene, nor even frown, with Neal's eyes always on me. Instead, I pretended to think him tired, and condoled with him upon his delicate con-stitution.

"Aw, now, Miss Jenny!" he said, plaintively. "How can you be so cruel? You know I could dance all night with *you* as a partner."

"No, indeed, I know no such thing. You have your eye upon Miss Collins. Shall we exchange?" To escape him gracefully, I would have thrown a better friend than Miss Collins to the wolves!

But he would not hear of it, and grew more amorous still, standing so close over me that he seemed to bear me down—a habit I detest in a man.

"Lord!" he whispered. "To think I had you once, and let you

216

go! I must have been mad to let that country squire bubble me so. I should have took my will of you, you little devil, and made you like it! You don't know what you're missing, Miss Archer. On my word you don't. I wish you'd let me teach you."

I sighed. The old song! How many men had sung it to me! You don't know what you're missing, my pretty innocent dear! Step into this dark bedroom, and let me show you. And afterwards? Why, you may cry and welcome. Nothing like a good shower to put out the last of a fire. And if you beg very hard, perhaps I may condescend to give you another lesson some day. My God! I wonder what man was clever enough to think of it first. *You don't know what you're missing!* We are all children, hungry for the forbidden sweets, jealous of those who have stolen into the pantry and eaten their fill. Curiosity, I daresay, has ruined more women than passion.

"Lord Gould," I said firmly, "I like and esteem you as a friend—" (I wonder my tongue did not wither at the lie!) "—but I am not one of your poplollies to be bought and set up in a house in Holborn."

Lord Gould turned very red and burst out laughing. "By God! Who has been telling tales?"

"Everybody," I said. "Such a person as your lordship cannot hope to escape scandal. And the ladies, you may be sure, would have me know the worst of you."

This brought him into a high good humour. "Aye, they are jealous, are they? And well they may be! By God, Miss Archer, you would wonder to hear how some of them go on. Yes, by God, one fine young lady not a thousand miles from here thought she had me last year. Caught me a bit high flown, don't you know, and pretended I had proposed. No, no, my dear, I told her. I'm too fly a bird to be caught so easy. Get my name on a bit of paper and I'll cry quits, but not till then. And now they see me taking a toss over a little red-headed minx without a penny to bless herself with, when I might have a girl this minute—this very minute, Miss Archer!—with forty thousand pounds."

"I felicitate your lordship. Forty thousand pounds is certainly a handsome sum."

"Aye, but I don't care for it. She has white gums. What say you, Miss Jennifer, shall we give 'em a real surprise, you and I? I'm in earnest, mind!"

Good God, thought I, is this a proposal? I stared up at his red grinning face, too taken aback to answer.

"Well, my dear?" he said, in what he evidently considered a highly insinuating manner. "Say the word and we'll give 'em all a surprise."

Announce it, here and now? Not even Lord Gould could draw back from that. One word, and it was all mine—wealth, security, position, My Lady for life, the high world of fashion, everything I had been taught to value, everything that had never been mine. It was all here before me in this fat, grinning, red-faced lord. True, I would have to endure him as a husband, lie with him in the same bed, do his will, and be his sweet Jenny. But that would pass in a year or two; then he would go back to the house in Holborn and I would be free.

It was not that the price was too high. It was not that. I do not know what it was. Or, if I know now, I did not know it then.

I drew my hand free and said, breathlessly, affecting to take it as a joke, "Nay, my lord, I will not take advantage of you when you are high flown. I will wait till you are sober enough to sign your name!"

He looked down at me with the queerest look—partly of relief, with something of affront, of frustration, even anger, and with something else too, something that for a moment was almost like real admiration.

"By God," he said, "I would not have believed it. Nobody would believe it. You're something new to me, my dear!"

The dance permitting, I swept him a deep curtsey. "Is honesty so out of fashion, my lord?"

He gave a grunt, shaking his head, putting out his hand to lift me up with a more courtly touch than he had ever shown me before.

"Clean unrecognisable, child," he said. "But, by God, Nick Gould will cut cards with anybody. Bring me your bit of paper, my dear, when you've a mind to be my lady, and I'll sign it."

There was good blood in the man. I had never seen it before, but I saw it then, and it was not altogether mockingly that I answered, "You do me too much honour, sir."

It was strange that *his* answer should be, "You have good blood in you, child. Dairymaid or no dairymaid, by God!"

Though so many old friends came to our lodgings in New Bond Street, George Parker never did. We sometimes encountered him elsewhere, however, at the theatre or somebody's house. He would speak when he could not help it, always with the courtesy of a distant acquaintance. All the old teasing friendliness was gone. I felt that he despised me, and I would gladly have despised him in return, but somehow could not.

Neal, who had always liked him, grew affronted at his continued coolness. "Why the devil does he never come here? I've asked him often enough. Have you quarrelled with him, Jenny? I used to think he was rather catched by you."

I fanned myself furiously. "By me, brother? Oh no. I think he used to admire Val."

Neal looked surprised, as well he might. "Val? I never noticed it. Then, if he has heard about Harvey, that explains—— But why should he hold aloof from *us* when she is not of our party?"

"Ask him," I said, hoping Mr. Parker would be cleverer in his excuses than I.

Neal laughed, a little annoyed. "That would be a question indeed! A man only asks a question like that, sister, when he wants to fight. *You* may ask him, if you like."

"Not for worlds," I said primly. But inwardly I was taking a very different resolution.

I had to wait some time for my opportunity. So long, indeed, that mere chance could not account for it. Mr. Parker must be deliberately avoiding us. The idea made me angry, and disappointed. I could understand that he might not wish to seek me out, but it was not like him, I felt, to bear so determined a grudge.

219

At last one night at the theatre I had my chance. We went into one of the boxes to pay our compliments to Mrs. Sylvester and found that she shared it for the evening with Mrs. Hamilton, Parker's aunt. Mrs. Sylvester greeted me as cordially as ever; Mrs. Hamilton only bowed. She was an aristocratic-looking old lady, with a fine aquiline nose, and dark, bright eyes that reminded me of her nephew. I felt that she looked on me distantly, as a person not suitable for approval, and my face flamed at the thought he might have confided in her.

This anger gave me courage when, a moment later, she said stiffly, "You are acquainted with my nephew, I believe?" and I turned round to see Mr. Parker enter the box.

He was as taken aback as I, and showed it more. The pleasant smile stiffened on his lips and he bowed formally.

"I have had that pleasure, madam," he said, as formally.

I curtsied in silence. Mrs. Sylvester, clever woman that she was, glanced quickly from one to the other of us, and said, in her pleasant, easy way:

"I believe Miss Archer was just going to return to her seat in the pit. I can't think where your brother can be, Miss Archer—perhaps Mr. Parker could escort you instead?"

I curtsied again. It was evident that her dear old friend, Mrs. Hamilton, was not grateful to her for the suggestion, but I could have kissed her. I felt that if I did not soon get the chance to exchange a few plain words with George Parker, I would burst.

"I shall return in a moment, ma'am," Mr. Parker said to his aunt. He politely opened the door and followed me out, closing it behind us. "The stairs are steep—will you take my arm, madam?" he said to me, with that same cool, maddening aloofness.

I glanced around me quickly. The play had just resumed. There was no one but ourselves in the narrow whitewashed corridor. Footmen were lounging on the stairs, playing dice; I could just see the tops of their powdered heads. They could not see us, and were too far away to hear anything. I would never get a better opportunity.

I said breathlessly, "I should like to speak to you." I did not

220

dare look at him; I don't know how he looked. But as I stood still, he perforce had to do likewise.

There was a perceptible pause, during which I wetted my lips and braced up my courage, before he answered:

"I am at your service, Miss Archer. But I do not know what we can have to say to one another."

"Why not?" I said, still with that same breathlessness.

"I was under the impression that we had said it all at our last meeting."

I felt the colour flame into my face. "Are you still angry with me for that? I did not think you would be so—so unforgiving."

"To what do you allude, madam?"

"Oh—don't be so *odious*!" I cried furiously. "Why should you treat me like this? Just because I believed ill of you once! I couldn't help it; I trusted the person who told me—then. And I —I said I was sorry!"

There was another pause before he answered, and then it was in a very different tone—almost like the old days.

"Jenny," he said, "it is not that. I have forgiven you for that, long ago."

Startled, I looked up at him. I had forgotten how brown his face was—browner than ever from the summer's sun. His eyes looked black, and their expression was strange to me. He had changed. His mouth was drawn up on one side in that quizzical way he had, but the old teasing glance was gone.

"Then what is it?" I asked, in a low voice. "Even my brother wonders why you never come near us."

"Don't you remember what I said? It was said in a somewhat theatrical manner, I'm afraid, but I wasn't feeling quite myself. And, after all, it was the truth."

"That—that it must be hate or love between us?" I murmured. "Oh, but that is foolish! Why must it? Cannot we be friends?"

He gave a queer little laugh. "Dearest Jenny, what a child you are still! All your toys bore you except the one you cannot have. Is that it? You have so many admirers, so many friends, why must you have me too?"

I turned away and looked blindly at the whitewashed walls.

The candles in their sconces were guttering in a draught, making our shadows strange and grotesque. Someone would come round to clip them soon. Below us, on the stairs, the footmen laughed and swore. I could dimly hear a raised voice from the stage, and a round of applause. Neal would wonder what had become of me. Perhaps he would think I had remained with Mrs. Sylvester. It was very cold and draughty here, and I shivered in my low-cut dress. I must not catch a cold. There were so many social events planned for the next few days and Val would be disappointed if I were ill on her birthday.

All these thoughts went vaguely through my mind while I stood staring at the black shadows on the white wall. I was seeing for the first time the shadow of the truth, and it was in a voice I hardly recognised that I answered him, at last.

"Because I liked you, and I used to think you liked me, too."

"Good God!" Mr. Parker exclaimed. He took me by the shoulders, forcing me round to face him. "*Liked* you! Jenny, you know it was more than that. You must have known how near I was to—to loving you."

I do not know what he saw in my face. Perhaps what I had seen in the shadows on the wall, for he let me go so abruptly I almost lost my balance.

"But that's all over," he said shortly. The black brows were drawn straight together, and his jaw set so that it spoiled the line of his mouth. "You liked another man better, and that settled it. I hear he's courting Miss Elin, by the way. I suppose he threw you over for the heiress. Is that why you have remembered how much you used to like me?" He checked himself and said more quietly and more coldly, "I'm sorry, Jenny. I ought not to have said that. But I won't take second place to Robert Haywood."

The contempt in his voice made me feel sick. I always get sick when I get very angry. I took a step away from him, feeling the grip of his hands still on my arms. The words came in a rush, without any thought.

"Why do you despise him so? You think he isn't a man because he is handsomer than other men. He's more of a man than you are. When he loves a girl he tells her so. He doesn't wait for her to throw herself at his feet! You want to be loved like a king! Why shouldn't you come second? How many loves have *you* had? Miss Kitty—and how many before her?"

I heard my voice getting shrill and managed to stop myself, biting my lip. Mr. Parker was curiously pale under his tan, looking at me fixedly.

"What are you trying to tell me, Jenny? You have a stab or two left to pay me back with. Go on, get it over."

"All right," I said steadily. I put my head back, meeting his eyes straight. "I have been Robert Haywood's mistress and would be again, if he asked me. You have always despised me, I know. You thought me a little better than Miss Kitty, that is all. And you see I am no better, just as bad. A wanton, as my father says. *You* might have had me for the asking. But you would not even do that. *He* asked and so I—I went to him. And now you can despise me as much as you like. Are you satisfied?"

He stood very still and straight, the black eyes on my face, looking blacker and blacker as his face paled. And every stab I dealt him turned straight back on myself, wounding me to the heart. Not till this moment had I known how much I valued what I now had lost for ever.

I finished with such a break in my voice I dared not go on. My head swung round. I leaned back against the wall, turning away from him. As long as I lived, I thought, I would remember how he looked then.

It was a long time before he spoke, low and hoarsely, like a man in pain.

"You would have been my mistress—— But, Jenny, I wanted you for my wife."

"Oh God!" I whispered. "Oh God—why do you tell me that *now*? When it is too late?"

It seemed to me my heart would break. "Oh God, I shall never forgive you, never! I wish I were dead. Don't touch me— don't speak to me. I'll never speak to you again as long as I live!"

I turned and ran from him as though my life depended on it. The startled footmen on the stairs jumped up as I came running past them, but I paid them no heed, not caring whether they saw the tears on my face. I only wanted to run and run and never stop until I had escaped them all.

It was raining softly. The pavement before the theatre glistened with wet, and the torches of the waiting linkmen made soft yellow splashes on the black street.

There were chairs and coaches in abundance, some waiting for their owners, some for hire. Several men pushed their way towards me, eagerly crying me for a fare.

"A chair, miss, a chair—— The finest coach, miss, not a leak, and a rug on the floor!—— A chair is quicker, miss, right inside your door and not a drop of rain on you."

The shock of rain and fresh air in my face steadied me a little; I stood hesitating what to do. I ought not to go home alone, it was not safe. And yet I didn't feel as though I *could* face Neal. He would be sure to see that something was the matter.

As I hesitated, one of the men from the theatre came out and spoke to me. I recognised him vaguely; he sold tickets for the pit, and of course knew me well by sight.

"Come inside, miss, pray, you're getting all wet!" he said urgently, and for the first time I realised that I had not even got my cloak on, the rain slanting down on my bare head and shoulders.

"I—I'm not well," I said desperately. "I want to go home. Can you get me a chair?"

"You can't go alone, miss!" he exclaimed, shocked. "Please to step inside and let me send for your brother."

But that was just what I did not want him to do. I could have wept again with frustration and despair.

"Oh, please, I *must* go home—don't you know any of these men? It's only a little way."

He looked doubtful. "You oughtn't to go alone, miss. But there's a woman here who sees to the ladies' shawls and cloaks. She's a very respectable sort of woman, miss, and I daresay she'd be willing to go with you—it's a quiet time with her just now."

224

God knows how little I wanted her, but a stranger was better than anyone I knew. I said wearily:

"Very well. I will pay her, of course, and you too for your pains."

"I'm sure you're very welcome, miss," the man answered civilly. "Won't you step in where it's warm while I fetch Mrs. Branch?"

I would not go back into the theatre, but stepped back under the portico where I was a little shielded from the rain, and stood there shivering till Mrs. Branch appeared. She was a nice plump body, well spoken and vastly respectable in appearance, like a superior lady's-maid.

"Good God, miss!" she exclaimed, "you're quite frozen. Run, you zany, and get one of the cloaks from my stall for the young lady. It's a wonder one of you wouldn't have thought of it before! —but then, miss," she added comfortably to me, "there's no use expecting sense from a man, now is there?"

I smiled faintly, but said the man had been very thoughtful for me.

"Lord, miss, he'd never have thought of it by himself! The gentleman sent him after you."

"The—gentleman?"

Mrs. Branch gave me a quick shrewd glance. "Yes, miss, the young dark gentleman in Mrs. Hamilton's box. He said you were taken ill and might come to hurt by yourself."

She would have been more than human not to wonder why the gentleman did not look after me himself; but she was at any rate well-bred enough not to comment on it, and I was grateful to her.

The warmth of the cloak, too, was grateful. I gave the man money, though Mrs. Branch assured me in a whisper he had already been well fed by the gentleman, and told him to send word to my brother that I had gone home with a friend.

Then, at last, I was free to get into a coach, with Mrs. Branch's warm bulk by my side, and hide myself in the darkness.

I would have been infinitely obliged to Mrs. Branch if she had accompanied me in silence, but at least she did the next best thing,

225

and talked incessantly without pausing for any response. Luckily, for I scarcely even heard her. As the coach rattled over the stones, her voice flowed on, equally without pause and, as far as I was concerned, without meaning. I was too dazed with misery to care. She could not talk loud enough or long enough to drown the memory of George Parker's low voice . . .

"Oh God!" I whispered. "Oh God!" I turned my face against the cold pane of the window, staring with blind eyes at the dark glass, on which, now and then, there fell a faint gleam of passing light. The coach was slow and, like most hired vehicles, wretchedly shabby, dirty and uncomfortable. Perhaps once I got home, and with Mrs. Frye, this ghastly sickness of despair would get better. But it was so slow, and I was so cold, and the woman wouldn't stop talking . . .

She was tugging me by the sleeve now. "Wake up, miss!"

The coach had stopped, and for an instant I thought we had reached home, but Mrs. Branch was still babbling, climbing over me, almost, in her eagerness to see out of my window. "Put the glass down, miss! There's been an accident. Lord, you don't think it could be a thieves' trick? Put your head out, miss, and see, but take care!" She lowered her own window with a crash and shrieked warning and advice to our coachman.

"What *are* you talking about?" I said, in irritated bewilderment. "What accident? Why are we stopping?"

"There's a coach stopped just ahead—look, miss, it's all on one side, and a horse down! Lord, miss, is there anybody killed, do you think?"

Startled, I let down my window and looked out. It was as she said: a coach lying tipped on its side, some yards before us, one horse down and still, its team-mate violently struggling, with a man trying to hold its head. By the light of the unbroken lamp I saw another man lying in the street, as still as the horse.

"Somebody's hurt," I said. I could hear our own coachman hoarsely bawling out enquiries and advice, without getting off the box. "Help me to open the door."

"Be careful, miss!" Mrs. Branch warned. "It may be a trick—don't get out!"

"Don't be a fool," I said. I managed to wrench the door open by myself, and jumped down into the street. The water came pouring over the tops of my shoes; the street was half flooded and the wrecked coach lay on its side in a river of water. It was raining furiously now, coming down in torrents.

As I waded past, our coachman called down to me that there was a dead man and a dead lady in the coach and if somebody'd come and hold these something horses, he'd help. I called to Mrs. Branch, and heard her shrieks of dismay as she came floundering out of the coach into the wet, but ran on without waiting for anyone.

It was the coachman who lay in the street; he was perfectly limp and I could not tell whether he lived or not, but he was half drowning in the gutter, and I managed to lift his head and thrust my rolled-up cloak under it, pulling a flap to protect his face. I could not see any wound, and did not know what else to do for him.

Meanwhile, the footman struggled with the desperate horse, in danger of having his brains dashed out, while the fallen horse lay quietly, poor thing, its big dark eyes staring glassily with the light in them.

I could hear my driver bawling advice from his box, and suddenly remembered an accident with a farm horse in my childhood. "Cut the traces!" I called to the footman, not daring to get too near. "Cut the harness!" But he could not manage this without help, and it was not until our driver finally struggled off his box and came at a clumsy trot, knife in hand, that they were able to subdue the terrified beast and cut it loose from its mate. Once loose, it became quiet, and stood trembling violently, head hanging. I judged him safe to leave, and ran to help the men get the lady out of the coach. I could hear shrieks and battering on the glass. "So she's not dead," I thought, idiotically.

One door was jammed against the street, but the men managed to force open the other, and dragged a woman out unceremoniously, head foremost, dumping her in the street, where she sat and sobbed hysterically. It was the maid, and the footman, turning a white face on me, called out that his mistress was still inside and he feared she was dead.

"We'll have to get help, miss, we can't right the coach, us two alone," my driver said, pantingly. He had been heaving at it from the other side.

"Wait!" I said. "Lift me in first. I'll help the lady if I can."

The door stood high and at an awkward angle, but they lifted me up till I could get a footing and scramble within. The footman was sobbing and my coachman cursed him and the hysterical maid impartially. Down the street Mrs. Branch, clinging valiantly to the horses, was alternately crying for help and calling advice which nobody could hear. "Run for help, you fool!" my driver said. "Your mate's dead, if I'm any judge, but maybe we can help the lady. Is she alive, miss?" he called me.

With caution, clinging to the seat. I scrambled down the steep cant of the carriage, afraid I might slip down and injure her further She was lying curled in the further corner, where the fall of the carriage had thrown her, and at first I thought she was dead. but I managed to brace myself in such a way that I could lift her shoulders and head into my lap, shuddering at the sticky feel of blood in her hair.

She was not dead. As I laid my cheek down on her breast, I could feel the heart beat. But she was barely breathing and in this awkward position I could not tell how much she was hurt, or whether the cut on the head were all. She neither moved nor groaned, and I had nothing to use as a restorative.

It seemed hours before assistance came to right the coach. Actually, I believe it was done very quickly. A wheel was broken, but they managed to prop it in such a position as to hold the carriage level while they lifted out the injured girl and helped me down.

"Shall we carry her into one of these houses, miss?"

"Put her into my coach," I said, after a second's hesitation. "We are nearly home. Yes, the maid too, of course, and the men——"

"Coachman's dead, miss," my driver said, in a subdued voice. "Went on his head and broke his neck, poor devil!"

I looked at the man lying still, with my cloak drawn over his face, and shivered. "But we can't leave him there!"

"They'll mind for him, miss, don't you worry. The horse is gone too—shoulder out. But you come along, miss, and mind the poor young lady."

I wonder poor Mrs. Frye did not faint dead away at the first sight of me as I burst into the quiet drawing-room, crying frantically, "Oh, come, come quick! there's been a dreadful accident and the coachman is dead and I'm so afraid she's dying!"

Mrs. Frye gave a cry of dismay, dropping her work all in a tangle on the floor, staring at me with horrified eyes. "Jenny, love! My dear! Are you hurt? What has happened?"

"Oh no, no, I'm not hurt," I cried, impatiently tugging at her hand. "*Please* come! I think she's dying and I don't know what to do."

"But you, Jenny——"

"Oh, never mind me—only come and help her——" I dragged her after me almost by main force, impatiently wondering why anyone should be concerned for me, while *she* lay white as death and almost as still on the bed in my room. (Afterwards, however, when I saw myself in the glass, I understood Mrs. Frye's concern.)

Mrs. Frye continued to exclaim and question me as I pulled her up the stairs, but the moment she saw the injured girl she became very quiet and entirely mistress of the situation.

"Send that silly creature away," she commanded, and the girl's maid was turned out of the room, still shrieking dismally and sobbing that her mistress was dead—was dead! "Get me a basin of warm water—not hot, *warm*. Jenny, love, some clean cloths— an old petticoat will do. Has anybody sent for the surgeon?"

The landlord had gone for the surgeon, and Mrs. Brown had the footman in the kitchen, attending to his bruises and soothing him: he was no more than a boy, terribly shaken by the accident and the coachman's death. My maid bundled off the hysterical abigail and I remained to help Mrs. Frye.

Very delicately, she parted the girl's thick hair, all matted with half-dried blood, and examined the injury.

"I am sure the brain is not injured," she said, thoughtfully, pressing with infinite care around the cut. "It is superficial only."

"Then why does she look so dreadful?" I whispered, staring with awe at the face which was whiter, I swear, than the sheets themselves.

"Loss of blood, my dear," she said. "But her heart is quite strong. Ah, here is Mrs. Brown with the water—good! Now, Jenny, hold the light and don't faint."

"I won't," I said indignantly, and I didn't, though I must admit that at the sight of that long gash in the scalp, my stomach heaved and I had to shut my eyes to keep steady.

"Hold it up, Jenny!" Mrs. Frye said sharply, and I stiffened obediently. "That's better. Mrs. Brown, take that basin away and bring another. I shall have to cut some of this hair—fetch some scissors while you are about it, please."

She snipped and daubed very cautiously, but gradually the stiff, caked mass yielded and she was able to treat the cut itself, using an ointment of her own preparation, and afterwards to bandage it. The cut was high on the side of the head, over the left ear; there would be no scar to show, the girl's face having luckily escaped injury from the glass.

"There!" Mrs. Frye said, straightening at last. I cautiously lowered my aching arm, setting the candlestick on the table. "That should do very nicely. Thank you, Mrs. Brown, you're a very sensible woman. Jenny, love, you were very brave and steady. But, poor child, how tired you look!"

"Will she get better?" I asked anxiously.

"Yes, I'm sure she will. Ah, here is the surgeon; he will be able to tell us with more certainty."

The surgeon was a gruff old fellow; he looked from under bushy brows and said roughly, "Too many women in here. I'll keep you——" pointing a stubby forefinger unerringly at Mrs. Frye. Before Mrs. Brown and I could get out of the room, he was bent over the bed, one hand on the girl's slight wrist.

Outside, Mrs. Brown and I looked at each other, she with growing concern.

"Oh, Miss Archer, you *are* in a sad state. Pray do put on a dry gown——"

"They're all in my room and I daren't go back—do you?" I said, laughing weakly, and aware quite suddenly just how wet and cold and miserably uncomfortable I was.

Mrs. Brown clucked her tongue. "The poor young lady! It's a mercy she wasn't killed outright. A terrible accident—terrible! The footman said a wheel came off and coachman was driving too fast—they were late for an engagement."

"Who is she, do you know?"

"She's Lord Burton's niece, my dear; the great heiress, you know—Miss Elin."

"Miss Elin?" I echoed blankly. "Kathleen Elin?"

"Yes, Miss Archer. Footman says she's the finest young lady that ever stepped, and Lord Burton will be wild when he hears the news. Why, Miss Archer, what's the matter?"

"Nothing," I said, leaning back against the wall and trying to check the wild laughter that threatened to become hysterical. "Nothing! Only—that it should be Miss Elin—and I——"

"I'm sure it was providential, miss, that you should come when you did! There, there, now, you're all to pieces and no wonder! Go into the drawing-room where it's warm and I'll fetch you a hot posset and then I suppose somebody had better take word to his lordship—maybe Brown can do that best," and off she bustled, leaving me clinging to the banisters, half laughing, half crying.

That was how Neal found me, flying home from the theatre in a panic after Mrs. Branch's return had filled the place with wild rumours. I fell into his arms, sobbing out the story of the accident, while he soothed me. He thought it a perfectly natural reaction, I suppose; he could not know how bitter my tears were, or how little for any shock or fright. The dammed-up misery that Mrs. Branch's presence had checked, and the accident had temporarily distracted, burst all controls, and I cried in his arms till I was sick and exhausted. I am not much given to tears; they never soothe or rest me; but this time I could not help myself.

They put me to bed in Mrs. Frye's room, for she intended to sit

231

up with Miss Elin. When I saw myself at last in a glass, I understood why everybody exclaimed at the sight of me—muddy, bloody, hair falling in a wet tangle, my dress sopping and all torn away at the hem, showing my legs dirty and scratched from scrambling into the carriage, my shoes a soaked and shapeless ruin, and in a white face eyes so enormous with tears and fatigue they looked as though put in with a charred stick.

I said faintly, "Oh, my God!" and, my spirit quite broken, let them undress and put me to bed like a child.

It seemed quite natural to everybody that I should not be myself afterwards. I received a great deal of undeserved credit for the delicacy of my nerves and the sensibility of my feelings. I know it is not the fashion for a female to admit it, but in fact my nerves are not in the least delicate, and if the accident had been all, I would have fully recovered from it with a night's sleep. As for my feelings, nobody could know them but myself, and I was grateful for the excuse to conceal them. I moped about the house for two days, petted and sympathised with by everybody and thoroughly sick of myself. Then my guest's recovery forced me to an appearance at least of my usual spirits.

They would not let me see Miss Elin the first day. She had recovered consciousness in the night, though somewhat confused and in great pain from headache. Mrs. Frye gave her a soothing draught which sent her into a sound sleep. Next day she was much recovered, but very shaken and not fit to see any visitors, though her uncle, Lord Burton, tiptoed in for a moment to kiss her forehead.

"A providential escape. Providential!" his lordship said afterwards in the drawing-room. "How shall we ever be thankful enough for it? And unscarred too! That lovely face—what a tragedy it would have been! Her hair—you are certain, madam, that her hair will grow in again?"

Mrs. Frye reassured him. Afterwards she said crisply that his lordship seemed more concerned with the state of his niece's hair than her head and, as long as she kept her looks, did not trouble himself what damage the brain might have received.

Luckily, the cut was shallow and Miss Elin did not suffer any permanent injury. By the second day she was well enough for me to be allowed to see her.

I would be hard put to it to describe my sentiments towards her. *Miss Elin, the heiress, has thirty thousand pounds. . . . he goes to Bath to make all secure . . .* This was the fortune that had bought my lover from me, and I hated her for it once. Something of the old bitterness still lingered, though I no longer loved Robert Haywood. And I felt guilty towards her as well, for I had robbed her too, and she would never know it.

It was with this mixture of emotions that I went in to meet her and congratulate her on a good recovery, and I'm afraid I did it awkwardly enough. Certainly I felt awkward.

She met my glance for a moment gravely, without replying, regarding me with the wide serious gaze of a child. Even now she was very pale, hair, brows and lashes looking almost black against that white skin, and I learned later that this was her natural complexion. Her eyes were unusually round and she was apt to hold them wide open, giving their expression something very young and innocent. She had a childlike trick, too, of holding her lips a little parted, showing fine white teeth perhaps a trifle small for her face. Her cheeks and short chin had a prettily rounded look, and indeed there was something soft and round and full-bodied about her altogether—a ripeness as yet far off from being over-blown.

So much I observed quite coldly, vexed at her gravity, drawing back under that serious, intense gaze. And then she smiled.

I never saw such another smile on any adult's face It was as open and candid as a flower, offering itself as a little child's smile will do—timidly friendly, anxious to be liked, deprecating judgment, utterly open. There was no doubt in it, no question, no reservation. No consciousness even that such feelings might exist. It would be a hard heart indeed that was not touched and astonished by such a smile.

When Mrs. Frye came in, she found us chattering nineteen to the dozen, and I saw she was surprised when I stooped to kiss Kathleen as I left her, for I am not readily demonstrative towards strangers. But she was gratified, too, by our quick friendship.

"That is a real lady, my dear. A great lady, though so young. I am glad you shall have such a friend."

But I was silent. I was thinking that if Kathleen Elin loved Robert Haywood and intended to be his wife, then I was the last friend she ought to have. There should be no intimacy between the girl who had been his mistress and the girl who might be his wife. I know there are such friendships in Society. Many a man's mistress is his wife's best friend. Men meet cordially every day with their wives' lovers, some in ignorance, some in wilful blindness, which we call sophistication. Why not? If there is genuine indifference, a little blindness, or at least near-sightedness, smooths things wonderfully. But I was not indifferent. I liked Kathleen Elin better than any girl I had ever met, and to base a friendship with her upon so gross a deceit would be impossible to me. All the more because I felt sure that if she knew the truth she would not hate me, nor even be angry, but only grieve for me. It must have been plain to a child that Kathleen Elin had never harboured a mean or unkind sentiment.

Miss Elin remained with us a week. Lord Burton came every day to enquire after her health, as did dozens of other gentlemen and ladies. The knocker sounded all day, and the servants ran up and down with messages and complimentary trifles. We had never had such excitement, nor heard so many illustrious names. The servants were all agog, and little Mrs. Frye in her element.

By the end of the week I think Miss Elin's uncle was very glad to get her away. He did not find the style of our establishment suitable to her station, and it was evident to me he was on pins and needles about Neal. A handsome young man, a pretty girl, thrown together in the most romantic way, and in company with each other all day and most of the evening—Lord Burton feared the worst and could hardly wait to get his niece away. Neal was as sorry as I to see her go, as indeed was everybody in the house, but I could detect no signs in him (or in her, for that matter) to throw Lord Burton into such a fright. He was an ambitious man, however, in a small way and looked for a better marriage for his wealthy and pretty niece.

Once he had her safely out of our clutches, he became gracious again, especially to me.

"My uncle is quite catched by you, Miss Archer!" Kathleen teased me. "He talks of you for ever."

"I am much obliged to his lordship," I said demurely, but secretly considered Lord Burton's good opinion as little worth having as that of any man I knew. There was no positive harm in him, but he was a creature of small virtues and large vanities, judging entirely by appearances, no doubt because he thought so much of his own.

My lord was still a handsome man, and had retained his figure and a good leg, but he had certainly reached a time of life when women at least are supposed to give over thinking of their own charms. Lord Burton was still very conscious of his. This was a harmless conceit in itself, but through jealousy led him to many small meannesses. I am sure part of his attitude towards Neal was simply the envy of an old beau for a handsome young man.

I do not know how much Miss Elin was aware of her uncle's character. She always thought good of everybody, if she possibly could, and was by no means critical in her perceptions, but neither was she in any way foolish. That wide childish gaze saw a good deal. Outwardly, she obeyed him in everything, but there was a certain steadfastness about her which inclined me to think she could hold her own in any matter she thought important. He quite underrated her, as vain men usually do, and never noticed the indulgent smile with which she pandered to his vanities and yielded to his advice.

I had determined, as much through guilt as pride, that all overtures to further friendship must come from the heiress, and not from me. She was rich, well-born, immensely sought after. All these things did not deter me from thinking myself good enough to be her friend, but they kept me from pursuing the acquaintance as naturally as I might otherwise have done. And though I never heard her speak of Robert Haywood, yet I could not keep from wondering at the relationship between them. If once I knew for certain that she regarded him with affection, then all this intimacy must come to an end. Meanwhile, I yielded to what was really very pleasant.

For Kathleen was determined in her affection. She came to visit me, and coaxed me to come to a party of hers. Lord Burton seemed pleased to have me of the company, and the company was certainly of the best. I could not help enjoying it, and Neal and Mrs. Frye were each, in their different ways, highly pleased.

I confess to a little dread that I might meet Robert there. I didn't; instead, that afternoon, I found myself vis-à-vis with George Parker at dinner. I did not know he was acquainted there, and the sight of him took me so utterly by surprise I could not keep my countenance. Luckily, there was a large party, so that I had only to bow to him, and need not speak. He saluted me coldly, and talked with animation all through dinner to Kathleen Elin and the lady on his other side, while I sat grimly resolved to get the better of my feelings if it killed me.

Lord Burton, like many gentlemen, had a habit of taking too much wine at dinner—and after. On this occasion, he was quite flushed before the dessert was brought in, and became so pointed in his attentions to me that I did not know whether to be more embarrassed or gratified, with George Parker's dark scornful glance resting on us both more and more often.

"Come, come, Miss Archer!" Lord Burton said, demanding an answer to a question I had parried earlier. "You must answer— I insist—the company insists. You must confess whether you more prefer a man to be dark or fair." As he spoke, he rested his eyes with no little complacency on his own blond image in a small hand-glass he kept always near him.

I daresay he expected a good deal more coquetry from me before I made the admission that was obviously required. Instead, pointedly *not* looking at Mr. Parker, I said:

"Oh, fair, my lord; a fair man for me always! I will confess to the weakness readily, if your lordship will admit to yours."

Lord Burton cast me a ridiculously languishing glance and

said that, for his part, he thought he had made his weakness evident.

"And so," said Mr. Parker in a low voice which carried plainly to me, "has Miss Archer." In a louder voice he added, "I see, sir, that we black men are out——it is you and Neal Archer and Mr. Haywood who carry the day."

Lord Burton, who had begun by smirking, looked annoyed.

"Oh——Haywood! That fellow! Upon my word, I can see nothing so vastly striking about him. Miss Archer, I appeal to you. Do you admire this Robert Haywood all the females have run mad over?"

There was an instant's silence. George Parker said encouragingly:

"Yes, pray enlighten us, Miss Archer."

I gave him one freezing glance, and turned to Lord Burton with an air of pretty deference.

"Why, my lord, you are a better judge; I know Mr. Haywood only slightly."

"Yes, but do you think him such a fascinating, irresistible fellow? For my part, *I* think him rather insipid. In a few years, he will be coarse."

He spoke with the peevish intonation of an ageing beauty denying the charms of a younger rival, and there were covert smiles around the table.

"Dear sir," Miss Elin said gently, "you could hardly expect to appreciate Mr. Haywood as we foolish females do."

She spoke as calmly as I ever heard a girl in my life. Both George Parker and I glanced at her involuntarily and saw her smiling and obviously untroubled. Whatever Robert's designs, I thought, with mingled triumph and relief, they had not been very successful.

Her self-control emboldened me to say, "I confess I do think Mr. Haywood very handsome."

"All glamour and fustian!" my lord exclaimed scornfully. "The man's a fortune-hunter, out to catch some woman with his good looks." Lowering his voice, but not much, he added to the elderly lady on his right, "Tried to get my niece, but I soon

237

put a stop to that. Luckily she was not so silly about him as some."

"Dear uncle," his niece said gently, "how severe you are! Pray recollect, perhaps Mr. Haywood is a friend of Miss Archer's. You are too hard upon him."

His little arrows of spite safely dispatched, my lord became good-humoured again.

"Very well, my dear, very well. I mean it all for the good, you know. I do abominate to see a fine girl taken in by some bold fellow, just because he carries himself well and has a girl's complexion. Don't you, Mr. Parker?"

In spite of my discomfort, I could hardly keep my countenance. I felt sure he could not have hit upon Mr. Parker's sentiments more exactly.

I thought George looked just a little ashamed of himself; he could hardly be very proud of his ally,

"I never think about another man's looks," he said shortly. "I don't care for Haywood particularly. He rides well, if that's a recommendation. Apropos, have you visited Newmarket Races yet this year, Lord Burton?"

This diversion proved highly successful, and the meal concluded without any more embarrassing moments. In the drawing-room afterwards, waiting for the men to finish their wine and join us, I had a few moments' private conversation with Kathleen, and thought she might mention Robert again. But she did not do so. I caught myself feeling piqued that she had been able to resist him so easily. Truly, there is no end to the vagaries of human nature!

At any rate, I need have no more qualms of conscience on her behalf. I had not robbed my friend of anything, and that was a great comfort to me.

When the gentlemen came in, the party grew noisy, and I began to wish that Neal would come soon to take me away. I could not be happy or at ease for a moment in any company where George Parker was.

Neal came, but to my horror he had Lord Dutton with him, and both were loudly invited by Lord Burton to take a hand at cards. My lord was upon the verge of being really tipsy, and consequently was friends with all the world, his suspicions of Neal temporarily forgotten.

Neal smiled at me, but did not catch my signal, and to my despair willingly agreed to join in a game of *vingt-et-un*. Lord Dutton glanced at the table, evidently reckoning up the stakes, shrugged disdainfully, and made his way towards me.

"Good evening, Miss Archer," he said, languidly. "They are dancing in the other room; would you care to stand up with me?"

"No, thank you, my lord," I said emphatically.

"Good, then I will sit with you," he said coolly, and flung himself into the other corner of the sofa with an air of arrogant possession. Wearing a powdered wig, he was dressed in the sombre magnificence of unrelieved black that he affected, and there were women, I suppose, who would have thought him handsome. "Of all the insipidities I detest," he continued, "an impromptu ball is the worst, though you will observe, Miss Archer, I was willing to endure it for your sake."

And he smiled at me blandly, with that devil's twist to his lips that made me both hate and fear him. I believe he perceived both emotions very clearly, and enjoyed them both. His smile broadened, and I said defiantly:

"I hope, my lord, you never put yourself out in any way to please me, for it's impossible."

He absolutely laughed. "I do admire your candour, Miss Archer. But why dislike me so much?"

I looked at him in amazement. "Good God—have you forgotten Vauxhall?"

The smile faded; he said meaningly: "It would be better for *you* to do so. You had the best of me there, and I do not like to be crossed, Miss Archer. I always make my opponents pay for it in the end. However——" he shrugged one shoulder. "I am willing to forget it if you take care not to remind me."

His arrogance absolutely took my breath away. I said, staring, "I think you're mad!"

"Not in the least," he said calmly. "I do not like to be annoyed over trifles, that is all."

"You call abduction a trifle?"

"Lower your voice, child! Do you want to lose your reputation?"

As I sat struggling to control myself, he rose languidly. "This is a damned dull party—by your leave, I'll go elsewhere. But do pray remember, my dear Miss Archer, that if you are not my friend, you must be the other thing, and you might find that most inconvenient. There are stories about me; I advise you to listen to them."

"Are you threatening me?" I said, in a low voice. I did not know whether to be frightened or angry.

He looked almost surprised. "Oh no. It is nothing to me—please yourself entirely. Good-night." And he made his way languidly from the room, deaf to Lord Burton's loud entreaties that he join them at cards.

"There is a man I *cannot* bear!" Kathleen Elin whispered in my ear.

I started, and shivered. "He is the most horrible man in London. I think he is mad."

"Perhaps he is. Everybody fears him; he has no friends."

"Except George Parker," I said bitterly. I saw how Dutton paused for a moment to put his hand on Parker's shoulder before he went out.

She looked at me in surprise. "Oh, but they are connected—did you not know? Yes, Dutton married Mr. Parker's only sister. She died years and years ago; she was much older than George Parker; but they say Dutton has a fondness for him because of her. He really loved her, I believe, and was quite different while she lived, and so Parker has some influence over him still."

"I see," I said slowly. "That explains it, then." My face grew hot as I thought of the times I had compared him to Dutton, and reproached him for the friendship. But there was no undoing that, nor anything else that had been done. It was too late.

In the chorus of admiration for Miss Elin, the only dissenting voice was Val's. She was a little jealous, perhaps, but the worst even she could find to say was that the heiress was insipid, and smiled too much.

"But if she would take Neal, it would be the greatest thing for him! Does she like him, do you think?"

"Yes, but I do not know how much. And Lord Burton would not like the marriage, I am sure. As he is her guardian, I suppose she must respect his wishes."

"When will she be of age?"

"Next spring."

"And then she may do as she pleases?"

"I suppose so."

"Then perhaps she would marry Neal, if she fancied him. We are talking of you and the heiress, brother," she added, turning towards Neal as he came in. "She will be of age next spring and may do as she pleases. I wish you luck!"

"Thanks, Val," Neal said, smiling. He sat down beside me, putting his arm around the back of my chair. "But I am being cut out, I'm afraid. Parker is the favoured suitor now."

I gave such an involuntary start that my chair creaked, and Val glanced at me sharply. "Is he?" she said. "Do you mean that seriously?"

"Oh yes. He is forever there, and escorts her everywhere. Have you not seen him at the house, Jenny?"

"Once," I said, shortly. I felt as though my stays were tightening, till all my breath was taken away. It was all I could do to sit still. To appear natural was impossible. But luckily Neal was talking, over my head, to Val.

"He is quite a favourite with Lord Burton. You know Parker's aunt, old Mrs. Hamilton? It appears she was a flirt of Burton's when they were both young, and I suppose he has tender sentiments towards the family. Anyhow, bets are being laid on it at White's, and Cory is sure it will be announced before Christmas. It will be a great thing for Parker. He needs the money, and she is a fine creature; I wish them joy with all my heart."

"You give up the heiress very easily, brother."

"Oh, I have no pretensions! I am only favoured as Jenny's brother. I am as well satisfied." He looked down at me with a smile and quick hug. "Miss Elin is charming, but she does not appeal to me especially. I would never marry a woman for her fortune alone."

"How noble of you," said Val, dryly. She changed the subject. "Are we going to hear the new opera tomorrow?"

"Of course. Did you think that we had forgotten your birthday?"

She smiled, and shivered in the same moment. "Only a week more, and Dangerfield will be home."

"Do you hear from him?"

"Oh yes. His business goes well."

"It would," Neal said. "He has the most odious gift for making money."

"He is not so noble as you, brother, in his means of getting it."

Nowadays, when Val grew waspish, Neal simply retreated. He did so now, saying that he would look in at White's to hear the latest odds on the marriage.

When he was gone, Val rose and came to stand in front of me, looking at me very seriously.

"Jenny," she said, "do you care for George Parker?"

I could not answer. I turned away, putting my face into my hands, and burst into tears.

I felt her touch the top of my head with her fingers. Caresses were rare with her, and meant she was deeply moved.

She paced up and down the room for a while, as I tried to stifle my sobs. I had not meant to betray myself, even to her. But the tone of her question, coming on top of the shock of Neal's news, had undone me. It was a long time since Val had thought of anybody but herself and Harvey.

"I'm so sorry," she said, at last.

I shook my head, sitting up and trying to dry my face

"But, Jenny—he used to like you so much! Yes, I could see he did. To tell the truth, I always thought you would make a match of it, though you were so shrewish with him. Was it that, that drove him away? He is more of a man than that, surely?"

"What does it matter?" I said, hopelessly. "It is done now."

242

"Why? You are prettier than she is! Fight for him, Jenny! I would—though she were ten thousand times my friend!"

But I still shook my head. "It is too late, Val. He doesn't love me any more."

She turned wearily away. "All goes awry with us, Jenny, doesn't it?" After a pause, she said grimly, "But if you can, Jenny, fight! Don't give in! All is not lost till one of you is married. I know now that a woman is a fool not to fight for what she wants. If I had given Harvey what he wanted, and what I wanted to give him, all this ruin would not have come upon me."

"I don't see that, Val."

"Yes. Because then I would have known better than to let any power force me into marriage with Dangerfield. And I would have had such a hold on Harvey that he would not have let me go. It does not pay, Jenny, for a woman to be good. They say it does, but it is all lies."

"Sometimes it pays," I said, in a low voice.

But she did not hear me. "Take what you want, Jenny, if you can get it. *They* do, why should not we? I wish I had learned that lesson long ago."

The next day was Val's birthday. She and Neal were both born in the dark month of November, though three years apart. He was now twenty-six, and this was her three-and-twentieth birthday.

We took tea with her, afterwards going to the opera. There was company at the house for tea, the usual crowd, and I thought Val seemed unusually arrogant with them, as though their presence fretted her unendurably. She was irritable and restless, moving from one chair to another. Harvey was not there. Now that she met him at his rooms, he seldom came here during the day. I am afraid he came far too often to spend the evening.

"Mr. Underhill used to be such a favourite with your sister," Miss Andrews said to me, simpering. "But we never see him any more. I hope there has not been a quarrel!"

"Not that I know of," I said coolly, damning her insolence to myself. "But there was so much tattle about his coming here, it was enough to drive anyone away."

Miss Andrews turned red. "La! I'm sure I don't know what you mean."

"Don't you? Perhaps you don't talk scandal, Miss Andrews. But it is a pity some of your friends have no better subject for conversation than my sister."

"Well, I'm sure——" Miss Andrews bridled. "People only get themselves talked about when they do something——"

She paused, and I said, "Something *what*?" so fiercely that she stammered and did not finish her sentence.

"You are mistaken," I said, when it was apparent that she had no intention of completing the insult. "People are talked about because they are handsomer, or cleverer, or happier than others. Scandal is the bastard of envy."

"La, Miss Archer, you are so outspoken!" she tittered, still very red. "I'm sure *I* don't envy Mrs. Dangerfield."

"Why should you?" I said contemptuously, and left her. After Kathleen Elin's companionship, I found these vulgar women still more difficult to tolerate.

Val dressed brilliantly for the theatre, and looked lovely. Colour burned in her cheeks and her eyes were as bright as the expensive necklace of brilliants that she wore. Between the acts we had numerous visitors in our box, and I never heard her so much admired before. Little Mr. Franklin could not take his eyes off her.

But once, when someone spoke unexpectedly over her shoulder, she started half off her chair and turned white with shock. I saw it with concern. She was strung-up to such a pitch that I was frightened. Something was amiss.

When the ballet began, before the last act, all the visitors left our box. Many people came only to see the dancing. Neal, who liked the music better, went away to pay gallantries to Miss Bertram in the pit. Val and I were left alone, and I felt sure she had some confidence to make me.

For a while, however, we sat in silence, both staring fixedly at the stage, although I doubt whether either of us saw the performance. Suddenly Val stretched out her hand and took mine, without looking at me. Her fingers were burning hot, and I saw her lips move nervously, as though she wanted to speak, but could not.

"Don't look at me, Jenny," she begged, in a low voice. "I have something to tell you. But don't look at me, look at the stage—or I shall break down."

I turned round obediently, with a strange clutch at my heart. Her hand held mine tightly; I felt how it twitched, and twitched again, with a kind of nervous reaction.

"What is it, Val?" I asked at last, softly.

She did not answer for a moment. With a shock, I realised she was trying not to cry and instinctively my own hand tightened on hers.

"Jenny . . ." she said, indistinctly. "Jenny—forgive me! I have so loved you!"

The tears sprang to my own eyes. In a moment, the lights, the stage, the dancers, swam together in a sudden blur, and I had to bite my lips to control myself. We were so conspicuous, here in our box, with all the lights burning, including those upon the stage itself.

"Val . . ." I could not say more. I *must* not cry here. But that little sorrowful voice had shaken me to the heart.

"I am going to leave you, Jenny," she went on, so low she was almost whispering. "I don't want to, but I must. I am going away with Harvey."

"Val!"

The little feverish fingers closed more tightly on mine.

"I *must*," she said, passionately. "Jenny, I *cannot* go on as I am. I can't stay when Dangerfield comes home. You don't know how I feel . . . I'll die before I let him touch me again. Anything is better than that."

"But what will you do? Oh, Val! Where will you go?"

"To Underhill Grange. Where else can we go? Harvey has no money to live anywhere else. I wonder if my father will still come to the Grange, when I am Harvey's whore?" she added, with a hard little laugh.

"It is he who has done it all," I said bitterly, remembering

245

how brutally he had forced this damnable marriage upon her. He —and Dangerfield, who had bought a desperate girl who hated him, just as he might have bought and brought home some beautiful, rebellious animal. The old resentment against my father rose bitterer than ever. "It is he who has ruined your life!"

But Val shook her head. "No," she said, with a curious, sorrowful wisdom. "We make our own lives, Jenny. Or they are made for us, but not by one another."

I was silent. It was coming over me, wave upon wave, what this meant. I should lose her. I should never be let to see her, when she and Harvey were living openly together. And he—how would he treat her, when she was dependent wholly upon him? He was such a fool! I distrusted him, not because he was a rake, but because he was a fool. As his wife, Val might have been able to manage him. But as his mistress, could she? And if not, to what ruin and despair would this elopement bring her? For when she left her husband for Harvey, she would step outside the world she knew, and it never would open to her again. Society will forgive much to a handsome woman with a vulgar husband. But this would never be forgiven. Live or die, she would be cut off from me for ever, or to be seen only in secret.

And yet, to live with Dangerfield, hating him as she did, to endure his possession of her, night after night . . . Anything was better than that. There was degradation there worse than anything this could bring.

She said slowly, with a humility that almost broke my heart— my proud beautiful sister!—"I've been thinking. I'm not clever like you, Jenny. I think I would always have made a mess of my life, whatever I did. But at least this way I'll be happy for a little while."

"Do you love him *so* much, Val?" I asked, sorrowfully.

"I am giving you up for him," she answered, simply, and something in that little answer broke me down at last.

I did not cry, but sat hopelessly with my hand in hers. I felt as though something in me had been broken. It had all followed too fast, one thing upon another. Everything had slipped away from me, one love after another, till now it seemed to me that I was all alone in a very desolate place. The winds blew cold upon me, there was a darkness and winter coming, with no escape . . .

I do not know whether Neal noticed anything amiss when he returned, but he asked no questions. Perhaps, if he guessed at something, he did not want to *know*. Men are much alike in that. As long as a trouble does not directly confront them, they will do anything to avoid it.

It was raining hard as we took Val home. The hired coach was dirty, and the roof leaked. Neal readily agreed to come in and warm himself before we went on. I wanted nothing so much as to be in my own bed, free to give way and cry as I pleased, but I followed silently. I might not have much more time with Val. It was queer to think, as we stood before the door while Val rang, that I might never come here again.

"Damm them!" Neal exclaimed impatiently, as Val rang, and rang again. "Where the devil are they? It's like their impudence to run off the minute your back is turned!"

"On a night like this?" Val said. "Perhaps the bell is out of order. Will you knock, Neal?"

He set up a furious tattoo, relieving his feelings. Presently I said I thought I heard somebody coming, while Val fretfully begged him to stop. "You'll wake the whole street, brother!"

"I'll wake this fellow when he gets the door open!" Neal angrily promised. It was pouring, and we were all three becoming soaked.

He stopped knocking, however, as a light shone through the chinks of the door. We could hear somebody fumbling with the locks and chains.

"Why the devil did they lock up while you were still out?" Neal fumed. "Hurry up in there, for God's sake! We're drowning!"

I heard the chain drop down, the bolts go back, and at last the key turning. The door opened, so slowly that Neal hastened it with an impatient kick. Then he gave an exclamation of surprise, as the door swung wide, and Val suddenly seized me by the arm with a grip that made me wince. For in the doorway, holding up a candle, was not a servant, but Mr. Dangerfield.

He had the queerest look I ever saw; I thought him much flown in liquor. He postured, bowing and grinning at us, giggling in apparent delight at our surprise, and waving the candle in extravagant gestures of welcome, while we stood, three images, staring at him.

"Come in, come in! Is this not a surprsie? A great surprise? You did not expect me till Tuesday, eh? But I could not stay away longer. I was called home. Did you enjoy yourselves? I did not think the opera would be over so soon. I sent the servants away, you see; I had to open the door myself."

"Well, then, let us in!" Neal said, pushing past him in annoyance. "Come in, Jenny; come in, sister, don't stand there in the rain!" He added, with an attempt at greater civility, "You have taken us all by surprise, you see."

"Yes," Dangerfield agreed. "I daresay I have! *Quite* by surprise." And he giggled on a sudden high note.

"He's drunk," Neal shrugged, not troubling to lower his voice. He turned to shut the door but the wind snatched it from his hand and slammed it, sending the chains rattling. You could hear the echoes slamming away through the house, through the halls and up the stairs, till they died away in the distance..

Dangerfield started violently at the sound. The candle in his hand tilted and a spot of wax fell on the floor. Instinctively he put up his other hand to shield the flame till it burnt strongly again.

"Good God, it's cold in here!" Neal complained. "Why did you send all the servants off? I daresay there's not a decent fire in the house."

Dangerfield, staring so fixedly that he showed the whites all round his eyes, said nothing. Neal shrugged in exasperation.

"Come, Jenny, let us go home. He's clean flown in liquor."

But Val, who had become very pale, said, "Something has happened. Something bad, or you would not look so pleased," she added to Dangerfield, with that mixture of disgust and disdain with which she always spoke to him. "What is it?"

"Happened?" he echoed, tittering. I noticed that he never looked at her, staring at Neal, or me, or at the floor, or anywhere but in her face. "Oh no, my dear, what should have happened?"

"Why have you sent the servants away?"

"To enjoy themselves, my dear. A little holiday, to celebrate my return. My unexpected return!" He tittered again, forcing his mirth. "Just like the farces, my dear! All husbands return unexpectedly, do they not?"

I saw Neal's brows draw down in a frown; Val stared at Dangerfield with a grimace of disgust.

"What the devil do you mean?" she asked roundly. She could sound very like her father sometimes.

"Never mind," Neal interposed. "He's drunk, he don't know what he's saying. You'd better get to bed, man. Sister, will you stay, or spend the night with Jenny and me?" He wanted to get away, I could see, but hesitated to leave Val. It had not yet dawned on him that Dangerfield was anything but unpleasantly drunk. I knew him better; I was sure that Val was right and something *had* happened.

Suddenly Val darted past Dangerfield, pouncing on a cloak that lay over a chair in the vestibule. "This is Harvey's!" she exclaimed, lifting it up. I thought she sounded relieved, but Neal's frown darkened.

"Harvey! Is *he* here?"

"To be sure," Dangerfield said brightly. "We have spent the evening together, waiting your return."

"You and Harvey?" Neal said, incredulously.

He smirked and rubbed his hands together. "Oh, we have had much to talk about. We have much in common, you know." His voice was full of meaning, and Neal exclaimed:

"Oh, the devil!" Above all things he disliked a scene.

"Where is Harvey?" Val demanded. "Has he gone?"

"Oh no, my dear, he would not go without seeing *you*. Such a very polite gentleman, Squire Underhill. Do you know, my dear, that he wants you to go and visit him in the country? I told him I was sure you would not want to rusticate like that!"

"Oh, good God!" I said, groaning for Harvey's rash tongue,

249

while Neal looked frankly bewildered. But Val, after gazing very fixedly at Dangerfield for a moment, suddenly ran to the stairs and called, "Harvey!"

There was no answer, but Dangerfield said, "He's in the drawing-room, my dear, waiting for you. Do go up!"

She ran up at once, gathering up her skirts in both hands, calling to Harvey again.

Dangerfield looked after her, grinning. He was ghastly pale, with big tallowy drops rolling down his face, though it was so bitterly cold in the house. But yet he grinned and grinned, as though he had prepared a joke with which to surprise her.

"Harvey!" Val called again, and I heard the drawing-room door creak open. It hung badly and always stuck and creaked in rainy weather.

It was strange how we all stood there expectant, as though waiting for a curtain to rise. Neal and Dangerfield both gazed up the stairs after Val, but I could not take my eyes from Dangerfield. I thought I had never seen a man look so loathsome. A worm, if it turned on you like a snake, would look like that—the blind swaying head, the fixed idiot's grin, the impression of an unnatural, nightmarish malevolence.

And then there came from Val such a scream as I never heard before, not even in the worst of her agony. Never, never have I heard such a cry.

"Great God!" Neal whispered. As we ran and jostled on the stairs he tried to put me aside. "Stay back, Jenny, stay back!"

But with such a cry as that ringing in my ears, I could not stay from her.

I do not know what I had expected to see, but it was a quiet scene we looked on as we came panting together to the open door of the drawing-room. The fire was burning low and there was no other light, but I could distinctly see Harvey sitting in a tall arm-chair by the hearth, his head thrown back a little, as though he rested, his hands hanging down over the arms.

Val had flung herself down on him so that her head rested on his knees. She was not crying so much as moaning, little stifled moans as though she could not get breath enough to weep. The firelight on Harvey's face gave it look of warmth, and he was faintly smiling. I could not imagine why he sat there like that, smiling so, letting her cry. I stood stupidly staring at them.

I heard Neal say, very rapidly, all run together, "Oh God, my God, my God!"

"What is it?" I said, stupidly. "What's the matter?" All I could think of was that they had quarrelled.

There came a gust of wind down the chimney. The end of a burning stick rolled off the fire grate and down on the hearth, flaring up momentarily like a torch, lighting Harvey's face brilliantly.

And then I saw that the round dark shadow on the side of Harvey's cheek, high near the temple, did not move, though the light burned up on it so brightly.

It was not a shadow . . . It was a small, round, dark hole with a very little blood smudged below it.

"Oh God!" This time it was my voice, rising hysterically. "Oh Christ, no—no, it can't be!"

Neal, stumbling as though he were drunk, crossed the room to Val. She was making horrible sounds now, tearing gasps like a poisoned dog. He tried to lift her away.

"Val, come away! Don't!"

She resisted him fiercely. Between them, the balance of Harvey's body was disturbed. He fell forward, almost upon her, and I saw the other side of his head, where Dangerfield's bullet had blown his brains away. And then the whole scene darkened and went out like a blown candle.

Once before there had been a dream like this, and Neal's voice had wakened me. It was Neal's voice that called me now, back from the silence and the darkness. But this time it was he who struggled in the nightmare and begged not to be left alone there.

I did not want to answer. For if I did, I would be in the dream too, and from this dream there would be no waking and no escape . . . but I could not leave Neal.

"Jenny . . . Jenny . . ."

I opened my eyes. I sat propped against the wall and Neal was bending over me a face so white that every drop of blood must have been driven out of it. Beyond him I saw the warm light of the fire, and the pair of them there by the hearth, with Harvey's shattered head in Val's arms. One of his hands dangled limply beside the chair and the fire glinted on a ring he wore. In the flickering light it was hard to believe he did not move.

"Is he dead?" My voice was quite clear, only very small and sounding far away.

"Dead? Oh God, yes!" Neal's grating voice broke on something like a laugh. He put his hand to his mouth to smother it; I saw him struggle fiercely to control himself.

I felt queerly calm and remote. Partly, I think, because I was stunned with shock, and partly because that moment or two of darkness had snapped my sense of reality. There was no escape from this dream, but it *was* a dream all the same. It must be.

"What shall we do?"

He shook his head.

I looked towards Val, observing her quite seriously and dispassionately, as though I were a nurse and she my patient.

"She mustn't do that. She will go mad. We must get her away."

"Get her away from him if you can," Neal answered, in that same strange harsh voice. "I can't."

I got to my feet. It surprised me that my knees should feel like that—as though I had been very ill. But I managed to steady them enough to walk.

"Dearest Val, come away!" I said, bending over her. "Neal will take care of Harvey——"

She did not speak, but looked up at me so terribly that I recoiled. I hardly knew her. It was a wild thing that crouched there, mad and dangerous with agony. A thing in a trap, a vixen with a broken back, snarling with hatred out of an unbearable torment, blind with pain, dying . . . She hugged Harvey jealously to her. I think if I had touched him, she would have flown at my throat.

"My God!" I whispered. Neal came up to me, his face ghastly.

"You see?" he said. "She is mad *now*. She——"

He paused, choking. There was a little giggle from the doorway. Dangerfield stood there, swaying back and forth like a drunken man, his fingernails scrabbling on the door frame. He looked at Val, and then at us, and giggled again.

"Why does she do that? She can't wake him, you know," he pointed out, reasonably. "I assure you he is quite, quite dead. Did you see his brains? They——"

"Christ!" Neal said. He took a stride forward and shook him fiercely. Dangerfield's head waggled. He continued to giggle, breathlessly. Neal raised his hand and struck him across the face, back and forth, hard smashing blows that snapped Dangerfield's head on his neck.

Abruptly the man's hysteria ceased. He put his fingers wonderingly to his face, seeming to feel the pain but not to understand the source. Then he sat down on the nearest chair and said, quite calmly:

"I didn't mean to do it, you know. But he was rude to me. He said she was going to leave me. She couldn't do that. She's my wife. And there's the boy."

A faint whine crept into his voice. "I had to do it! Because of the boy. After all, I had the right. They were lovers. He said so. He told me so. That was why he was taking her away."

Neal and I looked at each other. He asked, slowly:

"Dangerfield—was there anybody here?"

"No. I sent all the servants away. Except the nurse. I could not have the boy left alone. But she could not hear anything. I shot him. And then I heard you knocking. I think there was something in between. I don't remember now. He fell over in the chair, but when I heard you knock I put him up again. I wanted her to find——"

His voice died away. At the memory of that cruelty to Val, I shrank from him. To my mind it was worse than the murder itself. I had witnessed Harvey's arrogance to Dangerfield often. And I could not help remembering that Dangerfield's mother had run away with a lover and left him to a miserable neglected childhood. God knows you cannot speak of *right* when you speak of murder. There is not anything to justify the taking of a man's life. Still, Dangerfield *had* cause. A better man might have done the same. But only a monster would have propped him there, looking like life, for the girl who loved him to find.

"There were no witnesses?" Neal persisted. "There was no quarrel?"

"Quarrel?" Dangerfield echoed, vacantly. "I don't know—he was very rude," he repeated. "I don't think I said much—— It was because of her going away, leaving the boy. That was why I did it." I got the impression that he repeated the excuse with a certain air of cunning, as though he were coming to himself and beginning to reckon up the possible consequences of his action.

"Why did you send the servants away?" Neal asked, frowningly. "Was that *before*——?"

"Yes." He made a vague gesture. "I don't know why. He was talking loud. I suppose—I thought they might hear what he said. I don't know."

Neal stood staring down at him, frowning more and more deeply. "If there had been a quarrel, any witnesses—— If he had a weapon in his hand—— We could say there had been a duel. But your sending the servants away—— They will say you planned it all." He looked around the room. "If we had another pistol, we could fire it, and then put it in his hand, to show there had been a duel . . ."

Dangerfield slowly raised his head, looking at him wonderingly. The queer protuberant eyes bulged more wildly than ever, like a terrified frog's.

"They won't hang me, will they?" The very word seemed to panic him. He gasped, and begged, "You won't let them do that? You'll say it was a quarrel? *You* knew they were lovers—you won't let them hang me?"

Neal grimaced. "You deserve to hang," he said coldly. "You shot the poor devil in cold blood. But you're my sister's husband. It will be bad enough if we can make it out to be some sort of a duel. They may hang you, even so. But for Val's sake, and the boy's, I'll help you get off."

"Neal, be quiet," I warned him, in a low voice.

He looked at me, startled, and then at Val. She had raised her

head. She still held Harvey's body in her arms. But she was looking at us and listening, and the firelight in her eyes made them
shine with a queer, horrible animal's glare.

Dangerfield cringed from that look, absolutely cringed from it,
putting up one hand to shield his face. With his other hand I saw
him fork his fingers. I have seen ignorant superstitious country
people do that when a humpback or an old crone of a woman
went by. It is the sign against the evil eye. If he had never feared
her before, he feared her now.

I could not tell whether there were any reason in her glance or
not, but Neal spoke to her reasoningly.

"You must see, Val," he said. "It's better. Harvey's dead——"

"For God's sake, Neal!" I begged.

"But she must see that it's better. If Dangerfield hangs, the
scandal will ruin us all. You don't want your boy to grow up,
Val, to know that his father was hanged for murder? You've got
to think of the child."

For a long moment she stared in silence. And then she turned
her head a little, looking down at the broken thing in her arms,
and not even Neal dared to speak.

Slowly, very slowly, she laid him down. The tears seemed to
be frozen inside me, or God knows I would have wept to watch
her. She bent down over him and laid her cheek on his. I thought
she whispered something, but perhaps it was only that her lips
moved. And then she stood up.

I dared not speak to her, and Neal too stood out of her way.
Dangerfield shrank from her, getting as far away as he could on
his chair. She paused beside him for a second, and I thought she
smiled, while Dangerfield thrust out his forked fingers to ward
her off. Then, very quietly, she went out of the room and we
heard her slowly mounting the stairs.

"Oh God!" Dangerfield whimpered. "Did you see her look
at me? It's no use—she'll swear my life away. She's always
hated me. She'll swear to anything to hang me! You'll stand by
me, Archer? For God's sake, you will, won't you? The boy—
your nephew—for his sake!"

"Be quiet!" Neal said, his voice harsh with disgust. "For the

255

love of God, man—and if you love your own life!—try to pull yourself together. I'll do what I can. If you have another pistol, get it, and we'll put it in his hand. We must send for the constable. We can tell him you quarrelled, and that he threatened you——— That will be best. Help me lay him down; we can't leave him sitting there."

"Oh Christ, no!" Dangerfield said, recoiling.

"Jenny—*can* you?" Neal said, appealing to me.

I was not at all afraid. Together we drew him from the chair and laid him down on the rug before the fire. I knelt beside him and put the hair off his face and straightened his hands. He looked so young and handsome and quiet, sleeping there undisturbed by our voices . . . Oh, Harvey, Harvey! I knew you would bring ruin on us, but I never dreamed it would be anything like this. And how can I be angry with you now?

"Jenny," Neal whispered, his hand upon my shoulder, "you had better go to Val. She ought not to be alone."

I stood up slowly. I knew Val did not want me, and yet it was true—she ought not to be alone.

"What are you going to do, Neal?"

"Send for a magistrate. The sooner the better. If the servants do not return soon, I must go myself."

"No!" I said quickly.

"You needn't be afraid, Jenny. There's no more fight in *him*," Neal said, with a contemptuous glance towards Dangerfield. The man seemed oblivious. He sat staring at Harvey, torn between a horrible fear and a still more horrible triumph. He looked half mad, but it would be like him, I thought, to feign madness to escape blame.

"It's not him," I said, with difficulty. "It's Val—I don't know. Only *please*, Neal, don't leave us here! The servants *must* come back soon."

He promised, and I added, shuddering, "And—and don't leave Dangerfield alone with Harvey." It was in my mind that he might commit some horrid indignity upon that quiet body.

Neal nodded, saying soothingly, "I'll stay here, Jenny, I won't go away. Don't worry, I'll take care of everything. You go to

256

Val, poor girl!" He caught me by the hand. "Darling Jenny, this is horrible, I know, but we'll pull through somehow. Try to make Val reasonable, if you can."

"Oh God!" I said, incredulously. *"Reasonable . . ."* But it was no use. He did not understand. Harvey was dead, and there was the scandal to consider, and therefore Val might as well be sensible and make the best of things. I suppose he thought, too, that it was greatly her fault.

It was too much for me. I only shook my head and turned away, skirting Dangerfield as widely as possible as I went to the door.

But he, squirming round suddenly, caught me by my dress as I passed.

"Miss Jenny!" he whispered. His lips worked so that he could hardly get the words out. Though his face was greenish, the full lips were as red as ever. There was something horrible about the way they twisted and twitched as though they had life of their own.

I tried to pull away from him, but he held me fast. He was sweating with fear and the clutch of his hands left dark stains on the delicate silk.

"Miss Jenny! We've always been friends! I've been good to you, you know I have. Money—I never grudged you anything. You won't let her tell lies about me? You'll tell them I was always good to her? Seven hundred pounds on silks and lace since we were married, and the real pearls, and the stomacher with the brilliants—as good as any duchess in town! I never grudged her anything. You know how she treated me. I was a good husband, wasn't I? A maid of her own——"

He should not have reminded me of Mrs. Betty. I said fiercely, "Yes, for you to lie with! How dare you talk of her having a lover? Good God, you slept with every woman in the house and God knows how many beside!"

I saw how his eyes hated me, but he went on fawning and trying to smile. I finally realised *that* was what his lips were trying to shape. But try as he would, he could not quite force one, with Harvey lying dead there beside the fire and Tyburn not so many miles away.

257

"Don't be hard on me, Miss Jenny! A man's pleasures——
And I didn't interfere with hers. You know I didn't. It was only
when he sat there and told me she was going to leave me, leave
the boy—— That was wicked. You must admit that. She ought
not to have thought of leaving her own husband and her little
baby!"

"For God's sake, sir," I said, desperately trying to break away,
"it is all done now, and you must answer for it. I will tell the
truth as best I can."

He lowered his voice, glancing round cunningly at Neal, who
had sat down with his head in his hands.

"Aye, that's all I ask of you, love, to tell the truth! That'll
save me. They'll believe *you*, so young and innocent—Miss
Jenny——" his voice dropped to a whisper. "There's a thousand
pounds you shall have, the day they say I am not to blame——"

I dragged fiercely at my skirt. "Let me go!"

"Two thousand!" He whimpered. "Five thousand! Anything! I'll sign a paper—— Only say you'll stand my friend,
Miss Jenny!"

The silk tore in his fingers and I was free. Neal looked up
sharply at the sound. "What is he saying to you, Jenny?" he
demanded suspiciously.

"Mind!" Dangerfield said, getting suddenly a very ugly look.
"Mind, I can speak too! I have plenty to say! Your fine sister—
aye, and you too, Miss Jenny, pretty innocent Miss Jenny! What
about your handsome lover? And you——" he rounded on Neal,
who rose abruptly, walking towards him with clenched fists.
"Mind you, I can talk too! Scandal! Aye, I'll make a scandal.
If *I* swing for it, they'll hang you and your damned whoring sisters
in effigy all around the town! They'll——"

"One word more," Neal said, "and I'll strangle you now. Do
you hear me? You filthy little worm!" Gasping with rage he
stood over Dangerfield with his fists clenched, and the man
instantly sank back, putting up his hands to protect his face, and
fell to whimpering again, saying that we always hated him, were
all against him, had no pity for his hard lot——

"Get out, Jenny!" Neal ordered me roughly. "You'll never

258

set eyes on him again if I can help it. Dangerfield, if you mean to tell lies about my sisters I'll strangle you now!"

I went out hurriedly, not much caring whether Neal did it or not, so long as he did not suffer for it. It seemed to me at that moment that we were all guilty because no one had thought of taking Val away from this monster until Harvey came.

As I stood in the dark hall outside, trying to get strength to face Val, I heard a sound and glanced up to see a dim figure standing on the landing above. For a moment I shrank in superstitious fear—in the dim light the figure seemed to have a ghostly, pallid radiance.

And then I saw that it was Val in her white dress, her powdered hair tumbling in curls down her back, a faint light from one of the rooms shining behind her.

"Jenny?" she said, and I started, to hear her speak. Her voice was a little hoarse, but quite calm.

"Yes," I said, looking up at her anxiously. It was dangerous for her to be so calm. The first thing I meant to do was force her to weep.

"Tell *him* to come out."

I hesitated. I needed no second telling to know who she meant, but I was afraid. I had a horrible fear that she meant to dash herself down before his eyes.

But she was so calm! "Call him, Jenny. I have something to tell him. And then you may come up, if you like."

Hesitantly, fearing to take my eyes away from her, wishing I could clearly see her face, I opened the drawing-room door a crack and called to Neal. I could not bring myself to speak to Dangerfield again.

The two men came out quickly. I saw how Dangerfield shrank from the sight of her, so strange and ghostly there above us in the dim light.

"Go up to her, Jenny," Neal bade me, and I began very slowly and quietly to mount the stairs. I felt as one does with a wild animal—it would not do to go quickly or make any sudden motion, or God knew what might come of it.

Val leaned over the rail to look at Dangerfield. His dread of her was only too apparent, and she gave a little low laugh, not pretty to hear.

"Is he not a brave sight, Jenny?" she said, almost in the old mocking way.

"I did it for you!" Dangerfield said, stammering and trembling. "You *are* my wife, you know, you ought not to have thought of leaving me. But—but I'll forgive you. And if you'll only be reasonable I'll give you anything you want. Anything!"

"*Anything?*" Val repeated, softly.

"Anything, anything, I swear it!"

"Oh God!" I said. I appealed to Neal. "Make him stop—take him away!" I turned imploringly to Val. "Val—don't!"

"Don't come up, Jenny. Wait. My husband and I will never talk together again. You must give us our moment now."

There was something *staged* about this—her words, her manner, the very pose she had taken up—that frightened me more than anything else. But she flung out her little hand to stop me with such fierce command that I involuntarily stood still. I dared not press on her too hard. There were fifteen or twenty steps separating us still. . . .

"There is only one thing you can do for me," she now said, very quietly, to Dangerfield.

"Name it!" he exclaimed prayerfully. I thought I saw a little complacent smile twitch at the corners of his lips. He was a merchant to the end. He thought everything had its price.

"*Give me back my love.*"

The little short words, spoken very gently, struck him like blows. He took a step back, the smile stiffening, the sweat starting out on him again. I could see how his face shone in the dim light.

"You cannot do that, can you?" she said, still very gently. "No . . . So there is nothing you can do for me. But there is something I can do for you. I can teach you how it feels to be robbed by a murderer."

"Val!" As I cried out, I began to run. But I never, never could have been quick enough.

She stooped down and lifted something lying on the floor near her feet. As she lifted it, disturbing it, it gave a little mewling cry. As she held it out over the rail, and dropped it, it cried faintly again, a little trailing cry . . . Then there was a soft muffled thud on the floor of the vestibule, two flights below, and silence.

I do not know how long it was before Dangerfield began to scream—high, thin screams, like a trapped weasel. He ran, screaming and stumbling, till he reached the bundle lying there below us, the small white limp bundle that might have been a roll of old clothes. He caught it up in his arms, tearing wildly at the wrappings. Even where I stood I could see how the head rolled on the neck, and such a ghastly sickness came over me I could neither move nor speak.

Then Dangerfield looked up. He shook the bundle at her and shrieked—curses, reproaches, blasphemies—while Val, leaning over the rail, answered with peal after peal of wild, shuddering laughter. I saw Neal clap his hands over his ears to shut it out, but I could not move even to do that.

This, then, was the thing I had seen long ago in my dreams, queerly distorted, like shapes seen in water, but clearly recognisable now . . . the face of absolute disaster.

It was on this scene that the servants opened the door, coming home merry and laughing from the pleasant evening at the theatre to which their master had dismissed them on his unexpected return.

The wind blows, the sun shines, the world wheels round unchanging, half in darkness, half in light . . . For how many does the world end each day? And there is not a mark to show for it anywhere on this earth that we call our own. The tides rise and fall, the rain comes, and the snow; the days grow short and then, as surely, grow long again . . . Once, they say, the streets of London were no more than stones in the forest with the wolves howling over them. Some day, maybe, the wolves will howl there again, and all that went to the making of a great city will be no more than a little scar upon the face of the earth. And from beginning to end, all that came between——the anguish and the joy, birthing and dying, love and laughter, the bitterness of longing and the still more endless bitterness of loss——will be of no more importance in Eternity than the turning of a single tide. . . .

There came down upon us, that rainy night in London, such a thunderbolt of destruction that our little world dissolved before it like a house of cards. But the great world went on just as usual, and all that we felt and suffered made no more mark than to provide a brief sensation and a moral for matrons. I see now, of course, that it must be so, or we would all go mad. But it was hard to bear at the time.

Hardest of all, I remember, was the approach of Christmas, when people's faces shone with a brief reflection of an old joy. All the while Neal and I were fighting for Val's life, there were carollers tramping the streets, bells ringing long triumphant peals, the sound of hope and laughter . . .

It rang in my ears like mockery when it seemed to me that God had forgotten us.

"No, no, my dear!" said poor Mrs. Frye, greatly distressed. "You must not say that. He never forgets any of us——no, not the weakest, the wickedest of His children."

I thought of Newgate Prison, which she had never seen, and which I visited every day. "Perhaps He does not forget," I said. "But He has turned His face away."

She protested in vain. Religion was her consolation in this darkness. But the light had gone out for me. Why should God remember us, when so many of our friends forgot?

To please Mrs. Frye, however, I went with her often to church, at odd hours when there was no congregation, and marvelled to see how she would rise from her knees rested and restored, when I felt only the soreness of my knees, and my weariness, and the gloomy chill of the stones. I had long since ceased praying for any other favour, but I prayed passionately for the gift of faith, seeing all that it could mean to one who possessed it. Mrs. Frye told me that this was the one prayer which never remained unanswered. But there came back to me only silence, and at last I went only to satisfy her. She, at any rate, had remained faithful to us, and deserved whatever favour I could do her.

There were not many others. Some retreated absolutely and instantly. Some drew their skirts away more gently and dexterously, protesting their sympathy to the end. Quite a good many promptly turned and reviled us. A few—a very few!—stood by us.

Kathleen Elin was not a friend to be driven away by scandal or misfortune. Though Lord Burton forbade her to see me, she came in spite of him, till he ordered her to accompany him to the country.

"In a few months I shall be of age and then, Jenny, we shall *never* be apart again!" she said, kissing me with tears in her eyes on that last visit. I clung to her speechlessly. If Lord Burton had known all that her companionship meant to me, I do not think he would have been quite so cruel.

She was the truest of friends. She asked no questions, made no exclamations, but came with love and comfort, bringing all manner of little luxuries for me to take to Val. She offered me money also, and I took it; I had to. We were already desperate for money. It was the only thing that could save Val, if anything could. Meanwhile it bought her whatever comfort and decency there was to be had in Newgate. Without money, she would have lain in the common cells where the worst women in the city were gathered, exposed to illness and God knows what depravity. With money, we were able to buy her a single room, fire and candles, decent food, and even some medical attention, rough as it was.

"Does she suffer much, Jenny?" Kathleen whispered.

I shook my head. "She does not know anything. She does not know me. She sits all day and stares. The wardens say she often sits so all night. I don't think she knows where she is."

"Thank God!" Kathleen said, but I was silent. It seemed to me that anything, even suffering, was better than the endless silence of the dark.

When I came to her, she would smile a little vaguely, let me kiss her, turning her smooth, cold cheek as dutifully as a child. She never spoke. She had not spoken one word since that ghastly night. The silence that fell on that terrible pealing laughter had been silence absolute. At first we thought it was shock and sorrow, that it would pass. But it did not pass. When all our struggles to save her from trial had proved in vain, and she was committed to Newgate, I thought perhaps the terrors of the place would rouse her. But there was no change, neither for worse nor better.

Once, in growing horror and desperation, I said Harvey's name to her. That unblinking stare did not alter. The prison that held her had higher, thicker walls than Newgate's, and no voice, not even mine, and no name, not even his, could penetrate it.

Only her fingers had motion. They were never still, moving with a curious delicate precision through intricate patterns, as though all that there was of sense or feeling had retreated into them, seeking expression in this way. There was something horrible to me in their motions. I would sit and watch, fascinated, till I felt I was going mad myself. They haunted my dreams. They spoke in a language I could not understand, but there was a ghastly eloquence in their eternal striving. Sometimes I wondered if they were trying to rid themselves of the terrible thing they had done. There were times, I believe, when I *was* a little mad.

The physicians observed her with interest, but shook their heads. "A shock has driven her mad," one said to Neal. "Another shock, as great, might cure her."

"And then she would remember?"

"Perhaps."

"God forbid, then, that she should ever be cured," Neal said, and the man said no more.

They all tried to keep me from going to Newgate, but I would not be prevented, and Neal could not bring himself to force me. They said that I could do Val no good, since she did not even know me, that I only tormented myself with the sight of her, and with what I saw of that ghastly prison life, and put myself and

264

all around me in danger of jail fever. It was all true, but I could not bring myself to listen. While she was there, I could not stay away. It was always in my mind that she might wake some day, and know where she was, and what had happened. As for the jail fever, there were times when I would almost have welcomed it, for her and for myself. When you have the spectre of Tyburn before your eyes, jail fever loses a good deal of its terror. And, characteristically enough, because I did not fear the disease it did not touch me, though I saw people dying of it round me every day. As for Val, they say the mad are exempt from ordinary illness. I do not know, but whether it was that, or the special care given her—even to a fire, with medicinal herbs burning in it—she ailed nothing while she was there.

Her cell, with its privacy and its comforts, was like a little island in hell. To reach it, I had to pass by the common cells on the women's side of the prison and I saw things I will not speak of, even now, and would forget if only I could. The wardens, of course, were all hardened. They had to be—that, or mad, there was no choice.

And indeed, it is strange what you can get used to. In a way, I did get used to Newgate—even to the smell. To my country nose, the streets of London stank like barnyards, and for the same reason. But the miasma of Newgate was something else. It was pure evil—sickness, and hatred, and filth, and sin, and despair. God, I can smell it still!

It clung to me always then. I kept special clothes for my visits to the prison, changing them the instant I got home, right down to the skin, and washing all over with vinegar. But the smell hung about me still, faintly, or so I imagined. At first I tried to scrub it off, till I very nearly scoured my skin off. Finally I accepted it, and at last scarcely noticed it.

For, as I say, it is curious what you can get used to. I was soon quite familiar with the workings of Newgate, and well known to the wardens there, who brought me gossip and pointed out the more notorious prisoners as they walked in the jail yard below. There are ranks and privileges, even in prison. Highwaymen were the aristocrats, and disdained any exchange with such vulgar fellows as forgers or coiners, or even such lessser thieves as pick-pockets.

The keepers pointed out one particularly handsome and arrogant highwayman—I forget his name now—who was hanged the second Monday after Val's committal to Newgate. He was well supplied with money and bribed the keepers for all kinds of luxuries, including his harlot, who spent every night with him. But on the last night before his execution he did not have to pay for his entertainment. A woman of title—they told me her name—visited him. It was not uncommon, they said, when I at first refused to believe this. When a highwayman was both notorious and handsome, he had often his choice of fine ladies. They found it titillating to sleep with a handsome fellow whose body would one night lie in their arms and the next be swinging on the gallows.

One way and another, the keepers made a very good thing out of their occupation, though jail fever made it a hazardous one. Prisoners who could not pay for any mitigation were treated barbarously, and not only by the keepers but by their fellow prisoners. The stronger stripped the weaker of clothes and robbed them of food. There were deaths every day from exposure, hunger and sickness. If there were not, Newgate would be even more hopelessly crowded than it is. In the common cells there was hardly a place to sit or lie.

Nothing but money stood between Val and such a fate as that. Never, until I saw inside the walls of Newgate, did I really understand all that money can mean.

Having money, however, I was treated with respect, and Val too, especially as the case had aroused great interest even in the fashionable world, and the keepers got good bribes from the curious to tell them about Val and me. The prisoners passed news around in the most mysterious way—any event was known in a flash from one side of the prison to the other—and I soon found that I was known to everybody, either by sight or description. I was often shouted at, sometimes in sympathy and encouragement, oftener in derision. I even got used to this notoriety. The one thing that really sickened me was the news that a number of men had offered huge bribes to the keepers to let them spend a night with Val. It must have been a source of bitter regret to them to have to refuse, but they did not dare. The case was too well known; it would cause too much scandal.

Prisoners from Newgate are tried in the court-room of the Old Sessions House, just down the road from the prison, better known as Old Bailey. Trials are held about eight times a year, I was told, a great improvement over many prisons where people are held for two or three years before their cases are heard.

The first hearing at Old Bailey after Val and Dangerfield were committed to jail was early in January, and of all the cases argued at that time it was by far the most sensational. It was, indeed, one of the most sensational heard there in many years, and was so fiercely contested as to last three days. Gallery seats were sold at such high prices that the Keeper of the Court grew rich, and was heard to wish that the trial might last for ever. Gentlemen, lords and ladies fought for six inches on a rough bench, where they would sit for hours, unable to escape, surrounded by common people, breathing all the vulgar airs they usually avoided so assiduously. Of course there were scent bottles and pomanders always at their noses. For that matter, the judges themselves held nosegays, a most incongruous note, and drenched themselves with scent to drive off the jail fever.

For the few days that it lasted, London talked of nothing but the trial. Neal and I, as secondary sensations, were stared at, talked of, written of, followed by crowds till we could scarcely get in or out of a carriage. Night and day our house had a crowd before it, staring and pointing. As the evidence grew more sensational, we were hooted and hissed. Neal grew white and frozen with rage, powerless to resent the insults the mob shouted at us both. He would have kept me from the trial, except that, as a witness, I was required to appear there.

Our few remaining friends were swept away from us in this tumult. We begged them not to expose themselves. There was nothing they could do now. All that money, influence and pleas could do had been done. Val's fate rested now with the court and ultimately, perhaps, with the King. For should the jury bring in a charge of 'Guilty' then the judges would have no recourse but to condemn her, but there was hope that the King might extend a pardon because of her madness, if he could be convinced that she was mad before she did the thing for which she was convicted.

God knows how Neal had struggled to avert this trial. He and I both swore, again and again, that the child had fallen by accident, jumping and slipping from her arms as she held him up in reproach to his father. Dangerfield, of course, swore the opposite, but was so deranged by grief and hatred, and himself accused of a murder he did not even deny, that I think the magistrate doubted his evidence. It was the evidence of the servants and his friends as to Val's behaviour *before* the night of the murder, since they were none of them there at the actual moment, that swung the scales of justice against her. They swore such dreadful things that the magistrate might be pardoned for supposing that a woman so lost to decency would do anything. The fact that she would not speak in her own defence—for at first it was considered mere obstinacy or fear—went against her too. And in the end she was committed to stand trial for murder.

When, after several days' delay, it was finally decided to put her on trial for her life, many friends who had remained uneasily faithful until then gave up and followed the earlier deserters. I suppose I should not remember this so bitterly. Apart from fear of social contamination, some of them must have been sincerely shocked by the magistrate's decision, for it is naïvely assumed by many people that justices do not make mistakes or have prejudices like themselves.

On the whole, the men were truer to us than the women. Mr. Cory came often, and lent Neal money he could ill afford. All differences between them were made up. Little Mr. Franklin, who had so adored Val, was penniless, but he had great connections, and wearied their ears endlessly to bring influence to bear. And the day after the thing was known, Mr. Parker came to the house. He did not ask for me, and I did not even know that he

268

was there, but he offered Neal everything he had, and he secured for us the services of a famous young barrister, who never sent in a bill.

It was bitter to Neal to have to accept aid for Val, but he had no choice. Every palm had to be greased, from the common keepers to the great man himself, in one way or another. He even sent to my father for help, but my father returned word that he had no money to spare. Valentine had played the fool, and now she must pay for it.

"I wish I had cut my hand off before I wrote to him," Neal said, blue-white around the mouth.

"I used to think he loved her," I said wonderingly, while Mrs. Frye shuddered at the thought of a father so lost to all affection. Poor soul, she had so much to learn of a family like ours, and both Neal and I lamented that she had ever been brought into it. But she would not leave us, and he felt her companionship to be so necessary to me that he did not insist.

She even accompanied me to the trial, as gallant a little figure as I ever saw, and held my hand tightly through all the ugly revelations of the Dangerfields' marriage, only getting a little whiter now and then. I would have spared her the ordeal, but she would not hear of it.

"You must have a companion, my dear. I will not let you go alone. If you can bear it, I can."

Mrs. Frye's companionship was indeed important to me, for she was the only decent female left to support me. Miss Elin was gone, and even kind Mrs. Sylvester had drawn off, saying very frankly that though she pitied me and my sister, she could not, for the sake of her relations, be seen in public with me. She sent me things for Val, and I believe always spoke well of us. In the great, growing tide of voices against us, that was a good deal.

Voices . . . I hear them still in my dreams sometimes. . . . A great crying of voices, condemning, insinuating, saying vile things, cruel things, lying with half-truths, lying completely and shamelessly . . . some men's voices, but chiefly the high, shrill merciless voices of women. . . .

The nurse. "She would have nothing to do with the child. She complained because it resembled her husband." ("A most unusual complaint!" some wit whispered, and a titter ran up and down the benches near him, till the bailiffs pounded for order.) "She never went into the room where it was, nor asked to see it. It's my belief she had as lief it were dead all along. She hated her husband.—Yes, I often saw her with Mr. Underhill. They were always kissing and fondling together.—No, of course I was not in the room with them, what should I be doing there?—No, the door was not left open, you may be sure of *that*!" (Laughter.) "I don't know what that gentleman means about looking through keyholes. I'm sure there was no need to put oneself out to see what was going on in *that* house! I'm a decent female. I've always nursed in the most genteel houses. It was a great come-down for me to go into a merchant's house and I only did it to oblige the poor man, who was at his wits' end.——No, I never was in the house till the night the child was born, but I know what I know. She was a bad wife to him and a bad mother to her child and I'm as sure she threw her own baby down as though I saw her do it and nobody shall make me say different, and calling names and saying I spied won't make her any less a murderess!—Yes, sir, I *was* asleep when she came in for the baby, alas the day! and I'm sure it's no wonder, the way I was up all hours with it, poor puny thing, but it's a wicked lie to say it was from drink, for I'm sure that I had no more than a pint of porter with my supper, and maybe a glass of spirits afterwards to settle my stomach, but it takes more than that to overset *me*.——Well, it was gin, if you must know, but what difference does it make?"

Mrs. Betty. "Yes, I was maid to Mrs. Dangerfield. No, she was not a good mistress, sir, she was very ill-tempered and hard to please. Very vain—everybody said she was so handsome! but I'm sure it was a great deal of work for me to keep her so. She was forever complaining of the master.——Yes, sir, to me, or to Miss Jenny, or anybody. She hated him and made no secret of it.——No, I never saw him do anything against her, nor say anything. He was a patient man, we all said that. She talked very pert and rude to him. He was very generous; she never lacked for anything; she had fine dresses and jewels too, a real string of pearls, and a stomacher of brilliants, I daresay it cost ten or twenty pounds.——No, I don't know what has become of it, how should I? No, of course he didn't give it to me. I daresay Miss Jenny has it.——Yes, I mean Miss Archer. Mr. Dangerfield gave her all sorts of fine presents too, but small thanks he got for it. She was against him every chance she got and made the mistress even worse.——I don't know what you mean by that question, sir.—— Yes, I understand what the question means, but I don't understand why you should say such a thing. I'm sure I never gave the master any favours that I ought not.——No, that's not true, I never did! He was a very good master and of course we all felt for him. I'm a decent female and I won't stand here to have my character taken away. It's that Miss Archer has told you all these things. Her tongue ought to wither in her mouth!"

Mrs. Morrow. "I was well acquainted with Mr. and Mrs. Dangerfield. I went there often. He was fond of company but she was very proud and scornful. None of us liked her. She fancied herself a fine lady and thought we was none of us good enough to keep her company. She treated her husband like dirt, but I'm sure he was too good for her. We was all surprised when he came back with a wife from the country. For my part I was always sure she would run off with a lover some day; she was for-ever making eyes at the men and of course they admired her, though for my part I never thought her so excessively handsome. ——Well, sir, I am trying to give evidence; I'm sure I thought you wanted to know what the household was like. It was very ill run; there was a great deal of waste. Mrs. Dangerfield was idle and extravagant and knew no more how to manage her house than a baby. She had the worst spoiled set of servants I ever saw.——Oh, you meant about her behaviour with Mr. Underhill? Well, I must say I never saw anything out of the ordinary, but then she was sly. I always thought her sly. I daresay she may have liked him, he was a very handsome, agreeable gentleman.

———I don't know what you want me to say.———Well, I *am* trying to tell the truth but I'm sure it's very difficult. I don't want to do anybody any harm. I never liked her, I will say, and certainly she was very strange about the baby; she did not even seem to be glad it was a boy, but then, she never thought of anybody but herself."

Mrs. Collins. "I knew Mr. Dangerfield well and I was often in the company of his wife after he married, but I cannot say I was intimately acquainted with her. None of us were. She did not think we were good enough for her. I never saw any outright bad behaviour except she was very rude and pert to her husband, which is a great fault in a wife. She had not a penny to bless herself with and ought to have been glad of any husband. He was good to her so far as I know, too good; she was spoiled and so was her sister, a most odious pert young female. I do not know Mrs. Dangerfield well enough to say what she might be capable of; she was ill-tempered, and ill-tempered people do dreadful things, but I cannot say more than that."

"Yes, sir, my name is Elizabeth Andrews. Yes, I know the accused very well. I called upon her after her marriage and saw her nearly every day after that. Yes, I saw her often with Mr. Underhill and I'm sure I don't know how anybody could be so brazen. She was forever talking and whispering with him; she never spoke to anybody else when he was in the room; they never paid any heed to anybody. Once I heard her tell her husband to leave her alone, he made her sick. He seemed to love her devotedly and I'm sure we were all very sorry for him. When I heard her talk about her own child as she did I knew she was capable of anything."

Women's voices . . . one after another raised . . . malicious, self-righteous, offended, jealous . . . And the men too, not so bitter, but as damaging in their way:
    "He was a fool to marry her; she had nothing and disliked him. She was a handsome girl but treated him badly. He should

272

have shown her the rough side of his hand, but I believe he was always very indulgent towards her. She was proud and haughty; I believe she only liked Underhill because she had known him before. She liked none of us. I don't know anything about their being lovers; I never listen to women's tattle. But Dangerfield should have shown him the door. He was always a fool."

"Mrs. Dangerfield was always civil to me; people said she was proud and haughty but I never had anything to complain of. I used to think she was very free with her tongue to her husband, but she was civil enough to others. She was a well-bred lady and knew how things ought to be, but somehow it was never a pleasant house to visit. I never saw her with her child; I know nothing about that. I heard she nearly died but that is all. I met Harvey Underhill at their house; he was an arrogant squire of a fellow; we had nothing to say to each other. Yes, I saw they fancied each other; my wife mentioned it first, but I noticed it myself. I said there would be trouble there. Dangerfield was always too indulgent. But I believe he made free with the maids; I daresay Mrs. Dangerfield might not have liked that. There was blame on both sides; it is a bad business."

At the close of the second day's session Val's counsel, Mr. Case, said very earnestly to Neal, upon our return home:

"Mr. Archer, it appears to me that the charges made against your sister by all these witnesses are motivated by more than common malice. I wonder, have you any enemy who might be directing this affair, in your brother-in-law's interest?"

Neal stared at him dully, while I could not help a start. I think Mr. Case's quick eyes caught me.

"Enemies?" Neal said, at last. He sounded quite exhausted. I do not think physical torture could have caused him more agony than this trial. "We seem to have so many. But I know of none in particular. Why should we have enemies?"

"There is no saying," the lawyer answered, smoothly. "But there is a very skilful, malicious hand behind all this, and I do not think Dangerfield himself is capable of directing it."

As he left us, I followed him to the head of the stairs.

"My brother has no such enemy, perhaps," I said, in a low voice, "but my sister and I have."

"Indeed, Miss Archer?" he said, looking at me keenly. "Who is it?"

I told him, and saw that it did not come as a surprise to him.

"I have heard as much," he said, stroking his chin. "They certainly wish you ill, and have considerable power. Lord Dutton is much discredited, but his sister still has influence in high quarters. They have taken up your brother-in-law's cause for their own ends. Thank you for being so frank, Miss Archer. It is always best to know whom you have to fight."

"How does it go?" I asked him, anxiously.

He was non-committal, as lawyers always are.

"Neither well nor ill, yet. Your testimony will be of great importance. So will Dangerfield's. If he makes a good impression——" He shrugged.

"My sister is mad," I said, in a low voice. "Will they not show mercy upon that account?"

"Not necessarily," he answered. "Madness is not in itself a defence, in law."

"Then the law is damnably cruel!" I cried hotly.

"It may be so, Miss Archer. But if she is condemned, we must ask the mercy of the King. That is where these great enemies of yours may tell against us."

When he had gone, I sat for a time thinking, making up my mind. It was not easy, even then, with Val's necessity so plainly before me. But I did it at last—wrote the note and sent it off.

Lord Gould came to me that evening. Neal was out, Mrs. Frye had gone exhausted to bed, and I was alone.

He looked awkward and hangdog as he came in, but I pretended not to notice, and greeted him warmly.

"It is good of your lordship to come."

"I got your note at home. Of course I'll do anything I can. This is a bad business, eh? I'm mightily sorry, you may be sure, but what can I do?"

I had dressed in the best of my mourning, made myself look as pretty as I could. Disregarding his looks and tone, I went up to him and held out my hand.

"It is very easy, my lord. Cut the cards, and let us deal."

For a moment he looked blank, and then, understanding, got very red in the face.

"Eh?" he said. "Look here, Miss Archer, I don't quite——"

I interrupted him. "I think, my lord, you will not deny that very recently you made me an offer?"

He shifted uneasily. "I suppose I did."

"And I refused it, and therefore have no right to expect anything more of you."

He looked relieved. "That's the way of it, I believe."

"But nevertheless I do ask it. My lord, as you know, we are in very great distress and trouble. Perhaps I have no right to ask any man to share that trouble. But my need of your support is so great that I cannot be backward. If you will repeat that offer, and make me Lady Gould, I will be grateful to you till the day I die, and I will be as good a wife to you as any woman can."

He stared at me for a moment under lowering brows. "It's because of your sister. You don't care for me," he said at last, accusingly.

I was silent. No woman should be honest; it is not expected and ruins all. But I could not lie to him now. I was asking him to take up a bad cause, for my sake, and I could not add deceit and pretence.

"You don't care for me," he said again. "I did care for you, most damnably! Yes, I did, I still do. But they are throwing mud at you, and mud sticks, and I want my wife to be—to be——" He fixed there, and could not go on.

I said gently, "I understand, my lord. Never mind. I ought not to have expected it."

He came up to me with a clumsy rush and took me in his arms, hugging me as though he meant to crack my ribs.

"I don't want to let you go," he said hoarsely. "You're the only girl I ever cared tuppence about. But—there's the title, you see, and the children, and I care about that sort of thing, though

275

you mightn't think it, and I always meant to be respectable some day——" He gave a kind of groan, rubbing his cheek to and fro on my hair. "Why didn't you take me that night, Jenny? You had me for the asking. Then it would be settled. I wouldn't have deserted you, curse me if I would! But I can't, *now*. I wish I could! Jenny—you'll always hate me for this——"

"No, my lord, not at all. Only please let me go, and go away and leave me alone."

He released me slowly and reluctantly. "Jenny—is it very bad with you?"

I turned away from him. I had humiliated myself enough. "We will do very well, I hope," I said shortly. "I bid you good-night, my lord, and good fortune."

"Oh, damme!" he said, with real feeling. "I wish I could, Jenny—with all my heart. You are too good for me."

"Good-bye, Lord Gould," I said, and left him, since he could not seem to collect himself enough to go.

In my room, I sat down and laughed a little and cried a little. So it was all over now, that brief time when a man like Lord Gould would think of making me My Lady! It was not that I wanted to marry him, God knows, or that I craved the title so much, except as a weapon, but it hurt abominably to think that now I was not good enough. He had not meant it, but his words stung cruelly—— "They are throwing mud at you, and mud sticks . . . There's the title, you see, and the children . . . and I always meant to be respectable some day . . ."

I did not mind having humiliated myself, for I think he really cared for me. But I minded, horribly, that even he, a rake and a whoremonger, should think me no longer good enough to make a man's wife and mother his children.

At any rate, he was gone, and with him was gone my last chance of helping Val.

Except for my evidence, given before a great crowd and listened to very carefully by the wigged judges and eagerly by the jury. Mr. Case had advised me exactly how to give evidence.

"Speak clearly, and slowly, so that everybody can hear and

understand. Say only what you heard or saw yourself, not what anybody told you. Do not answer any questions without thinking, but do not pause so long you may be supposed to be lying. Do not be bitter against Dangerfield, or anybody, it will damage your standing as a witness. You look young and innocent, and may do your sister more good than anyone, so the prosecution will shake you if they can."

As to the truth of what I was to say, he had no advice. I suppose he did not wish to know how much was truth and how much lies. He left it to my wit to decide what to say, and afterwards merely told me that I had done well.

I said very simply all that I had to say. I had lived with the Dangerfields some five or six months, until I went to live with my brother. No, we did not part in anger; it was merely that my brother wished a mistress for his household. That had been intended since my first coming to London.

Yes, there were quarrels between my sister and her husband. (No use blinking that fact.) I did not suppose any married couple lived together in complete amity. They were not violent quarrels. She did not like his conduct with the maidservants.

No, I never heard him object to her conduct with any gentleman. He liked her to be admired. She was very much admired. Mr. Underhill was an old friend of my father's from the country; my sister had know him for half her life. Yes, it was true there had been some talk about my sister and Mr. Underhill before her marriage, and while his wife was still living, but it was idle malice. When his wife died he came to London, and naturally sought out his old friends. I did not think that he and Mr. Dangerfield liked each other especially, but there was never any objection made to his coming to the house. No, my sister and Underhill never met at my brother's except in the most casual way, as they might have met anywhere. Not more than two or three times at most.

It was all nonsense that my sister hated her husband or the child. She was gay and liked going about, and the child was delicate, so that the nurse had naturally the most care of it, but she often spoke of him and I was sure loved him dearly.

"On the night in question it was my sister's birthday. We went

277

to the opera for the occasion. Upon returning home, we found Mr. Dangerfield had returned unexpectedly from his business in Liverpool. He appeared very strange, which we set to being flown with wine. He had sent all the servants away, and opened the door to us himself. When we discovered Harvey's body, he raved and ranted very strangely, made no denial of guilt, and begged my brother and myself to save him. He blamed my sister, who was greatly shocked and distressed at this horrible affair. She ran upstairs to get her child, and held it up to him, protesting her innocence. The child woke and gave a great jump of fright, slipping from her hands. When she realised the child was dead, she became as you see her now. And Mr. Dangerfield, raving, declared that she did it on purpose, though my brother and myself were nearer and saw otherwise."

The prosecuting counsel then asked me many questions, against some of which Mr. Case protested bitterly, the judges inclining their heads to the argument and finally ruling one way or another. Answering those that were allowed taxed all my ingenuity. I trembled for an hour afterwards, not from fear, but simply from strain.

Was my brother-in-law good to me?—— Yes, he gave generously and was never unkind.

Did I think it sufficient repayment of his goodness to encourage his wife to be false to him, and to try to lie away his life afterwards?—— I did not encourage her to be false to him. I would not admit that she had been. He frankly admitted to the murder at the time, whatever he said now.

Had I ever had relations with my brother-in-law?—— If by that, sir, you mean what I suppose, it is a shameful insult to Mr. Dangerfield as well as to myself.

Why had I left his house?—— To live with my brother.

It was not because Mr. Dangerfield felt you to be so bad an influence on his wife that he would no longer have you in his house?—— No, it was not. He encouraged us to meet every day. No ban was ever put on her coming to me, and I was always welcome in his house.

Will you tell us upon your oath, Miss Archer, that you yourself have never had a lover? (This question was hotly contested by Mr. Case, and the judges at last ruled it was not germane to the issue and need not be answered. "Miss Archer," the Recorder stated, "is not on trial. Her morals do not affect this court." "They might, my lord, have affected her sister's." "Is it the prosecution's purpose to prove that Miss Archer's lover, if any, had some influence on the crime with which the prisoner is accused?" "No, my lord, only upon the wanton nature of both sisters, and the manner in which Mr. Dangerfield's confidence was abused." "It does not seem probable that a woman of twenty-two, married, with a child, would require her sister's example before she took a lover, that sister being four years or more her junior and, for any allegations made to the contrary, an innocent young girl. The question does not apply, and the witness may pass it.")

Thank God, I thought. I was more certain than ever that Mr. Case was right, and that someone was directing the questions who knew what the answer should be. No prosecuting counsel would put such a charge to a girl he believed to be innocent. It was too likely to react against him in public opinion; as in fact it did do, the judges taking my part.

It was over at last. Neal took the stand, and briefly testified to all that I had said of the night of the murder. We had decided on the story between us and, so far as I could, I tried to force myself to believe it. But I could not look at Val as she sat (by special permission of the court) and twisted her fingers endlessly, staring vacantly before her, a grim-faced officer standing behind her chair in the dock.

It had at last been accepted by everybody that she could not speak. While she was in prison many trials had been made to trick or startle her into speech. My visits had been spied on. But in the end even the most suspicious had been forced to admit that she was never heard to speak during the six weeks she spent in Newgate. Ordinarily prisoners who 'stand mute' and refuse to plead either Guilty or Not Guilty are found Guilty without more ado. (Not so very long ago, they were put to the torture to force them to plead—taken to the Press Yard and there piled with weights until they died or consented to plead.) But Mr. Case managed to be allowed to speak for her, and answered "Not Guilty" on her behalf when the charge was read.

And during the course of the trial, sitting hour after hour in the dock under the gaze of all those curious, pitiless eyes, her behaviour was such that again even the most suspicious were forced to admit that if it were acting, it was acting of such a high order it was almost as good as innocence.

Following Neal's evidence, they brought new witnesses—Harvey's landlady, coachman, chairmen, servants—anybody and everybody who could say damning things against Harvey and Val. They brought up servants from the country who testified to old scandals. At the end, they certainly had proved Val and Harvey to be lovers, flagrant lovers, and a certain tide of feeling set in towards Dangerfield. But even yet nobody could believe that a mother would wantonly destroy her child, even in revenge for her lover's death.

And at last Dangerfield testified against Val. This was the cream of the proceedings—the spice of the whole scandal. That afternoon the court-room was crowded to the roof to hear a man swear his wife was a whore and a murderess, the destroyer of his child.

I had not seen him since that horrible night. They said he had raved like a madman in jail, now against Val, now pleading for his life, then turning violently religious, so that many ladies' hearts were touched for him and they sent him Bibles and handsomely bound tracts.

A deceived husband is apt to be a ridiculous figure. But a betrayed husband who has killed his wife's lover is something of a hero, and a bereaved father is certainly a tragic figure. If Dangerfield had taken his part with any dignity or sense, I think he might have saved himself—popular opinion was certainly with him—and destroyed Val.

But instead, so terribly and insanely did he rage against her, that he brought public opinion round to her side again, and destroyed himself.

In vain his counsel tried to stop him. Even the judges, upon

280

the bench, protested with the demented man on his own behalf, having in mind his trial which was to follow immediately. He would not be silenced. He brought ghastly charges, he raved obscenely, he boasted of the murder, he reviled his wife, and he swore that she had murdered her child in cold blood and that "that bloody little wanton Jenny Archer and her damned whoreson brother had lied like devils in saying otherwise".

One thing he said that made my heart stand still. It was a "friend" he said who warned him of what was going on behind his back and suggested that he come home thus unexpectedly to catch the lovers together if he could.

I felt Neal, at my side, start. His face flushed high and then turned very white and set. I was as sure who that "friend" had been as I could possibly be of anything, and my heart turned cold at the thought that Neal might find out. It was Dutton or his sister, I felt certain, and if Neal also surmised this he would look for revenge some day, and God help us then!

In the end, both Dangerfield and my sister were separately found guilty; he, of the murder of Harvey Underhill; she, of the murder of her child. Both were condemned on the next day to be hanged.

Never have I seen anything so ghastly as Dangerfield's face as he turned it upon the black-capped judge and heard his sentence. They put a loop of string around his thumb and pulled it tight in a horrible imitation of the rope that would soon tighten around his neck. He looked down uncomprehendingly and then gave a scream and fell on his knees, shrieking to the judges for mercy. The turn-keys could not get him to his feet. They had to strike his hands off the rail, and drag him between them. He had lost the power to walk.

My sister turned her fair face on my lord, as he commanded her, and smiled that little vague smile. I thought he hesitated a second before he read the sentence, and a sort of groan, half pity, half horror, went through the court-room. They had heard her charged with every crime in the calendar, but as she stood there, playing with her fingers like a child, turning that childlike, empty, wondering stare upon her condemner, I think there was not one among them, even the women, who would not have saved her if they could. But it was too late. They had damned her amongst them, and now she must die for it.

As Neal and I left the court, Mrs. Betty threw herself upon me. She was weeping and blubbering, swearing she had meant to do no harm, had not meant to condemn her mistress, had not meant to . . .

The crowd hissed her, with angry eyes. Neal tore her hand away and thrust her fiercely back.

"You have had your way," he said. "You have destroyed both your master and mistress. Now go and say your prayers, but leave us alone."

In the next two weeks I do not think Neal slept more than a dozen hours. Every person who could or would help him—George Parker, Mr. Franklin, Mrs. Sylvester, even Miss Elin, whom he travelled all the way into the country to see—was pressed into service. He saw people of influence at Court, carrying letters from their friends. Mr. Parker induced his aunt, Mrs. Hamilton, to seek an audience with the King on Val's behalf. She had at one time been Lady-in-Waiting to the late Queen Caroline, and was well known to His Majesty, who favoured her for his wife's sake. Mr. Case drew up petitions, which many well-known persons signed. At last the King agreed to review the case; and then there ensued a pause more agonising than anything which went before.

"I don't know," Neal said, pacing up and down. He was never still now; he could not rest. "They say the King has already been much influenced against her—— Jenny!" He turned sharply and took me by the shoulders. "Do *you* know who these enemies of ours might be? Parker keeps telling me not to think of enemies, but I can't get it out of my head what that lawyer fellow said. He was shrewd—— Jenny, what do you think?"

"Dearest Neal," I said, putting my arms around him, "I think you have done all and more than anybody could do. If we have enemies, so does everybody. Mr. Parker has stood our friend; listen to him!"

"Yes, George has been a good friend," Neal said. His face worked. "I wish I could repay him!"

"He does not want repayment, I am sure of it," I said, steadily. "Only do not look for quarrels, Neal, and ruin all."

It was always in my mind, a terror, that he would learn the truth about Dutton. Nothing then could stop a duel, and nothing could save Neal.

I learned from Richard Cory that Dutton had lately returned to London, having suffered a serious violent illness in the country. I shivered at the thought of his return, though I did not fear him quite so much as long as Parker was here.

I had seen George Parker briefly at the trial. As I gave evidence, I saw his dark eyes fixed on me; he smiled encouragingly whenever I looked his way, but I thought his face showed the strain almost as much as Neal's. He did not come near me. I heard he had spent Christmas with the Burtons. No doubt it would all soon be settled between him and Kathleen Elin. Curious, I thought wearily, that I had once been so afraid of her because of Robert!

At last, late one night, there was a loud knocking and ringing at our door, and Neal went down to admit a messenger from Parker. The King had made up his mind; Mrs. Dangerfield was not to die. Next morning he signed the reprieve which took Val from Newgate and the gallows and put her instead into the asylum, Bethlehem Hospital, called by everybody Bedlam.

It was a mercy of a kind, I supposed, but the very word struck me with horror. I knew that people went there as a favourite sport, to poke and strike and torment the mad into fits, and then giggle at their antics—just as they visited the wild beasts at the Tower, only there it was not permitted to torment the animals.

Neal was so thankful, and he had worked so hard for this respite, that I could not say to him what was in my mind. I admitted it to Mr. Cory, however, and he reassured me. Money, he said, had influence at Bedlam as well as Newgate. We could certainly secure private quarters for Val, and all the comforts she needed, and when the furore had died down would probably be permitted to remove her to a private mad-house, where she might even recover her senses.

I was comforted, and God knows the day that saw Val out of Newgate was one of the happiest days of my life. It was a pale sunny day for January, and when she came out into the sunshine she smiled a little, and put up her face to it, like a child who has been ill and is let out of the house at last.

We took her to Bedlam in a private carriage, though a King's officer rode outside; and saw her housed in moderate comfort—no worse than Newgate, as far as that went, though so much worse in every other way. People say that the mad are happy. It is not true. I have seen more of Bedlam than most, and I say it is not true. Even those who ran free, relatively harmless to themselves and others, preaching, lecturing, laughing or singing, according to whatever delusion ruled them, were not happy. Do not look at the grinning faces, the meaningless laughs, the wild antics—look at the eyes. A child, lost in the dark, swept away from his friends and everything familiar and known, wandering helpless and terrified in strange streets—such a child, secretly despairing, looks out of all the eyes in Bedlam. Worse even than the sounds, the sufferings, the mockery and cruelty, is the memory of those eyes.

All I could think of, at first, as the doors opened to us and the sound swept out, was a barnyard, a barnyard gone mad—a barnyard in hell. Hissings, groanings, gruntings, crowings, one man going about yapping busily like a dog—some of the sounds were ludicrous enough in themselves. Taken together, they were hideous and terrifying. And under it always, to my ears, there ran the sound of weeping.

I do not say they do not try to cure some of the inmates. No doubt the physicians do the best they can. Most of them, at any rate. But nevertheless Bedlam is ruled by force. There are as many chains in Bedlam as in Newgate, and more bruises.

They are all jammed in together—the young and old, strong and weak, violent and helpless. In theory the sexes are divided; actually the inmates wander very much as they please, except at night, when they are shut away into wards or separate cells. There are plenty, of course, chained or locked into cells; but the greater number wander about quite unchecked, unless they make trouble, when they are chained or shut away in their turn. There are as many degrees as kinds of insanity. Bedlam is open to the public, yes—but not all of Bedlam.

The ward into which Val was put was on the gallery, a woman's ward with each inmate in a separate cell, for these were cases thought to be dangerous to themselves or others. Except that they were chained, they seemed to be better off than those who lay in the filthy straw beds of the wards down below, in that hellish din —and many of them chained also.

It did not take Neal long to persuade the keeper that Val needed no chains. They put her into a cell at the very end of the ward, with even a tiny barred window that looked into a courtyard. All these cells were bolted on the outside, and none of the women allowed to wander freely, though they said I might come and take her for walks, if she proved to be docile.

The keeper himself seemed a stupid, loutish fellow, a great oaf with ham hands and carrot-red hair. He was by no means slow to take a hint, however; as long as Neal kept putting money into his hand, he agreed to everything we said.

"The Governor has given us a pass," I said, lingering, though I could see that Neal was sickened by the place and longed to get away. "May I come and see her at any time?"

"Any time, miss, any time at all!" he agreed cordially. "I daresay you'll find her much better after a time. She'll get the very best of care, miss, I do assure you."

And he went on to boast of Bedlam, its great reputation in the world, its many cures, the happiness and good health of the inmates . . . And I listened, and simpered, and agreed to it all, with that devil's cauldron boiling under my feet . . . It seemed to me I *could* not go away and leave her there.

But Val herself was as insensible of her surroundings as she had been in Newgate, and we left her there at last, smiling the perpetual vague smile, sitting on the edge of her narrow bed, the little fingers, wasted now almost to the bone, forming soundlessly and endlessly their delicate patterns.

So far as we could tell afterwards, she was well treated. She was so quiet and easy to manage that they at last let her walk with me out in the grounds. The keepers were no more averse to having their palms crossed with silver than the warders at Newgate, and treated her, at least in our presence, with some deference as the source of all this wealth. Neal was running deep into debt, but what could we do? Better Newgate, better the gallows, than to be chained down there in the common wards, where the helpless and the friendless suffered out their terrible days, teased and mocked at by every City oaf with twopence to pay at the door. God, that men should be so ghastly cruel to one another!

The keepers swore that she should not be exhibited, and the porter at the door told me this promise had been kept. I do not know whether he lied or not. Very likely he did. Big bribes would be offered for a sight of the beautiful and notorious Mrs. Dangerfield. But for their own sakes, as a good investment, they would protect her. As long as we paid. If Newgate first taught me the real value of money, it was Bedlam that drove the lesson home.

Following Val's reprieve, still more efforts were made by his friends on Dangerfield's behalf. He was twice reprieved, so that it was the end of January before the sentence was carried out. I think that to the very last moment he believed a pardon would come. They say that on the gallows he could not stand alone from terror, and made such a poor show, whimpering and shrieking, that the crowd hooted him and threw filth. When he was turned off, the men hired to pull on his legs and end his agony quickly tried to get to him, but the malice of the crowd held them back, and the wretched man danced and writhed a long time upon the rope before he died.

"Don't tell me!" I begged Neal, who had heard it all from Richard Cory. "I don't want to hear. Poor wretch!"

"He deserved it," Neal said, viciously.

I said nothing. I was thinking that it was a long way from the assembly rooms in Ashton, where he first saw Val, to the gallows in Tyburn, and yet he had come that path in less than two years. We are all so helpless! I suppose he could not help being the man he was. His childhood was miserable; his mother a whore who deserted him, his father by turns brutal and indifferent. Perhaps it was that easy desertion that made him so mad against Val for thinking of leaving her child. No one would ever know how much Harvey might have insulted and provoked him, till he took up that pistol to silence him. And afterwards, I think he was in his way as mad as Val. The greatest crime of all had been my father's, to marry her to such a man. And for that crime there was no punishment. Not even remorse, for my father was not that kind of man.

"It has all been so hideous," I said at last, slowly. "Now it is over, Neal, let us not talk about it any more. Perhaps Val will get well, and we can take her away. Meanwhile, what shall we do? We can't stay here."

"No. We'll take lodgings somewhere else—nearer Bethlehem." He hesitated. "The fact is, Jenny, we must save money. If you can manage with one or two servants——"

"With none; but what about Mrs. Frye?"

"Miss Elin has offered to take her as her companion. Of course she does not want to leave you, Jenny, but I think it would be for the best."

So the little lady went away in Lord Burton's carriage, weeping bitterly at leaving me. I did not cry. I was past it. Every change, and every loss, only hardened me the more. One blow had come so quickly upon another that I felt a kind of indifference. Happiness was so far off, and forgotten, that I did not suffer so much from its loss as I had done. Only to have the worst over, and be alone——

We took cheaper lodgings presently, in Holborn, within easier distance of Bedlam. I left the Browns with regret. They had been kind, civil people, even at the worst, and we had certainly cause to be grateful to them. Because of the notoriety, I imagine they were not sorry to have us out of the house, though too kind to ask us to go.

Our new landlord was a surly, independent fellow, who paid us little attention, being chiefly occupied with quarrelling with his wife, a big noisy harridan. We kept Neal's manservant, and took a new maid, who lodged in the attic. The landlord's wife cooked and served our meals, and our own servants did the rest.

At first neither Neal nor I would go out, but at last people ceased to follow us and stare, and presently he began to visit the coffee-houses again, and even spend the evenings with a friend or two. He repulsed fiercely any attempt at sympathy or curiosity, and would have nothing to do with any friend who had not been true throughout, like Franklin and Cory.

We were both changed, Neal and I, but he more greatly, I think. He had lost half his good looks during that dreadful time, and never gained them back, remaining haggard and nervous. I fear his friends found his company somewhat trying. He was morose one moment, and even quarrelsome the next. The old gaiety, the old sweetness and spirit, were all gone. His pride had suffered such dreadful humiliations that he could no longer bear himself easily, but was always on the look-out for an insult, and always fancying an affront where there was none.

Cory was himself too spirited to bear it, and at last their friendship was quite broken off, but little Andy Franklin was always faithful. What would we have done without him? He came every day to see us, bringing me presents, paying me compliments, cheering Neal up, urging us both to come with him to the theatre, or some public place, and get the first appearance over. I thought his advice wise, but Neal said grimly, "My sister has been stared at and talked of enough, Franklin. Home is the best place for her."

He was not exactly bitter to me, but very dark and silent. Sometimes he would caress me so passionately that it troubled me, and then for days hardly speak. The visits to Val were torture to him, and yet he would not let me go alone. And if a man so much as dared to glance at me, Neal's hand was at his hip in a minute. His sisters had been his pride, and he was beside himself with the agony of having seen them publicly shamed. He minded it far more than I.

So things went very wearily with me through that cold, dark winter. I had no companionship except Neal's, and his did not give me much comfort. The landlady was a gross, common woman, much below the level of Mrs. Brown, and I would not stoop to make a gossip of my servant, who in fact was too stupid to fill the role. Neal had chosen her, I believe, simply because she *was* too slow and stupid to talk. His own manservant, a very superior fellow, was entirely faithful to him and, I think, not a little sorry for me. He would often linger in the room to bring me news and tell me little items of interest about our neighbours, trying to amuse me.

"I do hate to see you so poorly, miss!" he exclaimed one day.

I shook my head. "I'm not poorly, John. It's only that I'm so tired."

"I'm sure I don't wonder, miss. I never see you resting."

"I'm so tired I *can't* rest. I wish I could drink gin, like that woman across the street. It makes her happy for hours at a time, and then it puts her to sleep."

He looked horrified. "Don't you even think of it, miss!"

I smiled faintly, shaking my head. "No, John, don't be frightened. I never will." I had seen in Newgate, and saw every day in Bedlam, what Madame Geneva could do for her disciples. It was better to suffer sober.

"I wish my master was of your mind, miss," John said, in a low voice, and at once went out as though regretting the liberty. But I could not have rebuked him. It was only too true that Neal was drinking too much, coming home quite overcome, waking to sickness and repentance and a darker despair, and then drinking again to find surcease for a little while. Franklin did what he could to check it, put Neal had something of my father in him—he was stubborn, and there was a natural craving for drink in him.

So, as I say, things went darkly and wearily with me, and if it had not been for Val, I think I might have gone to the river one of those gloomy winter days simply to have it all over. It did not seem possible I should ever be happy again.

Even a proposal from Mr. Cory, who came secretly to the house when Neal was away, did not lighten my spirits. I thanked him with sincerest gratitude, but told him I was in no state to be wife or sweetheart to anybody. I was, in truth, astonished at his offer, and when he went away, seeming much cast down at the refusal, could only wonder that he had been loving me all this while.

With Neal gone so much, our lodgings were intolerable to me. When I got over my first fear of being recognised I took to walking a good deal, going out late in the afternoon when the dusk concealed me but before it was dangerous to be abroad. I used to go and walk in Lincoln Inn's Fields, and scarcely anybody disturbed me. Now and then men spoke to me, but I always repulsed them, and I spoke so shrewishly and showed so little inclination to be agreeable that they usually made off in short order.

One day, however, I noticed that a man was following me. I walked more quickly, but he persisted, and at last I turned right round, meaning to repulse him and have done with it, or call for help if necessary. There was always plenty of traffic in Holborn.

As I stood still, he came quickly up to me. It was already dusk, and I could not plainly see his face, but I suddenly recognised his figure, and my heart began to beat as I never thought it would again. It was Robert Haywood.

"Jenny!" he said. "I thought it was you. I have been searching for you everywhere."

"Why?" I said, fiercely, putting out my hand to keep him away. But he took it in his own, and the very touch of that warm strong hand made me want to cry for the comfort of it.

"My darling," he said, "forgive me! I have missed you so!"

And with that, without any more ado, I was in his arms, sobbing as though my heart would break, and he stood bending his tall head to mine, murmuring soft words of comfort, holding me tightly, warming me through and through . . . Oh God, I had been so cold, and so alone!

It was not like the old happiness. That was lost, and never could come again. But in the darkness that surrounded me, this was the only warmth there was. I think, if it had not come soon, I would have died of the cold. I had no friends, Neal neglected me, and I was not meant to live unloved and alone.

I did not deceive myself any more. I made no reproaches, and asked him for no excuses. I knew that I gave myself into the keeping of a man weak as water, a man incapable of true love, seeking me only for pleasure as he had sought me before. But at least he *did* seek me, and in his arms there was something of the old bliss, and of something I needed more—oblivion.

There was nothing else left to me. I had lost, by my own folly and wantonness, a man I really loved. There was not even his dark-eyed ghost left to haunt me. Any day I expected to hear of his engagement to Miss Elin. Only the illness of his father, of which I heard through Richard Cory, must be preventing its announcement. His father, Lord Linfield, was at the point of death, and all his family was with him at the country estate. Following a decent period of mourning, the marriage would no doubt take place. And I loved Kathleen Elin so well, I could not even hate his wife.

Once, and once only, I spoke of Kathleen to Robert. "I heard she received you with favour."

"Oh!" he smiled. "Did you? But Lord Burton, you see, objected, and the young lady is his ward."

"They say she is to marry George Parker."

He shrugged. "I wish him joy. She is charming. Too good for him."

There was no love lost between the two men. There must be an instinct that teaches them to know a rival. But so far as I could see, Robert neither regretted his loss of the heiress nor had any intention of seeking another. He seemed perfectly content with me; he was never a day away from me; we were together all the long hours that Neal was from home.

He did not make any offer of marriage, and I did not expect it. I went to him in plain wantonness, desiring him only, without love, but at least in honesty. Was it any worse than offering to cut at cards with Lord Gould simply for the money and prestige he could give me?

At any rate, it was all I had. Love I had to give, in plenty, but the man I wanted to give it to did not want it.

   .   .   .   .   .

Robert took rooms in Drury Lane, near Holborn, and I met him there nearly every afternoon. It was Val and Harvey all over again. But now I understood better the desperation that had driven her. It was so lonely and dreary at home, the hours so long, the four walls and my own thoughts such miserable companions! What must it have been for her in Dangerfield's house, seeing before her a lifetime of imprisonment and petty persecution? We women are so formed that we *must* have a home somewhere, if only in a man's arms.

When I was in Robert's arms, there returned to me something of the old bliss. God knows it was tired and tarnished almost beyond recognition, but, shabby as it was, it was still brighter and more beautiful than anything the world promised me now. I took it for what it was worth, and was grateful.

Once he said, "Darling Jenny, I used to think we were very happy together, but never so happy as this!"

I smiled, and was silent. Of course he was happier, for I had become more reasonable. I no longer asked anything of him, no longer demanded lies and protestations. I suppose it never occurred to him that in my reasonableness I might love him less. He took the moment, and did not enquire into the motive. He was wise, no doubt. How many of us can be so wise—or so indifferent?

At the end of February the weather suddenly turned and there was a warm, sleepy thaw. In the fields near Bethlehem there were blades of green, and even the rash little pale faces of snowdrops. I found one, and brought it to Val.

She took it obediently when I held it out to her. She would always take whatever you handed her, and hold it awhile gently before letting it fall. But today, after she had looked at the flower and then at me, with that wide, vaguely puzzled stare, she suddenly raised her hand and tucked the flower into her hair, turning to me again with her childish smile, as though she hoped to have pleased me.

The little action took me totally by surprise. For just a moment there was a shadow, an echo, of the past. And then it failed, and all was blank again. The small wasted hands fell into her lap and at once began to twist into those horrible, delicate fingerings. A blankness ghastlier than any grimace passed over the lovely face, fixing the eyes in that endless, unblinking stare. A gate had opened, for one brief instant, and then slipped shut again. Through such a gate, perhaps, come the fleeting visions that we call ghosts, and no ghost could have risen upon me with a greater shock, or a bitterer reminder of loss.

"Val!" I said, whispering, in a kind of terror. "Val!" For a moment I *couldn't* believe it was all gone. If I called, she *must* answer me; it was impossible that there should be nothing— *nothing*.

I seized her wrists, forcing into silence the eloquent speech of her fingers. She was not startled or frightened, but looked at me wonderingly. "Val!" I said hoarsely. "My darling! *Val*——" But she was gone. The wide eyes passed from my face and became fixed on the wall beyond. And in the grip of my hands her hands moved, and still tried to reach each other.

"Val . . ." It was no use. I let her go and laid my face down on my arms and sat so, in silence, until the keeper knocked on the door to say that the time was up.

He bolted the door behind me and grinned in acknowledgement of the coin I always gave him.

"She seems quite happy, miss," he said, falling into step beside me, looking at me with an admiration he did not trouble to conceal, at once stupid and insolent. He was a great, tall, strong fellow, with carrot-red hair, perpetually grinning.

"Yes—quite happy."

"They often are, miss. I often say they're happier than what we are, what have got all our senses.——Fine weather for the time of year, miss!"

But that night the weather broke, in a flurry of rain and even a few flakes of snow, hardening in the morning to bitter frost. Winter had come again.

One morning, as I sat over breakfast with Neal, I was taken with a sudden dizziness, followed by a violent attack of nausea. I was scarcely able to get out of the room in time, the sickness was so sharp and wrenching. Neal, who followed me in great concern, insisted that I must have a physician.

"No, Neal, please!" I gasped. I shut my eyes against a new whirling attack of sickness, and protested desperately, "I ate too much of the fish last night. You said it was not fresh—— But it's nothing. You know I'm never sick. I——"

"You're sick now. Jenny, you look very ill! Let me send for a physician. The landlady will know of a good man."

"Oh no, Neal, *please*! You know how I hate being doctored. I'm all right, I tell you! See, it's all over now."

He hesitated. "You do look much better," he said, doubtfully. "But, mind, if you don't feel well, we must have somebody." He took me by the arms, drawing me fiercely against his chest. "I *must* take care of you, Jenny! If anything should happen to you——"

I freed myself, somewhat abruptly. "Nothing is going to happen to me, Neal, don't be foolish. I was never so well in my life. It was that wretched fish, that's all."

But when he was gone to Will's, quite reassured by my tart tone, I leaned against the wall, shutting my eyes, swamped by wave after wave of terror and despair. Now, oh God! *now* what was to be done?

There was a slight sound behind me and I turned round, hastily trying to compose my face. The servant girl stood in the door, as slouching and stupid-looking as ever. But her eyes were on my face, and for once they were not stupid. They were bright with curiosity and malice. *She knew.*

I caught my breath. "Well?" I said, more sharply than I had ever spoken to her. "What is it? What do you want? Don't stand there watching me! Have you no work to do?"

She looked sullen, but with a sort of knowing resentment, as though she thought, 'Ah, my lady, I know what's the matter with *you.*'

"There's a gentleman to see you, miss," she said. "I'm sure I didn't mean to be watching you. I thought maybe you was not feeling so well."

"I feel perfectly well!" I snapped. "Show the gentleman in at once."

God knows, I was in no mood to see any visitor, but I wanted to get her out of the room.

She went, returning at once to curtsey in the doorway and announce, "Lord Dutton."

I leaped up, with an exclamation, but it was too late. He was in the room. And the maid, lingering as long as she could to stare from one to the other of us, went out slowly and closed the door.

We stared at each other for a moment in silence. He looked more natural, and more nearly handsome, than I had ever seen him, dressed in riding clothes of dark olive-green, with a heavy-caped cloak of black slung over one arm. The enforced rest in the country had done him good, evidently. But nothing could change that death's-head black and white, the hair and brows so smooth and shining in contrast to the pale face that they appeared to be lacquered, like a stage mask. It gave him the look of a very devil.

At last he smiled faintly. "You appear surprised, Miss Archer. Surely you didn't think you had seen the last of me?"

With coolest effrontery he tossed his cloak across one chair and sat down upon another, viewing me with a sort of cynical amusement, to see what I would do.

I was in two minds: briefly to walk out and leave him, or to ring for the servant and desire her to get a constable. A very little reflection showed me the folly of the latter, and since the first course was always open to me, I decided it might be wise to discover his purpose, if I could. So, thanking God silently that Neal was out of the house for the next hour or two, I sat down likewise, and returned his glance as calmly as I could.

The wolfish smile grew. He said, "I knew I had not misjudged you, Miss Archer. You are not given to what I believe is called *female sensibility*. I daresay you have never had strong hysterics in your life, whereas some ladies of my acquaintance indulge them every day. Nothing could be more tedious."

"I cannot say how gratified I am, my lord, to meet with your lordship's approbation. Surely no one could be a nicer judge of behaviour!"

"Don't be ironical, child," he said, indulgently. "It is not at all good style."

He crossed his arms and leaned back, glancing around him.

"This is a very ugly place. I am sorry to see you in such surroundings. It is true, then, that your brother spent all his fortune upon Mrs. Dangerfield's trial?"

I gasped for breath. "You—you must know! How much did you spend, my lord, upon the other side?"

He shook his head calmly. "Not one penny, my dear. I have no money to throw away in that fashion. I attended your brother-in-law's hanging, and have rarely seen a countenance that looked better upon the gallows."

I was much taken aback, and stared at him frowningly. Ordinarily I would not have credited his word under oath, but there was something in his manner of speech now which curiously inclined me to believe him.

"If it was not you," I said at last, suspiciously, "then who was it?"

"Oh," he said, carelessly, "I thought you would recognise the hand. 'Tis a very characteristic one. There is a family likeness, which I suppose has misled you."

"Mrs. Allison!"

"Of course. Surely you must know, child, how she hates you. It is positively a compliment, for I do not think she has ever taken the trouble to dislike anyone so much before."

"It is a compliment I am not aware of deserving," I said, trying to speak calmly. "I do not know what I have done to merit such enmity."

"Don't you?" he said, smoothly. The black eyes, narrow, opaque and bright—snake's eyes—regarded me expressionlessly. "I am sure, if you take the trouble, you can guess."

"Because of you?"

He gave a short laugh. "She is not such a devoted sister as all that! Come, come, try to guess! Why, Miss Archer, how many lovers have you had? Only one, to my knowledge, but perhaps you are even cleverer than I think."

I gazed at him, thunderstruck. "She—she is jealous? Because of——"

"Robert Haywood. Don't be shy, my dear. Your little affairs don't shock me in the least. Yes, Mr. Haywood, the beautiful, the all-conquering, has conquered my poor sister also. She is consumed with the flames of jealousy over every younger woman with whom he sleeps. And since he has slept with you longer than anybody—and quarrelled with her upon your account—she hates you worse than any woman alive. And my sister is a woman who does not, at best, love any other female!"

"But she—— Good God, she assisted us!"

"When you are forty-five years old, child, and love a man twenty years younger than yourself, you may be surprised to find what you will do to please him. But you will not, I think, love your rivals any the better for the humiliation."

I could not speak. Liar that he was, I knew he was not lying now. He had spoken of his sister with boundless contempt, but also with something of pity, and it was that touch of pity I never expected him to show towards any human being which told me he was speaking the truth.

It was a truth that almost choked me with its ugliness. I saw, in one lightning flash of understanding, why she had done so much for us, and why she had told me with such cruel glee of his betrayal. That painted, hoarse-voiced drunkard was his mistress as well as his bawd. All the while that I had known his love, thinking it a thing too splendid and beautiful to be really wicked, *she* had known it also. Those hours I spent with him, while she waited in the carriage—*she* had shared them, as surely as though she had been there with us——

Humiliation——good God, there was no word strong enough for it! I writhed, and even from Dutton I could not conceal my agony, though he could not know the full depth of it, and the horror that overpowered me. It was for Mrs. Allison's lover that I had thrown George Parker's love away, and it was her lover's child that I carried in me even now.

"I have shocked you, Miss Archer," Lord Dutton drawled, at last. The black eyes were fixed on me with a kind of cold-blooded curiosity. "I did not realise you were still so innocent. Pray tell me, what—or who—did you suppose Haywood lived on?"

"I never thought about it," I admitted helplessly, struggling to recover my poise. It was intolerable that I should expose myself to Dutton like this.

He smiled. "No wonder Haywood considers you the ideal mistress! Two innocents together! He is as simple as a child, you know. That is why it is so impossible for any woman to get the better of him. Stupidity is its own defence."

"He is not stupid."

"Good God! Surely you're not in love with him?" he asked, in apparently genuine surprise.

"Of course I am," I said, defiantly. "Do you suppose that I—that I sleep with a man if I do not love him?"

"You offer me an ungallant choice, Miss Archer. I must insult either your character or your intelligence. Valuing intelligence so much more highly, as I do, I admit frankly that I cannot believe a girl of sense like yourself can possibly love Robert Haywood. But admitting that he is a handsome idiot, and, I hear, makes love prettily, I think it quite possible you might be induced to enjoy what he offers."

"Lord Dutton," I said at last, as he waited smilingly for me to speak, "did you come here merely to insult me? Or had you a purpose beside?"

"My dear, I am not insulting you. I am merely putting the truth plainly before you. It has been a charming idyll. But I do you the credit to believe that your heart will not break when I tell you that it must now come to an end."

"*You* tell me!" I exclaimed contemptuously. "What is your authority, Lord Dutton? Or do you merely speak for your sister? I suppose she would have ended it long before, if she could."

"Undoubtedly," he agreed with unruffled politeness.

"I can assure you that it will take more than her orders to separate Mr. Haywood and myself!"

"Do you think so? I think Mr. Haywood will do very much as she tells him, as long as she pays the bills."

"Then why has he not done so before?"

"You will recall, child, that he once left you somewhat abruptly. What he has done once, he will do again. The fact is, Miss Archer, it is only recently that my sister learned he had returned to you. He was wise enough, at any rate, to keep that a secret!"

I could not and would not believe him. I *dared* not believe him—now. Now I must believe in my lover's good faith, or throw myself into the river at once.

I said, slowly, "Whatever he does or does not do, it is surely no concern of your lordship's. I have listened to you patiently, my lord, and now I beg you will go."

"My dear girl, I have not yet concluded my business with you."

"You can have no business with me, Lord Dutton. If you will not go, I shall leave you."

His hand darted out and caught me by the wrist. The thin bony fingers had a terrible strength in them.

"Miss Archer," he said, "you have run away from me too long. Now I am tired of playing, and we shall settle this affair once and for all. You can surely see how very much it is to your interest to oblige me!"

"Are you threatening me, Lord Dutton? I shall appeal to George Parker! You cannot silence him as you can me."

He laughed, the cruellest of laughs. "So you rely on George, do you? I believe he did have a weakness for you *once*. But since I have been able to inform him that he was no sooner out of London than you threw yourself into your old lover's arms, he has lost interest. I doubt if you can rely on his protection my dear, I really do. I am afraid he thinks you deserve none."

"George . . . You told him?"

"Of course. I am quite fond of the boy, you know. I couldn't see him deceived by a little baggage like you. Especially if you stood in the way of so excellent a young lady as Miss Elin.——— My dear, you are faint! Let me pour you a glass of wine."

I recoiled from him. God knows, George could think no worse of me than before—and what difference did it make now? But yet it seemed to me that I could forgive Dutton anything but this.

"Don't come near me!" I said, hoarsely. "Good God, I wish— I wish I could kill you! Let me go! Don't touch me! Don't———"

I struggled fiercely to throw him off without having to scream and rouse the house. It was always in my mind that I must keep Neal from any knowledge of this. But he was very strong, and my recent illness made me dizzy. I could not break his hold, and could only turn my face desperately from side to side, trying to avoid his mouth.

I saw him poised over me, bending me back so fiercely that my waist ached, the black eyes hooded like a snake about to strike. He was really horrible to me—repulsive beyond words. I thought I would die if I did not get free before that devil's mouth fastened on mine. And still I struggled in silence, trying to get one hand free to claw his face.

Next moment I felt him stagger from a violent blow, and, almost before I knew what had happened, he dropped me right to the floor, swinging round to ward off a second blow.

The fall did not hurt me. I scrambled to my feet and threw myself on Neal, screaming, "No, Neal, no! He'll kill you!"

My brother put me away from him, very gently but strongly. I had never seen him look like this. Never so handsome, even smiling a little, a kind of bright hardness about him, as though all the non-essentials had been suddenly stripped away. And I knew, though I had never seen it before, that this was the look of a man ready to kill—or to die.

"Sister," he said, distantly courteous, "will you do me the favour to leave us?"

I looked at Dutton. He had recovered himself and stood disdainfully returning my brother's gaze. Neither of them spared so

300

much as a glance for me. I, the cause of the quarrel, had already ceased to exist for them both. Till that moment, I never knew how far apart men and women can be.

Remonstrance was useless. The affront had been given, a blow had been struck. Neither man could turn back now and hold up his head again among gentlemen. Dutton, no doubt, was sure of himself, and my brother past caring.

I went dumbly to the door. Neal was going to die, and I could not even speak a word of protest. All I could do was let him go with dignity. Tears and protestations would only distress and humiliate him.

They stood in silence until I went out. Indeed, they did not speak for a minute or two after I had gone. I know, because I threw myself on my knees, careless of who might see me, and listened at the crack of the door, bending every nerve in my body to hear what might be said.

I have very keen ears, and the door sagged and fitted ill. Though they spoke so low, especially my brother, I heard nearly every word distinctly, and could guess what I did not hear.

Neal spoke first. "You will meet me, of course," he said, politely. It was not a question.

"It will be my pleasure," Dutton returned. I could tell by his voice that he was smiling. The wolf smelled blood.

"If you will be so good as to name your seconds, my lord, I will send my friends to wait on them."

"Oh, Alverson will do. He can find some other fellow," Dutton said carelessly. "I suppose you won't want to delay."

"No more than your lordship."

"I am quite at your command, Mr. Archer. I only need an hour or two to make arrangements for leaving the country."

The inference was plain. He expected—and intended—to kill Neal, and therefore would find it necessary to leave England for a while.

Neal gave a short laugh. "Then I will bid your lordship good morning."

I heard Dutton walk across the room, and sprang quickly to my feet, ready to run before the door opened. But he paused. I could hear so plainly I could even recognise the rustle as he lifted his cloak from the chair.

"You know, Archer," he said, "it's really a pity you struck me. For if you had not done that, I might have been willing to explain."

"Explain!" Neal said, in tones more of insolence than astonishment. "What the devil do you suppose needs explaining? You have been dangling after my sisters ever since they came to town. Your character is too well known, Lord Dutton, for your conduct to require any explanation."

Perhaps the profound contempt in his tone nettled Dutton. There came into his voice that peculiar rasping drawl I had heard once or twice before.

"You mistake me, Mr. Archer. It was not *my* conduct about which I proposed to enlighten you, but that of Miss Archer."

"My lord, if you say one word regarding my sister, I may forget myself."

"How very touchy!" Dutton drawled. "I merely wished to explain that she is not worth dying for. Really she isn't, you know. Or if you don't, you are the only man in London who doesn't."

"Get out!" Neal said fiercely. "Get out, unless you want to be horse-whipped here."

"Gently, Mr. Archer. I am not so easily handled as you think. One word only. On the night you lost your pretty sister at Vauxhall, did it never occur to you to ask her where she left— *this*?"

I heard Neal draw in his breath. Very gently, I lifted the latch of the door and looked through the crack. If I had pulled the door down, I do not think either of them would have noticed me.

Dutton stood, somewhat in the manner of a master showman, with his cloak opened and swirled out before him. Black on the outside, it was lined with a peculiarly lovely and vivid shade of flame silk, a silk very distinctive and fine. Val's cloak! I recognised it instantly, even in this bizarre setting. Good God! Would any man but Dutton conceive such a fantasy, carrying the reminder of his humiliation always with him? He *was* mad. But that would not save Neal.

My brother too recognised the cloak. He had his back to me, while Dutton stood in profile, but yet I knew he had recognised it, even before I spoke.

"That was Valentine's," he said, slowly. "She lent it to Jenny that night. How do you come by it?"

"She left it in my room," Dutton said calmly.

I held my breath. Of all the things he could allege against me, in this at any rate I was innocent. It would be ironic indeed if Neal believed the proof of this!

He said bitterly, "My lord, you are so great a liar that I can scarcely insult you by telling you so. Wherever my sister left that cloak, and however you came by it, I know you lie in what you are hinting. My sister is innocent—hardly more than a child. Any man but you would be ashamed to speak evil of her."

"Oh, I am not speaking evil," Dutton assured him cheerfully. He swept the cloak over his arm again. "I yield to no man in my admiration of Miss Archer's charms. They are not so innocent as you think—that is all."

"My lord, I will give you one minute to leave by the door. After that I will take great pleasure in pitching you out of the window."

"Very well," Dutton drawled. He turned so suddenly that I had scarcely time to close the door. I do not know whether he saw me or not. At any rate he gave no sign. "I am sorry for you, Archer," he continued. "It is a pity to die deceived. If you should decide after all that you would like to know the truth about Miss Jenny, I suggest you ask my sister, Mrs. Allison. She can tell you all about the meetings she has arranged—and all about the gentleman who has been the young lady's lover since last spring. Ah—ah, Mr. Archer! You can't threaten a man you've challenged. It simply isn't done."

I felt his hand upon the latch on the other side of the door, and fled down the hall, concealing myself in the open door of the dining-room.

The drawing-room door opened. For the benefit of anyone

303

who might be within hearing, Lord Dutton said with artificial politeness, "Good day, Mr. Archer. I have enjoyed our conversation. Pray let me know when I may have the honour of waiting on you again."

He walked briskly down the hall. Drawing back, I caught a glimpse of him as he passed. He was smiling. With one foot upon the stair he turned back, evidently facing Neal, whom I could not see.

"My compliments to Miss Archer," he said. "She is even cleverer than I thought her."

He saluted Neal and then, with insolent irony, bowed to me as I stood half hidden within the doorway. As he walked quickly down the stairs, the cloak floated open and showed its lining, like a tongue of flame coiled round his arm.

For a moment I stood in the dark dining-room, afraid to move. With the bang of the front door an absolute silence descended on the house, as though already someone had died and the rooms were hushed in mourning.

It took all the courage I had to break that silence, and go to him. I could not do it at once. I stood there in the dark, the curtains drawn against a wintry sun, staring into the shadows. Never, never would it have occurred to me to save Neal in this way. But now that the way had been shown me, why should I not take it? It needed only courage. Val's life was ruined, and mine, but something might still remain to Neal.

He was at the desk, writing, when I went in. My feet were silent on the rug, and when I laid my hand on his shoulder he started, instinctively shielding what he was writing.

"Jenny! I didn't hear you come in." He smiled at me, that artificially cheerful smile with which men lie to their women-folk. "It's fortunate I came back when I did, isn't it? You were so ill this morning—I could not be easy about you. But, Jenny, you should have told me before about Dutton. He won't trouble you again."

"Neal," I said, slowly, "you mustn't fight him."

"Fight him?" he said, with an assumed look of surrpise that

304

would not have deceived an idiot. "My dearest child, don't be absurd! Of course we aren't going to fight. He apologised, and that was the end of it."

"It's no use, Neal. I listened, and heard it all."

"Jenny, you ought not to have done that," he said sternly, his smile fading. "You had no right."

"You are all I have in the world, Neal," I said, struggling to speak calmly. "What will become of me if anything should happen to you? What will become of Val? How can you say that I have no right?"

He got up abruptly, jerking the chair out of the way with an impatient hand.

"Nothing will happen to me! Very likely Dutton will apologise before we meet, and that will be the end of it."

"Oh, Neal," I said, wearily, "what is the ust of telling me such things? Dutton is a killer, and he would be torn in pieces before he apologised to anybody. You struck him. He'll kill you if he can."

He shrugged, lifting his eyebrows. The worldly pose was good, but I knew him too well.

"My dear sister," he said, "you seem to have very little faith in my power to defend myself."

I went up to him and laid my hands upon his arms. He stood very still, looking down at me. I could feel how tense he was, deliberately withdrawn.

"Neal," I said, "it is not only your life that Dutton will take. It is mine, and Val's. He will never apologise; but cannot you?"

"No, Jenny. I cannot. Not even for you. Not even for Val."

The words were very gently spoken, but I turned away from them hopelessly, my hands slipping from his sleeves.

"I *cannot*," he said again, almost in apology. He came up behind me, his grip gentle on my shoulders. "Dearest Jenny, you would not wish to see me dishonoured?"

"I don't understand honour," I answered bitterly. "I only know that he wants to kill you, and that you are going to die to please him. But I want you to live. Oh God, God, I can't bear it if anything happens to you!"

305

"Dearest Jenny! Darling Jenny! Don't cry. You mustn't despair. I'll do my best to make a fight of it, you may be sure. But if I die—" his tone was studiedly light, "—it will be in a good cause, little sister. The best I could ever have."

It seemed to me my heart stood still. I disengaged myself from him with a kind of violence.

"No! Neal—it isn't. It isn't a good cause. That's why you mustn't fight."

"Jenny, you don't understand what I mean."

"Yes," I whispered. I stood with my back to him because I dared not look him in the face. "I understand. It's because of me. But Dutton was right. I'm not worth fighting for. Neal . . . everything he said was true. It was all true."

"You don't know what you're saying," he answered at last. There was a curious deadness in his tone.

I twisted my hands together. The pain gave me courage to go on.

"I'm *not* innocent or good, Neal. Ever since I came to London I've been deceiving you, and Val, and everybody. I've had lovers——"

He seized me fiercely by the arm, twisting me round to face him. I thought he was going to strike me, and hung back in fear. I had never quite forgotten that terrible night at Val's. I thought he would kill me then, and for an instant I thought he would kill me now. His face was all distorted, with a white line around the lips.

"Be still!" he said, gratingly. He shook me furiously. "Be still! Don't say such things! You don't know what you're saying."

He drew a long breath, trying to steady himself. "That's it," he said, as if to himself. "You don't know what you are saying, Jenny. You want to stop me fighting. But you mustn't say such things. Don't you know I'd rather die ten times over than hear you say such things of yourself?"

It was as if he begged for mercy. And looking into his distorted face, my resolution wavered and fell. Not from fear. As God is my witness, not because I was afraid of him. But because I could not bear to strike him such a blow.

306

"Neal . . ." I began hesitantly. Even as I spoke, I still had not made up my mind what to say. And now I never shall know.

For, interrupting me, the maid came suddenly into the room with a glass of something in her hand. "Oh, miss——" she began, breathlessly.

Neal turned on her with a fury that showed the stretch of his nerves. He damned her, and told her to get out and leave us alone. But she persisted, the dull eyes bright with that same malice I had observed before.

"Oh, sir, I'm sure I beg pardon, but as Miss was so sick this morning I made bold to bring her something for the ease of her stomach."

"Your mistress is perfectly well now," Neal said impatiently. "Take it away. Or leave it, and go."

Instead she drew a step nearer, holding out the glass with that irritating persistence.

"Do try it, miss. I'm sure it will ease you. The lady in the house where I was before always partook of it in the morning when she was in your condition."

The words hung in the air for a moment in absolute silence. Neal frowned at her. "What the devil do you mean, girl?" he said. "What condition?"

And then the common meaning of the word penetrated his understanding. He swore, choking, and leaped at her, striking the glass out of her hand. It was some queer dark liquid, and it splashed high into the air, staining the walls, the floor, and even the ceiling. He followed up the blow with another and another, she screaming and trying to cover her head with her arms, struggling and falling towards the door.

"Fool! Idiot! Whore! Slut! Bitch!"

She screamed and screamed, while his heavy blows fell anywhere, head, shoulders and back. With one hand he beat her, with the other he thrust her towards the door.

"Get out! Out of the house! Never come back, or I'll kill you, do you hear? Get out!" As she scuttled through the door he slammed it after her so violently that the house shuddered with it. I could hear her wailing and sobbing her way down the stairs.

Then he turned and came slowly and quietly towards me. I tried not to cringe, but Dutton himself never looked more mad, or more deadly.

"Now, Jenny," he said, speaking very softly, standing right before me without touching me, "tell me the truth. No lies now! The truth. Is that fool right? Are you with child?"

I could not speak. I simply nodded.

"It crossed my mind this morning," he said, after a pause more horrible to me than any violence. "It was so like Val as she was—— But I was ashamed of myself for the thought. You, my little sister! My innocent little sister!"

"Neal . . ."

The powerful hands were around my neck. Shaking me, choking me, the same cruel grip with which he had so terrified me before. But this time, I thought, he won't relent . . .

Black and red waves washed over my vision. I clawed at his hands helplessly. And as the blood tightened in my brain till I thought it would burst, I knew how it felt to die by hanging, and suffered the agony and terror that Dangerfield must have known.

And then he let me go. He must have thrown me into a chair, for I found myself there, gasping and gasping for breath, the sweat running in streams all over my body. I had never quite lost consciousness, but I have no idea how long it was before he let me go.

When I had any thought to spare for anyone but myself, or could hear anything except my own hoarse crowing breaths, I became aware that Neal was still in the room. He sat in a chair near me, his head bent down on his arms. He seemed to huddle upon himself like a man broken. The very brightness of his fair hair had faded. When at last he raised his head the handsome face looked pinched and old. I had meant to save him, and this was what I had done to him instead.

His eyes avoided my face as though he could not bear the sight of me.

He said, in the curious flat voice of exhaustion, "I'm sorry,

Jenny. But you might have spared me this, I think. The chances are I will be dead by tonight . . . I would have died happier."

I could only whisper, "I meant to save you. Neal—you won't fight Dutton *now*?"

He smiled faintly. The saddest smile I think I ever saw.

"Now? Because I know the truth, you mean? If I withdraw, all London will know it for the truth."

"Does it matter? I don't care. I'll go away to the country . . . Neal, if only you could forget us—Val and me!"

He laughed bitterly. "If only I could! One sister mad and the other a whore!" And then, as I winced in silence, he added hastily, in a low voice, "Tell me one thing. Who is the man?"

I was silent still, and he repeated, with a touch of his former fierceness, "Who is it? If I live after this meeting with Dutton—— Or *is* it Dutton?"

"No," I whispered, dully. "Not Dutton. No one that you know. Someone that I met—through Mrs. Allison." It was only half a lie.

He seemed curiously relieved. "He must marry you, Jenny. Does—does he know?"

I shook my head. He hesitated, and then for a while sat silent, staring before him. At last he rose, with a heart-breaking attempt at his old gaily swaggering carriage.

"I must be about my business. Dutton will think I have turned craven."

I sat speechless, almost emotionless. I had ruined myself, and broken his heart, and all for nothing. As he said, I might have let him die happy.

"Jenny——"

I started a little, finding him so close beside me. I believe he thought I flinched in fear, and a flush came into his pale face.

"I didn't mean to hurt you," he said in a low voice. "Forgive me, Jenny." He paused an instant and then, very briefly and gently, touched my hair with his hand. "It is my fault too," he said. "I left you alone too much. I thought—it would be better——" He checked abruptly and turned away.

He was at the door before I could speak. "Neal . . ." He

309

turned back reluctantly. I saw how he dreaded a scene, and yet I could not let him go without one word. I whispered, at last, "Neal, I have never loved anyone as I love you."

I saw his face break. He put up one hand, as if to ward off a blow, and turned, fumbling blindly at the door latch. For a moment I thought still that he would turn back. But he did not. The door opened, and closed behind him. He was gone. And I was left to wait till they brought me word that he was dead.

The landlady came upstairs sometime during the afternoon with my dinner. She was very cross, and very curious. Torn between the two emotions, she fussed about the room, scolding and complaining, and thrusting a shrewd series of questions at me between her complaints. I hardly even heard her, and my silence defeated her at last.

"Well, I'm sure!" she said, flouncing to the door. "A body might expect a civil word, after all the trouble I've gone to, and I'm sure it's not my business to be fetching and carrying, all because your brother has a temper. Poor girl, she was half dead, and I must say I advised her to have the law on him, for abuse is what I don't hold with, miss, whether it's your brother or another. And those that can't pay for better service, to be sure they might have to be content with worse. I hope you won't be expecting me to run and fetch for you, for I won't do it, and that's flat. If you want your supper you may come down and get it yourself. And let me tell you, miss, that your brother owes me two months' rent, so it isn't for you and him to be putting on airs, and if he comes home in *that* condition much oftener he may just walk, and you with him, for I'm a decent respectable woman, and I won't have it in my house, and I've told my husband so." She fetched breath. "And if you don't mean to eat that good chicken, miss, you'd better tell me, for I scrimped my poor man, and if it isn't to be appreciated why should he go without?"

"I'm not hungry," I said, as she at last paused for an answer. "Take it to your husband, by all means."

She snatched up the tray and slapped it on her great wedge of a hip. "Well, I'm sure," she said, staring at me with both dislike and avid curiosity on her fat red face, "there's some mighty odd things happening about here, and I only hope to goodness there's no talk or scandal, for we've always been respectable, and if we'd known when you came about the trial and all——"

"That's a lie," I said, flatly. "You knew it all. There was no one in London who did not know it. You took us because my brother paid twice what the rooms were worth."

"And cheap to you at the price!" she cried shrilly. "Nobody else would have you! And you may walk, miss, do you hear, walk! I've had enough. You can tell Mr. Archer so when he comes home, if he ever does."

It was merely a slap at random, but I caught my breath. Grinning triumphantly, she waited for me to speak, but when I did not answer, she repeated her threat, a trifle less vigorously, and went out, slamming the door. Before her steps died away on the stairs I had forgotten her.

How long before I could expect news? Neal had left me at noon. It would take two or three hours for the seconds to meet and arrange details. Duels were more often fought in the morning, because of the better light, but I was sure this one would not be delayed so long. They would fight before dusk, and dusk still came early. By four o'clock—by five at the latest—I should have news.

I sat by the window of the shabby drawing-room, watching the street. There was no one but Franklin to be his second, and it was Franklin who would bring me the news. Neal must have taken his manservant, or John would have waited on me before this, but Franklin would not leave me to hear of my brother's death from a servant.

I never had the slightest hope for Neal. I had heard duels described, and a thousand times on that dark afternoon I watched them fight, and saw him die . . .

They would meet in some secluded place, both parties saluting each other formally. There would be a surgeon, and perhaps the grooms watching from a distance. Neal and Dutton would be wearing dark clothes, to form as small a target as possible. I felt certain it would be pistols. Dutton was the challenged party and therefore had the choice of weapons, and he was a deadly swordsman. But he was still more famous with the pistols. In fence there is always a chance of a slip—a moment's relaxation, a stumble, an unexpected dangerous thrust—and Neal was the younger man by many years. But pistols equalise everything: age, strength, determination. Neal was high-strung, and Dutton deadly cold. He could not miss.

The pistols, long-nosed and deadly, would be brought unloaded in their box and loaded on the ground by one second in the presence of the others. Dutton would take first choice. Back to back, the two men would pace off the distance, stand for the count, and turn on Three! to fire.

I saw it all so plainly. As plainly as though I were there, and could see it done, and hear their voices. I heard the command given, saw the men wheel, heard the shots fired together . . .

And afterwards I saw always the same scene—Neal lying quietly on the grass, his face pale against the dark turf, a little blood, perhaps, on his coat . . .

Dutton would not be disturbed. He had killed two men in duels before this. It would be necessary for him to leave the country for a while, but, as he had assured Neal, his plans for that eventuality would be already made. No one could punish him. He would go beyond the reach of the law for a while, and the law would be glad to forget him. No gentleman would think of condemning him for what he had done. It was what they call a fair fight. The fact that one man had scarcely ever held a pistol in his hand, and the other could snap out the pips on a playing card at twenty paces, would not be held an argument against it. Dutton was not a popular man, and his popularity would not be increased by my brother's death, but why should he care for that?

The little clock on the mantelpiece whirred, choked and struck the hour. It was four o'clock—only four! It seemed to me that all the days and hours I had spent in London were shorter than this one afternoon.

Four o'clock . . . Somewhere else, a long time ago, another

girl in another world and another life had promised to meet her lover at four o'clock . . . Robert would wait a while, and wonder, little dreaming what had occurred to keep me from him, and how much he himself had contributed to it.

It seemed to me that the bright figure of my lover grew dim and far-away, even as I thought of him. My lover—Mrs. Allison's lover. The hours of this endless day had driven him so far from me that I could not even remember clearly how he looked. The vision of my brother's pale face rose between us, and blotted Robert out. We would never meet again without Neal between us. For between us we had broken his heart, and driven him to his death . . .

There was a hackney coach being driven at a furious gallop down the street. People walking by turned to stare. It stopped in front of our house, as I knew it would, and little Franklin jumped out, staring up at our windows with a pale, distressed face.

I stood up. I had a curious feeling that it would be better if I took the blow standing, as a duellist turns to meet his death. When Franklin rushed into the room, he paused, evidently taken aback by the sight of me. I am sure I looked wild and white enough.

I had some idea of sparing him, and said hoarsely, "I know he's dead. You don't need to tell me."

But little Franklin crossed the room at a run and took me in his arms.

"Not Neal!" he said urgently. "My darling—*not Neal!* He's all right. It's Dutton. He's not dead yet, but they say he will die. A shot in the chest. He fired straight at Neal and God alone knows how he missed—a miracle! It shook me up, I can tell you!" He added, with sudden consternation. "Jenny—Miss Archer! Don't faint! *Please* don't!"

But there was nothing I could do to help it.

They put me on the sofa, gave me hartshorn and water, slapped my wrists, and at last brought me round. Franklin's frightened white face, as he hung over me, showed me how long I had been unconscious. As he said later, he thought he had killed me.

The landlady, now that she had a finger in the pie, and could bustle and meddle to her heart's content, softened her tone towards me somewhat. She was sure, she said, that she had no idea the young lady had had such a thing on her mind. To be sure, it was enough to frighten anybody. Duels were horrid things, and she was sure gentlemen ought not to fight them, but of course they would have their way. To be sure, any young lady of sensibility would swoon to think of her brother being in such danger. And was Mr. Archer really quite safe? We should all thank the Lord for having preserved him. And the gentleman he fought with—— A Viscount, was he? Only think of that now! To be sure, she had always supposed us to be well connected.

She appeared to think that duelling with a lord implied considerable social stature, and she was ready to assume all manner of reflected glory.

Mr. Franklin got rid of her at last, though she would not depart until I was sitting up. It was not decent for a gentleman to be alone with a lady who was reclining on a sofa.

"Do lie down, Miss Archer," Mr. Franklin implored, when she had gone. "You look dreadfully white still!"

I felt dreadful also, with a curious sandy pain behind my eyes. The glass of wine he made me drink helped a little. It did not occur to me that I was partially faint from hunger, and the woman was too stupid to think of any assistance as practical as a dish of hot food.

Leaning my head against the hard back of the sofa, I said imploringly, "I'm all right. Please tell me everything!"

"Are you sure, ma'am? Lord, I never was so frightened in my life. I thought I'd killed you, and was going to cut my throat before I told Neal."

"No, no. It was not your fault. I have not been well today. And I thought—I never thought Dutton could miss!"

"I can't think how Neal came to let you know about it beforehand," little Franklin said, with strong disapproval. "Must be touched in the head!"

"He couldn't help it," I said absently. "I listened." Seeing his shocked face, I added bitterly: "Sometimes, Mr. Franklin, females don't wish to be protected. Sometimes we even think we have a right to know the truth in matters of life and death." I saw that he was still more shocked, though he would not disagree with me at such a moment, and checked myself from saying any more. What was the use? He had been very kind to me.

"At any rate, sir, you would do me the greatest favour if you could tell me now what happened. Is Dutton really likely to die? I suppose I cannot be thought so interested in his welfare that I may not hear the truth about *that*?"

The irony quite passed him by. He said, "Oh no, ma'am, there can be no objection to your knowing about *that*. Not that there is much to know. Your brother's ball entered the chest—high—and the surgeons were in doubt whether they should try to remove it. His friends took him away."

"Was he conscious?"

"Yes, throughout. He cursed the surgeons for fools, and said he wanted to be taken to his country house. When they said it would kill him, he cursed all the more. A terrible fellow, Dutton! I shouldn't be at all surprised if he lived in spite of everything."

"And Neal was not touched at all?"

"Not a hair of his head. The ball passed so close by his throat that it clipped off part of a button. My lord was aiming for the head, you see. 'Tis the surest shot, if you are certain of your hand—— Lord, what a fool I am! Miss Jenny!"

I managed to open my eyes and smile at him. No doubt he was more convinced than ever that females ought to be protected from the truth. He looked ready to fly for the landlady's assistance, and I caught him by the hand to prevent him.

"No! Please don't. I'm quite all right. Forgive me for being so foolish. It was only that I could see it, so plainly—I did not realise how near——"

"Oh, it was a near thing. But a miss is as good as a mile, you know," he said cheerfully, watching me with anxious eyes, holding me tightly by the hand. Suddenly he became aware that he did so, and dropped it, becoming bright red. "Miss Archer—I beg pardon!"

I was touched by his shyness, and said impulsively, "Mr.

315

Franklin, you have been a good friend to my brother and to me. I hope we can make you understand how much we appreciate it."

From red, he got quite white. "Miss Archer," he said, "I couldn't prevent Neal. A gentleman must fight, you know, when—— But I was thinking of you all the while. I was thinking I had to come back here to face you. And I was going to promise you that I'd call out Dutton myself and try to kill him. I'm not a bad hand with the pistol," he said, with a lapse into boyish boastfulness.

Really, there is no limit to the absurdity of men! Or to their vanity. But the offer was seriously made, as it was seriously meant, and I could not help appreciating the spirit, if not the purpose.

"I am so glad it was not necessary. Thank God, Neal was preserved! But, sir, where is he? Why doesn't he come home? Or—surely it has not been necessary for him to leave the country yet?"

"No, no," he said, appearing embarrassed. "I did think that he would surely wish to—— But the fact is, he seemed to prefer to be alone. I am sure you can understand that, Miss Archer."

I could understand it only too well, and my heart sank. Neal was alive. He had been miraculously preserved from death—perhaps because he had no particular wish to live. But he had been left to face the fact that I had betrayed him. There was no escape for him now, in death or anywhere else. And no escape for me from the bitterness of his reproaches and his pain. The reproaches I could bear, but I dreaded inexpressibly the sight of his pain.

Mr. Franklin mistook my expression, and rose, saying that he was wearying me. I was sorry to see him go, dreading solitude again, but did not know how to keep him. I asked him, as calmly as I could, to beg Neal to come home, if he should chance to meet him anywhere.

"I shall tell him you are not well, and of course he will hurry home at once." The young man smiled at me shyly. "It makes me wish to have a sister, when I see you and Neal together."

I concealed my wince as best I could, and he left me, promising to call the next day.

316

After he was gone I sat alone in the gathering darkness, hardly knowing whether to hope for or dread Neal's step on the stair.

He was alive. That was the great thing, the greatest thing of all, beside which everything else paled into insignificance. But I could never again be to him what I had once been. The bitterness of that truth seemed to grow bitterer moment by moment as I faced it, and saw at last plainly and clearly the thing I had done.

"Jenny?"

Neal spoke low, but I woke from my doze with a start. He had come into the drawing-room so quietly I had not heard him. The candles were burning low, and the fire on the hearth was nearly dead. I blinked, and glanced involuntarily at the clock. It was upon two in the morning. I had slept, upright in my chair before the hearth, for more than an hour.

"Yes," Neal said, following my glance, "it is very late You should have been in bed long ago. Why have you waited for me, Jenny?"

He sat opposite me, his legs stretched out, his fair unpowdered head resting against the chair back. In the dim light I could see that he looked tired, but could not be sure whether he were drunk or not. He used to get a curious stiffness around his mouth when he had drunk too much, which always betrayed him. It was not there now, and his articulation was natural, if a shade too precise. But I could smell the liquor, and his hands moved on the arms of the chair with a troubled restless motion quite foreign to him, reminding me painfully of Val.

"Why did you wait for me?" Neal repeated. His tone was hard, and instead of avoiding the sight of me, he stared steadily into my face in a way that made me uncomfortable.

I knew this hard mood of his. It meant a concealed unhappiness, a trouble he did not want to admit. But what was the use to conceal it, when we had already spoken so plainly of it?

I moved nervously on my chair. The awkward posture of my nap had made my back ache. I wished that he would stop looking at me like that. Once or twice he had turned that hardness towards Val, but never before to me. I thought, sorrowfully, that

317

it was natural his manner towards me should change. It is harder for men to pretend. Once your value is lessened in a man's eyes, be he brother or lover, he will show it in his voice and look, whether he strives to conceal it or not.

"I could not go to bed and sleep until I had seen you again," I said at last, in a low voice.

Neal raised his brows. "I thought Franklin had assured you that I was safe?"

"Yes, he did so. I—I congratulate you, brother, with all my heart."

"Thanks," he said, curtly. "I aimed to kill, but I am an indifferent shot. I suppose I ought not to complain, since Dutton's aim was even less good than mine."

"It was a near miss, Mr. Franklin told me," I went on, hesitantly.

He shrugged. "Far enough," he said, with what seemed genuine indifference. "I cannot conceive what made him miss his shot. They say he never did so before."

"You sound as though you were sorry!" I said, reproachfully.

"I am glad not to have given him the satisfaction of my death. Otherwise——"

"No!" I said passionately. "Don't say that! You know you don't mean it. Why should you wish to die?"

He stood up abruptly, leaning one elbow on the mantelpiece. The movement cast his face into shadow.

"Can you think of *no* reason, Jenny?" he said.

I looked away from him, into the fire where the last red coals were slowly cooling into darkness. You could still see the pattern of the logs in the feathery greyness of the ashes, looking so substantial you could not believe a touch would shatter them.

"No," I said defiantly. "I know of no reason sufficient to make you want to die."

He put one hand suddenly over his eyes. I thought the hand trembled, and so did his voice.

"You take your fault lightly, sister."

"I hope not," I answered. In spite of all that I could do, my voice too shook. But in the long hours of that night, as I sat wait-

318

ing for him, I had resolved that I must say these things to him, and I knew I had better say them while my courage still endured. "I have been very foolish, I know, and very wrong. Perhaps, as my father used to say, I was born a wanton."

He struck out savagely with his foot, jarring one of the iron fire dogs. The log of ashes shivered in an instant into nothing.

"Don't quote my father! It's he who gave you the notion. God! Living in his house, how *should* you know the meaning of decency?"

"I *do* know the meaning! Do not be unfair to me, Neal." There was a pause, in which he was silent, his face turned away from me, his head bent down as though he were staring fixedly at the fire. "I know that I have done wrong," I went on, "and it is very likely that I will pay for it the rest of my life. I do not say that it was worth it, but the thing is done. But I wish you to know I am not so bad as Dutton painted me—not as bad as I have painted myself. I said I had had lovers. That is not true. I have had but one lover, and he would marry me if he could."

"He is married now?" It was my turn to be silent. Neal gritted his teeth. "Tell me who it is. Jenny, I *will* know."

"Not from me," I answered resolutely.

"I will find it out somehow. Why should you try to protect him?"

"Because there will be no more fighting if I can help it. I have died a thousand deaths today. *You* may not care for your life, but I———!"

I stopped abruptly, and Neal said, in somewhat softened tones, "I sent Franklin as soon as I could. I know you care for me. More than I deserve, no doubt."

"Perhaps we are both at fault in that," I said, unsteadily. "But, Neal, do not say that because I have been a fool life has lost all pleasure for you. How can I live with myself, if you cannot endure to live with me?"

"It is not that," he said rapidly. "It is not that. It is——— Oh God, must I tell you what it is? Don't you know? Don't you understand what it means to me that you—that a man has known you?"

"But I am not different, Neal! If I had married, it would be the same. Many women have lovers! Is it such a crime? How can you say that it is? Neal, have you never loved anybody? I am sure you have! You know what it is. A great pleasure—a great joy—but you are not changed. You are the same person afterwards. I am sure you have many times known love, brother! But you are my own dear brother all the same. Not changed to me. Must *I* be changed to *you*?"

In my eagerness I jumped up, and drew near him. I felt how he moved away from me, and the involuntary shrinking wounded me cruelly.

His head was still bent down. I could hardly hear him when he answered, "Yes—— Changed. Lost."

I had no pity for him in my own pain. I said bitterly, "Then you have never really loved me. It was only pride—not love.'

He turned violently and looked at me. A great change had come over his face. I was frightened to see it, not knowing what it meant, staring at him in wonder and dismay. He looked so dreadfully tormented!

"Not love?" he said hoarsely. "Not love? My God!" His voice broke so queerly I could not tell whether it was a laugh or a sob. He sat down abruptly and put his head in his hands, his face hidden from me. "You don't understand," he said, hopelessly. "Jenny—you don't understand. Oh God, it would be so much better if I were dead!"

"No, Neal," I whispered. I went back a step, leaning against the mantel, staring down at him with a kind of terror. "No . . ." But it was not his words that I was denying, though he misunderstood me.

"I tell you it would be better! We can't go on like this. Don't you see we can't go on like this?"

There was such a violence of despair in his voice I had no words to answer him. I stood in silence, staring helplessly at his agony, while wave after wave of sickness came washing over me. I well remember the harsh feeling of the stones under my hands, and how I needed the support, clinging to them as though the floor were falling away from under my feet.

I heard my own voice say, faintly, "Neal, you can't mean—you *can't*——"

"Don't say it!" he interrupted, with that same abrupt violence. "For God's sake, don't say anything. Only let me think what we must do."

My head was whirling, so strangely and horribly I did not know whether I was going to be sick, or faint, or die. I could not speak; and I dared not move; I felt as though disaster waited there in the room with us, a beast crouching ready to spring.

And all the while, in flashes like lightning strokes, one incident after another came back to my remembrance . . . the terrible scene after my abduction from Vauxhall . . . the jealousy . . . the reluctance to have me marry . . . My God, had it been there always, and I had not seen it?

It was a long time before Neal spoke again. His voice was flat and quiet; he had somehow got himself under control. "If Dutton dies, and I think he will die, I must leave England for a while in any case. It will be better if I go at once."

"Yes . . ."

"But what will you do, Jenny—as you are now?" He stumbled over the words, and though he raised his head, he would not look at me.

I saw what it cost him even to speak of it and, forgetting myself, said quickly, "Oh, I am not afraid, and perhaps I am wrong, you know. I can take care of myself."

"The difficulty, as usual, is money," he said bitterly. This was an old trouble; he could talk of it more easily. He got up quickly and began to walk up and down. "Perhaps I can raise another loan. I must be out of England for at least a year and you must have something. Perhaps you could go into the country. It is less costly there, and it would be better—for a while."

"But . . . Val?" I reminded him, hesitantly.

"Val!" he repeated despairingly. "My God, I had forgotten Val." His voice shook again, in spite of his efforts. "Would you think we three could come to so much ruin in one short year?

321

Dangerfield dead, Harvey dead, Val mad, and you and I——"

I put my hands on my throat. I was choking with an agony not at all like tears. "*Please* don't, Neal, I can't bear it!"

He looked at me at last, and I saw his face constrict. "Jenny, your throat! Your pretty little throat! Oh God, what a brute I am!"

"No, no, it doesn't hurt!" I assured him hastily. In truth, I had forgotten the bruises that were beginning to blacken around my neck, though my throat ached and was sore, and the bruises were tender enough when I pressed them.

"Are you sure?" He touched them, carefully. "Perhaps a physician should look at them. We could contrive some story——"

It was my fault, all my fault! but I began to tremble under his touch, I couldn't help it. And he suddenly began to tremble also. I tried, unobtrusively, to move away, but I could not escape his hold. I saw his face change again, as though something had broken beyond his control, and then I was in his arms, his face against mine, burning hot, the desperate broken voice saying my name over and over, as though it were some charm that still could save him.

Despite all my efforts, there ran over me shudder after shudder of recoil. It was all I could do to stay quiet in that frantic grasp. I wanted to escape—to run away. There rose up in me an instinct so powerful it could not be denied, so powerful that for a moment all the old love was forgotten in the panic of that involuntary recoil.

And he felt it; he felt and understood it all, I know that he did. It was he who drew away, with an effort as though he tore away part of himself, turning so that I could not see his face.

He said, so low that I could hardly hear him, "For God's sake, Jenny, go away . . ."

I did not know what to do; I stood hesitating; and he repeated, more strongly, "Go away, Jenny, go to bed. Tomorrow—tomorrow we will talk about what we must do."

And so, because I did not know what to do, because I was

afraid and faithless and told myself it would be best, I obeyed him and left him there—all alone.

It was incredible to me that I should sleep, and yet I did—deeply and without dreams, lying fully dressed on my bed where I had thrown myself. When I woke, and it all came back to me, I could not believe I had slept like that. But there was the sunshine on the floor to prove that it was morning—a bright winter's morning, with the first early-day sunshine we had had for weeks.

I woke with a fierce sense of urgency. I must see Neal at once. I ought never to have left him like that. If I had had my senses about me—— But it was so late, and I was so tired, and the whole day had been so like a ghastly nightmare, one shock after another—— So I excused myself.

And Neal too; of course he had not been quite sane either. He had been drinking; he had not meant all he said. It was strange how that bright patch of sunlight brought everything within reason, so that I could look at it sensibly. Perhaps it would be better if he went away for a while—because of Dutton. But he must not go thinking I shrank from him.

We would talk tomorrow, he said. And it was tomorrow now. I jumped up, with that fierce sense of urgency on me, to go to him. I would not hesitate; I would go, just as I used to, and sit on the foot of his bed, and talk to him, and make him see that I would never forsake him.

"Never, Neal! Never, never!" The words were on my lips as I ran down the hall to his room.

John, the manservant, was standing in front of the bedroom door as though he had just come out and closed it, his back to me.

"Oh—John!" I said quickly. "Is my brother still asleep? I must see him—let me wake him!"

For a moment I thought he had not heard me. He still stood, his back turned, his hand upon the latch of the door. And then as I stared, puzzled, I saw that he leaned forward with his forehead against the wood, as though he were ill, his hand closed so hard upon the latch that the knuckles showed white.

"John! What's the matter? Are you ill?"

The man turned slowly round. His face was ghastly; his eyes wide and fixed. His teeth were chattering so that he could hardly speak. "Miss—miss!" was all that he could say.

"What's the matter?" I sprang forward, and instinctively his arm rose to stop me.

"No, Miss Jenny, no! You mustn't go in! *God!*" The word seemed jerked out of him, like a sob.

I seized his arm and shook it. "John? Are you mad? What's the matter? Is my brother ill?" My heart almost stopped. Perhaps he *was* ill. Perhaps last night had been the first ravings of delirium. Smallpox . . . He had not had it, and the city was full of it. No wonder John looked so terrified, though his own face showed the scars that made him safe. "*Is* he ill? John, let me in! I'm not afraid!"

"Oh, miss!" the man groaned. His face worked; I thought he would never get the words out. "He's—oh God, he's *dead!*"

He lay in the sunlight, turning his face towards it with something almost like a smile, as though he welcomed it. But it was in the night that he had died. It must have been soon after I left him, for the cheek I touched was cold as a stone. All the old lost beauty had come back to him, and something almost of the old gaiety. He had never looked so young, never so handsome, as he lay there with the sunlight warm on the cheek that it would never warm again.

As I knelt beside him, frozen and silent, I thought of Harvey. Not even Harvey had looked quieter or more at rest than he. One had not felt the bullet that killed him; and the other had welcomed it. It was death that he had turned his face towards with that look of smiling welcome—as he had so often looked at me. And it was death that had laid that curious young beauty on his face like a promise of immortality.

Later in that day I lost the child that I had begun, and was very ill. I cannot imagine why I did not die. I felt as though the bullet in Neal's heart had killed me too, and I could have lain down there beside him and died—so gladly!

But for everyone there is his day and his hour, and this was not mine. There is a stubborn streak in our bodies that will not let us go for the wishing of it. I lived—to weep and wish that I had died.

Sometimes those who seem most our enemies do more for us than our friends. The landlord and his wife, in being cruel, had no wish to help me, but they tormented me out of the hopeless lethargy into which I had fallen, which was more than the kindness of others could do.

I had been in bed a week, and felt as though I would never leave it again, when the landlady, Mrs. Evans, burst in on me one day. John, who had been nursing me as tenderly as a woman, tried to prevent her, but she turned on him savagely and drove him out of the door.

"Now, miss!" she said, standing over me with her red fists on her hips. "I've been patient since you've been so poorly, but you're as well now as need be, if you'd give over cosseting yourself and mewling about what can't be helped."

I stared at her sullenly, out of eyes so swollen with weeping they could hardly see, and was silent.

"It's no good your sulking and looking pathetic, miss! If you've got the money to pay the rent of that bed, why, it's yours and welcome, and you may sprawl and howl in it the rest of your life if you please, but, by what I hear, your fine brother left nothing but a wagonload of debts, and two months and more rent owing us!"

"Don't you dare say a word against my brother!"

"Highty-tighty, miss! I'm sure I've no wish to say anything against the dead, though, to be sure, a suicide is a horrid thing and to have one in my house is a thing I never *will* get over and I'm sure I hope it mayn't give the place a bad name, though I daresay it will. I suppose you can't help it, nor your misfortunes neither, though by what I hear you haven't been the discreetest young lady alive, however I'll throw no stones as want none thrown. All I want from you, miss, is my rent money, and you may stay here and welcome, though there's many as would turn you out, for the trouble and scandal you've brought. But I told my husband I'm sure it's not Miss's fault her brother should do such a horrid thing and she's cried her eyes out for him as though he'd died like a decent Christian, and a fine peck of trouble he left her in, to boot. You men, I said, never think of anybody but yourselves. For you must know, miss, that if it weren't for me he'd have had you take up your bed and walk—though, to be sure, the bed is ours as well, and if you haven't the means to pay for it, miss, we'd be obliged if you'd vacate as soon as may be. Though you won't step a foot outside the house till your quarter's rent is paid, and so I tell you flat. I'll have no moonlight flittings, or the bailiffs shall come, sure as eggs is eggs! By what I hear, you know the inside of Newgate pretty well, but I daresay you won't like the Fleet much better!"

At this threat of the dreaded debtors' prison, I found the strength to face down the horrible virago.

"You shall be paid."

"I suppose you can sell some things," she acknowledged, her eyes wandering around the room. "There's that ring, and your brother's watch, and his clothes. I know some that would give you extra for the clothes, just for the sensation, you know."

I would have killed her if I could. I said, hoarsely, "You shall be paid. Never mind how. I will get up and—and write to my friends. But leave me alone. I don't want to see you. Do you hear? Don't come in here again. You'll be paid, every farthing."

She retreated, muttering about insults, and I got trembling out of bed and tried to dress. I could not quite manage that, but I put on my wrapper and sat panting in a chair, wondering what in God's name I would do. And, for the first time since Neal died, I thought of Val. I must have money for her. That was the most important thing of all.

John brought me my supper. He complained bitterly of the landlady. She would have stolen away Neal's things to sell to the crowds for sensation, if he had not prevented her. She and her husband were no better than thieves, and the man such a brute he would have thrown me into the street at once, if the physician John had called had not threatened him.

"Mr. Franklin, miss, has been here time and again. I do believe he'd do anything to help you," John hinted, hopefully.

I leaned my head wearily against the pillow. I knew, only too well, how little power Franklin had of helping anyone out of financial straits.

"Are your wages paid, John?" I asked him.

He hung down his head, and muttered, but was at last forced to admit he had not had his half-year salary.

"I must sell my things, John. Will you help me? Do you know an honest man?"

"Oh, miss!" he begged. "Please don't trouble your head for it now. You do look so pale and weary it goes to my heart to see you. Have a good night's rest and think of it in the morning. I daresay things will seem brighter, and perhaps Mr. Franklin may call again."

"He is poorer than I am, John," I said, but I could see that John did not believe me. With the hopeful obstinacy of ignorance, he clung to the belief that Mr. Franklin would come riding to the rescue—and carry me off to the altar, as like as not. I was too weary and sick at heart to try to explain to him. Instead, I took his advice and went to bed. A few hours of sitting up had exhausted me completely.

But next day I felt much stronger for it, and I was able to get up and put on a loose morning dress by the time Mr. Franklin called.

He paid me compliments upon my good recovery, but I could tell by his distressed glance how greatly I was changed. Stammering, meaning it in all kindness, he began to say something about Neal, but when I almost screamed out, "No—no—don't!" he desisted, and sat looking at me in compassionate silence, while I tried to control my shivering. I could not bear any touch—not even a touch so diffident and kind as this.

I don't think I could have brought myself to speak to Franklin about my difficulties, but I believe John must have taken the liberty of a hint, for Franklin brought up the subject himself, with some self-consciousness.

"I'm afraid you are not very well off, Miss Archer? Pray forgive me," he added hastily. "You will believe, I am sure, I do not ask from vulgar curiosity, but only from a very great wish to be of service."

Though I found it so difficult to talk, I managed to say that I knew he meant nothing that was not friendly.

"Then you must let me help you, Miss Archer. You will not deny me the pleasure?"

I thought of Val, and said, hesitantly, "If—— If you could go to the hospital, sir, and see whether my sister is cared for, or wants for anything, it would mean more to me than anything."

I had forgotten, in my own troubles, his old passionate adoration of Val. I saw that he shrank from the thought of seeing her again, and was sorry, but what could I do? John might go, but a servant has so little authority, and a gentleman so much.

"I am sorry to ask you——"

Recovering himself, he would not admit that it was any trouble. Of course he would go, that very afternoon.

"It is very good of you," I said, on a long breath of relief. Now that I had Val upon my mind again, I could not rest easy till I had seen or had report of her. "You will give something to the keeper? And pay for the room? She cannot go in the common room, you know, and they will put her there if we do not fee them."

"God, no!" he said, shuddering. "Depend on me, Miss Archer, I will see her well cared for."

"I hope some day to repay you," I said, hesitantly. What use to make the offer, when I had so little hope of ever redeeming it?

"It is my pleasure, I assure you," he answered earnestly. "For your sake, Miss Archer, and—and for Mrs. Dangerfield's." I could see he did not know how to ask his next question. "She—has anyone sent her news of—— Does she *know?*"

I shook my head, and said, not without a struggle for self-control, "It would be of no use to tell her. You will understand if you see her. But the people there will have heard, I suppose. Pray assure them that—that there will be no difficulty about continuing the special payments."

328

He said, sympathetically, "Surely there is someone to assist you, ma'am. You have a father living, I believe?"

"Yes," I said briefly. I did not wish to appear wholly destitute. But I knew it was of no use to appeal to my father. He must know by now of Neal's death. The physician, at John's instigation, had written him. I did not imagine he would be much distressed. He had never cared for Neal personally, and he was certainly not the man to care much about having an heir to inherit after him. He was more likely to wish the world and everybody in it to perdition, once it could be of no more use to him. He had already refused to assist Val, when her very life depended upon it, and as for me, he would probably be rather gratified than otherwise at hearing of my distress. He cared nothing for his other children—not even Val, as he had proved— but he actively detested me.

I did not try to explain this to Mr. Franklin. He was himself so kind-hearted and generous, I doubt whether he could have believed me. I merely said that my father had a large family and was not able to do much for any of his children. Mr. Franklin, himself one of a large family, accepted this with a sigh.

After he had gone, promising me once again all the assistance that was in his power (poor fellow, I feared it was not very much!) I sat for a great while thinking what I must do. And though the more I thought, the more troubles I saw ahead, it was an indescribable relief to have something positive to fill my mind with. While I was wondering how much my watch and trinkets would bring at pawn, and whether Mr. Franklin could possibly lend me enough to pay the rent, I could not see so clearly the pictures that had haunted me so relentlessly through the days and still more terrible nights of my sickness.

Upon his return from Bedlam that afternoon, Mr. Franklin was good enough to call on me with his report. John was on an errand, so the landlady ushered him in, and I could see by the way she looked at us, and the affable manner in which she proffered refreshments, that she thought herself in a fair way to get her rent. I was long past caring what she thought of me, and was only in a hurry to get her out of the room so that I might hear the news of Val.

I could see that his experience of Bedlam had shaken Mr. Franklin a good deal. His voice trembled with feeling as he described the effect Val had had upon him.

"I saw her at the trial, you know, but it was at a distance, and under those horrible circumstances, who could wonder at how she looked? But now! Oh, Jenny, I did not think she would be so much changed!" His voice broke. After a pause he went on, unsteadily, "I paid for the room and fee'd the man, as you directed. An odious fellow!"

"A great hulk of a man with red hair? Yes, he is odious."

"He is a brute!" Franklin said vehemently. Not without hesitation, he added, "I thought—it seemed to me that—that your sister was afraid of him. Yet she seemed well cared for. They told me that she was."

"Afraid of him?" I repeated slowly. I did not like the train of ideas that suggestion brought with it. I tried to think whether I had ever observed him come into the room while I was there, and could not recall.

"I don't know, perhaps I was wrong." I could see that he spoke with reluctance, yet was driven by an impression that evidently troubled him. "I thought she shrank when he came near her."

It was not a pretty picture. I thought of the brute, and his great heavy hands. If he had ever struck or hurt her—— But how would we ever know? She could not tell us.

"I think—I wish that you might take her away," Franklin said, frowning in distress.

I stared at him. "Take her away! I cannot. She was confined there at the King's pleasure. How can I take her away?"

"Don't you think—if you could confine her in a private madhouse? Surely that would not be forbidden."

"I don't know, Mr. Franklin. I do not even know how to set about finding out. I suppose the lawyer might find out for me."

"What is his name? Let me ask him," he said eagerly.

"Indeed, Miss Jenny, she ought not to stay there! It is a terrible place. My God, I did not know there was any place so terrible! And people go there for sport!"

I thought that there was something in his tone almost of blame, and said bitterly, "Believe me, Mr. Franklin, it is better than Newgate. We were glad enough to take her there. It was that, or the gallows."

"The gallows might have been better," he said, very low.

I bit my lip to check an angry answer. He had been so good to me! After a moment he seemed to recollect himself, and flushed, saying apologetically:

"I beg your pardon, Miss Archer. I should not say that. I should not add to your troubles. But—if you could only get her away!"

"Do you know how much a private madhouse would cost, Mr. Franklin? One, I mean, that was not as bad or worse than Bedlam? I have not the means in the whole world to keep her in one for a month."

He looked downcast. "I wish I might help. But, to own the truth, Miss Archer, I am pretty nearly rolled up myself. I—I would not have you think I failed from lack of friendship!"

"The day when I would think that of you, Mr. Franklin, I will go to Bedlam myself," I said firmly, and saw that he flushed with pleasure. And I meant it. He had been our one true friend.

"They had not heard," he said. "About—about your brother, you know. So I did not tell them. I thought—perhaps they might be less kind to her if they knew."

"But they will surely hear the news some time?"

"I daresay. But I did not tell them," he repeated obstinately. "I don't like—— I wish they need never know. For then they will know they have only you to deal with, Miss Archer."

"Yes," I said, slowly. "Perhaps it was as well. Thank you." For it was in my mind, too, that things might be different for Val when they knew they no longer had her brother to consider.

Mr. Franklin had no sooner gone than the landlady came puffing to my door with another visitor. "An old friend of yours, miss," she quoted, meaningly. It was evident she thought matters were looking up.

As for me, I rose with a great leap of my heart. I do not know why I should have thought it was George Parker—except that I wanted him so much! But Parker was far away in Suffolk, and it was Robert Haywood who came in—the last man I expected or wished to see there.

He stood for a moment in the doorway, a bright apparition from which I shrank with a kind of superstitious horror. It was for his beauty that I had thrown my brother's life away, and the sight of it turned me sick with guilt and remorse.

He came forward quickly, taking my hands before I could escape.

"Jenny! My darling! I am so sorry! It was only this instant that I heard the news. I was angry with you because you had not come or sent word, and then, just now, I heard the news—— Dearest, what can I do or say to comfort you?"

There was always about him a brightness, a warmth, which was his greatest charm. It was to that I had clung even when the old passion was waning. And I felt the draw of it now, though I shrank from him, wrenching my hands away.

"Jenny—what's the matter? Are you angry that I have not come before? I tell you, dearest, I only heard this moment, at Will's. I came on the instant."

It did not seem to strike him, as it struck me with such a bitter pang, that this was the first time he had dared to come to me openly—now that Neal was dead and beyond reach of our treachery.

"What is it?" he persisted, with genuine distress. He really hated to see anyone unhappy, because it made him uncomfortable. Nevertheless, he *had* come to me, on the instant—though he must have known that I would grieve and make him uneasy. "Oh, Jenny, my little love! I can't bear to see you look so heartbroken! I'm so terribly sorry!"

It was hard to resist the old allure of his voice, deep and warm with pity. But he could not be content with pity. He tried again to take me in his arms, and again I forced him away, almost savagely.

"Jenny—what is it? Are you angry with me for coming? I suppose it *was* indiscreet!"

"No—— It was good of you to come," I said, with an effort. I could not blame him. I had never blamed him, and it was of no use to begin now. He simply did not understand. It was not in him. From the first I had known it was not in him to feel anything that was not purely physical. "But I—I can't see you any more, Robert."

He knit the straight, fair brows, only a shade less bright than the golden head, looking at me with puzzled astonishment.

"Not see me! But, Jenny, dearest, why not? Surely now——" He checked himself on the word, being not *entirely* without sensitivity.

But I knew what he meant, and it turned me once more against him, more violently than before.

"I can't explain," I said roughly. "You wouldn't understand if I did. But I won't see you any more."

"Jenny——"

"No! Leave me alone! Oh, Robert, can't you *see*? He's dead, and can't prevent me. That's what you were going to say, weren't you? But that's just why I can't see you again. And now please go away and leave me alone!" I could feel the tears coming, bitter as gall. "*Please*, Robert, if you ever loved me at all!"

He hesitated a moment, and then said gently, "Very well, Jenny, if you wish. But this feeling will pass. When it does, I will come at a word; you know that. Meanwhile, if there is anything I can do——"

I shook my head, mutely, and he went away without another word. I do not suppose he really understood my reasoning, or believed in it, but he understood perfectly—as he always did such things—that for the moment I was lost to him, and that neither cajolery nor reasoning would serve his purpose. And so, because he never wasted effort, he went away at once, without troubling me further. I was so grateful to him for doing so that part of his purpose was already accomplished.

333

At least, it pleased me to know he had not deliberately neglected me. As soon as he had known my trouble he had come to me. To that extent, at any rate, he had been true. More it was foolish and hopeless to expect from him.

There was only one man in the world who could be of any comfort to me now, and he was utterly lost to me . . . Robert Haywood had been curiously fatal to my happiness. Perhaps I could not directly lay Neal's death at his door. But it was in his arms that I had lost George Parker, and there were times when this loss seemed almost to outweigh the other. And I was equally guilty in both.

On the next day I was strong enough to go out. I asked John to procure me a coach. I could ill afford the hire, but I could not go all the way to Bedlam in a chair.

As I passed through the vestibule, the landlady darted out of her quarters and intercepted me.

"Where may you be going, miss, might I ask?"

I longed to tell her she might not, but I owed her a full quarter's rent now, and therefore answered, coldly:

"To see my sister. I shall return in an hour or so."

"And how do I know that?" she said, assuming her favourite pose, stomach stuck out and fists on hips. "For all I know, miss, you may be of a mind to flit, and I tell you flat I'm not a woman to be bilked."

"I have no intention of flitting!" I cried angrily. "All my things are here. You may go upstairs and see."

"Your things! Trumpery! I want my rent. It's of no use to keep putting me off, miss. Won't that fine lover of yours pay up? I'm sure he's here often enough!"

"Mind your tongue, woman!" John ordered, indignantly.

"Mind your business, long ears," she retorted viciously. "If you weren't as big a fool about Miss as the rest of the men, you'd have her in charge for your wages. I dare swear *you'll* never see the colour of her money! But I'm not a great fool of a man, miss, to be gulled by your bright eyes, and not a step out of this house do you stir till I'm paid! Hired coaches indeed! If you've money

334

for them, you've money for me. Let's see the colour of it, miss, and pretty quick too, or you'll not see the outside of the house this day!"

"How dare you!" John began, but I laid a restraining hand on his arm. I was bitterly angry, but this virago was dangerous, and she had the law on her side.

"Mrs. Evans, I cannot get your money by staying in my room——"

She muttered something obscene, with a grin, but I ignored her, going steadily on:

"I must visit my man of business and see what income I shall have. There is more than enough in my rooms to pay your rent, so you need not fear to be bilked. And as for going out, you have no power to prevent me, so pray step aside."

She glared at me, seeming ready to seize me by force, so that John bristled and growled like a dog, but at last thought better of it.

"Aye, miss, you say true, I can't stop you going out, so go and welcome. But my man shall have a word to say to you when you come back."

"I shall be very glad to discuss business with Mr. Evans when I return," I said, with what dignity I could, for I feared the silent, sullen man more than the shrewish wife. She grinned jeeringly, but stood aside to let me pass. As I went down the steps into the sunshine I heard her laughing behind me. I did not care for the sound of it.

"I'll split the old witch from crown to heel if she insults you again, miss!" John exclaimed, flushed with wrath. After a pause, with something of a loss, he added, "How *are* you going to pay her, miss, if I may make so bold?"

"I will see my man of business," I said, with an air. "But first I shall see my sister. Tell them where to go, John, please. Perhaps I may be late, so you may take the day as a holiday."

"I'm coming with you, miss."

"It's not necessary, John. I don't need you."

"I shouldn't think of letting you go alone, miss! In a hired coach!"

335

I wrong John when I say that Mr. Franklin was my only friend. *He* was quite as faithful, with less cause, and even more to his own detriment. The woman's gibe about his wages had cut me. Those should be paid, I swore, if I went to the Fleet for the rest. He should not suffer for his own faithfulness.

It was a fortnight since I had seen Val. Only a fortnight! It seemed such a long, long time. Last time I had come here Neal was with me. The sight of Val always distressed him, and he had waited for me outside in the sunshine, on that day that seemed so much like spring. I saw the very tree where he had waited, lounging and unhappy, but turning towards me, when I came at last, that look and smile always specially reserved for me. *Oh God, God, it can't be true! It cannot be true—that I have lost him. Only two weeks——— And they have buried him in a shameful, unmarked grave, because of me———*

"Miss, miss, are you ill?" John said, anxiously, catching me by the elbow. "Pray, miss, sit down for a moment. I'm sure you are ill."

I steadied myself on his arm. "No . . . Only a little dizzy . . . for a minute . . ."

"Will you come again another day, miss? You're not properly strong yet."

"I'm all right now. I must see my sister today. Wait with the coach, John, I shan't need you."

He agreed, reluctantly, and I went into the hell they call Bedlam, showing my pass to the porter at the door. For a fee, anyone can enter Bedlam and enjoy the spectacle, but my note from the Governor of the asylum gave me admittance to Val at any time.

It was strange how I dreaded seeing Val again. I knew she could not reproach me, would not comprehend nor even listen when I made my confession. But so bitter was my sense of guilt that at first I hardly dared look her in the face. It seemed to me that she must somehow *know*, and ask, 'Jenny, where is Neal? What have you done? He was my brother too, more my brother than yours, and I need him, and you have destroyed him . . .'

But there was nothing there, neither knowledge nor reproach. When at last I looked at her I saw the same hopelessly lost blankness . . . the faint little smile that never altered or deepened or took on any meaning . . . the wide, fixed, empty eyes . . . the delicate bones, holding their beauty still, a changeless, immortal beauty . . . And I saw Neal. Never, never had I seen before how much she resembled him. It was as if they both stood there before me, silent, smiling, utterly remote . . . lost to me for ever, gone away together into some far country of silence and sleep, leaving me alone in the terrible noisy misery of the world . . .

I stood dumb and helpless before the blank wall of that silence. In life, as in death, it shut me out completely. There was no gate in it that I could see, and no one to open to me if there were . . . All the paths ended here.

The keeper touched me on the shoulder and I looked up slowly, into his red grinning face.

"Beg pardon, miss, I'm sure, but I thought you'd gone off to sleep, you sat so quiet."

"I was . . . thinking," I said, turning sharply away from his inquisitive glance. I bitterly resented his interference, his familiarity—above all, his touch—but I dared not, for Val's sake, too much affront him. It came into my head to add, "I was thinking that my sister seems much better."

His reaction was a curious one. He shot a startled glance at Val and said, "Do you think so, miss? But sure she can't *talk* to you?"

I was silent for a moment. There was something in that question that frightened me.

He came a step nearer, staring at me with a look half ugly, half placating. "I hope, miss, she don't complain of me?" Then, recovering himself, he shook his head knowledgeably, explaining, "They do that sometimes, miss, pore things, having their fancies, you know, not responsible like you and me, and upsetting to their relations, as aren't up to their tricks."

I looked at him steadily. "Why should you think my sister has

337

complained of you? I am sure you have taken very good care of her. You know that we pay you to do so."

He was himself again, wagging that great flat face at me. "To be sure, miss, the best of care! Never you doubt that. Why, I've seen mothers with their babies that weren't so choice nor yet so coshering. But still and all, miss, we've had a bit of trouble with her, off and on, and I thought she might have taken some fancy in her head against me."

"Trouble?" I glanced at Val, sitting quietly on her bed. They would not take the pains to dress her, so she wore always a straight white gown over her shift. I had plenty of these made, and took them away with me to be washed, returning them on my next visit.

"Oh, they're sly!" he said, following my glance. "You wouldn't think it to look at her now, mild as cream, you might say, but you'd be surprised the tempers she can fly into when she's crossed, and if the nurses can't manage, of course we have to help."

Every nerve in my body bristled and stood at the alert. We were coming to it now—we were coming to it now—I could feel it, like the cold wind from a door slowly opened——

I stared at Val because I dared not look at him, for fear of what he might see in my eyes. And yet—and yet she sat there quiet and indifferent, not seeming to have noticed that he had even come into the room.

"I am sorry to hear it. I hope you do not have to put her to any restraint?"

"Oh," he said, meaningly, "being as you are such a generous young lady, we don't like to chain her, but we can't have one up here disturbing the others, so times I or one of the other keepers have to sit with her a bit, holding her still, as you might say, just to quiet her down like."

"I suppose that is extra trouble," I said, politely, and put one hand to my purse, as though I meant to reward him.

Watching eagerly, he became still more affable and less cautious. He laughed meaningly. "Well, to be sure, miss, with such a handsome lady as your sister! But still, it *is* a trouble, say

338

what you will, and of course she don't like it, so I thought she might have complained to you a bit, being, as you say, better."

"Oh, do you think so too?" I said, ingenuously. I lifted my eyes to his face, making them as round and innocent as I could. "But I hope, sir, you never have to *hurt* her?"

He laughed more loudly than before. "Hurt her?" he echoed, as though he had never heard the word before. "Lord, miss, we wouldn't hurt a pretty one like this!"

I tittered. "La, sir, I do believe you are catched by my poor sister!"

"Oh, we're good friends, aren't we, my dear?" he said complacently to Val and, taking a step towards her, he laid his great red hand on her shoulder.

The next instant he snatched his hand away, with a muttered exclamation, but it was too late. Plainer than words could speak, more damning than any accusation—the terrible dumb flinching of the flesh, the instinctive crouching of the body that has been hurt and fears to be hurt again. She did not know his voice or his presence, but she knew his touch. She knew that. The delicate hands flew to protect her breasts; her whole body, shuddering away from him, seemed to shrink and grow smaller.

Over her crouching head our eyes met. In his I saw fear and guilt and anger. I do not know what he saw in mine, but he took an abrupt step backward, and some of the red went out of his face, leaving it unpleasantly pale under the thatch of carrot hair.

Then, as I turned swiftly towards the door, he made a jump and put himself against it.

"All right!" he said quickly, his voice hoarse and angry. "So we've had a bit of fun with her. She's a loony; she don't know the difference!"

"But *I* know," I said softly. I felt a curious quiet deadliness in myself, and I saw that he felt it too, and feared it.

"All right—you know. What are you going to do?"

"Let me pass."

"I suppose you're going to see the Governor."

"Open that door and let me out, or it will be worse for you than it is now."

"Stop a minute, my lady! Stop a minute!" he said roughly. "I know more of the ways here than you do. You'll do yourself no good, nor her neither." In a quieter voice, but much more viciously, he added, "Remember, miss, when you go out of here, there's not a soul to know or care what happens. The loony there can't tell them. The others can't tell. *And the keepers won't.*"

He saw that the threat had told, and his tone took on more and more confidence. "Your word against mine, miss, and no proof— D'you think the Governor will care for you? I'm a good keeper; there's not many can keep order as I can, and there's not many as wants this job. You'll tell your brother, I suppose. Well, what can he do? He's nobody; he's got no influence; no, nor much money left, from what I hear. That little fellow that was here yesterday —d'you think the Governor'll mind *him?*"

As I was still silent, his tone became more confidential, almost its old familiar self. "Not a mark on her, miss, to speak of. Remember that. *You can't prove anything!* And who cares what happens to a loony? By rights she ought to have been hanged!"

"If I could see you hanged," I said in a low voice, "I would die happy."

"There's no need to be disagreeable, miss. We've always got on very well. After all——" he paused, and leered hideously, "from what I hear, miss, in her right mind she liked a man well enough. Why shouldn't she have a little fun now?"

There came over me such a sickness of hatred and horror that I thought my head would burst. And through the pounding in my ears, I heard him add, insinuatingly:

"To be sure, miss, I'd as soon take my bit of fun with a female that's got all her buttons about her. Like yourself, miss. I think you'd find, if you was nice to me, my dear, that I wouldn't care to trouble your sister."

I said, gaspingly, "Open that door and let me out!"

"Oh, I won't stop you, miss," he assured me. "For you're in your right mind, you know, and that might make it a bit awkward for me if you was to raise a fuss. But if you've a mind to come round, and get down off your high horse, we might strike a bargain agreeable to both. But if not——" he thrust his head forward, the grin swept off by an ugly look of triumph and cruelty, "if not, miss, I'll just make do with what I have. D'you understand me?"

"I understand you," I said hoarsely. "Open the door."

"To be sure, miss," he said, obligingly, and stood aside. As I passed him, ready to scream if he touched me, he added very softly, "So run along to the Governor, miss, if you won't be warned. But I wouldn't, if I was you. Really I wouldn't."

I did not go to the Governor. Down below, in the common cells where the friendless lunatics were kept, men and women, young and old, suffered out their terrible days, loaded with heavy chains, sleeping on bare boards, or filthy straw, matted with their own voidings, worse off than animals. The poorest stable in England was not kept so foully. The keepers, brutish men with an impossible task, beat and starved them into quiet. The public came, at twopence a head, and poked them with walking-sticks to make them shriek and gibber again. A peaceful lunatic is a dull fellow. When the curiosity seekers went home, the keepers beat the frantic, tormented inmates to docility once more. And the authorities, whose duty it was to administer and protect, saw nothing wrong in any of this. Once Bedlam was the admiration of the world. Now it was the devil's circus. Nobody cared. I knew that only too well. Would I have ever thought, or cared, before Val came here "by the King's mercy"?

I *dared* not go to him. If I made my charge, and failed to make it stick, then the keepers would punish me through Val. I could not risk it.

There was only one thing to be done. Mr. Franklin had suggested it, and the thought had been on my mind a good deal since. I must get Val out of Bedlam, and into a private madhouse. But it would take money, and influence exerted through the proper channels, and for this I needed help. I did not lose a moment in seeking it in the only place I knew.

"John, tell the men to drive to the Temple. I want to see the lawyer, Mr. Case."

As we rattled along on the tedious drive, I sat clutching at the coach straps, trying to get it all clearly into my mind so that I might present it most tellingly to Mr. Case. At the back of my throat there was a bitter taste of nausea, but I choked it down resolutely. Now was no time to weep and rave. From what I remembered of my previous experience with the young barrister he was precisely the man to detest and distrust any sort of scene. If I were to influence him, I must be very collected. But once or twice, as the memory of that revelation rushed back on me, I gulped and had to swallow quickly and put my hands upon my mouth to keep from vomiting then and there. It was curious. I was quite calm, and had no desire to cry or faint, but I had a great desire to be sick, as though I had swallowed something that was poisoning me.

Mr. Case was not at all pleased to see me. I realised that at once. He did not keep me waiting long, and he greeted me politely, expressing some half-finished regret about my brother's untimely death. It was the sort of remark that needs no acknowledgement, and I made none. But I saw very plainly that he was disturbed by my visit, and wished me at the devil.

The barrister was one of those men who, while still young, have no appearance at all of youth. He was tall, well made, and handsomely dressed. In court his wig and robes had sat well on him, and though so young he appeared quite the equal in dignity and self-consequence of the great men on the bench. He was reputed to be one of the cleverest counsels now appearing in court, and it was a stroke of fortune for the defence if his services could be procured. He had handled Val's case with great skill, considering the damning evidence against her, and had worked tirelessly to procure a commutation of her sentence. But not once in that long while had he ever expressed any sympathy for her; and in private he had made it quite plain both to Neal and myself that her cause was odious to him, and that he had taken it only as a favour to George Parker.

342

I did not waste his time now. Coming straight to the point, I told him that I knew Val to be abused and unhappy in Bedlam, and I wished his opinion on whether I might secure permission to have her removed to a private madhouse.

I think he was relieved it was no worse. "It is not impossible," he said, cautiously. "Have you any reason for such a request?"

I stared at him. "Is not abuse a sufficient reason, sir?"

He shrugged slightly. "Can you prove it? No one supposes Bedlam to be an agreeable place."

"Have you been there, sir?" I asked him, levelly.

"Once," he replied indifferently, "as a matter of general curiosity. But your sister, I believe, is not housed with the common lunatics?"

"No, Mr. Case. But wherever she is, she is at the mercy of the keepers. If you had a sister or near relation in such a condition, helpless and sick in mind, could you rest easy knowing her to be mishandled by such brutes as those?" I tried to put the question calmly, reasonably, but my voice trembled.

Mr. Case seemed to find the question offensive. "I am happy to say there is no lunacy in my family," he said coldly.

I sat silent a moment, struggling with myself. "I am not so happy," I said at last, in a low voice. "My sister is mad, and I am her only protector. My brother is dead, and my father will not assist her."

"He should be forced to do so."

"If you wish to make the endeavour, Mr. Case, I cannot prevent you. Force may prevail with him. Appeals I know to be useless. You must take my word for it that there is no one to help her but myself. I am very ignorant and powerless. I beg you to advise me how best to proceed. More than that I do not expect; you may rest easy."

For the life of me, I could not keep that back; but Mr. Case did not at all resent it. He appeared to feel the assurance quite in place.

Leaning back in his chair, and placing his clasped hands delicately upon the lapels of his coat, he began to explain in a bored voice, and very rapidly, the functions of various Commissioners,

Chancellors and I know not what, with regard to such a request as mine.

I stopped him, as politely as I could. "I cannot follow you, sir; I am too ignorant of the law. Please be so kind as to tell me plainly—Can the thing be done? and will you do it for me?"

Getting a plain answer to a plain question out of Mr. Case— or any lawyer—is a hard struggle; but I persisted, obviously annoying him very much, and at last he answered that he thought it could be done, but I must have a better reason. I must say that I begged leave to remove my sister for the benefit of country air, or to be near some responsible relative; in short, for any reason, or none, but the true one. Bedlam must not be criticised. And mere brutality—to a lunatic—was no reason at all.

"Choose any reason you like, then," I said shortly. "I'll swear to it, whatever it is."

He looked affronted, but said it might be done.

"Only, Miss Archer, it will take a considerable sum of money. Not for myself, of course——"

"Why not?" I interrupted. "I am sure, sir, you do not take cases out of charity."

Again the point of the thing missed him; he assured me solemnly that he never did. "But Mr. Parker, as you must be aware, has repeatedly assured me that all expenses in the matter— that is, pursuant to my own endeavours—shall be borne by him. I assume these orders still hold good, though of course I must advise him of this further expense——"

"I beg you will do no such thing!" I said hastily. "Mr. Parker has done enough. I know his own fortune is small."

"Of course I cannot discuss his private affairs with anyone, Miss Archer."

"Then pray do me the same favour. I shall find the money somehow. I will call on my brother's man of business now, and let you know as soon as possible what sum of money I have at my command."

"Do so," he said, and politely bowed me out.

Unpleasant as it had been, the interview had still answered my

344

hopes as much as I dared expect. The thing could be done. I saw it all quite plainly, in spite of Mr. Case's cautious replies. It could be done. It only required—as usual—that a number of palms be greased. And since some of them would belong to gentlemen with high-sounding titles, the grease must be of the best kind, and used liberally.

Money, always money! If you have enough, you can do almost anything. Without it, you are helpless.

My brother's man of business was as unlike Mr. Case as anybody could be. A little hunched attorney, he had never been in a criminal court in his life. His affairs dealt exclusively with land and money, trusts and estates. Occasionally his clients fell into litigation, and then they engaged someone like Mr. Case. As far as I can understand the hierarchy of the law, Mr. Enderby only got up briefs; he never argued them.

Unlike Mr. Case, too, he received me kindly and cordially. His office was huddled away under the eaves of Lincoln's Inn, the darkest, dingiest place into which I ever set foot, the windows blotted out by files and books, his desk a sea of papers, islanded by metal boxes with the names of his clients printed on them in white block letters. From the low ceiling hung two or three strips of syruped papers, clotted with last summer's dead flies. I am sure no duster had ever visited the room. At every step the worn drugget under foot gave off a puff of dust, and every time he moved papers he raised a perfect cloud.

But there was no dust or confusion in Mr. Enderby's intellect. Poking with a long stick, he fetched down the box marked "ARCHER" from the top of a heap, lifted the lid, and took out a small package of papers, neatly tied with tape. He went through them very quickly, as if to refresh his memory, and then slowly tied them together again, not looking at me.

"Miss Archer," he said, "I would soon have called on you, if you had not come to me. I was only afraid to obtrude too soon on your grief. But——" He took the little package in his hand and pushed it across the desk to me.

"Shouldn't you keep them, sir?" I said, hesitating.

M

The little man looked at me, as I thought, compassionately. He had a small wrinkled face, with bright eyes sunk into the wrinkles, and the lines fell into still deeper folds of melancholy as he said gravely:

"You may return them to me, if you wish, but I think you should show them to some other person—a friend whom you trust, or some other lawyer—to assure yourself that everything is in order."

"No, indeed," I said, astonished. "Neal always depended upon you. I am sure he was not mistaken."

"I wish that *I* were," he said, with energy. "Miss Archer, I should appreciate your having other advice upon those papers, before——" He hesitated.

"Before what, Mr. Enderby?"

"Before you burn them," he said in a rush. The wrinkled face twisted. "I am sorry, my dear! Believe me, I am very sorry. But all that is left of your brother's estate is there—those papers. And they are worth no more than as though they were just—paper."

"It is all gone?" I said, trying to steady my voice. But I could not steady my hands. I had to close them tightly on the little packet to conceal their trembling.

He nodded, pityingly. "The estate, as his mother left it to him on her death, was small but valuable. It has steadily decreased in value. During the past few years he borrowed upon it heavily. And now it is gone. At his death, without his having made a will, it returns to the Clarke family."

"And—and there is nothing else?"

"Nothing. If he had not been your father's heir, he would have been sold up by his creditors long ago."

There was a long silence. Mr. Enderby's chambers were very still, high under the eaves that almost shadowed them into darkness. And very cold. I shivered and pulled my cloak closer around me. The afternoon was drawing on, and the day growing cold as it faded.

At last I said, slowly, "That is not the worst, is it? There are debts?"

He answered reluctantly, "These past months were very expensive for him. But his debts need not concern you, Miss Archer. You are not responsible for them."

"If I were, I could not pay them. I have nothing, you know."

"Miss Archer, I am indeed sorry. If there is anything I can do—— I was very fond of your brother. A loan, perhaps? I should think myself honoured!"

I thanked him, but shook my head. "I am afraid youi fees have not been paid, sir; I am already in your debt."

He waved that aside. "You will go home, Miss Archer?" he said, hopefully. "Back to your father's home, I mean?"

Home? I almost smiled as I thought of it. But I could not explain to him why.

"It is not for myself that I am concerned. It is my sister."

"Ah, yes. Mrs. Dangerfield. Her husband was so very rich; is there no one there to help you?"

"His family would not give us a penny if we were starving," I said bitterly.

He sighed. "Natural, I suppose, natural! Well, my dear, if I can help you in any way——"

I rose, thanking him for his kindness. I took the papers with me, though I knew it was no use. I was so staggered by the blow that I hardly thought what I was doing. It had never occurred to me that Neal's estate would not come to Val and me. Encumbered as it was, it would have been something. I might have raised yet more money on it. But it was gone, and I might think myself fortunate not to be held responsible for his debts.

As Mr. Enderby held the door for me, bowing, he said, hesitantly, "Miss Archer, I am troubled to see you so alone in the world. You are, if I am any judge, a particularly captivating young lady. Is there any possibility that an advantageous marriage might settle your difficulties? I should be very glad to think so!"

"No, there is no possibility of it," I answered resolutely. The suggestion, however, reminded me of a favour he might do me, after all. "Sir," I said, "my brother's servant, John Mullins, is still with me, and has been faithful through all this trouble. I have no need for a manservant, and cannot afford his wages. I

347

wonder if, in your household, you could possibly find a place for him? or put him in the way of some other position?"

"To be sure," he said, readily. "My daughter or her friends are always in need of a good servant. Tell him to step round and see me at my home tonight. But you should not be left all alone, Miss Archer?"

"Oh," I said hastily, "I have friends—— Do not be concerned for me. I am greatly obliged for all your kindness. I will send John round this evening; he may as well begin at once."

It was growing dark when I came out to the coach again. The driver was getting impatient at so much standing about, and muttered about his fare. I paid him what I already owed, which pacified him, though it nearly exhausted the small store of money in my purse. Arriving near our lodgings in Holborn, I alighted and paid him off, explaining to John that I did not wish the landlady to be further annoyed by my driving up in a carriage.

He and I walked the rest of the distance home, but on the way I explained Mr. Enderby's offer, and told him he had better go round at once to his house.

"I'm afraid you will have a long walk, John, but I knew you would not let me come home alone."

"No, indeed, miss! But must I leave you?"

"Yes, John, you must," I said firmly. "Some day I hope to be able to pay the wages owing you——"

"Don't speak of it, miss!" he begged. The good fellow was almost on the point of crying. God knows I was sorry myself to see him go. But my mind was resolute on other matters, and John's absence was essential to my success. He could no longer help me, and I might easily do harm to him. It was a weight off my mind to know him provided for.

He left me at last, reluctantly. I hoped they would keep him over night. If not, it could not be helped. He would, at any rate, be gone several hours.

We parted at the door of my lodgings, and John, of course, supposed that I would go straight inside. It was quite dark now, six o'clock or after.

348

But instead I waited till his steps had died away, ringing faintly for a long time in the cold evening air, and then turned in the opposite direction, towards Robert's lodgings near Drury Lane.

I walked quickly, in the cold and dark, turning the hood of my cloak up over my head and drawing it close round my face. The cloak was long and dark, but not very warm, and I had grown thoroughly chilled in the coach. Walking warmed me again, and steadied my head. I was not very strong yet, but I hardly noticed the effort, thinking instead of what I must do.

Robert lodged, very comfortably, upon the second floor of a largish house, set back from the street and its neighbours. The landlord did not reside there, and the other tenants were discreet. I was not the only visitor who had the keys to the house.

I let myself in, feeling gratefully the warmth of the house, and went quietly up the stairs. I did not knock on the door, but again used the key. Robert's manservant was odious to me, not so much through any fault of his own as simply because I felt ashamed of his knowing so much about me. The less he knew of my comings and goings, the better.

Closing the front door cautiously behind me, I crossed the vestibule and peeped into the drawing-room. It was empty, but a good fire still burned on the grate, and the familiar smell of Robert's tobacco hung on the air. A bottle of brandy and a glass stood on a table next to the comfortable chair. At this hour, very likely, Robert was dressing to go out.

As I stepped into the vestibule again, I heard faint sounds from the kitchen, and a subdued voice, singing something low-key and hymn-like. "Can the poor fellow be a Methodist? What a shocking situation this must be for him!" I thought, idiotically, and had to stop and bite my lip to keep from giggling aloud. I was far more strung-up than I realised.

Robert's bedroom door was closed, but I heard faint sounds inside. I tapped softly, and heard the familiar voice call, lazily, "Come in! And bring the brandy while you are about it."

He thought I was the valet. I smiled as I opened the door, picturing his surprise and delight.

349

He was surprised, certainly. But no more so than I. For my lover was not alone.

There was a pretty low sofa before the bedroom fire. I had often sat there with him. He sat there now, long legs stretched to the fire, shirt loosely unbuttoned at the throat, head thrown back in complete relaxation. Beside him, leaning on his shoulder, one hand thrust into his shirt, gazing at him with a curious mixture of possession and adoration, sat Mrs. Allison. She too was half undressed, her gown loose almost to the waist, showing her breasts, her shoes kicked across the room, her hair in disorder, like the bed. If they had still been between the sheets, the nature of the scene could not have been more explicit.

Robert looked round and saw me first. He stared for a moment, paralysed, his mouth open, looking for once somewhat less than handsome. Then he leaped to his feet as though on fire, rudely jerking Mrs. Allison from his shoulders. She gave a little shriek of protest, astonished, before she caught sight of me and also paused suspended, her mouth falling open.

They both looked so ludicrous that a baleful amusement took the upper hand of my jumbled emotions. I walked into the room, shut the door, and put my back against it, bursting out laughing in their faces. If the laugh had a slightly hysterical note, I don't think either of them was in a condition to notice it.

"Pray don't get up, Mr. Haywood!" I gasped, between paroxysms. "Don't stand on ceremony, I beg!"

It was evident he did not care for whatever ground he *was* standing on. If I had not had my back to the door, I believe he would have bolted through it. I can hardly blame him. The situation was one in which the gentleman concerned is less likely to come off well than anybody.

"Jenny!" he said hoarsely. "How did you—— Where is Anderson?"

"In the kitchen. He should have been at the door with a flaming sword. But really, Mr. Haywood, you should not give your keys out so indiscriminately! With so many interests as yours, this was bound to happen."

Goaded, he said passionately, "Jenny, it was you who threw me over! You never wanted to see me again, you said so. It was not I!"

"I am not reproaching you," I pointed out, unfairly. I made a curtesy, mock-ceremonious, to Mrs. Allison. "Good evening, madam. Or should I pretend that you are not really there? I fear I am sadly ignorant as to the etiquette on these occasions. Pray enlighten me."

Mrs. Allison stood up. Without her excessively high heels, she did not appear a very large woman after all. With a certain dignity, she made no attempt to lace her dress or repair her appearance. She seemed, indeed, quite unconscious of any absurdity, and thereby carried off the situation far better than Robert, who I am sure had never appeared to so little advantage in his life.

"Throw the little bitch out!" she commanded Robert, her hoarse deep voice taking on a rougher edge.

"Jenny——" Robert said imploringly. "For heaven's sake, go! I—I will see you later. Surely you——"

"You will not see her later," Mrs. Allison cut in, her voice rising. "Either she or I will go out of this room tonight, and never come into it again."

"Oh, my God!" Robert said. "Clara, be reasonable!"

Reason, however, was precisely what Mrs. Allison did not now possess. As I smiled, it completely deserted her. She broke into a kind of hoarse scream of execration—cursing me, cursing Robert, calling us names so filthy that I did not even understand some of them, mud from gutters too dirty for me ever to have waded in.

Robert looked first dismayed, then aghast, and at last angry. To my amazement, he abruptly walked up to her and struck her—not lightly—across the face. So hard, indeed, that his fingers chipped the mask of paint she always wore. Great cracks appeared in it, breaking away at the edges. She looked in a moment horrible, and horribly old. I do not exaggerate when I say that the white lead and rouge must have been laid on by the spoonful, a quarter of an inch thick, at least.

She gave a kind of whimper, her hands flying to her face, and then she straightened, with a return of her old command. It astonished me that she should bear the blow from him. He had an even stronger hold over her than I imagined.

"You have been lying to me," she said. "You swore that you had not seen her since last summer. You have been seeing her regularly, haven't you? She has the keys."

"Yes, I lied," Robert said sullenly, like a little boy. "What can I do but lie, when you are so unreasonable?"

The horrible white and red mask was convulsed for a moment; she drew a long shivering breath.

"Yes—unreasonable. Of course you would think so."

"You know how great my regard is for you," Robert said, placatingly. He was regaining his self-command; he had got his shirt buttoned up and his hair smoothed down, and was his old handsome self. "But you *are* unreasonable, Clara. You cannot be my only friend."

"No," she said calmly, though her breath sounded through her nose in a way that ought to have frightened him. "Of course one woman could not be enough for you. Nor, I daresay, two, nor perhaps half a dozen. Miss Archer's is not the only other key. You must have them made wholesale."

Then, with a shriek, she launched herself at him, her nails at his face, kicking, biting, like a cat turned demented. The attack came so suddenly he staggered backwards under it, for a moment only trying to keep her nails from his eyes.

In the end, however, he had to subdue her, while I stood watching aghast, with no humour left in the situation for me. My knees began to tremble, and I wished myself anywhere else. But I could not go—not yet. Pride, dignity, and sense, all demanded it; but there was no room left now in my world for any of those virtues.

He flung her hard into a chair and held her there, not scrupling to hurt her. "Stay quiet, or I'll tie you down," he said, his breath coming unevenly. "By God, Clara, I think you are mad!"

Suddenly she collapsed, falling inwards on herself like a thing of rags. She did not weep, but sat rocking herself to and fro, groaning softly, nursing her wrists.

Robert released her, though he still watched her cautiously, and wiped his forehead. "Jenny, you had better go," he said, in a low voice. "Good God! Leave me to manage."

"No!" Mrs. Allison said, speaking so sharply that we both started. She sat up, turning the dreadful marred face away, but speaking with all her old incision of manner. "This thing must be settled, once and for all."

"Not now, Clara!"

"Yes, now. Get me a glass of brandy."

He brought her the bottle and a glass from a cupboard next to the hearth. She drank two straight tots, almost without drawing breath, and you could see her shoulders straighten after the second. Quite calmly now, she relaced her gown, pulling the torn sleeves into place, resettling the valuable lace that hid the half-bare bosom. Her hair was settled too, and her jewels put straight, until at last, except for the face, cracked and peeling like a broken wall, she looked almost normal.

When a woman takes time to consider her appearance, the worst of the situation has probably worn off. Robert evidently thought so, for he glanced at me and shrugged.

"Will you stay, Jenny? I do not know what there is to be settled, but——"

Mrs. Allison looked at me with a brilliant smile. "But we know, don't we, my dear? Sit here, opposite me. Robert, sit there, between us. Appropriate, Miss Archer, don't you think?"

"Very," I said, sitting down with composure and arranging my skirts.

She stared at me fixedly. "I always said you were not a fool. Or only so much fool as we all are, we women, about such a man as this."

Poor Robert writhed under the contempt in her voice. Too late he was realising what he had let himself in for. Wrath, screams and hysteria he could deal with efficiently enough. No doubt he had often encountered them before. But sarcasm left him helpless. Most men are at a loss before a woman when she is clever and merciless with her tongue, and Robert was never very quick.

I was in no humour to rescue him. I felt suddenly very tired, and was content to let Mrs. Allison play the game her own way for a time. The more vicious she was to him, the more readily he would turn to me.

"So, here we are, we three," Mrs. Allison said. She let her glance sweep over us. "It has been three, many times before you, Miss Archer, but always in the end it was two, and *I* was the one who remained in his arms."

"I felicitate you, madam."

"But your charms have been strangely persistent, my dear," she continued, ignoring me. "I knew, the first time I ever saw you, that there were men who would be mad for you, more than for your sister, though you were not half so handsome. I did not think then that my lover and my brother would be among them."

"Lord Dutton never cared for me," I said, scornfully. "It was only because I resisted him."

"He is dead, you know. Yes, he died two days ago of his wound. And it is you, Miss Archer, who killed him."

I stared at her speechlessly. It was irony upon irony—that *she* should reproach *me*, and in those words!

"And you, madam," I said, hearing my own voice flat and exhausted. "What have you done to us, that you should reproach *me*?"

"All that I could, you may be sure," Mrs. Allison admitted. "But that is bygones and need not concern us." Thus lightly she threw off the death of four men and my sister's madness. "What does concern us is the present. You are a sensible girl, Miss Archer. Let me put it to you plainly. You cannot afford Robert. I *can*."

I laughed, I could not help it, and the unfortunate Robert squirmed in misery.

"You put it quaintly, madam!"

"Let us say practically, Miss Archer. He is too poor to keep you, and far too poor to marry you. From all I hear, you are badly in need of a protector of some kind. I am prepared to assist you to one, to the best of my power. If you had listened to me the first time I made you that offer, you would not be in so much trouble now."

I regarded her with genuine wonder. Were there *no* limits to the woman's incredible hardihood?

"I'm afraid you must cut your joint a little lower now," she continued. "Lord Gould is married. But I was discussing the matter with him the other day. He is willing to set you up in a house of your own, a carriage, a good household, and everything nice. Be advised by me, Miss Archer, and accept. You are not likely to do better."

I glanced at Robert. "Well?" I said in a low voice. "What do you say, Robert? It is a handsome offer, you must allow. Have you no counter-proposal?"

He looked at me doubtfully, the blue eyes distressed. "Jenny— you know that I love you."

A flicker of rage distorted Mrs. Allison's face, and she thrust her hand into the firelight, turning it sharply to and fro so that the colour of the jewels on it made little rainbows.

"Can Robert give you these? Lord Gould can. He is a fool, and a fool about you; there is nothing you cannot get from him," she said contemptuously.

"One or two things, Mrs. Allison. But you would not understand those." I turned to Robert and laid my hand on his arm, forcing him to hold my eyes. "Robert, listen to me. We have been very happy together. I think that you must know that you are the only man who—whom I have known. I do not mean to reproach you with it, nor yet to hold you to any obligation——"

With the suddenness of a snake, Mrs. Allison darted forward and pressed her hand upon my waist. I struck it away, with angry disgust, but she sat back, satisfied.

"There's no brat *there*," she said, "so don't let her hoax you, Robert."

So that humiliation at any rate was spared me. With some men it might have been a weapon, but not with Robert.

"I know you are not rich, Robert," I went on, as though she had not spoken. "But you have enough to live on, to make a home for me. I would not ask for much. For myself I would not ask it at all, though I think we might be happy together."

"Very happy, I am sure," he said, in a low voice. "But, Jenny——"

"Wait, Robert. It is not for myself I ask it. There are other resources open to me, as Mrs. Allison suggests. It is for Val. Robert, they are killing her! I can't tell you—it is too horrible! But she will die in that awful place unless I can get her away. Robert, it's not as though she were really *mad*! She is only quiet and gentle, and never speaks. She is nearly as beautiful as ever. If we could make a home for her, I think they would let her be with me. Robert, there is no one else to help me. We have been very happy with each other. If you will do this thing, I will be grateful to you all my life. I will never ask what you do, or where you go; I won't be expensive, I promise I won't! Only your name, and a little house somewhere for Val and me——"

"You fool!" Mrs. Allison said. "Gould can give you all the money you need—enough to buy Bedlam!"

"But he cannot give me a name. She is the King's prisoner. They would never release her to a whore—even Lord Gould's whore. But if I were Robert's wife—— Don't you see? Mrs. Allison, it is you who put Val there. She would be hanged, if you could have done it. Why should you be so cruel to her? She never harmed you. Help me now to get her out and I promise you I will never interfere between you and Robert."

I might as well have appealed to Dutton himself for mercy. She showed her sharp, yellowish teeth in the wolfish grin that always made her so much resemble her brother.

"Lord, my dear!" she said. "You ought to be upon the stage. I never heard a prettier piece of fustian! Why the devil should I care what happens to your sister? Or why should Robert, for that matter? A pretty picture of marital bliss! A tiny cottage somewhere in the slums—you, he, and the madwoman! God, 'tis delicious!" She went off in peal after peal of affected laughter.

I looked straight at Robert. "If you do not do this thing, I think you know what may happen to Val—and to me. What is your answer?"

356

But I knew it by his face, even before he said, with a kind of groan—"Jenny—forgive me—I *can't*."

"You idiot!" Mrs. Allison cried, between peals. "I could have told you so. Appeal to Robert for chivalry! God, I shall die!"

"I wish you would," Robert muttered fiercely.

I sat very still for a moment. I do not think I ever had much hope of success, but the knowledge that I had failed seemed to numb my senses for a moment.

Then I got up slowly. All my bones ached, as though the fever had come back; I could hardly straighten my shoulders. But if it killed me, I would go out of that room with whatever tatters of pride remained to me.

I turned to Mrs. Allison, and curtsied slowly and carefully. She ceased her laughter, but sat regarding me with delight, showing all those jagged, yellowish teeth in a grin.

"Madam," I said, "you have won. I wish you joy of your success. Sir——"

But Robert caught me by the arm. "I will go with you to the door, Jenny," he said, and though Mrs. Allison cried sharply, "I am waiting for your apologies for this scene, sir!" he thrust me through the door and slammed it behind us.

With an effort, I wrenched my arm away and walked to the front door. My hands shook so with weakness I could scarcely fumble for the keys, but I found them at last, and put them down on the table.

"I won't need these any more. I daresay you can always find a use for the extras. Good-bye, Robert."

He put himself before the door, taking my hands very firmly in his.

"Wait, Jenny. There is something I must tell you."

"There is nothing I wish to hear."

"I know you hate me just now. But I am not quite as bad as you think. It is not that I *will* not marry you—— I *can* not. I am married already."

He looked at my astonished face, and laughed, a little harshly. "You must keep my secret, Jenny. At least for another month. I know you will."

"Married! How long have you been married?" I gasped, at last.

"Since last summer, when I was at Bath."

I stared at him, utterly bewildered, my mind groping for something that was almost in its grasp. "Last summer—in Bath? But I thought—— It was Miss Elin you courted then!"

"Well?" he said, with a faint smile. "And it is Miss Elin that I married. We slipped away one day and were married by special licence. I'm afraid it was something of an irregular marriage, but legally tied. Kathleen will be of age in April, and will then make it known to her uncle. There is no saying but what he might procure an annulment, somehow, if he were to hear of it before. You *will* keep our secret, Jenny? Kathleen is so fond of you."

I reeled back against the wall and stared at him silently. The floor seemed to be unsteady, and his face loomed and then receded, as faces do when you are fainting, or have drunk too much wine.

"Jenny—I'm sorry! I didn't know it would be such a shock! Of course *she* mustn't know," he said, jerking his head towards the door behind which Mrs. Allison sat and fumed. "She'll raise the very devil when she does! But it can't be helped, and I think Kathleen will stand true to me."

"Yes," I said, hoarsely. "Yes, I am sure she will. But you—you! Oh God!"

"Jenny, what's the matter?"

"Don't you see? She's my friend! She has been good to me—trusted me—— But, no, no, you can't see, you can't see anything!"

He was, in his turn, bewildered. "Dearest Jenny! I am very fond of her, but of course I don't love her as I do you. And we have done her no harm. It's not as though she and I could live together."

"No. No. And you could not live faithful to any woman, could you? Oh God, Kathleen, what have you done? And you —what have you done to me? I can never look her in the face again! Oh God, no wonder George despises me! If he ever should know this, I will die!"

358

His hands suddenly tightened fiercely on mine. "It is Parker," he said. "It has always been Parker you cared for, not me. *You* betrayed *him*—what right have you to be so hard on me?"

The question struck me hard, so hard that I think in an instant he repented of it, and would have taken it back. But I nodded my head. It was true.

"Oh, Jenny," he said, sorrowfully, "I didn't mean it to end like this. You are the loveliest thing that has ever come into my life. And now I feel as though I had harmed you terribly, without meaning it."

"It is not your fault," I said, in an exhausted voice. "I did fail George, and that was my fault. But for God's sake, Robert, do not you do the same thing. You have a girl a thousand times better than I am. Don't throw her away for another girl like me. You will be sorry all the days of your life, if you do."

He agreed to everything. "For your sake, Jenny——! I shall never love anyone else as I have you."

Then he tried to press money on me, but I would not take it, guessing its source.

"Don't lie, Robert. I know you take money from Mrs. Allison. If this is *hers*——"

"Money is money, Jenny, don't be foolish!"

But I could not take it. I felt as though it would burn my hand if I touched it.

"Jenny—say that you forgive me."

"Oh, yes," I said, wearily. "It is not your fault."

Nor was it. No man lived truer to his nature than Robert Haywood, or sought less to conceal what that nature was. And I could not even plead blindness or stupidity. I had seen it from the first. For the gratification of a pleasure, I had wilfully chosen to accept it. What was the use of crying out upon him now?

He stood in the door, looking after me as I went down the stairs. I turned once, and looked back. He was as beautiful as ever, standing tall and fair under the light that made his hair shine like the old red gold of the Saxons. As beautiful as ever— and it seemed to me strange and impossible that I should ever have cared so much for that beauty that I had turned aside from all others to follow it.

Only a child can love a doll, however beautiful, a thing bright and shining but without the mind and capacity to love in return. I had been a child for far too long. Now, all in a moment, I was grown up, looking back in wonder and dismay at the delusion I had cherished. It seemed to me that I had never known the full bitterness of my lost love until that moment.

I do not remember walking home. If I saw anyone, or anyone spoke to me, I do not remember it. I found my way without conscious volition, seeing and hearing nothing that was around me. Instead, there rang in my ears without ceasing the same words, over and over again . . . Lost, lost, lost! Lost my love, my pride, my honour . . . Even my delusions were gone, swept away into the darkness, vanishing pale and dim, without a rag left of the old deceitful brightness. . . . Neal was dead—in hell, they said, for taking his own life. Val too was in hell, and lost was every chance of rescuing her. What then remained for me? Why should I not go where Neal was? One leap into the dark, and it was done. I would be on the other side of the wall. And whatever was there could not be, it seemed in my unutterable misery, any worse than where I was.

. . . I came to myself at my own door. I was leaning against it, sobbing, and the wind tore at my cloak. Above me, the house creaked and groaned, and beyond the eaves the stars were being blotted out, one by one. The wind was coming from the sea now; it was going to rain soon.

Why should I go in? What was there for me to return to? The landlady's insults? The silent lonely rooms, where Neal had died? The things that were not even mine, and the roof that I could not even pay for? What was the use of going on? There was nothing . . . nothing. Around me was the wilderness, and before me the blankness of that unrelenting wall. I had my choice. Should it be Lord Gould, and after him, Mr. Smith, and after him, perhaps, Madame Polly's house, and whoever chose to take me for a few shillings? Should it be the wilderness, and the taste of gin, and the sound of cheap laughter, and the brutal hands of men, driven to take what they themselves despised?

Or should it be the river?

The wind was blowing hard now. Slowly, I turned away from the door and let the wind drive me. It seemed to pour around me, like the current of a dark river. And I was whirling down that river, fluttering a little before I sank, all my bright yesterdays done, and before me the dark drowning embrace of the sea. . . .

I do not remember clearly the way I went. Once I seemed to wake, and wonder that I should be near Lincoln's Inn, where I had been, so long ago, to see Mr. Enderby. I have a dream-like recollection of walking through many streets, passing once by Temple Bar. It seemed a very long way, and it had begun to rain, so that my cloak hung heavily on me and dragged me back with its weight. Yet I was very hot, and the cool rain on my face tasted pleasant . . . The river would be cool too, I thought, dreamily, but I was in no hurry, now that it was decided, and I was so very tired. . . .

The next thing I remember is seeing an open door, at the top of a flight of steps, and the yellow light of candles shining through the rain. I must have been quite near the river, but I was really exhausted now, and so bewildered by the wind and rain that I hardly knew where I was or what I was doing. The light drew me. I dragged myself slowly up the steps, and looked in at the open door.

I saw a little narrow hall, the worn floor scuffed and splintered, with one very large splinter gouged out near the wall, as though something heavy had been dropped there. At the end, opposite the door, there was a rough shelf with a large candle, of the cheapest kind, burning in a heavy brass candlestick. It was of such inferior make that it guttered constantly and filled the air with the smell of hot wax. Just below there was a small box, with a slot beneath which was clumsily lettered, 'For the Poor . . . Give of thy Bounty in the name of the Lord'. The word

361

'bounty' had first been misspelled and the correct spelling lettered over, but you could still see the error underneath. There was nothing else, not even a bench.

It was a church. I felt a pang of bitter disappointment. The light had misled me. There was no warmth here, and no comfort. Only too well I remembered those long sessions with Mrs. Frye, the coldness of the stones under my knees, the sense of chill and misery and hopelessness with which I had risen from them. There would not even be a service held at this hour; the church was empty. The candle was a false light, promising a comfort which did not exist.

Yet I went in. A sense of great physical misery was coming over me, and like a sick animal I sought shelter, even so cold and comfortless a shelter as this.

I went in and sat in one of the rear pews. The light from the candle in the vestibule filled the church with a soft twilight. I did not kneel. What was the use, when I did not believe, and if I *had* believed, I was so soon to disobey and be damned?

The shelter and silence had a numbing effect upon me. I laid my arms on the back of the next pew, and my head on my arms, and I believe I must have dozed, for I woke suddenly with a great start, my back and neck aching from the awkwardness of the position.

It was a curious awakening. I had a sense of rest and peace; no, more than that, almost of happiness, as though in my sleep I had dreamed something beautiful. It was so long since I had wakened with a light heart that I felt queerly unlike myself— almost like the old Jenny—and wondered vaguely what I was doing here, in this strange place, and why I was not at home.

And then it came back, wave after wave, so that I shrank back, trying to huddle in upon myself, as one does from a physical pain. I had grown a little dulled to unhappiness, and now this one unguarded moment had come and undone it all.

"Oh God!" I whispered. "I *can't* bear it!"

The whisper ran round the empty walls of the church, sound-ing more like a prayer than the defiance I had meant it to be. I found myself stiff and silent, listening—— But there was no answer. There was never any answer. I hated myself because I still was deceived enough to listen—to hope——

I stood up abruptly, steadying myself with a hand on the pew railing. There was no answer here. I was only wasting time. The answer, if there was one, was at the bottom of the river. The old resolution returned, ten times stronger than before. That one moment of forgotten brightness had shown me exactly what I had lost. Not all the dark rivers of the world could cut me off more completely, but, if I were lucky, they might blot it out. Talk of hell! What is hell, but remembering the happiness you once had, or might have had?

The little vestibule looked very bright, after the dimness of the church, even with its one candle. Someone once said that candles in church were like bright hands pointing upwards to God. I thought of that now, bitterly. I was ashamed of myself because I could not die in charity with the world, but I *could* not. I didn't want to die. I didn't want to turn into the dark while the candles still burnt so brightly. It was simply that I didn't see any way to go on that was not worse.

The lettering on the Poor Box ironically caught my eye. "Give of thy Bounty . . ." I took out my purse. There were a few shillings left in it. With all that money means in this world, there was no use wasting them on the floor of the Thames. There might be somebody to whom a few shillings would make all the difference.

My last will and testament, I thought grimly, dropping them one by one through the slot. The estate of Jenny Archer, left in full, with no entail or restrictions, to the next beggar who came this way.

The coins dropped with little clinking sounds to the bottom of the box. Others must have contributed here recently, as well as I. By the sound, the box was quite respectably paved. It was improvident of them to leave it here unguarded. There were plenty of thieves who would not stick at robbing the poor. . . .

As I stood there, looking at the crude lettering of the box without really seeing it, it seemed to me that the whole plan came clearly into my mind, as though someone stood beside me and spoke the words into my ear. It could be done. It *might* be done. It was a chance—the last chance of all. If it failed, neither Val nor I could be worse off. And while there was any chance at all, I could not leave her. The river could wait. It would always be there.

Slowly, feeling like a thief, and worse, I approached the box again. The slot was too narrow for any hand to go through; there must be another opening. I lifted the box from the nail on which it hung, and turned it over. There was the opening, a swinging door in the back, fastened only by a hook and eye.

I knelt down on the floor, spreading out the corner of my cloak. Shutting my eyes, I turned the box upside down, shaking out its contents on to the cloth. I shook, till there was not one rattle left in the box. And then, for a moment, I knelt there with my eyes still closed. When a gambler puts everything he has on the turn of a card—his hopes, his future, and his past—I doubt if he finds it very easy to watch while the pack is dealt.

I opened my eyes . . . It lay there, in a tumbled heap on the dark cloak, a little handful, mostly copper and silver, but with here and there the gleam of gold. I took up the coins slowly, one by one, with hands that trembled so that I could hardly manage them. I tried to count—I remember that I kept counting to two pounds, three shillings, and then falling into confusion and starting again—but all the while I knew it was not necessary. There was enough. For what I meant to do, there was enough. . . .

In the end, I put back the four shillings I had found in my purse. Call it superstition, or what you will; if it had meant the difference between success or failure, I still think I would have put them back.

When I came out of the church, the clocks were striking the hour. It was eight o'clock—still early, though it had been dark so long, on this stormy day. All the parts of the plan seemed to be falling smoothly into place in my mind. I knew just what

I meant to do, and there was still time tonight to do it. If I could help it, she should never spend another night in that place.

"So you've condescended to come back, miss, have you?" the landlady said, barring my way to my rooms. "You were a mighty long time with your *man of business*!"

The meaning she threw into the words brought the blood to my face. She laughed when she saw it.

"It's to be hoped, miss, you've something to show for your *pains*!"

"I have no money, if that is what you mean," I answered quietly. As her grin changed to a scowl, I added firmly, "But I have something better than money. You may look, if you like." And I held out the bundle of legal papers that Mr. Enderby had given me.

At the sight of the ribbons and seals, her eyes glinted; she recognised legal documents when she saw them. But she made no move to take them. Instead, almost with fear, she said:

"Indeed I won't, miss! You might be saying I had taken some. I want no trouble with lawyers and such."

"I suppose you *can* read?" I asked, ironically.

She bridled. "To be sure!" But I knew, if she could read, she would have taken them in her hands long since.

I turned on my heel. "If your husband wishes to look at them, he may. *He* can read, I know." And I laughed, disagreeably, for I had upon two occasions found him looking through my letters, on the pretext that he wished to amend a drawer which stuck.

I do not know whether it was the papers, or my changed attitude—which I suppose she might think resulted from my coming into possession of an estate—but she moved aside and let me go unmolested up to my rooms. Soon afterwards, her husband came up.

He was a surly fellow, at best, but making an attempt to be civil, wished me good evening and said he had heard I had some papers he might look at.

"It's your brother's estate, miss, I suppose?"

"My brother's estate, and I am his heir," I said, and handed

365

him the bundle. If they were not *all* there, it was no concern of his. Those that remained looked promising indeed—titles to Neal's properties, lists of rents, etc. He thumbed through them slowly, grunted, and handed them back.

"I wish you joy, miss, I'm sure," he said, sourly. "I hope, miss, as it won't be long before you can lay your hands on a bit of money?"

"I shall have some next week," I assured him. "You, Mr. Evans, will have the very first of it."

He unbent somewhat farther. "I'm sure that's very handsome, miss. I hope your brother's bit of trouble hasn't given you a misliking to the place?"

I felt a hysterical desire to laugh in his face. Bit of trouble—my God!

"I shall see. I thought from something your wife said that I might not be welcome."

"Pay no heed to her," he said contemptuously. "She's as big a fool as bitch, and that's big enough, God knows!" He rapped his chest with the knuckle of his thumb. "*I'm* master of my own house, miss, and if *I* say you stay—you *stay*! Understand?"

"I'm sure I'm very much obliged to you," I said primly.

When the man had gone I collected very rapidly the things that I needed, and did them neatly in a bundle wrapped round with two of Val's clean nightdresses. Then, as quietly as I could, I went downstairs and out again into the night. I had no fear of being stopped now, but neither did I wish to be observed.

It was still raining and blowing very violently. I had not troubled to change my clothes, and indeed there would have been little use, for I was soaked through again in a minute.

I battled my way to the silversmith's shop down the street. He was surprised to see me abroad alone, so late, but was willing enough to send his boy to fetch me a coach; and I had not long to wait, though every minute seemed an hour.

The coachman was owlishly drunk, but I could not wait for anyone better. As it was, it worked out very well; for he was still able to drive, and yet had no curiosity as to my destination. After repeating it after me several times, mispronouncing

366

it differently each time, he nodded solemnly and said, "Le'sh go—gi-up!"

Luckily his horses did not move too quickly, or he would have driven off leaving me standing in the street. As it was, I wildly scrambled into the seat, and a lurch of the carriage slammed the door after me.

They admitted me at Bedlam without demur. The pass from the Governor was still potent. The porter at the entrance did remark, "You're a late visitor, miss!"

I smiled at him, slipping a coin into his hand. "Not too late, I hope? You see I have brought some clean linen for my sister."

"Ah, she's a lucky one," he said, shaking his head. "There's not many here, miss, as are cared for like her. To think of your coming out so late only for that!"

"Oh," I said, looking him very steadily in the face, "my brother and I were driving this way. I daresay he will come in presently."

"Is he in the coach?" he said, peering out. But the rain and dark defeated him. "God sakes, miss, it's a foul night!"

"I'm afraid you're cold."

"Cold? You may say so, miss! Christ! One of these days I think I'll get myself a decent job. You wouldn't be wanting a manservant, miss, would you?"

"I might," I said, smiling on him again. "This is a very cold place. I hope you'll drink my health?" And I added another coin.

"That's handsome of you, miss, I must say! I'll keep a lookout for your brother and let him in if he rings, for the others won't let him in this time of night without that paper you've got."

"Oh no, don't trouble! I daresay he will not come in at all. I shall only be a minute. Don't stand here in the cold for me. I'll ring when I want to go out."

"As you like, miss. You're not afraid to go up alone? They're all shut up for the night by now."

"I'm not afraid," I said, and slipped past him, hearing him jangling his keys in his eagerness to shut up and be off to the keepers' quarters, where he could buy drink.

.   .   .   .   .   .

I kept my word, and was not long. But long enough for him to have drunk my health several times over. When I rang to go out, it took him some time to answer, and he came wiping his mouth, breathing warmth and good cheer at a distance of several feet.

"I didn't hear you ring at first, miss. Very faint this old bell is—— Good Lord, sir, I didn't see you come in!"

He stared at the tall figure beside me, and then slowly began to fumble at the door, seeming half fascinated by my companion.

"Oh," I said, "one of the others let him in. I'm sorry you should be troubled so often."

"He looks pale," he said, swaying near to breathe confidentially in my ear. "White as a ghost he is!"

I started; I could not help it. Up there, in the dim light of one lantern on the gallery, it had seemed to me too that I had raised a ghost.

"I'm afraid he is not well," I said, dropping my voice also. "A little too much—— You understand!"

"To be sure," he said, chuckling, and making very hard going of it with his keys and bolts, while my fingers twitched to help him. "To be sure, miss—I know." As if to give point to his claim, he belched loudly, and modestly tried to cover it with a cough. He pulled open the door and swore as a great drive of rain came in all over him.

"Come along, my dear," I said to my silent companion. I *could* not call this ghost by Neal's name. "We'll soon be home."

"And none too soon for you, sir, eh?" the man chuckled, giving me a great nudge with his elbow. He meant it for my companion, but I kept myself always between the two of them. Then he swore again, as the wind slopped a puddle over the edge of the door, and almost pushed me through it to get me out of the way.

Without waiting till we reached the coach, he slammed the heavy door again behind us, leaving us to grope our way in total darkness towards the bulk of the coach.

This time I saw us both safely mounted into the coach before I called and woke the driver. With a good deal of grunting and muttering, he gathered up the reins and gi'upped his horses on their way. In a second the faint lights of Bedlam were blotted out behind us in the driving rain. And I slid down on my knees in the wet dirty straw of the coach and wept with my head in Val's lap.

"I want two places on the Essex coach—for Ashton," I said. "For—for my brother and myself."

The clerk peered around me. He saw a tallish slender figure in boots and breeches, with a heavy cloak coming half-way down below the knees, its wide collar turned up, and hat pulled down, till only a blur of white cheek showed, and short fair hair tied back with a broad black ribbon.

"Your brother doesn't look very hearty, miss!"

"He's quite well, only tired; he's but a boy. When does the coach leave?"

"Not till six, miss. Four in summer, six in winter, and it's winter still out, by the looks of it. Will you want a private room to wait?"

I said yes, and something to eat and drink. A yawning servant showed us a room; another brought up a tray of food; and after that we were not disturbed until somebody knocked to say that our coach was loading and we had best to hurry.

It sounds easy; it was easy. But never so long as I live will I forget the hours we waited in that room. When I looked at myself in the glass I would not have been surprised to see my hair whitened.

With luck, she would not be missed until tomorrow. With luck, with luck! Perhaps not till late tomorrow. They were careless enough about letting the patients wander, only checking from time to time to see that nobody had crawled off to die in a corner. The bars and walls of Bedlam were safe. Nobody could break out.

And when she was missed, how long before they guessed the truth? The porter would lie to save his job. He had let two out, when he had admitted only one, but he could swear that both were known to him. On the other hand, nobody else had seen me and if necessary he could deny the whole affair. The coach driver, if he could be found, was far too drunk to remember anything. It might be they would never know exactly how she had left the hospital. But when they began to look for her, it would be very apparent who had helped her get away. And then the hunt would be up for us both. Nevertheless, I did not know anywhere to go but the place where I was going. I could only see that far ahead.

At six o'clock on a rainy spring morning it was still dark; but the rain was slackening away to a drizzle, and there was a faint lightening of the eastern sky.

The passengers stood about in the courtyard, cross and shivering, while the men loaded the coach and put in the horses. Last of all the coachman strolled out, taking his lordly time, his nose very red from being buried in a mug of mulled ale. Coaching in a cold spring dawn is hard work, and many drivers start so drunk they can hardly get the coach out of the inn yard. Luckily the horses know their business, and almost drive themselves.

At last all the passengers were loaded, climbing up the flight of wooden steps to the high musty interior of the coach. Two or three of the poorer sort were put into the basket with the trunks and mailbags. Val and I were squeezed beside an old woman, with our backs to the horses. Opposite was a surly man with a sad-faced little boy, who never spoke a word the whole way, and a shabby-genteel female of middle years, who never stopped, even to fetch breath. She was a midwife, as she at once informed us, and between London and Ashton told us some of the horridest stories I ever heard. I once ventured to ask if she had ever heard of men who went about delivering difficult cases secretly; and she assured me that there were no such persons, the whole story a mere rumour to discredit the honourable profession of midwife. She was one of those ignorant good bodies who will swear to anything they tell themselves, and pooh-pooh as nonsense stories told by anybody else.

Even with her incessant chatter, the frequent stops, the

coming and going of passengers, and the scenes to be observed from the windows, it was a very long and wearisome journey. Tired as I was, I dared not doze, for fear Val might betray herself in some way. I was very much alarmed how she would seem in the daylight. That fixed stare was almost unmistakable. But the cold gave me an excuse to keep her huddled up, and God knows she was easy to manage, though you had to tell her everything. She would put food into her mouth, at my direction, and chew and swallow it, and then let the fork lie idle till I gently put something upon it, and urged her again to eat.

"Your brother looks poorly, miss," the midwife whispered to me. "Is the poor lad ill?"

I told her he suffered very much from fits, and often would sit still without speaking for hours at a time.

The old woman sitting beside me overheard, and exclaimed anxiously, "Lord, miss, sure to goodness he won't have a fit in the coach? For I'm sure I couldn't a-bear to see it!"

I reassured her, and the midwife explained, in a superior tone, that these were *still* fits. "I've seen the like many a time. Hysterical young gals and boys what have outgrown their strength, mostly. Goes all frozen like, does he, and afterwards don't remember a thing, isn't that it, miss?"

I said it was, but was hard put to it to answer all her questions, and at the end of my inventions she shook her head and said it was a remarkable case and she'd never heard of another just like it. Which may certainly have been true.

In one way, Val's stillness and indifference served us. I never yet saw a woman in man's clothes but that she betrayed herself by voice or gestures or a certain something of femininity—whether on the stage or elsewhere. But Val sat so quiet, and never spoke, and the long cloak and boots changed her walk, so that you might have thought her sick and strange but I do not believe it would readily have occurred to anybody that here was a girl dressed as a boy.

Long before we reached Ashton, too, everybody else in the coach except the midwife was frozen almost as stiff as Val with cold and exhaustion, in no case to be curious or critical about anything. To the folk in the inns I daresay it looked peculiar to see me assist my supposed brother in and out of the coach, and do all the ordering and management of everything, but nobody had any right to interfere with us; I had enough to pay our way decently, if not lavishly. Only the midwife was too inquisitive for my comfort, but thank goodness she was easily distracted.

There were certain difficulties I could almost have laughed at under other circumstances. Of course poor Val could not ease herself like a man, and so we had the devil's own struggle with those breeches whenever the coach stopped for relief. Each time I had to take a private room and beg the use of a close stool, and by the time we stumbled out at Ashton I had not a penny left for hiring a chaise nor so much as a cart. But Lord! I was glad to see the coach rumbling off in the distance, with all those people carried away with it. To the very end it seemed to me one of them would throw off disguise and declare himself a constable, come to carry us back to London and Bedlam.

I was so tired by the time we reached Ashton that I hardly felt any emotion at seeing it again, only a curious kind of unreality. It was not possible that we were here, with London twenty miles behind us, and yet here we were. Dusk was coming down again, for the coach travelled slowly, taking the better part of a day to come thus far, and I stood in a kind of daze, holding Val's hand and watching the soft candlelight blossom here and there along the quiet streets of the little town. I never realised how quiet the country was—even a country town—until I had lived a year in London. where it is never truly quiet by night or day. And I had never seen before what a little retired place Ashton was, hardly more than a great village, though I used to think, when I went there, that it was a mighty fine, big, bustling town. Now it seemed to have shrunk away to nothing, a handful of houses and people that would not have filled one street in London. Of course Ashton was not changed; the change was all in myself; and it made me feel lost and strange to think what a gulf lay between myself and the girl who had waited here so eagerly one night for the coach to London.

At last I roused myself, our present coach having creaked away

372

into the dusk, and tugged Val by the hand. We had no money for hiring a conveyance, and therefore must walk, and hope for the good luck of a ride.

"Come on, Val," I said. "Let's go home." And it came over me with a great wonder that we *were* nearly home, and that I had actually done that incredible thing, and carried her away out of Bedlam like the ghost she looked to be.

Home! I could have wept for the strangeness and sorrow of it all. Never in all my imaginings had I dreamed of any homecoming like this, and God only knew what lay at the end of it, or whether there was any home for us anywhere, any more.

We had the luck to be picked up by a farmer returning home from Ashton, after we had walked only about a mile, or I do not know what we would have done. Val had already begun to limp in the heavy boots that fitted her so ill, and I could feel every rut and stone in the road biting through the papery soles of my town shoes.

When I hailed the farmer for a ride, he seemed much amazed at the sight of us. Country people, however, do not ask so many impertinent questions as Londoners. Having room for only one beside him on the box, he bade us climb up behind, which suited me very well, and, after enquiring our destination, drove on without a word the whole way.

As he let us down at my father's gates, however, he leaned over and studied our faces by the pale light of a new moon in the clearing sky.

"I have no money, I'm sorry," I said, hesitating.

"I don't want money, thank 'ee," he replied, in the slow country way that sounded so restful after staccato London voices. "I be'nt in the habit of taking coin for a small kindness."

I blushed for myself. In a year I had forgotten so much!

"I thank you kindly for your help," I said, and put up my hand.

He shook it, very carefully and rather doubtfully. Then he looked again at Val, standing drooping and motionless beside me. At last he asked, awkwardly:

"Beg pardon, miss, but are you expected?"

373

I turned round to look up the avenue towards my old home, seeing the distant gleam of lights. It made me feel queerer than I can say, to be there in the dark, so near it, and feeling so utterly an alien.

"No," I admitted. "We are not expected. Is the Squire at home?"

"He's at home, miss. He be almost always at home nowadays. They do say he be a hard man to deal with now, and the Lord knows he never was easy. He's had misfortunes lately. But maybe you know about that."

"Yes, I know about it."

He slowly gathered up the reins, staring at me from under the brim of his broad hat.

"It's no business of mine, miss. I was only going to say that if so be there should be any trouble yonder you might come down the road to Farmer Carter's, and my missus and I would make you kindly welcome."

Before I could thank him, he clucked sharply to his horses and the wagon rolled rattling on its way.

I stood looking after him for a moment. Then, greatly heartened by this unexpected kindness, I took Val by the hand again and, pushing open the wrought-iron gates, led her up the avenue towards the house.

There was not a foot of the way unfamiliar to either of us, but I could not see that she took any notice, nor seemed to know where she was. My heart sank with the disappointment, for I had counted more than I would admit even to myself upon this return to her old home and the old familiar things. I had always said that I did not expect, nor even wish for, a cure, but in my heart I was always hoping for the miracle. If it did not come now, it would never come.

The maid who opened the door was a stranger to me—taken on since my time. She was young and pretty, staring at me with insolent curiosity almost equal to that of a London servant.

"Master won't let anybody in this time of night," she said, pertly. "What's your business with him?"

374

"It has nothing to do with you," I answered coldly, and stared her down until she at last fell back sullenly, and let us enter.

"I tell you Master won't be disturbed this time of night."

"Then I will speak to Minnie. She is still here?" I added, with a sinking of my heart as the girl hesitated.

"Oh yes. She's still here," she said, with a contemptuous twist to her voice that puzzled me. Minnie used to rule her staff with a rod of iron in the old days. "I don't know if she'll come, but I'll tell her." And, with a last long stare at Val, she flounced off.

The hall had not changed. There was the same smell, the smell that all old houses have, each peculiar to itself, the dozens of animals' heads around the walls, the long bench beside the door. I gently pressed Val down on this seat and she remained there obediently, drooping a little with weariness, oblivious to everything around her, only glancing at me now and then with that childlike, anxious stare, as though she vaguely knew there was something expected of her, and wished to please.

Minnie did not keep me waiting long. She came trotting from the back premises with the nervous, bustling step of a housewife interrupted in the middle of getting supper.

"Well, what is it?" she said, peering at me. The hall was only dimly lighted by two horn lanterns, and she was always shortsighted. "Is it a message for the Squire?"

"Don't you know me, Minnie?" I asked gently, putting my hood back from my face.

She gave a smothered exclamation and both hands flew to her mouth, her eyes rounding over them in alarm and amazement.

"Miss Jenny! Dear God!" And then her natural warmheartedness conquered and she caught me into a great hug, crying, "Oh, my dear, and is it really you, after all this weary while? Oh, Miss Jenny, I never thought to see you again!"

I was touched almost to tears, but I dared not let myself give way, and so said, trying to joke:

"It is such a great while, Minnie, that I thought you had forgotten me!"

"Oh, my dear———" she began, and then she broke off with a smothered shriek, turning white as her apron and starting back in terror, flinging out one hand as though to ward off some horror. "Christ, *Master Neal . . .*"

And I turned and saw Val standing under the dim lamp, her great eyes fixed on Minnie looking so like him in this light that even I shrank for an instant from the ghost that I had raised.

"No, no, Minnie, it's Val! See!" I pulled off the hat and untied the bow, letting the pale cropped hair fall around Val's face.

The poor woman collapsed on the bench, gasping and sobbing, with her hand to her heart.

"Dear God! Dear God! Oh, Miss Jenny, how you did fright me! Oh, poor Master Neal!" And she wept bitterly.

"I'm sorry, Minnie. I forgot how she was dressed."

"But why should you do such a cruel thing, Miss Jenny? It'd be the death of the Squire, if he'd seen her so and taken her for—*him.*"

"I had to, Minnie. I can't tell you now. First I must see my father."

"My dear," she said solemnly, looking up with her face all blotched and swollen, "it's as much as your life is worth. To be sure, he blames it all on you."

"Does he?" I said, and laughed. The irony was too much.

She flung out her hand again, in almost the same gesture, and with almost as much fear.

"Don't! Don't, Miss Jenny! Oh, you *have* changed," she went on, peering up at me apprehensively. "Almost as much as—as Miss Val. It's enough to break one's heart to see you both now!"

"Minnie." I said. "I *must* see him. You're not afraid to stay here with Miss Val, are you? She is very quiet and gentle; she never troubles anyone. Only stay with her, and tell her what to do, and she will be as good as gold."

"Nay, I'm not afeared. Poor young lady! But it's you, Miss Jenny—I'm feared for you with him. He'll kill you, like as not."

"I'll take my chances——" I began, when suddenly Minnie hushed me with a fearful gesture.

"He's coming. *She's* bringing him. I knew she would—the spiteful bitch! *She* sleeps in the big bed now," poor Minnie said, her face twisting up with sorrow and resentment, and remembering the pretty, insolent face of the maid, the whole story became clear to me. This was my father's new whore, and Minnie was only one of the servants now.

The girl—Cora was her name—pushed into the hall ahead of my father and stood pointing at me.

"There she is! Asked to see you, and then changed to Minnie, and they've been whispering together ever so long. Ask her what she wants. I daresay it's the spoons."

"I'll kill you for this," Minnie gasped, struggling to her feet. "Miss Jenny—run!"

But I stood my ground. I had not come thus far to run now. As my father followed Cora into the hall, staggering very much in his walk, I pulled Val forward so that what light there was fell on her face, and stood beside her, holding tightly to her hand.

Momentarily my father peered at us, much as Minnie had done, swaying so much he had to paw at the girl's shoulder for support. She confronted us with an insolent smile, expecting, I suppose, to see us thrown out next minute.

My father's reaction must have considerably surprised her. For, all in a moment, the sight of Val struck him sober. I mean that literally. One instant he was too drunk almost to stand; the next, he was more cold sober than I had ever seen him. The red flush drained out of his face, leaving it stony grey. He stiffened and stood as though turned to rock, staring at Val.

The maid was foolish enough to jerk his arm. He swung instantly and knocked her away so roughly she fell against the wall and began to whimper.

"Get out!" he said. "Get out! You too." But Minnie, shaking all over, stood her ground, even when he started towards her with his fist up. It was I who thrust her aside.

"Go on, Minnie," I said. "Please!" And she went reluctantly, Cora sobbing after her, leaving the three of us alone together.

"Val!" he said hoarsely. "Val!" He went up to her almost timidly, bold, fierce man as he was, and stood in front of her, staring at her, not seeming to dare to take her hand. "Val!" An

N

imploring tone crept into his voice. You could see that he believed she could answer him, if she only would.

Anyone might have pitied him in that moment. Even I felt a kind of pity, and judged it best to stand back in silence and let him learn for himself the hard lesson that Neal and I had had to learn—that there was no answer, not even of reproach, and no remembrance, not even of love.

At last he turned to me in appeal, seeming hardly even to notice who I was.

"Does she know me?"

I shook my head. It was evident he could not believe me at once; he appealed to her again, and seemed to shrink within himself when there was no answer. She stood, docile as ever, one hand still clasped in mine, the great wide eyes that never blinked fixed straight before her. She looked, not *at* him but *through* him, as people will do when their mind is turned inward, without even realising that their gaze is fixed on anyone. Whatever it was she saw, or wherever she wandered, it was in a world so remote from ours that all sense and feeling were shut off, making no more impression than drops of water upon glass.

"Is she always like this?"

"Yes, always," I said, wearily. "She has never been any different, not since——" I stopped abruptly. It came back upon me violently sometimes—the memory of that moment, and the white bundle on the stones, and Dangerfield's high thin screaming. It was when I remembered most clearly that I knew I was a fool to hope or expect she would ever wake from this sleep that they called madness.

I suppose he saw something in my face, for he asked huskily: "They say she killed the child. Did she?"

I looked him steadily in the face. "It was an accident. She was holding it—it woke and gave a jump—and fell."

He could not hold my gaze. His own eyes dropped away; he said hastily:

"Yes, of course. But, God!—is she *always* like this?"

I turned to Val and pressed my hand gently on her arm, showing that I wanted her to sit down. She did so, obediently, and I

378

drew the cloak more closely around her shoulders. It was cold in the hall, the lamps flickering constantly in the draughts from the high, beamed ceiling.

Then, standing beside her with my hand on her shoulder, I said, "Yes. She is always like this. She will never be any different, any better. They were cruel to her in Bedlam, and therefore I have brought her away. If you will keep her, I think they will let her stay here. She is very quiet and gentle and never gives any trouble. But she will never get better. I think perhaps it is best if she never does."

Again our glances met, and this time he did not evade mine. At last, he nodded. And in that gesture I saw that he understood as much as he ever intended to understand; and that he accepted it all.

Quite suddenly my knees buckled under me, and I was obliged to sit down beside Val. I had never let myself think what might happen if he refused to take her in. But I felt, in that moment of relief, as though I had been carrying for a long time some load too heavy for me, and now at last I knew how tired I was.

There was to be nothing too good for Val. That was obvious at once. Every servant in the house—including Cora, sullen and dismayed at this turn of events—was sent scurrying on errands. A fire was lit in the best bedroom—her old chamber was no longer good enough—bath prepared, fresh clothes brought, trays of dainties sent up, and two or three maids ordered to do nothing but take care of her. There was much exclaiming and to-do-ing and cosseting, as the servants saw which way the wind was blowing. My father could hardly bear to let her out of his sight; he declared that she should have a new wardrobe, and the doctor must be sent for, to say whether she might ride, and he would soon get these cobwebs out of her brain.

I said nothing. There was never any turning my father from his purpose, once that purpose was set to a thing. It was all to Val's advantage. Neither fine clothes nor dainties nor doctors nor riding lessons could work any change in her, but she would be safe and comfortable and pampered. And my father would fight to the death, as much from obstinacy as love, before he would let them take her away from him.

She was safe. I had done all that it had seemed, that night in London, so impossible that anyone could do. And as I stood there, watching her led away without a backward look, it seemed to me that my heart would break. She did not need me any more. There had been nothing left of the old love except that need. Now it was gone too, and I had lost her utterly. The light on the landing shone momentarily on the fair head and then she was gone out of sight into the darkness. She had not once looked back. Not once.

"Are you finished?" my father said, coming into the dining-room, where I sat with Minnie over the remains of the hearty supper with which she had been consoling me.

"Yes."

"Come into the library, then," he said, and turned on his heel, walking out.

Minnie caught me by the hand. "Be careful, love!" she whispered. "For God's sake, don't cross him! Don't cross him, he can't bear it, you know. He'll be all the harder to you for being soft to *her*."

"He always was," I said, and followed him, but not before I kissed and thanked her for her pains. I left her clearing the table, sighing and muttering to herself. We both recognised that the Squire was himself again.

He was waiting impatiently for me in the library, standing behind the desk where he kept his papers, paid the servants, and did business with the people of the estate.

"Come in," he said. "Shut the door."

I obeyed him, and came right up to the table opposite him, waiting for him to speak.

He had some money in his hand—notes and gold. He leaned over and put it on the table in front of me. He smelled strongly of liquor, and the familiar flush had returned to his face. Except for that unnatural redness, which coloured even the whites of his eyes, he might have been a handsome man still. He was not yet old—not yet fifty—and, despite the way he had used himself, retained the vigour and almost the build of a young man. Only that flush of the heavy drinker, and the coarsening of all the lines of his face, betrayed him.

"There's twenty-five pounds," he said. "It's all the money I have in the house. Take it, and get out."

I did not speak, or move, and he repeated loudly, "Take it, and go. It's all you'll get from me, and more than you deserve."

"Where shall I go?" I asked quietly.

"Anywhere you please," he answered, scowling. "To London, or Bath, or Hell, or anywhere you like, so it is away from here. I never want to set eyes on you again. If you come back I'll turn the dogs on you."

"You've always hated me," I said, slowly and wonderingly. "Why?"

He leaned over the desk, his face darkening with rage, the veins standing out on his forehead. I remembered so well that danger signal, and how we children used to run from it.

"Why? *He's* dead, and *she's* mad, and you stand there and ask me *why*?"

"Do you blame me for that? I loved them better than you ever did. They would be alive and happy today if it were not for you. *You* made her marry Dangerfield," I reminded him bitterly. "Everything followed from that. If it were not for me, she would still be in Bedlam. You would have let her die there."

"It's only remembering that that keeps me from wringing your neck. But don't try me too far."

"I'm not afraid of you," I said, contemptuously. "I used to be, but not any more. I've seen worse things than you dream of. I don't care if you do kill me. But you won't like being hanged, I can tell you that. I heard about Dangerfield's being hanged, and for all you did to help her, they might have hanged Val as well."

He stared at me almost with wonder. "By God!" he said at last. "You were always a hard little devil. I remember you never cried however much I beat you. I don't believe you *would* care if I *did* break your neck."

"I don't care what you do. I knew you wouldn't keep me. I

381

didn't think you would send me away tonight, but it doesn't matter. I only want to know why you hate me so. I can't help being your daughter. God knows, I wish I could!"

"Why, you little fool, that's just it! How many times must I tell you you're no get of mine?" The words jerked out of him savagely.

I stared at him incredulously. "I know you always said so," I said, at last, "but—— Is that why you were so cruel to my mother? But why did you keep me?"

"Hell, was I to tell everybody I'd been left with a cuckoo in the nest?" he said shortly. "That bitch, your mother, was the only woman who ever made a fool out of me. And you're one just like her. I don't know why I didn't wring you neck in the cradle. God knows I wanted to. That damned red head of yours—when was there ever an Archer with a head that colour?"

"I wish I could believe you——" I whispered, at last.

He shrugged, and laughed grimly. "It's true," he said. "When she was dying she admitted it. God damn it, she flaunted it! And laughed! Christ, I can hear her yet! She paid me back for everything. Soft—you'd think, to look at her, butter wouldn't melt in her mouth—like you. And then she tricked me, like any fool of a husband, and lay there laughing at me while she died."

"Who—who was it?"

"Hell, how should I know?" he said, sullenly. "There was a fox-headed lord spent a fortnight here for the hunting—— And old Underhill—you had a look of him sometimes. But one thing I do know, you're not mine. I've kept you all these years, but I'm damned if you'll spend another night under my roof. You can have the twenty-five pounds. That's about the dowry she brought me."

I stood speechlessly looking at him. One thought kept going round and round in my head—— *Then Neal needn't have died.* He needn't have died! Oh God, if I had only known! But bitter as the thought was, there was comfort in it too. It seemed to bring him back to me as he used to be, the mark of that horrible night all washed away, gay and smiling . . . "You see, Jenny, my darling, I had a right to love you after all . . ."

.   .   .   .   .

"Well?" the Squire said loudly, and I came to myself with a start, finding him staring at me curiously. "Are you struck dumb, or what? You're not going to pretend to cry about it, I hope."

"Cry about it?" I burst out laughing in his dumbfounded face. "Oh, my God! It's the only good thing you ever did me—*not* to be my father. What do I care what blood I have in me, so long as it is not yours?"

And, still laughing, I caught up the gold and notes that had lain all this while on the desk, and ran out, leaving him standing frozen behind me, for once without either word or blow with which to answer me.

"But, Miss Jenny, what will you do? Where will you go?" Minnie asked, gazing at me anxiously, her face puckered up with anxiety. "Oh, he is a wicked man! But I was afraid of it, Miss Jenny, indeed I was. It seems he always did have a spite against you."

"Never mind, Minnie," I said cheerfully. I had the most curious feeling, compounded, I suppose, of shock and fatigue and overstrain, quite light-headed and gay, as though I had drunk too much wine. "Look, I have twenty-five pounds! It was my mother's dowry, so I have taken it. I never was so rich before."

"But, miss, where will you go? Tonight in the dark and cold?"

"Back to Ashton, I suppose, if I can get a ride from the village."

"Will you go to London, miss?"

"I don't quite know," I said, sobered. "I don't want to. I feel as though I never want to see London again. But what else can I do?"

"How will you live, miss, when you do get there?"

"By my wits, I suppose."

"I know what that means, Miss Jenny, and it isn't your wits you'll live by! Dear God, I wonder the Squire can face himself in a mirror. He'll drive his own daughter to be a whore, he will."

"Perhaps I can buy a husband with twenty-five pounds," I said gaily.

383

"I did hope, miss, as you would be married. Did nobody ask you, so pretty and gay as you are?"

"A lord asked me, but I would not have him. No, Minnie, that is the truth!"

"Then you must be crazed," she said frankly.

"I think I am. I think I was. Oh, Minnie, what do you do to make a man love you again?"

"If he's given over loving you, there's nothing you can do. But if he's just angry, maybe he'll come to you again. Was he really a lord?" she added, wistfully.

I laughed and kissed her. "There was really a lord, and he really did offer—once—though he took it back again. But he's not the man I loved, Minnie. *He's* gone, and he'll never come back again, for he's stopped loving me. Minnie, I wish I were dead!"

"Oh, my dear! Maybe he's only angry. Love, don't cry!"

"I'm not crying. I don't think I'll ever cry again. Never mind, Minnie. You've been very good. I'll write you from London. You must let me know about Val. No matter what happens, you must let me know."

She came running after me. "Miss Jenny! Wait! I've a notion. Why don't you go to your grandfather for the night? I daresay he'd be main glad to see you."

"My grandfather!" I said. I stared at her bewildered in the light from the open door. "Who do you mean?" I was thinking of the fox-headed lord.

"Why, Farmer Lake, to be sure. Your mother's Pa. He's still alive, the last I heard, though his grandson runs the farm now. That's your cousin, miss. To be sure, they're not grand folk—— He came here once, they tell me, when you were little, to see you, but the Squire wouldn't let him in, and he's never been back since then."

"Do you think he'd take me in?" I said, doubtfully.

"To be sure, he would. Of course, they're only plain folk, Miss Jenny, not what you've been bred up to."

Perhaps it was as well she could not see my face more clearly in the half-light. I only said, "Better than I've been bred up to. But how far is it? Can I walk?"

"Stay a moment," she said mysteriously, and bustled away again.

She was back in half a minute with a tall young man in farm breeches and gaiters, who came shyly behind her, trying to smooth down his curly hair, looking at me out of the corners of his eyes.

"It's Harry. You remember Harry, Miss Jenny? You were always romping with him in the old days. Make a leg, man; this is the Squire's daughter!"

He bowed awkwardly, but broke into a wide grin when I went up to him and held out my hand.

"Do you remember the strawberries, Harry, and falling out of the hayrack, and the whipping we got for chasing the cows? Or are you so grown-up you've forgotten me?"

He took my hand clumsily, looking down at me half bashfully, half pleased.

"I've not forgotten you, Miss Jenny. But I wonder you should remember me."

"You've changed," I said, trying to remember my boyish play-mate in this shoot of a young man. "But I couldn't forget all our romps, Harry."

"He'll take you to Farmer Lake's on a pillion, miss," Minnie interjected. "He lives over that way, and the Squire'll never know."

"I don't care if he does," Harry said, sturdily. "I'd do Miss Jenny a favour if he was to send me off next day."

"Well, he won't, for he won't know," Minnie said, practically. "You don't mind riding, Miss Jenny?"

"I'll do anything," I said, "but walk. I can't walk another step."

"Then you bide there, miss, and I'll bring the pony," said Harry, taking me literally. And in five minutes he returned with his little sturdy cob, and I was up behind him and trotting away, with Minnie waving from the kitchen door.

385

On the four-mile ride to my grandfather's farm I had plenty of time to break down Harry's shyness, and he was soon talking freely. He gave me all the gossip of the place since I had gone away—nearly a year now, and it seemed like ten, at least. Minnie had been deposed as my father's mistress after he got a good look at Cora. As Harry put it, "She was surely crazed to hire a wench like that with the Squire the man he is!" But opinion in the servants' hall was that she was too sullen and wilful to last long; whereas Minnie's housewifely abilities were unparalleled. "Mrs. Minnie'll be back in the big bed afore long, miss, and then Cora will have to walk."

"How about yourself, Harry? Have you a sweetheart? Or maybe you're married already?"

"Not yet, miss, but I've bespoke Jane Carter from over Ashton way, and we'll be married after harvest next year. Master has promised me one of the cottages. I don't say as Jane is the handsomest wench in the world but she's none so bad for all that, and there's not a woman in Ashton with a better hand at the stove, though I say it myself," said Harry, with complacency.

I wished him joy, amused to see how practical he was in his choice. I suppose among working people, where a husband's comfort—and digestion—are entirely dependent upon his wife's skill, domestic gifts are bound to rate higher than grace or wit or charm.

"Harry, I wish you would tell me about my grandfather."

"There's not much to tell, miss. Lord, it seems strange that he should be your grandfather! And young Lake—I suppose he's your cousin?"

"Of course. Do you know him, Harry?"

"Aye. Some. The fact is, miss, the Lakes are good, tight farmers and hold themselves a bit above the rest of us. I daresay that's partly on account of having married into the quality. They do say young Lake's mother was a bit above them, and his father only got her because Miss Mollie married the Squire."

"Then I hope," I said bitterly, "that he got a better bargain than my mother did with the Squire."

Harry squirmed, obviously shocked. "I don't know as to that,

386

miss. But Bob Lake has more book learning than the rest of us and holds himself a bit off, though I will say he never puts on airs. They say old Lake is a warm man, and it's a good farm; none better. You'll be comfortable there, Miss Jenny, though it's not what you're used to."

I was silent, leaning my head wearily against his broad back. It was as well, I thought, that Harry could not know some of the strange places I had grown used to since I saw him last. A comfortable, tight farm sounded like Heaven—if they would only take me in! But why should they? I was nothing to them. They had never even seen me. I had scarcely ever thought of my mother's people (except to be somewhat ashamed of them) until this moment.

"Here we be, miss," Harry said, presently, turning up a long broad lane, and I peered around his shoulder, seeing two or three low-lying lights ahead of us. As the pony's hoofs clattered on the ruts the farm dogs rushed out barking. Harry shouted at them, as the pony shied, and they retreated, woofing in a casual manner, as though to show they had not meant anything by their original demonstration.

It was too dark, of course, to see much. I had an impression of a long, low farmhouse, an orchard coming up close on two sides, but with something of a garden in front, sufficiently unusual on farms to show that the Lakes were indeed a cut above their neighbours. There was a soft golden light of candles in several windows to the rear, but the front was dark.

Harry pulled up in front of the door and jumped down, lifting me down.

"Stay with me, Harry!" I whispered, in a panic. "Perhaps they won't keep me."

"Don't you fear for that, miss," he said. "They're proper hospitable folk."

He marched up to the door and rapped on it smartly, whistling at the dogs, who came crowding round us, sniffing. Harry had the proper farm smell and they soon left him alone, but they found so much interest in my skirts that I was almost knocked down by their friendly crowding. I was engaged in trying to repulse their advances when the door opened, and I looked up startled in the flood of light.

"Get away there, you idiots!" a man's voice commanded, friendly but masterful. "Don't be frightened, miss; there's no harm in them. Is it you, Harry? Come in, then."

I was disposed to hang back, till Harry could explain, but had no chance. A powerful hand reached out and drew me in, Harry following, and shut the door.

I found myself standing in a small square hall, whitewashed and very neat, with a boxed staircase in one corner, and an open door, leading away into a long passage, low, dark, and flagged with stones. A large lantern hung from a hook overhead, making a good clear light, its brass clean and polished till it glittered.

The young man who had opened the door was dressed, like Harry, in heavy breeches and leggings, with a short thick coat, and a handkerchief tied loosely around his neck. But his clothes were of a much better quality, quite new and scrupulously clean. There was even a suggestion of frivolity in the neckerchief, which was of fine quality and the same shade of blue as his very blue eyes. He did not look like a gentleman, but he looked like a straight-backed yeoman with a good opinion of himself and no fear of anybody else. He was not so tall as Harry, but very well and strongly made, with a short round neck, round head with very small ears and closely cropped curling fair hair, and a countenance not precisely handsome but comely enough.

I never had the slightest question but that it was my cousin, and I must confess his appearance was a relief to me. God knows I had small cause to be particular, but yet I could not help being pleased that he was so much less rustic than he might have been.

He looked at me with quite as much frank curiosity as I at him, and I could not see that he was in the least surprised when Harry said:

"Bob, this is Miss Archer—Miss Jenny, you know, the Squire's daughter. 'Twas her mother, Miss Mollie, that married the Squire."

"Aye, I know," my cousin said. He had a short, resolute way

388

of speech, not precisely hard or rough, but in the manner of a man used to ordering and having his own way, with no time for nonsense. "I bid you welcome to Lake Farm, Miss Archer."

"Thank you, cousin," I said, and held out my hand.

He looked at me for an instant with something almost like a frown, then took my hand and shook it with a quick, hard handshake, as if it were a man's.

"I suppose we are cousins," he said. "I'd almost forgotten it. And to tell truth, we thought maybe you'd be best pleased to forget it altogether."

I felt myself colouring as I answered, "I don't blame you. I should have come here long ago to see my mother's kin."

"We do not hold it against you," he said shortly. "I know the Squire would not let you come. None of us have set foot on his place since he told my grandfather he was not welcome there. But that's not your fault."

"The Squire has driven her out, Bob," Harry said, in a low voice. "He won't let her bide."

My cousin scarcely glanced at him. "Why?" he said, pointblank to me.

Harry looked horrified, but I thought it a reasonable question. "He has always hated me," I said. "Now he is angry because my brother is dead and my sister is—is not well."

"Is that your fault?"

"No. But if you knew the Squire——"

"I know him as well as I wish to," my cousin cut me short. It was plain the affront to my grandfather had never been forgotten or forgiven. "It's a house you're better out of, Miss Archer, if I may say so."

"Mrs. Minnie thought," Harry explained, "that maybe old Mr. Lake would like to see Miss, being his granddaughter and all, and she could bide the night."

"She can bide as long as she pleases," he said, in his abrupt way. "You'd better come and see him now. Harry, you'll stay and sup with us?"

"Nay, Bob, thanks kindly all the same, but my old woman will be on the look-out for me," Harry said.

I walked out with him to the pony to thank him, leaving my cousin waiting in the hall.

"You've been very kind, Harry. I'll never forget it."

"I've done nought, miss. Bob's a bit of a hard fellow, but he means well, and they'll make you comfortable. You mustn't mind the way he talks."

"I don't mind it. I feel quite safe now. Good-bye, Harry. If I bide, will you come and see me sometimes? Bring me news from Minnie."

"Aye, Miss Jenny, I will." He hesitated, gathering up the reins, and then, with half a laugh in his voice, leaned down and said, coaxingly, "I don't suppose you'd kiss me, Miss Jenny, like old times?"

"I'd do more than that for you, Harry," I said readily, and put up my face. But his kiss was not the boy's kiss I remembered, and I drew away, so that he said, rather sulkily:

"You used to do better than that in the old days, miss!"

"That was before you bespoke Jane Carter," I said, teasingly, not wishing to affront him. "Good-bye, Harry. Remember to come soon."

"Aye, I will. And—and I'll drown Jane Carter if you'll kiss me like the old days!" he said, with a rush, and driving his heels into the pony's sides trotted off down the lane.

I don't know how much of this my cousin caught. He was waiting to lock and bolt the door when I returned, looking at me levelly and dispassionately, seeming neither to approve nor disapprove what he saw. I judged him to be a man who was careful in making up his mind, but probably absolutely immovable once his opinion was fixed. And in this I was very nearly right. Such was certainly his character in general.

"It's this way," he said, after securing the door, and lifting the lantern down from its hook. "Mind the steps at the end. This is a rough place, not like Archfield."

There was an apology in his tone. It was a simple statement of fact. But it contained a hint that I thought it best to face at once.

"I was never happy for a day or an hour in Archfield. I have lived in fine houses in London, and been very unhappy there. I would rather be here, if you will make me welcome, than in any other place."

He did not answer me directly. He said, "My grandfather is an old man. He forgets sometimes, and gets confused, especially in the evening. He may take it hard, seeing you. He talks a deal of your mother lately. But no doubt he'll be glad to have a sight of you."

He led the way down the long stone-flagged hall as he spoke, holding the lantern so that I could see, and I followed him without attempting any reply.

At the end of the corridor he pushed open a door and I found myself in a big farm kitchen—the biggest, and best kept, and most inviting I ever saw. The kitchen at Archfield was not half so agreeable a place.

Farm suppers are late, after the barn and dairy chores are performed. There was no one in the kitchen now, except an old man sitting by the fire, but I heard voices echoing from a room beyond, where the maids were packing eggs and butter for next day's market. The room was long and low, with heavy darkened beams, the walls whitewashed, the stone floor scraped so clean you could see your face in it like a mirror almost. Copper and brass pots and pans hung round the walls, and there were two beautiful silver milking pails hanging from hooks driven into the stone chimneypiece. I learned later they had been given to my mother as a girl by her doting father, to make her fond of her dairy work, and never touched, except to be polished, by anyone since her marriage.

There was a good banked fire burning on the hearth. High-backed settles stood on either side, and an old man, with very white hair, as curly as my cousin's, sat nodding in the corner nearest the fire. He wore leggings like Bob, with a long white smock covering everything else.

"Grandfather!" Bob said, rather loudly, going up to him and shaking him gently by the shoulder. "Grandfather, wake up! There's someone here to see you."

He woke up slowly, muttering to himself, as old people often do. He seemed very aged to me at first, but looked less old when his eyes were open, for they were still bright and blue like Bob's. The fresh country colour was still in his cheeks too, but he had lost most of his teeth, so that his cheeks fell in, and he had the typical fine tremor of head and hands.

"Eh—what—what?" he said jerkily. "Bob—is it you, Bob? Time—is it supper time?"

"No, grandfather, not yet. It's only eight. But there's somebody here to see you. A young lady."

As Bob stepped aside, old Mr. Lake saw me, and with natural, dignified courtesy, hobbled to his feet and gave the country tug to his forelock.

"Servant, miss," he said politely, adding reproachfully, "You oughtn't to bring a young lady into the kitchen, Bob! Where are your manners, boy? Ask the young lady to step into the parlour."

But I went up to him, half laughing, half crying, and kissed him.

"Don't put me in the parlour, sir! I like it much better in the kitchen."

He looked at me, all amazed and bewildered, and then suddenly caught me by the shoulders and turned me around so that all the firelight fell on my face. He said, quite harshly and loudly, "Ah, Mollie, Mollie!" And then he fell back into his seat and shut his eyes, so that I was frightened at what I had done.

"Dearest grandfather, it's Jenny!" I said, kneeling down in front of him and rubbing his hands. Bob was beside me in an instant, with a glass of wine, and between us we helped the old man to drink it.

He revived at once, but at first could do nothing but hold my hands, the tears running down his face, saying over and over, "Mollie! Mollie's girl! Oh, Mollie, Mollie!"

"He will be all right," Bob said, in a low voice. "I told you it would be a shock to him."

"I was too sudden," I said, self-reproachfully. "But I didn't know—I didn't realise he would recognise me so quickly."

"You are like her, I suppose," he said calmly. "Never mind, it's all right, only we had better get him to bed."

He stepped to the farther door and called out, "Rachel!"

A big, strong-looking girl answered the call, and stared in astonishment at me, and at her old master in tears.

"Rachel," my cousin said, in his calm way, "this is Miss Archer, who has come to stay with us for a while. She is my Aunt Mollie's daughter, you know, and grandfather is a little upset. Can you get him to bed, do you think?"

"To be sure," the girl said, bobbing me a curtsey. She was a good-looking girl, in a rustic way, with round, firm red cheeks and arms, a fine bosom under her plain stuff gown, and a general air of health and strength and good humour. She helped my grandfather to his feet, addressing him kindly and respectfully but firmly, like a good nurse. "Come along, sir, you'll be best in bed, and I'll bring you a bite of supper presently."

"Mollie—Mollie!" the old man said, catching imploringly at my hand.

"You'd best to come too, miss, if you will," she said, in low tones.

"I won't leave you," I told him gently, and I walked on his other side, his hand tightly and pitifully clutching mine all the way. He would not even let go while she undressed him down to his shirt and tucked him into bed. He, his room, and everything about him was as clean and neat as the rest of the place.

Because of the stairs, he had the best bedroom, off the little-used parlour, with a good fire, and by day a pretty view of the orchard. I sat there with him while Rachel fetched his supper and coaxed him to eat, all but feeding him by hand like a baby in his weakness, and stayed there till at last he dropped off to sleep. He hardly spoke, but could not seem to leave off looking at me, holding me fast till he slept, and murmuring now and then, "Mollie's girl! Little Jenny!" so that the tears rose to my eyes.

"Will you be pleased to sup in the parlour, Miss Archer?" Bob said to me formally. "I'll ask Rachel to serve you there."

"Where do you have supper, cousin?"

"With the men and maids in the kitchen," he answered.

"Then, if you please, I'll join you there."

He stood looking at me with that frowning consideration. "It is not necessary," he said. "It is not what you are used to."

"Cousin," I said, "let us settle this once and for all. If I bide here——"

"There's no doubt of that," he interrupted, "if you wish it. My grandfather is still master here."

"And if you were master, cousin?"

"You are kin to us," he said shortly. "For all of me you may bide as long as you will."

"Well, then, you must treat me like your cousin in truth. Don't call me Miss Archer. I don't consider the Squire my father; he has sent me away; I have no home at Archfield. Call me Jenny, or cousin. And let me follow your ways. I do not mean to be a trouble to you. I know how to keep house; I can work."

Abruptly he took my hands, and turned them over, looking at both sides. I thought he smiled a little, in contempt, and I pulled my fingers away angrily.

"I *can* work!"

"You do not need to work for your keep, cousin. We are not so poor as that. But if you would rather take your meals with the rest of us, it will be easier."

"I would much rather."

"Come along, then. Afterwards Rachel will show you your room. We go to bed early here, and get up early, though you may lie in bed as long as you please."

There was the same careless contempt in his tone, and I made up my mind to teach Master Lake a lesson, if I killed myself doing it. At the moment I said nothing, but followed him meekly back to the kitchen, where he introduced the servants and farm hands to me before we all sat down to an excellent and bountiful supper. My cousin took the head of the table and said grace. It was evident that he was master of the house in all things but name. His people were stiff and shy because of me that night,

394

of course, but afterwards I observed that though they addressed him as one of themselves, and he himself made no distinction, they had just that little deference towards him that set him off as master.

There were half a dozen men and as many women—Lake Farm being primarily a dairy farm. Two of the men were middle-aged, the others about my cousin's age. All of the women were young, there being no married couples on the farm, nor accommodation for any. Rachel was head girl, by virtue of ability rather than age; the others were much alike, healthy, hearty farm wenches, who eyed me surreptitiously and giggled at sallies from the men.

Besides being shy, they were all tired and sleepy from the long, hard farm day. The meal was taken in silence for the greater part, the women eating quite as heartily as the men. I was hungry myself, and did the meal justice, but had an invalid's appetite compared to these hard-working folk.

When the last mouthful was down, my cousin pushed back his chair and said, "Rachel, will you show my cousin her room? John, I'll lock up tonight. Good-night, all."

He nodded generally to all, without heeding my "Good-night, cousin," and walked out. The others rose, and stretched, speaking among themselves in low tones, straggling off to bed, while Rachel took up a candle and showed me upstairs.

"It's a small room, miss, but the only spare," she said apologetically. "I've lit the fire to take the chill off. Would you like a hot brick in your bed?"

"No, thanks, I'm not cold. It's a very pretty room," I said, looking appreciatively around the little chamber, which was simply but neatly furnished, a bright woven rug on the floor, a handsome quilt on the bed, and plain but snowy curtains at the window. It was directly over my grandfather's room, as I later learned, and had the same pretty view of the orchard, with a vine at the window that always gave me pleasure to open my eyes and see in the morning.

As I had obviously no extra clothes with me, Rachel shyly offered me a clean shift, which I took with thanks. It was clean rough linen, smelling sweetly of lavender. I never in my life saw a house where everything was so well kept and orderly. Harry said rightly that it was the best farm in the county. I have seen fine London houses that were sties by comparison, and Archfield was never half so cleaned and polished, though Minnie was a notable housekeeper.

The bed, too, was rough and clean and smelled of lavender. I laid my head on the pillow with a feeling not only of utter thankfulness, but of complete security, and went to sleep almost before I had time to enjoy it.

Life on a farm is always hard, and on a dairy farm hardest of all. Winter or summer, there is never any let-up from the demands of the stock. Cows must be fed, watered, and milked, butter made, stalls cleaned, equipment scalded, and a thousand and one details carried out every day—not excepting Sunday. Cows are hungry and let down milk without distinction as to holidays. Winter brings no respite, as it does to crop farmers. It simply increases the discomfort of the work. Because milk and butter taint so quickly, dairies must be always kept cold. Even Rachel, who feared hard work as little as anybody I ever knew, used to look grim at the remembrance of winter milking and churning.

But at the time of my arrival spring was well on its way. Coming earlier in the country than in London, it had already laid its softening touch over the orchards and meadows. The little garden in front of the house, where my grandfather delighted to sit on sunny days, was bright with early flowers, the grass green with that almost enamelled brilliance which never comes again when the first days of spring have passed.

I used to sit here with the old man, holding his hand while he chatted or dozed, and feel as though I were being newly made over, like the flowers and grass, all the taint of London gradually sloughing off.

At first he could scarcely bear to let me out of his sight. He surprised me, the morning after my arrival, by the sense and strength with which he spoke, recollecting me perfectly and not confusing me with my mother, though he talked of her with tears in his eyes. But by evening, as he grew tired, he rambled and lost the thread of his speech, and at last was content merely to hold and stroke my hand, until Rachel came to help me tuck him up in bed.

All his days followed this pattern. It was in the morning that I learned, little by little, the story of his life, and of his children, particularly my mother. She was his only daughter, and his darling. From one or two things that he said, I collected that he had never been quite the same since her early death, and that first Bob's father, and then Bob himself, had taken over the farm even before my grandfather was so very old.

Bob's mother had been, as Harry said, a cut above her husband's family. "She was a good lass, a very good lass," my grandfather often said. "Aye a bit short-spoken, and sensible to a fault, if you take my meaning, child, but a very good lass! She was a good daughter to me, and did her best, and she made a fine lad out of Bob. 'Twas she gave him a taste for lessons. He has a bit of Latin, you know, and used to do algebra with the Rector, and can tot up a row of figures as quick as any of those chaps in the shops at Ashton. Algebra! Do you mind what that is, child?" the old man said, with great pride. "To be sure, it's no use to a farmer, nor Latin neither, but Bob's a good lad, with no foolish notions; I daresay it's done him no harm," he would say, with a great air of tolerance, which ill concealed his bursting pride. "Are you much book-learned, Jenny, my dear?"

I told him I was a very indifferent scholar.

"But the Squire gave you lessons?"

"My stepmothers used to do so. I can read and write——"

"So can I—a little," my grandfather said, wistfully. Indeed, it's none too common a talent among country people.

"—and talk a bit of French, and read music; but nothing else."

"I doubt you'll look down on Bob a bit, poor boy, after the fine gentlemen you've known?" he said, anxiously.

"No, indeed," I said; adding petulantly, "It is he who despises me because I can't milk a cow."

My grandfather looked at me with a trace of amusement.

"Bob's a very practical lad," he said. "But I daresay you'll get the better of him, Jenny, in the long run!"

As soon as my grandfather grew a little used to having me in the house, and did not so constantly crave my company, I set about proving to my cousin that I was not so useless as he supposed.

I told Rachel I would be glad to help her in any way I could. She was obviously doubtful of me at first, though too polite to say so. Now I will confess that I am not much good at hard, plain work, not having been brought up to it. But Minnie had taught me much about the ordering of a household, and I did not see why some of her methods should not apply to a farm as well as Archfield. So after I had shown Rachel the best way to make soft soap, and a new way to bleach linen, and rearranged the linen room to better advantage, and taken over the still-room, turning out all sorts of washes and purges and waters, she began to assume a very different attitude towards me. She was an intelligent girl, eager to learn and improve herself. She came from a very poor family, and had had no advantages, going out to work at the age of eight, and still sending the better part of her wages home to support the younger brothers and sisters. Lake Farm had been her home for five years, and it was due chiefly to her that it presented so immaculate an appearance. But she had never had an opportunity to pick up any but farm ways, and it was almost pathetic to see how eagerly she learned everything that I could teach her, yearning after pretty ways and graces as hungrily as most women.

I liked Rachel. She was clean-minded and honest and intelligent, and we became friendly. She was terribly over-respectful at first, but two girls working together can always find a good deal to laugh at, and I soon laughed her out of her 'misses' and 'ma'am', making her call me Miss Jenny.

For about a month my cousin persisted in his aloof attitude towards me. He called me, stiffly, 'Cousin', and persisted in treating me like a guest and a stranger long after his own people had forgotten I was Squire Archer's daughter.

I let him alone for those first few weeks, and then I began to

398

take liberties with him. I saw to the laundering of his shirts, and taught the errand boy a better way of polishing his master's boots. I had hot possets waiting for him when he came in from work, and when he happened to complain of a touch of ague, I dosed him with Lady Binion's Ague Water, that Minnie had taught me how to make. I made delicacies for the table and forced him to admire them. I put flowers in his room, and upon one Sunday, as we all walked to church, I put a flower from my nosegay into his buttonhole.

He turned very red at this, and said, with that awful stiffness, "I thank you, Cousin Jenny." Watching him surreptitiously during the sermon, I saw him several times glance down and adjust it carefully. As we walked home, he caught me looking at it, and promptly snatched it out of his buttonhole and threw it away, muttering something about "looking like a fool." I could hardly keep from laughing, but managed to preserve my countenance, and, giving him a wounded look, fell back and walked with Rachel and the other women, leaving him to march on ahead. During the rest of the day I was as stiff with him as he with me. That night there was no special posset for him at bedtime, and next day I carefully removed all the flowers from his room.

He came in just as I was carrying away the last posy. I saw him cast a quick glance around the room. "Are the flowers dead so soon?" he said, with an attempt to appear at ease.

"No, cousin," I said. "But I thought you did not like flowers and so I am taking them away."

He got very red again. "I never said so! I—I am very fond of flowers."

"Oh," I said, keeping my eyes downcast. "Then it is only that you don't like flowers I have given you. Well, that's easily mended." And I marched away, laughing to myself to hear him give a groan, as men do when women appear more than usually unreasonable.

For two or three days I ignored him. There were no more special delicacies and I let one of the maids use stone soap on his shirts. At dinner one day he complained pointedly of feeling agueish. Rachel said, "Miss Jenny must give you another potion, sir, for I'm sure nothing ever did you so much good."

"Well, I don't mind," he said, graciously.

I smiled sweetly at Rachel. "I have forgot the recipe," I said. "And I have always heard the best cure for the ague was to eat moderately. "It is often brought on," I said, gazing stonily at my cousin's well-heaped plate, "by gross feeding."

"Hell!" my cousin exclaimed loudly. He pushed his plate away, got up and stalked out. All the others looked uncomfortable—they were not used to see the master crossed about anything —but I went on serenely eating my dinner.

"Have you really forgot the recipe?" Rachel asked anxiously.

"No," I said, with a wink at her. "And neither has your master got the ague. He only wants attention."

She looked quite shocked; and after that there was a change in her manner towards me, which I was stupidly slow to attribute to the right cause.

That night, as I went up to bed, I met my cousin on the stairs. I thought at first he was going to pass me without a word, but he hesitated, and then suddenly reached out and took my hand.

"Jenny," he said, "I do like flowers. Especially if you give them to me."

I was somewhat taken aback by the seriousness of his manner. I only wanted to force him to be friendlier with me. Feeling a trifle ashamed of my stratagems, I said smilingly, "Forgive me for teasing you with my nonsense, cousin. It is only that I want you to notice me a little."

"Notice you!" he exclaimed. More soberly, he added, "I am dull company for you, Jenny. I am not used to—to anyone like you. I don't know what to say to you."

This confession from my self-assured cousin both surprised and touched me. But I only said, lightly, "Perhaps if you were to practise at it more, cousin——!"

"Well, I will," he said, with the air of one taking a great resolution. "I daresay there is a good deal you could teach me."

I pretended great astonishment. "I, cousin? But you know I have no abilities. Only think! I don't know how to milk a cow."

"Well, I will allow you know more of housekeeping than I thought you would," he admitted. "The house is more agreeable since you came into it."

"Then you *have* noticed!"

"Of course I have. Do you think I am blind? I don't know how to thank you, that is all. By the way," he added, with a sudden mischievousness, "what *have* they been doing to my shirts? You are very revengeful, cousin!"

I laughed, and begged pardon, and ran upstairs, well pleased at having made so considerable a dent in his armour. He was a very human young man after all, only serious and solemn beyond his years because of so much responsibility.

After this, Bob and I got upon much easier terms. He fell into the habit of coming into the parlour to sit with me in the evening —his one hour of leisure, after the late chores were done and supper was being prepared. I sat there because it was next my grandfather's room, and I could be near him and hear him call if he wanted anything, and yet have a light to read or work by. Since my arrival he always supped early with me, and went to bed, and I joined the others at their meal only to be friendly.

The parlour, like all farm parlours, was exceedingly formal and unwelcoming, used perhaps two or three times a year, when the Rector called or upon some other great occasion. Nevertheless it was a pretty room with its white mantelpiece and bow windows, and I set about loosening it up, till at last it was almost as agreeable as the rest of the house. There was even a spinet, bought for my mother as a child. It was old and out of tune, but I sometimes played on it softly to please my grandfather, who sat humming and nodding to its tinkling old tunes.

When Bob first came in, he looked around in a puzzled sort of way, and at intervals he kept looking around again, like a cat in a strange garret. "It's different," he said at last, "but I don't see what you've done."

"You don't mind, cousin?"

"I used to hate this room," he said, musingly. "It's odd what a difference a woman makes in a house."

I laughed. "Why, cousin, the house is full of women!"

"Not like you, Jenny. Rachel is very good, and she works hard, but somehow she doesn't know how to do differently. Of course," he added, with a return of his old stiffness, "we are common folk to what you are used to."

"Cousin," I said, "if you say that again I shall leave you! You don't know how much better you are—all of you—than the people I have been used to. You know yourself that the Squire is a brute and a bully."

He could not deny it. "I suppose, though, you won't want to stay here," he said, hesitantly. "I mean, not for always."

"While my grandfather lives," I said, slowly. "But if you should marry, cousin——"

"I'm not going to marry," he interrupted shortly. "I have no such thought."

"Well, but you will some day. And then your wife might have something to say about it."

"This is your home for as long as you choose to stay. No one has any right to say anything else."

"I won't borrow trouble, cousin. I did not think I should ever be as happy again as I am here."

"*Are* you happy, Jenny?" he asked eagerly.

"Yes," I said, stoutly. It was true, in a way. I had come so near to absolute disaster that the peace and security of the place was like Heaven. It was more than I could ever have hoped for. Let us say that I was contented. That is a long way from happiness, as anybody who has been really happy knows. But as I never expected to know that kind of happiness again, it was no use pining for it.

Harry came now and then, bringing me word from Minnie. He reported that the whole household revolved around Val. The doctor came every day, and my father swore that she was improved, though nobody else could see it. He sent for a dressmaker and had a beautiful new wardrobe prepared for her, and she was dressed by the maids two or three times a day. Minnie would not let Cora wait on Val, she was so vicious towards my sister. Shortly afterwards, Harry reported with great glee that my father had overheard Cora calling Val "a drivelling idiot" and had promptly thrown the girl out of the house and reinstated Minnie as his mistress. Everybody was pleased at this—except Cora.

"Do you see my sister ever, Harry?"

"Sometimes, Miss Jenny, when the Squire takes her out for a walk. I thought at first she was just the same as ever—just as handsome, you know. But I got close to her once and I saw how it was with her. But nobody minds, for she never does anything to fright anybody, nor makes any trouble. Poor young lady!"

It was no use asking if she missed me. It was foolish even to think it. Now and then, when I thought of the Squire's revelation, I tried to understand that she was not my sister, any more than Neal my brother, but it seemed to make no difference. Blood or no blood, she was my sister still. I remembered that last time we had talked together—the very last—in the box at the opera, when she had told me how dearly she had come to love me. Nobody could take that from me. However terribly I had failed Neal, I had at any rate never failed Val.

"The farm agrees with you, Miss Jenny. You've got colour back in your face," Harry said, on one of his later visits. "You looked mightily peaked that night you came home."

I smiled complacently. There will never be a time, I hope, when I cease to care for my appearance. It was undeniably a consolation to look into the mirror nowadays and see that the old colour and softness and roundness had come back. Farm life is healthy, and I had plenty to eat, plenty of rest, and long sunnings on every fine day. The very colour of my hair was brighter, the texture silkier.

He looked at me, half sullenly, half admiringly. "I wish you'd not be so stand-offish, Miss Jenny! You used not to be so disagreeable about a kiss or two."

"Now look here, Harry," I said severely, "I like you very much, as I always have, and I like kisses well enough too. But

403

you're betrothed, and I'm a grown-up woman now. You wouldn't ask it if I still lived in Archfield," I added, with something of bitterness, for I could not help feeling now and then that I had come down in the world, and that the people round about regarded me with a good deal less respect than when I had been Miss Archer and lived in the big house. For myself, I did not care whether the house I lived in was big or small, but nobody likes to be thought of less regard than they were.

"I would too," Harry said indignantly. "Don't talk so silly!"

"All the same, you ought to be thinking about kissing Jane, not me."

"I can kiss Jane the rest of my life," he pointed out.

I laughed so much that my cousin came out of the house. I thought he scowled a good deal at the sight of Harry, and spoke so coldly that Harry shuffled with his feet, and at last said, "Well, good-bye, all," and hastily rode off.

"Why does he come here so often?"

"To bring me news of Archfield."

"It's just as I thought," my cousin said, kicking a clod violently. "You always wish yourself back there."

"I do nothing of the kind. I hate Archfield. But I want news of my sister."

He made some sort of an apology. "If you are going for a walk, cousin, I will walk with you as far as the lane."

I accepted this peace overture, and we strolled on together. "This is a muddy walk for you," he remarked, as we turned into the lane. "And in summer it will be dusty."

"I don't mind."

"Do you know how to ride—would you rather ride?" he offered unexpectedly. "There's a nice little mare that would just do for you."

I accepted joyfully, and went at the next opportunity to Ashton to order a riding dress. The first day it came home I went out on the mare. My cousin had bought a pretty new lady's saddle for her, and, somewhat to my astonishment, he had the bay cob saddled for himself, and rode with me. I had never before known him to do anything so frivolous—and in the middle of the morning, too!

After that, we rode together often. On a horse he looked his best, and it seemed to do him good to break away from the routine of the farm; he was gayer and livelier on these rides than I had ever seen him. Indeed, there were plenty of men to do the work; he had no need to labour so hard himself, but it was a point of honour to work side by side with his men.

"A farm never comes to any good, Jenny, when the master does not work with the men," he said gravely. Nevertheless he managed to absent himself for an hour or two nearly every day to ride with me.

One morning when we returned from a long ride he was greeted with bad news—a prize heifer had fallen in the stalls and injured herself. He rushed off to the barn at once, and was there all day, without even coming in to a meal, but that night the heifer died.

The animal was valuable, and by way of being a pet of his, a pretty spoiled little creature. I was very sorry and waited to tell him so when he came in, looking tired and stern.

He replied curtly, so I said no more, but made him sit down and urged him to eat, giving him first a strong sack posset to relax his nerves.

After supper he said, abruptly (there was no one else with us in the kitchen at the time), "It was my fault for being away. I have always handled her because she is nervous and frightens easily, but they had to take her out, and John is no good with animals, and so she was alarmed somehow, and tried to bolt, and fell. It would not have happened if I had been here."

"I'm sorry, cousin."

"It is not your fault," he said. He got up and moved about restlessly, not looking at me. "But the fact is, I have been neglecting my work to go about with you, Jenny."

"I am sorry," I said, again.

He turned and faced me abruptly. "Jenny—will you marry me?"

I was clearing the table, while the maids worked in the dairy. At his words I let fall a large spoon which covered the cloth with a spreading berry stain.

"Oh Lord!" I said desperately. "Get me the salt dish, quickly!"

He brought it, and stood beside me while I sprinkled the stain. Suddenly I felt his arm around me, and he said, very softly but urgently, "Jenny—answer me! Will you? I think you must know that—that I want it very badly."

"No," I said, breathlessly. I felt something almost like terror in his nearness, as though I were being crowded into a corner. What a fool I was, not to have seen this coming! But I never dreamed he would care for me. And now—now what on earth was I to do?

"I'm not a good marriage for you, Jenny, I know. You have been bred up a lady, and I'm only a yeoman. But we are kin-folk, and I have had some advantages, and I would better myself to please you. You should have the ordering of everything in the house. There is plenty of money. You would always be comfortable. And—and I love you, cousin."

He had made his little speech with considerable dignity, facing facts but not apologising for them. And the break in his last words was surprisingly eloquent. I felt perfectly desperate; I did not know what to do.

"You must give me an answer, Jenny."

"Not now, cousin," I said, frantically. "I—— You have taken me by surprise! I—I never thought——"

"Didn't you? But you don't dislike me, Jenny?"

"I like you very much," I answered, troubled.

"Is it because I am not a gentleman?"

"No! I'm not such a fool as that, cousin. Good God, you have everything, and I nothing. No dowry, no connections——"

"I don't care about that."

I felt trapped, at bay. I owed him everything. It was the most reaonable, the most fortunate conclusion to the whole affair. Who was I, a bastard of no name, thrown off by my genteel relations, to worry about whether I stepped down in the social scale or not?

And I truly did not care. Lake Farm was a place where a woman might be very happy. and my cousin would no doubt make a kind, affectionate husband. But——

I said, at last, in a very low voice, "Do not be angry with me, cousin. It is because I love someone else."

He stepped away from me as abruptly as if I had slapped his face. After quite a dreadful pause, he said, "A gentleman, I suppose? Someone in London?"

"Yes . . ."

"Will you marry *him*?"

"No. I never expect to see him again."

"Well, then," he said, with renewed eagerness, "why shouldn't you marry me? You're fond of me, cousin; that's enough."

"No, no, it isn't—not for you. It is robbing you."

"If *I* don't mind, cousin, *you* needn't. Come, Jenny—it would make grandfather so happy. You will think about it, at least?"

"Yes, I will," I said at last, reluctantly. I felt as though I had bound myself with even that little, and I resisted his embrace and would not let him kiss me. And all the while I felt so guilty— they had done me nothing but good!

I at last induced him to let me go, and ran upstairs to my chamber in great disorder of mind. I found Rachel just turning down my bed and stared at her in astonishment, for she had long ago given over waiting on me.

She stared back at me defiantly, with red eyes. "I thought, seeing you are to be mistress here, I'd best get in the way of serving you," she said bitterly.

A great light burst on me. She had been so cold and difficult to me lately! "Oh, Rachel! You love my cousin!"

"Yes, I do," she said, and with that sat down on the side of the bed, threw her apron over her head, and cried bitterly.

I sat down beside her and consoled her as best I could, all the while ready to tear my hair with dismay. Just as I was learning to be contented! Now this—and what should I do? Everything in reason argued for the marriage. It was safety, security, comfort, for the rest of my life. I had nowhere else to go, nowhere else to turn. I liked my cousin and he was a fine young man; he would make a husband not to be ashamed of in any company. But——

There was always that great *but*—— George Parker was gone, lost to me. I should never see him again. But what difference did it make, when I still loved him so desperately I dared not even think of him, it made me so unhappy? How could I think of marrying anyone else while I still felt like that?

I consoled Rachel more easily than myself. We parted friends and she went off to cry herself to sleep. But I lay and tossed all night. What was the use of it? Why should I torment myself with hope? Rid myself once and for all of that dark-eyed ghost, marry my cousin, and be, if not happy, at any rate safe and contented? That was the thing to do.

But——

"I wish you could make up your mind to Bob," my grandfather said, wistfully, one morning as we sat together in the warm spring sunshine. He nodded, as I looked at him startled. "Aye. He did tell me about it. 'Twas just what I was wishing for, Jenny, my dear."

"Did he tell you why I cannot take him?" I said, turning away from the anxious glance he fixed on me. I was so fond of him, and wished so much to please him!

"Aye, my dear," he said, sadly. "Bob says you've a fancy for a gentleman in London. To be sure, the lad's not a fit match for you, the Squire's daughter and all——"

"It's not that! Grandfather, you must know it's not that!" I desperately declared. I was almost ready to do what they wished, simply for fear they would believe this of me—that I thought Bob not good enough.

"Have you a very great fancy for the gentleman, Jenny?" he persisted. "For, to be sure, if there's a chance he might marry you, it's only right you should have the chap you like best."

"There is no chance, grandfather. It is not that. But I—I cannot get over it. It would not be fair to Bob."

"Well, my dear," he said gently, "I won't pretend to tell you what's best to do. But I've known many a lass that thought she'd never get over some fancy of hers, and yet married another fellow, and was happy enough with him in the end, aye, and learned to laugh at her old fancy too."

"Perhaps so, grandfather. I will think about it. I wish I could, for your sake———"

"Nay, nay, child," he exclaimed, with much feeling. "Not for the world, not for the world! Don't think of me. Think only of yourself, or of Bob, poor lad! I never thought to see him so set upon a thing. I always reckoned he'd marry cold, as the saying is, and late in life. But you were too much for him, Jenny. I told you so."

"I didn't mean to be," I said, troubled, thinking of my teasing, and how I had forced myself upon his attention. "I am sorry for it."

"Ah, well——— But, Jenny, if you *could*! He's a good boy, you know, a very good boy——— And when I'm gone, Jenny, there's not much I can leave you, and you couldn't stay here with him unless you were wed——— What will you do, child?" he asked, very gently, but as though he wished to open my eyes to the future.

I sat silent. Once upon a time I had looked into my future and seen nothing there that was not darker and uglier than the dark face of death. I was not likely to forget that moment. Even here, in this safe warm garden, I felt a chill come over me, and shivered under the remembrance. The frost had touched me once, and the mark would never come quite off again.

He patted my hand, and sighed. "It's hard to be young," he said simply, with unexpected acuteness. "I would not be young again, for all the strength and pleasure of it. Maybe I didn't ought to speak to you, Jenny, child———"

I exclaimed in remonstrance, but he shook his head. "It's never right to interfere. But, Jenny, love, I keep remembering your mother——— *She* married her fancy, and a sorry old time she had of it, and there never was another suitor of hers but would have made her happier than the Squire, though she never would have believed it then. And I was proud for her, Jenny, prouder than I ever was for myself, and thought it a great thing she should marry so high——— Bob'd never be a cruel husband, Jenny, nor

409

false. But there, I'll say no more. You're a good child, a good lass."

A week went by, while I swung endlessly round from one decision to another, never quite fixed enough to speak out. When it was morning, and the sun shone, I was braver, and thought that I never could marry where I did not love, and that it was better to gamble and lose all than take your first small winnings and run home. Late in the afternoon, as the sun went down and the shadows lengthened, my courage began to slip from me. It came back with fires and candlelight. And then, in the middle of the night, it would leave me altogether, and I would wake wild with terror from my dreams, ready to run to Bob that very moment and beg him to take me and hold me and never let me go back into that wilderness from which I had escaped. . . . But when morning came, and the sun shone, my courage returned, and it was all to do over again.

My cousin did not press me for an answer. He was very quiet and reserved, hardly ever looking or speaking to me. I am sure there was not a soul about the place who did not guess how things were, and I got plenty of reproachful glances. Rachel, poor girl, having betrayed herself, was no longer sullen towards me, but went about hangdog and red-eyed. She would have made him so much better a wife, adoring the very soles of his shoes. . . . Why must we want what we cannot have, and pass over so scornfully the thing that comes easily?

One morning, after they had all gone out to the dairy, I was passing to and fro in the kitchen, putting away dishes and making all tidy, singing to myself as I did so, for the sun shone and my courage was at its highest.

Suddenly I heard the sound of a horse being ridden hard, and went to the door in time to see Harry gallop up the lane. He jumped off the cob, as I waved, and ran up the path, obviously in a state of high excitement.

"Miss Jenny! Minnie bade me come—— Lord knows what'll happen if the Squire finds I'm gone at this time of day!"

"What's the matter?" I asked anxiously. "My sister is not worse?"

"No, not worse, miss, but there's a gentleman from London come for her!"

"Oh God!" I said faintly. I clutched the sides of the door till the splinters ran into my hands, and Harry caught hold of me.

"Don't take on so, Miss Jenny! He didn't get so much as a sight of her—the Squire saw to that! Sent him off with a flea in his ear! You'll not see my daughter, he said; get out and be damned to you! Swore up and down she wasn't there, Minnie said, and at last he went off and the Squire said he'd set the dogs on him if he ever came back."

"Dear God!" I said again, and sat down on the step with my head on my arms. Harry knelt beside me.

"Don't, Jenny! I didn't mean to fright you so. You don't think anybody can take her away from the Squire, do you?"

"The King can," I said grimly. Harry looked doubtful. The King was merely a name to him; but he knew from experience the power of my father's hand.

"Well, I don't rightly know. Miss Val's his daughter. I don't see how the King has any call to interfere."

I could not help smiling faintly, and Harry cheered up at once. "Don't you fret, miss! Minnie said you were not to fret. Only she thought you ought to know."

"Yes. It was very good of her. Harry—you must go back or you will be in trouble. Only—I *must* know what is happening! Will you promise to bring me word every day?"

He swore he would, bade me again not to fret, and rushed off, far more apprehensive of my father's wrath than the power of any King's bailiff.

I sat for a while in the sunshine, feeling very cold in spite of its warmth. The Squire would fight—yes, but would he win? Perhaps he might frighten off a bailiff or two, but sooner or later there would come a power he could not defeat. Cursing and threatening an official was certainly not the best way to go about proving himself a suitable guardian for Val, but it was the only way he knew to win an argument.

411

Somehow I had never really faced the possibility that they would come after her. It had always been in my mind that, once she was gone, they would let the thing drop; perhaps even pretend she had died in Bedlam. But it was not so. Dear God, surely, surely they would not drag her back? It was too cruel, too damnable.

I steadied myself at last. She was not gone yet. The man had retreated; perhaps there would be no more trouble. At any rate, there was nothing I could do. It was in her father's hands now and, little as I loved him, I knew he would fight obstinately if not wisely.

I went back to my dishes finally, but there was no more singing. I could not get that feeling of cold off my heart . . .

Turning round at a step, I saw my cousin at the door, his straight fair brows drawn together in a frown almost of pain.

"Is there no one else to do that?" he said roughly. "It is not fit work for you."

"Oh, nonsense, cousin!" I answered cheerfully, determined to be easy and natural if possible. "I am not so high-stomached. I am learning to be quite at home in the kitchen, and like it very well."

"I will not have it!" he said, loudly and angrily, taking a step towards me. "Do you hear? Somebody else shall do it. . . . I'll not have you."

He spoke so unreasonably that I did not attempt to answer, but stood regarding him doubtfully, the dish clout still in my hand. As I did not move, he gave a wrathful exclamation and, striding up, snatched the cloth from my hand and threw it furiously into the corner of the kitchen.

"You do it to anger me! As though I wanted you to work your way, because you will not——" He stopped, choking, and I said sorrowfully:

"Oh, cousin, I have spoiled everything for you. I wish I had never come here."

"I wish you never had!" he said, with a passion I would not

412

have suspected of him. "Jenny—I can't wait any longer. Say Yes or No, and have done with tormenting me."

"I don't mean to torment you," I said, in a low voice. "It is only that I am in doubt what to do. I am fond of you, cousin, and of Lake Farm——"

"Then marry me! You shall never come into the kitchen again, Jenny, if only you will. I'll have the house done over. I'll make it as good as the Squire's——"

"Oh, Bob! Don't—don't!"

"Then it's No?" he said hoarsely. As I did not answer him at once, he swung on his heel. "I knew how it would be. Some damned fellow in London who'll never think of you again!"

"I can't help it, Bob. Any more than you can."

"Look here," he said shortly, after a pause. "I can't go on like this. I've always been meaning to go and see a bit of the world. If you won't have me, Jenny, I'll go."

"And leave the farm!"

"My grandfather's not so old yet," he said, sullenly.

"I won't drive you away, Bob. I'll go myself."

"Where will you go?" he said, turning on me sharply. "To *him*?" I did not answer, being angry, and he came up to me with a rush and seized me in his arms. "Jenny—don't be angry! I'm off my head about you, and that's a fact! Only say the word and I'll make you forget all about that fellow. I swear I'll be good to you!"

I stood passively in his arms while he kissed me. His arms were strong and his kisses clean and pleasant. A woman could not desire a man stronger or better able to take care of his wife. He was good, kind and masterful. I did not shrink from the thought of him as a lover—in bed, too, I was sure, he would be both masterful and ardent.

This was what must be. What was the use of dreaming any longer? With that cold on my heart, I had no courage left, even in the sunshine.

I said, stumbling because the words would not come easily, no matter how I forced them:

413

"Cousin—I will not drive you away. If—if you want me, I will try to make you a good wife——"

"Want you!" he exclaimed, staring at me flushed with triumph. "Jenny, do you mean it?"

"Yes," I said, trying not to mind that look of triumph, trying to force my mind to stay steady.

Then he kissed and caressed me with such passion that I was at last forced to drive him off—not very easy, since he had the muscles of a hard-working farmer. He stood looking at me, laughing triumphantly. And I stared back at him, trying to smile, and conscious only of a dreadful panic. So this was to be my master, this fair, bull-necked fellow, who flushed high and lustfully with a few kisses, crying imperiously:

"Now you're my lass! D'you hear, Jenny? And I'm a bulldog for holding what I want, so don't you think to put me off now! We'll have the banns cried this Sunday and next, and then——"

I did not deny him. What was the use of straining at a gnat? I escaped from him at last, however; he luckily recalling that he had to go back to the barn.

"Out of the kitchen, my girl! I'll not have *my* wife a kitchen slavey! I'll make you as good a lady as anybody could!"

I stood looking at him hopelessly. His whole manner had changed; the man's naturally masterful nature had come uppermost in triumph, all the more for being made to bend before. He would be kind—but, oh God, what chance would his wife have before this calm, self-assured, humourless nature, that had probably never doubted, and certainly had not a grain of imagination in it?

But I had given my word. Now the best thing I could do was carry it out quickly, and think about it as little as I could.

Before he went out, he said, "I'll ride with you later, love. Don't you go out this morning. I don't like to have you riding about alone."

'You're not my master yet,' I thought sullenly, and as soon as he was gone to the dairy I slipped out to the stable and had the boy saddle the mare. I felt, as I did so, a kind of defiance, as

414

though already I was oppressed, and had the need to revolt. And yet I kept hoping all the while my cousin would not suddenly appear. Good God, I was not going to be afraid of him, surely? I set my whole self in defiance at the thought.

Galloping along the lanes, some sanity returned to me. The wind whipped my face, sweet with the smell of orchards in bloom. This was a good life. I had made the right decision. There was nothing against it, nothing to make me hesitate—only a ghost, the ghost of an old love that no power could bring to life any more. . . .

And at the thought, I pulled in the mare so suddenly she stumbled, and, dropping the reins, I sat with my face bowed down in my hands. It was no use. No use. I could not help it. Oh God, this was the strongest thing of all, the only thing that mattered . . . and I had lost it.

I must get away. That was the only thought my mind would fix on. It was cowardly, it was wrong, it was foolish . . . but I must get away. If I stayed here, I would sooner or later marry Bob Lake. And then, one day, there would be disaster. Maybe it was in some women to love one man and marry another, but it was not in me. I had sinned enough against my love . . . denied it, fought it, betrayed it with Haywood. That was a little thing, a light thing, compared to this—that I should marry an honest man and cuckold him every night in my dreams. . . .

The mare, shaking her head petulantly, strayed towards the hedge and began to crop at the short, soft grass, rolling her bit noisily as she chewed. The hedge was full of may, soft and white, smelling so sweet . . . They said it was unlucky to bring it in the house. Years ago, as a child, one of the maids had screamed and rushed me outdoors again when I came in innocently carrying my arms full of it. Curious, that anything so harmlessly lovely should be thought so unlucky. . . .

Slowly I straightened in the saddle, taking up the reins, resolutely checking the mare as she stretched her pretty neck for one more bite. "I will not bring the may into your house, cousin . . . I will not be the one to bring you bad luck. It is of no use to try to be sensible and wise—I *know* that bad luck follows where the heart does not go——"

I spoke to the mare. "Come up, Jincey! We'll go home and face him. If there is anything left of us afterwards—— Well, then it will be time to plan and be wise."

She pricked her ears, liking to be talked to, as most horses do. I patted her neck. "Come along, Jincey. I don't suppose you and I will go a-riding any more. . . ."

But even as I swung her head towards home, I checked again. It was the old story. Val was on my mind once more, all the heavier weight for having been for a while removed. If she needed me—I could not rest easy nor think wholly of myself until I knew the truth of this new trouble. I was not far from Archfield. I would go there and see Minnie and maybe even talk to the Squire. I was not afraid of him, not if I could do Val any good. At any rate, I would know the worst. After that, it would be time enough to face Bob.

There is a long incline to the west of Archfield that cuts off all sight of the house except the chimneys. Top the incline, and you look down on the whole spread of the roofs and windows, lawns, gardens, stables and barns, like a stage carefully set. Often, as children, we hid here among the thick holly bushes on the crest, away from my father's anger, until we saw him ride off or one of the maids came out waving a white apron to show the danger was over.

I guided the mare cautiously up this incline, planning to reconnoitre carefully before I went down, going if necessary on foot. I was not afraid to meet the Squire head-on, if need be, but first I wanted a word with Minnie. There was no use battling with him if I could do no good by it.

The turf was thick and springy and Jincey's little hoofs made no sound. I reined her to a walk as we approached the top, meaning to tie her to one of the bushes. If she saw the horses down below she would whinny, like as not, and give me away.

And then, suddenly, my hands jammed down on the reins,

checking her in her tracks. There was somebody here before me. . . .

He stood among the holly bushes, half concealed, staring down so fixedly at the house that he did not hear or sense me come. His whole pose was eloquent of watchful, relentless patience. He looked as though rooted to the ground. . . . So might an enemy, in the old days, have looked down on the house, still and implacable in his waiting, yet alert always, to seize on the chance he looked for.

It was fear and despair that made me so angry. This was no casual watcher, no enemy to be easily driven away with threats or frightened off by the dogs. This was a real danger. It was Val he looked for, and sooner or later he would see her, and then——

If I had had a weapon, I believe I would have tried to kill him. Frantic with rage and despair, I tried to drive the mare upon him, but the holly leaves stabbed her and she shied, trampling sideways into the bushes, though I lashed her with my crop.

The hidden watcher whirled, the flying hoofs missing his head by inches. The sunlight fell full on his face, and I saw him to know him. It was George Parker.

He said, "Jenny!" so loudly and passionately that it seemed to ring all around me with the exultant sound of trumpets. And then, somehow, I was off the mare and into his arms, my arms around his neck, clinging to him as though I could never let go, sobbing and laughing together, saying his name over and over . . . my own true love, come at last to lay all the ghosts . . .

"There is one thing I will never forgive myself, Jenny."

"I wish I had only one," I said sorrowfully. He gripped me harder than ever, shaking me.

"No! Not even one It was all my fault, Jenny, all my fault from the beginning. I have never forgotten what you said—that I wanted to be loved like a king. How could I be such a fool? Such a fool! But I've paid for it, Jenny. I can never forgive myself that I was not there when you needed me so much."

"There never was a time when I didn't need you," I said, in a

417

low voice. "Only I didn't know how much, until I thought—I thought I should never see you again."

We sat on the sunny hillside, safe among our holly bushes as in a fort, while his mount and Jincey cropped the turf peaceably together. He was thinner than I remembered him, and looked tired, but even as we talked the grim look began to fade, from his face, and the old teasing brightness return that I loved so much.

There, in the quiet and the sunlight, I told him everything—everything, I think, there was to tell. At first he tried to stop me, but I begged him to let me go on.

"If I could only tell it once, George, all of it, just as it was—I think I could forget it better."

And even as I told him, the old pain grew easier, even the pain of Neal's death . . .

"You mustn't blame yourself, George, because you weren't there. I think, perhaps, I *had* to help myself."

"It was a great thing that you did, Jenny," he said, almost with wonder.

I shook my head. "It wasn't me. At least—I don't know. I can't explain. It all seemed so clear, as though someone had stood beside me, and told me what to do."

"I wish it had been me!" he said, with a kind of curious jealousy. I saw that the thought of it made him unhappy, and so I said no more of it, but told him the rest of the story quickly, concluding:

"So you see, I haven't even a name nor a father, let alone a dowry. Oh, George, I'm not a fit match for you! You'd better let me marry my cousin."

"I will, if you can say you like him best."

"Ah, you know better than that. But do you really and truly not mind my being a bastard?"

"Having met your father, dearest love, will you think me impolite to say that I rejoice at it?"

I could not help laughing. "And you know, George, perhaps it was the fox-headed lord and I am really an aristocrat after all!"

"Perhaps. But I don't care if it was a fox-headed poacher. The story begins with you, Jenny! begins and ends with you."

Well, there it is. There is only one more thing to tell now.

Not about my cousin—though telling him was really almost more than I could screw my courage up to. Poor Bob took it very well, and I'm afraid that my grandfather was so much gratified he forgot to be as disappointed as I thought he would be. The old pride that had led him to agree to my mother's marriage with the Squire was not entirely scotched—he said, "It's better to marry with your own kind, child, if you can; and for sure you were always too spirited for Bob. He needs a fine sturdy girl, with no nonsense about her——"

"Not like me, grandfather!"

"No," he agreed, quite unconscious of my teasing. "Your gentleman will manage you very well, Jenny. He's a match for you. Poor Bob would never have been that."

"I hope he's not *very* sorry."

"Aye, he is; but he'll get over it," my grandfather assured me, calmly. "He's not one to die for love."

And not even about our marriage. It was not long delayed. When Minnie discovered that the London gentleman, instead of coming to take Val, had come for me instead, she declared that she had known it all along. "And it was pure spite of your Pa to hide you from him, and try to keep you apart. But Lord! the Squire has met his match for once!"

"I thought perhaps you didn't want to see me," George said. "But I was determined you should—I would have stayed in those holly bushes till Christmas, if need be. And then there you were, like a thunderbolt out of nowhere, trying to ride me down, you little virago!"

"I thought you were after Val. George, do you think they'll let her stay?"

"Rather than admit somebody could escape from Bedlam, and throw the whole city into a panic? Don't worry, Jenny. They are well satisfied to let things stay as they are. Damn that prig of a Case! He'll hear from me for having given you so little help when——"

"No, no, I don't want any revenge. Not even that horrible man at Bedlam, though I think he ought to go—I only want to forget it all, and never think of any of it again."

"And so you shall," he said grimly. "I will make it up to you, Jenny—I will make it all up."

So we were married almost at once, and went back to London because George said you must always try to ride again a horse that has thrown you. Mrs. Hamilton accepted me with a good grace, after all. We stayed with her for a little while, till we could find a house of our own. George, at his father's death, had inherited a small but sufficient income; he wanted to go into Parliament, and his aunt said he was sure to make a success of it. "He is so clever, you know! and whatever he does, he does with all his heart. When I saw his heart was set on you, my dear, I knew it was no more use throwing Miss Elin in his way. And now I hear that she has been secretly married, to that sad rake Haywood! What a pity! But I am glad, child, that we are to be friends. You and he shall have everything, when I am gone."

But still, the thing I have to tell has nothing to do with all this, nor even with George.

After we were married, and returned to London, I told him there was a debt I had to pay, and we went accordingly to the little church near the river. A service was just concluding, and we remained for the end, going out last of all to introduce ourselves to the clergyman. His name was Hall; a round-faced agreeable little gentleman of middle years, who appeared quite gratified by the story George told him.

"And so my wife, you see, feels she must repay her debts," he said, with a smile, and gave him a roll of money, folded up in paper.

The clergyman, with the most innocent naïveté, immediately unfolded and counted it. Then he looked at us quite astounded.

"Oh, but this is too much!"

420

"No, indeed it is not. We repay our debts with interest. Especially such a debt as this."

"But, my dear sir," he said, looking from one to the other of us. "My dear ma'am! You could not possibly—— There has never, to my knowledge, been more than a few shillings in the box at any time."

George looked at me; I said eagerly, "Oh no, there was more, a great deal more, than five pounds."

"Five pounds! My dear Mrs. Parker! It would be a miracle—a miracle, I assure you!—if there were ever so much as five shillings!" He smiled on me most kindly. "My dear young lady, you must be mistaken! It was some other church."

I looked around me in silence—the little bare vestibule, the deep splinter gouged out of the floor, the bare shelf with the candle, now of course snuffed, and the Poor Box, the error in spelling more conspicuous than ever in the flood of June sunshine. I said nothing, but my husband was watching my face closely.

He turned to Mr. Hall, and smiled. "Never mind, my dear sir," he said. "I am sure the poor of your parish can use our offering."

"To be sure," he said hastily. "To be sure. I shall put it to good use—*good* use."

We left him staring after us, and went out into the sunshine. I said, in a low voice:

"George—it *was* the same church. I could not be mistaken. And there *was* all that money——"

I stopped, almost afraid to go on. He put his arm around me very tightly, and said:

"I know, Jenny, I know. But it is a thing to think of, and to believe, not to talk of."

And so I never have, until now, when I have remembered it all again, just as it was, for the last time.

WE COME APART

WE COME APART

SARAH CROSSAN
BRIAN CONAGHAN

BLOOMSBURY
LONDON OXFORD NEW YORK NEW DELHI SYDNEY

Bloomsbury Publishing, London, Oxford, New York, New Delhi and Sydney

First published in Great Britain in February 2017 by Bloomsbury Publishing Plc
50 Bedford Square, London WC1B 3DP

www.bloomsbury.com

Hardback ISBN 978 1 4088 7885 9
Export ISBN 978 1 4088 7886 6

MIX
Paper from
responsible sources
FSC® C020471

Typeset by RefineCatch Limited, Bungay, Suffolk
Printed and bound in Great Britain by CPI Group (UK) Ltd, Croydon CR0 4YY

1 3 5 7 9 10 8 6 4 2

For Alan, Richard and Daniel – S.C.
For Ian and Catherine – B.C.

Part
ONE

Caught

You have to be quick,
none of this pretending to be browsing business
that some shoplifters go for.

It's in
       grab what you want
and out again.

But the others don't get it.
They take ages making decisions,
like they might be legit buying,
so I know before we're done
       that
we're done for.

And I'm right.

We don't make it two steps out of
Boots
before a security guard
nabs me by the hood of my jacket.
Liz and Shawna are
legging it up the high street
       and away,
while Meg and I
get dragged back into the shop
and up to an office.

'Empty your pockets,
you little scrubbers!' the security guard shouts.

'Can't make us,' I say.

'You want me to call the police?' he asks.
'That what you want?'

'No!' Meg says,
and as quick as a heartbeat
turns her coat pockets
                    inside out.

But they're empty.
No lipstick or nail varnish,
none of the mini chocolate eggs I saw her
stash away either.

'I didn't even do nothing,' she says.
She bites her bottom lip,
starts to well up.
Looks all sorts of pathetic
            really.

'Now *you*,' the security guard says,
poking the air around me with his fat finger.

I turn out my pockets
wondering if all the gear I tried to nick

will somehow disappear too,
like Meg's did.
But it doesn't.

Everything clatters to the floor:
lipstick, blusher, mascara, nail varnish
and
bloody mini chocolate eggs.

Mini chocolate eggs that *I* didn't nick.
Mini chocolate eggs that Meg can't get enough of.

She winks.
She winks to tell me to keep schtum,
to make sure I don't tell it as it is –
that she somehow managed to stuff *her* loot
into *my* pockets on the way up to the office,
that she's meant to be my mate
but is stitching me up
and letting me take the rap
for everyone else's thieving.

Again.

'What's all that?' the security guard asks,
pointing at the gear on the floor.

'Never seen it before,' I say.

'Really?' he asks.
'Well, it just came out of your pockets.'

'Can I go now?' Meg asks.

I stare at her,
hard.
Is she for real?
Like, is she actually going to leave me here
            on my own
with some mentalist security guard
and the threat of juvenile jail?

'Mum'll be expecting me,' she says.
            'I ain't nicked nothing.'

The security guard picks up the phone.
'Yeah, you can go,' he tells Meg.

Then he grins at me,
well pleased with himself –
Captain Catch-A-Thief.
'But *you*.
You're going down to the station.'

HERE

In the one month
since we
arriving to live in
London North, England,
it rain most
of days,
and sunshine only a few,
which is funnier because
we come here in
summer.

Tata say we here for
short time
only
to make the Queen's cash

then

return back
to our city, town, village
for to buy:

house mansion

then

car with top speed

then

fashions for impressing

then

gifts for my older brothers and sisters
who we leave in Romania.

Tata lucky he have connections
to give him strong job.

On some days after we
arrive
I helping Tata with his
tough work.
He driving his white lorry van
around streets,
spying
seeking
searching
for the metals that people in
London North
not wanting.

We put every items on lorry and
top man pays Tata hand cash
for metals.

It good for me to helping Tata
because now I am main son
and need to
quick learn
how to make family monies
and be
provider for all.
This is what my peoples do.
Roma mens
become cash provider,
for keeping all family happy
in clothings and food.

I am fifteen
and man now,
so my working in lorry van
make much sense.

Real reason we come to
England
is because I am
older,
and cannot be without
working
wealth,
or
wife.

And Tata must to make
sacks of cash
for to pay
family
of girl
back home.

And then
we can to marry.
Which make gigantic hurt in my head.

Caseworker

You can't even get into the youth offending services
    building
without going through
a series of locked doors
and signing yourself in with
two different doormen.

Along every corridor are
blue plastic chairs
arranged in pairs,
kids in hoodies slumped in
them so you can't see their faces.
Some of them are with their parents,
some aren't,
but there's this low rumbling
of rage in the place.

You can smell it in the air.

I don't have to wait long to meet my caseworker
– 'Dawn Green' according to her badge –
who's got the smug look of someone
who thinks
she knows
more than most people.

But Dawn Green knows jack shit
about me.

She tilts her head to one side
like she's talking to toddlers:
'So . . . taking part in a reparation scheme
would save Jess from getting
a criminal record.'

'Reparation scheme?' Mum asks.

'Yes. As this is her third offence,
the police can't turn a blind eye.
She has to show a willingness to change,
to give back to her community.'

'So it's like community service,' Mum says.

Dawn bites the insides of her lips.
'It's helping out in parks
and attending self-development sessions.'

Always quick with an apology, Mum says,
'Well, she *definitely* wants to show she's sorry.'

'And she'll do what she's told,' Terry adds,
like he's my dad
and this is any of his bloody business.

12

What is he even *doing* here?

'Great, so,
the police have proposed
a scheme lasting three months.
What do you think, Jess?'
Dawn turns to me,
finally,
and I know that
I'm meant to tell her
how sorry I am for being such a drain on society
and
    of course
I'll pick up crap down the park
to make up for it.

But a massive part of me
wants to say no,
wants to turn to Dawn and go,
I'd rather do time
and get a record
than
hang out with no-hopers
and do-gooders
for the next twelve weeks.
Thanks all the same though.

But I don't get a chance to speak.

Before I can open my mouth,
Terry leans forward and grabs Dawn's hand,
shakes it like they've just done a deal
and says,
'When does she start?'

ENGLAND IS THE STRANGER OF PLACES

Some peoples
smile and say hello
in street or on bus.
Other peoples
not like my face
and don't returning
the smile I sharing.

Mămică feel same as me.
Sometimes I see her
feeling sad
or
I can hear her
anger conversations with Tata:

> 'This place isn't for us, they don't want our kind
> here,' she say.
> 'We won't be here long,' Tata say.
> 'Don't make promises you can't keep.'
> 'For God's sake, Miri, we'll be home by
> Christmas.'
> 'We don't fit in here.'
> 'I know, but I'm making good money.'
> 'So when we've made enough, we'll go home?'
> 'As soon as we've the money to pay for a wife
> and some left over.'

15

'Christmas?'
'Christmas.'

And I hate hearing these conversation
because many times
I not wanting to return there.
Most times
I not wanting to think about
old life.

Or
new wife.

Bad Parent

Terry's out.
Dawn's got Mum and me
sitting at the kitchen table
with cups of tea,
pretending we're having a friendly
chat when really
she's checking I'm not living
in a shithole.
'We've got classes we can offer parents too,' she says
    to Mum,
'Empowerment for Women and other things
you might be interested in.'

Mum won't even consider it. 'Don't think so,' she
    says.

Dawn raises her eyebrows. 'We find that young
    offenders
are reacting to situations at home
when they commit crime.'

'I'm not a bad parent,' Mum says
quietly,
though she doesn't believe it.

'And no problems between you and Jess's dad?'
    Dawn asks.

'He left,' Mum tells her.

'And her stepdad?'

'He stayed.'

Dawn turns to me.
'Anything you need support with, Jess?'

'No.'

'You don't just have to pick litter
and plant flowers.
We have loads of courses you might like.'

I take Mum's lead,
shake my head
and say, 'You're all right,'
when inside
a little voice is screaming for Dawn Green
to open her eyes and figure out
who the real offender is.

THE PETROL STATION

Every eye watch me because
one: my hair, clothes, skin, shoes
is differing from people here.

Every eye watch me because
two: I not have car, cash, friends, trust.

I walk in petrol station
to *Magic Trees* department that give cars flower
    smell,
newspapers with many hard words,
magazines with many pictures of dirty beauty girls
and
celebrities with all the sexy muscle and money.

Then I see them
close to the pay area
and near the exit get away.

I spy candy sweets.
My stomach do see-saw.
My eyes pop.

Too long since I eat
any chocolate bar,
all sitting in rows like little sparkle soldiers
making technicolour in my eye.

Which one?
Which one?
I know shop workers want to catch thief in red
    hand
so I must act
super rapido:
grab
snatch
steal
bolt.

I do the quick nab,
open door and
Usain
Bolt fast.

Security man
sprint faster.

I tumble.

Security man's big hand
dig in my shoulder.
Big carrot fingers
rip my trackie.

Tata will go off his bonkers
because he telling me many time
never let them catching you.

But they always catching me.
Three time now they catch.

That's why
I cry and have massive press in the chest.
Not because another arrest
or security man sitting his arse on me,
but because I don't want to be getting Tata's
left right
right left
jab
to the abs or head.

I see it all in my imaginings:
me on floor,
Tata snorting nose steam like bull,
Mămică helping my
tears
and
blood.

I am terror full.

That's why
I hoping police will be my protect
when Tata come get me
from
cell station.

Good Mates

First day back at school
Liz is like,
'God, that was *so* bad.
I totally thought we were gonna get *done*.'

And Shawna goes,
'We were *so* lucky.'

And Meg's like,
'Yeah, close call, weren't it?'

I almost laugh,
not
cos anything's funny –
it's cos I can't really believe what I'm hearing.
'It's not a close call if you *actually get caught*,' I say.
   'It wasn't my first offence, was it?
And now I've got to do this stupid scheme thing,
like, every Saturday.
How fucking lucky is that?'

Meg puts her arm around my shoulder.
'Yeah . . . but . . .
what they're saying
is that only *one* of
us got caught,
innit?'

'Yeah . . . *Me.*'
Meg sighs like I'm too stupid to get her point.
'Look, Jess,
your mum doesn't
care about that stuff,
does she?
If *I* got caught,
my mum and dad would blow a nut.'

'I'm picking up shit,' I say.

Meg smiles.
'I know.
You're a well good mate, Jess.'

But I'm not.

I can't be.

If I were a *good mate*
I wouldn't be thinking about
how to get my own back on Meg.

THREATS AND PUNISHMENT

After my arresting
they threatening me with young people jail.
They tell me I'll be *bitch boy*.
'Look at you,
all dark skin,
dark eyes.
It'll be a bit of exotic for them,' Security Man One
    say.
'They'll be gagging to get their hands on you,'
    Security Man Two say.
'Good looking lad like yourself,' One say.
'Foreign,' Two say.
'Pretty boy.'
'Fun boy.'
'Lovely.'
'Bit of crumpet.'
They scare me too much with bitch boy story
so that I tell to them all truths about my
steal.

But when real police come
they not send me to
young people jail.

For goodness gracious sake no.

They send me to something called
'reparation scheme',
head down,
tongue shut
with other
terrible teenagers.
They also tell Mămică and Tata that I must go to
    school
because 'as parents' they have a
    'Duty of Care'
and
    if we are living in this country
our family
    'must adhere to the laws and rules in England.'
They say at end:
    'Is that clear? Got it?'
If not *got it* Tata must go to man jail
or pay heavy cash fine.
And who will be the blame?
Me, that's who,
    like all other times.

School!

Night . . . mare.

Just in Case

I've been stealing stuff for ages.
Can't remember the first time any more,
but it was way before
I started secondary school.

Small stuff back then –
        other kids' rulers,
        fags from Mum's bag.

And I hang on to loads of the stuff I've nicked,
not because I'm one of those freaky hoarders
you see on TV
or anything.
It's cos I don't steal stuff you can sell,
nothing of any value:
I mean,
who wants to buy a pair of Top Shop tights,
cheap mascara,
gloopy nail varnish
or pencils pinched from a teacher's desk?

I take the gear out now and then,
and I
can't help feeling proud of all the times I got away
   with it
before they finally caught me. . .

then caught me again and again
            and gave me my very own caseworker.

There's a knock on the door,
and before I can throw everything back into the
    shoebox,
Mum's in my room.
'I got KFC for dinner,' she says,
        then stops,
        stares at the stuff
        piled on the bed,
        frowns.
'What's all that?'

'Just some things I found,' I say.
I chuck the stuff back into the box,
push it underneath the bed.

She rubs her forehead,
letting a load of worry trickle into her face.

Thing is,
that's not the box she should be worried about.

See,
I've got a different one on top of my wardrobe.
I've got a box filled with supplies:
a toothbrush, tampons, spare T-shirt, socks, knickers

and a couple of crisp fivers
just in case.

Like,
just in case,
      I ever need to get out of this place

      in a hurry.

HIGH VIS

At reparation scheme
they make me dress in
high vis vest
in piping hot park.

Me and many criminal others
cleaning muck,
sweeping leaves,
picking up, picking up, picking up
crisp packet,
fizz can,
half kebab,
booze glass,
butt cigarettes.

The lives of the pollute people.

Breathing Down our Necks

Mum and I are watching
Jeremy Kyle
which
makes me feel way better about my life,
looking at a bunch of losers
and knowing that no matter how
horrible everything is for *me*,
I'm not
      them;
I'm not in the gutter just yet.

'Shouldn't you be picking litter, Jess?' Terry asks.
He cracks his knuckles
because he can.

'Just Saturdays, isn't it, Jess?' Mum blurts out.

Terry leans on the doorframe,
sniffs
and sips at his can of beer.
'But did I ask you, Louise?' he says.

'Sorry,' Mum whispers.
She turns off the TV,
jumps up from the couch
and scurries into the kitchen.
'I better get started on dinner.'

Terry peers down at me.
'You know,
getting into trouble at school is one thing,
but having the police breathing down our
    necks
is something else.
I don't like it.'

I nod.
'I know.
You already told me, Terry.'

He sniffs hard.
'You being cheeky?' he asks.
He cracks his knuckles again.

Mum is standing behind him,
shaking her head,
her eyes wide and terrified
cos she knows that if I do anything
to annoy him,
she'll be on the receiving end of his boot.

'No, Terry. Sorry,' I say.

I go to my room,
curl up on my bed
and wish it weren't Monday,
wish I were

picking litter instead of here
in this house,

with
him.

PERSONAL DEVELOPMENT

Some Saturdays we do the job
of servant men,
when body sweats and hand sores
with hurting.
They calling this 'Personal Development'.

'Personal Development' help everybody to
    becoming
decent peoples again.

In park
I am part of team,
but not the same like
when I was strong member of
wrestling team in my village.
In park I am not
captain;
here I am in
Offenders Boy Team.

One Saturday
ex-Army man, Bicep Andy,
take my team to pond,
shows us giant bag of plastic,
many woods and strings.
   'Right, lads, your task is to use only
the wood, string and plastic bottles

to build a raft.'
All faces confusing.
Much puffing of air.
  'A raft?'
'Yes, Lee, a raft,' Bicep Andy say.
  'What for?' other guy say.
'Well, Rick, it'll improve your
communication and collaboration skills.'
Bicep Andy tap Rick on back.
  'Doubt it,' Lee say.
'Your raft needs to take one member of your group
from this side of the pond to the other.'
Bicep Andy point to other side,
where girl team make also.
  'Whatever,' Bill say.

I tying strings
tighter,
better.
Rick and Lee do
design control and
building of square boat.
  'Right mate, hop on,' Bill telling to me.
And I thinking:
I could show him my skill.
Grab
flip
hold.
Learn him the respect.

But this would be very bad communications.

I jump on tiny boat.

It not float.

Faffing Around

It's like these caseworkers pull ideas
out of their arses
and all agree
it'll do us the world of good.

This morning I'm sitting with the other girls
whinging about
how tough it
is to be female.
Dawn reminds us
how important school is –
'And I don't mean sitting in the inclusion unit,
    girls!'

And now here we are,
up against the boys,
but on the other side of the pond from them,
faffing around with
rope and wood
and arguing about which one of us
has to sit on the stupid raft we're building
once it's in the water.

Fiona goes, 'You ain't getting me on the *Titanic*.'
Jade is like, 'The raft's tiny, you moron.'
Fiona goes, 'Whatevs. I ain't doing a DiCaprio,
    right.'

And Jade is like, 'Well, I got my period, innit. I
    can't go swimming.'

Dawn sighs. 'The key is cooperation.'

Fiona rolls her eyes. 'Yeah, right.'
Jade crosses her arms over her chest.
'You know what, Dawn,
I reckon health and safety would
be all over this raft-building bullshit.'

'*I'll* do it,' I say, just to shut them up.

From the other side of the pond
come hoots
and whistles.

'He got soaked, man!' Rick shouts.

One of the boys is in the water,
his head bobbing up and down
like a beach ball.

When he comes up he shakes his hair out
like a dog,
laughs
and splashes the other boys on the bank
as though it's nothing at all
to have fallen into the pond.

'Who's that?' I ask Dawn.

'That's Nicu,' she says.
'Good egg, that one.'

WOMAN LONGING

Mămică tears because she missing her other
   childrens.
Daughters
back in village with tiny babies,
sons being mans of house.

I wanting to give Mămică my
super son hug,
for remember her that she have me,
her very own younger boy,
in this country.

But I am older now for
super son hug.
I watching her at table
with photos,
with tears,
with suffer.

Always she saying same thing:
'I want all my babies in one place.'

Always she talking of return to our village;
'I want to go home to Pata.'

That is why I only looking,
not speaking,

caressing her tearing
or
soothing her feeling.
Mămică not want to listen to
my need.

That one day my whole family can come to
visit
 here.
        Live
        here.
        Working
        here.

In my new country.

When Liam Left

Liam just left.

I woke up one morning,
saw his bedroom door was open,
but not him in among the squalor
with his
bare legs dangling out of the
      side of the single bed.

'Where's Liam?' I asked Mum.

'Gone.'

'Good riddance,' Terry said,
and I had to bite both my lips
really hard
to stop myself from saying something
like
Yeah, you *did this, Terry.*

Then
I left for school like normal
but didn't go in,
hid between
the recycling bins
in the Queen's Head car park.

And I couldn't stop crying,
couldn't even breathe properly,
because without Liam
I was on my own.

Completely and utterly
on
my
own.

LANGUAGE

When I hearing this
fresh English language,
I think I will be
able
never
to speaking in same tongue,
to telling my joke
or
showing my imaginings
or
being the great listening ears to peoples.

But.

English is the tough watermelon to crack,
a strange language with many weird wordings:
heart in your mouth
fall off the back of a lorry
if you pardon my French
and
too many more.

We have ways to understanding though:
Michael Jackson helping Tata with learning.
Celine Dion helping Mămică with learning.
YouTube and Jay Z helping me.
Breaking Bad helping everyone.

I working hardest than ever
to being in this England world
fluently.

I not wanting to
start school
with too much
foreign tongue.

Recording

Terry stands in front of the TV even
though I'm watching it.
I don't shout, 'Get out of my bloody way, Terry!'
I say sweetly, 'You all right, Terry?'

He holds out his phone
and I go cold,
look around for Mum.

'Film me
doing my press-ups,' he says.

He pulls off his vest.
I take the phone.
'Why?'

'I wanna examine my technique,
you know?'
He flexes his muscles.
Rolls his neck.

I press the red button,
watch him as he hits the floor
and counts to fifty,
each press-up punctuated by a grunt:
'One, *argh*, two, *urgh*, three, *huuu*, four . . .'

By the time he's finished
his face is as red as a battered pizza.
He stands up all sweaty and panting,
pleased with himself.

'How did I look?' he asks.

'You looked *great*, Terry,' Mum says.
She's wearing a bathrobe,
her hair hidden beneath a towel.

Terry snatches his phone from me.
'Make me a cup of tea, Louise,' he says,
and falling down into an armchair,
turns the TV off
and watches himself
puff and pant
all over again,
with an ugly
grin on his face.

NASTY WEATHER

My clothes is heavy with raining.
My feet squash and slip
in my shoes.
My hair stick to me like I step out of
deep blue sea.

In England it rain
all times.

Reparation scheme is zero happy when wet.
Every other delinquents
shielding under shed hut,
smoking, spitting, stone kicking,
bantering.

All delinquents except two:
me
and
girl.

Not us.

I am under umbrella tree.
Girl hide below kids' silver sliding tube.
She seem lonely.
She seem lost.
She seem total tragic sad.

And I want to rush to her feelings,
show her my smiles,
make conversation chit-chat,
peace her mind.

Maybe tell some tale of my land,
how stars shine so bright,
how wild horse tame with one kind hand.

But
for this girl of perfect visions
I remaining under umbrella tree
and follow only with my eye.

Eyes

I know he's watching –
Nicu,
the boy who fell in the pond
and didn't moan about it.

But
what does he see when he looks at me?

What does anyone ever
see?

BAD SHOES

So we go to garment shop to get
a tie,
grey shirt,
clunk shoes,
and I ready for going to school.
It feel like I dressing for wedding,
and I wonder
how everyone put on these elegants all days.
School in England must be like
big song and dance
or
the military with these uniform.
Students all looking same.
And I hoping
it be more easy
now
to be one of them.

School happens on
Monday
Tuesday
Wednesday
Friday
and
Thursday.
Phew!

School and reparation scheme my new life,
but I still don't miss my old –
no way.
Never going back,
where people like us
always
under attack
from the rich-wealthy and those born of plenty.
Here
everyone is Romanian in all eyes,
but
back home
we are the Romani Roma gypsies
and we are kept in gutter.

No chance.

Here
with school, reparation scheme
and bad shoes is better.

Safer and sounder.

Pretty Good

It's weird
cos
I thought that
getting nicked
would be one hundred per cent
horrendous.
And I guess it is at home,
with Terry going on about it all the time
and Mum tearful.

But at school it's not like that.

At school
everyone looks at me
like I'm some big celebrity.
And since I started the scheme,
I haven't had to queue for lunch
        once.

It's like they're all afraid of me.

Like getting in trouble with the police
is a shield –
  or a weapon.

And it actually feels
pretty good.

OLD HOME

Back in Pata, in my bed,
I listen to the
Tip . . . tap . . . tip . . .
On the old house tin roof.
Every night I listen to these sounds.
Sometimes when raining is too much,
the
tip . . . tap . . . tip . . .
fall on my head, nose, cheek,
tongue.
Fresh clean water in my mouth,
falling from our sky,
which is better than the muck water that
fall from our filth tap.

The toughest of times.

Winter hurt our bones.
Summer hurt our skins.
No money hurt our bellies.

Tata say political man
    not give a shit about us.
They give:
no road,
no light,
no house.

Mămică say they treat us
   like the world's disease.
They take:
our land,
our dignity,
our choice.

Here is decent good.

But sometimes,
when I look from window
or
go for long street walk,
I see something same between
old village then
and
new place now.

Many peoples with much miserable in their heart,
many peoples with little monies,
all walking
up down
down up
stopping
starting
again
again,
smoking in huddle group
and

chatting in small circle.

Everyone watching everyone do same things.

Peoples with no place to go for laughing and be
    happy.

    Same as my old village.

The atmospheres, buildings and peoples

in London North

is like giant rainbow.

But

not beautiful colours

    with golden treasure at end.

Is the rainbow with

white to grey to brown to black.

Sometime when I walking past

high sky houses,

I thinking that maybe some

politician take also:

land,

dignity,

choice

of these London North souls.

Arse

We're not long back at school
before
I'm thrown into inclusion
for telling my form teacher
to kiss my arse.

It was a joke.

And
like I'd let her near my arse.

What the hell is her problem?

WELCOME

The lady teacher
give no smiles.
She keep everything serious.
I think maybe her man go with too much women
or
someone die in her family.

Then I understanding:

Lady teacher is angry annoyed with *me*.
Her boobs expanding.
She is full with irritating.
'Your name?'
'Nicu Gabor,' I soft say.
She huff like wolf.
'Right. OK.'

She writing and move paper on table.
'I doubt you'll be able to catch up.'
Her voice turn to whisper,
    'Just keep your
head down and behave.'

Her eye go to my eye.
She say, 'OK . . . erm . . .?' fighting for find my
    name.
I don't tell her again.

She point her finger to chair.
'Right, sit there for now. But when the others get
    here
you'll need to find somewhere else to put yourself.'
I walk to chair
without giving lady teacher
my smile,
my thank you.

That Bird

We sit in the Sainsbury's car park passing a bottle
of cider around.
Meg acts like she's pissed before she's even had a sip,
and once she's had a few mouthfuls
she flaps about and asks Dan who he fancies,

hoping he'll say her,

which he doesn't.

'Know that bird in lower sixth
with the massive tits?' he asks.

Kenny laughs.
Ryan snorts.
Meg tries to look interested.

'There are like a hundred girls in the sixth form,'
I say.
Dan looks at me,
        down at my chest,
and I wish I hadn't opened my mouth.

He smirks.
'Nah,
but there's this one bird
and she's pure porn material.'

His mates laugh again.
Shawna swigs at the cider.
Liz looks at her phone.
'What a whore,' Meg says.

'Here's hoping,' Dan says,
hooting,
high-fiving his mates
then
grabbing his crotch and squeezing it.

Like anyone wants to see *that*.

FIRST WEEKS

Things no one do on first weeks:
say hellos,
give smiles at me,
say sorry when chucking pens . . . and other stuffs,
understand my confusing,
show me the way for doing lessons,
ask me to joining in with their fun times
and
be friendliness.

Things I do on first weeks:
say my morning, afternoon hellos and goodbyes,
give smiles at all teacher,
try harder for to become part of England,
say sorry when they shoulder bump,
hide when I hearing big laughs close by,
look out of window because no one explaining
    school education to me
and
close eyes for wishing new life get better.

These Sessions

Dawn drags her chair so close to mine
our knees touch.
'So, Jess,
how are things going?'

I open the App Store on my phone
to look for updates.

Dawn's proper pissed off.
She breathes loudly through her nose.
'You have to take this seriously.'

'Do I?'

Dawn puts down her clipboard
and sits up straighter.
'This is about your future, Jess.'

Yeah, great.
Whatever.
I mean,
what sort of future can I have with Terry around?
Cos he's furniture now.
And as immovable as wallpaper.

'Everyone takes part in these sessions,' Dawn says.

'What, even the one who doesn't speak English?'

'Even him.'
I roll my eyes to
show Dawn how boring this is.

I'm not like that guy, Nicu.
I can't get excited about
raking leaves
and doing all that self-esteem rubbish.

I can't put on a brave face and pretend that
at the end of this
things will be different.

Maybe for him they will be.

But for me
they won't.

Nothing's ever going to change.

Part
TWO

WORSE THAN DEATH

At school I am
the boy worse than death.
Me,
the boy people won't waste breath on.

Teacher puts me in no-hope group.

No-hope group is for kids who don't know
numbers,
words,
history,
science,
facts,
neat writing,
behaving,
more.

I do know things.
But teachers never question,
they never ask.

But
I know many things:
books,
music,
ideas,
horses,

more.

      Even much English in my head
but
not so well out of my mouth
yet.

Teachers not care because
they only see disorder not student.
Also
I almost went to young people's jail,
      so I always criminal.

The Half of It

Mr Morgan passes out the test
and tells us to sit as
     far apart
from one another as possible.

Suits me.

Then he says,
     'You may look up for inspiration,
     down in desperation,
     but *never* side to side for information.'
He laughs at his own hilarious joke
like we haven't heard it
a hundred times already.

Meg smiles at me and rolls her eyes
like she couldn't care less what Morgan says,
but as soon as the test is slapped down on to her
   desk
she goes white
and gets scribbling.

I look at the numbers and letters,
maths that might as well be Chinese,
and spend the rest of the lesson
doodling in the margins –
messy circles mostly.

Morgan collects the tests,
looks at mine:
first name at the top
followed by empty boxes
meant for answers.
He winces
and
when the bell rings, asks to see me,
and comes so close
I can see his nose hair.

'You're a smart girl,' he says,
which is a lie.
It's what all the do-good teachers say:
you could be anything,
you could go anywhere.
Try really hard
and all your dreams will come true.
But we aren't in Disneyland, are we?
And anyway,
          what could any of them know about our
    dreams?
I bet they don't live on grey estates and
eat Mars Bars for breakfast.

His eyes glint with delight,
like he's about to bag a big secret.
'I hear you've been in trouble with the police,'
he says.

'Sorry, sir, but what has this got to do
with algebra?'

'Just wondering if everything's OK.
You used to be good at maths.
If I knew what was happening, maybe I could help
get you back on track,' he says.

Just then I spot Meg standing by the door, listening.
I stand up and
push the desk away,
give Morgan the look I usually save for Terry
when he isn't looking
and say,
'You think I care about maths?
You don't know the half of it, sir.'

COOL NAME

The girl from reparation scheme,
I see her in school.

My heart rat–rat–rattles.

    Does she see me?

We never speaking to each other.
Today is day we do?
I put loose books in bag,
hide behind locker row.
I watch.
Imagine.
Dream.

She's never said
hello.
Good morning.
How are you?

But I swearing my heart is in her mouth
when I seeing her.
I dreaming of chat introduction:
    'Hi, my name's Nicu.'
    'Nicu, that's a cool name.'
    'You thinking?'
    'Totally.'

I'd like to have the *cool* name.
Me,
Nicu,
the boy with the cool name.

The Girl with the Camera

Terry makes me hold the phone
and record every moment of him
beating the crap out of her.
That's my job,
though I never applied for it.

I *could* throw it at him.
I mean,
I could use the phone to crack his skull open,
smash his brains to bits,
instead of recording what he's doing –
beating Mum
with such steam
you'd think it was an Olympic sport he was
    training for.

I gag
a little bit
whenever he glances into the lens.
Or maybe he's looking at me,
making sure I *am*
    holding the phone steady,
doing my job.

I don't want to let him down,
or I can guess what'll happen:
it'll be my belly under his foot,

my face against his fist.
Or worse,
Mum'll get it again.

Afterwards he goes out,
   down the pub
   to his mates,
who all think he's a right laugh,
      a right geezer
for having a bird who cooks and cleans,
wipes his arse
if he asks her to.

And Mum?
She heads for the bathroom,
locks the door and cleans herself up,
then into the bedroom where she
covers the bruises with a turtleneck and too much
   foundation.

That'll make him mad too.
Can't she learn a lesson?

When she comes into the kitchen
I'm sitting there
at the table,
pretending to finish off my French homework,
verbs drills,
lists of words

that start the same
but end
         differently
depending on who's doing the talking.
And I wonder whether my life could be like verb
   endings,
whether things here would be better if Mum
   weren't such a
wimp all the time.
Like,
if she was someone braver,
would Terry give up and go away
and hurt someone else instead?
Would we get to have happy endings
sometimes
instead of a constant stream of shit?

'You want some toast? Cereal?' she asks,
really gently,
and I hug her,
scared it'll hurt her,
but so sorry for not stopping Terry.

WHO I AM

When I watching television movies
all actors
speak too speedy
for my comprehendings,
and I thinking
it be mission impossible
to learn this language
with fluent.

It so much frustrating
when words can't escape my head,
when peoples not
understand my meanings.
All I want
is for them to see how
I am fun,
clever
and
nice guy.

I afraid no one
ever know who I am.

On the Rob

Mum sighs and lights a fag.
'This is the end of the trouble, Jess,
innit?
I don't think I could take another
incident.'

'I'm late,' I say,
which isn't an answer,
but I can't promise I'll be good for ever,
and she knows that.

When her back is turned
to the toaster,
I rob a few fags from the freshly opened packet
and have one lit before I'm out the door.

And then I'm inhaling
great gulps,
like it's oxygen,
like I've never had a smoke before,
and by the time I reach the youth offending
    centre
I've finished off all three,
and I've got nothing to do except
pick actual litter.

Dawn
sort of smiles at me when I arrive,
like we might be friends.

But she hasn't got a clue who
she's dealing with.

And
she doesn't know it was Rick who keyed her car
   last week,
and Fiona who nicked her phone.
She's so gullible,
thinks she's helping to
reform,
rehabilitate,
reissue us into society,
all scrubbed clean and ready to make nice.

The only one she can probably trust is
Nicu.
He's the one we all avoid.
Can't understand much anyway.

And he's weird.

An immigrant gypsy boy
who looks half-wolf
if you ask me,
picking litter and leaves like it's cash,
greedy for it.

'You want my helping you?'
he asks today,
trying to team up
before I've even had a chance to get my gloves on,
and I sneer
as best I can.
Sneer at him
and his bullshit English.

Gypsy wolf boy.

A BUCKET OF SPANNERS

Everyone laugh and make jokes.

I stay far,
picking
dead leaf,
cut grass,
pongy food,
sharp glass.
Many caseworkers never speaking to me.
They just wave and point to filth I should see.
'Understand?'
I nod my head
Yes, I understand.
I'm not the real no-hope.

Lady Dawn swings her flower dress around her
    bum and
hums tunes.
I think she is liking me.
She not believe I am wild animal
        like other delinquents.
Because
I not wild animal.
I am pussy cat.

I come out from massive tree,
do the baby step to go nearer to girl from my school.

She stands not with the others.
No laughing or making joke.
Her eyes on ground
in deep thinkings.
She look depressing,
eyes all puffy red.

Her sack is empty
of rubbish.
Dawn can add days if we are lazy dogs,
if we don't helping our community.

Maybe she need my rescue.
A friend.
A man for muscle work.

My baby stepping bring me metres from her.
Two red eyes flick up to me.
I shine my smile.
She sniff hard.
Empty sack is no good.
   'You want my helping you?' I ask.
She look in air
and does a snigger laugh,
which is good because
laughing is the medicine for not being sad.
'You talking to me?' she say.
'I talk yes.'

'What do you want?'

'You want some my leaves?'

'No thanks, creep.'

I not know *creep*, but her voice tell me it's same as

dick

knob

wanker

prick.

'I am Nicu.'

          I say my name to show my friendly.

'I *know* who you are.'

'And your name, please?'

'*Nicu*, what sort of name is that?'

'I from Romania,' I say.

'Romania! Long way from home.'

I do laugh because I *am* long way.

She do laugh from belly also.

She ask me for cigarette,

I tell her no way because I not

want to die.

She do more laughing.

'You're as weird as a bucket of spanners.'

I pretend I know her meaning.

I want to tell her how much beautiful she is,

not like village girls

Tata wanting me to marry.

Sorry, not *wanting*.

Forcing.

Vermin

Terry's in a top mood,
frying up pancakes
and whistling like a postman.
But I don't ask what's got into him,
what the good mood's for,
cos that would be
stupid.

And there's
no reason why anyway.
Never any reasons.
Not real ones.
Not ones to hang your coat on.

'Hey, nip down the shops and get us a little bottle
    of lemon juice,' he says,
all cheerful,
and slides a fiver across the countertop
with a wink.
A wink
and a smile,
like a real dad.

The bastard.

I take the cash and go to the corner shop.
The old guy knows me there,

keeps two bald, beady eyes on me.
Like I'd nick anything
with him watching.
In broad daylight.
Cameras everywhere.
I might be a thief, but I'm not a moron.

On my way home, I stop by the park.
Not to litter pick,
just to have a smoke
without Terry finding out
and giving Mum a clattering for not
taking better control of me.

It's empty,
the park.

Quiet.

I sit at the top of the slide
and puff away
when wolf boy appears
out of nowhere,
climbs up next to me,
hands over his bag of pick 'n' mix –
cola bottles,
chewy fried eggs,
sweet 'n' sour snakes.
'Will kill you more slower,' he says,

grabbing my fag and firing it down the slide.
'Oi, you're paying for that,' I say.
'Paying where?' he asks,
cos he doesn't really understand much.

Not words anyway.

But he says,
'Life shit pile today?'
And I laugh.
'A right shit pile every day, Nicu.'

BYE BYE BAD BOY

The jelly egg and sugar snake sweets
I eat
make my nerves better,
giving my heart a break.

And I smile when I spy her,
high on kids' sliding tube,
smoke up in the air, puffing from her head.
That girl has to know cigarettes make her dead.

I do the sneak walk,
like a spy.
I'm behind her.
I act like flash man.
I flick her fag down tube,
offer her a sugar snake.
'Will kill you more slower,' I say.
I become brave and sit beside.
Again I see her sad eyes.
    'Life is shit pile today?' I ask.

She laughs.
        Hip hip hooray!

'A shit pile every day, Nicu,' she say.
I laugh also
and feel warm because she speak my name.

It sound weird coming out her mouth,
lovely weird,
make-my-stomach-tickle-weird.
    'Snap!' I say, because our living is the same.
    'Snap? What you on about?' she say,
with trouble eyes,
but eyes anyway that could be on a Christmas tree,
twinkling
twinkling
      brightly.

I look.

Secrets Shared

He acts as though secrets can be shared like sweets.

But I hardly know him.
Not sure I can trust him.

I mean, I don't trust anyone,
usually,
and definitely not with stuff about *him:*

Terry the terrible.
Terry the terrier.
Terry the twat.

'You can talking with me,' Nicu says.

And for some reason
I know he'll be good at keeping secrets
so I start to speak.

But I can't tell him everything.

STRUGGLINGS

'Jess,' I say.
'What?' she say.
'My life too has strugglings every day.'
'Really?'
'Big strugglings.'
'Sorry to hear that, Nicu.'
'Thank you.'

We laugh in same time.

'My family too is arse pain,' I say.
'Yeah, but I bet you don't wish any of them were
    dead.'

We look
to each other.

Breakfast

Terry's pancakes are cold
and his mood has cooled down too.
'What took you so long?' he asks,
but I can't say
Nicu,
can I?
Nicu? he'd say.
Sounds foreign. Is he foreign?
Thought we'd voted them all out.
Dirty immigrants.
Rat scum.
Knock those boats outta the water before
they arrive, I reckon.

So I say,
'They didn't have any lemon juice.
I had to walk to the Co-op.
Took me ages.'
But it doesn't matter what I say now.
I've riled him.

'Louise!' he shouts.

GOOD CITIZEN

Even though we here in this country,
Tata think for ever of home,
his peoples,
his cultures,
of village with no road or toilet.
Every day he talk of return,
always of the past.
'As soon as we find enough money for a wife,
we'll go back,' he say.

I wanting to
remain:

learn my English,
be the good citizen – no more thief,
wave bye-bye
        to bad boy.

When day come to return home
to meet wife from village,
I will cry.
I will hide.
I will disappear like magic.
Lots of cash
Tata say
he have to pay,
for finding me honest wife.

But
I am not the cow on market day.
'I want to stay here!'
I tell to Tata in high voice.
I need to
go to school,
work the hardest,
have a job like businessman, making clean money,
find my own wife.

Tata puts finger in my face.
He screaming with the loud mouth:
'You're going.
    You do what I tell you to do
    and that's the end of it.'
His breath pong of
booze and
fags.
The screaming go on more –
Mămică start
when she come through the door.
'Do you believe this boy, Miri?' Tata say.
'Nicu, listen to Tata.'

His finger touch my head.
His breath touch my tummy.

'Nicu, Tata knows best,' Mămică say.
'But I want to stay here.' I praying to them.

'*Here*, what is here?' Tata say. 'People hate us *here*.'
'Nicu, people *here* only see our skin, not the thing
   within,' Mămică say,

thumping her bosom,
        two times.

We continue to
shout
scream
roar
yell
until I have no more voice.

The Dregs

They say
we are the dregs
and
pack us off to the park to teach us a lesson,
where we
pick up crap
and
talk crap,
pay back
our society,
which we
so
wounded.

But take the rest of them – the other wrong'uns.

Rick's got a temper,
might batter you if you
talk dirt about his mum
or whatever.

And Fiona's a bit of a crackpot,
tattoos up her arm like a footballer.
She's only here
cos some slag tried to bottle her
outside a nightclub.

Lee was done for selling weed
to kids in his class
(but looks like he smokes most of it himself).

Bill nicked a BMW
and was caught joyriding down the A10
like Lewis bloody Hamilton.

And Jade tagged tonnes of tube trains,
too stupid to realise they had the whole thing on
    camera.

So,
yeah,
we're not exactly angels,
probably a bit yobby,

but the dregs?

Do me a favour.

EYES OF JESS

Many day at reparation scheme
Jess try to helping with my
English.

She say to me lots of important informations:
FAG BREAK
BUNK OFF
KEEP AN EYE OUT
COMPLETELY KNACKERED.

Rick, who is like *top boy* offender,
tell me that passing womens are
WELL FIT
but
I hearing *WEALTHY,*
which make Rick
and others
hyena laugh and friend–slap my back,
though
Jess give me special eyes
when peoples are
TAKING THE PISS.

Rick
definitely taking my piss when
he ask me to shout
CAN I WARM MY HANDS IN YOUR MUFF?
to Dawn.

And when these *TAKING THE PISS* things
happen,
I always search for the special eyes of Jess.

Always
I
search.

Pairing Up

I spend two hours
scrubbing graffiti from a kids' climbing frame,
then meet Nicu by the park gates.

We seem to be doing this a lot,
and I can't remember how it happened,
how we paired off from the others,
and I stopped smoking cheeky fags
with Fiona and Rick,
started sharing a bag of
Maltesers with Nicu instead.

'You want I walking you home?' he asks.
'I protect you from bears.'
He growls and flexes his muscles,
kisses both fists.

I laugh. 'Ain't no bears in Wood Green, mate,
and you know it.'

He laughs too. 'I protect you from
bad boy robbers instead,' he says.

'How about I walk *you* home
to protect *you* from bad boy robbers,' I say.

'Sounds like first class deal to me,' he says,
and tries to take my hand,
like,
actually hold my hand
as though we're going out together
or something.

I pull away.

I don't need anyone touching me.

'Unless you plan on walking out in
front of a car,
I don't think
we need to hold hands,
do you?' I ask.

He smirks. 'Worth trying, Jess,' he says.

'Yeah,' I say. 'It was worth a try.'

MISTER INVISIBLE MAN

Woman are complicate.
One day
up,
one day
weirder.

At school I thinking that
maybe Jess has really
two peoples
inside her brain.

She don't return my smile.
She don't give me the Jess special eyes.

I am Mister Invisible Man.

But I not want to make for her
difficult time
in case
she has boyfriend in the lad crew.

Mostly I not want Jess to lose her
pride
dignity
honours
if she friendly chatting with me.

I can be her protect from this.

Still,
it not feeling lovely to be
Mister Invisible Man.

All Smiles

After litter picking
we go to the cheapest caff on Wood Green
   High Road.
I get a Coke.
Nicu orders a mug of tea
and smiles.

He's got a nice smile, Nicu,
even though
his teeth are a bit
        crooked.
His face sort of
   scrunches up,
         his eyes shine.
And I watch him slurp at his tea
while he tells me all about his life
back home,
how he lived in a house with no proper floor,
just dirt and dust on the ground,
and he rode donkeys and horses,
cos they didn't have money for a car.
   'And no skateboardings,' he says,
and smiles again,
        all shiny.

The woman behind him gets up
and goes to the counter to pay,

but she leaves her bag right there
on the seat,
   wide open
like a bloody invitation.
   'The bag,' I whisper to Nicu.
   'Tea bag?' he whispers back.
He looks into his mug,
stirs it with the spoon.

I don't hang about.
I sit next to him,
pretend to put my arm around his shoulder,
then slip my hand into
the woman's
fake Gucci
and find her phone.
Job Done.

Nicu doesn't have a clue what I'm doing,
thinks I'm trying it on,
and leans into me.
   'Relax, mate,' I tell him,
and drop the phone into the pocket of his blazer.

The woman comes back,
      grabs her bag
and is gone.

And then we're off too,

up the High Road to the Italian,
where we order meatballs
and salad,
a pizza with extra olives.
And for dessert two slices of tiramisu.
Thank
you
very
much.
'I like these eats,' Nicu says.

The waiter gives us the bill.

I rummage and rummage around my
bag,
pretending to look for my wallet.
'I left it at school. It's at school.
Oh, crap.
Have *you* got any money?'

'No.'
Nicu looks like he might
cry.
I told him it was my treat.
'I tell to you this.
I *tell* to you I have no monies!'
He's almost shouting,
frantic,
while the waiter looks on.

'Give him your phone,' I say.
I manage a wink.
Nicu blinks.

'Give him your phone.
It's in your pocket, Nicu.'
I point.
Nicu reaches into his blazer
and finds the iPhone.

I snatch it
and wave it at the waiter.
'Can we leave this here and come back?
I'll bring you the money for the bill in an hour.
No.
Half an hour.
I promise.'

I do a drama on him.
Make my voice *EastEnders* shaky.

He nods
and
lets us leave,
lets us swagger out of that place
without paying a penny.

'You make me bad boy,' Nicu says
when we get to the park.

We're on the slide again,
at the top of it,
chewing on liquorice laces.

'*I* made you a bad boy?
Oh, come on, Nicu,
I think you were a bad boy well before you met
    me,' I say.

And he gives me that smile.

NEW TEACHER

On top of slide
I think I should say to her *my* secret,
my special confidential.
But I am afraid
in case Jess not understanding,
in case Jess slide away
and
         never come back.

I can't tell to her
how one day
I dream to escape Tata and Mămică
because of person *they* want me to become.
And
how I have too much shock thought every day
in and out my head
of seeing future wife in white bling dress.

Jess is the danger girl.
She is the danger to big plan that
Mămică and Tata have for me.

But she is also the helper girl.
She say she is going to teach me to speak proper
if it bloody well kills her.
'This will be the most help,' I say.
She say,

'You can't speak like a twat, if we are going to be
    mates, Nicu.'
'I agreeing, Jess. I not wanting to be twat.'
She puts her hand in face and giggling.
All this tell me one thing:
Jess is kindness.

When I ask:
'Jess, what is *mate*?'
she tell me
a mate is someone you can chat with.
'You know, about anything, secrets and that.
Stuff you don't tell your parents.'
'Like dreams?'
'Yeah, I suppose.'
'Confidentials?'
She rub my hair
        and butterfly float in my belly.
'You do this to mate?' I say.
'Only if I like them,' she say.
Maybe if I kiss her I can say:
And this too?
But I'm OK that Jess is my mate
(my first English mate),

so I stop thinking about kiss.

Bad Friday

He sits in the library
at lunch,
flicking through books with loads of pictures
in them.

I see him on Wednesday
when I go in there with Shawna to
copy her homework.
He looks up,
but before he can wave or call out my name,
I turn my back on him.

And then on Thursday
Liz wants to photocopy some form for her mum
and he's in there again,
different book,
       same lonely look.

I just peer through the window on Friday,
and of course he's there again,
turning the pages
of some big book,
his eyes really wide.
'What you staring at?' Meg asks,
spooking me from behind.
'You know him or something?' she asks,
spotting Nicu.

'No,' I say quickly.
'Why would I?'
She snorts.
'Yeah, it's not as if you speak Polish or anything?'

'Exactly,' I say,
and we laugh,
like friends,
so loudly that Nicu turns.

He sees us.

And so I stop.

I stop laughing.

THE BUTT

Before I coming to school
in new country,
I not understand how hard
it will be.
Education is very important thing
here.
Very important thing
for to get jobs,
cash,
houses,
holidays,
cars,
shoes.

Back in village,
going to school not so important for us children.
Political persons don't
care if I go or not.
Parents
same.
But,
back in village,
no person does the laughing at me
behind my face.

Even in front of my face
it happening.

In class,
out class,
in corridor,
out corridor,
in yard,
out yard,
in canteen,
all place.
Snigger, snort, chuckle,
chuck paper,
pens,
pretend knives, guns, bombs,
weapons of massive destruct into my feelings.

But
they don't seeing
what I seeing.
They don't hearing
what I hearing.
They don't emotion
what I emotion.

I think maybe Jess is different.

I want to know an answer.

The Three Bitches

Liz is all like,
'That pikey's staring again, Jess.
I reckon you're in there!'
She smirks and
and Shawna goes,
'Eww, man, I think he really fancies you.'
She sticks out her tongue,
blue from the gobstopper she's been sucking,
and waggles it.
Meg lets out a laugh and says,
    'Maybe he wants to show you a good time in his
    caravan.'
Everyone in the corridor can hear,
and she thinks
it's well funny,
like we haven't heard the gypsy joke
a hundred times today
already.

She reaches into her locker and
    pulls out
a book,
holds it up:
Big Fat Gypsy Weddings.

Where the hell did she get that?
'Really?' I ask.

'What?' Meg high-fives Shawna,
and they squeal
like ugly sick pigs,
like nasty little witches about to brew up
something poisonous.
'Gonna cut out some pictures and post them around
the place,' Meg says.
'Might give a few to Dan, so he can
put 'em up in the changing rooms.'

Liz is like, 'That's *hil-ar-ious.*'

And I could say,
But is it?
Is it hilarious?
Cos I think it's boring.
I think you're boring.
All of you.
And anyway he doesn't live in a caravan.
He lives in a flat.

But I don't say anything
cos I don't wanna be on the receiving end
of Meg's bile.

'I've got French,' I say instead,
and turn away.

Behind me I hear whispering.

Nothing else.

I keep walking.

TOSSING AND TURNING

I sleep bad these nights.

The *tip-tap-tip*
in my head
still happen in new country
because too many times
I thinking of Jess.

I thinking what Mămică and Tata would say
if they knew Jess was so much
in
my
mind.

Inside and out,

she is beauty full.

Shag/Marry/Dump

'Right,' Meg says.
'Mr Pitcher, Mr Morgan and Mr Betts.'

Shawna screams.
'That's just *nasty*.
Can you even imagine?'

Liz laughs.
'No. Cos I'm not imagining,
but you must be.
Rank!'

The bell for the end of break
rings
but
Meg drags on her fag
like she hasn't heard it.
Everyone else smoking behind the drama block
leaves for their lessons.
'You've *got* to decide.
Shag, marry or dump?
Go!'

Shawna shrugs.
'Shag Mr Pitcher, marry Mr Morgan, and dump,
definitely dump, Mr Betts.'

Meg turns to me.
'You're quiet,' she says,
like it's a crime.
'This one's just for Jess.
Right,
Dan, Kenny and . . .'
She pauses.

Shawna and Liz wait with their mouths open.

I see the horrible machine of Meg's mind
as she searches for the name.

His name.

I cross my fingers that it won't be him,
that she'll say Ryan,
cos he's the most obvious choice.

Then she finally says it:
'Nicu.
Go on then, Jess.
Shag, marry, dump?'

It's a trap.

I mean,
I know it's a trap,
so I say,

'I'm not getting married, Meg.'

'Why? You a lezzer?' she asks.

Shawna moves away from me,
          just a bit.
Liz chucks her fag.

'It's a crap game,' I say.
'We played it in Year Eight
and it was crap then,
too.'

Meg throws her fag butt on to the ground,
grinds it to dust with the heel
of her shoe.

'Do you fancy Dan or something?' she asks.
I almost
crack up laughing.
That's what she thinks?
That I fancy Dan?

'Know what, Meg,
you can shag them *all*.
But it's a good job it is a game
cos I don't think anyone'll
be queueing up to shag you.'

THE LAST LAUGH

Big Fat Gypsy Weddings pictures
are in everywhere:
school changing place,
canteen,
locker,
and
teacher board.

Many photos of
wives with
epic dress and comic hair
or
husbands with
golden smiles and diamond eyes.

I don't rip pictures away.

I don't rip away
because
these gypsy weddings are
not my peoples,
not my weddings,

not my me.

So
I have last laughing.

After very short timing
Big Fat Gypsy Weddings pictures
look sad,
like death sunflower.

Finally,
they flop down
dead.

And
I have one more
last laughing.

A Quick Word

I'm washing gunk off my hands
after pointlessly playing with
papier mâché for two hours,
when Dawn moseys over.
'Can I have a quick word, Jess?'

I show her my sticky palms and say,
'One sec,'
knowing her *quick word*
will totally turn into some
clock-watching psycho session.

'Just wondering how you're finding the scheme.
Any positives from this whole thing yet?' she asks.

'Uhh, like what?'

'I don't know. Have you learned anything?'

'Dunno.'

'Or maybe you made a friend?'

I sneer.
'Friends?
With that lot? Yeah, right.
You must be joking.'

Nicu is on the other side of the room.
He waves a papier mâché pig
and gives me a thumbs up.

I guess Nicu is my friend.
In a way.
We hang out,
I can rely on him and he's never tried
to hurt me.

So why haven't I given him
my number?

I mean,
what would be the harm?

NUMBERS

On eat and fag
break at
reparation scheme,
the others message
on phones with
fast fingers.

Everyone do swapping of numbers.
Not me.
I go to pond and
swap sweets with swans.

I hear foot crunching on stone.
  'Hey, you didn't give me your number,' Jess say.
My breath become heavy weight.
'You want *my* number?' I say.
'Yeah, what is it?'
I tell it to her,
and
she tell hers to me.

And I photograph hers in my head.

Quite Nice

I've no shortage of boys
wanting me,
after me,
telling me
I'm the golden sun
and bloody silver moon.

In Year Seven
   Keith Woods
passed me a note
in science
that said
'*Your reelly cute!*'
and I let him
kiss me with
his mouth open
more than once,
his tongue
far too flappy
for my liking.

In Year Eight,
   Michael Mensah
asked me out,
and I said *yes*,
and spent the next three weeks
battling with him

while he fought to
get my bra off.

In Year Nine
    Noah Stein
told everyone
I was hot,
and I liked that,
and when he put his
hand up my skirt
I didn't say no.
Not the first time anyway.

And this year,
    even though I'm still in Year Ten,
    a load of sixth formers have been
        chatting me up after school,
    messaging me,
    saying stuff that would make Mum's eyes
        water.

But it's all the same.

It's all about *them*.
What they want.
What *I* can give.

Down the youth offenders' place
    Nicu Gabor

talks to me
and listens to me
and wants to do things for me.

His voice dances
with words that are all messed up
but actually mean something,
and whenever we're together
he makes me
laugh
and laugh,
sometimes until my ribs hurt.

Nicu:
> he's more than quite nice.

GIFTS AND TALENTS

How do English boys impressing the girls?
Chocolate?
Cider?
Car?
What is the secret?

I want to impressing Jess with being
her listener,
her joker,
her doer.

Maybe if she see me back in Pata
as talent wrestler,
making throws
and
takedowns,
she be in the full impress with me.

Cleaning

I know I was young
cos I couldn't
work Terry's phone properly.
I took a ten second video of my own face
before he snatched it back.
'Are you stupid? This. Here. The red button.'

He hadn't beaten Mum up,
just given her a toothbrush and told her
to clean the toilet
while he watched.

But then he got bored,
wanted to see the end of some Spurs match,
so that's when he had the idea to give me his phone,
to record it,
save the memory of Mum on her knees.

'And next time the bathroom's a pigsty,
I'll make you clean it with your tongue,' he warned
    her.

Mum didn't answer.
She just nodded
and reached for the bleach.

'Record until she's done,' he told me. 'Got it?'

'Yeah,' I said,
and as he left the bathroom
Mum glanced up at me,
and I knew then that Terry had forced
me to be on his side,
    leaving Mum on the other,

            leaving Mum alone.

I knew right then
that Terry had found a
very important
role for me.

HATE PAGES

On my mathematic book
some peoples write:
Isis Slag.

On my science book
some peoples write:
Taliban Gooooooo Home.

On my French book
some peoples write:
Voted out of Britin Fuck Off.

On my mathematic book again
some peoples write:
Rat Boy Gypsy Scum.

On
English
geography
history
book
they write:
Stinking Gyppo.

I do ripping of hate pages.

Scribble

Nicu and I are only in one lesson together –
design technology,
and
while he's up at the teacher's desk
getting something checked,
Dan grabs his work book
and scrawls
Stinking Gyppo
across it.

'Dick!' I say aloud.

Meg sniggers into her hand.
'Yeah, you should tell Dan to write that on his
    maths book
next lesson.'

I don't bother telling her I'm actually talking about
    Dan.

'Dick,' I say again,
this time
looking right at Meg.

BAD TACKLE

If you not do school homework
you do
detention
for to write
punishment words.

But

I don't write punishment words.
I look out window at P.E. teacher playing football
    with crew lads.

I see.

I see
crew lad football tackle into Obafemi.

I see
geezers laughing,
Obafemi foot holding.
Teacher doing the five highs with Dan and other
    crew.

I see
everything.

Don't Make It Easy

Terry's got the paper open in front of him
on the kitchen table
and he's jabbing at some article
with his finger,
prodding a picture of
a slightly scruffy bloke
like he might actually be able to hurt
him a bit
by attacking the newspaper.
'They're only here five minutes
and the council's putting them in houses
down Lordship Lane.
It's disgusting.
Taxpayers' money
putting up scroungers
who'd pimp out their
own kids for a pound.'

I want to roll my eyes
and make Terry
tell me exactly where these foreigners
are living.
Because I've *seen* the estate where
Nicu lives and it's worse than
this one –
windows covered in
bed sheets,

gangs of kids everywhere
and loads of people with dogs on chains –
a total hellhole.
I say,
'Yeah, it's terrible, Terry.'

'Are you taking the mick?' he says.

'No,' I say
quickly.
'No, I mean it, it's terrible.
Loads of foreign kids at school too.'

'Well, I hope you don't make it easy for them,' he
    says.

I shake my head.
'Nah, I don't make it easy,' I say,
thinking of Nicu.

And actually,
this isn't even a lie.

THE GHOST

At school I try to be so much low key,
to not catch her gazing
or
have my body in her space.

Sometime I follow like ghost
to where she goes:
I sit behind in canteen,
so I can watching her without notice,
spy her hair flowing,
her shoulders dancing when she laugh.

One time I see her white skin between
jumper
and
trouser.
A dream!
Like desert oasis.

And she never see my follow,
my spy,
my ghost.

But my voice, hair, skin
don't make easy my blending in.
Maybe
I need to do

gel style hair
like Dan and his crew,
show my undergarments
above tracksuit,
walk more like
gangster man.

Maybe then I can becoming
important
part of here.

Big
question mark.

A Bit Much

Liz is all like, 'He keeps *staring* at you!'
And Shawna says,
'Doesn't he wash his hair?'

I take a bite from my limp pizza
and say, 'I'm doing time with him
     down the park.
He said he used to ride a pony or a horse or
   something back home.
He's funny.'

'You mean he actually *is* a pikey?' Meg says.
'I never said that.'
'Yeah . . . he's probably one of them Roma ones.'
'Maybe. So what?'
'So *what*? So *brilliant*.'

One side of Meg's mouth twists into a smile and
I know then
I should've kept schtum.
Information like that is jackpot gold
to a bitch like her.

'Oi, gypsy boy! Oi, gypsy boy!
When you gonna show us your donkey kong?'
Meg shouts across the canteen.

Nicu doesn't look up.
Just keeps chewing on a roll,
gazing out the window.
But Dan and his gobby mates have heard,
sidle over.
'What's happening?' Dan asks.

Meg cups her hand around Dan's ear
then puts her lips to it,
whispering,
whispering,
thinking she's so hot and mysterious.

And I know what comes next.

'*Ee-aw! Ee-aw!*'
It starts with Dan.
Not that loudly.
Then his mates join in.
'*Ee-aw! Ee-aw!*'
Then Meg too.
'*Ee-aw! Ee-aw!*'
Nicu still doesn't know that this crap is
aimed at him.
He's smiling at a dinner lady now,
with that puppy smile
that makes her *well* happy –
I mean, she's like forty years old.
Why wouldn't she love that face?

Dan picks up his plate
and marches over to Nicu.
He thinks he's Kanye bloody West.
Everyone knows Dan lives with both parents in a
    massive semi
up Crouch End way.
Thinks he's a rude boy.

I watch.
Can't look away.
Know I should leave.
Know I should tell someone.
Know I should do something.

But
come on,
this is Dan Bell-end we're talking about.
Standing up to him would be
one hundred per cent suicide.

Nicu looks up.
        At last.
But smiles
        too sweetly,
        too innocently,
        too much like a typical foreigner
        who just doesn't get it.

Until he does.

Until Dan tips his chips over Nicu's head.
Until they are tumbling down his shoulders.
Until ketchup is slathered through his hair and
Dan is laughing,
and his mates are laughing,
and most of the idiots in the room are laughing.
Then
Meg saunters over and casually launches half a
    muffin
at Nicu's face.

'A bit much,' I murmur.

And Liz is like, 'So what? He's *weird*.'
And Shawna says, 'I think the hair's an improvement
actually.'

Nicu is silent.

His hand curls around his carton of apple juice.
The sparkle trickles out of him,
and I'd bet anything
that in his head he's telling himself to be
a good boy, a good boy.

I mean,
what else can he do
with Dan and his boys surrounding him,
hoping it'll kick off?

I can't stay.
Can't see any more.

'Fuck this,' I say
and, leaving my tray where it is,
go for a smoke behind the drama block.

RED FACE

I see on floor
chips and
red
ketchup.
Happy is not my blood.

My only happiness.

I see the angry in Jess face,
angry not at me,
at them.

I see her push door with
aggressive and leave.

Leave everyone in the laughter
at my pain.

Picking

I blow smoke rings into the air.

Without turning around I know
Nicu's there,
ketchup in his hair,
and he's looking at me.

I pretend not to sense him,
concentrate on my fag.

I pick
at a thick, hard scab on my hand.

I just know he's not
    looking away
or curling up his nose
or going to say, 'Don't pick, Jess, so ranking,'
or do anything else to
make me feel
disgusting
– which I am
    sometimes.

Not to him
though.

Not ever.

And
I don't know why
but
it doesn't feel good.

I keep waiting for him to see through me
or just see me
as I am,
and when he does
he'll be pretty
disappointed.

HATING THINGS

I hate
morning interval,
lunchtime eating,
afternoon break,
people looking and jokes they make.

I hate
P.E. lesson because I can't kick ball
like lads here.
Crazy teacher howls, '*Nicu, Nicu, Nicu!*'
Some do fouls on my legs
with purpose.

I hate
P.E. showers because
I don't want
them
seeing
my naked.

I hate
Dan and crew doing cock helicopters
near to my face,
slapping my arse with towel.
I can't to scream
cry
freak

run out of the place.
That would
tell crew
I'm the easy prey.

I hate
the day someone put note
on no-hope table:
Brexit!!!

I hate
being target board for
their every
dart.

As If Nothing Happened

Standing around waiting
for Nicu at the youth centre
my mind is going mental:
I'm so over
these team-building activities,
I'm so bored with
Dawn's sessions
and
I've had it with
all this reparation bullshit.

Nicu bounces out of
Bicep Andy's office,
which makes me feel
even worse.

'Hi, Jess,' he says,
as if nothing ever happened
in the canteen the other day,
like he's forgotten all about it.

'Nicu, I'm sorry. I was well out of order,' I say
    quickly.
'Sorry? For why?'
'For what happened in the canteen.'
'You do no bad to me, Jess.'
'Shut up. You know I should've said something.'

150

'Jess, if you walk with wolf, it not mean you *are* wolf.'

He nods.

I don't really get what he means.

Doesn't matter though.

I already feel a bit better.

'Thanks, Nicu.'

'No thanking me. You are not my evil, Jess.'

ACTIVITY CIRCLE

Boy team activity circle
have also Dawn and Bicep Andy
as our lead.

We do many talkings about
home,
school,
futures,
fears.

Rick say he want to be footballer.
Lee say he want to be millionaire.
Bill say he want to marry model.

'What about you, bruv?' Lee ask.
'Yeah, Nicu, what you want to do, mate?' Rick
    ask.
All heads eyeing me.
I say:
    'I never want go to man prison.'

All boy team big time laugh.
Me too.
'I hear that, Nicu,' Bill say. 'I hear that.'

When Dawn and Bicep Andy
leave circle,

Rick come to me.
Standing over.
'Oi, Nicu.'
'Rick.'
'Question.'
'OK.'
'How do you say *fuck this shit* in your language,
    mate?'

When I telling Rick answer
all boy team big time laugh
again.

Me include.

My Future

Now we're studying for proper exams,
it's not just Mr Morgan
banging on about us fulfilling our potentials.
Every teacher is like,
'It's about time you lot took school seriously,'
and
'If you applied yourself, you could
blah blah blah,'
and
'What do you want to do after your exams anyway?
Have you thought about college?'

I could say,
'Well,
I wanna be a doctor
with my own practice down
Harley Street
and make four hundred quid an hour.
But
if that isn't possible
maybe I could
work in films,
and make stuff
that everyone watches.
Or
if,
you know,

like,
I don't get great results,
I could do an apprenticeship or something
like my aunt Helen
who works as a hairdresser on a cruise ship.'

But
the thing is,
it doesn't matter what I want,
how smart I am
or what results I get —

    people like me
    never get out
    of places
    like this.

HANDS

When I exit Bicep Andy office,
Jess is there again,
sitting in plastic chair.
She wait for to meet Dawn.

My body goes wobbly.
'All right?' she say.
'I all right,' I say.
'Crap this, innit?' Jess say.
'Suck job,' I say.
Jess does laughing.
'Suckest job ever,' I say.
'Exactly.'
'You want chocolate button?' I ask.
'I'll have two,' Jess say.

Jess looking gloom.
              I sit down.
'What is matter?' I ask.
'Nothing,' she say.
'Tell to me.' I friendly punch her.
'Just leave it, Nicu.'

I want to find her world,
to see what she see,
to pain with her pain.

Most of all
I want my hand to touching hers,
but I just
        leave it.

Why Won't He?

I can't persuade him
to even take one drag
of my fag
and
it sort of pisses me off sometimes
that he won't do it,

that he won't keep me company.

'You're such a baby,' I say,
which is a bit weak,
but it's cos I don't really know
how to insult someone
who has his
own mind.

THE WRESTLER

After park workings
my bones are exhaust,
my back is shatter
and
my stomach sing for Mămică's soup stew.

I thank all gods we have
only one week to finishing.

This work make me never stealing from any shop
ever.

When I coming in my home
I don't smell Mămică's soup stew,
or
hear clatter of cooking.
My belly rolls with groans.

Out of the nowhere,
laughing hit my ears.

Mămică and Tata.

Mămică and Tata
in living room.

Alone.

      Laughing.
      Alone.
        Noising.

      Sexing?

I freeze to my spot,
and I wanting so much that black hole
swallow me up.
      No. No. No. No. No. No. No.

'Nicu!' Tata shout.

I schtum it.

'Nicu!' Mămică shout.

My breath schtum.

'Nicu, come here,' Tata shout again.
'We want to show you something.'

My heart almost schtums too.

'Nicu, get your arse in here,' Tata say in louder
   voice
because he think
I am far.

On my enter all is
OK.

I see them looking at
Tata's phone,
bodies together, eyes watching, faces sunny.

'Look, Nicu,' Mămică say, 'look what we found on
    Tata's phone.'
'It's from last year,' Tata say.
'You look much younger,' Mămică say.
'But strong as a bison,' Tata say.

Over shoulders
I look also the phone and see it.
See me.

Body low.
        Head up.
Feet wide.
Ready to do classic takedown move.

'You could have been a proper champion,' Tata say.
'A national champion,' Mămică say.
'An Olympic champion,' Tata say. 'First famous
    Gabor ever.'

And I was dreaming this too
long times ago.

Gold,
silver
or
bronze.
Any of three.

But dreams flutter high in air.
       Bye-bye
wrestling butterfly.

Hello
husband.

Looking for an Excuse

I won't miss Dawn, or Bicep Andy
or any of the navel-gazing crap
they make us do here.

But I hate it ending

cos,
like,
how am I gonna find an excuse to be
with Nicu?

PARTY

Fiona
Bill
Rick
Jade
Jess
Lee
me
   everyone say *see you laters* in shed.

So much noise,
laughing,
piss-take,
smoking.
I not understanding chat banter
but I understanding
the happy face on guys
for
final day of youth offender work.

In shed party
Fiona and Jade sink cider,
Bill and Rick spark roll-up,
Lee pump tunes from iPhone.

Me and Jess
share good time
conversation.

When Terry Is Out

I find one of
Terry's old phones hidden
      at the back of his wardrobe
and watch
through films I helped make.

Pan shot of the living room:
TV, sofa and sideboard.
A normal enough flat until
there's the
zoom shot of Mum screaming –
then
cut to
Terry laughing and kicking,
      his fists flying
      and
      my
      voiceover saying quietly,
      'Please stop, Terry.
      Please stop.'

Finally it
fades out.

      He's telling Mum
what set him off,
and she's saying sorry

again
     and again
     and again.

My finger hovers over the delete button,
but I don't do it.

     I can't.

I put the camera back in its hiding place
and
go out to look for Nicu,
who isn't anywhere.

He can't always be there

and I shouldn't
expect him to be.

PHOTOGRAPHS

There is
X
in calendar
in big, thick pen.

When we have
wedding day
celebration.

On coffee table
they spreading photo of marriage girls
night
after
night.

I will need
all my skills for
wrestling out of damn situation.

See,
they want me to tell who I pick.

I can't to tell.

And
I can't to tell Jess.

Falling

It's the first free Saturday for three months.
And I don't have to,
but I spend it with Nicu
on a patch of grass
behind his flats.

He won't stop messing around,
making faces,
telling jokes,
and then he
unlaces his right trainer,
does the same with my left.

I don't shoo him away
or smack the back of his hand.
I watch
as he ties our laces together,
binds us.

'Up! Come with me,' he says,
and tries to stand,
but of course he can't
cos
I stay sitting like a stone
with my eyebrows raised,
being as cool as I can.
'Bit old for three-legged races,
aren't we?'

'Come. I want to try,' he says,
so I stand,
finally,
our legs pressed up against each other.

He throws one arm around my shoulder.
'For to balancing,' he says.

I put my arm around his shoulder too.

And we shuffle,
his left foot forward
          my right foot forward,
then
my left and his right together.

We walk slowly,
          awkwardly,
          laughing and on the
verge of falling.

We don't get far.

But we do manage to move.

          We do get
          somewhere
          tied together like that.

DOUBLE OH SEVEN

On Internet I see the old film of James Bond.
This spy man have all he want:
the girls,
the fashions,
the cars.

I practise my James Bond,
chatting up ladies
in front of mirror.
> *Hi there, girl, would you care to share cocktail drink?*
> *Do you like to be in my car?*
> *Can I unzipping your garment?*

Then I change,
I am special agent
Nicu Gabor
and I imagine asking to Jess:
> *Do you like to be in my pleasure?*
> *Can you show me to your world?*
> *Would you enjoy dating day with me?*

This final question is what I will ask to Jess.

No Answer

My phone
pings.

> Wanna go 4 a Macky Ds l8r
> wiv me, Shawna + Liz?
> Meg xxxxxx

A few months ago
I would've said
YES.

Now I don't even bother answering.

I text Nicu.

ICE NATION

When Mămică and Tata tell to me about
all the peoples who will be gifting me
presents for wedding,
I have great fear.
I think that one day
I will returning from school to become
Victim of Kidnap Plot.
Hood on head.
Gag in mouth,
taken away to old place for to be
meeting and married to
stranger.

I know that this will happen.
I know I have not the power to stop.
But.
I need Jess.
I must to make her my
only and one.
It is essential for offer myself to her.
First to be date partner.
Second to take my heart:
   for Jess to be my kidnapping.

Sometimes

I wanna say to Nicu,
'I'm way out of your league,'
or
'Look at me, and look at you,'
but I don't.

And I'm not sure why.

GOOD FUN TIMES

The day I ask to Jess is like
World War III
in my chest.
I am too much shitting my bricks.

'Tell me you're having a laugh, Nicu?' Jess say.
'I not laughing, Jess. I dead serious.'
'What, like a *real date*?' she say.
'It will be nicest of days,' I say.
'With *me*?' Jess say, looking with her demanding
     eyes.
'We will have good fun times.'
'Suppose so.'
'Proper dating. In night-time,' I say.
I swear Jess eyes
fill with the
tears.
She kick stones,
small,
big,
bigger,
away into the distance.

'And I like your gorgeous physical,' I say,
because all the girls need knowing this.
'That's sweet.'

'So we go on night date then?' I say.

'We can go out at night,' she say. 'But it is *not* a date.'

WE CAN GO OUT!

I want to

jump,

cheer,

whoop.

Sit on nine clouds.

Jess

say

YES.

'I thinking Burger King

or

greasy spoon,' I say,

because these are

English date places.

'No,' Jess say. 'Let's do something better.'

I swallow grenade.

Does Jess meaning that we do . . .?

That we should to . . .?

That we . . .?

'Let's go up Ally Pally,' she say.

'Ally Pally?'

'Alexandra Palace.

They've got a massive ice rink there.

Can you skate?'

'Yes.'

I tell white
little lie.

Effort

I don't wear much make-up usually,
can't be bothered with bright lipstick or thick
  eyeliner
that all the other girls go for.

I never normally wear perfume.

But I do today
because I'm going out with Nicu.

And I don't want him to
think
I didn't make an effort.

ONE BOY FALLING

On bus to Ally Pally
I can smelling my Tata's
man–splash
that I tap on
cheek and chin.
My date clothes have condition washing,
and my
special occasion leather jacket
make me handsome man.

Jess smell of
summer day in lovely garden.
She have skinny jeans,
red lips,
black lines under eyes,
hair like the girl band.
Bus people stare
because she is complete
wow vision.

We don't do much speaking on bus.
We staring at world outside.

The skating is not graceful romance like Olympics.

Music DJ plays
doof

        doof

                doof!
Lights flash
red,
green,
blue.
   'Hey, guys, welcome to Ice Nation!' DJ shout.

Boys, girls, dates, friends, gangs
ferocious fly in their skates,
zip zoom.
Ice spraying every place.

I hold on to side.

'I thought you could skate?'
Jess saying with snigger.
'It is different ice in Romania.'

I fall
five,
ten,
double ten
times.
My clean clothes and leather

get
wet.

Jess does *whoosh* circle alone
and backways skate too.
She could be professional ice woman.

I leave holding side
and bang my bum arse.
　'Come on,' she say with hands out to me.
I reach for her.
She slide closer.

We touch
fingers.
　　　Fingers become chain link.

They snake.

We touch
hands.

No . . .
We *hold* hands.

And the electric
flows
between our skin,

bones,
bodies.

We make three big circle around rink
with hands holding –
always holding –
and it's the most
magic amazing minutes of
my life.

I want so many more.

And
more.

Same as You

A few days after Ally Pally,
after skating around the rink like
happy
kids at Christmas,
Nicu and I meet near the Tube station
and I tell him exactly what to do.

'You watch them coming through
the barrier,
and if they put a ticket in
and it
       pops out
again,
it's probably a Travelcard,
and *that's* what we want.
You understand what I'm saying?'

He nods. 'I understand, Jess.'

'Good.
Then, just as they get out of
the station,
you ask if they've finished with the card
cos you have to get to Holloway
to see your sick dad or whatever.
You get me?'

He nods again. 'I get you, Jess.'

'Then you give the cards to me,
and I'll sell 'em on to
the people at the ticket machines
for half of what they'd usually pay.
Right?'

He gives two thumbs up. 'Right, Jess.'

And then we get going,
blagging tickets,
selling them on,
making a fiver a time
until I've got fifty quid
in the back pocket of my jeans
and Nicu has two spare
Travelcards to get us into London.

So we take the Tube,
the Piccadilly Line all the way to
    Leicester Square,
and from there straight into
Häagen-Dazs, where I order the fattest cone
they've got and four scoops of
cookie dough ice cream.
'What do you want?' I ask Nicu.

'I want same as you, Jess,' he says,
eyes so fixed on my face that
I blush.
'All time same as you.'

RHINO HANDS

Metal collecting give Tata dirt and oil hands,
like rhino skin.

I can't to keep eyes off those rhino hands.
Mămică stand behind
with palms in pray position.
It like
Heaven and Hell
are standing in living room.

Tata have two photo picture,
one for each dirt hand.

I scare to look.

Mămică and Tata have sunbeam on their faces.

'We've found her, Nicu,' Mămică say.
'Well, we're down to the last two,' Tata say. 'Two
   lovely girls.'
   He holding these *two lovely girls* up to my eyes.
'Have a look, Nicu, and tell us who's your
   favourite,' Mămică say.
'I've spoken to both families. They're happy with
   what I've offered them.'
'So it's down to you now, son.'

Right rhino thrust:
   'She's called Ana–Maria.'

Left rhino thrust:
     'She's called Florica.'

I look
at both photos
with concentrate.

But I seeing only
Jess.

Liam

Nicu flicks my ear and I scream out,
try to give him a dead leg
and we bust our arses laughing
until a shadow appears over us.

'Jess?'
It's Liam.
He's got a bit of a goatee,
brown with flecks of ginger,
but he looks good.
As usual.
   'You all right?' he says.

I feel Nicu watching,
wondering who this bloke is,
this mad-good-looking bloke
who can get any girl he wants.

'I heard you got nicked,' Liam says.
'It was ages ago, Liam.'
'Yeah.'
He pulls out a packet of fags and offers me one.
I take it
and we walk away,
Nicu's eyes burning into my back.
I feel them,
and I wish he wouldn't do it –

look at me like that all the time —
like I'm
Someone.

'Where the hell have you been?' I ask Liam.
'It's been over a year for fuck's sake.
You didn't even tell me you were going
and now
it's a nightmare at home.
You have to come back.'

Liam shakes his head,
flicks ash at some flowers.
'Terry still around?'

I nod.

'Still knocking Mum about?'

I nod again.
    'Way worse than ever.
You've gotta come home, Liam.
He'll kill her
if you don't come back.'

Liam looks up at the sun.
Right into it.
    'I got my own problems, Jess.
Leila's pregnant.'

Leila,
the girl on the estate
who did drug runs for everyone?
That Leila?

'I'm living with her over in Tottenham now.
You could visit,
if you want.
Sometime.
That's what I wanted to say.
I wanna see you more.
I mean,
I wanna see you again.
I feel like a total dick for leaving,
but I couldn't stay.
Someone would have ended up dead.'

'OK.'

'Council gave us a flat.'

I look up at the sky myself
but the sun's gone –
heavy clouds hang low overhead.

He roots around in his pocket and pulls out a
    tenner,
stuffs it into my hand.
    'I'll see you around, yeah.

I'll call you,' he says.
But I know he won't call.

'Who was heart throb?' Nicu asks
when I walk back.

'Mind your business, Nicu,' I say,
and punch him in the arm,
when what I really want
is for him
to give me hug.

THE CHANGING PLACE

Teacher of P.E.
blows whistle,
scream my way,
   'Come on, son, toughen up!'
I rubbing my knee because some idiot dick
kick it hard on the purpose.

P.E. teacher does fast walking to my direction,
swinging arms,
steam in ears.
My knee blinks with pain.
'What is it?' he say when closer.
   'My knee hurting,' I say.
'What?'
   'My knee.' I try to tell to his ears and eyes.
But P.E. teacher don't care of my agony.
'If you knew the difference between a ball and a
   kebab then maybe you wouldn't get yourself
   hurt,' he say.
   'Yes, sir.'
Asad and Bilal look at grass.
Dan and mates do evil stare.

'Get up off your arse,' teacher say.

Red come to my face.
Fists get tight.

No reply.
Instead
I fast run to changing room.

P.E. teacher screaming more until I hear fading in
    his voice,
like I run inside cave.

After what happen in changing room
I don't do more football lessons.

After what happen in changing room
I don't want to go to school.

After what happen in changing room
big part in my heart
think Tata could be right when he say:
    'People here will never accept us.
They treat us like animals.'

But other part in my heart
think not all people see us like that.

Jess, for number one,
because she tell to me,
'The way I see it, if you're a dick, you're a dick,
so it doesn't matter what country you come
    from.'

But Dan definitely disagreeing with Jess
because
in changing room
he call me,
'a filthy, fucking thief,'
as he can't to find
his pen.
His pen with words *Chelsea Football Club* on it.

One mate with neck muscle say,
    'I bet he nicked it,
when he pissed off from football earlier, Dan.'

Two mate with the punk rock hair say,
'They'd rob from the
blind given half the chance.'
But I not know what he mean.

Three mate with fat belly say,
'Yeah, my old man's right about them lot.'
But I never one time meet his old man.

Dan and crew make the circle around me.
I try to put my sock on
but Punk Rock Hair
yank it
from my toe
and try to

throw on top of locker.
      It miss
      and hit wet floor.

Neck Muscle say,
   'You should do him, Dan.'
Punk Rock Hair say,
   'Break his nose.'
Fat Belly say,
   'Or his fingers.'
Then all I hear is
RA
RA
RA
because every boy shout in
my face,
so very close that I feeling their
mouth spit as it hit my
cheek
chin
eye
ear.

Then another great
yank come.
Massive yank on my hair.
Dan's hand is
strong and mighty.

My head is pull back,
my eyes see roof,
my heart like music:
Boom!
Boom!
Boom!
Dan come close like maybe he want to
kiss.
'If I find out you robbed my Chelsea pen,
you stinking gyppo twat,
I'm going to slice you
from here
to here.'
He do finger line across face
from ear
past cheek and mouth
to destination other ear.
'Got it?' he say.
'Got it,' I say soft.
But I don't
got it,
his stupid football pen.

'Right, come on, lads,' Dan say.

Before leaving changing room
Fat Belly kick my knee.

The sore shoots
between my legs,
but I stay silence.

Neck Muscle sniff up until his face become red,
his mouth full.
He spit
on side of my head.
But I again silence.

Punk Rock Hair do nothing,
laughs only.
Still I silence
while
my blood boiling with angry
and violence.

After they going
I pick up my
sogging sock.
The toe part is dry
so I use for towel
my eye sockets
and
clean Neck Muscle spit
from my head.

As I leaning to pick up bag
I spy it.

Like long plastic cigarette
lying dead under bench.
I roll it over with my
toe,
all the way
until *Chelsea Football Club* shine
up at me.

On the Grass

Ally Pally again.
But not to skate,
just to sit up there
and watch London
spread out below us like an untouchable 3D map.
'Weird, isn't it?' I say.

Nicu is next to me on the grass
pulling apart dead leaves.
'What so weird?' he asks.

'I dunno.
Just that there are millions of
people in London,
and everyone thinking they're so important.
But if,
like,
a giant came along
and
squashed them,
hardly anyone would care.
Everything would go on as normal.'

'News reporting would care,' Nicu says.
He cups his hands over his mouth,
making his voice dramatic.
'Killer giant squash all citizens in London.'

I laugh.
'Yeah, but you get what I mean?'

He is silent. Maybe he doesn't understand.
Sometimes it's like that,
and not just cos of the language.

He rests a hand on my knee.
'You meaning *we* not important, Jess.

You wrong.

We both *very* important
enough.'

THREE SEATS

Tata is not computer man.

I showing him much times
how to delete
his
Internet History Browse.

Tata is not strong student.

When I get computer
time,
it not the
sexy site
Tata looking at
that
shivers up my skin.

Skin shivers begin
when I see
the buying of
three seats
to Cluj-Napoca.

Three seats to take us away
from
here.

Three seats in three weeks.

To take me away from
Jess.

Accused

I see it happen.

I mean I'm standing right there.

And what happens is
nothing.

One hundred per cent
zero.

Meg is taking her books out of her locker,
moaning about some physics test,
when Nicu walks by,
brushes her with his bag,
and she turns
like a wild cat,
like a witch,
and pushes him against the opposite wall.

'Did you just touch my arse?' she shouts
in his face
and loud enough for the whole
corridor to hear her.

'What's going on?' my form teacher,
Ms Allen, wants to know,
coming out of her classroom.

'He touched me, Miss,' Meg says,
and starts to cry,
like,
proper tears.

'I not touched her,' Nicu says.
He holds up his hands
as if the truth were written
on to his palms.

'No, he didn't,' I say.
I stand forward.
I stand up
for Nicu for the first time.

'*Yes*, he *did*,' Meg says,
and gives me a glare.
A warning.
I look away so she enlists Shawna and Liz.
'Didn't he?
You saw him.'

They nod,
and if Ms Allen
wasn't standing right there
I'd claw them both.

'Right, everyone, come with me,' Ms Allen says.
Her face is flushed,

with pleasure, I think;
            she likes a good crisis.

'But Nicu didn't do it,' I repeat.
And
as though
Meg's conjured him up using black magic,
Dan appears.

Great.

'What's happening?' he asks.

'Him. He touched my arse,' Meg says.
Tears again.
Sobs.
Choking sounds
I've never heard from her before,
not even when her nan died
last year.

'Yeah, a thief and a perv,' Dan says.
'A little dickie bird told me he was on some
youth offenders' thing.'
He turns to Nicu.
'Rape you were done for,
weren't it, mate?'

Students slow down in the corridor –
stare and smirk
like it's some show at the O2.

Ms Allen's way out of her depth now.

'He. Didn't. Touch. Meg,' I say.

Dan puts his mouth to my ear as Ms Allen
tries to calm Meg down.
'That don't matter, Jess,' he whispers.
'What matters is that everyone *thinks* he did.'

INNOCENT

It is filth lie what they say to me,
filth lie.
I do no arse touch
or
what Dan accuse.

I can't to prove
because I have no words for
defend myself.

So
I stand like stupid man in the train lights,
listening to Jess
doing
my defending.

Then I can't be stupid man no more.

I bolt away from all voices,
down long corridor,
past canteen
and find
my comfort.

In library.

The Right Thing

Meg says, 'Oh my *God*,
did you see his face, though?
Classic.'
And they all crack up laughing
like an army of idiots.

I know there's nothing
I can do
to make them
more human,
but at least,
for once,
I didn't stand and watch
like someone had his hands around
my throat,
stopping me from speaking
      out.

For the first time in my life
I did the
right thing.

VERY KIND

In library peoples are always giving Ms Nimmo the
    headache
because they don't stay in silence
or
they are giggling to their phones.
But Ms Nimmo doesn't do crazy off her nut at
    them.
Always she remain cool calm.
She smile,
throws eyes to sky,
tuts lips,
but never crazy nuts.

One day Ms Nimmo asked me about good things
    of Cluj,
the big city near Pata.
She sit with face near me.
I tell to her lots about my city:
our dramatic sun,
our photo panoramic,
our church cathedral.
    'Wow, I must go one day. It sounds beautiful,
    Nicu,' she say.
And she grinning.

On other day
she ask me to help lift

heavy box into office.

'You're very kind, Nicu,' she say. 'Very kind
indeed.'

And I grinning.

Today she say, 'You don't seem yourself, Nicu.
Everything OK?'

And even though I hearing only lies and jangle
voices

inside my head,

I seeing too

Jess being my defence.

And I grin

the most

than ever before.

Where Nicu Lives

'You sure they won't get
back early?' I say,
as Nicu turns the key
in his front door
and we step straight into his living room.
A kitchen runs along one of the walls.

'Don't worry, Jess.
Dad working
and Mum shopping to find bargains.'

The flat smells clean.
All the furniture is brown.

'I just don't want them going
nuts if
they find us
here,' I say.

'They go nuts only if
they finding us
doing sex,'
he says.

'Idiot,' I say,
but can't help snorting
into my hand,

trying to muffle the sound
like there could be someone else
at home.

I follow Nicu across the room
where he
opens the fridge and hands me a cold Coke.
I peer inside,
clock a big Tupperware box
filled with what look like sausage rolls.
'What are they?' I ask.

He takes out the box and opens it.
'Mum make herself.
Better than buying.'

'Yeah, but what are they?'

'It called sarmale. You never hear?'

'Never.'

'Very tasty.
I make one for you.'
He grabs a mushroom-coloured bowl from the
    countertop
and carefully
puts two rolls into it.

I wander away,
sit on the sofa,
stare at the coffee table
and the gleaming glass ashtray in the centre of it.

'Your parents smoke?' I ask.

Nicu looks over at me,
his eyes soft,
his lips pressed together.
'Dad smoking always.
It make Mum
so annoying.'

I laugh,
consider taking out my own fags
and lighting up,
but I don't
cos I know Nicu
wouldn't like it.

The only other thing on the coffee table is a photo
of a girl
in a flowery headscarf,
two plaits woven with coloured ribbons
at the front of her face.
She's pretty,
maybe our age,
maybe a bit older,

but she's staring into the lens
like it's a mugshot.

'This your sister?' I ask,
and wave the photo at him.

Nicu comes towards me holding the bowl.
He stops and stares.
'No,' he says,
'she not my sister.'

He puts down the bowl,
looks at his feet.

'Shit, she isn't your dead girlfriend or anything, is
    she?'
I ask.

But he's not laughing.
He looks at me again.
'Is not my fault,' he says.
'I not choose her.'

'What you on about, Nicu?'

'They choose wife for me,' he says.

'What? Who did?'

'Parents.
This girl in photo is name Florica.
She is the choose.'

'Wait a minute, so you're telling me that she's . . .'

'Florica is the wife choose.'

'Sorry, what? Your *wife*?'

'No, no. She is becoming wife after wedding.'

The rolls are steaming in the bowl.
I'm starving but
I suddenly don't like the look of them.

'My wedding.
They want us to getting married in nineteen days.'

SAD WAVES

After I telling to Jess
story of Florica,
story of my cultures,
the gloom wave is over us.

I know she takes it hard to understanding
our ways,
our young age weddings,
our sarmale.

I finding it seriously hard too.

Life in England
make it all harder.

Jess make it the hardest.

Nineteen Days

Who cares he's getting married?
It's not like *I* wanted to marry him.
It's not like I even fancy him.
He's a friend.
He can do whatever he likes.

But what sort of parents make their
kid marry someone they don't even know?

I keep thinking he's just like me,
that we get each other,
but I don't get this.

What is this?

It's bullshit, is what it is.

Nineteen days?

He can't though.

He just can't.

DREAMLAND

And I dreaming of you last night,
but my eyes don't close for sleeping,
and it raining in my stomach,
and it storming in my heart.

And I thinking.
Thinking.

Thinking
of
us
together
for ever
and ever.

We never get lost
and
when I wake
I fear that our love will never be
found.

Unheard

Shadows moving behind the front door.
A leg,
a head,
and I hear it too,
a thud,
a scream
and when I go in
Mum's lying in the hallway,
blood seeping into the rug,
Terry standing over her,
his phone on the hall table.

I'm afraid to help Mum.
But I can't just stand here and do nothing.
I can't be his accomplice any more.

'I'll call the police
if you touch her again,' I say.
My voice wobbles.
I know she's in for it now,
and that my big mouth has caused it.

But I'm wrong.

Terry sniggers,
looks like he's been expecting me to say
something like this,

and in one sharp movement
his hand is around my neck,
pressing me up against the wall.

'You speak to me like that again
and I'll give you something
to go to the police about.
You hear me . . . sweetheart?'
he hisses.

I can't breathe.
He holds me there,
squeezes.
'Now *fuck* off!' he shouts,
and pushes me away.

I walk backwards to my room.
'Mum,' I croak.

I don't think she hears me.

SWISS ARMY

At the swan pond
we have throwing bread competition.
I throw most far,
my swan swim
fastest.
I am winner.

'All right, Nicu, calm down,' Jess say.
'I win prize?' I say.
Jess dig deep into her bag.
'Here,' she say, holding big green apple.
   'Not exactly a gold medal, but it *is* a Golden
   Delicious.'
'We share it,' I say.
Jess toss apple high. 'It's all yours.'
I catch one-hand. 'No, we share.'
'It's all right, really.'
'I insisting,' I say.

I do my own deep dig,
take out my
Swiss Army,
flick open
knife section.

'Jesus, Nicu,' Jess say.
'What? Swiss Army for surviving in wilderness

not for being town hooligan.'
'Right.'
I chuck Jess piece.
She catch one-hand.

When apple hitting our mouths
we look each other,
we nod each other,
we agreeing.

It true golden moment.

But gold moment like these
always
have black shadow in ceiling,
always
have thick fog in feeling,
always
have wedding and **X** day in my head.

And I can't to enjoying our
apple time.

Transformation

I find a long piece of orange ribbon
Mum used to wrap the present she bought me
for my last birthday,
and cut the length of it
    in two.

Then I thread the pieces through my hair
and into long plaits
which lie against my face.

I take a towel from the radiator
in the bathroom
and wrap the back of my head in it,
try turning myself into the girl from the photo,
Florica – his wife in two weeks –
but I'm too pale to pass for her.

I'm studying my creation in my phone
when Mum comes into the room
looking for her hairdryer.

She blinks.
'Oh, you look nice,' she says.

I yank the towel off my head,
chuck it on the floor.
'I look ridiculous.'

'No. You look different.
Colourful.
You look pretty, Jess.'

She has sad eyes:
even when she's trying to be cheerful
she's a picture of misery.

I untie the plaits,
pull out the ribbons.
'Shut up, Mum.
I look like a dog
and we both know it.'

BEWARE THE SILENCE

I curse myself
because it best to take
the end urinal for to
pee.

Not
middle one.

Stupid!

Here Dan and crew
can make easy
human sandwich
of me.

Here I can't escape them
because I peeing
streams and rivers.

Dan and henchman
say no swear,
do no shoulder pushing.

They let me pee.

I listening to splash from urinal,
sound of water fall

and
echo of our three
sounds.

I hearing crew breathings,
their whisper and laughing.
Like all is normal,
all is fine.

No speaking assaults.
No threaten.
No wicked eye.

It is worser.

It hitting my knee,
thigh,
shin.

Dan shake dry and exit with henchman.

When I hearing his giggle outside door
my body entire tremble.

I Used to Walk to School with Meg

Not now.

I message Meg most mornings to say
I'm gonna be late,
I'm still in bed,
I'm not well,
so that she walks on without me,
and I prefer it.
I way prefer not having to make
small talk
with
someone
I wouldn't touch
to scratch.

PING

My phone pinging,
Jess messaging
all times.

Question

Wanna go cinema?
J x

TOUCHING

We go to cinema to see
funny movie
romcom.
Jess show me how to sneaking past
without ticket buying.

In movie we drinking
massive Fanta.
We sharing
bucket popcorn.

In movie we touching
elbows together:
gentleness,
delightness.

And it feel like
voltage
speeding through my body.

Proper Dates

We're going on dates now.
Like, proper dates.

But what's the point?

DEEP GUILT

If Mămică and Tata
find out that I dating with Jess
their mercury hit sky high.

If family of Florica
finding out this,
they make sausages from me,
     put extra cash charge on Tata.

          Whole lots of shit
          hit
          fan.

I should to feel
in the deepest of
guilt
for being with Jess,
but
I don't.

I will never.

Know Each Other Better

Terry's sitting on my bed
flicking through a battered copy of
Matilda.
He grins when I come in.

I'm not sure what he wants.

'All right?' he asks.

He closes the book,
        leans forward and
carefully puts it
        back on the shelf
between a scrapbook
and some old CDs
Liam gave me years ago.

'I've been thinking,' he says.
'You and me never do anything together.
We should start.
We should get to know each other better.'

I take an almost invisible step
back
into the hall.
'You've known me since I was eight, Terry,' I say,
as happily as I can.

232

He nods, stands, comes forward
                    and takes my hand
so he can pull me into the room,
then
uses a foot to kick the door closed.
'Yeah, I know that.
But when you're a teenager you change, don't you?
I've seen the changes in you.
I wanna get to know who you are now.'

He sits back down on the bed
and cos
he has my hand, I've got no choice but to
sit down too,
when what I really want to do
is run,
            get out of that room
as quick as I can.

But why am I suddenly so afraid?
Terry's never hit me.
He's never put me in one of his films.

'Maybe we could go swimming or something,' he
    says.
'Do you like swimming?'

'I suppose so.'

'Maybe you'd be shy in a bikini though.'

'I don't know, Terry.'

'Nah, it's hard to know how you'd feel
about that sort of thing until the
time comes.'

He pats my knee
then
goes to the door.
'We'll find something fun to do.
Just don't tell your mum.
You know what a sulk she is
when she thinks
we've ganged up against her.'

He closes the door.

I stare at it
and know only
one thing:

I have to get out of here.

I SPY

At bus shelter
we hide from England rain.
Two people
too close
that we make connect with
shoulder and thigh.

Jess crush closer
like I am cosy cushion.

She cuddle tight
like she fear this rain too much.

She squeeze my arm
like priests hold bibles.

I thinking,
this body talk is not because of England weather.

So I try to cheer
with game she teach me.

I search.
        I looking.

I seeing,
one Ford car,

one flag of England
and
one flower shop.

'Jess?' I say.
'What?'
'I spy with my little eye something beginning
with . . . F.'

Jess don't do eye spying.
She look at feet.
'Fucking family.'

I want to reaching her hand,
be her calm.
Because I knowing who she speak about.
'You mean Terry?'

And she lift her
face from feet.

The Things He Does

'See, he's not really a normal person.
He's an animal
and you can't tell when he's gonna bite.
Not that he ever fights with me.
Not, like, directly.'

Nicu listens
without looking shocked,
without interrupting,
without making me feel like
a freak.

'It's Mum who gets it.
You wouldn't believe the things he does
    to hurt her –
the punching and kicking –
and he makes me film everything
like he's making a bloody documentary.'

Now Nicu winches.
'I'm sorry,' he says,
and reaches for my hand.

IN THE FEAR

When Jess tell me things
he do –
    smacks Mum around
    and
    punches her black and blue
    and
    boots her like a football
– I wanting to wrestle him hard.

Wrestle him to ground,
wrestle him to pain,

to pieces.

For Jess
Terry equal terror,
Terry equal terrible.

Jess should not be in this fear.

Nothing Like Him

I don't tell Nicu
about Terry
sitting on my bed
and
offering to be my best mate
cos
I can't really explain
what it was
that made me so afraid.

Not in actual words.

And when Terry's out
and I try to tell Mum,
mumbling and getting confused
about exactly what he said,
she frowns and scratches her forehead
like I've asked her an impossible
University Challenge question.
'He said he wanted to take you swimming.
    So what?'

'So, it's weird, Mum.'

'Is it? He's like your dad, Jess.'

'No. No, he isn't like my dad.

He's nothing like Dad.
Dad wasn't a total prick.'

She sighs.
'He was to *me*,' she says.

'Mum . . .'

I can see she knows what I'm trying to say
but she doesn't really want to hear it.
She can't hear it
cos of what it'll mean
for both of us.

'If we keep our heads down, Jess . . .' she whispers.
'Look, he hasn't laid a hand on me for ages.'
She bites into a custard cream.
There's a yellow bruise on her forearm.

'You're never gonna leave, are you?'
I ask.

She stops chewing the biscuit,
blinks hard.
'We've nowhere to go,' she says.
'And even if we did . . .
            he'd find us.'

STUPID THINGS

Tata say stupid things:

'You'll soon be the head of your own family.'
'A good wife should always make you feel strong
in the stomach.'
'Only ten days to go.'
He point to **X** on calendar.

Mămică also say stupid things:

'She's so lucky to be getting someone like you,
Nicu.'
'A good wife should always make everything
happier.'
'Ten days will fly by.'
She point to **X** on calendar.

I hate this bloody calendar.

An Idea

He sits next to me in detention
and pulls his chair really close.

He smells of salt and vinegar crisps.
The sleeves of his blazer are
   too short.

'What do you want?' I murmur.

But it isn't his fault everything looks like hell.
He's the only thing in my life
I even like.

Nicu stays where he is.
'Why you being not my mate
all of a suddenly?' he says.

Mr Tierney looks up,
points a red ballpoint pen at Nicu.
He didn't notice him walk in.
   'Who are *you*?' he asks.

'My name is Nicu.
P.E. teacher tell me I must to come
because I not have proper football shoes.'

'I've no idea what you're talking about,

but just sit down.
And sit away from *her*.'
Mr Tierney circles his pen in my direction
like a wand.

'You act like tough cookie.
But you not cookie,' Nicu says.

I can't help laughing.

Even when I'm fed up
he breaks me down
somehow.

Nicu takes the seat in front,
opens his bag and pulls out a book.

I stare at the back of his head,
his neck
brown and freckled,
his hair
hardly even brushed.

'Oi,' I whisper.

He turns.

'I've got an idea.'

AT THE BACK GATES

So when she whisper
   'Oi'
I feel the blessing in my
bones.
Jess has the serious face on.
No smile,
no teeth,
no eye diamonds.
   'I've got an idea,' she say.
   'What idea?' I say.
   'I'll tell you after this crap,' she say.
   'OK.'
   'TURN AROUND, BOY!'
Teacher shouting at me.
       So tell me the new.

I stare at clock –
tick-tock.
It is longest twenty minutes
in life.

'Right, you can both beat it now.'
We sprinting to back gate.

'God, it's bloody Baltic.'
Jess cuddle her body.
But it not *too* cold.

I *know* cold.
When blood is frosty inside you.
When it hurting to walk.
When it better not to wash.

Jess blow
      little cigarette circles.
I try to pop them with my
      finger.
  'What is big idea, Jess?'
She does shuffle foot dance,
flicks fag
far in distance.

'What is idea?' I say.
'OK, you hate this school, right, Nicu?'
'In most times, yes,' I say.
'But you don't want to go back to where you came
    from
to marry some stupid girl
you've never met either, right?'
'Not in the chance.'
'Well, you're running out of time, Nicu. You've
    only got, like, a week.'
'Not week, Jess. Eight days.'
'And your dad's basically forcing you to do it.'
'He force.'
'Being a bit of a dick, if you ask me.'
'He is dick when talking of wife for me.'

'Well, that's just like me too, innit?'

'What?'

'My stepdad's an utter bastard.'

'You tell me before, Jess. And I sorry to listen.'

'And, this school . . . I can't stand it any more.'

'I understand.'

'That's why I think we should get out of here.'

'The school?' I say.

'No, not just the school,
     away from everything.
          you and me, Nicu.'

'You and me?'

'We could take a train somewhere.'

'Where somewhere?'

'I dunno. Warwick, Bristol, Glasgow?'

'This is idea?'

'Yeah, we should do it.'

'What?'

'Do a runner.'

Do a runner?

So me and Jess together for all the days?

Shitting sake!

Madness

I mean,
he could turn out to be a Terry
once we're together all the time.
Maybe underneath that puppy dog face
there's a madman
bubbling with rage
and ready to do me in.

When I get home
my phone pings:

**I think yoor ideer
is most Einstein
ever. Ciao Nicu xx**

But that's the thing —
running away was all my idea.

So maybe,
actually,
I'm the one who's mad.

CHAT TIME

'You need to wash your hair
and
put on these
clean clothes,' Mămică say.

My white shirt with big collar
is hanging on room door.
My fresh trousers
lie straight on my bed.

'You'll need a bath too,' Mămică say,
'The water's hot.'

Tata is silence.
His finger clicks at computer.
He get better and better
with tech work.

'Why? What's happening?' I ask.
'Tata has something he wants you to do.'
'And I need to wash my hair for it?'
'Don't be a smartarse, Nicu,' Tata say, his body
    swing to me on seat.
        'Just do what your mother says.'

I stare at them
like baby boy,
with teenage angst.

'Your dad wants you and Florica to meet,' Mămică
    say.
'He thought it would be a good idea
if you both had a nice chat
before next week.'

My angst go wilder
and
every organs inside me
skip a jump.

I thinking that maybe Florica,
any seconds,
will pop
from wardrobe
or
fly
through door.

'What? Now?' I say. 'She's coming *here?*'
'No,' Tata say. 'I've set up a Skype call for half seven.'

Mămică barber my hair
into Justin Bieber style,
but this not my look,
this
not me.

We wait for Skype music to
call us.

I wait to hearing Florica say,
  Hi, Nicu, nice to finally meet you,
but this girl is not my desiring.

This, all this,
is
not me.

Packing

Terry knocks on my bedroom door
like a real gentleman,
      like someone you could trust.
Funny that,
cos
with the same knuckles
      he knocks Mum out.

Flat.

'Yeah?' I say.

He puts his head around the door.
'What you up to?' he asks.

I hold up a sock.
'Nothing. Just sorting some stuff out.'
What I don't tell him is that I'm packing,
getting out of here,
taking a train somewhere – anywhere – with Nicu,
and sticking two fingers up to him and
waving goodbye to life here.

On the bed I've got a pile of clothes:
trainers,
grey knickers,
jeans

and a hoodie.
Plus, every single thing I own that I might get a
    few
quid for:
a couple of old phones,
a hair straightener,
gold earrings Liam got me one Christmas.

'Where's your mum?' Terry asks.
His voice is sort of sing-songy,
chipper,
but I can tell from his twitching temples
he's about to explode.

'Dunno,' I tell him,
which is true.
I haven't seen her since yesterday.
She wasn't up when I left for school,
and the house was empty when I got home.
And cold.

My gut starts to flip.

Did she leave?
Did she clear off without me?
Before me?

'Can you see now why I get so mad with her?'
Terry asks.

His fist flexes.
Oh, God,
if Mum doesn't come back maybe I'll get it.
Maybe I'll be the one with a broken rib
and bruises where no one can see them.

'She probably went to Asda,' I say.

'Then why's her phone off?' he asks,
like I should know.

'Dunno,' I say again
and shrug.
'Want a cup of tea?'
I add,
because that's how Mum diverts him –
with food and drink,
and sex sometimes.

Keys rattle in the front door.
'Hello?'
It's her.
She hasn't left at all.
And I take a deep breath,
relief,
until Terry marches into the hall,
his feet hard on the floor.

I follow.

His fingers seize Mum's wrist
and he puts his face so close to hers
their noses touch.

And then,
very gently,
he presses his lips to her lips and kisses her.
He kisses
and kisses
and kisses.

'Shall we put a bottle of wine in the fridge
and watch a film tonight, love?'
he asks.

'Sure,' she whispers.

Terry turns to me.
'You still here?'

I squeeze my own hands into fists
and go back to my room to finish packing.

RUNNERS

This what I thinking:
Jess is exact right,
it *is* time to do
a runner.
Runner from Mămică, Tata, Pata.

Runner from Florica.

It *is* time to
bugger off.

This what I also thinking:
I dream of
my heart
beating
on top of
Jess heart.
So we beat
like one.

Not a Clue

In afternoon registration
I don't even look at my so-called mates.

I sit away from them,
at the back,
with my feet up on the desk,
and roll my eyes when Ms Allen calls my name.
  'Jessica *Clarke*,' she repeats, eye-balling me.

'Well, if you're looking right at me,
I must be here, Miss, innit?' I say.
I want her to notice me,
see I'm in school
and definitely *not* call my mum to tell her I'm
  bunking.

A few of my classmates snigger.
Ms Allen goes red and blotchy.
  'Do you want another detention, Jess. Is that it?'
  she asks.
She's a young teacher
who doesn't have a clue
about teenagers.
And small scuffles like this get her all hot and
  bothered.
I love watching it happen.

'I don't mind a detention,' I say and shrug.
She can do what she wants.
I won't be here at three-thirty anyway;
by the time the bell goes,
I'll be miles away.

           With Nicu.

I leave registration and go straight out the
front gate.

Every other time I've bunked off
I've just headed to the park for cider
instead of going to science or whatever,
but today it's different.
I'm leaving.
For good.

I feel sick and dizzy,
so I go straight
to the corner shop to get a drink.

And then
I wait.

CREEPING AROUND

Busy.
Busy.

Tata go out metal collecting
most days.
Mămică stay and do sausages, stews
and clothes.

Busy.
Busy.

So it good timing to become
ninja boy.
Creep around boy.
Bunk school boy.

Do a runner.

If they nabbing me in this act
I know
I'm the goner.

But
X
day
is getting
so closer.

Bloody wife!

The day Jess nerves
shatter
to end of her rope
is getting
so closer
too.

Bloody Terry!

Now is time for preparing
to do runner.
Now is not time for
delaying.

I go where Tata keep his
metal collecting cash.
His wife buying cash:
in bedroom,
top of wardrobe,
deep at back,
in box for shoes.

I lift box,
open,
and reach my hand inside.
Hand disappears in
tens

fives
fifties
oranges
blues
reds
      monies
      cover all my skin.

I stuff my bag with
all my needs.

I take much wedge
and
in bag
squeeze shove
it under
jeans and jumper.

My stomach do
churn spin
thinking if Tata catch me he do
left hook
      right hook
on it.

But I must to escape
X
day.

I must.

With bag on my back
I become the mouse,
        tipping toes
           on creaky floors.
I stop even from blinking
in case Mămică listen from kitchen
and know I not in school like usually.

I aching to hug her for last time
but
I fear to see the hurt in her eyes.
In eyes of Tata too
when they know
I not wanting
their life
for me.

And it vital important
I go to Jess
waiting
now.

Batman

I'm outside Nandos
when I see him shuffling up the road,
a backpack over one shoulder.
He waves at me.

But . . .
       Oh, God.

He's wearing a cape.
Like a proper cape –
black and buttoned up at the neck.
Where the hell did he get it?
And
what exactly did he think I meant
by doing a runner?
Maybe he thinks we're gonna fight crime
instead of commit it.

Jesus.

'All right, Batman,' I say,
pulling on the cape's collar.

He frowns.
'Might get chilling at night, Jess,' he says.

'You look like you're about to go to a bloody

Dungeons and Dragons convention,' I tell him.
'Talk about conspicuous.'

'I not understand these words,' he says.
          'I ready for running though.'
He lifts up a foot, so I can see he's got his trainers
    on.

He's beaming
but I don't know what he's so happy about.
Does he even know what we're doing?
Does he get that we're not running
          to anything
          but
          running *away*
          with nowhere to go.

'Everything hunky dory,' he says,
twisting his arm around
and
patting his backpack.

'Don't say hunky dory,' I snap.

'Hunky dory proper English words,' he says.

'Well, coming out of your mouth
it sounds like bullcrap,' I say.
I'm being mean

but
I can't help it.
He doesn't seem to be taking this seriously and
I'm not running away with him
if all I'm gonna be doing is spending the next year
stopping him from sounding like a complete
    moron.

'How much pounds you have?' he asks.

I reach into the pocket of my blazer
and pull out a handful of tenners.
Nicu stares at the notes,
the Queen's superior face glaring at us.

'That all you find?' he asks.

'Well, what have you got,
Prince of Romania?'

He throws his backpack on the ground,
digs deep into it
and shows me.
'Where the hell did you get all that?'
        Wads of cash –
more money than I've seen in my life.

'It not good?' he asks.

'Good?
It's nuts, Nicu.
You *are* bloody Batman!'

He zips up the backpack
and puts his hands on his hips
like a real superhero.
'Glad I making you happy, Jess,'
is all he says.

EYE BLINK

The guilt give me goosebump.

For cash in my pocket,
for destroying dreams of Mămică and Tata.
Also
for stealing Tata's
treasure coat,
the one he wear to village festivals.
But here is cold and chilling most of times,
raining and greying every day,
so
I needing
this
treasure coat for my own.

Jess make joke when
she see treasure coat first time
but that is OK
because
big part of her is piss-taker.

Her eyes wide open when I show my cash.
She tell me I am
superhero.
But I am greedy –
I want
handsome, smart superhero
AND

gentle kissing,
lip locking,
hand hugging.
Now, that would be
amazing.

We don't do any tender stuff.
No time.
We go quick
                away.

But
it not so easy.
Sometimes London North
is too small enough
and we can't be
alone.

And we not alone
because everyone school bunk today.
Dan and his crew –
Punk Rock Hair,
Fat Belly
and
Neck Muscle –
bump us in street.

When seeing crew
Jess tight squeeze my arm.
    'Shit,' she say.

I feel all her finger press me.
Crew come close.
I pulling her stiff to me.
Body guard her.
   'Don't worry, Jess,' I say. 'I protect.'
My hand wrap around,
pressuring her waist.
I am Jess steel suit.
   'You not worry, I have you,' I say.
Crew come close.
   'No, you leave this to me, Nicu,' Jess say.

This is what I understanding:
   'All right, Jess?'
   'What you doing with that little thief?'
   'Where you going?'

This is what I also understanding:
   'Pikey twat.'
   'Immigrant wanker.'
   'Smack him.'

Crew do circle on me again,
so near
I smell the pong of booze and smoke.
   'Leave him alone, Dan,' Jess say in terror voice.
   'You stay out of this,' Dan say.
   'Slapper,' Fat Belly say.
   'Gyppo lover,' Punk Rock Hair say.

'Gyppo shagger more like,' Muscle Neck say.
Too many laughing.

People in street
seeing,
hearing,
witnessing,
but flick eyes on ground and
quick step past circle.

It just me and my Jess.
Alone on tiny Island.
With no person to
save us.

Dan flick Jess hair,
come close to her ear.
Very close.
Too close.
His mouth, her ear.
He make whisper.
Jess pull back.
    'Fuck off, Dan, will you?' she say.
Her hand squash me more harder.
    'Come on, Nicu.'

And we fast walk to small street,
away from crew,
away from whispers.

To leave the noise behind.

But Dan and crew don't to leave.
They follow.
Behind us in silence street.

We walk quicker.
They speed follow.
We stay in silent.
They don't quiet.
We don't run.
They move so fast to be in front of us.
All bodies stop.
I hear words I half understanding:
   'Plunge the prick.'
   'Yeah, go on, Dan.'
   'Right in his fucking eye.'

And this boy, Dan,
who
I have never did hurting to
ever,
listen to these wordings.
He listen well good
because
he pull sheen blade from behind jeans.

Jess does banshee scream.

I feel fire
and fear at same time.

Blade come to me fast rapid.
I dance
jerk back
slip slide
touch
tap
wrestling days back.

My hand go deep in Tata's treasure coat.
I feel for my Swiss Army,
my protect.

Shuffle feet
left
          right
reveal my *own* blade slash.

One
          two
like in movies.

The wild man take my body
to crazy land.
I see target,
hard advance,
charge,

271

arm straight,
lunge,
plunge.

My protect
rips
deep

in and
       out.

          And it sink softly.

Stab happen in an eye blink:
Dan falling,
crew frozen,
Jess calling
my name,
and
us

running . . .

      running . . .

          running . . .

Part
THREE

Jess-Jess-Jess

I'm shouting and running,
and Nicu's
  behind me
shouting back,
and running too,
but I can't really hear what he's saying
except my name
— *Jess Jess Jess* —
over and over
like a bloody
siren.

MR WOLF

Huffing
puffing
I hearing still his yell
inside my ears.

Huffing
puffing
I seeing still my Swiss Army,
one-two, in-out.

Its picture won't leave me.

I can't to breathe.

Eating air.

I can't to breathe.

Hurry
sprint
speed
lights of shops shoot past eyes,
blinding.

I can't to breathe.

Blood on Our Hands

'What the *fuck* was that?'
I'm screaming
and Nicu's
    behind me
screaming back.

What just happened?
Did Dan get stabbed?

I mean,
Wood-Green-gang-stabbed
like the proper hood boy he pretends to be?
Yeah,
he deserved to get hurt,
but why did Nicu have to be the one to do it?
And why now,
just as we were getting away,
just when I thought things were looking
up?

We round a corner,
leg it down an alleyway
and almost collapse at
the end
of it,
hiding between a pair of wheelie bins.

'How badly did you hurt him?' I blurt out.
'Did you *kill* him?'

Nicu can't speak.
He's just gasping, panting,
then punching one of the wheelie bins to bits.
Punching and
hollering and
punching and
hollering.

I've no idea what he's saying.

'Stop!' I scream
and grab his hand.
'Your hand's bleeding,' I say,
feeling the blood's slipperiness between my fingers,
coughing up a little bubble of sick.

He exhales.
'Not my blood, Jess,' he says.

I close my eyes, thinking.

Thinking.

What do we do now?
Where do we go?
Mum? Dawn?

The police?
That's it:
we go to the police.

It was self-defence,
broad daylight.

I hold on to Nicu
tight,
two hands gripping his shoulders.
'We have to give ourselves up.'

'No.'

'If we run away
it'll look well suspicious.
They'll think we meant it.'

He shakes his head,
pulls his cloak
up to hide his face.

'We *have* to, Nicu.
We haven't got a choice.'

He steps away from me,
eyes filling with tears,
looking like a little kid.

'*You* have choice, Jess,
because police believing
white girl
speaking good English.
But me.
They seeing only
gypsy boy
with
criminal paper.'

He kicks the wall.

'Shit,' I say,
because he's right.
The police wouldn't believe him for a second,
and not just Nicu;
with my offender's record
they wouldn't believe me either.
We're textbook delinquents.
Guilty before we've even
opened our mouths.

'We must to go far away now,' he says.
'We can cutting hair and
changing names
and nobody remember
us
after.
OK, Jess?'

He wipes his hands on his cloak,
shudders when a dog in the distance
barks.

'Yes,' I say.
'I think we have to go
away like we planned.'
I take his hand.
I hold on tight.
'Let's get you cleaned up
first,' I say.
'Let's wash this blood off your hands.'

SALTY SWIMMING POOLS

She pour the water bottle over my
blood hand.
I not hear what she say,
her tongue, mouth, words
all
happening too much fast.

Jess is angry,
in devastation,
totally pissed-off with me.

She is correct to be.

But
I want for her to give me
tight hug
and tell me
    everything going to be all right.

Instead
she do the big panic.

I try rub blood off my hand.
Again Dan's liquid
drop
one

two
on my shoe.

Blue and red lights
blur past,
and I thinking of Dan, poor guy,
and me without brain,
and why I always do the stupid thing.
Why?

What idiot idea
to using my protect.

And it come . . .

Like Falls of Niagara it come.
I can't to control
the tears.
My stomach and shoulders
bouncing
bouncing
bouncing
like the
doof
doof
doof
on the night of our
ice skate
date.

And I *still* can't to breathe.

'Come on, Nicu,' Jess say.
And she making her thumbs do car wiper on my
    eyes.
'Jesus, don't cry.
It was self-defence.
I saw it.
There's CCTV cameras all over the place to prove
    it.
I'm telling you, it was self-defence.'

Jess move closer.
Arms out.
We become one,
hugging.
She is warming.

Her touching help peace my mental
and my body.
'I only want to scare on him, Jess,' I say.
'I know you did.'
'It happen fast.'
'Exactly.'
'Maybe I make just little hole in him.'
'Whatever it was, we better get out of here.'
'Where?' I say.

The mobile phone shine light on
Jess face.
'Liam,' she say.
'Liam, is that you?'

Clean Up

'Ok, see you later,' I say and close the phone.
I didn't tell Liam
why
I
so desperately
have to see him,
and I know he must think it's
something to do with Terry,
something to do with Mum.

In a way
it is
because if it weren't for Terry
I'd never have tried
to run away.
I'd never have been
in that place
with Nicu.

'My flat's not far,' I say.
'Let's go there first
and change
so we don't get clocked.
Quickly.'

I never knock on the front door,
but I do today,
to make sure Terry's not about.

Mum opens it and before she can talk out loud
I slam my hand against her mouth.
'Is he out?' I hiss.
She nods.
'Come on, Nicu.'
We slide past her into the hall.

'What's going on?' Mum asks.
She is staring at Nicu,
at his blood-spattered hands,
his face streaked with tears and sweat.

'Cape off. Trainers off,' I tell Nicu.
'And you have to change those trousers.
Mum, you got anything he can wear?
Anything Terry won't notice is gone?
When will he be back?
Did he say?
Is he out for the day?
Mum!'

She puts her hands over her eyes
and starts to cry.
'What's happened? What's going on?'
She takes Nicu by the arm.
'Who are *you*?' she screams,
like we've time for *her* hysterics.

'Help us or piss off,' I shout.

She runs to the kitchen and comes back
clutching a spray and cloth.
She picks up Nicu's trainers and starts to
wipe away the blood.
'I'll be back in a sec,'
I tell them
and dash into Mum's room,
where I rifle through Terry's stuff
until I find a pair of
tracksuit bottoms
and a T-shirt
that'll fit Nicu.

We might be OK,
I think.
We might get out of here,
get to Liam's place,
keep our heads low for a while
and finally make it out of London
where we'll be free,
all of this behind us,
all of this a stupid bad dream,
a new life.

Mum has finished wiping
Nicu's trainers
and he's just standing there,
sort of shaking,

staring into the distance,
being useless.

I click my fingers in front of his face.
'Stay cool,' I say. 'Don't go all weird.'
'OK,' he says. 'I try.'
I hold out the tracksuit bottoms.
'Go into the bathroom and
put those on.
You've got one minute.'

He nods and disappears.
The door clunks shut.

I bolt to my room
and pull out something completely
different to wear plus
a cap to cover my hair.
Mum has followed me in.
'What have you done?' she whispers.
'Oh, Jess, what the hell have you two done?'

I want to confide in her,
this woman who loves me more
than anyone in the world,
but before I can,
the room door rattles
and

Terry
is there,
standing and
watching us.

OLD RED EYES

He stagger in hall.
I seeing
the red eye,
lip licking,
bull sniffing,
the predator animal ready to make kill,
this guy who does
trampoline on her mum.

'Who's this?' he say.

He zigzag to me
at bathroom door,
looking my body
up
down.
His finger goes below my
neck apple.

Prod.
Jab.
Stab.

'Why-the-fuck-are-you-wearing-my-stuff?' he
     asking.
'Terry, the boy's had . . .' Jess mum start.
'Was I asking you?' he scream at her.

'Nicu's my mate from school,' Jess say.

'Yes, I friend,' I say.

'We're just going out. We're in a bit of a hurry,' Jess
    say.

'I don't think so.' He growl.

Jess Mum try:

'They were just heading to . . .'

'Louise!' he bark. 'Stay out of this.'

All time he keeping finger and red eye on me.

'*Nicu?* What sort of name is that?'

'It is Romanian name,' I say.

After everything that happen
to me
now this.
This bastard man.
So close
he nearly kissing me.
His smell shoot into my nose
like poison.

'Well, there'll be no foreigners in this house.'

'We're just leaving,' Jess say.

'*He* is. You're not.'

'You don't tell me what to do,' Jess say.

'Wanna bet?'

'We go now,' I say.

'You better believe it kiddo,' Terry say.

   'But before you piss off back

to where you come from,
get those clothes off.'

He put big hand on my hip,
tug
and
yank
at my T-shirt.
'Get it *off*!' he shouting.
Jess shout, 'Leave him alone!'
And still he pull,
assault
and
attack.
But I no more have
my Swiss Army.

Threw it in drain hole.

I am protectless.

I hear sirens
in distance
outside.
Nee naw
Nee naw
Nee nawing
in my brain.

What to doing?
How to escaping?

His hand pressuring my neck.
'See you and your type –'
'Terry!' Jess mum scream more.

I seeing Jess body tight,
her mum face full of fright.

His pressuring gets stronger
until Jess grab his arm.

Sirens
screams
shouts
brain
pain.

Jess kick his knee with all her muscle.

In super slow motion
it happen.
Terry's hand
exit my neck
and
connect with eye of Jess.

Sirens

screams
lights
blue
red
      mist arrive.

I think to using my other self-defending.
Wrestling days again appear.

I escape from the hold,
then
advance my head with full force
and
connect with Terry's
nose.

Crack
break
bleed
fall
howl
and again we're

running . . .

      running . . .

        running . . .

Understanding

'Come on, Jess,'
Nicu says,
dragging me down the
    stairwell
    so fast I think I might fall.

But even when we're halfway
down the street I can still hear Terry howling,
shouting over the balcony
every last bit of abuse
he can fit into his mouth and
hurl at us.

'We must to run quicker,'
Nicu says,
    tugging at my arm.

I make him
    stop
at the zebra crossing.

'Why did you hurt Terry?' I shout,
and then I punch his shoulder
again and again and again,
hoping it'll hurt *him* –
hoping it'll knock some sense into his head.

He looks like he might cry again
and it only makes me angrier.
I shove him hard,
almost
into an oncoming car.

We squat between two white vans
to get our breaths.
'He want to destroying us, Jess.'

'But, my mum,' I explain.
'*She'll* be the one who
gets it. Don't you understand?
Isn't there *anything* you understand?'

He holds my fists, so I won't hit him again
and presses his face up close to mine.
'I understand we have to run now.
I understand Terry is total bastard.
I understand I making your life
more terrible than before.
Tell me what I *not* understanding?'

Now I feel my own tears come.
And I hate it.

I hate crying
because that's not me
and that's not what we need right now.

We need to go,
get to Liam's
and figure out what we're going to do.

But we don't move.
I just stare at Nicu.
'No one ever stood up for me before,' I tell him.

He nods. 'You preferring I didn't do?'

'No,' I tell him.

'What you want us doing now, Jess?'

I take his chin between my fingers.

We come together.

ON CLOUD TWENTY-NINE

When her lips touching mine
all
siren
and
screaming
noise

     stop.

It seem her kiss
sprinkle the magic
diamond dust
on my fear
and
my panic.

All of a suddenly
I'm in hot-air balloon.

Floating . . .
     floating . . .
far away
into different land.

I am in peace.

I am in
love.

When kiss ends
I returning
into the now.

Into

here.

U with Nicu? Call me.
Dan's at the North Mid.

Unde ești?

Like WTAF U DOING?

Sunâ-ne acum. Poliția îi la ușa

WHERE R U JESS?????

Te rog sună acasă Nicu

No Junk

We can't get a bus
cos they've got cameras on them,
and in some taxis too,
and even along the high street
to stop gangs and muggers
and whatever,
so we walk
hand in hand,
quick as we can,
breathing hard,
thinking harder,
wishing it were different
and glad it isn't,
past the tube station,
all the way along Lordship Lane,
miles it feels like,
miles and miles,
until we get to Tottenham High Road
and walk up towards White Hart Lane,
the Spurs' ground,
Torrington Gardens,
Liam's estate,
and the red door to his flat,
which has a sign across it that reads,
NO JUNK MAIL.

TEARS AND FEARS

Jess drop my hand
to *knock–knock*
soft
on red door.

When Liam open
I seeing his man face,
strong
like warrior Viking,
hair sea wave cool.

They have same eyes:
colour of sky
on sunshine days.

Liam look me once over,
same as Terry –
down
up.
His face tell me that he can't to see
past my
skin.
My foreign.
I want to say:
Hello, Liam. Please to meet you.
But no chance.
I look at my feet

and seeing Dan on my toes.

Still.

'Can we come in, Liam?' Jess say.

Liam step out of door and we step back.

'I can't help you, Jess.'

'But I thought . . .'

'I spoke to Mum.'

'Mum? When?'

'She called a few minutes ago.'

'Is she OK?' Jess say in the desperate.

'She's fine, she's with a friend.

Apparently

she bolted and left that arsehole

snorting on his own blood.'

Liam looking me with serious.

'Nice job, by the way,' he say.

'Where's Terry?' Jess say.

'Who gives a shit?'

'Liam, we need help.'

'There's no way. Leila will go nuts.'

Liam nod head to me.

'We'd be screwed if they nabbed *your mate* in here.'

'What do you mean?'

'Mum told me everything.'

'Mum doesn't know shit.'

'The police were at the estate, Jess.'

'And what?'

'Well, she sees blood on his hands and

both of you changed your clothes.'
'And what? Two and two make . . .'
'What? Big coincidence, is it?'

I looking at Jess.
We pressurise our hands to become one unity.

'What the hell will we do, Liam?'
'I can't help.' He step back inside red door.
'Please.'
'I'm sorry. I just can't.'
'Where will we go?' I hearing the shaky in her
   voice.
A volcano ready for the erupt.
'If I were you, I'd get out of London,' Liam say,
before closing door.

Slam.

Thud.

Lock.

Action Plan

'Liam!' I shout through the letterbox.
'Liam, *please*!'

It's not like I thought we were gonna
live
with my brother.
I just thought that maybe Liam would know what
    to do,
that maybe he'd wanna help
after running out on me
like he did.
But he doesn't feel guilty about leaving.
He's taking care of himself
like he always has.

Like he should.

And
I'm on my own
again.

Except,
        I'm not
        alone at all.

My mind sprints.

We need an action plan.

'You've got money,' I tell Nicu.
'Tottenham Hale Station's not far.
We'll get a train from there.
Go anywhere that isn't London.
It's what we were gonna do anyway,
right?
That was always the plan anyway.
Right?'

He's staring at me,
or squinting,
trying to figure something out.

'What?' I ask. '*What?*'

'It OK to changing your mind,' Nicu says.
'You OK to calling police
and staying here with
family and friends and normal
life.
It me who make mistake, Jess.
Not you.'

I shake my head,
take his hand,
his nails still dirty from Dan's blood.
'You aren't leaving me,' I say.

FOR EVER

'You aren't leaving me,' she say.

No.

I want never to leave Jess.

For
Ever.

Lucky

A siren blares out somewhere close by
as a high speed train
      zips through the station.

God,
I wish we were on it,
wish we were heading for Stansted, then Spain,
somewhere so different
we'd hardly recognise ourselves
when we got there.

'Shit, there isn't another Cambridge train for forty
    minutes,'
I tell Nicu,
looking at the timetable,
my hood covering my face to hide it from
station staff.
'We should go somewhere quiet to wait.'

And we do.

We go outside
and find a bench by a burger van,
where we sit with our heads down,
thighs pressed against each other's,
sweating hands
holding on tight.

Everything disappears.

The cars and people,
the planes above and
the trains along the track.

It's just him and me.

All quiet.

And I think
for a second
how lucky I am
to have found him.
How lucky I am
that he came into my life.

'You not so worrying now, Jess,' he whispers.

'No,' I say.
'I'm not so worrying at all.'

PLATFORM

'I need toilet,' I say.
'What? Now?' Jess say annoying.
'Yes, I needing now.'
'OK, go. Hurry up.'
'OK. Look after my stuff.'
'Fine. I'll meet you on the platform.'
'Platform. Yes.'
'Make sure no one sees you.'
I do little laughter.
   'I'm serious, Nicu.
   I'm really serious.'
She soft touch my cheek
and look me eyes to eyes.
Hers say
You are my heart
without the speaking
and
I try to swallow massive lump in throat
because
we have sharing
heart.

'No kissing stranger blokes,' I say.
'Shut up and go,' Jess say and does
punching of arm
again.
She could be champion boxer if she want.

She could be
anything
if she want . . .
if I didn't make problem for her.

Anything she want . . .
if only without me.

Time Sharing

Prison wouldn't be too bad
   if Nicu were there.

If we shared a cell.
Shared time.

I mean,
   he'd get on my nerves
   trying to tell stupid jokes
   or throw chat up lines at me
   which just wouldn't work with his English.

But he wouldn't hurt me,
   would he?

We'd be locked in,
   and locked up together
and he'd keep me safe,
   I reckon.

Prison wouldn't be that bad
   if Nicu were there.

But prisons don't work like that.

They aren't bloody love shacks.

And if we get caught
I'm all on my own.

MIRROR MAN

I look at my
phone:
many missing calls.

I look at Cambridge train time:
five minute.

I look at face in toilet mirror:
I want no more reparations
for self-defending against Dan.
How many jail years?
Five?
Ten?
Twenty?

I look my fingers in light.
Dan won't wash away
From them.
I scrubbing and scrubbing and scrubbing.
But still.

I Can't See

He's been ages.
What can be taking so long?

The train approaches.

I can't see him.

The train pulls in.

On time.

I can't see Nicu.

TEXTING

I can't to see my face in mirror.
My eyes are glass with wet.
A force is on my chest.
I am in wood worker's vice,
turning
tightening
twisting
tensing.

PING!

Where R U? Train here. ♥

I send text.

I arive now. C U on train. ♥

PING!

OK! J X

I remain looking in mirror.

Train leave in
three minute.

I can't to move.

Train leave in
two minute.

PING!

**I CANT C U.
R U ON TRAIN???????**

Phone tight in hand.

Train leave in
one minute.

PING!

IM ON TRAIN...U???????

My fingers shake.

My heart break.

Yes. Stay. I come to u. Ever ♥

I listen to train.
Doors beep-beeping.

Train leave in
zero minute.

I feel for the courageous

in my heart.
The brave decide
that I make.
Time to self-defending
Jess.

Engine is louder now.
Wheels squealing.
My heart is the wheels.

PING!
PING!
PING!

Time to set Jess
free
from
me.

And Nicu,
always stupid.

ALWAYS STUPID.

Plan to go on platform
after train has vanishing.

But
        train still there.

And I see her.

Jess

through door,
through window

and she see me.

Her eye
meet
my eye.

She see.
We see.

Train moving . . . and moving,
and we don't to
hold hand,
have kiss,
hug tighter.

We don't to say
goodbye.

Goodbye, Jess,
I whispering and waving.

*Goodbye
my Jess.*

320

Train to Nowhere

'NICU!'
I shout,
much louder than I did when Liam turned his back
   on me.

'NICU!'
I bang the window,
kick the door,
so mad and so loud everyone in the carriage is
   staring,
not knowing
why I'm freaking out.

But it doesn't matter what I do,
     I can't open the door –
the button won't work,
even though I punch it and punch it and punch it.

And

the train is moving slowly,
leaving,
chugging up to Cambridge
without Nicu.

And he isn't doing anything to stop it.

He's just
watching me,
waving,
almost smiling
and crying too,
like a bloody big baby,
watching and waving,
sobbing,
and I know,
          then,
seeing the look he's giving me
that
there's no point
in texting him and
telling him to meet me in Cambridge
in a couple of hours
because he did this on purpose.

He let me leave.

'You *dickhead*!' I shout.
Doesn't he know how much worse everything is
     now?
He thinks I'm going to Cambridge, but I'm not,
          I'm going nowhere
and when I arrive he'll be
somewhere else —
on his way to prison probably.

'Why?' I ask,
but he doesn't hear me,
and I know the answer anyway.

I look for him but
the train is out of the station.

I am gone and
there's nothing else to do except
say his name
over and over in my head like a spell.
Nicu, Nicu, Nicu, Nicu, Nicu.

I sit,
stare down at his bag by my feet.
His cape is rolled up at the top.

I take it out
to cover myself in him –
his smell,
        his stupidity.

'Nicu,' I hear myself saying
and look into the bag again,
where I see
the cash –
        wads and wads of his dad's cash.

'You dickhead,' I say again,
and I can't help it:
　　　I smile.

IN THE DISTANCE

I watch
Jess
go *clack-clack*
down
train line
track.

I see train disappear.
Two lights
wink at me
in long distance.

Everything now in long distance:

hands in mine
ice skate laughs
sweets on slide
running
hugs
lips
tears

every dream in long distance.

Life is all
clickety clack.

We come together.

Now

we come apart.